It Was Only Ever You

KATE KERRIGAN lives in County Mayo,
Eire, with her husband and children.
Her novels include *Recipes for a Perfect
Marriage*, shortlisted for the 2006
Romantic Novel of the Year Award and
Ellis Island, which was a TV Book Club
Summer Read. She is also the author of
the highly acclaimed novel *The Dress*.

ALSO BY
KATE KERRIGAN

Recipes for a Perfect Marriage
The Miracle of Grace
Ellis Island
City of Hope
Land of Dreams
The Lost Garden
The Dress

It Was Only Ever You

KATE KERRIGAN

HEAD
of ZEUS

A catalogue record for this book is available from
the British Library.

ISBN (HB): 9781784082413
ISBN (XTPB): 9781784975906
ISBN (E): 9781784082406

Typeset by Adrian McLaughlin

Printed and bound in Great Britain by
CPI Group (UK) Ltd, Croydon CRO 4YY

MIX
Paper from
responsible sources
FSC
www.fsc.org   FSC® C020471

Head of Zeus Ltd
Clerkenwell House
45–47 Clerkenwell Green
London ECIR OHT

WWW.HEADOFZEUS.COM

For Rosie
because we're rocking and rolling now.

It Was Only Ever You

Prologue

Riverdale, New York, March 1941

SAMUEL KLEIN clicked off the radio and leaned back into his low, soft chair. He sucked deeply on his pipe, releasing a ball of smoke into the still air, then said through clenched teeth, 'You've got to love the British – but they could be right, you know? Churchill reckons that now the Yanks have agreed to come on board we are finally coming to the end of this wretched war.'

His wife Anya shot him a warning look but it was too late. Their niece Sheila was at the door and had already heard him. Samuel did not like to be shushed by his wife, especially not in his own home, but he immediately realized his terrible mistake. He laid his pipe down in the large wooden ashtray on his armrest and leaned forward in his chair.

'The war is ending?' said Sheila.

Samuel and Anya loved their fourteen-year-old niece as if she was their own child. Samuel's brother had been a German opera singer, living in Berlin when Hitler came to power.

1

Klaus had intended to move his whole family to America, and had sent his young daughter over to New York for an extended 'holiday'. He had kept his son behind so he could finish his studies at the Mendelssohn Conservatory of Music. Then war broke out and it was too late.

Sheila had learned not to think about what was happening to her mother and father and brother. She had been so impatient to see them again that the waiting for them to come had been almost unbearable.

'Soon,' was all they had ever said. 'After the war.' After a while, she could see that her continued enquiries hurt Auntie Anya and Uncle Samuel, so she made herself stop. When her family's faces came into her mind's eye she put thoughts of them to one side, reassuring herself that she would see them again when the war was over. Until then it was best to do what Auntie and Uncle told her to do, and live in the day.

But now, the war was ending! Everything would change. They would be coming home? Five years had been a long time, but now it was over!

Samuel watched Sheila as she stood in the doorway, her arms crossed and her bony shoulders in their long, brown cardigan hunched. She had a strong face, like her father. A long aquiline nose gave way to a broad, generous mouth – alight when smiling, markedly downturned when not. Her eyes were dark brown with luxurious lashes, but their heavy lids gave her the appearance of being slightly bored. Sheila's habitually serious expression made her look older and wiser than her years. An unfortunate fact, in Samuel's opinion, that was in direct contradiction to her sweet, open nature.

Sheila's face was now lit up with such an expression of hopeful delight that it seemed to Samuel as if she held the world in her eyes. If they could only see her, Churchill and

Roosevelt; if they could only see the expression of pure innocence and hope on this child's face they would put an immediate end to this war and find a way of bringing her family back to her.

'Come in, bubula… sit down.'

Sheila looked at her uncle and there was something in his face that made her not want to do as he said. Why was he not smiling too? He had said it himself – the war was ending and yet…

She stayed where she was and said, 'When the war ends, then Mama and Papa and Hans…'

The words trailed off.

Why could she not finish the sentence? Anya and Samuel said nothing. Anya's face was as pale as dough.

The terrible silence hung in the air between them in unspoken words, in assurances. *Mama and Papa and Hans will be here. Soon. After the war.*

The war was nearly over. So surely it was safe to say it now.

But they weren't saying it, or telling her that everything would be all right. Why weren't they saying it? Why did she feel unable to say it out loud herself?

'Sit down, bubula,' Samuel said. 'I have something to tell you.'

Sheila looked at her uncle's face with its grey, pointed beard. Her own father wore his beard short and brown. She knew that from the photograph, although she could not picture it from memory now. She could not recall the feel of it pressed against her cheek. Uncle Samuel's eyes were sparkling with tears. Not tears of happiness, like when he listened to Mahler on the gramophone. This was something else. Something she did not recognize and yet she knew what it was. She couldn't look at him, didn't want to look at him. She looked to her auntie for comfort, for a shred of hope, but Anya's face was equally stricken. Sheila felt sick. She steadied herself in the doorway and looked around the room, searching for something to alleviate that awful fear crawling its way into her conscious mind.

This small drawing room was her home. For five years it had been her sanctuary, the safe place where she had come to find salve for the torn skin on her knee from Auntie's medicine box, or to tinker on Samuel's piano. But in that moment it felt as if the room itself was shrinking away from her; the polished mahogany sideboard clung to the flowery wallpaper, the large radio with its constantly flickering light was silenced in shame, the piano lid shut tight as if the keys beneath it were paralysed with dread.

They were dead. Her family was dead. Hitler had killed them. That was why they hadn't written. That was why nobody ever talked about them or the war ending any more. Even as she thought it, Sheila kept telling herself that it could not be true. She was a bad, bad person for even imagining such a thing. You shouldn't tell yourself people were dead unless...

'Bubula,' Samuel said. 'Come, sit down. We must talk...'

He reached out to her, his long fingers outstretched. Tears were streaming down his face and in a sudden moment, as suddenly as if she had been slapped, Sheila recognized the look in his eyes. Pity. They were not the tears of emotion inspired by music or art that she so often saw in her uncle's eyes. They were tears that told her her parents really were dead. Not only that, they told her that she was not loved, only pitied.

Anger flashed through Sheila as she ran from the room. She heard Samuel say to her auntie, 'Leave her, Anya. Give her some time.'

Sheila ran to her room and locked the door. Her heart was

pounding. She felt sick. Where were the tears? She waited patiently for a few minutes but they didn't come. Why wouldn't they come? She wanted to shout out and scream, 'It's not fair! None of this is fair!' but she could not. If she let any of the words out she was afraid they would be too loud, and the whole world would hear her.

Sheila felt a sob building in her chest. Not the kind of sob that comes from having a torn hem or a scraped knee, but something huge and frightening. Black and unknown. If she gave it voice she would pull the house down around their ears. So she took a deep breath and kept it to herself, inside her head. They were dead. All of them. Mama. Papa. Hans. How did they die? By a bomb? How long had they been dead? Why had they not told her? The questions made her feel angry. There were so many of them and yet she did not want to know the answers to them.

Five minutes ago her life had been good. Her parents were not here, but she had everything else that she needed. Five minutes ago there was kugel for dinner and, afterwards, she would be allowed to stay up to listen to a play on the radio with Uncle Samuel. Tomorrow she would go to school and do that rotten maths test, then afterwards go to Margaret's house and flirt with her Irish cousins. In five minutes everything had changed. Her family was dead. They were never coming for her. She was alone. Five minutes ago the people downstairs were her beloved auntie and uncle. Now they were strangers who had lied to her. She hated them. She hated them for not telling her the truth. And she hated them for not lying. They could have told her that her family was still alive. That they would all be coming for her. Soon. After the war.

The pain in her chest just kept getting bigger and bigger but as Sheila lay on her bed and waited for the tears, she realized that she could not cry alone. She had never cried alone. When she was small, she would go to Auntie, wrap her hands around her waist, press her face into her large, soft bosom and weep into the buttery smell of her cooking apron. Or her uncle would sit her up on his lap at the piano and teach her how to play 'Für Elise', complaining and laughing when her frizzy black curls got caught in his greying beard.

But that seemed a long time ago now. Now, in the last five minutes, everything had changed. Love was not the same as pity and she would *not* go downstairs and endure the pity of the two people she had decided, in her sudden, shocked fury, were strangers now.

Big girls don't cry, and she was a big girl now. Her family was gone and she was on her own.

There would be no tears. Not today.

1

County Mayo, Ireland, Summer 1958

I T WAS a hot day and Patrick Murphy was heading down
to Gilvarry's lake for a swim with his friends. The small
lake was easily accessible from the town, a twenty-minute
barefoot stroll across three flat green grazing fields. However,
that month Mickey Gilvarry had taken possession of a new
stud bull so his fields were out of bounds. The lads had to
walk forty minutes at a brisk pace along the stony road in
their boots. It had been a good summer, with spells of hot sun
between the rain, so the boys' faces and chests were weathered
from a hard week's work. Brendan Kelly had been picking
and bagging potatoes, his brother, Tony, cutting turf and Patrick bringing in hay on his father's small farm. This was the
three young men's day off and as the dusty air stung their
burnt skin, they cursed Mickey's bull for making their journey to the cold water of the lake longer than it needed to be.

They stopped at the roadside to strip off their shirts and
Brendan pulled a packet of Woodbines out of his breeches

and passed them around. 'I've half a mind to take these trousers off,' he said. 'I'm roasted alive.'

'We'd rather you didn't,' said Tony, who, despite his burly physique, had the manner and wit of an old woman. 'I caught sight of your bollocks once and I'd just as soon not repeat the experience.' He pulled a small hand-corked bottle from his shoulder bag.

'Is that tea?' Brendan asked as Tony perched himself on a stile at the side of the road. 'Isn't your mammy great altogether?'

'She's grand, surely,' Tony said coyly, 'and this is the finest and sweetest tea my mammy ever made me.' Then he took a swig from the bottle and grimaced wildly.

'You fecker – it's poitin! Give us a swig!'

The other two made a grab for the flask, as Tony dived under their arms.

'It's tea, I'm telling you!' he said, walking backwards down the road, waving the bottle at them and laughing, urging them to follow.

Brendan chased after him, but Patrick held back and started to pull his shirt off. Of the three, twenty-five-year-old Patrick stood out as the eldest and by far the best-looking. His luxuriant black hair was slicked back from his forehead in a heavy quiff and his white shirt-sleeves were rolled up to his shoulders to reveal muscular tanned arms. He had the tall, broad physique of his father, but unlike other men whose bodies were built more for labour than for love, Patrick carried himself with a nonchalant charm. However, while his peers envied Patrick, they could never hate him. Although he looked like a Hollywood idol and had all the girls round about driven pure daft chasing after him, Patrick was sound as a pound. There wasn't an ounce of arrogance about him, unlike the la-di-da local gobshites that went off to London for a summer working the sites and came back with big ideas and cockney accents. Patrick, with his singing talent and his good looks, could easily go off abroad and make his fortune. But he didn't. He was happy at home, working on the farm, and singing whenever he was asked. He wore his gifts lightly and was always sure to direct attention away from himself. Only last month, at a dance in Pontoon, he had cornered Mary McCarthy and gazed searingly at her, then, just as she was fit to fall into a swoon, gently delivered her to Tony Kelly who had been plucking up the courage to speak to her for six months. Tony didn't mind that she had fallen in love with Patrick first. It was a rite of passage for almost all the girls in the town anyway and, sure, Tony was a little in love with him himself. Mary was engaged to him now and Patrick had made that happen.

Patrick laughed, watching big Brendan make a grab for Tony's poitín flask, but as he went to place his shirt on the stile it fell on to the high soft grass on the other side. Reaching over the wall to get it, something caught the corner of his eye. It was a girl, standing stock-still in the middle of Mickey's field. Facing her, not twenty feet away, was the bull.

'Mother of God,' Patrick whispered to himself. Without thinking, he clambered over the stile. Cautiously but steadily he began to walk towards the girl. Her body was paralysed with fear, he could see that from here. She was doing the right thing, standing still. As Patrick inched closer, the girl turned her head towards him. It was Dr Hopkins's daughter, Rose, his younger sister Sinead's best friend. There was a look of terror on her pretty face.

The bull seemed transfixed by a small, blue bag dangling from her arm. Rose must have been heading down to the

lake for a swim and not known to avoid the field. Her flowery dress had a solid red ribbon around the hem, which was
fluttering slightly as she struggled to hold her shaking legs
steady. One gust of wind, and the red hem might set the
bull charging.

As their eyes met, Patrick raised his palms up in front of his
face and shook his head. He wanted her to stay exactly where
she was. He was twenty feet to the other side of her now and
knew he had to act fast. So he opened his mouth and he sang.

'The pale moon was ri-sing, above the green moun-tain...'
Patrick's broad, impressive baritone reverberated across the
empty field.

As soon as she heard his voice Rose felt the frozen edge
of her fear melt away. For a few seconds the bull just stood
there, confused, then, slowly, he turned his head towards
Patrick. As soon as he did so, Rose began to run.

Still distracted by Patrick, the bull scraped the ground
with his left hoof. Once Patrick was sure that he had the
animal's full attention, he began to wave his arms wildly.
Then, still singing 'The Rose of Tralee', he did a little dance
before shouting, 'Come over here and get me, ya big hairy
bastard!'

As the bull started to charge, Patrick turned and ran as if
all hell was after him. He could feel his heart banging in his
chest as the galloping hooves of the heavy animal reverberated through the soft ground beneath him. His friends were
shouting frantically from behind the wall, 'He's up your arse!
Run!' Patrick had barely made it over the stile when the bull
stopped a few feet short of the stone wall. His nostrils flared
as he shook his flat square head.

'Jesus, Patrick, you pure lunatic, you could have been
killed,' Tony said.

As the bull began to turn, his adventure over, Patrick picked up a stone from the ground and threw it at his ear.

'Feck. What the hell are you...?'

'I have to go back for her,' Patrick said to his friends, 'make sure she's safe. Keep him busy.'

Before the other two had the chance to object, he climbed over the wall back into the field. As he ran across the flat meadow of daisies and dandelions towards the mirrored glint of the still lake, Patrick could see that Rose was well clear of danger, but he still followed her.

He caught up with her at the old boating jetty where they all swam. She did not seem surprised by his sudden appearance. Perhaps she knew he would follow her. Patrick felt a pinch in his stomach when he thought that.

'How'ya now?' he said.

She looked up at him shyly from beneath long black eyelashes.

'Grand,' she said.

Rose had the type of elegant, refined beauty about which his mother might remark, 'That girl has a touch of Grace Kelly in her.' Sleek blonde hair sat in lush waves across her delicate shoulders. Her skin was pale silk, and her cheeks and lips were tinged with soft pink, as if God had remembered the rouge. She had an almost overt perfection to her appearance, which, when she was younger, had made her appear prim. As she grew into a woman it had made her astonishingly beautiful. He remembered his father and his pub cronies saying about Grace Kelly one night, 'That woman's face is a caution. It doesn't do for a woman to be too beautiful.' 'You wouldn't know what kind of trouble they'd lead you into.' 'A plain woman will never stray too far from the house.' 'Marriage makes a woman plain in any case – that's the proper order of things.' 'All the same, I'd do time for a kiss from them perfect lips!'

Rose was his sister's wee friend. He had never paid any attention to her before now. She was just the blonde quiet girl in the background of his life. Yet now he was noticing that her rosebud lips were set in a closed smile, pouting. He thought of reaching across, touching them gently with his thumb to see if they were as soft as they looked. He had done that a hundred times before with other girls, but with Rose he felt unable to. She was too much for him. Too beautiful.

So, he looked down at his feet and said, 'That was some bull.'

'It was surely,' she replied.

He looked up at her again and she was smiling. Her teeth were straight and white and her blue eyes turning sapphire in the sunlight.

'Yeah, that was some bull,' he continued, gravely adding, 'It might have killed you.'

'Might have,' she said brightly.

'And me too. Did you see the way he was chasing me across the fields? I tell you, he was going at some speed.'

She shrugged, and smiled a little bit. Not a big smile. Just a small one, her eyebrow raised slightly.

She was mocking him!

'That was some stupid thing you did coming through the field like that with everyone in the town told there was a bull in it.'

The happy glint dimmed in Rose's eyes and she lowered them.

He had upset her and immediately felt sorry.

'There was no sign,' she said, still looking at her feet.

Patrick remembered that, being part of the professional

class, Rose's family lived slightly apart from the ordinary town people. As the local doctor, her father was liked and respected, but his wife was aloof. Mrs Hopkins was not interested in local news and Rose was never let out to dances or to the pictures like other girls. It was possible then that she had not picked up news from around the town about Mickey's new bull.

'Well anyway,' he said, making his voice as soft and gentle as if he were talking to a child, 'you're safe now.'

She rewarded him with a smile as dazzling as a film star's and Patrick felt that his legs might go from under him.

'Are you going in for a swim?' he asked.

It sounded like such a stupid thing to say now, but she laughed, as if he were the wittiest man in the world.

'I don't know,' she said. 'What about you?'

Spurred on by her smile and the aftermath of his bull-chasing, Patrick ripped off his shirt, breeches and pants, and then right there, stark naked and in full view of Rose Hopkins – the doctor's daughter – he ran down the jetty and threw himself into the freezing water. When he came back up to the surface he saw her standing there on the edge laughing and clapping. Patrick felt as if he was the funniest, cleverest man in the world.

'Come in,' he shouted. 'It's warm, I promise.'

Rose took off her shoes and laid them carefully on the mossy wood, then sat down on the edge of the jetty and dipped her toes in the water. She let out a shiver. 'It's cold as ice!' she squealed, then said, 'I'm not as adventurous as you.'

He swam towards her, making long broad strokes with his arms, trying to impress her. He trod water in front of her, his breath heavy with the cold. He could feel every inch of his naked body tingling, the chill of the water fighting the heat of his nakedness. Rays of sun bounced off his skin and look-ing down at his arms he saw how tanned he had become. With his long narrow face, broad nose and coarse curls, Patrick was told he was the most handsome boy in the town. He didn't care much about that, but he also knew when he fixed his vivid blue eyes on something, be it girl or bull, what effect they had.

He fixed them on Rose now and said, 'You're as adventur-ous as any man, I'm thinking.'

'What makes you say that?'

Patrick's limbs were getting tired and he suddenly regretted his spontaneous urge to strip naked.

'Facing down a big bull, there's not every man would do that.'

He felt stupid having a conversation, with her fully dressed in the warm sunlight and him naked in the freezing lake. What had he been thinking of?

Then Rose did something entirely unexpected. She closed her eyes, pointed her toes and slid herself, fully dressed, into the water with the smoothness of a raw egg sliding down the edge of a cold plate. Before her head went under, Patrick heard her say in a clear voice, yet not much louder than a whisper, 'Save me. I can't swim.'

Rose didn't know why she did such a reckless, stupid thing. It was the same passionate impulse that had led her to take the back route down to the lake, after she had seen Patrick Murphy and his friends taking the road in that direction with their swim bags. Her parents had gone down to Galway for the day and she had stayed behind in the house on her own.

Her mother had wanted her to go with them. She was quite insistent but Rose had said she would prefer to stay at home and sketch. Eleanor Hopkins had no reason not to trust her daughter. Rose was a quiet, studious young woman who, aside from a friendship with young Sinead Murphy stretching back to their first years in school together, spent most of her time drawing and sketching, for which she had some considerable talent. There had been talk of sending her up to Dublin to art school, when the time came. But the idea of that made Eleanor uncomfortable. Rose had grown into a beauty and Eleanor knew all about the great responsibility beauty could bring and the terrible pitfalls that came with male flattery. Including a backstreet abortion in a filthy room above a shop in Dublin's seamy streets, which had robbed a demure young girl of her capacity to have children. It was a dark secret that, as a medical man, her husband suspected, but never referred to. Rose was adopted from a convent shortly before the Cork doctor moved his practice and family to this Mayo town. Rose did not know she was adopted and her parents never discussed it, even between themselves. Although their daughter's astonishing beauty was a constant reminder of her provenance, they kept it a secret from her. It was their shame, not hers.

Eleanor loved Rose even more than if she had given birth to her from her own broken womb. Now she was determined to keep her daughter away from boys for as long as she could.

Perhaps, then, it was a rebellion against her mother's anxiety and persistent cloistering that had caused Rose to chase Patrick Murphy and his friends down to the lake that day. The very moment her mother's back was turned she had faced off a bull and then slid into a lake in the hope that a young man would save her from drowning.

Rose felt the freezing water creep through the roots of her long thick hair as the ends floated up to the surface then, as she sank, tangled about her face in a slimy curtain. She struggled to hold her breath and after a few seconds felt the panic rise up in her, willing her to flail around and struggle against the water to reach for the air again. As she was about to open her mouth, she felt the force of Patrick's body push against her as he carried her in his firm arms up towards the surface of the lake. They burst out of the water and sucked in great breaths together, gasping and clinging to one another.

Rose had not intended to drown. All she had known was that she had wanted to embrace the moment, to keep the adventure alive. When Patrick had saved her from the bull, the feeling of having been rescued was sweeter than she could have imagined. In those moments, as she was running across the fields, heart thumping, blood pumping through her small breasts, her feet running so fast across the soft grass, she felt as if she was flying. So, she thought, this is what love feels like: to surrender and be saved. She wanted to do it again.

Rose had pretended to drown because she had wanted to find a way to make Patrick touch her. She knew she was pretty but she also knew he would never look at her. She was his sister's friend, younger than he was. Rose was the doctor's daughter, and she also knew that put her out of bounds, not just to Patrick, but to all the boys in the town. Rose was considered 'posh' and she hated that. Apart from Sinead, all the other girls thought her standoffish and strange, because she preferred to paint and draw than to talk to people. Sinead said they were just jealous of her because she was beautiful, but Rose didn't think she was especially beautiful. She knew she looked 'different' from the other girls, with her ash-blonde hair and pale, delicate skin. She longed to be earthy and 'ordinary' in the just plain pretty way that the boys liked. She wanted to be teased and tickled and danced with, but it seemed that the local boys were somewhat shy of approaching her and the girls just ignored her. Sinead said not to mind them. She said that Rose's drawing was a special talent. She understood people with special talents because her brother was able to sing like John McCormack. Sinead said that her brother found it hard because people didn't always understand how important singing was to him. Patrick once confided that the only time he was truly happy was when he was singing. Sometimes, he told Sinead, he dreamt of having enough money to go to America and become a big star, but he was afraid of saying it to people in case they laughed at him.

Rose could not imagine Sinead's older brother worrying about anything. But then, no one could imagine Rose Hopkins, the doctor's daughter, being worried about anything either. She was the girl who had everything, and Patrick was the boy who had everything. Yet Sinead had told her that Patrick, too, had that strange space inside him: the space she could only fill when she was drawing.

That was what had started Rose off looking at Patrick Murphy in a different way. Up to then he had just been the good-looking bad-boy in town. Now, it seemed, he was a sensitive artist, like her. An unlikely soulmate. Rose had followed him that day, hoping she might draw him away from his friends and, perhaps, strike up a conversation. She had not banked on the bull. Frightening as it was, the encounter with it had worked to her advantage. She had certainly got Patrick's attention.

Underneath his blather, she knew that Patrick was not the type to put his hands on a girl uninvited, especially not his little sister's friend. Which was why she slid into the water and put herself at risk of drowning.

She had known he would save her. When she felt his strong

17

arms lift her up towards the air again, towards breath, towards light, she felt the thrill of being saved as acutely as if she had actually fallen to her death.

Patrick put his hand under her torso and swam the few strokes to the edge of the jetty and then told her to hold on to the wooden stilt. He should have asked her why she had done such a stupid thing. She might have got tangled in weeds, he might not have been able to see her in the dense lake water. He should have been angry that she had recklessly put them both in such a dangerous situation. But when he looked at her face and her glistening wet skin, her eyes glittering with the reflection from the lake, with the excitement of simply being alive, he was flooded through with a painful desire. Reaching out, he ran his thumb along her bottom lip and as her eyes half closed, he kissed her, his naked body folded around her, keeping her afloat.

In that moment, the fierce cold and the adrenalin rush dropped away and all Rose could feel was him.

'His clothes are here, he's after going in without us... Murphy! Where the feck are you?'

They had not heard the lads coming down the jetty until they were on top of them.

'Shite,' Patrick whispered.

Rose wasn't worried about getting caught. Nothing in the world mattered to her except being kissed by Patrick Murphy. Nonetheless, she was glad to see that he was worried for her reputation.

He whispered at her, 'Follow my lead.' Then, 'Down here, lads!' he called out. 'She fell in – she can't swim so I came in after her.'

Neither of the boys commented on the fact that he had stripped before diving in for this daredevil rescue, or asked why Rose Hopkins came down to the jetty with a swim bag when she was unable to swim. Either they didn't think of it, or they were too shocked to believe that their friend was forward enough, or stupid enough, to go after the doctor's daughter.

For the rest of that afternoon Rose lay on the jetty with the three lads playing and talking around her; jumping in and out of the water, showing off their smooth, strong bodies. They were kind and respectful towards her, feeding her sweet biscuits and allowing her a taste of their poitin – which burnt her lips. She lay on the jetty, her clothes drying on her skin. When the others were in the water she and Patrick looked across at each other. His blue eyes gazed at her with something she could not name but which made her feel as if her limbs might dissolve with longing. Rose turned on her side and felt the hot sun bake her damp dress. The secret kiss and the passion of her rescue seemed to burn into her very soul over the course of that afternoon. She longed to kiss him again, and again, and to never stop kissing him, but she knew that could not happen while the others were watching. They would have to wait, and Rose knew her life from then on would be spent counting the moments until she saw Patrick Murphy again.

2

Yonkers, New York, 1958

AVA BROGAN was doing the jitterbug, zigzagging with her unnaturally long legs and large feet, and flicking her arms out to her sides in time to the Jack Ruane Band. The dance floor of the Emerald Ballroom in Yonkers was packed tonight, but Ava's limbs were so long that the other dancers left a wide circle around her in case she gave one of them a dig. Another person might have been more self-conscious about flinging herself around like that, but, despite her height and build, Ava was a good dancer, and she knew it. The only place where she had confidence in how she looked was on the dance floor. It didn't matter if she was pretty or not, or that she was wearing pants and a sweater instead of a dress, when she was dancing, it was just her and the music.

Tonight she was mostly dancing with Jamsey Collins, an Irish guy who cleaned windows in her father's office where she and Myrtle worked in the typing pool. Even though Ava was the boss's daughter, she had no airs and graces. Her father was a self-made man, Irish himself, and didn't mind who his only daughter dated as long as she was happy. Her mother was a different story. She didn't think Ava should be working in an office at all, or wasting her time learning to dance when she should be busying herself finding a good husband. Ava shrugged off her mother's concerns but in truth she was hoping that one might lead to the other.

Ava and Jamsey had just done two jives, a cha-cha, the stroll and now the jitterbug – back to back. She could tell he was ready to stop after that crazy jive to 'Rip It Up', but she had challenged him to two more. At one point he had her laughing so hard, messing about during their stroll, that she thought she might have to stop and be sick! Jamsey was a funny-looking guy, gangly, and even taller than she was. He wasn't a looker but he was a charmer all right, what the Irish called 'great craic'. Ava liked him but, more than that, she thought she might be in with a chance – none of the girls in the typing pool was interested in him and so she felt they had that in common. Perhaps he knew what it was like to be left out too.

When they were done, Ava threw herself down into the banquette next to her friend Myrtle, exhausted.

'You are one hell of a dancer young lady,' Jamsey said, panting. 'You have me worn out.' Ava laughed. She felt her face redden with a flush of hope, and was glad to have the excuse of the dancing to cover it. 'Can I get you ladies a drink?' he asked. But as he stood up, the slow set started with a smoochy waltz. Jamsey held out his hand and said, 'May I?'

Ava blushed and was about to accept when she saw that he wasn't holding his hand out to her, but to Myrtle. This had obviously been his intention all along: being friendly with Ava in order to get close to her prettier friend, who would never have looked at him otherwise. It hurt.

Ava flinched then gathered herself before Myrtle sensed her disappointment.

'Do you mind?' Myrtle mouthed as she hopped behind him, her hand in his.

Ava shook her head and made a funny face. Jamsey turned and gave her a friendly wink, as if Ava were one of the boys.

'I'll go and get the drinks,' she said, then called after Myrtle, 'Watch his hands – he's cheeky!'

She felt a stab of rejection, and then shook it off by reminding herself it was always the same.

Ava was the most popular girl in the room for the fast dances, but she never got asked up for the slow set. Even the boys that nobody else liked weren't interested in her. It wasn't their fault. How any boy could take a girl of her height and build seriously, especially, as her mother was constantly at pains to point out, since she insisted on wearing 'those dreadful pants' instead of a dress.

She went up to the bar and ordered two coffees for herself and Myrtle. Jamsey could buy his own drink. Ava was sore, but she was no pushover. He hadn't meant to be cruel but even so, it was a nasty game he had played getting to Myrtle through her. There was no need to reward his cunning with a drink.

She stood looking out at the vast wooden dance floor. The resident band was playing a medley of old-fashioned Irish waltzes. Couples clung to each other. The older men wore suits and ties, only taking their jackets off to dance, draping them on the backs of the chairs. The younger men wore the smart-casual look that was all the rage – slacks and collared sweater-shirts. Many of the younger girls were wearing tight pencil skirts that had just come into fashion. Myrtle was poured into one, which showed off her full bottom and wasp-waist to full effect.

Despite her friends cajoling her to embrace fashion, Ava disliked dressing up. Everything she put on seemed only to draw attention to her height and broad build. As a teenager in those innocent years when she did not realize quite how unattractive she was, she had experienced the humiliation of being left out. So now, during the slow sets, while the other girls sat prettily smoking, waiting for their turn to be asked up to dance, Ava always went straight to the bar. She got asked up occasionally, but only ever by the desperate or the drunk.

Kind-hearted by nature, Ava had endured being fondled and stepped on by the very worst the Irish-American dance-hall scene could throw at her. One night, about two years ago, after a particularly treacherous waltz with a man who had more hair growing out of his ears than on his head, she was slapped on the bottom and told she was 'a fine big heft of a thing that would be a welcome addition to one of the biggest cattle farms in Mayo'. The girls in the typing pool were in stitches when she relayed her ordeal the following morning during coffee break, but as she reached twenty-two, Ava could feel that the self-deprecating humour and her plucky nature had begun to fail her.

She watched the couples on the dance floor. The older married ones gliding in the old-fashioned style, the younger ones with their bodies pressed against each other, shuffling slowly in search of intimacy. A murmured suggestion, a breathless request, might be given permission to slide outside and canoodle in a car before being dropped home. Some girls would be left on their parents' doorstep with the promise of new love. Others would go home alone, carrying with them the hope that next Saturday the handsome prince would find them. But that was never how it was for Ava. Not tonight, or any night.

The Emerald Ballroom was where the Irish came to find love. When immigrants stepped off the boat from Ireland it was the first place they came. The huge dance hall had four bars and was a Mecca not just for the Irish immigrants, but for the children who had been born here. The Irish showbands were just taking off. They took the music that had shaken America – the rock and roll of Bill Haley and Elvis Presley – and were feeding it back to the dance-crazy Irish. While conservative priests preached about the moral dangers of rock and roll, the Irish carried on going to mass and courting each other in dance halls, as they had done since the 1940s.

The New York Irish showbands scene was like a home-from-home for Ava. She and her friend Myrtle were here every Saturday night, without fail. Ava knew most of the staff and many of the band members. The resident band comprised, largely, classically trained musicians. Dating back to the old Glenn Miller days, they kept the regulars busy waltzing and foxtrotting throughout the week. On weekends, the visiting Irish showbands came to town and shook things up; with their sparkly suits and cheeky, cheery grins, they toured a circuit that ran from London, Leeds, across all of Ireland, then to Boston, Chicago and New York. Many of these dance halls were owned by Iggy Morrow – a Kerry man and entertainment mogul who was friendly with Ava's father, Tom Brogan.

Jack Ruane and his lads had cleared the stage and the resident band was playing an old-time waltz. The jiving was over. The rest of the night would be given over to romance.

Ava looked across the crowded floor to see how Myrtle was getting along. With a bit of luck her friend would have shaken off Jamsey and would be ready to go home.

'Worn yourself out, Ava?' the barman quipped as he slid her two coffees.

Ava smiled but found herself at a loss to think of a smart comeback.

It was not that she particularly liked Jamsey, only that she had been foolish enough to think that he had liked her when he hadn't.

'On the house,' the barman said.

Did he feel sorry for her? Ava didn't even mind – she was feeling a little sorry for herself, if truth be told.

As she was walking back to the booth she spotted Myrtle and Jamsey in amongst the mash of couples. Jamsey whispered something into Myrtle's ear and she threw her red curls back and laughed. A wave of sadness washed over Ava as she felt that moment would never belong to her.

Leaving the coffees behind, she picked up her bag and her cardigan and walked back out on to the broad suburban street where she hailed a taxi home.

3

'IT'S AN investment.'

Nessa Brogan had said it straight out, while explaining to her husband, Tom, over breakfast that morning, why almost two hundred dollars of his salary was being spent on a Sybil Connolly gown for their daughter, Ava, to wear to a wedding that wasn't her own. P. J. Dolan was a high court judge and one of the most powerful people in New York Irish society.

Tom Brogan was a successful insurance broker, one of the rising middle class of Irish Americans, but his real passion was his philanthropic work with young Irish immigrants, many of whom came to be employed in the dance halls owned by his friend Iggy Morrow. Tom and the judge knew each other vaguely through their charitable work for the poor immigrant Irish, but it was apparently well enough for the Brogans to be invited to be one of their eight hundred or so guests at PJ's eldest daughter Gloria's wedding. Nessa was determined to make an impression.

The famous Irish fashion designer Sybil Connolly was renowned for her classic designs using the finest Irish tweeds and linens. Jackie Kennedy was a customer. The Brogans were not in the same league as the Kennedys but being invited to Judge Dolan's wedding was a start and Tom could afford to splash out every now and then to keep his wife and daughter happy. Or rather, his wife. His daughter hated shopping.

Nessa opened her eyes wide and nodded conspiratorially. 'It's a big day, Thomas, an opportunity. There will be a lot of important people there.'

Then she mouthed the word 'husband'. Tom shook his head and blushed, embarrassed. He didn't see what the problem was. So Ava was taller, broader and not as delicate and pretty as her cousins, but she was still a great girl. She was sensible, practical and as smart as any man he'd ever come across. She could fire through a crossword in an hour and count as fast in her head as any of the young men he had working under him. Ava was a good, kind person too – worth a thousand of these silly American girls with their bows and big busts and their wasp-waists. As far as Tom Brogan was concerned, any man would be the luckiest man alive to marry his daughter. What she needed to find was a good, solid Irishman, like himself. The fact that she insisted on working in the typing pool of his insurance firm didn't help. She was too independent by far, and men didn't like that either. Ava could afford to buy her own clothes, but most of the time she didn't bother. This was her mother's way of trying to fancy her up a bit. Tom could have told her it wouldn't work. Ava just wasn't that kind of girl.

Tom loved his only daughter more than anything and told her she was beautiful every day. The problem was, she didn't believe him.

'You can stop talking about me finding a husband,' Ava said to them. 'I'll find my own when I'm good and ready.'

Tom laughed. 'There now, Nessa, will you leave the poor girl alone?'

Nessa smiled, taking temporary comfort in her daughter's show of confidence.

'The fitting is in the Plaza at eleven, we'll have time for lunch afterwards in the Palm Court...'

'Steady,' Tom said.

'Perhaps your father might call in with one of his colleagues?'

'She never gives up!' Tom said, smiling, bringing the paper back up to his face.

'And I never will,' said Nessa, picking up her bag, 'until our daughter is as happily married as we are.'

Tom pulled a face behind his paper so just Ava could see and she winked back at him.

It was important to Ava that she let her parents know that she neither noticed nor cared that she wasn't especially pretty. Except that Ava did notice and she did care. Her nose was too long, her eyes were close together and her face was broader than it should have been. She had good hair that set easily – but it was a dull shade of mousy brown and she was nervous to dye it a shade darker for fear of looking ghoulish. Glamorous 'Hollywood' blonde would have been a ridiculous notion on a girl of her size – almost six foot tall, with broad shoulders and long limbs. She was slim, but not curvaceous. Ava had long since decided that she was not going to apologize for her size. She did not want to make herself invisible and shrink into the corners of the dance hall to become a wallflower. She had lots of friends, and people liked her – men liked her too, just not in a romantic way. At least, not the ones she liked.

Ava's favourite film star was Doris Day and since she was a young girl she had tried to emulate the star's feisty, independent manner. Doris had shown her that a girl didn't have to be sultry like Lauren Bacall, seductive like Marilyn Monroe, or romantic like Grace Kelly. She could be tomboyish and plucky and full of fun. But she still had to be pretty if she wanted a man. If she wasn't pretty, a girl didn't stand a hope in hell of finding love. Ava knew, from seeing how happy her parents were, that without love, life was nothing.

The lavishly decorated suite was on the tenth floor of the Plaza Hotel. It had panelled walls and heavy silk drapes at the windows that were closed to preserve the client's modesty. Light was provided by occasional lamps with large yellow shades that threw off a warm, flattering light. Twice a year, Sybil Connolly would take a suite here and New York's wealthiest and most discerning fashion lovers would make appointments to be fitted with her elegant, classical designs. Ava left her clothes in a pile on the thick, navy carpet and came out from behind the ornate Chinese screen in her undergarments. Her long pale limbs were shivering, less from the cold than from the shame of being almost naked in front of a complete stranger.

Sybil's assistant pulled out a magnificent evening gown for her to try on. It was made of Connolly's trademark pleated linen, in a shade of soft, dove grey. Her mother had wanted her to have this dress since reading about it in *Harper's Bazaar*. The handcrafted effect was produced by closely pleating up to nine yards of handkerchief linen to produce one yard of delicate fabric. It could be packed away in a bag then shaken out and emerge as good as new. *Harper's* had declared Sybil's evening dresses both 'modern' and 'practical'.

'Just like you,' Nessa had said, hopeful that the cutting would light a fire under her daughter's lack of interest in how she dressed. Ava had agreed to give it a try and Nessa remained optimistic that this expensive dress would turn her daughter into a princess.

'There now,' Sybil's assistant said, holding open the huge, pleated skirt. 'Step into this, like a good girl.'

Ava loved the way the Irish talked. As if they had known you all their lives. At least half the people at their church were 'full Irish' not just born to Irish parents, like she was. The assistant talked in a kindly, matronly way, although she couldn't have been much older than Ava.

Ava stood in front of the full-length mirror as the assistant pulled the bodice up over her slim hips and narrow chest. The grey dress had a skirt, which spread out in a soft triangle from the waist. The bodice crossed over her bust and the fabric felt as soft and sublime as a cloud. It was, truly, a magnificent gown. However, it looked the same on her as all the magnificent dresses her mother had been making her try on since she was a little girl. Just ordinary. She glanced across at her mother and saw the shadow of disappointment flicker across Nessa's face before she plastered on her usual hopeful smile.

The dress was beautiful, but her daughter Ava was not. Another expensive mistake, she thought. The more elaborate the dress, the plainer her daughter seemed to render it. Ava was plain, and as each year passed, getting plainer. In the year since she had been home from finishing school she went about the house in slacks and her father's weekend sweaters, only putting on a skirt and blouse when her mother forced her into them. Nessa didn't want to destroy her confidence but if her daughter didn't smarten herself up she would never find a husband, and without a husband Ava would never be happy.

'Oh no.' Sybil Connolly swept into the room and stood behind Ava, her dark hair swept back from her face in a high set, her severe eyebrows raised in a look of thoughtful disapproval.

'Oh no – I do not like this dress on you, young lady – at all. This is all wrong.'

Nessa began to bristle. She was paying a lot of money for the dress and did not appreciate the woman's tone. It was one thing for Nessa herself to comment inwardly on her daughter's unremarkable looks, but quite another when somebody else did it.

'We want the finest dress for our daughter,' she asserted. 'Money is no object.'

Sybil smiled at her curtly. 'I don't doubt it – but this dress is all wrong on her.'

'But it's this season,' Nessa objected, adding sharply, 'And the most expensive you have.'

'Seasons mean nothing,' Sybil said. She gave a formidable glare. 'And price is of little interest to me.' Nessa blushed, regretting her faux pas.

Sybil turned her attention back to Ava. 'What this young lady…What is your name, my dear?'

'Ava.' She had never met anyone like Sybil before. So outspoken, so… certain. She reminded Ava of some of the stricter nuns in her boarding school but with lipstick and coiffed hair.

'What Ava needs is something to suit her own style. Isn't that right?'

Ava was not aware that she had a style.

'I suppose.'

'Tell me, my dear, do you like this dress?' Sybil said as

she stood behind her, smoothing down the exquisitely soft pleated skirt.

'Well, it's beautiful.'

'Of course it is. As your mother tells me,' and she arched a perfectly painted eyebrow, 'it's the most expensive dress money can buy. But do you like yourself in it?'

Ava wasn't sure what she meant. She didn't like how she looked in anything and avoided looking at herself as much as possible. Standing in front of a full-length mirror like this was torture. She thought she should answer truthfully if she wanted to get out of it so she shook her head and said with certainty: 'No. No, I don't.'

'Good,' Sybil said. 'So we will find something else.'

The older woman clicked for an assistant to come and undress Ava as she walked across to a clothes rail by the window and instructed another assistant to pull out items for her one by one.

She flicked past dresses, rejecting them with a 'No – not that one, wrong colour. Again…'

Ava felt a curious wave of depression come over her. She had been in this position before. Hours spent in the dressing room of Saks, Fifth Avenue while Nessa and a bevy of shop assistants passed in dress after dress, nothing ever fitting her properly, and nothing ever looking quite right. Hope followed by the humiliation of just not being quite pretty enough, not quite feminine enough to pull anything off. Now this was happening in the rarefied atmosphere of the Plaza and in front of this very important woman.

'STOP!' Sybil said, and then dramatically added, 'Now – what have we got for you here, Ava?'

Her assistant was holding up a tweed suit. It had a straight, slim skirt and a fitted jacket, nipped in tight and flaring into a waved pelmet at the waist, all pulled smartly together by eight mother-of-pearl buttons at the front. But by far the most unusual thing about the suit was its colour: an exquisite shade of pink.

'It's the colour of a rose,' Ava said.

'Well yes,' Sybil said. 'How charming of you to notice. As a matter of fact this tweed was commissioned by me from the wonderful nuns in Foxford Woollen Mills on the west coast of Ireland. It is a match for the wild roses of Mayo, the most delicate flowers you will ever see.'

While her assistant held the skirt open for Ava to step into, Sybil herself pulled the jacket over her bare shoulders and buttoned it up the front with confident speed, pinching the fabric with her strong manicured fingers.

As Sybil stepped back and Ava saw herself in the mirror in the rose suit, she could not quite believe her eyes.

Encased in the structure of this skirt and jacket, her tall gangly limbs looked statuesque, almost royal. She lifted her chin and noticed how the V of the neckline seemed to elongate her neck and make her look slimmer. Holding her own gaze in the mirror, Ava turned to one side and, arching her back slightly, checked her profile. She had miraculously acquired curves. The rose colour of the tweed was unmistakably feminine and yet it did not look ridiculously out of place on her broad shoulders. It was a wonderful outfit. More importantly, she was wonderful in it.

'I look so different,' she said. She smiled nervously at herself in the mirror.

'You look beautiful,' Nessa said.

'What she looks,' Miss Connolly added, 'is stylish. A sense of style will carry a woman much further than beauty, if she knows how to use it.'

Nessa looked at the designer, wondering if she was being negative about her daughter's appearance, but she seemed not to be. Although she was, indeed, a very stylish woman, Miss Connolly was no great beauty herself.

'Beauty fades with age, Mrs Brogan. Style matures. If a woman has the right clothes with the perfect fit, she will never be without confidence and grace.'

All Ava knew was that, for the first time in her life, she felt beautiful. She had never wanted anything as much in her life.

'We really were hoping for a dress,' Nessa said. 'It's for a wedding, you see. My husband's colleague—'

'I prefer the suit, Mother – please?' Ava pleaded.

'A suit is perfectly acceptable for day wear at a wedding,' Sybil asserted, pulling out a lace blouse from her rack. 'And this will dress it up for evening wear – I assume you have pearls?'

'Of course she has pearls,' Nessa said, anxious to reassert her status, and resigning herself to lending her daughter her own pearls in the interests of fulfilling her husband-finding potential.

Ava was barely listening.

She could not take her eyes off her own reflection. She did not think she was beautiful. Indeed, that would never be the case. But in this suit there was no denying she had something. Style, Miss Connolly had called it, but it was more than that. When Ava Brogan looked at herself in the mirror she saw somebody she recognized. Neither the gawky girl of her childhood, nor the gangly tomboy of her young adulthood – but the person she was always meant to be.

For the first time in her life, Ava looked and felt like a woman.

4

AFTER SHE discovered her parents had died, Sheila escaped into the radio, listening to it obsessively, every minute that she could. The joyful twinkling jazz piano of Count Basie, the comedic lyrics of Fats Waller and the harmonic bebop of the Delta Rhythm Boys were able to cheer her up in a way nothing else could. The pleadings of Louis Armstrong spoke to her soul and listening to music was the only time Sheila was able to be herself.

Uncle Samuel deplored swing. When Count Basie or Eddie Condon came on the radio, he would rage and fluster. 'Turn off that rubbish!' he would shout. 'Music is Mahler and Mozart – never forget that, Sheila.'

Samuel hoped Sheila would develop more sophisticated, classical tastes as she grew older but his pompous pronouncements only made her even more determined to pursue her love of modern music. She bought records and hid them in her room. There was no point in trying to explain to her uncle that this was the music that moved her. Not the droning misery of Mahler who reminded her only of her dead family and all she had lost. This was the music that made her feel alive. It was new, exciting. Swing music was who she was now – and that was all that mattered. Classical piano made her recall learning 'Für Elise' on her uncle's knee and Sheila had closed the door on those times. Good or bad, she did not want to remember.

As she grew into a young woman, Sheila fulfilled her family obligations by being a grateful little orphan and a good Jew. Samuel and Anya Klein hoped she would meet a nice boy in school whom she might marry. A doctor, or an accountant, perhaps, not a musician like her father, or a poor professor like Samuel. A good Jewish man with some status and a little money. Sheila deserved a nice husband who could give her a good life, after all the poor child had been through. She went along with their wishes because she was grateful for all they had done for her. At the same time, she could feel something wild smouldering inside her. She knew that, however happy it would make Anya and Samuel, a cosy life in Riverdale was not for her. At nineteen, during her second year of college where she was studying pharmacy, the fire broke out inside her. She went to see Charlie Parker playing at the Three Deuces and that night, in the velvet-red underbelly of New York, Sheila grew up. She sat on a leather banquette in a smoky corner swaying from side to side, a cigarette expertly falling from full scarlet lips, and she felt as if she was at home. Shy of dancing in public, she hid in the corner, watching as couples twisted their hips and swung their partners, pretty skirts swooping and smart boys smiling. Black and white, rich and poor – everybody wanted to dance.

This was where she wanted to be, not in some dusty college.

Sheila's quick academic mind enabled her to fly through her college work at double speed. The rest of the time she spent in the jazz clubs around 52nd Street: Three Deuces, Onyx Club, the Famous Door. She stuck out her degree to keep Anya and Samuel happy, then, as soon as she could, got a job in a diner in the city and left the house in leafy Riverdale.

'Where will you live?' Samuel said. He was sorry she was leaving but Sheila was an adult of twenty. She could go where she liked.

He could see she was aching to get away. She was escaping her past. She needed to do that.

'I'll find somewhere in the city,' she said. 'I'll be back every weekend.'

Anya wept like Sheila was dying. Sheila knew she should feel bad at leaving them but, in reality, she felt relieved, and that just made her feel more guilty.

She took a room in Times Square, above Al's Diner.

Sheila felt at home in Times Square with its huge, Technicolor advertisements urging people to 'Relax with Camel Cigarettes' or improve their lives with Admiral Television Appliances. The transience, the constant moving, was in such sharp contrast to the leafy, closeted environs of Riverdale, yet, for some reason, the crazy pace made her feel at ease. This was a no-man's land, a commercial hub where people came to see a show, eat a meal, or dance their socks off for a few hours before going back to their suburban lives. Times Square offered New Yorkers a brief interlude in their dull lives to be entertained and indulged. Anxious for adventure and escape, Sheila turned that series of sweet, brief interludes into her life.

Sheila soon got bored working in the diner. The daytime hours didn't suit her. So she got herself a job in the Twilight

Ballroom, an old-style dance hall, right across the street. She lived from one work shift to the next, from one man to the other, club-to-club, dance-to-dance – snatching meals when she remembered and going back to her shabby apartment.

Sheila started out waiting tables, then worked behind the bar and eventually, after five years, was promoted to manager. The Twilight had a resident band who stuck to ballroom and swing. It was a good job and it enabled her to live the nocturnal life she enjoyed, but as the years went by, Sheila's heart remained firmly in the jazz scene. Part of her felt that she should be working in the jazz clubs and not some schmaltzy outdated ballroom. However, she also knew that if she worked in the clubs where she socialized, she might go into a hedonistic free fall. Sheila knew how to party but she knew her limitations too. She loved her black musician friends but loving things too much could lead to trouble, so she kept a respectable distance, working hard in the ballrooms then relishing her rare nights off in her precious jazz clubs. Ballrooms and jazz clubs and even the up and coming dinner-dancing venues were worlds apart from one another. Those musicians who worked in the ballrooms were mostly white and classically trained. The self-taught musicians in the jazz/R&B clubs were mostly black. They overlapped, of course. Good musicians were always welcome in both camps, and it wasn't unusual to see a middle-aged white saxophonist in an all-black jazz band or, indeed, a black trombone player in a big band.

However, all of this was about to radically change, and Sheila wanted a piece of it.

Sheila had bought a record the year before called 'Crazy Man Crazy' by a white kid called Bill Haley. The record had a wild beat, and she liked it. So when she heard that this kid from Michigan had just got a regular gig in New Jersey in a dance bar, she decided to go and check him out.

As soon as Sheila walked in the door she could tell this was a country bar. Not her scene at all. Nice girls in pretty dresses with full skirts – boys in Sunday-best shirts and slacks. Not as formal as the ballrooms – but all white. She got a drink and stood at the small bar and watched the crowd. As they waited, Sheila could feel their excitement in the air. But then, she thought, country people always got a bit excited when they were out. Eventually, a bunch of white boys came on stage. The chubby front man had a big smile and a cowlick in his hair. They all wore long, tartan jackets and dicky bows. Pure hick. The singer was carrying a guitar and as he closed his eyes and reached his head back to release the first note, Sheila braced herself for the cowboy yodel. What came out surprised her more than anything else she had ever heard. As the band broke into 'Rock Around the Clock', her hips started to swing.

Sheila was a cautious dancer. In the jazz clubs, she never felt she belonged on the dance floor. She sat, clicking her fingers, tapping her feet, smoking laconically, enjoying the music that way. But with this new, strange rockabilly sound she found her hips were swaying from side to side at a speed that felt fast – too fast – and yet she was compelled to move in a way that felt utterly natural. It was as if the beat had injected her, and everyone else there, with a kind of electricity. Her body seemed to understand what to do in a way it had never done before now. By the time the lead singer roared out 'put your glad rags on', Sheila had grabbed the hand of the nearest stranger, not noticing or caring who he was, and was allowing herself to be swung and twirled around the floor in his expert grip, her feet stamping out the one-two beat as if she were born with it inside her.

Then, as Sheila moved around the floor like a wildcat she realized she had heard this very song being played before. It was a proto-rock song called 'Rock the Joint' that she had as a Jimmy Preston recording. She had always enjoyed the beat of it and yet she had never actually danced to it before. However, the way these hillbilly boys were playing the tune she simply had no choice but to dance. It was like a tribal drum, as if something old and terribly familiar was instructing her to get 'with it'. When the song ended her body was hungry for more and she joined the crowd in baying for Bill and his Comets to play it again, and again. Three times the crowd danced to that tune as if they had never heard it before. While the band took a break, Sheila leaned against the wall, and it hit her like a thunderbolt. This was black music for white kids. These hillbilly kids and their crazy white R&B could change the world.

The next day she went into work and marched straight into Dan's office.

'You have to book this band, Dan,' she said, 'Bill Haley and His Comets. They are calling it rock and roll; it's going to change everything.'

Dan looked across at her, narrowed his eyes and gave a hollow laugh.

'I heard of them, bunch of kids from Michigan. Waste of time. It'll never take off.'

'But...it's like black music for white people, Dan. This is what we've been waiting for. You didn't see the crowd there. They were going nuts.'

Dan shook his head.

'I heard about it. Jumping up and down and going crazy like savages. The kids are going wild – it's a phase. It'll never catch on.'

'Well I think it will!'

Dan smiled at her, although she could sense he was getting irritated.

'I had a meeting with the boys in the band about it last week.'

'Without me?'

'Sheila, darling, I've told you before, leave the music to the experts. As manager, you are in charge of keeping the books straight and making sure the cloakrooms are tidy…'

Sheila would have walked out if she thought she could have got a manager's job anywhere else. If she left the Twilight, she'd be back to square one selling cigarettes in some other dive. How she wished she could be in charge of the whole place. In charge of her own life…

'Me and the boys have been looking into it and, let me tell you, rock and roll ain't never going to hit the mainstream ballrooms and dance halls. Not in New York – not anywhere. The big bands are going nowhere. This rock and roll nonsense is a flash in the pan. Dancing cheek-to-cheek is here to stay. Let the lunatic kids wear themselves out in their living rooms and underground dives, they are not coming in among the respectable folk in the Twilight.'

If Dan McAndrew had been a respectable, churchgoing, God-fearing man, Sheila might have understood his resistance. But he was anything but. He drank like a fish and cheated on his wife. However, he was also funny and charming, so he got away with it. In the years that she had been working for him Sheila had come to care about his business, and a little bit about Dan himself. Sheila knew she was right about bringing in rock and roll. Unfortunately, being a woman meant that she could never be right when it came to a man's business. However, knowing that just made her even more determined to keep trying.

A month later, 'Rock Around the Clock' was all over the TV and radio. Still Dan and the resident band would not change their minds. The old guard would not let down their guard. If they let this reprobate music into their ballrooms, all hell might break loose.

Sheila decided to try and persuade Dan one more time.

At one a.m., after the bar shut up and the club closed for the night, Sheila ran into the ladies' restrooms to get changed out of the pencil skirt, blouse and heels Dan insisted she wear at work. She pulled on pedal pushers, low pumps and polo neck sweater, all black – her off-duty uniform. Briefly, she checked herself in the mirror. Shaking out her bun and pulling her eyebrow-length fringe down, she squinted through it as she quickly slicked a slash of red over her full lips. She barely looked at herself before moving on. Time in front of the mirror was wasted time. Sheila was puzzled by women who spent time fussing over themselves. You couldn't change how you looked any more than you could change who you were. Men said they preferred pretty faces so women spent a lot of time trying to make themselves look prettier for them, but Sheila had sussed out long ago that it was all just a game. Seduction had very little to do with beauty, and everything to do with sex. Sheila wasn't 'easy' for the sake of it. She was discerning about whom she slept with. The guys she had sex with, she liked. Sheila needed affection and the human touch as much as the next woman, but unlike most women, she was not prepared to get married to have it. As soon as she felt a guy was getting to like her too much, getting soft on her, she made sure to blow him off. Sheila did not want to shackle herself to one man. She found the very idea boring and frightening. If she could find a man who was her equal, one who would let her work and be herself, then that would be fine. But if there were guys like that in New York, she never met them. She always made her position clear with all her lovers. No strings. Strictly sex. Most men didn't believe her. They convinced themselves that she must be in love with them and sometimes got very offended when they found out that she had not got the least intention of marrying them. Sometimes men fell in love with her. She broke some hearts but, as long as she gave them a warning shot, Sheila did not feel she was doing anything wrong. Intimacy, and the hurt that went along with it, was beyond her. That was the way she liked it.

When Sheila walked into his office, Dan was slightly taken aback. He had never seen her with her hair down before. She looked a bit wild tonight. Untamed. Angela, his wife, was on holiday in Italy for the month. Angela's family were old mafia. They all met in Naples once a year and Dan was never invited. It bugged him how her brothers were always lording it over him as if they were something special. Tough guys. He could tell they thought his wife was too good for him. Nonetheless, Dan had promised himself he would be good while she was away, this time. Plus Sheila worked for him and that had never played out too well for him in the past. She was on about the rock and roll thing again.

'It's not just about the dancing,' she insisted. 'If we get in on the rock and roll scene we could back our own band. Make records. Make a fortune!'

'We're fine as we are,' he said.

What did Sheila know about business? She was a woman. Albeit a smart one and, he had always suspected, a bit of a firecracker.

'But if you don't move with the times, Dan, we'll get left behind and—'

'I'll tell you what, sweetheart,' Dan said. 'Why don't you try and persuade me over dinner?'

'It's one a.m., Dan. There's nowhere open.'

'This is New York, doll,' he said. 'There is always somewhere open. Besides, I know a place.'

Sheila knew what place he was talking about. His place.

Dan was incorrigible but there was something irresistible about him. It was late but Sheila was wide awake and the adventure of doing something illicit was calling her. Maybe it was time to get to know the devil she already knew a bit better.

'OK,' she said, 'but just dinner.'

'Just dinner,' he said. 'I promise.'

Then he smiled and pulled up his crossed fingers from beneath the desk. She laughed.

5

THE AFFAIR with Dan lasted four years. If you could call it an affair. It was a casual arrangement based on attraction and need. There was a kind of fondness, by dint of having known each other for as long as they had and working together. The fact that he was married suited Sheila. When she was a kid, Sheila had known that staying at home making soup and rearing children would never be the life she wanted. The affair with Dan bore out that her early instincts then had been right. Although their affair was sporadic, this was the longest 'relationship' she had had with a man. It taught Sheila that she was too selfish, and not cut out for pandering to a man's needs. Both Dan and Sheila knew that she would never be a threat to his marriage. She would have been horrified if he had left Angela.

Sheila was discreet and accommodating. Dan was great in the sack, and always on hand for company while Angela was tied up with her huge, Italian family.

She was not in love with Dan, nor he with her, but there

was a kind of equality that suited her. Having worked with her through ten years, Dan knew her. He knew what she was capable of, what she wanted. There was loyalty and respect there. At least, that's what she had thought until a week ago, when Dan had called her into his office and told her his fiery Italian wife had found out they had slept together. Sheila was horrified.

'Just once,' he said. 'That's all she knows about.'

'How did she...?'

'She got it out of me,' he said. 'She can be very... persuasive.'

Sheila closed her eyes and grimaced. She was sorry that she had betrayed Angela but mostly sorry that she had found out. She had known the woman, if not exactly liked her, for a long time. Angela knew that Dan was a philandering pig. He had slept with every bar girl, every waitress that had ever come through the door of the Twilight. In fact, his wife would have thought it miraculous that Sheila had managed to hold him off for as long as she had. And just once. That wasn't too bad.

'I'm sorry, Dan, that's a bummer.'

'Yeah,' he said. 'So we better, you know?'

'No, totally. I get it.'

That was that. It was back to business and how it had been before. However, when you sleep with a man, even if he is your friend, especially when he is your friend, everything changes.

Today, less than a week later, Dan called her in to say he had brought a new manager in over her head.

'Angela doesn't like us working so closely together. She doesn't mind you tending bar or being around, but not in a management position. I'll keep you on the same wage but...'

Sheila was seething with hurt rage. She looked across at him.

Her boss, her lover looked sheepish, small, scared – but at the same time his eyes were mean and determined. He meant it. He held all the cards.

'You can't fire me because I don't give a rat's ass about your stinking job! I've had enough anyway! I'm outta here!'

'Baby, please – I wasn't trying to fire you I just need...'

But he was trying to fire her. They both knew it. Dan had deliberately brought the new manager in. Sheila Klein was the feistiest, proudest woman he knew. He had known she would walk out.

Sheila stood and, arms folded, glared at him.

She wasn't leaving empty-handed. She didn't even need to say the word 'severance pay'. Dan reached for his cheque-book, and as he looked up sheepishly she just said, 'Make it hurt.' It sickened her to see him so pathetically sorry.

Sheila snatched the cheque out of his hand, and shoved it in her pocket without even checking the amount. Then she turned on her heels and stormed out of Dan's office, slamming the door behind her.

Sheila ran out the stage door on to Times Square and immediately fumbled in her bag for her pack of cigarettes. As she found them, she realized she was still holding a lit one. The long ember nearly fell into her open purse. 'Shit,' she cursed, and threw it on to the ground. She pulled a fresh one out of the pack and shoved it in her mouth. Her hands were still shaking with rage as she shook and flicked the Zippo half a dozen times before getting a flame. Finally, she drew the nicotine down into her lungs and felt herself begin to calm down.

Sheila thought now of all that she had done for that man. All that energy to try and persuade his lazy ass to get with the times? She had actually cared about his business. It made her feel sick at how damned stupid she had been to believe he might think he owed her something for her trouble. Loyalty? Respect? No. They were things men gave to other men in business. Women were for waiting tables. Sure, make the girl a manager, give her a few extra dollars, but respect a woman for doing a man's job? Nah. Never going to happen. And now he was flinging her out on the street like trash?

She threw her cigarette on the ground, lit another, and walked across to her apartment.

Inside, she went straight to the fridge and took out a cold beer. She flipped the lid of the bottle with her teeth then sat on her small bed, looked out the window and thought about what she was going to do next.

Part of Sheila was raging again at the injustice of having worked all of those years and leaving with nothing but some lousy cash. Money was never the point. Sheila knew that she had forgotten more about music than Dan and his ballroom-owning business buddies would ever know. Yet they were the ones who held all the power. She had tried to help Dan make more money by getting hip to the new scene, but he had laughed in her face. And, as she looked across at the sunlight flashing off the lit-up Pepsi sign, Sheila had a thought, as powerful as the revelation that night when she first heard Bill Haley. Rock and roll was here to stay and so was she. To hell with Dan – he had done her a favour. Losing her job at the Twilight was an opportunity. She was over thirty now. A spinster, for sure, but she wasn't ashamed of the fact. Sheila had known from a young age that she couldn't rely on anyone except herself. However, because she had been working for him for nearly ten years, she had come to rely on Dan more than she ought to have done. She didn't love him, and had only slept with him out of comfort because he was there, and she knew him, and couldn't be bothered to try and find a new, more exciting lover. Worse than that, she had become complacent about her work. Her passion for music had become dulled by time and familiarity.

In the ten years since she had left college, Sheila had never really thought about her life, where it was going or what she was doing.

But that, she decided, was all going to change.

Sheila had always wanted to be a music manager. Out there, on the scene – finding new talent, then bringing them along, turning them into stars, making hits and making money.

She was going to take this slap in the face from Dan as the kick she needed to make it work. There wasn't anybody to push her forward, but that meant there was nobody there to hold her back. She'd flown in the face of convention already just by being a single Jewish woman working in a white man's world. She was going to get herself out there, find herself an artist and start making hit records.

If she got to stick one in the gut to Dan McAndrew and his fuddy-duddy ballroom while she was doing it? Well, that would be a bonus.

She made a start the very next day.

Sheila made a list of all the great musicians who she knew were without formal management, or who would be willing to switch to somebody with her kind of fresh ambition. If she could manage a few established jazz musicians, offering them good bookings and better deals on their existing pay, Sheila believed that would give her the basis from which she could seek out and make investment in completely new talent.

She was delighted to see that the list was long, ten to fifteen definite-maybes – she knew a lot more people than she had realized. The list done, she washed her face, took off her bra and lay down for a nap. Seasoned night worker that she was,

Sheila always rested in the afternoons so she would be ready
to work hard in the hours when most other people slept.

But this time, she could not sleep. For an hour, she lay there,
just staring at the heavy blinds. She noted the slice of sunlight
at the sill that settled on the dusty floor like a ray of hope.
Sure, she was alone – at thirty-one, Sheila figured that was,
more or less, a given now. She had hoped to find love, just like
everybody else, but she knew she wasn't most men's idea of
romance. She was too tough, too outspoken. Plus, she liked
sex for the sake of it, just like a man. Men loved her for that
and all of her best friends were men, but they didn't fall in
love with her. How could they? She was too much like one of
them. Some afternoons, lying alone in her single bed above
the diner, Sheila felt sad about that. But not today. Today
she was going to put them all aside and follow her dream.
Her first love was music, it always had been. Until now she
had been flirting from the sidelines; today, she was going to
jump right in and join the game. Sheila Klein: Talent Manager. Hell, Sheila Klein – Music Impresario. She was only mad
at herself for not doing this years ago, irritated by the part
of her that had set her own ambitions aside out of loyalty to
Dan and – yes – perhaps a bit of fearful laziness too. Those
days were over now. All she had to do was find herself some
talent, and if there was one thing New York had in abun-
dance, it was talent. There was nothing to hold Sheila back.
Not a man, or a job or responsibilities of any kind. She was
as free as a bird to pursue her dream and, hell, was she going
to fly.

She leapt out of bed and checked her watch. Four o'clock.
Her friend Frankie the Sax had a regular gig playing with
a five piece at a dinner club up on Lexington. Frankie was
old-school. He had no manager – he worked all the time

on word-of-mouth and more or less lived in the places he worked. He'd be up there now in the small club kitchen, eating his main meal of the day with the kitchen staff buzzing all around him. Then he'd march out to the bar and drink a few beers, followed by three whiskey chasers, then slide nice and easy over to the stage where he'd be mellow and smiling before the punters came in for the pre-theatre dinner bookings at six.

Frankie was a great place to start and with that knowledge Sheila felt a kick of excitement in her stomach.

Frankie was in the kitchen of the club, as she expected. His long black coat hung down over the edge of the tall barstool, his porkpie hat was perched on the side of his head, white hairs powdered his temples.

'I don't know if that's such a good idea, honey,' he said. 'There's already too many managers in this town.'

'But I know music, Frankie.'

He laughed and shook his head. 'I know that, girl, but I'm telling you – this town's gone crazy. Everything's changed. Soon as a boy opens his mouth to sing these days, there's a man there wants to make money outta him. My day we played for love and whiskey – if the punters threw you a few bucks – well then we got to eat. Now they got every two-bit kid singing before they can barely talk. There was a kid here; I was bringing him along, slow like. He had some talent but I said, you gotta bide your time, boy, wait until your voice matures, until your soul matures. You know what I mean? He ran outta here in a huff. He had heard about some English kid who was writing songs in a "music factory" downtown. I swear, they producing music in a factory now...' He shook his head in disbelief before continuing, 'Would you believe that same kid came back in here last week lording it up in a Mercedes-Benz? Some man from Decca give him a deal.'

'Who's looking after you these days, Frankie?' she asked.

The wily old charmer shook his head again and laughed her off.

'I'm too old and ugly for you to manage, honey. Besides, I don't need no management. I roll along just fine as I am.'

Sheila gave him a peck on the cheek. He helped her put together her list, but didn't seem too hopeful about anyone taking her up on her offer.

However, she was undeterred, and spent the following week diligently trawling all her favourite haunts. She headed out at six every evening, and visited every club, large and small, on the island of Manhattan. She talked to every musician, those she knew and those she didn't know. By Friday, to her disappointment, she realized that Frankie was right. All the great artists she admired already had management and all of the new, younger acts that were worth their salt had already been snapped up.

They were all really enthusiastic for her but nobody wanted to be managed by a girl with no track record and none of them knew anyone that was still looking for management. She talked to just about every musician in town, even the old jazz-hands, but even they had lost their laid-back edge. Suddenly, music had become all about the money. People had been buying records for years, but since rock and roll came along, they were buying a lot more. Music lovers were still packing the dance halls and they were still listening to music on the radio, but now, nearly every home in the country had a record player. This was not simply the 'music business' any more, it was now the 'recording industry'. There was money to be made and, when it came to money, New Yorkers didn't hang around. The club owners, the managers, the music producers and the record companies were all in cahoots with each other. It was one big boys' club. There was a party happening and Sheila was not invited. Making money was a serious business and she knew that being a woman meant she would never be taken seriously. She began to see that while she had partied behind the scenes in the jazz and R&B clubs over the years, she had never actually worked in them. She was, after all, little more than a fan. A groupie. If she had left the Twilight all those years ago, when her instincts told her to, when she had first heard Bill Haley, she could have walked into any club and put together her own rock and roll band. But she hadn't had the guts.

But Sheila was determined. For as long as her savings would carry her, she followed every lead, rooted out every possibility. She kept going to the clubs looking for her star. However, as one week turned to two, and three weeks turned to four, she saw a pattern emerge. It seemed that the more she pushed her friends in the music industry, the more the musicians pulled back from her until, politely, backstage became off limits. Nothing was openly said, but it became clear to her that behind the scenes was not an area open to Sheila any more. Curtains began to be drawn, special areas were cordoned off for 'friends' and 'record executives'. All her old friends were suddenly busy, running off to the next gig as soon as she walked in the door. After trailing around her favourite haunts trying to charm a break out of somebody, Sheila became not only disheartened, but puzzled.

Was she imagining it or was there something else going on?

She cornered Frankie again, this time waiting for him in the diner across the road until she saw him heading into the

Cotton Club. He saw her coming and rushed towards the alley and the kitchen door, but she headed him off on the corner.

'What is going on, Frankie?' she said.

'Nothing, honey,' he said, but his voice was flat and he looked, Sheila was surprised to note, frightened.

'Why is everybody avoiding me? Is there something flying about that I don't know about?'

Everybody knew everybody in New York City. Manhattan was an island, the music industry was a family. When you were flying high it was like being at the best party in the world. When things were bad, it could get very small. Sheila could see in Frankie's face that something bad was going on.

Frankie looked behind her to check if they were being seen talking together. There was only one reason people in New York looked around the streets like that. Suddenly, it hit her. Angela – Dan's wife. Angela McAndrew – formerly Angela Balducci of the notorious Mafia clan.

Frankie shook his head. 'I know you didn't mean no harm by it, honey, I know you don't like trouble. But they are bad men, Sheila – you know who I'm talking about?'

Sheila nodded. 'I know who you're talking about.'

Frankie put his arm on her shoulder and said, 'Sweetheart, they are saying some bad things about you right now.' She looked up into his old face, his eyes were kind and rheumy with sadness. His pity was so gentle, paternal almost, that it didn't offend her. She felt like crying. Like she might collapse into his great coat and stay there for a while.

'It's not just the Balducci brothers neither. They got some Irish mob in their pocket, too. Guy called Joe Higgins been sniffing around asking questions. He owns a small club in Hell's Kitchen but he's trying to work himself up into the big time and looking for the Balduccis to back him. I hear he's real mean, Sheila. Maybe it's best if you left town for a while.'

Sheila nodded and smiled, but her heart was breaking. Leave the city? Was she being chased out by Dan's bully-boy in-laws? Was it possible? But the Balducci boys were a bad bunch all right. Sheila looked at the stern, worried face of her old friend and realized with a growing sense of alarm that this was really happening.

If Angela's brothers were going about town warning innocents like Frankie the Sax off her, no wonder she was persona non grata in the clubs.

'Thanks, Frankie,' she said. 'Maybe I'll do that.'

She kissed him and he said, 'You take care now, honey,' before tapping twice on the big steel door and being let in by the janitor. As Sheila watched him go into the kitchen she knew she was saying goodbye, not just to Frankie, but to a part of her life.

As she walked back towards midtown, Sheila let the reality of what she had just learned sink in. Aside from her dream being shattered, she had run out of money and she needed a job. Nobody would take her on as their manager right now.

There was no point in even trying. If Angela's brothers had got to the smaller club owners, then there wasn't a dance hall in Manhattan that would give her a job washing dishes.

She wouldn't give up. She didn't know anything else. But she would have to get out of the city for a while and figure out how she was going to make this work.

Sheila had made a big mistake. She knew that. Dan was the married one but the woman was the one who always paid. It wasn't fair but she would be dumb to think it would be any different. She had screwed the wrong guy, with the wrong wife, from the wrong family and now – she was screwed.

There was no sense in crying over it. She just had to move on. Where and how, she had no idea. The only one place she knew she could go at that moment was the last place she wanted to go.

Back home to her aunt and uncle in leafy Riverdale – the Bronx.

6

ROSE'S BEDROOM was on the first floor and looked out on to the courtyard at the front of the house. It was just short of midday and a small breeze was tickling the tall bamboo plants that sat in huge exotic pots on the cobblestones. A gang of swallows were swooping across towards the gooseberry bushes in her mother's walled garden.

Rose lived with her parents in a large, stone-fronted house about a mile outside Foxford, on the Ballina road. Dr John Hopkins was the general practitioner in the town and tended to the medical needs of the people of Foxford with great kindness and efficiency. He and the local priest owned the only two cars in the small town.

The courtyard was surrounded by a high stone wall covered with ivy. The stone arch led to a narrow public road down which cars rarely passed. From her window Rose could see the small wooden gate, which led to a hilly field, circled by shrubs and trees. It was part of their garden, but semi-wild. A man came to mow it throughout the summer, but otherwise her mother had her hands full with the rose garden and the walled fruit garden and rarely ventured across the road to 'the hill'.

Rose was sitting by the window, painting, with her easel propped up on the wide, deep sill. The weather had cooled in the last few days and there were droplets of condensation on the inside of the glass. Rose was trying to capture the drops of fluid, with their sparkle and shadows, in a charcoal drawing. She looked across to the field and, from behind a bank of hydrangea to the left of the hill, she saw Patrick's hand waving a blue shirt.

Excited, she grabbed her cardigan from the bed, and ran downstairs. 'I'm going out, Mother,' she called into the kitchen.

'Where are you going?' Eleanor called out anxiously.

'Just taking a walk across the fields to do some sketching. I'll be back within the hour.'

Rose was always careful never to stay out longer than she promised in case her mother became suspicious and followed her. They would keep her boarding with the nuns in Crossmolina till she had finished her Matriculation exams at nineteen, then they would decide what was for the best. But Eleanor wondered sometimes if it was right to keep her daughter so cosseted. Rose saw nobody these days and only went out for the walks she took across the fields with her chalks and pencils. She made rough sketches which she would later turn into beautiful watercolours at home.

What Eleanor did not realize was that Rose's notepad was already filled with detailed drawings of flowers ready to show her mother when she got in after a deliciously clandestine hour with Patrick Murphy. Now, Rose sauntered casually from the house, crossed the road and, as soon as she was out of sight, ran over the hill to the bushes at the back of the hill where Patrick was waiting. She was so happy to see him that she simply tumbled into the arms and began kissing him.

'Did you miss me?' she said. The line of her white neck was taut, her face bent back, lips parted, her blonde curls tumbling down her back, eyes sparkling with unashamed joy. Every time he laid eyes on her Patrick was shocked anew by her beauty. More than that, she seemed to understand him. Rose's passion for drawing was as strong as his own love for singing.

'I missed you madly every minute of every hour and well you know it!' he said, laughing.

'I felt like I was going to go mad these last two days – I was furious when my mother told me we were going to Galway for the day. You do realize it has been nearly a full forty-eight hours since I last saw you? I was afraid you would have forgotten all about me.'

'Never! What was your name again?'

Rose punched his arm, reached up and kissed him briefly on the lips then all over his face, pulling him down with unexpected strength on to the ground until the two of them were laughing and rolling around on the warm, soft grass.

Patrick touched her tenderly, tentatively – running his long, browned hands over the bare skin of her neck and her arms, then, finally, slipping back the strap of her cotton sundress, the creamy curve of her shoulder. After the christening touch, he gently kissed each place in turn before kissing her mouth, reaching into her with a hunger that made her whole body ache. She felt passion race through her in a wave – as if she was drowning again and he was the only one who could save her. Rose knotted his fingers with hers then reached their intertwined hands and arms out to their sides. The push and pull of pushing their hands away from their bodies was a dance of discretion; a way of holding each other while stopping themselves from taking the next step. Their young, vital bodies hurt with a yearning but they both knew they could not go too far. While Rose, at only eighteen, was recklessly in love, she knew it was her responsibility, as the girl, to hold herself back from luring her lover into trouble. They were in enough trouble already just seeing each other.

Rose knew that she would never experience a love this strong, this certain ever again. This was the love Hollywood films were made on. The instant passionate knowing you have, one for the other. Rose would do anything she could to protect it.

In the last few weeks she had even withdrawn from her dearest friend, Patrick's sister Sinead, because she was afraid that she would have to confide in her and Sinead might confide in her own parents. The easy-going Murphy family would probably be delighted to see their son happily in love with their daughter's friend, but Rose's parents would be a different matter altogether. Deep in her heart, Rose knew they would not approve. To supplement their small farm, Patrick's father worked in the local woollen mills, and his wife and six children lived in a two-bedroom smallholding with three cows and a handful of sheep and two small fields just outside the town. They were respectable, but they drove a horse and cart and did not own a car. They were not the sort of people the Hopkinses would invite to take tea in their drawing room and they would certainly not allow one of them to marry their precious only daughter.

Rose pushed Patrick back then shook her head quickly from side to side to break the spell. She sat up and straightened her hair then leaned back against the bark of the narrow tree and took out her pad.

Patrick ran his hand in frustration through his thick hair, puffed out a deep breath and let out a short, angry sigh. He lay on the grass in front of her and Rose felt the gaze of his blue eyes on her as she reached into her pocket for a pencil.

'Stop looking at me,' she said. 'I'm the one with the pencil. I'm the one looking at you.'

'You're so beautiful – I could look at you for ever,' he said, and meant it.

'Well don't,' she said smiling. She felt thrilled when he told her she was beautiful. 'Look over there at that tree while I draw your profile.'

Reluctantly, he turned his face, his eyes rolling back towards her.

'Stop,' she said. 'I'm serious, I want a drawing of you.'

In the shadow of the tree, his face relaxed, his deep tan revealing white crow's feet around his eyes. His nose was strong and his browline high, his eyes glinted shards of blue and grey. In that moment Rose could see and feel that Patrick was not simply a young man, but nature itself. He was the earth beneath them and the sky above. As complex and beautiful as a tree or a flower – as significant as a single blade of grass in an endless, lush, green field. While she sketched the lines of his face she tried to capture not simply a likeness of his good looks, but the essence of who he was. Deep, sensitive, artistic. Other girls saw the handsome, dark-haired bad-boy. None of them could know what lay underneath. None of them could know what she knew about him. None of them could feel his spirit the way she could. Rose wanted to define his spirit in a drawing so that she could show him how much she not only loved him but could see him for who he was. If Patrick saw himself how she saw him, if he knew how well she knew what lay inside him – he would love her for ever.

He would never look at another girl. She would be the only one.

Under the dappled sunlight she looked so perfect Patrick could not believe he had found a sweetheart as delicate and beautiful as this girl was. The wind touching the leaves sent dappled flecks of light across her pale skin and the blonde curls tumbled over her shoulders. Patrick watched Rose as her eyes flicked across and then down at the page. Something about the way she was so absorbed in her work, the confident skill and the way her small hand moved across the paper, brought such a stab of love in his heart that he said what he was thinking out loud.

'I love you.'

As the words came out of his mouth he wondered if he should be saying them. Although he could feel that he loved her in his heart, it was the first time he had ever said it to her. Indeed, at twenty-five, it was the first time he had said it to any girl – and he had been with plenty. It was always worth thinking carefully before you gave a girl ideas. Otherwise she might think you wanted to marry her.

Patrick reassured himself that he was only telling the truth. He had meant the words fully when he said them and, oh, but she was beautiful, so beautiful.

He sat up and reached across, gently taking the pencil from her hands. Then he gave a broad smile, before taking her face in his hands and kissing her softly on the lips.

'I love you too,' she said.

Patrick was visibly relieved. It was out now – she loved him back. They loved each other. She was the girl for him – it was settled. They could date now, and all the others would leave him alone. He could take her to the pictures in Ballina and show her off to his friends and family.

Patrick did not question the ease and speed with which she had replied.

'I'll come down and talk to your father,' he said brightly, 'so we can put a stop to all this secretive nonsense and start courting properly.'

He hadn't noticed the way that Rose's hand halted on the page when she heard him say 'I love you', or how she had begun drawing again as she said, 'I love you too'. Neither did he sense that her kiss was not as passionate as he might have imagined it should be after the first declaration of love. When the kiss was over she prodded him playfully in the chest and said in a firm, gentle voice, 'Sit back how you were – I'm not finished drawing you yet.'

She smiled at him, dazzlingly, which he took to mean utter happiness. In fact it masked the fact that Rose did not know quite what to say. The very fact that he had told her that he loved her was, for an older lad like Patrick, tantamount to a marriage proposal. Patrick was not some stupid boy of eighteen, mooning over her. At twenty-five it was time enough for him to get married and if you told a girl you loved them, especially a girl like Rose Hopkins, the doctor's daughter, that was what you meant.

Until now she had assumed that Patrick understood that the secrecy was because her parents would not approve of him, not because her parents would not approve of the fact that they were courting without serious intention of marriage.

She could not hurt his feelings by telling him that her parents would not think that he was good enough for her. Of course he was good enough, he was too good. Rose knew that she would never find anyone who understood her as he did.

Never find anyone who would complete her the way that Patrick did. She had not realized that she had been incomplete without him until that day at the lake when he had swooped her up out of the water and kissed her. Now, she could not go back to being without him. She would only be half of who she was. Rose didn't know why that would be but in the hours she was not with him a terrible ennui descended on her. When she was with Patrick she felt powerful, fulfilled, whole. Just being with him rescued her from herself. They were soulmates, she knew that. Much as her parents loved her and wanted her to be happy, they did not understand her as Patrick did: the life and death nature of her drawing, the passion she felt for nature, but mostly, the all-encompassing love she felt for this man. There was no way that her pragmatic father and anxious, snobbish mother could begin to understand Patrick and Rose's love for each other. Her parents would find a way of putting a stop to the romance if it became public.

'Let's run away,' she said.

As she said it Rose had no idea what she was suggesting. All she knew was that she could not have Patrick going to her parents' house and talking to her father. She could not bear the thought of seeing the disappointment in her father's face or the fear in her mother's eyes when she found out her precious daughter had been 'running about' with 'that Murphy boy'.

'We could go to Dublin: I finish school in a year.' An idea began to take shape. 'You could go ahead of me and get digs and a job. I could go to art college and you could sing. You know you'll never get work singing around here.'

The more she spoke, the more Rose started to believe that it could be true. They could go away and start a life together in the city. It was where they both belonged anyway – the artist and the singer, there was nothing for them around here. They would have to get married, of course. But once it was a fait accompli and her parents saw how happy she was, and that Patrick was a good man, they would come round to the idea. They had already agreed to let her go to college, more or less, so this would be the perfect solution. If she and Patrick started dating here, now, in the small town of Foxford, her parents would disapprove. That would not stop them, of course. Their love was too strong. Nothing would stop them. But nonetheless it would taint the beauty of what they had. If they ran away and got married her parents would have no choice. They would have to continue as normal and, in time, they would come around to loving Patrick too. Rose knew it would all work out. It had to all work out, it was just a delicate situation and she knew she had to be clever about how she would make it all happen.

'It sounds a lot simpler to me to just tell our families that we are doing a serious line...' he said. 'Besides, I hate all this creeping around, putting charcoal stains on your dress so your mother thinks you are drawing flowers – we're not doing anything wrong.'

Rose began to panic.

'My father would be really upset,' she blurted out, 'because you are so much older than me. I am still his little girl and—'

'—he's afraid I'm not going to be a gentleman and that I'll defile you.'

Then he leant across and grabbed her by the waist. 'Maybe he's right about that too, aghrá!' And he tickled her so hard that she dropped her pad, clutching at her skirt with her charcoal-covered hands and squealing with delight.

Patrick settled his body in behind hers, putting his arms around her neck so that they hung, temptingly, in front of her breasts. 'So that's why I should go and talk to him,' he said, kissing her neck and adding, 'I can reassure him, tell him we're serious. Tell him that we're to be…'

Patrick frightened himself, coming so close to saying the word 'married' out loud.

Rose was happy that he had left the word hanging in the air. She turned around and sat, with crossed legs, facing him, patting down her skirt between her legs so that her pants weren't visible, the light cotton tucked into the curve of her thighs.

She said, 'Let's just keep it the way it is for now. I'll be nineteen in a few months and, if they don't push me into the convent in the meantime, we can talk about it then.'

Patrick smiled and nodded. 'Sure,' he said.

In truth, Patrick wasn't ready to get married. To Rose or anyone. He was still waiting to see if his father could get him a job in the Foxford Woollen Mills so that he would have a steady enough income to help him pursue his singing career. Not that he had any idea how he might go about that. All he knew was that he could sing as well as John McCormack and everyone said he was as much of a fine thing as Elvis Presley. He had his regular gig in Ballina town hall playing the Saturday-night dances, which made him a big deal locally. But although his skiffle-playing friends were happy with that, Patrick dreamed of bigger things. The world was changing – Bill Haley and Jerry Lee Lewis had seen to that. In the past year, rock and roll had started to creep into the dance halls around Ireland. Even the priests had been powerless to stop the jiving, jitterbugging revolution. Everyone Patrick met told him that he was so good it was only a matter of time before he was 'discovered' and became a famous singer. Patrick always laughed off the accolades but, deep in his heart, it was what he wanted. At twenty-five he had finally come to realize that it wasn't going to happen for him in Mayo. He had to get himself somewhere – London, Manchester, America, anywhere that he might be discovered. In reality, he had never travelled any further than Galway. His father said he didn't have it in him and Patrick was starting to wonder if perhaps his father was right.

Maybe it was the time just to bite the bullet and move away. Perhaps Rose was right and the move to Dublin wasn't such a bad idea. He could pick up some casual building work, he was a decent enough carpenter when he wanted to be. Although where would they live? How would they live? A lot of lads went to London but he had never managed to scrabble together the fare. The Hopkins family had money. Perhaps her father could loan them the passage over. Although, they'd have to be engaged before he could even ask for anything like that – and if they went to London, or even Dublin, they would have to marry for sure.

Patrick looked at her sideways for a moment and a small feeling of doubt crept into Rose's heart. Perhaps he was changing his mind about the whole thing. Perhaps her reticence about telling her parents had upset him. Had he guessed at the truth? Should she go ahead and tell them, and to hell with the consequences? Then they could run away together. It would be crazy but they loved each other so much, she knew they'd manage somehow. That would be the right thing to do: honour their love. Be brave. Be fearless as lovers should be.

But before she had time to put words to her thoughts, Patrick said, 'We'd best be getting back.'

He helped gather her things as she shook down her skirt, then as he leaned in to kiss her goodbye, Patrick stopped and picked out a daisy head from a tangle of curls on her shoulder.

As he looked at her face he felt overwhelmed by the sheer wonder of how beautiful she was. He desperately wanted to pick her up in his arms then lay her down on the grass, give in to his most base desires and take her, right there in the open country. He knew from her pleading eyes that she would not stop him. In fact, he believed she wanted it too. But she was too young, and they had already taken things far enough. Even if he didn't feel like it, even if it went against every natural desire in his body, Patrick knew he had to be a gentleman.

So he simply smiled, then they kissed and parted under the tree, as they had done a dozen times before.

As she walked back over the hill towards home, Rose felt a sheet of melancholy fall down over her heart, although she could not say why. Their kiss was tender, and sweet but nonetheless it had felt, to Rose, like an ordinary goodbye.

7

ELEANOR HOPKINS was preparing dinner when she looked out the window and saw Rose coming towards the house from the small hill across the road. Her appearance was messy, as usual. Her cotton dress was crumpled, her slim athletic legs, on which she refused to wear stockings, were doubtless spattered with muck where she had trudged through a puddle in her flimsy plimsolls. And, Eleanor noted, her hair was not tied back in a neat bun like her own, but instead it tumbled around her shoulders, probably full of tangles that she would have to try and brush out that evening.

Eleanor tutted to herself disapprovingly but, at the same time, felt a flash of fear. Although Rose was a good girl, with her quiet demeanour and her love of art and her good manners, she had a savage beauty that worried her mother. She looked untethered – wanton. Eleanor had always tried to keep Rose tidy as a child, tying back her hair and containing her growing curves in smart clothes. Now that Rose was eighteen, Eleanor did not have any jurisdiction over her daughter's wild beauty.

She often felt powerless over her adopted child and worried about her growing older in a way she believed she might not have done if she had been her own. Rose did not have Hopkins blood so how she turned out was God's department. Eleanor could only hope He knew what He was doing. Sometimes, anxious Eleanor wished she was more like the ardent rural Catholics. They seemed to get great comfort from their faith, with their whispering confessionals, endless chanting novenas and statue-turning, candle-lighting, medal-kissing rituals. Eleanor was reluctant to leave her daughter's welfare to God alone. She loved her too much. She could barely express her fears for her daughter, even to her husband. He would have said she was being irrational, but he only half knew the truth about his wife's experiences before they met. He would not have wanted to know more, even if she could have told him.

As her daughter neared the house Eleanor thought Rose looked more pensive than usual. These days, she came back from her walks fresh-faced and happier than usual, as if refreshed and invigorated by the combination of open air and creativity. At first, Eleanor had been worried that Rose was sneaking off to see a boy. But, on reflection, she didn't believe her daughter would be that duplicitous, or that she would be afraid to confide in her mother about such things. Eleanor kept her own fears away from Rose. She always kept her voice breezy when she talked about young men, encouraging Rose to get to know that nice Anthony Warren, who had just got a place studying law at Trinity, or Bishop Richard's son, who would be home from Harvard this summer. Middleclass Catholic men from educated homes were thin on the ground, but then, no girl in Mayo was as beautiful and as cultured as Rose Hopkins. Eleanor knew that her daughter would not be stupid enough to throw herself away at some local boy.

In any case, Rose never stayed out later than an hour and always came back with charcoal stains on her fingers and dress. She generally left her sketch pad on the kitchen table and, while she washed her hands in the scullery sink, Eleanor made a point of having a quick flick through. It was always filled with exquisite pictures of flowers and trees. Eleanor fretted about her daughter's ambitions to be an artist and how it would affect her chance of securing a nice boy. The uncertainty brought a tightness to her chest.

'You worry too much about her,' John would say when Eleanor voiced her concerns. 'She's a good girl and it would be a terrible shame to waste that talent. Let her go off to Dublin and see what happens. She has to learn to make her own way in the world.'

When John talked like that, Eleanor knew he did not have the first idea about Rose. She could not say why she felt that her daughter was heading for trouble. Only that her maternal instincts told her Rose, her beautiful Rose, was more sensitive than most. 'Artistic' was how her husband described the raw spirit that seemed to inhabit their daughter: driving her to spend hours alone, drawing. Only Eleanor could see how vulnerable she was. She had none of the practical grounded ways of her friend Sinead. She was winsome, imaginative – not of this world. The idea of her going up to Dublin terrified her mother.

When she came in from her walk today, Rose seemed different, somehow. Her eyebrows were set in a small frown and her lips were tight, as if she was worried about something. She was quieter than usual, and barely greeted her mother as she came in the kitchen door. She was holding her sketch pad and there was charcoal on her skirt.

'Go and wash your hands, darling,' Eleanor said. 'Would you like a sandwich for lunch?'

Rose felt vaguely irritated with her mother. Everyone else in the town had their main meal or 'dinner' at one o'clock, then 'tea' in the evening was bread and jam or a boiled egg. The Hopkins were the only people who had 'lunch' and their dinner in the evening. Her mother said it was because of the hours her father worked, but Rose knew that this 'European' routine was just another way of Eleanor establishing herself as a cut above everyone else. How Rose hated her mother for standing in the way of her love for Patrick. For being such a snob.

'I'm not hungry.'

Eleanor looked devastated, so Rose said, 'I'll just put my sketch pad away then come down for tea.'

Eleanor watched her, clutching her sketches as she walked up the stairs. There was something wrong. Rose was usually very anxious to show her mother the drawings she had done while she was out. Something was not right.

They chatted pleasantly over tea and discussed the upcoming fundraiser for the new church roof. Rose was having some of her small watercolours framed for sale. She brought a selection downstairs so they could decide which ones would be best, but left her pad with her drawings from the day up in her room.

Later that evening, Rose went for a drive with her father. The Catholic bishop was sick and John was called out to the palace. Rose went along so she could sit in the kitchen of the impressively large, if somewhat ugly building, where she would be fed biscuits and gossip by the old housekeeper, just as she had done since she was a child.

And John treasured these outings with his beautiful daughter.

John had adapted better to Rose's maturing than Eleanor had. Their relationship, if anything, had blossomed over the years and when Eleanor saw it she felt a pain and sense of estrangement that somehow she felt powerless to reverse.

As soon as the car pulled out of the drive, Eleanor rushed up to Rose's room, and grabbed her sketchbook from the bureau by the window. She quickly flicked through to the last pages and was relieved to see the usual pictures. There was a sparsely drawn page spotted with poppies, the next had intricate sketches of wildflowers, another page was generously swiped with black charcoal marks identifiable as blades of grass, and then a close-up of a tree trunk that was so extraordinarily detailed Eleanor leaned in to look closer. As she did, she noticed that the page was standing back slightly from the spine. Rose's sketch pads were made of thick, expensive paper. They bought them by post from a supplier in Dublin. Eleanor held the pad close to her face and carefully studied the spine. There was a sliver of black space. The page after the tree trunk had been torn out.

Eleanor checked the dustbin where Rose threw her discarded work. It was empty. She ran downstairs to check the kindling basket where Rose sometimes put her paper waste – also empty. She hared back upstairs and began opening and closing drawers. She searched behind the bureau, lifted the cushions on the window seat and the rug until, finally, she found it, under the bed. A sheet, hurriedly thrown, discarded like lost rubbish. However, the mere fact it had been hidden told Eleanor that it was far from rubbish. It was a secret. When she lifted the page and saw what it contained, her worst fears came to life.

It was a portrait of a devastatingly beautiful young man, his eyes seeming to flicker off the page, gazing out mournfully into the distance. Eleanor recognized him instantly: that useless good-for-nothing, slick-haired gutty-boy Patrick Murphy.

Eleanor put her fist to her mouth and cried out in anger but also in pain. She did not know if she was more afraid of the fact that her daughter was in love, or of the man she was in love with.

Furious, every instinct made her want to march over to the Murphy house and tell the young man to keep his filthy hands off her precious daughter. But Eleanor had enough sense to know that would not work. How many times had she herself been warned as a young woman? It had made no difference to Eleanor and would surely make no difference to her daughter either.

She would have to be smarter than that.

Her hands shaking, Eleanor put the room back into order, carefully placing the picture under the bed in exactly the same position she found it so that Rose would never find out that her mother knew her secret.

Patrick was delighted with himself. Tony had given him a lift into Ballina on the tractor that morning, and he had been in to see the manager of the town hall, Liam Brennan, about securing a regular Saturday-night slot. Liam fancied himself as a music impresario and was bringing in a showband from Athenry the following weekend. He wanted to know if Patrick and the lads could support them.

'Come in an hour earlier than usual. The good news is, we're charging double on the door and so we'll be able to throw a few pounds your way.'

A paid gig. It wasn't much, but it was a start. Patrick was

humming 'Singing the Blues' to himself as Tony dropped him off at the bottom of the lane to the house. As he turned in the gate he stopped singing. There was a car outside the house. That could only mean the priest or the doctor, neither of which, as a rule, brought good news. His mother had been ill last year and had been sent up to Galway for a stay in the hospital. When she came home, nobody exactly knew what had been wrong with her, her being a woman and all, but they had known it was serious because his father had said it was a miracle to have her back at all. When Patrick saw Dr Hopkins's car he instantly feared she might have had a relapse, but then, as he came towards the house he saw his mother at the front door saying goodbye to the doctor, and she looked fine. Another, even more ominous, thought began to form in his head.

Patrick nodded a greeting at the doctor, taking his hands out of the pockets of his blue jeans, trying to look more respectable. He wished he had worn his trousers and jacket into town, but he had wanted to look with-it meeting Liam.

'Patrick,' Dr Hopkins said, nodding at him cheerily.

'Grand day, Doctor,' he said.

'It is that, Patrick – I hope it holds for you.'

Patrick thought to himself, That wasn't so bad. If there was anything wrong the doctor wouldn't be passing the time of day with him like that.

'And you, Doctor, you might take the roof down on the car and give her full tilt one of the days before the summer is out.'

The good doctor laughed and said, 'Indeed!' before tipping his worn trilby and getting into the car.

There, Patrick thought to himself. A grand man. No mention of Rose or anything like that at all. Probably just calling in to check up on Mammy and she looks fine so...

As soon as he got into the house, however, Patrick sensed all was not fine.

His mother's smile, so radiant for the doctor, disappeared the second they were inside. His father was puffing on his pipe at double speed.

'Have you been carrying on with Rose Hopkins?' he said, before Patrick's mother had even closed the door behind them.

Patrick didn't know what to say. He had never been caught out lying like this before. In truth, he had never yet lied – or done anything very much that was worth lying about. His parents were easy-going people. His father had taken him to the pub for his first pint when he was sixteen and, aside from teasing the odd bull over a wall, or, when he was very small, stealing the occasional cigarette, Patrick had no reason to lie to his parents about anything.

He had no reason to lie about this either, except that Rose had not wanted people to know. Or rather, had not wanted her parents to know, for some reason.

'I don't know about carrying on. We've been very careful…' That sounded awful. 'I mean, I've kissed her and that…' Why was he sounding so guilty? 'There's nothing illegal about it – I'm a man of twenty-five and she's eighteen – a woman.'

'She might be of legal age, Patrick, but she is still a girl,' his mother shouted at him. 'The same age as Sinead! Your baby sister!'

Patrick was confused now.

'Sinead's been dating Tommy Fleming since she was sixteen, and he was only a year behind me in school.'

'That's not the point!'

'Well what is the point?'

'The point is, you shouldn't have lied…' his father said, still tut-tutting hard on the pipe.

'I know, Da, I'm sorry, it's just that Rose didn't want people knowing. She wanted it kept secret for a while.'

His father just raised his eyebrows; his mother was flustered.

'Look, son,' she said. 'It's just that you can't go about...' She paused, then seemed to gather herself up into a fury again before saying, 'You can't just go about the place messing around with the doctor's daughter.'

'We weren't messing around – I already told you—'

'I mean – dating the doctor's daughter. You can't go about dating her.'

'Why not?'

His mother looked to his father for support and his father shrugged and looked back at her, raising his eyebrows, then looked Patrick straight in the face and said, 'Because you just can't.'

He looked back at the fire, as if ashamed of the outburst, then released a long stream of smoke from his barely opened lips, before tapping some of the ash on to the stone grate beside him. Slowly, he picked up a snifter from the tobacco tin by his side, and pressed it down into the smouldering bowl. His father only ever relit a finished pipe immediately when there was something wrong.

Patrick knew what was being implied here. He just didn't want to believe it. It wasn't her age that bothered them. It was her social status.

'You think I'm not good enough.'

His father continued to look into the fire.

'It's not that, Patrick,' his mother pleaded. 'Please try to understand.'

Patrick was her eldest child. Her blue-eyed baby boy. A laughing, sweet-talking charmer of a boy, he had been star of the church choir. When his voice broke at fourteen, the priest and organist had been distraught. By sixteen he had developed a deep baritone.

Mary's eldest son had owned her from the day he was born. She adored him. There was not a woman alive good enough for him. But even so, the humiliation of the doctor calling to say that her son had been carrying on with his daughter was terrible. Dr Hopkins had been such a gentleman about it too. Not even saying how wrong it was or anything – just did they know? It was clear, though, that he didn't approve. In all fairness, Mary Murphy thought to herself, how could he approve of his daughter going out with Patrick?

'Oh, I understand all right,' Patrick said, and marched out of the door. He grabbed his bicycle from the front yard without a backward glance and cycled into Foxford. He wasn't going to be told by anyone that he wasn't good enough for their daughter. His family were hard-working, God-fearing, honest people.

Twenty minutes later Patrick walked into the Mayfly, the small hotel in the centre of town. Dr Hopkins looked up from his sandwich and coffee and his face flickered with something like disappointment before setting itself in a grave, but friendly way.

He said, 'Patrick. Won't you sit down. Can I get you a pint?'

'I don't drink,' Patrick said, then realizing how ludicrous that sounded, added, 'During the week,' which was true.

'Tea? Coffee?'

Patrick shook his head. He felt nervous. Perhaps this had not been such a good idea.

John Hopkins's face was benign and comforting, full of concern and kindness, as it was when you went to him as a patient. Suddenly Patrick felt bad for carrying on with his daughter and not telling him about it.

'I know why you are here, Patrick.'

'Dr Hopkins, I'm sorry that we've been sneaking around but—'

'Patrick, it's all right, really.' Patrick was relieved. This was a lot easier than he had thought it was going to be.

'I understand that you love my daughter and want to marry her.' Patrick tried to keep the surprise off his face. He had been expecting some kind of a ticking off.

'And while you are a very fine young man, Patrick, I am just concerned, as any father would be, as your father would be if Sinead was being asked for her hand, as to how you are going to look after her?'

This was way more than Patrick could deal with on the spot. He tried to steady himself and come up with something, anything, to get himself out of, or indeed, into this fix. He wasn't entirely certain what he wanted any more. Did he want to be with Rose and married? Or be with Rose and not married? Had he, indeed, asked Rose to marry him? He was sure he would have remembered if he had. What had Rosie told her father? Had she sent him here to put pressure on Patrick to get married? No. She was the one who had wanted to keep it a secret. This was clearly why. Patrick was certain he loved Rose but how could he say to Dr Hopkins, 'I love your daughter but I am not sure if I want to marry her'?

Or, perhaps, he did want to marry her but, like the good doctor, was unsure how he would keep her? Patrick had had an idea about that too – what was it?

'If I could just know, Patrick, that you had prospects, abroad even, then perhaps we might come to some kind of an arrangement.'

There it was!

'Well, sir...'

'Please call me John.'

'Well, John, I had been thinking about going to London. Perhaps getting something set up over there and then sending for Rose, when she was finished school, of course, and after we were ... you know ...' John looked at him quizzically until he said, 'married.'

'And you'll need some money to help you set up first?'

The way he said it, straight out like that, made it sound cheap, as if Patrick was begging for money, which he wasn't. Then, the good doctor smiled, his kind, soft features sort of crumpling in on themselves, and Patrick knew he didn't mean anything bad by it.

'I may be able to help you, Patrick,' he said.

Then he leaned over and he patted Patrick's hand, as he had done when he was a child, to comfort him before an injection.

Dr Hopkins had a cousin in New York who owned a large golf course and clubhouse. They held a lot of functions there, weddings, dances, 'that type of thing', he said. John was going to contact his friend and see if he could get Patrick a job there. Of course, he would have to start doing some work in the kitchens and waiting tables, but his friend was very well connected and would surely help him to get on in his singing career.

If things worked out, which of course they would, because John had always known Patrick Murphy to be a bright, intelligent and ambitious young man, Patrick would let John know when he had things set up, then he could send for Rose. John would organize everything from this end. But there was one proviso: Patrick was not to tell Rose he was leaving.

'She will be so upset,' John said, 'and you know what the ladies are like, Patrick. They don't always know what's best for them. Look how she kept you a secret from us.'

It was true. If Rose had been out in the open about their relationship from the beginning, this could have happened ages ago and his parents would have been spared their upset.

Patrick left for Dublin the following week. He wrote Rose a letter explaining everything and saying goodbye. John assured him he would deliver it as soon as possible, and pass on his details in New York.

'She will be upset at first, but you know you're doing the right thing, don't you?'

Patrick explained it all to his parents. His father said nothing. His mother was upset that he was leaving, but told him he was right to take the opportunity when it was handed to him.

As he left the house for Dublin with his small suitcase strapped to the back of his bike, he kissed his mother and said, 'Don't cry, Ma, I'll be back soon. I have to come back anyway, to get my Rose. She'll be mad as hell at me – but she'll know it was something I had to do.' Then he turned to his father. 'A man's gotta do what a man's gotta do, Da – isn't that right?'

His father raised his pipe at him, winked and smiled as his mother wiped her tears away with the hem of her apron.

'Back soon,' he shouted as he wobbled down the drive on his bicycle, 'with my first million!'

If he had turned round in that moment, Patrick would have been hurt to see that neither of his parents looked entirely convinced.

8

THE SUIT was delivered to their home in Yonkers three days before the wedding. Ava hung it on a hook behind her bedroom door then opened the bag. It was as beautiful as she remembered it, but she didn't try it on in case she didn't ever want to take it off again. Ava was afraid the reflection she had seen in Sybil Connolly's Plaza studio might have been a mirage, a fluke of lighting that made her appear better-looking than she was. So she decided to wait until the day of the wedding before putting it on again. In the meantime her mother's years of nagging paid off. Ava decided her new suit needed a new hairstyle to do it justice. She made an appointment with her mother's local hairdresser, Miss Parrish, where she picked out a picture from a magazine of a hairdo similar to Miss Connolly's – a short, ear-length bob. Two hours later, Ava's mousy hair had been dyed a few shades lighter, cut short and set into rollers. As Miss Parrish took Ava out from under the dryer and began to brush out her curls, even the matronly hairdresser was shocked at how different her young client looked. From a gawky lump of a girl to a sophisticated young woman.

'We have found your style at last,' she said, delighted with herself. Then Miss Parrish went to her handbag and took out a compact and well-worn Revlon lipstick. She patted Ava's nose and chin with the powder, applied a slick of pink and said, 'There you are. The prettiest young woman in Yonkers.' She felt a tear come to her eye. Turning ugly ducklings into swans was her calling.

Ava smiled at her own reflection. She could not help it. Everything about her face looked different. Her neck longer, her nose shorter, and her skin creamier. First the suit, and now this. How her life had changed in just two days.

'Thank you,' she said to Miss Parrish. 'I feel like a new woman.'

Ava indeed felt like a different person walking back towards her car. The new Ava. She was the sort of woman who could walk into a shop and buy a new outfit for herself, just like that. Could acquiring this new confidence really be as simple as knowing her own style? It seemed so. Ava flicked her new hair and held her chin high, proud of her tallness and the elegant demeanour it gave her.

She could not wait to get to the wedding to show off her new self.

The following morning the Brogans drove to Our Lady of Dolours Catholic Church in Westchester County to Gloria Dolan's wedding. Nessa was in a bad mood with her husband and he was not sure why. Earlier that morning she had said to him, 'Doesn't Ava look wonderful?'

'Very smart,' he had replied, barely looking up from his paper.

The two women had been fussing around the kitchen

putting on lipstick and readjusting their outfits and he was worried they would be late. On their way out to the car Nessa had taken him to one side and berated him for not making more of a fuss of his daughter's new look.

'Can you not see how she looks so much better?'

'Better than what?' he asked. Ava joined them before she had the chance to tell him off any more, but Nessa gave him the silent treatment all the way to the church.

As they got out of the car Tom finally got the message and awkwardly told Ava, 'You look lovely.'

Ava laughed and said, 'Thanks, Pop,' and winked to let him know she knew Nessa had put him up to it.

Tom was flooded with such love in that moment for his little girl that he said, 'You always look beautiful to me, Ava – you know that, right?'

'I'm your daughter,' she said. 'You're prejudiced.'

But still, it felt good to be told.

After the church service they followed the other cars to the Westchester golf club where the lavish reception was being held. Tom was a member here, although he played seldom. His position as chairperson of the Connaughtman Association kept him busy most weekends. The charitable organization ran a supper club in their local church centre once a month to help support young Irish immigrants. They raised funds and gathered clothes and care parcels to send back home to the impoverished communities, as well as providing support to help them find work and settle in New York. Barely a week went by when Ava and her parents were not at some function or another. Most of these family events were held in the half-dozen Catholic church halls and Irish clubs around the area of Yonkers/Riverdale where they lived. However, this wedding was fancier than most.

The Irish community was tight-knit, so Ava saw plenty of people she knew. One or two of them passed her by, seeming not to recognize her, which delighted her even more. The style was top drawer; all the men wore expensive suits and the women were filling the room with wide new-look skirts, and some in candy-coloured day suits like herself; the older women in hats, the younger women wearing jewelled headbands cut close to their coiffed hair. Ava was delighted that she could match any of them. So was Nessa, who was dressed head to toe in an emerald-green ensemble. She was in her element. Ava knew what was on her mother's mind but, for once, it didn't bother her. In fact she was delighted to see her mother so happy.

As they entered the lobby, Nessa nodded at a passing hat and said out of the side of her mouth, 'There's Kitty and Kevin Flanagan – the crème de la crème,' then seeing her husband was about to remove his jacket hissed, 'Don't even think about it!'

Tom raised his eyes to heaven and headed towards the bar, while Nessa grabbed her daughter's arm and rose up on her toes exclaiming, 'Holy God! Is that Rose Kennedy?' then deflated. 'No. Bridie Connor. Same hair – similar height – still,' she said, taking heart as they walked through the elegantly laid-out lobby with its swirling patterned carpets and Formica side tables, 'with this upmarket crowd I wouldn't be at all surprised.'

They wandered over to the seating plan and Ava saw that she was at a different table to her parents, at the same table as Niall and Dermot Dolan, sons of the judge. Nessa was temporarily dumbstruck with excitement and before she had the chance to open her mouth Ava gave her a look that said, 'not a word'.

Ava knew Niall Dolan from her Thursday nights at the Emerald Ballroom. While he was great fun and they liked each other, like all of the young men she was friendly with, Ava knew he wasn't interested in her romantically.

She had never met his older brother Dermot before, although she had heard about him from her mother's endless gossip of who was (and wasn't) eligible in the Irish community. Dermot was eligible. A lawyer, he had followed in his father's footsteps, graduating with honours in law from Harvard five years before, and his star, as a brilliant young defence attorney in the New York District Attorney's office, was rising. He was known for using his charm and legal skills to great effect when representing the underdog, and had a reputation for compassion as well as a sharp mind. However, he was still single at pushing thirty, which meant he was probably a charmer and an impossibly good-looking womanizer, like his younger brother. The mere thought of sharing a meal with a dashing man who would doubtless dismiss her, would normally have made Ava feel inadequate and sad. However, today was different. Today, Ava was feeling hot-to-trot.

Walking away from her mother, towards her table, Ava could feel her body inside the armour of her outfit; the prickle of the snug lace against her skin, the movement of her buttocks as they brushed against each other in the tight skirt, the broadness of her shoulders against the smallness of her waist – it all made her lift her head and straighten her back with a poise that felt unfamiliar and yet, utterly as it should be. Ava found herself walking with confidence and grace; like a panther in pink. As if the instruction from her frustrated deportment teacher in finishing school had finally sunk in!

She got to the table early and when she saw she was sitting next to Dermot Dolan she reached down to move her place card to another part of the table. She was feeling too good about herself to be ignored by some snooty lawyer. However, she caught the cuff of her silk blouse on the name placeholder. As she went to release it she noticed the white lace of Sybil Connolly's blouse peeping out from under, and the perfectly turned cuff of her pink suit with its three pearl buttons, and she felt a clip of pride again at her beautiful outfit.

'Won't you sit down?' Dermot Dolan appeared next to her. 'It's Ava Brogan, isn't it?' he said. 'I think we've met before.'

Dermot was an ordinary-looking man, not at all like his dashing brother. He was also stout, a few inches shorter than she was, with a large, soft face, full of good humour and warmth. He was certainly not handsome, but he seemed kind, and Ava was relieved. He looked like the sort of man it might be fun to have lunch with.

Ava saw something in his eyes, too, that she had not seen in any man before. A sparkle that said he found her attractive. Inside, she smiled – a broad, triumphant smile. On the outside, however, she fought to keep her face aloof and somewhat imperious. She was in a Grace Kelly suit and she was going to play this ice-princess cool. That was the way to get a man. At least, that was what Myrtle always said. Ava hadn't a clue herself.

'Have we?' she said, raising one eyebrow slightly before sitting down. 'I really can't remember.' He looked crestfallen and Ava felt bad and quickly said, 'Oh yes, I remember you now,' even though she didn't. 'You're a lawyer, aren't you?' For once she was glad of her mother's eligibility briefings.

Dermot pulled her chair out and once he was sitting next to her he let out a large sigh saying, 'Ah – that's better. We're the same height at last!'

Even though she was trying to play it cool, Ava could not

help but let out a loud, impulsive laugh. Immediately she regretted it, thinking he might think she was laughing at him.

'I'm sorry,' she said.

'No need to apologize,' he said. 'Thankfully my ego is as diminutive as my body.' Which made her laugh again.

'You have a beautiful laugh,' he said. Nobody had ever said anything like that to her before. Ava thought it was strange, but also sort of wonderful.

'Would you like a cigarette?' Dermot's younger brother Niall sat down on the other side of her and held out a box of Lucky Strikes. Ava did not especially enjoy smoking, but she took one anyway. Dermot had his lighter ready and clicked it before Niall had the chance to strike a match.

Niall gave Dermot a murderous look. Was it possible her new look had engaged Niall's interest too?

'There's a really fantastic band booked for later, Ava. They'll be coming on after all the old folks have gone to bed – it should be a blast.'

'Fool,' Dermot said. 'Does Ava look like a teenybopper jiver to you? She's a sophisticated lady – a woman of taste, am I right?'

Ava took a drag of her cigarette and smiled at him sideways. She could feel the excitement bubble up through her. Was it really possible that two of the most eligible brothers in the room were fighting for her attention?

'Ava and I know each other, actually,' Niall said. 'We are regular dance partners, isn't that right, Ava?'

Ava smiled and nodded – enigmatically, she hoped. She was enjoying this. How she wished Myrtle was here to witness her debut as a flirt.

'All girls love to dance, Dermot, and if you didn't have two left feet you might know that.'

Dermot blushed, and set his chin defensively at his brother.

'I can waltz,' he said, and then turning to Ava explained, 'That's the only dance a true gentleman needs. It is the dance of romance.'

'Back in the eighteen hundreds maybe,' Niall said, winking at Ava. 'Dermot has broken more bridesmaids' toes than I've done the jitterbug!'

Then another young man butted in from across the table, 'Lots of rock and very little roll – that's what they say about Dermot Dolan!' And another joined in: 'Remember the time you twisted your back pulling Mary Murphy under your legs at Josie Kane's wedding?' The whole table laughed.

Dermot was red-faced with embarrassment and mumbled to her, 'I'm afraid dancing is not my forte.' Ava decided that she definitely liked him. There was something soothing in his gentle manner and the way he was happy to put himself aside. Most men were such boastful bores.

Over lunch Dermot told her all about his life. She knew most of it already from her mother and from general gossip in their social circles. He told her about his volunteer work ministering to the legal needs of the poor in the area. He was proud of his Irish roots and asked how she felt about the Republican cause back home and how they were fighting to get their land back from the English oppressors.

'My father fundraises for Sinn Fein,' she said.

Ava knew a good deal about Irish politics from her father. She read the Irish newspapers as well as the American ones. Dermot seemed impressed that she knew something about both things and kept questioning her. The conversation made her feel clever and important in the way conversations with her father did.

During the speeches, Dermot had to get up and give gifts

to the bridesmaids. His speech was witty and articulate. And as the room filled with laughter she felt a small snap of pride. As he praised the bride's beauty his eyes moved across the room to her. When he came back to the table he rested his hand gently on Ava's as if to apologize for having left her for so long and continued to attend to her, lighting her cigarettes, pouring her coffee and passing her petits fours.

The band came on stage and began to warm up for the bride and groom's first dance.

'I believe the singer is very good,' Dermot said. 'He is recently arrived from Ireland, so I believe.'

'No rock and roll then?' Niall butted in. 'Will I have to wait until later, Ava, before I steer you away from my selfish brother?'

The opening verse of 'Down by the Salley Gardens' came floating across the worn, wooden dance floor and the bride and groom began their first dance.

'Aha,' Dermot said. 'A nice slow start. May I...?' He stood up and reached for Ava's hand.

'This song is my father's party piece,' she said to Dermot.

'And it's a waltz,' he said. Then clasping her hand added, 'Could it be any more perfect?'

It was Ava's turn to blush. She could barely believe this was happening to her. Being asked up for the first dance, and a waltz! She did not even dare look across the room at her mother. Nessa would have to be hospitalized with sheer joy.

As they joined the wedding party on the dance floor Dermot placed his hand firmly on the small of her back and clutched her right hand awkwardly in his left. Ava's initial thrill waned somewhat when she realized that Dermot was, indeed, a clumsy and disjointed dancer. With a terrific confidence that his skill did not warrant, he clunked her about on the dance floor with a heavy foot, bruising the tips of her toes with almost every step, and driving her off in a straight line away from the dance floor. Ava redirected him firmly just as the singer came and took his place at the front of the stage. Ava could see that he was around her own age. He was wearing a deep green velvet suit. His hair was soft black curls, his eyes – she could see even from here – were a striking blue.

She could not say if his face was handsome or not because he wore an expression of such ecstasy as he sang 'Down by the Salley Gardens' that she could almost feel his emotion sliding over her skin.

The deep, glorious sound of the young man's singing voice affected her so deeply that Ava could feel her legs weakening beneath her, as if she were about to faint. She loosened her back and arms and sank her head on to Dermot's shoulder.

Delighted with the intimate gesture Dermot relaxed his footwork so that the two of them were simply shuffling on the spot in a sideways embrace. He closed his eyes and drank in the perfume of Ava's hair. He distracted himself from the closeness of their bodies, her breasts against his chest, her breath on his neck, by planning how he could capture her affection. Perhaps he would make a statement and take her for lunch during the week to the Law Society Club. That would impress her. It would show Ava, and her family, that he was serious in his intentions.

9

'I DON'T WANT him in Dublin, or even London where he might come back,' Eleanor had said. 'I want him as far away as possible.'

John had persuaded her that New York was the best option because his cousin owned a golf course. 'He can give him a job and we'll be able to keep an eye on him.' Although he had said it to appease her, Eleanor knew that John had wanted to keep an eye on the lad to make sure he was all right. She would have sent him to Australia or South America and let him fend for himself without a second thought. She felt certain, too, that the wretched boy would have just taken the money and gone anyway. Although she was more afraid of him coming back.

John did not say anything directly to her, but she knew he thought she was being too hard on Rose and the lad. If it had been left up to him, Eleanor felt certain that he would have let the romance play out, right there, in front of all their neighbours. He didn't know how these things could come to a sorry end. He had married the first girl he had fallen in love with, which was her. He could never know the pain that bad decisions in love could make when you are young.

John felt guilty, about lying to his daughter as much as about banishing the boy, but Eleanor knew that they were doing the right thing. In time, Rose would forget this silly lad and Eleanor would fix her up with a nice man from a good family. Someone with a profession. A lawyer or, ideally, a young doctor who could join her father in the practice. In the meantime she would indulge Rose by letting her go to art college. She might even rent an apartment in Dublin and join her there so she could keep a close eye. Eleanor intended to keep a very tight rein on Rose until she felt confident that her daughter's future was certain and safe. This business with the Murphy boy had been a warning shot across the bows. They had caught it just in time, it seemed.

It had been almost six months since they had banished Rose's young man to America. A week after he had disappeared Rose was due to go back to boarding school in neighbouring Crossmolina. She refused point-blank to leave Foxford when the summer ended, saying she would prefer to sleep at home and had no interest in the company of the other girls. Her parents knew it was because she was hoping that Patrick would appear under her window one night, and she wanted to be there. As it was her final school exams year, her parents conceded. So John was forced to drive her to and from Sligo each day for her studies. It was an hour's drive there and back, very disruptive for his working day, but he felt so guilty that he conceded. As each day passed, Rose grew more and more silent and withdrawn. It broke John's heart to see her suffer so, and every day he felt an increasing compulsion to confess. But the lie seemed to grow larger, his actions more difficult to explain. As time went on, and she didn't get better, his cruelty was less easy to justify. John felt he had no choice but to try and draw her into jolly conversation, with less and less success until they simply sat in a terrible sad silence, Rose nursing the secret of her broken heart alone, and her father knowing what was happening, that he had caused it, and yet unable to do or say anything about it.

Christmas came and went, but the pining didn't go away.

Rose was listless and sad all the time, with barely the energy to pick at her food before going straight up to her room after dinner. She withdrew from her parents completely. They tried to persuade themselves that she was upstairs drawing, fighting to deny the fact that she was no longer coming downstairs to show them each finished piece as she had done since she was a child. In truth, both of them knew that she was simply sobbing into her pillow after Patrick Murphy. Both of them had expected her to be upset, but as two months turned to four and Rose grew thinner, John became genuinely worried that his daughter was losing her mind. Even Eleanor was beginning to doubt that she had done the right thing.

One evening, after they had made a particularly excruciating effort to please her with a coq au vin dinner and her favourite fresh cream sponge from Clarke's in Ballina, Rose had stumped up to her room immediately afterwards. Her face was stricken with grief. John was heartbroken, watching her slowly climb up the stairs as if her navy school stockings were too heavy for her legs.

As soon as she was out of earshot he turned to his wife and said, 'It's not right, what we are doing, Eleanor. I have to tell her the truth.'

His wife's reaction was so immediate and so strong that it frightened him.

'You will do no such thing.' Her voice was an angry growl. 'You think you know, but you know nothing. She's upset, but she'll get over it. If she carries on with him...' She stopped abruptly and began clearing the plates.

Eleanor was prone to hysterics so John didn't push any further, but he resolved to find a way of talking to Rose over the coming days.

Patrick had been sending letters to Rose, care of John, as they had arranged. As the letters came through, Eleanor had, of course, absolutely insisted that they should not be passed on. So, when Eleanor went to stay with her sister for a few days, John decided to act. He knew his daughter would be angry and upset, but she would see sense, he was sure, and in any case this terrible situation had to end. By the time Eleanor came back from her sister's house, the situation would be sorted out. So, before he called Rose down for her breakfast on this Saturday morning, he went into his office and unlocked the bureau drawer where he kept cash and confidential documents. But, as he reached to pull out the unopened letters from Patrick, the telephone rang. Dr Hopkins ran quickly out of the hall to answer it. His was one of five telephones in Foxford, including the postmistress's and the priest's. If it rang on a Saturday morning, it was probably an emergency.

'Come quickly, Doctor, Enda fell down – he's not breathing.'

Katherine Pryor from just down the road. Enda's second heart attack – he could save him again, but he'd have to act fast. John grabbed his bag from the hallstand and ran out the front door, without even closing it behind him.

When he started up the car, Rose looked out the window and saw him leave.

It was safe to go downstairs.

Weekends were hell these days. She could not stand to be around her parents. Even though they had not known about her relationship with Patrick, some part of her felt that if they had known the cause of her misery they would have been pleased. Possibly even gloated. The mere fact that she could not tell them about this huge, consuming sadness that she felt in losing the great love of her life was enough, in itself, to carve a huge chasm between them. How could they possibly understand the pain she was feeling? It was as if somebody had cut off one of her limbs. She had not known how much a part of her he had become until he had gone.

His family had told her. Sinead had said, quite casually one day, 'Patrick's gone to Dublin. It's all very mysterious. Somebody offered him a job in America and off he went. Just like that!'

'Just like that.' Rose's heart was broken.

She didn't believe it at first. Patrick would never leave her, and if he did, he certainly wouldn't do it without saying goodbye. Without offering some kind of an explanation, a note, something. But there was nothing. Nothing but a big empty hole where love had once lived. And not just love, it seemed now, but hope and her future and all the dreams and ideas she had of them being artists together, out in the world, painting and singing. Two beautiful people in love, ready to set the world alight. Without him, she wasn't beautiful any more. Without Patrick she had no fire, no heart. She was a shell. She wanted to die.

How could her parents possibly understand? Anyone understand? Except him. And yet he was the very person causing all of this. She had loved him, she had trusted him with her heart and also with her soul. And now, in breaking that trust, he had not only broken her heart, but scooped out her soul too. Rose was lost. Bereft. Broken.

However, she was also occasionally hungry. Just never in front of her parents.

So as soon as her father's car took off at speed down the drive, she knew it was an emergency – probably a heart attack. They were the most popular emergencies around here. Her father did love saving lives. The glory of it kept him going, so he would probably be spending half the day driving to the main hospital in Galway and back. With her mother away, that gave Rose a full day on her own in the house. This meant that she could be depressed, but without the pressure of knowing that her parents were watching her. She couldn't enjoy her cake with her parents gazing at her, wondering if her eating was an indication that things were getting better. Which, of course, they weren't.

As Rose came down the stairs she noticed that the front door was open. While she was closing it, she noticed that the study door was wide open too and the drawer on her father's bureau was pulled out. John always kept his desk drawer tightly locked because he often kept a lot of money in there. He banked most of his takings but liked to keep a good deal of cash in the house as well, for paying the gardener, or getting the car fixed – although she often heard her mother complain about it. Rose had an immediate fear that perhaps they had been burgled, and that her father had rushed out in pursuit – before reminding herself that he would hardly have taken the car. Somewhat intrigued, she walked in and laid her hands on the brown leather desktop and, as she did so, she saw an envelope just tucked into the drawer, as if it had been half pulled out when her father was disturbed. Picking it up, she was confused to see it was addressed to her and in a familiar hand. Under it were two more. Her stomach sank and her hands shook as she tore open the first envelope.

MY DARLING ROSE,

By now your father would have told you about our wonderful plan to set everything up for our future together.

He has sent me over to America to a cousin of his, a big, important man called Desmond, who runs a golf course, and I'm going to work there for a while until the singing takes off which please God won't be too long. America is the home of rock and roll, Rose, and I'm so happy to be going there as you can imagine! The English lads like Tommy Steele and Cliff Richard, well they're all right but America is where it's all happening! If I am going to be discovered, that's the place to be. Jerry Lee Lewis? Sure, he'll only be trotting after me once I get going! I might be the new Elvis yet! Now, I know what you're thinking, Rose – you're thinking but if he's the new Elvis he'll have all the women screaming after him and there'll be no room for the likes of me! Well you know that will never happen. You are the one for me, my wee Rosie Hopkins. Here I am sitting on an aeroplane, up above in the sky among the clouds – looking down on Ireland which is smaller from up here than you can imagine. I should be off the head with excitement and looking out the window and thinking of all the adventures ahead of me. But all I can think about is you, my darling girl, aghrá. It has been so hard these last few weeks, pretending I didn't want to see you. I hope you got my last note saying I was away up to Dublin for work and that, and you didn't go thinking that I had abandoned you altogether – although you would know me by now that that would never happen. That was the hardest thing of all, not seeing you or being able to tell you where I was going and what I was doing.

But your father knows you the best of all. Better than me even, I'm thinking, and he said you would try to stop me going. But, Rose, my darling Rose, this is the best thing for us, and that is certain. I've nothing to give you back home (except all my love and kisses and more besides!) but in a few short months I'll be able to send home for you, pay back all the money I owe your father for his kindness in sending me here although I know he did it for you, more than for me, because he wants you seen right with a man with prospects, someone you can rely on. That's what I want too, so that's why I came without stopping to say goodbye. I hope you'll forgive me – and I know that you will.

My darling Rosie, it will be so hard to not see you again for a while. And oh! How I have been longing, this long time we've been apart, to wrap my arms around you and feel you breathing into my neck and the joy of knowing your kisses, time and time again, all over my face, and when I am thinking like that, of what I am missing, even though I'm a man, I could surely cry. But I won't cry, because it will seem a short time coming, with all the work I have to do, before we see each other again. You will have your school to finish and your drawings to do, maybe for art school in New York this time. Although there will be no need for you to work when you're married to a rock and roll star!

Write back to me as soon as you can to let me know you're not mad with me (and if you are take it up with your father ha, ha!)

All my love,
For ever and ever.
Only Ever Yours
PATRICK

P.S. I wrote a song for you. It's the first song I ever wrote, but that day and you drawing me I thought how you inspire me too.

It's not very good, I'm thinking, but I am sending it anyway. I hope you don't think it's silly. The air I had in mind was 'Treasure of My Heart' as I know you love the air. You made me sing it for you often enough as we sat in the field in front of your house. I'll be closing my eyes and singing this out when I want to bring you to mind. You are never far away in my dreams, aghrá.

On a separate piece of paper, with several crossings out he had written:

It Was Only Ever You

I ask myself are you the one I dream of night and day
Are you the reason why this yearning never goes away
I ask myself are you the one whose face I can't forget
Your name hangs gently on each breeze I still can hear it yet
I ask myself are you the one whose gentle fingertips
Caressed my skin and kissed me like an angel on the lips
I ask myself are you the one who filled me with desire
Are those the eyes that once searched mine and set my soul on
*   fire...*
Could it be true... could it really be you... the one I search for
*   in a song and waited for so long... was it only ever you?*

I tell myself that you're the one who fills my every day
Your name your face your touch your smile... you take my
*   breath away*
I tell myself you are the very reason I exist
And when you look into my eyes your love I can't resist
I tell myself that on each breeze I'll call your name aloud
And wrap you in my arms each night through every stormy cloud
I tell myself that without you my life would fall apart

Each season will roll round again each memory break my heart
And now I know that you're the only one who makes my life
complete
And when you whisper in my ear... how my heart skips a beat
There's nothing in this world that makes me feel the way I feel
When I'm with you because I know this love I have is real...
Because it's true... it was only ever you... the one I love with all
my heart... and have done from the start... It was only ever
you... my love... yes... It was only ever you

Rose stood in her father's study, clutching the letter, her head swirling with conflicting thoughts and emotions. Frantically, she tore open the next letter in the pile. It was dated less than a week later, 'The place where I'm working isn't in the city at all but in the countryside – like at home...' She skimmed it and grabbed the next one dated less than a week later. 'The lads in the kitchen are great craic...' then the next, 'I sang at a wedding last night. I bowled them over. It put me in mind of our own wedding darling girl...' then on until she reached the last one. Dated early in November it read, 'Why won't you write me back my Rose. I am so lonely over here without you. Have you forgotten me entirely?'

Rose let out a sob, then a terrible rage ran through her as she realized her parents had tricked her, lied to her, and banished her beloved to the other side of the world. But despite the fury at her mother, who she knew, somehow, was behind this, and the hard slap of hurt she felt at being betrayed by her father, Rose could feel her heart pumping with happiness. This letter meant that Patrick had not abandoned her after all! He still loved her! He had written a song for her! 'It Was Only Ever You'. He had written, 'Only Ever Yours' on each of her letters. It was right here in her hand. She kissed the paper and tears of joyful relief poured down her face. Then she remembered that the date of his last letter was November. Three months since he had written to her. Surely he had not given up? Surely he could not think that she didn't love him?

There was only one thought in her mind now. Rose had to find Patrick and be with him. There was no time for consideration, no time even for anger or regret. She had to get to Patrick and let him know that she still loved him. Rose reached into the back of the desk where she knew her father kept cash and found two fat lumps of bank notes. She had no idea how much was there, but she was certain it was enough to get her to wherever she wanted to go. In any case, she couldn't think about that now. Then she rummaged across to the top shelf of the bureau where she knew he kept family documents and found her passport.

She rammed the cash, passport and the bunch of Patrick's letters into her deep cardigan pockets and ran up the stairs. Taking down the small suitcase she used for school, she stuffed whatever came to hand in there: a few random items of clothing, her sketch pad and pencils. The case being only half full, she had a small revelation realizing that she didn't need very many things after all. But she did need Patrick.

Before she ran out of the house, Rose realized that her father might be home soon and would try and follow her. So to put him off the scent, she ran into his office, found the key to his bureau drawer, and locked it. She then wrote a short note saying that she had gone for a walk and not to wait about for her. As she left it on the kitchen table she had a jolt of conscience, then reminded herself angrily that her parents had been lying to her in the filthiest way possible for the past month. She had every right to lie right back at them.

As she quickly pulled on her boots, cursing at the laces taking ten precious seconds from her escape time, she checked her watch. If she cycled like the clappers she would make the lunchtime train from Castlebar in just over an hour. It was too risky going from Foxford or even Ballina. If she was seen getting on the train, her father could get word of it then be ahead of her in the car and waiting to meet her when she got off the train in Dublin. This way she could abandon the bike and slide on to the train without ever getting caught.

Only after she was in New York and reunited with her true love would she get in touch with her parents and tell them she was alive.

Then they would be sorry for what they had done.

As her bare legs pumped the bicycle pedals as hard as they could, pebbles and mud dashing up from the dirt lane that led her on to the Swinford road, Rose astonished herself with her own strength. This was what love was: this speed, this strength, this certain, unfailing, single-minded knowing that she was on the way to Patrick. He was her match, her prize, her everything and she determined to find him, and keep him – and never let him go again.

10

AVA AND Dermot began dating. Their first date was, as Dermot had planned, lunch at the Law Society Club. They had a nice time, talking easily and laughing loudly into the dark, dusty dining room. However, Ava was considerably less thrilled than her mother at his choice of location and worried that he was trying to impress her parents more than her. He dropped her back to the house just before five in the afternoon, and there was an awkward moment when they stood on the doorstep before he leaned in to kiss her. This was Ava's first kiss. Breathless with excitement, she closed her eyes and puckered up, only to be rewarded with a perfunctory peck on the cheek, followed by Dermot whispering in her ear, 'Sorry, this isn't a sweet nothing but I think your mother is watching us through the window.'

While her heart sank with disappointment, Ava couldn't help but laugh and said, 'Well why don't you kiss me anyway and give her something to tell her friends about.' He swooped her down and kissed her on the mouth. Although

Dermot's arms felt strong and sturdy, Ava was still nervous that he might drop her on to the wooden porch. In any case, the performance being entirely for her mother's benefit, it did not feel as a proper kiss should and Ava felt somewhat cheated after he left.

The following weekend he took her out for dinner. They went to a very nice Italian restaurant in the city. Ava would have liked to have gone dancing as well, but given Dermot's lack of grace in that department she did not suggest it. Throughout dinner, despite his efforts to talk about her, she insisted on grilling him more thoroughly about his work, which she found fascinating. As far as she could gather, he defended criminals, which she thought was terribly glamorous and exciting, although once he got going, much of his talk was about the intricacies of the law and court procedure and she could barely make head or tail of it.

'I'm sorry,' he said. 'I'm an awful bore when I get going.'

'Not at all,' Ava said. Although, truthfully, she had been a little bored. For the first time in her life, she had the feeling that she had met a man who liked her a great deal, and although she liked him too, an awful lot, she was not quite so sure how she felt about him romantically. Was there something missing that should be there?

If Dermot had been able to see inside Ava's heart, he would have been dreadfully upset, although not entirely surprised. He knew what he was good at, and that was The Law. When he was in court he could be clever and charming. With his law friends and negotiating almost every area of life, he was a titan of a man. But when it came to girls, he fell down. He was able to make them laugh and generally enough girls liked him and enjoyed his company. They just never seemed to fall in love with him. Dermot, with his keen, lawyer's detachment, knew he wasn't good-looking like his brother and he certainly wasn't a good dancer. Also, he wasn't 'dangerous'. Dermot was the sensible option, considerably more popular with girls' mothers than he was with the girls themselves. There was never any shortage of young women interested in him. Nice girls who were keen to do as their mothers told them and try to win over the unremarkable-looking, pragmatic but very successful lawyer who could offer them a good life in exchange for warming his slippers and cooking his suppers, and hanging off his arm at the occasional law-society dress dance. But Dermot wanted to choose for himself. And he chose Ava Brogan.

The fact that Ava was Tom Brogan's daughter had only registered the first time he had seen her, six months previously, at a Connaughtman fundraiser. His attention had been caught first by her laughter. The delightful sound of a woman letting out a broad, raucous guffaw had arrested him from across the room. When he looked across, he saw this fine woman, with her head thrown back, standing head and shoulders above a group of small, delicate, rather silly-looking creatures. He thought she looked magnificent and immediately had a feeling that this was the woman that he wanted to spend the rest of his life with. It was as simple and as complicated as that. He had fallen in love, and he had not the first clue what to do about it. So, lawyer that he was, Dermot thought it through. She was relatively unadorned – no fancy hairdo or jewellery – wearing a dress that seemed nondescript next to the fluff and froth of puffy skirts and the jewellery of her friends. She looked like his sort of girl. The sort of girl who wasn't embarrassed to throw her head back and laugh. Perhaps, as she didn't seem to set great store by glamour, she might not mind a man being somewhat stout and ordinary-looking.

'Who is that tall girl with the loud laugh?' he asked Bridie Flaherty, a rather annoying friend of his mother's who was always trying to pass herself off as Rose Kennedy.

Bridie grimaced. 'Ava Brogan, Tom Brogan's daughter.' Then, assuming he was more offended than interested, added, 'They only had the one, thank God!'

Dermot didn't even hear her. Already he was marching over to Tom, his hand out in that convivial Irishman-about-to-do-business pose, asking for an introduction to 'your charming daughter'.

Ava had held her hand out politely, and said, 'How do you do.' But her voice was flat and uninterested. Of course, asking to be introduced by one of her parents had been a stupid thing to do. So unadventurous. So mundane. The act simply complemented his ordinary appearance. How, Dermot thought, could the cleverest lawyer in New York have done such a pedestrian, obvious thing? Before he even had time to register her total lack of interest, the wretched band struck up. There was a second when Dermot could have grabbed her hand and whisked her on to the floor and shown her what a fun-loving, exciting, downright hilarious, good-time guy he was. He wanted to do it so badly, that he could almost see the action unfolding in front of him. Except – it did not. Dermot could not dance. He had no sense of rhythm and was, in fact, so clumsy and self-conscious that he knew he was not just an uncomfortable partner, but downright off-putting. So Ava rushed on to the dance floor in a frenzy of excitement without him. She was immediately grabbed into a wild, skilful jive by his brother Niall.

When Dermot saw what a great dancer she was, his spirits fell. She was laughing, and thrashing and bursting with joy. His own heart was bursting watching her, but after a few moments of despair, he resolved that he would find a way of getting through to her. He would just have to bide his time and be smart.

So when his parents were making plans for his sister's wedding, Dermot made sure that the Brogans were on the guestlist, and that their daughter was sitting next to him. He had to agree to Niall sitting on the other side of her because he did not want to alert his parents to his plan. He also paid the band to make sure the first three dances were waltzes.

Meeting Ava again at that wedding, and wooing her, had been the greatest night of his life. The fact that she had been more sophisticated, and somewhat more elegant, than he had remembered her just made Dermot feel all the more pleased with himself for having successfully secured a second date. Now he just had to make sure he could keep hold of her long enough to get her to marry him. He had no doubts. Ava Brogan was the girl for him. She was funny and clever and seemed to have the same steady outlook on life as himself. He could not say that she was beautiful, or not beautiful – only that when he looked in her bright, interested face, he understood beauty in a way he had not done before. From that first afternoon, Dermot felt a warm glow of recognition in his heart that told him they were meant to be together.

By the end of their second date, he felt that he might be starting to win Ava over. And, to a certain extent, he was.

The food in the restaurant was excellent, and Ava did love her food. She ordered spaghetti and Dermot watched, delighted, as she scraped up every last piece of the tomato sauce with her bread.

'What?' she said, blushing slightly as she noticed him gazing across at her with his chin in his palm. 'Am I making a show of myself? It's just so delicious.'

'I'm just thinking that's the most satisfying two dollars I've spent in a long time. I love hearing you laugh, and I love watching you eat. Is that strange?'

'Yes,' she said, waving a piece of bread at him. 'Very!'

She shook her head, smiled and kept eating. She noted that she felt as comfortable as if she was eating at home with her own family, and wondered if that was a good thing.

After the meal they drove up to a parking spot he knew. It was half an hour from the city, so she realized that he must have planned it. He took the roof down on his car and they sat and looked down on to the city lights.

Ava sat and waited to be kissed. Properly this time. But first he asked her if she would like a boiled sweet, he had some in the glove compartment. She was so irritated by the suggestion that she nearly exploded, but just then he leaned across and kissed her tenderly on the mouth. It was different from the kiss on her parents' porch. That had, really, just been pretend. This kiss was soft, and sincere and full of feeling. It was not the passionate, earth-shattering experience she had been expecting (and perhaps rather hoping for), but rather a gentle heart-melting. After they had kissed for a while, he took a small rug off the back seat and laid it over her legs, saying, 'To stop the night chill troubling your knees, m'lady.' In actual fact, he needed to cover up her lusciously long legs to keep his desires in check.

On the way back to Yonkers, Ava rested her head on his shoulder. She felt warm, safe and thoroughly happy. She was with a nice man who liked her and had kissed her. Life was good, better than she could have dreamt it would be.

When Dermot dropped her home, he kissed her again, more passionately, with an urgency that suggested he would have liked to go further. Ava felt reassured and flattered by his desire. They made an arrangement to meet again the following weekend. Then midweek for a movie, then the following weekend for dinner again, and another midweek movie.

Six dates in a row meant that they were now officially sweethearts.

On their seventh date, as he was leaving her on the doorstep of her parents' house, Dermot turned back and said, 'Ava, I want you to know that I'm serious about my intentions towards you.'

Ava smiled, and then bowed her head modestly, although in truth she was smiling inside at his formal use of language. 'Thank you, Dermot,' she said. She knew what he was driving at. 'Serious intent' was the precursor to marriage. Her mother would be thrilled. So would her father, even though he was less anxious to see her settled and away from home.

Dermot put his hands on her shoulders and patted them reassuringly.

'You know, this is not a casual affair for me. It is no fling.'

'Oh, kiss me like you mean it!' she said. Then he laughed, and did.

Once inside, Ava thought about Dermot's use of the word 'fling'. She did not feel particularly 'flung', to be honest, and doubted he had ever had a such a thing in his life, although, of course, neither had she. They were not 'flinging' types. And the realization that she was dating a man who was as pragmatic and unromantic as she was made her feel slightly sad, for a moment. Was this, really, what love was like? Even their dates were becoming routine, starting at the same time, and ending in the same way, with a single kiss on her parents' porch.

No question of anything more than a kiss either. Dermot's hands were always firmly on her waist when he kissed her. He was as reserved and controlled as his conservative, Catholic background had taught him. Ava was bound by the same religious and social conventions, but she understood too that such rules were to be broken. If one didn't feel like breaking the rules, what was the point of them at all?

Only Dermot knew how much he truly wanted Ava. How he ended each date deliberately early with a demure kiss in order to spare her the full force of his desire. Only he knew how much he longed for them to be married so he could take her in his arms each night and make a true, natural woman out of her.

'How are you and Dermot getting on?'

When Ava got in after their seventh date, Nessa ambushed her in the kitchen. She had finally cracked. Tom had repeatedly warned her not to say a word, but the tension had got too much for her.

Ever since she had ruined her first kiss, Ava was getting beyond irritated by her mother's meddling.

'He says he has "good intentions" towards me, Mom. I assume that means he wants to marry me.'

'Now, Ava, let's not get ahead of ourselves. It's early days yet. But you seem to like each other and that's the most important thing. Just relax and enjoy being in love.'

Ugh. Typical of her mother to try and use reverse psychology tactics.

'Thank you, Mom. You're full of good advice.'

'You're welcome, darling,' she said with a false calm. 'Sleep tight.'

From the kitchen, Ava saw her mother do a little dance at the bottom of the stairs then leap up them two at a time to tell her father the good news.

But Ava was feeling flat. Was this what falling in love was supposed to feel like? She did enjoy being with Dermot.

He was very funny and kind, and it was lovely to get the attention from a man. She liked going out for dinner, and getting dressed up – but in truth, Ava enjoyed her nights out at the Central Ballroom with Myrtle too. She was beginning to wonder if perhaps it wasn't a very good idea, after all, to fix up with the first man who fancied her.

11

DERMOT PLANNED the proposal as if he was preparing for a case.

He found it hard treading that fine line between respecting Ava as a lady and showing her his true feelings. Coming off all manly wasn't the way to go, but he feared, at times, that his acting the perfect gentleman had made him appear mundane. He knew Ava was intrigued by his connections to the underworld and that she loved it when he told her about some of the criminals he had defended. One of his clients, Joe Higgins, had been nagging him to come and have a night out in his club in Hell's Kitchen. It was a risky option, but Dermot wanted to make this evening memorable. Also, Joe Higgins was a silent partner of the golf club in Westchester, where they had first met, and Dermot had an idea about that too.

Dermot called for Ava at seven p.m., as usual. Ava decided to wear her Sybil Connolly suit.

As he opened the car door for her to get in, Dermot said, 'Oh, you've worn your suit. That's nice.'

Ava immediately felt irritated. Then he looked at her oddly and said, 'It's a strange thing to wear for dinner. Any particular reason for it?'

Sometimes, he could just be so infuriatingly blunt.

'Shall I go and change?' she said. 'I can go put on something more suitable.'

He did not seem to notice the sarcastic tone in her voice but said, 'No, it's fine. Actually, I'm taking you somewhere a bit different tonight. We're going over to the bad end of town. One of my clients has a club there and he's always on at me to visit. It might get a bit rowdy.'

Ava could not help herself from thinking, I certainly hope so.

She had once asked him, 'Don't you feel awful – getting these gangsters off from their crimes?'

'I'm not getting them off, darling. Everyone has a right to be defended properly in court. It's how democracy works. Only the very best, thoroughly moral lawyers get chosen to work with the very worst criminals.'

Ava remembered his saying that and how stupid and a little pompous she had thought it was. Sometimes, it seemed as if Dermot thought he knew it all. Like her father.

Dermot drove the car towards the city. Ava looked out the window at the Hudson glimmering over on her right. As she sank back into the comfortable leather seats of Dermot's Corvette and watched the evening sun dropping down behind the water, she realized how fortunate she was. It was wrong of her to be bored with Dermot. He was a good man. He was respectful and thoughtful and had perfect manners. He opened the car door for her and presented her with small gifts of flowers and chocolates on their dates. If he did want to marry her, she wouldn't find anyone better.

She certainly wouldn't find anyone that would make her parents happier.

They drove through Manhattan and into the area that Ava knew to be Hell's Kitchen. This was where the Irish mob – the Westies – operated. She had been there once or twice over the years, accompanying her father in his charitable work. Nobody ever bothered Tom Brogan down here. He was a solid Irishman, a devout Catholic and had a good name across the whole community – including the criminal fraternity. The Westies did not approve of Tom Brogan's do-gooding any more than he approved of their money-laundering and strong-arming, but they nonetheless maintained a healthy respect for each other.

Tom negotiated with Westie bosses to get fairer rents for Irish tenants, with some success, and tried to win back lost souls, with less success. He had seen how easy it was for young men to come straight off the boat to the Irish-centric village where they knew their muscle and drinking and Irish bravado would be welcome. Within weeks the best of them would fall into bare-knuckle boxing, gambling, or some other such criminal activity. What nobody told them was that you couldn't move on from the Westies. Once you were in, you were in for life. The gangster code was unbreakable. Tom tried to make sure young Irish men arriving in New York stayed as far away from Hell's Kitchen as possible, and to settle them into the more suburban areas of the Bronx. Sometimes it worked, sometimes it didn't.

Dermot drove them down a quiet street in what seemed to be a particularly seedy area. As he opened the car door for her, he said, 'I hope you don't mind slumming it tonight, my darling. There is no need to worry. I've kept the owner out of jail so many times, he owes me. We'll be looked after.'

He handed the keys of his Corvette to a huge, rough-looking man who nodded deferentially. Ava felt a small thrill as she realized that her sweetheart was able to command the same respect from these gangsters as her own father.

Inside the door they walked up a narrow staircase into the nightclub. It was a small, dark, seedy room, already filled with cigarette smoke and the chatter of Irish drinkers. This was a very different part of Irish New York to the dance halls: people didn't come here to dance, they came here to drink and to gamble and, very probably, fight. The stage was backed with silver and green tinsel and a paper shamrock banner. There were heavy green drapes on every window, the carpet was green and even the small tables at the front of the stage were covered in green baize. It was like being in a green womb. Dermot and Ava were shown to a table at the front of the stage and a rather shabby-looking waiter brought them a bottle of champagne.

'Courtesy of the management,' the waiter said and Dermot nodded his approval. Everything was going to plan. The waiter poured the champagne; he wondered if perhaps now was the moment. No. He would hold off. Wait for the romantic surprise he had planned.

'This is nice,' Ava said. In truth it was thrilling to be here. She looked up hopefully at the small dance floor in front of the stage.

'I thought you'd like to come somewhere a bit different,' Dermot said. Then he leaned across and whispered, 'I know how interested you are in my contacts in the criminal fraternity, so I thought you'd like to see what a proper joint looked like. I hope the food is decent.'

Ava smiled and said, 'I doubt it – but it is certainly unusual.' She sipped her champagne and looked around, fascinated.

'How was your week?' Dermot asked.

As he was looking across the table at her Ava thought that perhaps she could talk to him about her doubts. Confide in him that she was worried that things were moving too fast. His eyes looked so concerned, so enquiring, so kind – she felt she could tell Dermot anything. As she was thinking this through, the lights dimmed and a man who was as round as he was tall, wearing a cheap tuxedo, came out on the stage and announced, 'Ladies and gentleman – we have a special guest in for you this evening to get the entertainment started. All the way from the county of Mayo, would you please put your hands together for Mr Paa-trick Murphy!'

This is it, thought Dermot. The moment had come. He watched Ava, waiting for her reaction as he slipped his hand into his pocket to reach for the ring.

There was polite applause as the young man came out on stage. Ava immediately recognized him as the boy from the wedding.

She felt her stomach lurch as he began to sing 'The Rose of Tralee'. Ava knew all the Irish ballads. This particular one meant nothing to her, but the way he sang it... his voice... his face... He drew something out of her she had not known was there. He sang with such passion that it was as if he was reaching inside her and making every part of her sing alongside him. With every word he sang, and every breath he took, Ava felt herself being transported to another place. She did not know this person and yet through his singing she felt as if she knew him absolutely.

Dermot loosened his grip on the small box. He had arranged with Joe for this particular singer to be here tonight. He knew how Ava loved Irish ballads and she had been so impressed with him at the wedding.

'It's the singer from the first day we met,' he said, leaning across. The box was out of his pocket, ready to press into her palm.

'Shhhh,' she said. She closed her eyes, ecstatic. Dermot thought she had never looked more beautiful than in that moment. He got a glimpse of how womanly she was. A promise of what the future might bring. He felt so emotional that he had to gather himself. He put the ring back in his pocket. Now wasn't the time.

As soon as the song ended, Dermot reached for the ring again but just then their host appeared at the table.

'Now here's my favourite lawyer!'

Joe Higgins was wearing a sharp, shiny blue suit with a broad-shouldered jacket and slim, straight trousers. A real spiv. 'And this is the beautiful lady you keep tellin' me about?' He took Ava's hand and, before she had fully extended it to him, kissed it.

'This is Ava,' Dermot said somewhat nervously.

'Ain't you going to introduce me?'

'Ava – this is Joe Higgins, he owns this establishment.'

'And several others.' Joe patted Dermot's shoulder. 'Thanks to this character, who got me out of a tight spot last month. I hope you know your fella is a kind of genius when it comes to getting guys like me off the hook?'

Dermot shifted uncomfortably in his seat. Ava smiled. He was inviting her to ask what kind of a guy he was. She wasn't stupid. She could see straight away he was a gangster. She could also see that Dermot was a little afraid of him. Ava wasn't. Her father had always taught her that if you looked a man straight in the eye and told the truth, the Lord would protect you.

'That singer you had tonight was very good,' she said.

'You think?' Joe gave Dermot a conspiratorial wink. It looked terrible. This evening was not turning out as Dermot had envisioned. Joe took a big cigar out of his pocket and clipped the end of it.

'I dunno, I'm not big into the serious Irish ballads. Give me Sinatra any day.'

'He's got a strong voice,' Ava said. 'I reckon he could do a pretty good Sinatra if he was given the chance. Seems to me all he needs is a break and a decent band behind him.'

Dermot stepped in then. 'Did you notice, Ava, he was the guy my father booked for my sister's wedding?'

'Really?' she lied. 'I hadn't noticed.'

Mention of Judge Dolan's name immediately altered Joe's aspect.

'The judge is a man of great taste. Would you like to meet the kid? I can bring him out to you.'

Ava's heart did a small leap. She looked at Dermot, shrugging as if she did not care one way or the other, but implying with a flash of her eyes that Joe might not like it if they refused his offer.

'That would be grand, Joe, thanks. Me and Ava would be happy to have a drink with him.'

That was the engagement off the table. Maybe as he dropped her off? They could go in and celebrate with her folks? Perhaps God was telling him not to try to be such a romantic klutz. Don't try and be something you're not, Dermot, he said. Be yourself. That's always the best way.

Joe went off and came back with Patrick Murphy. His green velvet suit was gone and he was now wearing a pair of shabby brown trousers and a white shirt that looked in need of pressing.

Ava felt a little sick. He had the same slightly lost,

down-at-heel look of the poor young Irish men her father helped. The stage suit had been borrowed, she now realized.

'These folks want to meet you,' Joe said rather abruptly, then clicking for a waiter to bring over another bottle of champagne he went off, leaving Patrick standing there.

'Won't you sit down?' Ava said. 'It's Patrick, isn't it?'

Patrick sat down, next to Dermot. In his shabby clothes he seemed diminished.

'You are a great singer,' Ava said.

'Thanks,' Patrick replied, then looked down at his hands. He clearly didn't want to be here and Ava was sorry she had called him out. He was completely different from the charismatic figure she had seen on stage. He seemed ordinary and out of place. 'Straight off the boat' was how her father described these boys.

'Where are you from in Ireland?' Ava asked.

'A place called Foxford in County Mayo,' he said. 'It's very small, you'll hardly know it.'

'Is that the place that has the woollen mills?'

His face lit up. 'It is surely.'

'Well would you believe it? This suit I'm wearing is made from fabric woven in Foxford Woollen Mills.'

'Get away out of that,' he said, and he leaned over and touched the arm of her jacket. Ava shivered, despite herself.

Patrick's hand lingered, his fingers stroking the fabric, until Dermot let out a small cough.

'I'm sorry,' he said, but Ava could see from his eyes that he wasn't sorry at all and she felt excitement unfurl deep in her stomach.

'Somebody belonging to me would have woven that tweed – it could even have been my father.'

'What a coincidence,' Ava said. 'I was told by the designer

that this tweed was a match for the wild hedgerow roses of Mayo, the most beautiful roses in the world.'

'They are that surely and more,' he said. 'And if I hadn't moved over to this wretched hole of a country six weeks ago there is a good chance that's where I'd be working myself.'

'You don't like New York then?' Ava asked.

'Let's just say it wasn't what I was led to expect,' he said.

Dermot began to feel uncomfortable. He patted his pocket. The ring was still there.

'Why don't you order Patrick a proper drink, Dermot? That champagne is awful. Patrick, what would you like?'

'I'll have a pint, thank you.'

Dermot's eyes narrowed slightly. A small pellet of rage began to flicker inside him, although he could not say why.

'I thought we were having dinner,' he said.

'Dinner can wait,' Ava said, firmly, matching his stare. 'I'm sure we are both interested in hearing what brought Patrick to America.'

Dermot was not interested. He should be – but he wasn't. Was this lad moving in on his girl? No. That was preposterous.

Over the next twenty minutes or so Patrick told them his story.

How he had been invited over to New York by a contact he had understood was a man of influence in the world of music, but who, in fact, was just the manager of a golf club that occasionally held functions. He was given a job in the kitchen and after a few weeks of pot-washing was finally given the 'opportunity' to sing on stage at a society wedding, where he might be discovered. Or not. That was the wedding they had seen him at. Joe, the boss of this place, had requested he come down here specifically tonight, to sing that ballad. He had no idea why. With no car, it was impossible for him to get into the city. If one of the chefs was coming into town, he was able to get a ride in with them. Otherwise, he was stuck out in Westchester County.

'Where are you living?' Ava asked.

He blushed. For the first time since she had mentioned Foxford he looked uncomfortable again.

'Patrick – where are you living?'

Ava knew that unscrupulous employers exploiting young men from Ireland often put them sleeping on the banquettes of their restaurants. They were paid their fares over from Ireland but once they arrived they found themselves doing manual labour and sleeping in their workplace until their fares were paid back. Her father had explained it was not simply a way of the bosses saving on rent money, it also ensured that the young men stayed under their control. They ended up being henchmen or pot-washers: slaves to their own people. These young men were usually too ashamed to tell their families back home the circumstances they found them-selves in and pretended they were doing grand.

Dermot looked at his watch. 'I'm sure Patrick has to be get-ting back.'

This was an absolute disaster. He felt bad for the boy and everything, but it seemed that his carefully executed plan for romance was built on a human rights violation. If Ava found that out, well – it just didn't bear thinking about. He would sort it out in the coming week. Have a word with Joe and make sure that the boy was found something better in the city. In the meantime he just wanted to get this evening over and done with as quickly as possible.

'And perhaps we should head downtown for something to ea—'

Ava cut him off. 'Are you sleeping in the golf club?'

Patrick nodded. 'Just until I pay back my dues – then I plan to get something better.'

'You are coming home with us,' Ava said.

A look of panic washed over Dermot's face and as Ava reached under the table for her bag and began to stand up, he leaned over and held her wrist.

'Do not make a scene, Ava,' he said. His voice was an angry whisper.

Dermot felt terrible, but he had no choice. He let go of her hand and whispered, as kindly but firmly as he could, 'You don't mess with these people, Ava. They are dangerous gangsters.'

Ava felt suddenly furious.

'Do you mean to tell me that you are going to let this injustice continue because you're afraid of some two-bit hoodlum?'

'He is not some two-bit hoodlum; he is much more powerful than that. Also, he is one of my clients and it will be the height of bad manners to make a fuss in one of his establishments.'

Dermot knew that sounded bad, but he was clutching at straws. Also, it was true. Sort of.

'Bad manners?' Ava snapped. 'Your client – the gangster – is clearly taking advantage of Patrick and goodness knows who else. Making them work for a pittance with not even a proper bed as payment? Well, if you won't help him, my father certainly will. My father,' she said, pointedly, to Patrick, 'is Tom Brogan. He helps young men in your situation all the time. If you go and get your coat I'd be happy to take you home with me now, this very minute, to meet him...'

This was worse than Dermot thought. Not only did he look dreadful in Ava's eyes – but would her father think less of him as well?

Patrick was confused as to what to do for the best. On the one hand he had not met anybody since he came to New York who would help him move on from the situation in which he found himself. On the other hand, this warring young couple did not seem like the best option. The girl was one feisty creature, that was for sure. Nice eyes. She was kind – but a handful all the same. The man, Dermot, was right – Joe was a very nasty piece of work. Patrick had been told as much by his workmates; he would shoot a man, or have him shot, for looking at him sideways. Everyone working out at the golf club and here in this dive in town knew not to upset their boss. Patrick sensed that Dermot would be able to look after himself but he worried about the young woman. Joe didn't like women too much.

'My lift is leaving soon,' Patrick said, 'so I'll go back to the golf club, if that's all the same with you. But it was nice to meet you and thank you for the drink, and your company.'

As he stood up to go Ava felt she had failed him. Had she humiliated or embarrassed him in some way?

'You are a wonderful singer,' she said, 'and if you can ever make it into the Emerald Ballroom in Yonkers, I am there most Saturday nights. I know everyone in there. I can introduce you to some people I know, if you'd like. And remember my father's name is Tom Brogan, 175 York Avenue, Yonkers. We're in the book.'

'Thank you for your kindness, ma'am.' Then he bowed slightly, turned to Dermot and said, 'And thank you for the drink. You and your wife are very kind.'

When he was gone, Dermot smiled nervously at Ava.

'Sorry for losing patience with you,' he said, reaching for her hand. 'Let's just get out of this place and head downtown for some spaghetti?'

Ava smiled back but barely heard him. She realized her heart felt a little broken. Patrick had thought she was Dermot's wife. He had not checked her finger and seen that she was not wearing a wedding ring.

12

NESSA HAD got herself into such a fluster organizing this engagement lunch, she began to wonder how she'd ever cope with organizing the wedding itself. Ava was being utterly useless. She had showed no interest in finding a dress to wear and seemed to feel that the lunch menu and choice of flowers were of no importance. How she was ever going to adapt to being an important lawyer's wife was beyond her mother's comprehension.

'Should we put canapes on the coffee table? Or up here with the corned beef?' she said, balancing a tray of pineapple and cheese cocktail sticks elaborately arranged around a radish centrepiece.

'You're making way too much fuss, Mom. Really – it's not like it's the wedding.'

'It is a dry run,' Nessa insisted. 'It sets the tone.'

'We've already had dinner with the Dolans. Wasn't that enough?'

Dermot had proposed to Ava while dropping her home

from their disastrous date in Hell's Kitchen. They had agreed to hold off on telling their parents, and make an official engagement announcement over dinner in the Law Society Club. Dermot, not wishing to appear fusty or old-fashioned to Ava, secretly approached Tom at work and asked formally for Ava's hand. He told Tom that he understood his beautiful daughter was extremely precious and that he intended to respect and honour her, and their family.

Tom was as happy as any doting father could be, having his daughter taken away by another man, and agreed not to tell Nessa before the 'official' announcement. Both sets of parents had guessed, when they received the invitation, and all were thrilled, except for Dermot's mother Donna, a rather snooty and very beautiful Italian woman with a contessa somewhere in her family background.

Over cigars in the smoking room after their meal, Dermot's father, Judge Dolan, said, 'I was delighted when Dermot told me he had decided to settle down with a nice, sensible Irish girl. So easy for men like us to land up with some pretty, money-grabbing flibbertigibbet.' Tom smarted at the inference that his daughter was not pretty, but he let it go. Ava seemed happy. She had adopted a serene sort of elegance lately, a smarter way of dressing, and seemed to have calmed. Tom was not entirely convinced by this 'new' Ava – he liked his wild dancing, joke-around girl, but he supposed this is what happened to daughters when they matured. You lost them.

They had passed a pleasant evening. Tom liked the judge well enough. He was a good man, and between politics and their philanthropic interests, they had plenty to talk about.

Nessa, on the other hand, had found herself overwhelmed

in such elevated company. Desperate to impress Judge Dolan's wife, she was unable to stop herself from babbling, 'Of course, we think of ourselves as "Educated Irish". I much prefer to read than watch television, even though we have two sets. One of them is colour.'

Nessa was not stupid. She knew she was being gauche but the more magnanimous Donna Dolan appeared in the face of her ignorance, the worse she got. By the end of the evening Nessa was in bits. Not wanting to give up easily, she became determined to create an occasion that would show her family to be suitable for the lofty Dolans. And so she planned an Engagement Luncheon.

'It gives the ladies an opportunity to discuss the wedding arrangements together.'

'It gives you an opportunity to show us off as posh.'

'Nonsense, we are every bit as good as the Dolans. In any case, it's very important that Mrs Dolan and her daughter don't feel left out.'

Ava had already sensed that Donna Dolan had very little interest in her son's wedding. She had been polite enough to Ava on the few occasions they had met. But Ava only had to look at her high cheekbones, her black glossy hair tied up in a perfect elegant chignon and smooth olive skin to see she was disappointed in her son's choice. In fact, Ava did not especially mind if her future mother-in-law did not fully approve of her. What she minded, very much, was her own mother's insistence on seeking out that approval for her.

However, it was too late to worry about that now. The guests had begun to arrive. Nessa had staggered her invitation times so that everyone would be waiting when the Dolan ladies came in.

First was Bridie Flaherty, their neighbour, stalwart of their local Catholic church – she would add an air of quiet respectability. Then there was Nessa's cousin Kitty, a widow. She could always be relied upon to turn up in a crisp blouse. Finally, there was Jean Brogan; Tom's troublesome younger sister was thirty-five and a spinster, although she insisted on calling herself single. Jean wore trousers and had a degree. Nessa did not approve, but thought her sister-in-law's presence would show them off as modern thinkers as PJ and his wife were intellectuals. Nessa placed her various friends and relations around the brown shagpile rug in a way that showed off the Formica surround on the fireplace to its best advantage. Just then the doorbell rang.

Patrick was a month in New York before he finally gave up on hearing back from Rose.

'The father was trying to get rid of you, man! Any fool could see that.'

For the first couple of weeks he had believed that Dr Hopkins had made some sort of private arrangement with the owner so that he would be given an opportunity to sing. When the big Irish wedding came, Patrick had been assured that it was his big break. But that very evening he was back in the kitchen washing dishes.

His fellow dishwasher, Juan, had drawn him into a conversation about his past. Patrick was feeling lonely that night and told him about Rose. How madly in love she was with him and how he had come here on the generous patronage of her father to build a life for them both. Even as he said it out loud, scrubbing dishes, side by side with this Hispanic lad from a poor background, he realized he knew how absurd it sounded.

'You been cheated, man. Man, that's bad. Sending you away like that from yo' true love. And he was acting quick too, getting you on a plane. Plane ride would have cost you rent for a year. He sure was in a hurry to get rid of you.'

Patrick went quiet. In his heart he saw it was true. He had been a fool. A stupid fool.

The next day he packed up his things and cadged a lift into town with one of the kitchen suppliers.

He didn't tell anyone where he was going and he went to the only other place he had an address for: Tom Brogan's. He had the price of a taxi fare from Manhattan out to the Bronx in his pocket, not much more. The house looked very grand, so Patrick brushed down his jacket, stood as straight as he could, and rang the bell.

Nessa opened the door with great flourish and her most charming smile, expecting to see the Dolan women, only to find a young man standing there. He was carrying a bag and had the apologetic look of one of her husband's unfortunates. Young men like this called to the door looking for her husband's help quite often – but today of all days! Tom was not due home for two hours. This was a disaster.

'I'm looking for—'

'I know well who you're looking for and he is not here. He won't be home for two hours – at least.'

The young man looked suitably mortified.

'You'll have to go home and come back later. After six o'clock this evening. He'll be able to see you then.'

He had that haunted expression they all had when they landed on her husband's doorstep. Broken dreams. Desperate pride. She felt bad but really – this timing was very unfortunate.

'Grand so,' the young man said. 'I'll call again later. Thank you, ma'am.'

Nessa looked anxiously up the road to see if there was any sign of the Dolan women. They weren't due for another ten minutes.

The man turned, walked down the steps, and then moved slowly towards the path. It was apparent he had nowhere to go from here. He was going to wait out on the street. Nessa started to panic. He could be loitering around when the Dolans arrived. What would they think of the area if they saw a destitute young man sitting under a tree outside their house? And then – if Tom brought him in later and they were still there? That would look even worse.

'Come back,' she called after him. Signalling wildly for him to follow her around to the back of the house, she let him into the kitchen and gave him a bottle of Coke, a chunk of leftover corned beef, some crackers and Tom's newspaper to keep him occupied.

Daisy, their maid, arrived at the back door just in time to serve the guests. She was in full uniform, but before she had the chance to apologize for being late, Nessa said, 'Thank *God* you're here. Arrange those chips around the onion dip and do not let him *move* out of here until Tom comes home. Ah! The door! That's them...'

Patrick could see that this lady, presumably Tom Brogan's wife, had the same fierce look of his own mother when she was intent on something. The big black woman in uniform now glaring at him was closer in age to his grandmother. He knew better than to cross either of them. For the first time since he had arrived in America, Patrick Murphy felt completely safe.

* * *

Ava picked out a red shift dress and cream jacket ensemble and teamed it with a pair of low cream pumps. It had caught her eye in her local boutique the previous week. Although she had developed an interest in clothes, and in presenting a smarter, more feminine image, she could still not quite bring herself to go into the large department stores on Fifth Avenue. She found the vast corridors of clothes and smarmy showgirls intimidating. In this smaller, friendly shop she was always able to find just one thing that suited her needs. She back-combed her hair at the roots, puffing it up into a wide bob, applied a little pink lipstick, and took a deep breath.

'You can do this,' she said to her reflection in the mirror, then looked back at herself quizzically. Why was she dreading this afternoon? This was a dream come true, surely? Dermot's family were going to become her family. She was about to spend the afternoon talking about dresses and flowers, choosing the hotel where she would have her wedding reception. Her parents would give her anything she wanted in order to see her married to a man who was educated, Irish, charming and from a good family. They would give anything to see her happy. She shook her head at her own silliness and headed downstairs.

'Here she is!' Bridie said, waving a cheesy pineapple stick in her direction.

Everyone turned to look at her. A flutter of panic caught in her chest.

Her Aunt Jean waved across wryly and said, 'Late for your own party in your own house, young Ava? I'm impressed. We'll make a rebel of you yet.'

Ava inspected the gathering. Her mother- and sister-in-law-to-be were seated on either side of the new fireplace, immaculately turned out. Gloria had her handbag neatly settled on her lap and was removing her gloves. Donna was cautiously lifting a glass of champagne to her lips. Daisy was standing in the corner, almost hidden behind the orange velvet curtains, looking extremely uncomfortable in the ridiculous uniform her mother made her wear when she was entertaining. As usual, Nessa had left her with nothing to do except look the part.

This whole charade was for her. This was her engagement party. Ava was getting married.

'Ava! At last.' Her mother's eyes flickered slightly in admonishment.

Cousin Kitty came over, grabbed her shoulders and gave her a big kiss. 'I can't believe you are getting married!' Kitty had been at the onion dip and the smell of her breath, along with the feeling of panic that was now pounding in her chest, made Ava urgently nauseous.

'Would you excuse me for a moment?' she said, and rushed towards the kitchen.

She ran through the swing doors and over to the double sink where she retched loudly. Nothing was coming, so she stood up, took a deep breath and reached for a glass to pour herself some water.

'Are you all right?'

'Jesus!' Ava jumped, dropping the glass.

'Sorry, sorry...' Patrick got down from his spot at the counter where he had been wondering if he should make himself known, and began picking up the broken pieces on the floor.

'Oh – it's you...'

'Patrick,' he said, 'from the club.'

'Ah yes, I...' She had been about to say she remembered him but, for some reason, stopped herself. Her stomach started twisting again. Whatever was the matter with her today? 'Be careful – the glass...'

A drop of red fell on to the grey linoleum. Patrick had not noticed the cut. Instinctively, Ava reached across for his hand. She opened his fist, lifted the shard of glass carefully out of it as a pool of blood gathered in the crease of his palm. She reached for a tea towel and gently closed his hand around it. All the time his eyes, those endlessly deep blue eyes, remained steadily fixed on her face. Ava had never been looked at in that way before. She told herself he was simply trying to be brave, although the cut was shallow. Her hand held his. She tried to make him clench his fist to stem the flow of blood, but it seemed he would not. He did not tense his hand. She did not want to let his hand go.

'What the *hell* is going on in here? I thought I told you not to…'

Speechless with fury at this tableau, Nessa said in an angry whisper, 'Get back out there this instant, young lady, and entertain your guests. *You, boy…*' she said, jabbing her finger into Patrick's face, 'get back up on to that stool where I left you and do not move an inch, or so help me God, I will put you back out on the street and you'll not get near my husband this night!'

Ava was so embarrassed that she did not know how to react. Patrick quickly stood up and did as he was told.

At the door Nessa paused and, seeing her good tea towel in his bloody hand said, 'I'll send Daisy in to look after that and clear up this mess. Lord knows she looks as if she needs something to do…' Then she swept out.

Now it was Ava's turn to be angry.

'How dare she speak to you like that!' she said.

Patrick was smiling, more amused than offended. 'She reminds me of Mam,' he said.

'You must miss your family.'

He smiled, gave a little shrug and said, 'What's the occasion?'

Why was he smiling? With a cut hand in a stranger's house? Could it be her? She didn't dare think such a thing.

'It's my engagement party.'

His smile faltered. 'You had better get back out to your guests, so.'

Ava regretted telling him she was engaged, then remembered that in the club he had thought she and Dermot were married. Then, the fact that she had made note of it at all made her feel uncomfortable. She forced herself to focus on her mother's terrible treatment of Patrick, who had, after all, come to their house, at her invitation, looking for her father's help.

She had an idea. 'Has your hand stopped bleeding?'

He checked his palm. 'Yes.'

'Good,' she said, then she ran to the back door, picked one of her father's smart hats off the coat shelf and threw it across the kitchen at Patrick.

He caught it, laughing. 'What's this for?'

'Put it on.' He did as he was told, cocking the expensive trilby over one eye and striking a Sinatra pose.

'Perfect,' she said. 'Now, follow me…'

'I'm not moving,' he said. 'I've upset your mother enough…'

But Ava grabbed him by his sore hand and dragged him through the kitchen door and out into the drawing room.

'Ladies,' she announced. 'I would like you to meet Mr Patrick Murphy – who I have invited along to entertain us with Irish songs this afternoon.'

Nessa's eyes were flaming saucers of fury. Ava was momentarily delighted with herself then suddenly realized she was still holding Patrick's hand. She let it go with a sweeping flourish, inviting him to take the stage in the centre of the room.

Patrick stood there, trapped in the glare of ten women. For a moment he wondered how he had found himself in this situation. The room was fancier, more opulent, than any he had ever been in before. But the lady of the house was Irish and her crazy daughter meant well in finding him an audience. So, Patrick did what he always did when he was uncertain, or nervous, or simply standing in front of a group of silent people: he opened his mouth and he sang.

'Oh, Peggy Gordon, you are my darling, Come sit ye down upon my knee...'

As soon as the words began to flow out of his mouth, Patrick fell into the powerful trance of the born musician. The women found themselves mesmerized as his voice lifted their spirits and carried them off into the world of Irish romance.

'And tell to me the very reason, why I am slighted so by thee.'

Bridie was transported back to her father's knee at the Irish homestead in Ireland she had left behind over twenty years ago; Kitty remembered the day she had married her late husband; Jean thought of the boy she had loved in college. How many years since she had lost him, pretending she didn't mind being on her own? But most struck of all by this young man was Italian socialite, Donna Dolan. She had never cared much for Irish music; her husband's love for fiddle music over classical violin irritated her. However, this young ballad singer had genuine soul and for the first time in her life she began to understand and enjoy the romance of the John McCormack records her husband was always playing. After a while Donna found she was leaning back in her chair, smiling. As the wine and the music began to mingle, she found herself humming along. What a lovely afternoon she was having. It sure beat making small talk with this slightly common woman and her friends. Nessa, seeing Donna's newly blissful demeanour, calmed down somewhat, although as the afternoon wore on, she began to feel uncomfortable about Ava, who seemed more taken with this young man than she ought to be.

She was very relieved when Tom arrived home earlier than expected.

'What's going on here?' he said.

Patrick was leading the guests through a somewhat raucous rendition of 'Home Boys Home'.

'…and it's home, boys, home' – clap-clap – 'home I'd like to be…' The women had all had a few drinks by now; even Donna was pink-cheeked and clapping along to the chorus.

Tom threw off his hat and joined in – '…home I'd like to be – home far away in me own country…' – until the song was finished, and the older women laughed and patted their hair, and began to gather themselves together.

'Hey – seems I've missed quite a party here…'

Ava went straight over to her father and gave him a hug, saying, 'Pop, this is Patrick – he needs your help.'

'Well now, I don't know about that. This young man looks as if he is doing just fine by himself.'

Patrick walked across the room holding out his hand. 'I'm very pleased to meet you, Mr Brogan. I have heard a great deal about you and your kindness from Ava.'

'I wouldn't believe a word this young lady tells you. She's a desperate blagger altogether!'

'I don't doubt it, sir,' the young man said. His eyes flicked across to Ava and he grinned. Tom saw the way the boy's eyes softened when he looked at his daughter. He also noted the expression of barely contained fury on his wife's face.

'Well, Patrick,' Tom said, putting his arm around the young man's shoulder and taking him off into the kitchen, 'perhaps you and I should go out and see if we can find you a job and let these ladies get on with their party?'

'Thank you, sir,' Patrick said. 'I'll just collect my bag from the kitchen.'

'No need,' Nessa jumped in, nodding for Daisy to hand him his knapsack and jacket, before herding the two of them out to the car.

'Perhaps I should go with you?' Ava said.

Nessa looked as if she might explode, so her husband said, 'No, Ava, you stay here and entertain your guests, my dear.'

This whole wedding thing really was bringing out the very worst in his wife. At the same time it was wisest to go along with her, so he gave her a reassuring nod as he put his arm around the young man and led him out through the front door.

As the door was closing Nessa remembered her manners and called out, 'Thank you for the singing!'

Nessa felt relief that this would be the last they ever saw of that wretched young man.

13

ON THE morning after the party Ava asked her father about Patrick, but he put her off, saying, 'I think it's just best for you to concentrate on your wedding plans, Ava.'

She knew that was because her mother was there, so she tried to talk to him about it again later but he simply said, 'Patrick is in gainful employ and living in the city, you'll be glad to hear,' then went back to his paper.

Her father was always eager to talk about his work and Ava was hurt by this rejection. That aside, she was anxious to know what had happened to her protégé. Where was he working and what was he doing? Bartending or washing dishes? Was he singing? If he told her that, then maybe she might be able to ask her father what he thought of Patrick. He had seemed to like him. What had they talked about in the car that day? Did Patrick ask about her? But the subject was not up for discussion and Ava didn't push it. She knew why Tom didn't want to elaborate and he was right. It was disloyal of her to be showing any interest in another man. Thinking about Patrick was the height of silliness. It was wrong. She was engaged to Dermot and things were all set. Dermot was a good, kind man and she wanted to marry him. The church was booked for three months' time and the reception was to be a grand affair in the Waldorf. She was having her dress made by Sybil Connolly, with her first fitting that very weekend. Almost every moment of her spare time since the engagement had been taken up going to see florists, and hat designers, and choosing stationery for the invitations with her mother. Dermot had been very busy with his work and so they had barely seen each other since the engagement. He seemed happy to let her mother, and his, make all the decisions. She didn't mind one way or the other about the arrangements, and she supposed this relaxed indifference was a sort of love. Although it felt like the opposite of passion, not minding one way or the other was easy. But was an easy life what she should aspire to?

Every now and again Ava could not help but think about that afternoon. Even if Patrick had wanted to kiss her, perhaps it meant nothing. Boys kissed girls all the time these days. Dermot had asked her to marry him and she had said yes. That was the promise she had to keep now.

'You do realize we haven't even been dancing for eight weeks?' said Myrtle, when Ava called to ask if her friend wanted to come to the dress fitting with her.

'I'm engaged, Myrtle,' she said. 'Why would I be going dancing with you? I'm not looking for a man any more.'

'Well I am.'

'Nonsense – you've too many of them after you, that's your problem.'

'You were never looking for a man anyway,' said Myrtle. 'You just loved dancing…'

'Love dancing…'

'Well it doesn't feel like it – all the gang are asking where you are.'

'Dermot hates dancing,' she said.

'You can say that again,' Myrtle said. 'I danced with him once, at Patsy Kenny's wedding. He took me round and round in one direction, over and over again. It was like carrying a tree trunk from one end of the dance floor to the other. An endurance test – I thought it was never going to end!'

Ava didn't like Myrtle saying what a dreadful dancer her fiancé was. Dermot may well be a klutz on the dance floor, but he was a good man and she didn't like him being laughed at.

'Come on,' Myrtle said, 'you come dancing this Thursday and I'll come to your wedding dress fitting on Saturday, even though I shall be sick with envy.'

'You could click your fingers and have any man you wanted, Myrtle. Not like me…'

'And yet you've ended up with Dermot, and the prize of a fancy lawyer husband.'

Dermot was nice, but he didn't feel like a prize. Ava pushed the thought aside and agreed to meet her friend.

After an hour on the dance floor Ava took a break at the bar, for the slow set. It wasn't like before; this evening it was by choice. It seemed that news of her engagement, as well as her change in style, had transformed the menfolk at the Emerald Ballroom. At least three of her regular dance partners had asked her to save a slow dance for them. One of them had even followed her back to the booth and made a lunge at her ear.

While she quickly put him off, Ava was enjoying the attention, although part of her felt sad that her time as one of the pretty, popular single girls would be coming to an end before it had properly begun.

'Hello, stranger,' Gerry said. 'I hardly knew you with the new style.'

'Thanks,' she said. 'Slumming it tonight?'

Gerry was the manager here and only tended bar on quiet nights or if they were short.

'Training in a new guy – he's on a break. What can I get you? Still on the coffee?'

'Thanks. How's business? No showband in tonight?'

'Cancellation – Big Tom and the lads got caught in Chicago for an extra night – bit of a mix-up with dates.'

'Bad luck. The resident band looks a bit short too.' It felt good to be having this conversation; like coming home.

'Singer has flu. Leo is normally on drums…'

Ava looked towards the stage where a bulky man in a tuxedo was making a very poor job of 'All I Have to do Is Dream'.

'God love him,' Ava said, 'he's doing his best.'

'He makes a reasonable fist of it usually, but I think he has a touch of the flu himself tonight— Ah, here comes the new boy. Excuse me, Ava…'

Wearing the staff uniform, a green waistcoat and bow tie, was Patrick.

Of course he worked here, of course, why had she not thought of that? This was the first place her father brought all new arrivals to look for work. Perhaps he had assumed Ava would have known that and come here looking for him anyway? Ava found herself completely thrown; her head was spinning, her stomach in knots – what had come over her? She needed to gather herself before he saw her.

She quickly turned her head back towards the stage and was about to walk away when she heard him say her name.

'Ava?'

He slid a cup of coffee towards her and smiled.

When he smiled, she smiled back at him – despite herself. The fear was gone in an instant. As soon as he spoke to her everything felt normal again. Everything felt right.

'That's me.'

'Fancy seeing you here,' he said. 'I wrote to your father and thanked him – did he get my letter?'

She shrugged. 'I don't know.'

'I suppose I should have written to you too,' he said. 'After all, you were the one who introduced me to him. You were the one who…'

He wanted to say 'rescued me' but it didn't sound very masculine.

'Oh no,' she said, rather too emphatically, imagining how Nessa would have reacted to her receiving a letter from the young man. 'There was really no need, it was…'

She wanted to say a pleasure, but then thought that might sound suggestive, which was ridiculously Victorian of her, and that made her blush and shake her own head and laugh, then Patrick started laughing with her. Gerry looked down the bar and saw his new young barman flirting with poor, plain Ava. Although she wasn't so plain any more. Wasn't it amazing what a bit of lipstick and a new hairdo could do for a girl?

When the song ended, a rush of customers landed up at Gerry's end of the bar so he called Patrick down to serve them. The band started up with 'Love Me Tender'. Leo, the drummer/singer, coughed loudly into the microphone and he blanched. 'Jesus, but Leo really is brutal tonight. I think we'd be better off going full instrumental tonight – although the girls do love the few words…'

The idea hit Ava like a slap to the head.

'I'm surprised you're letting Leo away with it when you have the best singer in all of County Mayo under your roof tonight.'

'And who would that be then?'

'Your new barman – Patrick. I saw him sing at a wedding a while back.'

'I thought you two looked as if you've met before…'

'Not like that, Gerry! He was really good…'

'Thanks, Ava, but I think I'd better stick with the professionals.'

'Really?' Ava said. 'How long have I been coming here? I know a good singer when I hear one and Patrick is very good.'

'I don't know.' Gerry grimaced. 'The band don't like strangers coming in. I don't want to upset Leo either – good drummers are the hardest to find.'

But Gerry had learned that it was sometimes worth listening to the young ones. In a business like this the crowd could grow old without you even noticing. So he handed her his list and Ava nodded.

'"Rock Around the Clock", "The Galway Shawl", and "The Locomotion" – nothing too complicated there. Sure, he knows them all…'

She could tell she had got Gerry's attention now.

'Leave Leo to me. You give that list to Patrick, and then take over the bar for an hour. I promise he won't let you down.'

Then before he had time to object, Ava ran across the empty dance floor to the front of the stage. All the guys in the resident band loved her. Ava's exuberant dancing got them through the sometimes humdrum business of playing to the same crowd night after night, week after week. As soon as he saw her, even though he was halfway through a song, Leo came to the front of the stage. The dance floor was nearly empty anyway.

After a few seconds, he stood back up, finished the song, and then announced, 'Ladies and gentlemen, we have a very special guest here tonight. You all know our favourite girl, Ava, and she's going to introduce her friend.'

He hauled Ava up the high step to the side of the stage. She was not even nervous addressing the peppering of dancers that was still there. She could not see the seated crowd beyond them over the stage lights.

'Ladies and gentlemen, I'd like to introduce a very special young singer, Patrick Murphy, from County Mayo. You know him from behind the bar here in the Emerald – the best ballroom in New York State…' A cheer went up, and she felt a wave of excitement at how easily the words came flooding out of her, despite never having been on stage before. 'Gerry is behind the bar for the next half-hour so you had better get the drinks in quick. Grab your partners – because our Mayo Man is going to start us off with a rocking jive – "Rock Around the Clock"!'

Once Patrick was on stage, Leo took off his sequin-collared purple jacket and gave it to the young singer before handing him the microphone.

From the bar Gerry watched in amazement. He didn't know what Ava had said to charm his truculent drummer, but she was some player, that was for sure.

Patrick did not have time to think or be nervous. Gerry had simply shoved the list at him, and then pushed him towards the stage. He didn't worry about the slow set, he knew every Irish ballad by heart, but rock and roll was new territory for him. Aside from that one time at the wedding, and once or twice in the Emerald, he had never really performed with a proper band – a big, professional outfit like this – and certainly never to such a big crowd. At that moment, Patrick was not even sure that he knew the words to 'Rock Around the Clock'. Before the panic set hold of him, he felt Ava grip his arm and she looked at him calmly and said, 'You've seen Bill Haley at the cinema – imagine you are him.'

Behind him the band were silent, waiting for his lead. Patrick stood for a moment that felt like for ever, watching as Ava walked to the side of the stage, then he put his head down on his chest, raised both his hands in the air, cocked his left knee up and pointed his toes to the ground and said into the microphone, 'One, two, three o'clock, four o'clock rock' – Leo bashed the drum – 'five, six, seven o'clock, eight o'clock rock' – another bash – 'nine, ten, eleven o'clock, twelve o'clock rock, we're gonna rock' – bash – 'around' – bash – 'the clock tonight…' Then all hell broke loose in the band. The vibrancy, the urgency in Patrick's voice set them alight. They were experienced musicians. They could feel that he had been waiting his twenty-odd years for this moment. They wanted to make the music come alive for him. And they did. Everyone rushed to the dance floor before the song took off. Every booth in the house was vacated, the bar stood empty. The dance floor was a heaving mass of bodies. Patrick sang the three songs on Gerry's list, and when he tried to go off stage the audience stomped the floor with their feet for him to stay. He ended with a slow waltz to 'Danny Boy'.

Ava was waiting for him backstage. She was jumping up and down with excitement.

'You did it!' she shouted. 'You were brilliant. *Brilliant*!'

As she pulled him into a friendly hug, Patrick's legs felt weak under him. Now that the whole thing was over, it was safe to be afraid. He had just entertained a crowd of almost a thousand people in one of the biggest dance halls in the world. Had that really just happened? Was that him they had been clapping for? It had all come upon him so suddenly – and now the girl that had made it happen had her arms around him.

She broke away from the hug and stood in front of him saying, 'Oh, Patrick – I didn't know if you could do it – but you did! You were—'

And then it happened. Patrick wrapped his two big hands around her face, pulled her over to him and kissed her, fully, on the mouth.

She gently broke away, and then laughed nervously.

'Oh,' she said.

He had not meant to offend her. He had just been overcome with gratitude. Realizing his mistake, he quickly drew back. He loved Rose, and perhaps would always love her, in a way. But Rose was not here. She had not written, and perhaps his friend in the golf-club kitchen had been right: her father had simply sent him to America to get rid of him. Even if that was the case, Patrick told himself, if she had wanted to get in touch with him badly enough, she would have found a way. He had fleetingly thought that perhaps Dr Hopkins had intercepted his letters, but, truthfully, Patrick couldn't believe he would be that conniving and cruel. It was far more likely that Rose had simply met somebody else now that he was 'out of the way'. Somebody more 'suitable', in accordance with her parents' wishes. Rose had let him go as surely as her father had banished him. The thought of that had left him lonely, hurt and afraid – but now Ava had come into his life. It seemed to him that in the short time he had been here, he had lived a lifetime. He had come out here, all alone in the big wide world of New York City, and had somehow survived. Which had been, in no small part, due to the kindness of this young woman and her father.

'I'm sorry. I just wanted to say – thank you.'

She smiled. She wasn't offended, after all. Ava's smile was so broad, and her eyes so bright, that Patrick felt he could see everything in the world that mattered in her face.

'No problem,' she said.

He leaned across again to kiss her, properly this time, on the cheek. But as his mouth was only an inch away from her skin, she boldly turned to face him and whispered, 'It was my pleasure.'

14

S HEILA DIDN'T telephone ahead. She didn't want Samuel and Anya making a fuss.

As she put her key in the door she guiltily wondered how long it had been since she had come to visit. Maybe six months? Now she was arriving with a suitcase.

Samuel heard the key in the door and was in the hall. He silently took her case from her and carried it upstairs to her old room. When Anya came down the stairs, a look of excited elation passed between them. Their girl had come home. Hope. Even though they both knew that Sheila arriving at the door like this meant there was a problem, a failure of some sort.

Sheila followed Anya into the kitchen and picked up the blue apron that was still hanging on the back of the kitchen door, as if waiting for her. Together they prepared the potatoes, Sheila peeling and passing to Anya, who cut them into thin slices and laid them in the baking tray.

'So – how is your life?'

'Good,' Sheila said.

'You have a boyfriend? You broke up with him?' Anya asked.

Auntie was always hungry for information and never minced her words. She was a tough old bird, but she seemed smaller, and more stooped since the last time she had been here. She could see love glittering in her aunt's eyes and felt uncomfortable.

'I'm thinking of leaving New York,' she said. 'Going to work somewhere else. I might only be staying for a few nights. Before I decide where I am going to go. What I am going to do…'

Anya's face hardened and they prepared the rest of the meal in silence before going to sit for a while. The drawing room had hardly changed in twenty years. The wind-up gramophone had been replaced with a record player. The old tube radio, however, was still there. Sheila looked at the ancient object, then at her uncle.

I should love it here, she thought. Knowing that Anya and Samuel were living a life filled with love, and contentment and easy domesticity, made her impossibly sad. She had never thought she wanted that life and yet she felt the loss of it when she was with them.

Being back here, like this, homeless and jobless, felt like a personal failing. At the same time, Sheila knew she was strong. She kept reminding herself that this was a temporary setback. She would move to Boston, or Chicago perhaps. Once she moved on she would start again, start a new life, in a different city. She would be anonymous again. Free. In some ways, perhaps, this extended visit was a goodbye to her old life and the start of a completely new one. Who knew when she might see the old couple again.

* * *

After they had eaten their meal, Anya announced she was going to the bakery.

'Cheesecake. My Sheila loves her cheesecake,' she said, touching Sheila's cheek. Her aunt's hands had always felt old to Sheila, but now they seemed gnarled and ancient. She felt a moment of fear at how old her aunt and uncle were getting.

Anya gave her niece's cheek a gentle slap. 'Look at how thin you are! We'll make you fat again. I promised them I would make you fat...'

She trailed off. Anya always found a way of bringing Sheila's parents into the conversation. She knew that Sheila did not like the truth, but she also knew that they had been wrong, back then, to lie about her parents. The truth was always better than a lie, even when it was done to protect somebody. Samuel nodded across the room at her irritably, but Anya was defiant. No matter how painful it was, the truth must be faced.

'You're in trouble?' Samuel asked Sheila as soon as his wife had left the house.

'Nothing I can't handle, but...' She looked to see if he would question her further, but his face was impassive. She felt grateful and simply added, 'I needed to get out of the city.'

'Well,' he said, 'this is not the city, for sure.'

She laughed. He knew how much she hated the cloying suburbia of Riverdale.

'I came to see you too.'

'I know that,' he said. Although he knew no such thing. Samuel wondered, for a moment, if he should apologize for Anya, but decided against it. Samuel believed that pain was something that everyone had to deal with in their own way. Sheila had her own way. He felt sad that she did not include them in her life any more. But he also knew that as guardians, they had to let her go. They were not her parents.

'You lost your job?'

'I quit.'

'You need money?'

'I've got enough to last me a while.'

Samuel walked across to the sideboard and took out a hundred dollars. She shook her head, but he pressed it on her. 'You know you can always come to me for help.' He paused, adding, 'You always have a home here, you know that. Stay as long as you like.'

'I'll pay you back,' she said. As she kissed him, she thought how she would never be able to pay them back for all they had done for her.

Samuel closed his eyes as her lips touched his sagging cheek. Inside, he allowed his heart to call her 'daughter'.

Sheila ate a large slice of cheesecake under Anya's careful watch, smoked a cigarette with Samuel, then said, 'I'm going to take a walk. Don't wait up.'

There was nowhere for her to go out here, but she needed some air, and to escape from the house.

She wandered into Riverdale, with its single row of shops, a hair salon, diner, small boutique and Jewish bakery. She walked past Joyce's Bakery, where Sheila's birthday had been written in a book and the same cake was produced every year, a chocolate and vanilla ring sponge. Philip in the salon hair was nearly as old as Anya now. He used to set her hair into tight curls every Saturday afternoon and had trimmed and set

Sheila's unforgiving frizz straight every six weeks. Walking these streets again plunged Sheila back into her childhood. She knew that this place should make her feel comfortable, happy and secure. But every perfectly trimmed lawn, and clean, painted house in this neat cloistered neighbourhood made her feel trapped and claustrophobic. Riverdale and her aunt and uncle's house made her feel like a child again: a victim of war. Sheila knew she was anything but a victim.

She walked faster away from Riverdale and towards Yonkers. As she reached the end of St Andrews Place she hit the corner of South Broadway. She noticed a large, square building with flashing lights out front and realized she was in the heart of Irish New York. She didn't know this part of town. The Jews and the Irish lived side by side in adjoining suburbs but never paid each other much attention. As soon as Sheila was old enough to escape Riverdale, she had headed straight towards the bright lights and glamour of Manhattan. Other areas in the Bronx were foreign territory for her.

The sign outside the building was flashing green: the Emerald Ballroom. Sheila didn't know much about the Irish but she knew they liked to drink. And she needed a drink.

She paid her dollar at the front door, but didn't bother to check in her coat. She would not be long. The place was thronged. It was a standard dance venue. It could have been the Twilight Ballroom, except it was much busier. This was midweek but it was as packed as if it was Saturday night. The long banquettes at the side were flanked by two big bars. Sheila bought a packet of cigarettes from a plump tray-girl in a hokey uniform emblazoned with shamrocks and went to sit at the bar.

She looked around at the crowd. They were all Irish.

She didn't know how she could tell except that she just could. The men were bigger and broader than usual. The women were plumper and they laughed more. It felt strange sitting in a place like this as a punter. The band was absolutely dreadful. Actually, the band was fine, it was the singer who was truly atrocious. Out of tune in an almost comical way. Service at the bar was dreadful too and as Sheila tried to order herself a whiskey, some kind of a kerfuffle started up and she was unable to get anyone's attention.

Frustrated, she lost patience and got up to leave. She congratulated herself for having left her coat on and was just about to push open the exit door when 'Rock Around the Clock' came on. It was still her favourite number, and she could use some cheering up. She lit a cigarette and stood, twisting on the spot, elbows by her side. The kid singing on stage was doing a good job, and he had a pretty good voice too. That being said, every damn kid in town could sing 'Rock Around the Clock' these days. When that final abrupt cymbal came down at the end, Sheila threw her cigarette butt on the floor, stubbed it out with her heel and pushed open the exit door.

A voice stopped her in her tracks.

The boy on stage had started singing a ballad in the deepest, sweetest baritone she had ever heard. She took her hand from the door and leaned against a pillar. Her knees felt weak. She did not notice what song he was singing, only his voice. It was such a powerful sound, it seemed to enter her body and make her tremble from the inside out. It created an emotion in her that was so powerful and so new she could not say what it was. All she knew was that she had never experienced anything like it before. It was as if somebody had torn open her skin, unzipped her so that her very soul was naked.

She felt utterly exposed. And yet it was not an uncomfortable feeling, but a glorious one.

Crowds had gathered around the stage and a hush came over the place as he sang. Sheila looked around her. It was the women's faces that struck her. They were all, without exception, gazing up at the boy on stage. He was barely through the first verse and yet each female in the room was mesmerized, seduced by the extraordinary baritone emanating from him.

And that's all he was. A boy.

Nice-looking, dark-haired and probably Irish. Not her type, of course, but he was oozing charisma, and talent and stage-charm. She knew he was a newcomer, a nobody. It was probably try-out night, judging by the atrocity that was on before him. He was wearing a cheap jacket that didn't fit right and was holding the microphone like a nervous amateur.

Put all that together and he almost certainly didn't have independent management yet. He would just be a part of the resident band. In which case it would be bad form to contact him directly. He was owned by the club and, if there was one thing she knew about the Irish, it was that they were territorial.

The Irish scene was quite different to the one she had worked in. They called their ballrooms dance halls, instead of ballrooms. It was typical of them to give a hokey name to what was actually a vast empire, owned largely by one man. Iggy Morrow. Sheila had never met him, but very few people on the ballroom circuit had. He was so elusive that some people said he didn't actually exist, but his clubs were so tightly run by a series of managers that it hardly mattered. The Emerald, she figured, was probably one of his.

In any case, Sheila didn't know, or care, who ran this place.

All she knew was that the guy up on stage had some talent. With a voice like that he could conquer the world. Hell, with a voice like that, she could conquer the world. She had to find a way of getting hold of him.

15

GNATIUS 'IGGY' Morrow was something of a legend. Despite rumours to the contrary, he did actually exist. The Irishman owned thirty-three dance halls across Ireland and Britain as well as the US. Other ballroom owners were astonished that he managed to juggle all of these venues. Dance halls, they all knew, were a hands-on business. The owner needed to be on site to make sure that nobody was pilfering from the till or slacking. Iggy's trick for keeping absolute control over his empire was a combination of well-paid, loyal managers and eccentric unpredictability. Nobody in the world knew where Ignatius Morrow was at any given time. One day he could be in Manchester, the next, Boston. Unmarried, he had no fixed abode, keeping hotel suites in his favourite cities and living out of a suitcase. He might swoop down on one of his businesses at any time without warning. This kept his managers on their toes and his staff on red alert at all times. In addition to owning the venues, Iggy also managed and promoted most of the bands that played in them.

He looked after them too. Unlike many of the ruthless managers who kept their bands on a meagre salary and milked everything from record sales to door takings, Iggy shared his good fortune and rewarded his bands with a percentage. He got rich – they got rich.

Everyone knew the rules. Managers had absolute autonomy. If there was a problem, they had to sort it out themselves. But whenever Iggy arrived, everything had to be tip-top, from the ladies' bathrooms to detailed records of bar takings. One night, legend had it, he walked into a dance hall in Liverpool, sacked everyone on the spot, and had the place open again three days later with entirely new staff and management. Nobody knew whether it was because the place was badly run, or because Iggy was keen to make a point. It worked.

Iggy's other obsession was the music. It had to be excellent. All managers had to stick to his rigorous booking schedule for his bands. Showbands were the future of the dance-hall scene, he believed. They could make records as well as draw crowds and the two fed off each other. Iggy kept his resident bands employed, partly out of loyalty, but mostly to fill in the spaces until he had enough showbands to move around his venues permanently. Resident bands were a thing of the past, although a lot of other dance halls kept them on for ease. Iggy was not afraid of a challenge and it kept him on the move.

Apart from the managers and bands, few of Iggy's staff knew what he looked like. At forty, Iggy was tall and thin, with an angular face and an attentive expression that made him appear curiously bird-like. He was not a man that one would pick out for his good looks. However, once you knew who he was, you would never forget him. As a punter in a crowd, he was invisible. As Iggy Morrow, music millionaire, he was memorable. Aware of this, Iggy was protective over his love life. Early marriage to a glamorous but avaricious English bunny-girl in his twenties had cured him of all idealism about romance. Money and business was his mistress. When Iggy needed female company, he could be a gentleman, but essentially, he was a loner. If you didn't know him and you found yourself standing next to him in a bus queue, you might think twice about starting a conversation.

Which was why he was very surprised when the woman standing next to him, near the exit of the Emerald, turned and asked, 'Excuse me – do you know where the manager's office is?'

He looked at her, somewhat taken aback at being spoken to in his own club.

The manager, Gerry, didn't even know he was in yet. This was obvious, because the place was a shambles. Iggy had been horrified to see that gobshite drummer, Leo, murdering 'Love Me Tender'. Now some kid had wandered up from behind the bar and was on stage singing 'Rock Around the Clock'. At least he was doing a decent job of it, the crowd were all up dancing, but hell, he wasn't even wearing proper stage attire. This was just not good enough.

'No idea,' he said adding, rather abruptly. 'What do you want the manager for?'

Sheila smiled inwardly. Her gut was telling her this guy was the manager. No drink? He certainly wasn't on a night out. And only a manager would look that anxious and defensive in a place of entertainment. Although, she thought, he should be defensive given the mess he was making of this place.

'I just wanted to congratulate him on the music tonight.' She took a drag from her cigarette and looked him straight in the eye. 'And the service at the bar was excellent.'

His face hardened. He was mad as hell, and not bothering to hide it either. He looked kind of mean. She liked that. He also looked like he might explode at her any minute and she liked that too. Suddenly, Sheila remembered herself.

She wasn't here to antagonize the manager. She was here to try and cajole a novice singer out of him.

The kid was singing 'Danny Boy'.

'Well,' she said, softening her tone, 'whoever does run this place has certainly got a nose for talent.'

'You think?' Iggy said, absent-mindedly, looking around for Gerry. 'Excuse me,' he said, abruptly. Sheila's eyes narrowed as she watched him walk over to the bar.

So he wasn't the manager after all. Could this possibly be Iggy Morrow himself?

There was only one way to find out. Sheila followed him to the bar, keeping a few feet behind so she couldn't be seen. Sheila had a crazy idea. As she watched the frightened collapse of Gerry, Sheila saw that she was right. They had words; Sheila knew what they were as surely as if she had said them herself.

'Get this sorted then meet me in the office.'

She followed him again, towards the black, felted door that led to a small corridor with two doors marked 'Dressing Room' and 'Office'.

Sheila took a deep breath before knocking. Iggy Morrow. She smiled to herself. This was some turn-up.

'Mr Morrow?'

The door opened so suddenly that she almost punched his nose with her still raised hand. 'Get in here,' he said. 'Who the hell are you? Are you a bloody journalist?'

'No,' she said, surprised to find herself even able to speak in the face of such unprompted fury.

'But then how the hell do you know who I am?'

'I guessed.' Her usual wry, clever caution seemed to have deserted her. He asked questions, she answered them. That was the way this was going.

'What do you mean, you guessed?'

'I saw the way you were talking to the bar manager so I guessed you were the owner of the place and also…' Why was she being so… so… submissive to this odious man?

'Plus you look like the owner.'

She could not imagine a legendary Irish music magnate looking like anything else. He looked powerful. Whatever that looked like. His clothes were modest, this scruffy office even more so. But his face had a cold, determined edge to it. She was in the presence of a man with absolutely nothing to prove and yet she could see in his eyes that somehow he still believed he had everything to fight for.

'If you're not a journalist, then who the hell are you? And what do you want?'

'I want the boy on stage,' Sheila said.

Iggy raised his eyebrows in surprise, and Sheila saw a trace of amusement cross his face.

She allowed herself a small smile.

'I'm a music manager,' she explained. She knew she was pushing it a bit, but hell, she was here now. She may as well go for it. She held out her hand. 'Sheila Klein.'

He took it reluctantly. Sheila had met some strange men in her time but he was one seriously charmless character.

'I am interested in taking him on.'

If she was a music manager, she wasn't a big one because Iggy had never heard of her. Probably just chancing her arm. The business was full of fly-by-nights these days. People trying to make a quick buck off the back of other people's talent.

But he had never seen a woman claiming to be a music manager before. Iggy was curious.

'What's so special about the kid?'

He watched her face closely as she answered and realized that he didn't really care about the lad. He was enjoying looking at her, watching the way her broad, full-lipped mouth pursed before she spoke.

'Well, he's got talent...' she said. Her eyes narrowed as she continued, 'His voice certainly has range, which means he can do rock and roll but he can also own a ballad. He's good-looking, that's a bonus...'

Iggy felt a flicker of jealousy that surprised him. She was hard, she seemed cold, but Iggy felt strangely comforted by her. As if she were a weaker version of himself. Weaker and yet, on some deep level, she frightened him a little.

'There is just something about him that would really add to my stable of talent,' she said, looking him straight in the eye, privately praying that he would not ask her about the other acts.

He didn't, but Iggy knew damn well she was a novice. Only the desperate or the naïve would come knocking on his door like that, talking bullshit about the kid owning a ballad. He had no doubt that she wanted to be a manager and he could also see that she had no idea of what that meant. She thought she was tough but she wasn't.

'So?' she said. 'Are you going to let me take this boy on for you? Or with you? Can we do a deal? What do I have to do to persuade you to talk to me?'

'I'm afraid it's out of the question.'

'But—'

'I'm afraid it my business policy, Miss Klein, not to form partnerships with anyone, and, as you said yourself, the kid has got far too much potential to let go.'

'Who is he?' she asked. 'The kid? What's his name?' He could see she was furious. Those dark eyes were flashing fire at him.

'That is beside the point...'

'You don't even know his name,' she said. 'Some manager you are, Mr... Mr Morrow.'

As an insult it was pretty weak, and inaccurate. It had been stupid of her to come in here and chase down the singer, especially with a man like this. She turned away and said, 'I won't say it was a pleasure meeting you, and the best of luck with your nameless singer. I won't be looking out for him because I expect he'll be disappearing without a trace under your careless hand. Good evening!'

She opened the door to go but to her absolute astonishment, Iggy said, 'Would you join me for supper?' adding, as an afterthought, 'Please?'

She looked at the inscrutable face of a man who was used to getting what he wanted, and found herself considering the offer for one second.

'Mr Morrow,' she said, smiling charmingly at him, 'I'm afraid it is my business policy not to have supper with people that I don't like.'

Then she gave the door a good slam behind her.

16

I T WAS Patrick who finally broke the kiss, saying, 'I'd better get back to work.'

'Of course,' she said. 'Myrtle will be wondering where I am.'

She did not give a jot for Myrtle. She could have stood there kissing him all night. Before they parted, Patrick took her hand and said, 'Thank you.'

She did not know whether he was thanking her for putting him on stage or for the kiss, or perhaps a combination of both. Stupidly, she wished he had said something else. Something that might give her a reason to change her whole life; to give up her fiancé and a secure future for an entirely insecure and barely formed dream.

For the rest of the evening, Ava watched him as he worked the bar under Gerry's watchful eye. She knew he would not be able to escape before the end of his shift, but nonetheless she sat in her regular booth to the left of the dance floor willing him to seek her out again. She refused several dances that night until Myrtle began to suspect something was up.

'Are you OK?'

'I'm fine,' she said, knowing that she didn't sound fine at all.

'I think you're up to something.'

Ava smiled casually, and said unconvincingly, 'What would I be up to?'

Myrtle stared at her and smiled. Ava could not help a small smile back.

'Were you canoodling with that singer backstage?'

'I most certainly was not!'

'I thought so. He's not a bad-looking buck...'

'Seriously, Myrtle, I would never do anything like that.'

Myrtle raised her eyebrows, and then shrugged her shoulders.

It was a small denial, but Ava felt bad lying to her friend. Myrtle kissed lots of boys, but then, she was not engaged to be married. Ava had only ever kissed Dermot. She was more afraid that Myrtle would encourage her than judge her. Ava was afraid of what she might do with her friend's backing.

Myrtle looked up and waved across the floor.

'Oh look – here's your favourite jiver... Hey! Niall!' She nudged Ava. 'Your brother-in-law-to-be – maybe Dermot sent him to keep an eye on you...'

The mention of Dermot's name sent a shiver through Ava.

She picked up her purse and said, 'You're right – there is something wrong with me. I don't feel at all well. I'm going to head home.'

In the days after it happened, Ava kept going over the kiss in her mind. She was angry with herself, barely able to admit that she had, in fact, not just allowed, or even encouraged, but rather had invited Patrick to kiss her. It was a terrible thing to have done. She was engaged to another man, a good man, and the man her family wanted her to marry. It was a terrible sin against her parents and God and even, surely, herself, to be kissed by another man. Not just kissed, but to feel such a fiery passion for him. And yet, no matter how much she prayed and asked God's forgiveness, no matter how angry and upset she imagined her parents would be if she called off her engagement, she could not make herself wish that it hadn't happened.

She was regretful, of course she was, but she was not remorseful. When Patrick Murphy kissed Ava, her whole body had come alive. More than that, she had felt a searing, absolute joy being in his arms. A belonging, a feeling of righteous pleasure that was the opposite of sin. They were meant to be together. For the time they were kissing, behind the stage of the Emerald Ballroom, shielded from the world by a navy velvet curtain, Ava felt as if she was, finally, in the place she had always wanted to be. There was no rhyme or reason for this, why she should want to be making love with a strange-looking Irish boy who tended bar and sang, rather than the kind lawyer to whom she was engaged, but that made the feelings she had for him all the more magical. The truth was, kissing Patrick had felt completely different to kissing Dermot. 'God makes his magic in the heart,' the Irish nun had taught them in convent school, 'and the devil makes his magic in the body.' She had felt the devil's magic when she was with Dermot, sometimes longing that he would touch her more intimately when they kissed. With Patrick her body was on fire and it ached with sweetness, a longing that was close to pain for the rest of that night. However, it was the craving in her heart, the fear that she might never be with him again, that was causing her almost unbearable pain.

For a full week Ava wrestled with herself. She could not sleep and barely ate. On the Thursday afternoon she excused herself from work. She had made several mistakes in an important document she was typing up for her father and he had noticed how preoccupied she seemed. And sad. Unlike herself.

Nessa, too, had noted her daughter's nocturnal wanderings and the loss of her normally hearty appetite that week. Her instinct told her there was something very wrong.

'There is no need to be nervous about the wedding, darling, everything is under control,' she said over dinner.

Ava threw her fork down on her plate and shouted, 'I wish you would just shut up about this stupid wedding,' and ran upstairs to her room.

'Think you might be overdoing it a bit on the arrangements, dear,' Tom said to his wife, but deep down he feared it was more than that.

Alone in her room, Ava felt she could not take another step in her life until she had sorted out the terrible mess that was in her head and her heart.

She knew what she had to do.

She went to her bureau, took out her best notepaper and wrote a short note which she then put into an envelope and addressed. Then she went downstairs, put on her coat and took her father's keys from the hallstand. She would not need to tell him she was taking the car – she hoped she would not be more than an hour.

Her stomach was in knots as she drove along the Hudson Parkway. The sun was sinking behind the dusty trees along the riverbank and the water was glimmering with orange and purple reflections and shadows. Its extravagant beauty made Ava feel all the more ashen inside.

Dermot opened the door, surprised at her unannounced arrival. He gave a big smile and stepped back. Ava stayed on the doorstep. Determined not to humiliate him with explanations or apologies, she took a deep breath and simply pushed out the words, 'I'm calling off the wedding, Dermot, I'm sorry. I just don't love you.'

Dermot felt the whole world collapse beneath him.

'I see.' He nodded. The words just came out automatically. As they did when somebody delivered terrible news at work, and he needed time to gather his thoughts before responding. Except there was no response to this. There was no solution. What came out of his mouth next was as automatic as the last. A type of negotiation to see if the deal was sealed.

'Is there somebody else?'

Ava was wrong-footed. She felt like lying. Dermot was such a good man. A solid man. A good friend. She didn't want to hurt him. But she owed him the truth. As much of the truth as he could stand anyway.

'Yes,' she said, 'there is.'

Of course there is, thought Dermot. He knew who it was too. That young Irish singer, Patrick. The lad was handsome, full of romance. Ava loved music and dancing; it suddenly seemed like the most natural thing in the world that she would want to be with somebody like him, instead of with a stuffy lawyer. Dermot thought of the first time he had seen her jiving wildly at the fundraiser, full of energy and life. And then her face as she had listened to the ballad. He had brought Patrick into her life that evening as a gift to express his love for her, but she had fallen in love with him instead. Dermot's world was shaken to the core, but he could not blame her for it. She was, as some part of him had always known, too free, too beautiful a spirit for a mundane man like him.

It hurt. It hurt more than he could possibly say out loud, but what hurt most of all was that it also made perfect sense.

'I expect it's that young singer Patrick? I could see you were keen.' Perhaps he shouldn't have said that last bit. But Dermot couldn't help himself. He was only human.

The pity and guilt Ava had been feeling disappeared. Not only was Dermot not going to plead or fight for her, but he seemed to know that she was carrying on with Patrick and had done nothing to discourage her!

Furious, she said, 'Well goodbye then!'

On the way home she drove to his parents' house and left the short note of apology she had written in her bedroom, then she went home to face her own parents.

In the time she had been gone they had speculated, and guessed, where she had been and what she was doing. Her mother had sensed Ava's reservations about getting married from the start of her engagement but had put it down to nerves and inexperience with men. Although neither Nessa nor Tom said it out loud, they had both instinctively recognized her fancy for the young Irish lad. Tom had an impulse to confess that he had placed Patrick as barman in the Emerald Ballroom, Ava's favourite dance venue. Nessa was furious.

'You stupid, stupid man – you haven't the brains you were born with! The last thing Ava needs now is a distraction like that. If she breaks off this engagement, Tom, it will be entirely your fault.'

'But if she doesn't love him—'

'Don't be ridiculous. Dermot is a good boy from an excellent family. He will make her happy.'

'Maybe the other lad would make her happy too?'

'Do you know nothing? Look around. This comfort is what Ava is used to. Dermot can give her all this and more.'

'Comfort isn't everything, Nessa.' Tom was worried he might have gone too far but he loved his daughter and it was important he had his say. Tom had really liked Dermot. He was a fine young man and personally, he had found him easy company. He reminded him a lot of himself as a younger man. Dermot was steady, honest and hard-working.

However, he was concerned only for his daughter. Nessa had no such compunction. She was determined to get her way and see her daughter married well.

She roared at him, 'That's easy for you to say. Have you forgotten what life was like before we came here? Four children sleeping top to tail in one bed? Stepping out into the yard littered with cow dung? No running water in the house? No electricity…'

'It wasn't so bad.'

'You have a short memory, Tom Brogan – you couldn't wait to get out of the place.'

'We were happy growing up in Ireland…'

'We are happier now.'

Tom raised his eyebrows.

'I had nothing when you fell in love with me.'

'You had prospects,' she said, 'an education – a middle-class uncle to sponsor you coming here…'

'I made a success of things because I had your support, Nessa – not anybody else's. My labour bought all this but I was only able to do it because of your love…'

'Love!' Nessa spat the word out. 'Love doesn't put food on the table. Love doesn't pay the bills.'

Tom knew it would not only be pointless contradicting her, but hurtful. The Brogan family had a bigger farm than Nessa's family, who were dirt-poor. His own mother had been disappointed when he married Nessa, and although it was never mentioned, Nessa knew it. That was why she worked so hard to elevate herself socially.

'If she breaks off with Dermot she'll never meet somebody else as good as him.' Nessa closed her eyes and breathed in on her panic. 'But we are worrying too soon. She loves him. Everything will be fine.'

Then they heard the front door open, and Ava came into the kitchen.

'I have broken off my engagement to Dermot,' she said and ran out again. Nessa wasted no time chasing her up the stairs.

Ava was already seated at her dressing table, applying make-up and fixing her hair.

'I know where you're going,' Nessa said, 'and I think you're making a very big mistake.'

Ava had suffered enough in the last week wrestling with her conscience; she would not be bullied by her mother.

'I don't love Dermot, Mom. It would be wrong to marry him.'

'And I suppose you think you love this other lad?'

Ava got a fright. 'I don't know what you're talking about – I've arranged to meet Myrtle at the Emerald.'

Nessa softened her voice.

'Don't do this, Ava. Dermot loves you.'

'I don't think he really does, Mom, I—'

'Of course he does. Telephone him now – tell him you've made a mistake. It's pre-wedding nerves. He'll understand. It's not too late.'

Now it was Ava's turn to get angry. 'I am not marrying Dermot. It's done. That's final, you'll just have to get used to it.'

'You'll never meet anyone as good as Dermot...'

'Perhaps I already have.'

But Nessa was ready for her.

'You think this young man loves you, Ava? Really?'

Of course Ava did not know if Patrick loved her. But she was certain, after kissing him, that she did not love Dermot and that she could not marry him. She also knew the only place she had wanted to be the last week was back in Patrick's arms and she owed it to herself to try. To at least see if he felt something of the same for her.

'Just you remember,' Nessa continued, 'that Dermot Dolan was the first boy that ever showed any interest in you.' Her voice was hard and clipped. 'You seem to have forgotten your tremendous good fortune, meeting someone upstanding, someone who could have anyone he wanted and yet he chose you. You could trust a man like that. You could trust him to his word...'

'What is that supposed to mean?' Ava said.

'You are very naïve, Ava,' her mother said. 'Most girls your age have more sense because they have more experience with men. This – Irish boy – this person...'

'Patrick.'

'Whatever – who is to say you can trust him? He comes over here from Ireland, penniless, then he meets you, with your important father, and your comfortable life...'

'What are you saying?'

'I am saying, Ava, that men like that cannot be trusted. They will make you feel as if you are the most beautiful girl in the world but...'

Ava felt a bubble of hurt rise up through her chest.

'But what, Mother? I'm not beautiful, is that what you are trying to say? Because I know that... I know what I look like.'

Nessa held back from comforting her. This was too important. Ava needed to understand what she was giving up.

Who knows what she would be letting herself in for if she ran off with this unknown gouger from Ireland? Nessa was suddenly furious with her husband for dragging all these needy young men into their lives. Nessa knew Patrick's type well. A charmer, with his singing and his black hair and twinkling Irish blue eyes – typical chancer. That whole romantic 'croppy-boy' nonsense was irresistible to the second-generation New York girls, but that didn't fool Nessa for a moment. If her daughter hooked up with him, she would be signing up for a lifetime of poverty. Ava would spend the next fifty years of her life waiting for that waster to come home from the pub. Nessa Brogan hadn't supported her husband while he worked his fingers to the bone making a life in America for her daughter to throw it all away on some foolish notion. The girl was 'in love'. Nessa had been in love a dozen times before she settled on sensible Tom Brogan. She loved her daughter and could not let her make the biggest mistake of her life.

Ava's face was full of defiant anguish as she blurted out, 'I know I am too plain to get a man, Mother, and yet here I am – with two of them after me!'

Nessa did not lose her temper, but took a deep breath, looked Ava steadily in the eye and said, 'That young man is after your money, Ava. You are too naïve to see it, but I've met chancers like him before in Ireland. He has no education and no qualifications—'

'Patrick is not a chancer, he is a singer and you don't need qualifications to sing.'

'I am sorry to say this, truly I am, but you are simply his ticket to an easy life.'

'Well,' Ava said, holding her mother's gaze, 'I don't care if he is after my money, I intend to be with him anyway. I love him that much and there is not a goddamn thing you can do about it. '

Nessa finally lost her temper.

'If you're happy knowing that he's simply after your money,

there is nothing I can do about that. Just don't come crying to me when it all goes wrong!'

'I won't!' Ava shouted as Nessa slammed the door behind her.

Tom heard the shouting from downstairs. He sat at the table with his head in his hands, wondering how two women could cause one man so much trouble.

17

AFTER HER mother had left, Ava fought back the tears and checked her face in the mirror. She had been crying, so her face was blotchy and her eyes were red. She took out her panstick and began the transformation. Eyeliner, mascara, rouge, lipstick – weapons she had recently discovered to help transform her appearance. She quickly smoothed down her bob.

'You are beautiful,' she said to the reflection in the mirror. It felt pointless and slightly mad to be talking to herself in this way but Ava was determined to prove her mother wrong. The feeling she had for Patrick was real. With Dermot, there had been no question of anything 'happening' before they were married. And yet both she and Patrick had been unable to help themselves. Kissing each other in that reckless way that they had was as immediate and natural and inevitable as rain on an April day. You didn't feel that kind of passion towards somebody unless the love was real. She had doubted her feelings for Dermot, but she would not doubt her feelings for

Patrick. She would not. No matter what her parents thought of him, Patrick was the real thing.

Ava opened her wardrobe and picked out her rose suit. It was her talisman now, her lucky-in-love suit.

She teamed it with a tight silk blouse in sky blue.

The tailored outfit was entirely unsuitable for dancing, but then Ava did not intend to do any dancing that night.

She was going in search of an altogether different kind of excitement.

Ava sat to the side of the Emerald's dance floor, in a banquette facing the bar, for almost the whole evening. Men came and asked her to dance but she dismissed them all, waving them away with a cool detachment that was, her regular dance partners observed, most unlike her. Instead, she simply sat smoking, nursing a single coffee, and looking over at Patrick. She did not smile brightly across, signal for his attention or acknowledge him in any particular way. As the evening wore on and she did not move from her spot, Patrick realized that she was waiting for him. Not to see him sing, dance with him, or engage him in conversation. She had come for him. She smoked, and stared, mostly into the middle distance. He had thought a lot about her since their last encounter. To be singing on stage and then to come off and engage in an endless kiss with a beautiful woman had felt like the perfect moment. Patrick had been unable to stop himself imagining she was his darling, Rose. He had believed that he would never kiss another girl that way again. With that urgent feeling in the pit of his stomach, rising up through him, making him feel strong and confident, warm and weak – all at the same time. But as soon as it came the moment passed as the taste of this new girl came to him. Patrick had thrown himself into the kiss with Ava and, in that glorious moment, had felt as true to her as ever he had to Rose.

Ava was his talisman too because when his shift was over, Gerry had come and told him that the owner of the club had been in and heard him sing. 'No promises,' he said, 'but he liked your style and wants to try you out as resident band singer.'

Patrick nearly kissed him.

'Don't get too excited,' he said. 'Same salary and we still need you behind the bar.'

'I won't let you down,' Patrick said.

Ava was the girl that had made that happen for him.

But Patrick also knew that the relationship which had begun with that kiss must end with it too. Ava was engaged. Plus her family were big shots, and even though he was from a good family himself, if he wasn't good enough for Dr Hopkins, he certainly wouldn't be good enough for Ava's family. He knew that Tom Brogan was a decent man, not a snob. However, he had been inside their house and seen the luxury in which Ava had grown up. They had two television sets and carpet on their walls. The Brogans would never accept their daughter taking up with somebody like him.

And yet, here she was. Waiting for him.

The bar closed at one a.m. and Patrick quickly went to the staff area and changed out of his uniform. When he returned, the band was finishing up with the Irish national anthem. As they came down on the last bar, everyone moved towards the wide double doors but Ava remained where she was. As he walked towards her he saw her face blanch as the fluorescent lights came up and she momentarily lost sight of him. By the time Patrick reached her table, 'hello' seemed too small a greeting somehow, so he said nothing. She stubbed out her cigarette and then, unable to hold his eye, simply looked down at her hands. He could see how nervous she was. Without saying a word Patrick simply took her hand. She led him out to her father's car in a corner of the parking lot. When they were both seated she looked at him and smiled, that glorious open smile, and they kissed for the second time. As the parking lot emptied, they moved into the back seat and made love.

Afterwards, Ava was surprised at how little shame she felt. In fact, she felt perfectly wonderful. Liberated. It was as if, for the first time, her body felt wholly alive. All those years of dancing, had, she now realized, merely been her body going out in search of this truth. And now she had found it. This was love. An infinitely bigger and more seductive feeling than the simple camaraderie she had enjoyed with Dermot.

Ava was not a girl any more. She was a woman. And she liked it. Gathering herself, she began searching around for lost buttons, while Patrick found himself half trapped in his own trousers. They laughed at the shocking recklessness of what they had just done.

Looking out on the empty car park, they talked.

They talked about Patrick's dreams of being a singer. He told her about the beautiful town of Foxford, in County Mayo, and his family.

'Mammy and my sisters cried and pleaded with me not to leave them but I knew I had to come. I knew I had to make it in America…'

He didn't mention Rose or Dr Hopkins and Ava didn't ask how he got the money for his flight. Patrick was relieved about that but then realized why she hadn't. Rich people didn't worry about things like that. He told her, then, in great detail about his boss in the golf club, embellishing his antics to make himself sound slightly heroic.

'I told him, "I will not work another day in this lousy place" – and I walked straight out the door without looking behind.'

Even though Ava knew he had effectively run away, and that it had been her introduction to her father that had saved him, Ava told herself he was just showing off, which was what men did when they were trying to impress you. Some men. Her father rarely showed off and neither did Dermot but then neither of them had been that bothered about impressing her. As Patrick talked, Ava looked at the dusting of hair under his open shirt, his firm square chin toughened with the day's stubble, his glittering blue eyes, his fine head of black curls, and she wanted to reach over and sink her fingers into them again, and tear back his head and engage him in a savage kiss. He was magnificent and he had been the first man to make proper love to her. He was her hero now. There was no going back.

'I know now I can be a big singer,' he said.

'You were wonderful,' she said.

He smiled and stopped short of thanking her. He had thanked her already. She knew how grateful he was. He did not want to diminish himself in her eyes.

'I know I can be a big star,' he said, 'and I won't stop trying until I get there.'

'I don't doubt it,' she said, smiling.

Patrick was so excited that he could have talked all night about himself. Making love was wonderful, but the thing he had missed most about Rose was having someone to share his dream with. Now he had met somebody else. He put the thought of Rose to the back of his mind and reminded himself that Ava was different. Not a girl like Rose, but a mature woman. Sure, hadn't they just gone the whole way? He had never gone that far with Rose. Rose was just a girl. A woman was what he needed now.

'What about you, Ava?' he asked. 'What do you dream of?'

Ava had never thought about dreams in that way. She loved life itself, not dreaming about it. Life was life and dreams were dreams. She enjoyed dancing, but had never been foolish enough to imagine she could make a life out of it. She had always hoped for marriage and children but being engaged to Dermot had never felt like a dream come true. It felt like the fulfilment of an expectation.

Of course, like all women, Ava had dreamt of romance. Of being held in the arms of an impossibly handsome man and told she was beautiful, even though she knew she wasn't in real life. It was this knowledge that made her the practical girl she was. Having dreams of being beautiful and experiencing romance would only lead to pain. And yet, here she was, being romanced by the most handsome charismatic young man in the whole of New York.

'Nothing really,' she said, 'except this evening feels unreal somehow, don't you think? As if we were in a dream?'

Ava immediately regretted saying it. She felt foolish. Immediately she wished for him to tell her that she was beautiful, that this was a dream come true for him. He hadn't a clue what she was talking about but as he saw her face fall, he quickly said, 'It is surely.'

Ava tried not to look disappointed and changed the subject.

'So how do you suppose you are going to become a famous singer?'

Patrick thought he detected a slight barb in her voice but then he looked at her sweet face and he knew that couldn't be the case.

'I shall just charm all the ladies of New York in the way that I have charmed you,' he said.

'Is that so? And it will be as easy as that?'

'Well,' he said, 'perhaps I will need some help, aghrá…' and he leaned over and kissed her again.

They drove around the city all night. Parking in different places; kissing, talking, making love.

When Ava got home that morning she found her parents sitting in the kitchen waiting for her. There was nothing either of them could say. They knew where she had been and who she had been with. They did not need to ask what she had been doing all night. She was not their little girl any more. They had known the time would come, one day, that she would leave them. Nessa had hoped that she would simply pass her on to another good family, into an easy, domestic life that she could share with her. Tom had only the father's hope that his little girl would never grow up at all.

Ava and Patrick continued to see each other. Shortly after that night, Ava moved out of home into a small apartment in the Upper East Side of the city. It was small and poky but near her father's office, where she continued to work. Tom bought her a second-hand car, and arranged a driving test for Patrick, greasing the right palms to ensure he passed it. On the day she moved out, Tom also took a day off work and helped her move in her things. Nessa had not spoken to Ava since their confrontation. However, she did leave a box of crockery and kitchen utensils at the back door. As her father lifted the box into the boot of his car Ava asked him, 'Will Mom ever come round, do you think? I love Patrick and I know I did the right thing in breaking it off with Dermot. Do you think I did the right thing, Da?'

'Now, Ava – you know there's not a man in the world good enough for my favourite girl.'

'Even Dermot Dolan?'

'Even Dermot Dolan.' He smiled warmly at her. 'Your mother will come around, one day, although I can't say when. She's stubborn – like you.'

After Ava left that evening, Dermot stood in his hallway, unable to move for what seemed like ages. Time stood still. Even though he had intuited her affection for another man, even though he understood her reasons for ditching him for somebody more exciting, the shock was terrible. Not so much that she had left him for another man, more the shock of what she had left him with. Which felt like nothing. Of course, he had always hoped that one day, he would find a wife. But he had never been prepared to compromise. He wanted to share his life with a woman, not simply take on a glorified housekeeper, which, as far as he could see, was what marriage meant to many of his successful lawyer friends. Dermot compromised a great deal in his work, defending gangsters who were sometimes guilty of the crimes he got them off on. He had to pretend to like people he despised. He never wanted to do that at home. He could have got married a dozen times over. He knew that as soon as news of his break-up with Ava became public the cream of respectable Irish motherhood would be throwing their daughters at him again. But he didn't want to compromise. He loved Ava. He had been disbelieving that she might love him back. But not so disbelieving that he had been prepared for her to leave him. When they had got engaged, Dermot had thought that his life had come together so wholly, he had taken his eye off the ball. Was there anything he could have done to have stopped her from running off in this way?

His thoughts were interrupted when the theme tune for *Search for Tomorrow* came on the TV. He wandered in to the living room to switch it off and as his hands reached towards it he wondered if this would be the week that Dick finally got together with Jane. He smiled to himself. It was Ava's favourite TV show. He had only bought this set to keep up with her. It was the best TV money could buy. It was going to go into their home together.

Dermot turned the knob and watched the picture disappear into a tiny white dot. As the screen went black, he sat down on his settee, put his head into his hands and cried.

18

AFTER THAT first night, Ava was very careful. She travelled across town to find a drugstore where nobody knew her and stocked up on contraception. It was embarrassing introducing the biscuit-coloured balloons into her relationship with Patrick, certainly not romantic in any way. But Ava knew how important it was that she did not get pregnant. Not until they had decided what was for the best.

Patrick kept his room in the apartment he shared with six other lads. It belonged to his boss and the rent was negligible as long as you were working for him. The boss was Ava's father's business acquaintance, Ignatius Morrow. He had seen Patrick singing the night she got him on stage, and was so impressed, Patrick said, he had promised to make him a star. It was great news, but it also meant a longer day, as rehearsals were in the afternoons and went right up until his night shift in the bar began. However, Patrick spent every spare moment he had with Ava.

Ava loved him. Or rather, she was a passionate and

voracious lover. Since that first full night together, Ava felt as if the floodgates had been opened. She was hungry for Patrick in a way she used to be hungry for dancing. She would get home from work every night and prepare the house, and herself, for his arrival after the evening work shift. More often she would be half asleep in bed, and feel him crawl in next to her. Already naked, his hands would seek her out in the darkness. After they had made love she would get up and pull back the curtain, and under the blue lights of the city she would trace the fine features of his face with her fingers and wonder how she had come to be making love to a boy so handsome and sweet.

There was a boyish innocence about Patrick that enchanted her. He was so different from the confident, pragmatic men that she knew. She felt he needed her to look after him and that made her feel wanted.

Two months after they had established this comfortable routine, Ava took sick.

She woke up one morning feeling nauseous and headachy. She vomited, something which she never did. Shocked, she stayed in bed for the day and found that she was fine later that evening. Patrick came round as usual and they made love. She got up before him, as she always did, but as she was applying her make-up, she vomited again.

Morning sickness.

Ava was not stupid, but she was so terrified that she tried to push it to the back of her mind and soldiered on. It was another three days before she went to the doctor. By that time the sensible, pragmatic side of Ava had already counted ten weeks back to that first night in the back of her parents' car. The other, wishful, optimistic side of her burst into tears when the doctor told her.

Ava and Patrick married within days.

Her parents did not object. This was, after all, the only way forward and at least she was getting married. Nessa had come to feel that this new Ava was a complete stranger to her. She had visions of Ava becoming one of those renegade 'beat-nik' girls she read about in the magazines. She might decide to live in sin and have the baby out of wedlock. Where would they be then! When news of her pregnancy and impending marriage threatened to unhinge her, Tom pointed out that they should be grateful that Ava was not running wild. Pat-rick, too, was a Catholic, and so, in some part, his decision to marry Ava had been made the night he made love to her in the back of her father's car. You didn't go all the way with a girl like Ava and then abandon her.

When she told him she was pregnant, Patrick was not as upset as he imagined he would be. In some ways, he was relieved. He had held off on asking Ava to marry him because he felt he was still engaged to Rose. Perhaps, he had been thinking, he should make more of an effort to contact her, break it off properly, even though he felt certain it was over from her side too, otherwise she would have found a way of getting in touch. He thought about telephoning Rose from the office at work. He felt sure they would allow him to do it if he explained it was a family emergency. But then, he would have to find her telephone number. He supposed he could ring the exchange in Foxford and asked to be put through, but then they would know who he was – and it all seemed so very confusing.

The moment Ava told him she was pregnant the problem of breaking off with Rose seemed to go away. His answer had been given to him.

The very next day, he asked Gerry for an advance on his

wages then took the afternoon off and shopped around the city until he found a ring he could afford. It was plain gold from a discounted and seconds jewellery shop. She smiled quietly as he placed it on her engagement finger.

'Are you sure?' she said.

'Yes,' he said. 'I have never been more sure of anything in my live-long life.'

She looked into his eyes and it seemed as if he meant it.

On their way to City Hall, Ava and Patrick passed through Columbus Park. They were early and sat for a moment on a bench. There was a small group of hipster students sitting on the grass. One of them had a guitar and another was singing, all under a cloud of pot smoke as Patrick lit his own cigarette.

Ava looked down at her legs, encased in tan tights, crossed at the knees, barely covered with the skirt of the cream woollen dress she had bought for the occasion. Patrick was wearing a suit he had borrowed from one of his friends at work. It was navy and slightly too long on the leg. Ava had made the decision to get married without her family there. Patrick had not written to tell his family about the wedding. 'They are so far away,' he said, 'my mother would fret. I will write after we are settled.' Ava was hurt that he didn't want to share the news, but when she pushed him on it, saying that she would arrange a telephone conversation, he put her off, quite abruptly. She didn't question him further. Perhaps there was some estrangement she didn't know about. She knew so little about Patrick's life. Although she knew all that she needed to know, which was that she was madly in love with him. And, if Patrick could not have his family there to support him, she decided to do without her parents. However, Ava did feel sad that she was taking this step without them. Seeing the hipsters cheered her up. People like that didn't worry about marriage or doing the right thing. Soon people would not bother getting married at all. Not that Ava would have wanted that. She loved Patrick and they were having a baby together. That was what you did when you felt strongly enough about somebody to make a baby with them. You married them. You pledged to spend the rest of your life with them. That was God's will.

One of the couples began making love, right there, under the tree. Kissing with a messy, wet passion, their hands exploring, crawling all over each other's bodies. The man's hand shoved under the girl's blouse and began kneading her breasts. Ava felt a sudden shiver of shame and embarrassment. She looked at Patrick, panicking at the thought that he had seen it too. He said nothing, only turned to her and said, 'We had better be making a move.' He took her hand then raised her fingers to his lips and kissed them.

This wasn't ideal. The baby, the shotgun wedding – any of it.

But in that kiss, as with every kiss Patrick gave her, Ava felt everything in her world come right again.

19

O N THE train to Dublin Rose read and reread Patrick's letters over and over again. Declaring his love for her.

My darling girl, you cannot imagine how hard it is for me not to be able to hold you in my arms. How I miss your face and the touch of your small hands upon me.

Begging her to get in touch.

I cannot understand why you have not written up to now. I can only imagine that you are busy with your studies. Please write to me and tell me you have forgiven me for leaving you behind.

Innocently recalling the machinations of his escape:

My mother had an awful job trying to find my birth certificate! Your father was great though – he made a phone call and got me a passport in double quick time. He could have sent me across on the boat like my grandfather, but he paid the full price of an aeroplane ticket. He is a generous man, Rose, make no mistake. A good man. I know this has been difficult for you, having me gone, but it is for the best. Thank your father again and tell him I will pay him back in full although he knows that we are both gentlemen and I won't let him down.

His family knew as well. Had they all plotted to keep them apart? No. They were nice people. It was her own parents that were behind this nasty trick. Rose's fingers tightened around the letters and her heart hardened with fury. Part of her wondered how Patrick could have been so stupid not to see what was going on. It seemed so obvious to her now, but then she thought how could she have been so stupid? She knew what a snob her mother was and how her father played man-of-the-people, but really was as much a snob as her mother. But this? Even she could not quite believe that they would go to these lengths to stand in the way of love. Who had told them? How had they found out? It didn't matter now. It was all over. She would never speak to them again. She would go to America and find Patrick and be with him, for ever. She was finished with her parents.

Rose looked out of the window at the passing countryside. It was a flat day, but the grey sky against nature's colours only served to make them appear brighter: the green grass of the grazing fields, the copper moss of the bogs and the messy yellow gorse that lined the train tracks. On another day, in another life, Rose would have snatched up her pad and started drawing. Not today. Today, the lacy outlines of the trees against the sky, the hares hopping across the fields, the whitewashed cottages dotted across the Mayo landscape like little rays of hope and home, were all invisible to her. There was nothing she wanted to do until she saw Patrick's face again.

She took the drawing of him out of her bag, and unrolled it to remind herself of what he looked like. She remembered pulling the drawing out from its hiding place between the floorboards, and realizing that her mother must have found it. Perhaps the first day she had drawn it, before she had time to hide it properly. That was how all this had started. Well, she determined, her parents wouldn't find her out so easily again.

Rose and her family had flown to London on a surprise trip the year before. Rather than book their flights by phone and risk his wife and daughter receiving them by post, spoiling the surprise, John had simply said they were staying in Dublin. After a night in the Shelbourne he had walked them down to the Irish Travel Agency on D'Olier Street and paid for the tickets in cash. They had issued them straight away, and it had been so thrilling going to the airport and on to her first flight. The three of them had been so excited, travelling by air for the first time. 'All you need to go anywhere in the world these days,' her father had told her, 'is a spirit of adventure, a passport and a ticket!' Once they had returned her father noted to her, with interest, that they were thinking of bringing a 'visa' system in to America for travellers, 'but it's a long way off yet', he had said. When the flights to New York from Dublin had launched the year before Tom had also pointed them out in the paper with the idea that they all might go on a family holiday there. Well, now she was going. On her own. Without them!

When the train arrived in Heuston Station, Rose went to the bathroom and changed into a smart dress and jacket, stockings and shoes. She tied up her hair into a tidy top-knot and applied some lipstick to make herself look older. In the cubicle she counted out the money she had stolen from her father. There was nearly six hundred pounds. She was shocked to find so much. It was an absolute fortune. Perhaps even a year's salary. She blushed and thought of how scandalized her parents would be to find she had taken such a huge sum. Then she thought of how much money her father must have spent sending her lover away to America, and her resolve hardened again. Rose took a taxi from the station down to D'Olier Street, went into the travel agency and bought a ticket for the following day. She had wanted to travel that day but the girl in the office, not much older than herself, had explained that the first flight out was in the morning.

'You'll need to give them the name and address of the people you are staying with in New York. It's very straight-forward,' she said. 'Once you have an airline ticket and a passport, there's no fuss. As long as you're not planning on getting work...'

The girl looked at her keenly, but Rose smiled and assured her she was only going on a short holiday. It was her intention to get a job and stay there for ever, with Patrick, but she would never be allowed on the plane if she said that, so she gave Patrick's name and the address of the golf club where he worked. Even if they bothered following it up, which she doubted, Rose knew that Patrick would sort every-thing out. The most important thing was to find him.

At the travel agent's suggestion, Rose stayed overnight in a small boarding house off O'Connell Street. She barely slept a wink, ploughing through the landlady's copies of Irish *Tatler* magazines in the dusty downstairs lounge, trying to keep herself distracted. Every inch of her body was simply fizzing to get on the plane.

The following morning, she took a taxi out to the airport. She went over to the Aer Lingus check-in desk and presented her passport and ticket to the ground hostess.

The woman looked her up and down. Moira had been working for Aer Lingus for ten years, and this route had only been opened a few months ago. This girl did not look like the typical transatlantic passenger. Only the very wealthy could afford to fly anywhere, let alone New York. To Moira's seasoned eyes, this young woman did not look rich. Plus, her passport said she was barely eighteen. Moira thought she had better check with her boss.

'Excuse me for a moment, miss.'

In the back office she found the new ground-staff boss, an Englishman called Mr Simpkins.

'Sorry to disturb your lunch, Mr Simpkins, but there's a girl out here that seems rather young to be travelling alone.'

'Is she eighteen?'

'Yes.'

'Is her passport in order?'

'It seems to be but—'

Percy Simpkins had only been in Ireland for a few weeks working the new transatlantic route. He did not like having his lunch interrupted.

'Can you not deal with it?'

'Well, I'd rather you checked her in.'

Moira was nearly thirty and one of the older ground hostesses. She was less easy to boss about.

Percy put his sandwich back on his plate, irritably placing his napkin down on top of it.

The young woman at the front desk had her back to him. He assessed her briefly, thinking that her jacket looked a little crushed. He was about to give Moira an approving nod when the girl turned. Her extraordinary beauty hit him so hard that he stepped back slightly. With her hair pulled back, the young woman had a gloriously striking face. High cheekbones, blue eyes glimmering out at him, she smiled and asked: 'Is there a problem?' Mr Simpkins decided she could only be from the highest European aristocratic stock.

'None at all, miss, just checking that your passport is in order.'

'Is everything all right?'

Rose gave him her best smile and Percy's jaw dropped at the sheer, Hollywood dazzle emanating from her.

'Just fine, miss. Where would you like to sit?'

He handed Rose a boarding card and her passport whilst not taking his eyes off her face.

'Have a good flight,' he said, regretfully, as he watched the slim, elegant figure walk away from the desk towards the departures gate.

It was not until Percy Simpkins was back at his desk eating his lunch that it occurred to him how strange it was that the young woman was travelling with only hand luggage.

When they sat down, the air hostesses handed everyone three picture postcards with their drinks. The first had a photograph of a jumbo jet on it, the second an illustration of the interior of the plane, the third a picture of the food they could expect to eat, arranged neatly on a little white tray. Rose put the three cards straight into her bag. She would not be writing to her parents and she would be seeing Patrick in person soon enough. The flight itself was very long, bumpy and quite frightening. The man sitting next to her vomited into a small paper bag for much of the journey.

Rose was exhausted, and managed to sleep a little on the flight. For the last couple of hours before they landed she revved up, not just with the knowledge that she would soon be seeing Patrick, but also with the excitement of simply being on this crazy adventure. Soon she would be in America! She was there for the sole purpose of seeing her lover; without him she would have no reason to go there. She took out his last letter and checked the address, repeating it to herself – Westchester Lakeside Golf Club, 500 Ridgeway – over and over again until the destination was seared into her mind. It sounded like a simple enough place to find. What a surprise he would get when she walked in the door! She couldn't wait!

They landed in Newark airport early in the morning. Rose changed her Irish money at the bureau and found she had less than fifty dollars left. The flight had cost a fortune. She wondered how far fifty dollars would get her in America. She had no idea about American money. She had little enough idea about Irish money. Her parents paid for everything.

She bought a map in the airport and looked up the address of the golf club in Westchester County but she could not find it on the map. She had no idea what the nearest train station was and decided that the easiest way to get there was probably by taxi. Even though her father had a car, she and her mother would often call a taxi to take them up to Galway for the day.

The taxi driver was black. Of course, she had seen black people in the movies – *Gone with the Wind* was her favourite film and the church sent money across to the priests who were working in Africa – but Rose had never actually met a black person before.

She sat in the back of the yellow taxi and told him the address.

'That's a long way, miss,' he said. 'It will cost you ten dollars, maybe more on the meter.'

That seemed to be a lot of money but Rose didn't mind. Even if Patrick wasn't there, she would wait for him until he came in. Then he would look after her.

'That's fine,' she said.

In the city the traffic got bad and the cab driver looked in the mirror to get the measure of his passenger. He was curious: it was a long drive to Westchester and the radio was bust. She was one pretty thing, but she wasn't a typical airport fare. For a start she was too young. Who travelled on an airplane at that age? She had no luggage, so maybe she had just been out there seeing someone off? In any case, there was something in her eyes, in the way she was gazing out that window, at the suburban clapperboard houses, the roadside diners and shabby motels, as if she'd never seen nothing like them in her life. He caught her sneaking sideways glances at him in the mirror. And not those kind of glances either. It was like she had never seen a black man before.

'Where you from, lady?' he asked.

'Ireland,' she said.

'You just fly in this morning?'

'Yes,' she said – and then it all came tumbling out. The dreamy boyfriend. The cruel parents. Stealing the money, running away. Donnie wished he hadn't asked.

'The flight was a lot more expensive than I thought it would be.' Then she got worried that Donnie might think she didn't have enough to pay the taxi. 'But don't worry, I've fifty dollars left, plenty to cover the taxi fare!'

Jesus! This kid was going around asking to get mugged!

'And are you sure your boyfriend still works in this golf club? He knows you are coming, right?'

The girl snapped, 'Of course' in a way that suggested she was not at all sure, then resolutely looked out the window, indicating that the conversation was over.

Donnie had a bad feeling about this kid but his wife was expecting their third child any day now and he needed all the fares he could get. The last thing he needed was a runaway ingénue in the back of his cab causing trouble.

Westchester was way out of the city. It seemed to Rose that they were heading for the middle of nowhere. They had driven for half an hour along broad roads that were wider and longer than any road had a right to be. Everything here seemed bigger. The cars, the vast hills with mountains beyond them. Even the trees seemed somehow taller and more leafy, more voluminous, than the trees at home in Ireland. There were sprawling buildings on the side of the roads with huge signs like 'MOTEL' and 'DINER' above them. Rose was beginning to feel overwhelmed when they turned into a long driveway, past an empty security hut, and into an open space covered in manicured hillocks dotted with little flags, stretching out on either side of the neat road as far as the eye could see. As they pulled up to the large, square building, with its white pillars and stucco carvings, she began to feel a little overwhelmed.

'Would you like me to wait for you?' Donnie asked.

'No thank you,' she said. 'I'll be fine.'

Rose had not liked the driver's earlier inference that perhaps Patrick had run away. In truth, she had been more frightened than annoyed by it. The black man asking all those questions had made her feel uncomfortable. Ill at ease. She wasn't sure if it was him or the questions themselves that unnerved her.

What would she do if Patrick wasn't here? Rose decided that was out of the question. She would have faith. In Patrick, and in herself for coming here to find him. If her parents had had faith in Patrick, and her, none of this would be happening. Although strangely, she was kind of glad it was. This was some adventure she was on. When she saw her love again, this lonely leg of it would be over, and they could begin the great adventure of their life together.

She took a ten-dollar bill out of her purse and handed it to Donnie. She barely stopped to thank him or to wonder about whether she should give him a tip. She just ran, almost skipping in through the grand front door of the clubhouse.

There was a large reception desk with an older gentleman in a smart blazer behind it. He eyed her suspiciously as she came across and said, in her best accent, 'Good morning. I am here to see Mr Patrick Murphy.'

'Certainly, miss. I'm afraid I don't recognize the name. Is he a new member here?'

Rose blushed. She was not ashamed. There was nothing to be ashamed of.

'No,' she said. 'He works here.'

'I see,' said the man. He had an English accent, and looked at her imperiously. Rose found her voice shaking as she said, 'In the kitchen.' Then, remembering why she was here, firmly added, 'If you just show me the way to the kitchen area I can find him myself.'

The man smiled. 'I'm afraid that won't be possible, miss. The clubhouse and the kitchens are all gentlemen only. If you would wait here for a few moments I will go and enquire after... Mr Murphy.'

'Thank you,' she said. Rose sat down on a leather chair and waited. She was shaking with nerves. The reason for her whole journey was this moment. The moment when he would walk out and see her. What would they do? Where would they go? Would he be able to kiss her, right here, in this strange, posh male-only place? Or would she wait here until he had finished his shift? Would the two of them go dancing out into the evening, then maybe call a taxi? Rose closed her eyes and tried to imagine how their reunion would unfold. With a rising sense of panic she realized that she could not envisage it.

The man seemed to come back just a few seconds later and she stood up.

'I'm afraid,' he said, 'that Mr Patrick Murphy no longer works here.'

Rose tried to sound steady.

'I see,' she said. 'Do you have any idea where he went?'

'None at all, I'm afraid.' The old man looked genuinely concerned. 'I asked around and, while one or two of the staff knew him, they said he left in rather a hurry and didn't give any forwarding details.'

That was no surprise, the old man thought, the way these Irish gangsters treated the kitchen staff. And now this pretty young thing was looking for one of them, probably all the way from Ireland. The poor Irish really were such savages. Still, nothing he could do. This was a very expensive private club. No women or blacks allowed in the building, and that was that. He wouldn't have let her in the door at all if she hadn't moved so damn fast.

'I'm so sorry,' he said, 'but I really am going to have to ask you to leave. We have a party due in from the course any moment now...'

He vaguely hoped she had a taxi waiting but, hell, that wasn't his problem. The clubhouse was his domain. If she was caught wandering about outside, that was gate security's problem. They should never have let a woman in in the first place.

Rose stepped out into the blistering sunlight. Patrick was not here. Where was he? He was gone? How would she find him? She was in a daze, absent-mindedly holding her bag, and took two steps before the magnitude of it began to hit her. She was in New York. Alone. Patrick wasn't here. She had to find him – but how? She had lost him. She would never find him. The tears came before a mixture of shock, exhaustion and hunger made her legs collapse and she fell. Before she hit the ground she felt herself being scooped up again by two strong arms around her waist.

Donnie pulled her up on to her feet and half walked her into his cab.

As he arranged her on the back seat she said, 'You're still here?'

'Yes,' Donnie said. 'I'm still here.'

He knew the girl was trouble but he couldn't abandon her without knowing she was safe. Donnie was a good Christian and never left a fare unless he knew they were safe. God was always watching.

20

'SHE IS not staying here!'

Donnie's wife Marisa was standing in the small kitchen next to the living room in their two-bedroom apartment on the top floor of the Harlem brownstone.

'Quiet down, honey – she can hear you.'

Marisa had her hands on her hips. She took one of them off to point accusingly at him, then wagged it in the general direction of the pretty white girl Donnie had brought home in his taxi not an hour before. He'd expected her to feed the kid. Marisa found enough food and just enough courtesy to give the stranger lunch but she was not having her stay under their roof. They had two small kids and another one on the way. No matter how good a Christian her husband was, no matter what their pastor said or Jesus himself said, Marisa had only just managed to move one useless cousin-in-law off their couch after a six-month homeless stint. She was not bringing another waif in under her roof. Not even a clean, pretty one. Hell, especially not a clean, pretty one!

'I don't care if she can hear me,' she said, bringing her voice down to an angry whisper. 'I told you before, Donnie, you can't go bringing home every bum that gets into your cab...'

'Aw, come on, baby. That girl ain't no bum.'

That was the wrong thing to say. Marisa looked fit to explode.

'I'm taking the kids to the store. I want her gone by five.'

'Where will she go?'

'Not my problem...' And before he could object, added, 'And not yours either!'

Marisa went into the room to collect the two children, and found them watching, transfixed, as the girl, Rose, sketched on a pad.

Marisa felt even more agitated. She had so little to give her children these days, this third pregnancy had hit her hard. It did her heart good to see them happy.

Flossie, aged three said, 'Mom, come and look.'

Marisa felt a stab of irritation but went to look at the drawing. It was a beautiful sketch of the small bunch of weeds and wildflowers, which Flossie had picked in the park that morning and Marisa had put into a jam jar. Tears came to her eyes. Everything made her cry these days. Half the time she didn't even know she was doing it. After this child, no more. No matter what the pastor dictated, or how much Donnie objected, she was getting contraception fitted and that was that!

'That's very good,' she said, brushing away her tears quickly and reaching for Flossie.

'Leave the children here with me if you like,' Rose said. 'I do so appreciate you bringing me into your home when...'

When what? She had been abandoned? Lost the lover she had come here to find? Was fearful she might never find him again? Rose needed to gather herself, to think about what her next step might be, but found there was such a fierce panic pounding through her that it was all she could do to keep herself from throwing herself out of Donnie's taxi at a stop sign then running aimlessly around the unknown streets screaming 'Patrick!'

In the end, she had steadied herself by concentrating solely on what was in front of her. Rose had always used drawing to calm herself down, and the first step in drawing was looking. Looking out of the window at the vast city, with its tall, looming buildings and teeming streets seemed too overwhelming. So as Donnie talked, Rose scrutinized the back of his cab, the polished screen between the cab and driver, the advertisement for hair colourant on the back of his seat, the worn, leather seats. When they got to his apartment, she was in such a daze she barely took in her surroundings. After a sandwich and some strong coffee, she began to feel a little more settled, but it was the two small children that grounded her. She took out her sketch pad to entertain them, and as she drew, she began to feel more like herself.

As her mind settled she began to think logically, for the first time since she had found Patrick's letters. Everything had happened in such a whirlwind and she had been so intent on getting here, that she could now see she had been caught up in a kind of madness. She supposed that's what they meant when they said 'madly in love'.

Patrick would not have told her he was leaving his job because he had had no reply to his letters. He might well think that she had jilted him. Her father had organized Patrick's job on the golf course. However, if Patrick had left there under a cloud, leaving no forwarding details, there was nothing to be gained going down that route. And besides, she was still so angry with her parents she did not want to contact them.

New York was a huge city but Rose knew that there was an Irish community here. It couldn't be that hard to find him. Patrick, as a true Irishman, would be with other Irishmen. With other men from County Mayo, if at all possible – people from Foxford. What she needed to do now was find out where the people from County Mayo gathered in New York City. She also needed to stay calm and spend the few pounds she had left carefully. This taxi driver and his wife were the only people that were standing between her and those tough-looking streets. Donnie was a kind man but Marisa looked cross.

'Well,' Rose said now, 'I do so appreciate your inviting me into your home. You are surely very kind Christian people, and your children are,' she looked down at the two babies and smiled genuinely, 'so beautiful.'

Donnie was due out on another shift and Marisa had been planning to kick the girl out with him as soon as he got back. She looked at Rose and her two children and thought how nice it would be to have an afternoon to herself.

'Well,' she said. 'If you don't mind?'

Marisa touched the heads of both her children and beckoned Donnie out into the hallway.

'On the way to your shift call into Pastor Wiggins. He'll know what to do. Tell him to call around after supper and if she stays here she sleeps on the couch and pays like a hotel, understand?'

Donnie nodded.

As soon as Marisa left, Donnie told Rose she could stay the night and that he was going to talk to his pastor.

'Are you Catholic?' she asked.

'Methodist,' he said, 'but we're all Christians.' He seemed like he was taking it as an insult.

'Oh no,' she said, 'I just meant that if he was a Catholic priest, he might be able to help me find Patrick.'

She sure was stuck on finding her man. Donnie knew that, of course, every woman needed a man, but he had a bad feeling about this guy. Such a sweet little thing she was, to be let down by him just disappearing on her like that.

'You might ask your pastor if he knows any Irish Catholic priests?'

Pastor Wiggins, an ancient black man with white hair, was curious to find himself being called upon to help a middle-class white Irish girl. Not pregnant, or beat-up – just that she was chasing some boyfriend over from Ireland on an aeroplane, if you don't mind, then had run out of money just in time to take charity from a poor black family.

The streets of Harlem were alive with needy families and if Donnie and Marisa Jones had not been such kind good people, he would not have bothered making the calls he did.

He took Donnie into his office and made a call to Father Moran, who was based in the parish adjacent to Harlem, that took in parts of Hell's Kitchen. He worked the 'poor Irish' shift, which was tough, but not as tough as Harlem. 'Poor Irish' were better than political Irish. But they were still white. And Catholic. The men maintained the veneer of professional friendship, but they were in fierce spiritual competition with one another.

'One of my congregation just took in a girl from Ireland, straight off the plane...'

'An aeroplane? Not the boat?'

'I know. Stole the money from her parents to get here and now she's stuck here with this family who can barely feed themselves. She doesn't know a soul. Straight out of a convent. I wouldn't call except that this family have enough troubles...'

Wiggins was getting the upper hand.

Never let it be said that the Irish didn't look after their own. A convent-educated Irish girl taking charity from poor black Christians in Harlem? He never heard of such a thing!

'Where is she from?'

'Ireland.'

Moran signed loudly. Now it was his turn to show Wiggins what Christianity was all about – Irish Catholic style.

'Where in Ireland? Have you a county? A town even?'

Wiggins conferred with Donnie.

'Oxford? Near a place called Mea-yowh?'

'Foxford, County Mayo. Give me the family's address. I'll get on to the Connaughtman's Association. I can't promise to have her out of there by tonight, but certainly we will get someone to collect her first thing in the morning. Of course, we'll remunerate the family for their trouble.'

When Marisa returned with the groceries, Rose helped her unpack and prepare a chicken and rice supper. After they had eaten Rose offered to look after the children again while Marisa went to visit her sister. Being with the children meant she did not have to explain herself, or stress about Donnie coming home with news. The children forced her simply to be in the moment with them, drawing or playing.

After she had put them both to bed, Rose went to her purse and took out three dollar bills. She tucked them in behind the wooden crucifix on the mantelpiece and said a silent, but heartfelt prayer that she would find Patrick.

At that very moment, across Harlem, Father Moran got on the phone to Tom Brogan.

21

AVA STARTED to 'show' early on in her pregnancy, partly because she quickly started to gain weight. She was happy to give up work in her father's office and concentrate on making the perfect home for her and Patrick and the new baby. Although her pregnancy was unexpected, she quickly became very excited at the idea of becoming a mother. An only child herself, it felt as if very soon her family would be complete. Although her parents offered to buy her a home, they decided that they would stay in Ava's small apartment which they were managing to pay for themselves. It was not pride so much as the feeling that, in some way, she had still let her parents down. She had a husband, and soon she would have a child. In a way, that was all her parents had ever wanted for her. Perhaps, also, it was all she had ever hoped for herself. And yet when she was with her parents she felt as if her relationship still fell under the shadow of the circumstances in which it had started.

The nursery was little more than a box room, a large

cupboard. She and Patrick had chosen the paint together in a hardware store around the corner from the house. For weeks, now, the paint pot had been sitting at the door waiting for Patrick to get a day off. Since the opportunity to sing had opened out for him at work, he had been working nearly all the time. Ava missed having him around, and with the baby coming, and the ongoing awkwardness with her parents, sometimes she felt lonely.

However, she knew how important Patrick's singing career was to him so she said nothing. Ava went ahead and picked out fabric for curtains and a quilt, a sky-blue cotton with small ducklings on it. She understood that men were not interested in such things, but nonetheless she wanted there to be a sense of occasion and excitement about the baby's coming. Perhaps because its conception had been unplanned it was all the more important to make plans now.

On this particular day, Patrick promised he would stay at home and paint the room.

He told Gerry that on no account would he come in early for rehearsals. He and the wife were going to spend the day together decorating the nursery and, later in the afternoon, go to the hardware store and buy wood and other materials for him to make a crib. In the evening, he had promised Ava that he would take her out to their local bistro for a spaghetti dinner.

The day before, he had come into the bedroom and found her trying on a dress for the occasion. She was struggling to get her arms into it. 'I'm getting so fat,' she complained. 'I have nothing to wear.'

As he attempted to zip it up, Patrick did experience a moment of alarm at how much bigger she had got in just a few weeks since the wedding. However, he had the good sense not to comment upon it, and reassured her as he helped tug her arms free.

'It doesn't matter what you wear, after all. It's only Tony's and they won't mind if you don't look fancy.'

She smiled. Patrick thought she looked a bit sad. Ava didn't always seem as happy as a new bride and pregnant mother should be. He worried that it was his fault. He worked long hours and while he wished he could spend more time with Ava, the truth was, when he was up on stage singing, even just in rehearsals, he was happier than anywhere else. Sometimes he stayed behind after rehearsals to practise on his own. He would put on a record player to the side of the stage and sing along to Elvis, mimicking his microphone holds, hip movements and practising his own passionate crooning face, which Gerry had told him 'sent the women crazy!' Some afternoons he became so lost in the music that the hours just slipped by him and he would forget to go home before his evening shift began. He worried, sometimes, that he was a bad husband. Although Ava never nagged him or criticized the amount of time he spent at work, Patrick often sensed that she was disappointed in him. This should have made him come home more but he reasoned that the harder he worked the quicker he would become a big star, and once that happened everything would be all right. They would have enough money to buy a nice house in the suburbs near her parents. Then she would be happy with her baby and her nice kitchen and all the things she was used to. In the meantime, he had to try and keep her sweet in the best way that he could. By telling her that he loved her and that everything would be all right.

'I still love you, darling, and besides, you'll lose the weight after you've had the baby.'

Ava wondered sometimes how Patrick could say such hurtful things without even knowing it.

The next day, Ava woke late. Patrick had already been to the bakery and she could smell fresh coffee brewing on the stove. She smiled to herself. Life was perfect after all. She tugged on her robe, went out to the kitchen and pulled him back to bed, laughing.

After they had made love, Ava realized it had been over two weeks since they had woken up together, and she wanted to lie on in bed, but Patrick was determined to get working on the nursery.

They both dressed in their working clothes, without even showering. While Patrick began preparing the bedroom for painting, Ava set up her sewing machine on the kitchen table and got to work on the curtains and coverlet.

She put on the radio. There was a repeat of a Jack Benny comedy show, *The Drive-In Movie*. She had listened to the bespectacled comedian every week, as a child, with her father. The comedian even reminded her slightly of him. She turned up the radio and said to Patrick, 'Listen to this – you'll love it! He's hilarious!'

Patrick pretended to listen. He was struggling to cover the carpet with the old sheet, having already spattered it with yellow paint. In truth, he was not a delicate house painter. The only painting he had ever done was in the cottage in Foxford, which was roughly whitewashed, inside and out. This room had skirting boards and picture rails and a carpet, which all had to be avoided. Angelo, the building superintendent, had offered to do the job for them for a small fee and he wished he had taken him up on it. Ava would be furious about the carpet, as any right-minded woman would be.

'Listen to this bit...' Patrick heard Ava call through from the kitchen.

'Oh, boss, you're not counting Tuesday night, are you?'

'Why not?'

'That's when I had my appendix taken out.'

'What's the difference, you didn't get home till three in the morning!'

As he anxiously dabbed at the fallen paint spots on the carpet, Patrick laughed as loud as he could, but it sounded fake.

Ava could tell he wasn't enjoying the show, and why should he? Patrick was Irish, after all. There was no reason why he should 'get' American humour. She turned the dial to music radio and Perry Como's voice came booming out.

She could feel Patrick's mood lighten through the half-opened door.

'You know,' he called out, 'I'm thinking of working "Catch A Falling Star" into Friday's set.'

'I think you should,' Ava shouted back. 'It's a great song and you would do a great job of it.'

'Will I sing it now for you?' he said, appearing at the door.

He had paint all over his face. Such a cheeky, handsome face. Ava laughed.

'Instead of painting?'

'As well as. I've nearly finished...'

'Let me see...' She got up but he stood in front of the door and closed it.

'Later,' he said, holding the brush up to his mouth like a microphone.

As he sang the first notes, the phone rang. Ava went over to it, laughing.

It was Gerry from the Emerald.

Her heart sank.

Patrick took the phone.

'You know I'm having a day off, Gerry – there is not a hope of me coming in today.' Then, winking across, he added, 'I have important business here with my wife—' Before he finished the sentence Gerry interrupted him. Patrick's face lit up, his eyes glittering with excitement. 'Sure, sure,' he said, before putting the phone down.

'I'm really sorry, Ava,' he said. She could tell from his tone that he wasn't sorry at all. 'It's just that this is a really big one. Something amazing has happened.'

Ava looked at him. She was angry but hid it. What could it possibly be that was more important than this? She couldn't say it out loud because whatever it was he clearly thought it was more important.

'Iggy Morrow called. He's on his way in and he wants to see me.'

'What about?' said Ava.

'I've no idea,' Patrick said. 'But he's the big boss man, and when he wants to see you…'

'If you want to see Mr Morrow, my father can just call him up.'

She was making him feel stupid. Her father was a big boss man too. It was her way of showing him her family were important. More important than him. Well, Ava didn't work there. She didn't know how elusive Iggy Morrow was, what kind of an important man he was. Her father might be important but he wasn't a music mogul. If Morrow wanted to see him, right now, then that's where he needed to be.

He didn't need to explain himself to anyone. He didn't need to explain himself to a wife who thought she was better than he was.

Patrick walked past her into the shower without saying anything.

Ava's anger melted away into a small pocket of despair at having upset him.

While Patrick washed and put on his good suit, Ava had a quiet, petulant cry in the kitchen as she finished hemming the curtains.

When he came out, Patrick came over and stood in front of her looking contrite.

'I'm sorry,' he said. 'I have to go. I'll call in to Angelo and send him up to finish the painting.' He kissed her on the top of her head and added, 'I'll be back as soon as I can.'

After he had gone, Ava turned off the radio and walked into the half-painted room. In the empty flat a terrible feeling of loneliness opened up inside her. She tried to remember that she was not alone, there was a baby growing inside her, but she could not get a sense of it.

After a few moments, Angelo called to the door. He was a swarthy Italian workman in his mid-forties who lived in the basement apartment with his wife and four children. Although he was about the same age as her own father, he always had a slight twinkle in his eye.

'How is my favourite Irish lady?' he said. 'Your husband, the big singing star, has left me to paint the baby's room.'

'Thank you, Angelo,' she said smiling.

She gave him coffee, and made him a sandwich for lunch so he wouldn't trouble his wife, who was still nursing their youngest.

As they sat at the table, she noticed a change in his attitude towards her. Normally she could rely upon Angelo to be openly flirtatious, offering up some lascivious remark with a wink and a smile. Today, his voice was flat and his warm eyes indifferent. Perhaps he had had a row with Maria, or lost a night's sleep with the baby. However, Ava read his dispassion as a personal slight. That was how it was when you were pregnant: even the most kind and good-humoured of men weren't interested in you any more.

'Maria says you must call down and she will tell you everything you need to know about babies,' Angelo said. 'How long have you got left?'

She didn't want to tell him she was not yet four months along. She felt so big and dowdy already.

'Soon,' she said. The birth was months away and she felt like a fool making such a fuss about having the nursery painted so early.

When Angelo had gone, Ava hung up the curtains and stood for a moment in the yellow room. Patrick had promised to make a crib, but she was beginning to wonder if it would ever happen. Everything was set up for their perfect life together and yet she felt as if there was something missing. She was lonely, and, in truth, also a little bored. Perhaps she should have stayed on at work? Although working while you were pregnant was widely thought to be unseemly. She should have enough here to keep her busy if Patrick was coming home every evening for dinner. But without a husband to look after, what was a wife to do? In Yonkers Ava had been involved in the church, with her mother, fundraising for poor families back home in Ireland. Since moving to Manhattan, she had been attending St Patrick's cathedral every Sunday. However, the cathedral was a large institution in itself, with an established committee, and it felt somewhat intimidating to start a relationship with them, especially in her current condition. She could get involved in the Catholic Connaught Woman's Association. As Tom Brogan's daughter she could pick and choose the district and role she wanted to play, but Ava was slightly afraid of the gossip that might ensue. The Brogans were mid-level Irish royalty and she had no doubts that her break-up with Dermot had spread through the grapevine already. Her marriage to Patrick had been very fast, and it would take only one smart Irish biddy to add up the weeks until the baby came for them to be dining out on her family's disgrace for years. It was better for her to keep a low profile, at least until after the baby came and things had settled with her parents.

In the meantime, she had to find something to do to keep herself busy – starting with this afternoon. The apartment was spick and span, and she was darned if she would go to the trouble of preparing a meal for Patrick. If he was not back in time to take her out for her spaghetti dinner, he could starve!

Ava wandered into her bedroom and looked at the clothes she had been trying on the night before, scattered across the wardrobe door and chair. Most of them didn't fit her, but even though Ava knew she would lose the weight after the baby was born, part of her just wanted to throw them all away. These were the clothes she had bought and worn before she had met Patrick. She was a different woman now, in a new life. The pedal pushers and sweaters she had worn dancing, all those dresses her mother had made her buy that she had never liked, the very sight of them irritated her. Perhaps it was time to let them go, and with them, her past. Remembering her work with her mother, and the clothes parcels they sent through the church across to Ireland, she decided to parcel them up and find a way of approaching her mother with them.

Opening her packed closet, Ava took a deep breath and began to plough through her clothes. She sifted out the items that no longer fitted her and put them into a pile on her bed.

Holding up each one, she noted sadly that most of them had been bought in preparation for being the lawyer's wife, during her courtship with Dermot. The smart navy cotton dress and jacket suit she had worn to meet his parents for the first time. The silk, pussy-bow blouse she wore on their third date. She only wore it once, regretting the high neck one evening as she had tried to unbutton herself to lure him into a more passionate kiss. The red shift dress she had worn to her engagement party and finally, her Sybil Connolly rose suit.

Ava stood in front of her dressing table mirror and held it up in front of her. It seemed like it belonged to another woman.

She thought about how much her life had changed in just a few months, how much her body had changed. She looked across at herself and almost jolted at the look of fear in her eyes. It was the prospect of how much more change she knew there was to come with this baby.

In that moment, despite being married to a man she loved, despite carrying the baby that she very much wanted, Ava felt overwhelmed by her own life.

22

IGGY COULD not get Sheila Klein out of his head.

As soon as she left the building he went out to the bar and gave Gerry a roasting. Gerry was convinced he was about to be fired. But in the end the only instructions Iggy gave him were to give the kid a regular slot with the house band three days a week and, 'Get him a decent stage suit, for Christsake!'

As his manager was sheepishly heading out the door, Iggy barked, 'What's his name?'

Gerry looked confused.

'The kid! The kid! What's his name?'

'Er – Patrick Murphy,' Gerry said. His boss's behaviour, and sudden patronage of Patrick on the strength of that frankly accidental performance, was puzzling. Iggy was a difficult boss in that he was exacting. But he was pretty easy to read.

Gerry could see he was off form, but he had no idea by how much.

During the next hour Iggy tried to go through the books, but the whole time he felt restless, as if something was missing.

He decided to go back out into the club to see if that Jewish chick had hung around. He was sure that she hadn't, but still, he thought he'd go out and check anyway. He wandered around, even going back to the place by the door where she had first approached him. Of course, she wasn't there. She had stormed out.

He went back to his office and opened the books again. Ingoings and outgoings, deliveries and overheads. Bar takings were up on last month, door takings were down on the last six-month period… Oh! To hell with it! He threw the books aside – who cared about them anyway? That chick had got the last word on him. And some cheek she had coming in here, to his club, pretending to be some kind of a bigshot manager when he knew everyone in town. She was a nobody, but she had knocked him back. Iggy didn't get knocked back by anyone. Not for a long time. Not by anyone who knew who he was.

He had asked her out to supper and she had said 'no'. The hell with her…

Iggy picked up the phone and rang old Hymie Baldwin across town. Hymie owned the Spotlight Ballroom in the East Village, where Iggy had cut his teeth behind the bar as a fifteen-year-old roughneck straight off the boat from Ireland.

'Work for a Jew if you can,' a man on the boat across had advised him. 'Work hard and they'll pay you properly. Only work for your own when you don't need something.' Iggy had learned everything he knew in business working for Jewish bosses. It was, he knew, what made him such a success. He wasn't afraid of upsetting his own. He wasn't beholden to anyone, or afraid of anyone. Wherever he was, Iggy remained an outsider and he liked it like that.

Now he asked his old friend straight out, 'Do you know a broad called Sheila Klein? Calls herself a music manager.'

'Ouch,' Hymie said. 'She worked for Dan McAndrew at the Twilight. Did more than work for him, too. His wife, Angela, is one of the Balduccis. I heard they were pretty mad. I was kind of hoping she might turn up here, looking for a job. She was one hell of a manager, by all accounts. More than that lazy, womanizing shyster deserved, anyway. But with those Italian gorillas after her, I'm guessing she skipped town. Why the interest? You looking for staff?'

'I'm always looking for staff, old man.'

They exchanged a few more words before Iggy put the phone down.

He was disappointed. Dan McAndrew was exactly the sort of lazy, louche character he despised. Ignatius Morrow was certainly not interested in his leftovers. Even if he were, he reasoned, women were enough trouble on their own, without the Mafia after them. Plus, Miss Klein had skipped town. So, that was that.

Except that Iggy had an itch now and he couldn't let go until it was scratched.

The next day he went to Boston to check on his establishment there. He rang round. Nobody had heard of Sheila Klein. From there he went to Chicago, and made a few more calls. Again – nobody had heard of her. Cincinnati, Fort Worth, St Louis – no one in any of the clubs in any of the cities where he operated had known of a dark-haired Jewish broad in her thirties come in looking for work. Furthermore, word was spreading that Iggy Morrow was losing it. Ringing around competitors, chinwagging and asking questions? Every stop, Iggy told himself he was being a fool. What the hell was he doing looking for this woman? He didn't even know her. Somehow, she had got right under his skin.

As the weeks passed and his enquiries led to nothing, Iggy

began to worry that something had happened to her. In a whiskey snooze on his regular long-haul flight to London, Iggy had a nightmare the Balducci brothers had found her. They were following her through the streets of Willesden in north-west London, and he was chasing after them, but, no matter how fast he ran, he couldn't catch up to their slow, menacing swagger. He woke up calling out her name. The air hostess, Linda, brought him over a blanket and coffee.

'Who's Sheila?' she said, teasing him.

He decided enough was enough. He visited Manchester, Liverpool and Cork on that trip. Returning to New York from Dublin he made a conscious decision to stop looking. He would not ring Hymie or other club owners to see if Sheila had turned back up on home soil. Enough was enough. She was just some woman, and if she was in trouble it was nothing to do with him.

There was one sure way to scratch the itch she had given him, but Iggy didn't call any of his girlfriends on that trip. He just didn't have the will for his usual enjoyable but ultimately pointless encounters. Next time around, next trip, he told himself. Or perhaps, he thought, I am just getting too old. Too old for all the travel and the cheap sex. Maybe, he worried, I am losing my mind altogether, chasing around after some woman I don't even know.

His flight came in early and Iggy decided to head straight to Yonkers for breakfast in Katie's, his favourite diner, before going across to the Emerald. It was closer to Riverdale than Yonkers, but he could use the walk. When he was done there he would head across to the club, get all his paperwork done before noon, then go back to his hotel, sleep and be ready for his flight to Boston the next morning.

The diner was busy, but that was no great surprise. It was a great place, popular with the Irish crowd. There were proper Irish rashers and sausages shipped in from home, and brown bread like 'your mother used to make'.

Not that Iggy had grown up eating rashers and sausages, or indeed had a mother to make brown bread for him. Home was a Christian Brothers orphanage, whose brutality ended when he ran away at thirteen to work in Dublin and save for the boat ticket to his American dream. Iggy reinvented the truth by re-creating the vision of Ireland for the Irish abroad, and the Irish at home too. And in doing so he was able to invent a pretty fiction for himself with the finest rashers and sausages and strong tea, never coffee, in a Yonkers diner.

'The usual, Katie,' he said to the woman at the counter. She gave him a mug and he sat down in his favourite booth with a copy of the *New York Times*. A waitress came over with the coffee jug as he put his hand over the mug – she splashed it with boiling coffee.

'Ouch!' he said and looked up at her angrily.

A somewhat defiant pair of dark eyes looked straight into his, and a broad mouth twisted in very slight but nonetheless unmistakably amused recognition.

'I'm sorry,' she said. She didn't look sorry. And she wasn't.

Sheila had hoped never to see the creep Morrow again, although she had also known that in taking a job in an Irish diner, on a die-hard Irishman's patch, was not exactly the best way of avoiding him.

She had needed the money and this gig was a last resort. It was near home and she had nowhere else to go. The knock-back from Iggy that night had thrown her, and she had decided to sit tight and try and save enough money to get herself to another city to start a new life. In truth, though, she didn't feel like running anywhere.

So she took this job, but Sheila hated waiting tables and frankly, she was lousy at it. People might forgive a young waitress for spilling coffee, but they expected a kind of home-spun charm from older servers, and Sheila was pretty short on that. The dim and dusty world of New York nightlife was what she knew. Over and over she told herself that if she could have that ten minutes in front of Iggy Morrow back again, she would offer her services. Hell, pulling pints or sell-ing cigarettes in an Irish dance hall was better than this.

So, here he was.

Still, they had parted on bad terms and Sheila didn't do apologies – empty or otherwise.

'It's you,' he said.

'You want some ice for that hand?' she asked, without making a move to help him.

'No it's fine,' he said. Then, remembering himself, said, 'It's Miss...?'

'Klein. Sheila Klein.'

Iggy felt pleased with himself. As if he had somehow clawed back some of the self-respect he lost while chasing around after her. At least she had no idea he had been looking.

Sheila shuffled from foot to foot.

'Hey, lady! Where's my coffee?' a fat regular called from across the room.

She arched her eyebrows at Iggy in an embarrassed apol-ogy and went off to serve the other customer.

Iggy watched her as she worked. Her skinny black pants with a matching black sweater made her body look even narrower than he remembered. Her hair was slung casually into a ponytail at the nape of her neck and her back was so straight as she walked across the room, it looked like she might snap in half. She seemed full of more energy than her thin body could contain.

Although she said little, and moved carefully, Iggy could sense something glittering beneath the surface of her reserve. An anger. A hunger. As his gaze carefully followed her he alarmed himself with the thought that she might walk out the door of this establishment at any moment and he might never see her again.

Katie brought over his breakfast herself.

'New girl,' he said.

'Worst waitress I ever had. Charmless. I'm doing a favour for her family.'

'She's local?'

'Nice old Jewish couple, the Kleins, German. She grew up with them. Her family died in the war.'

So this is where she was from. She hadn't moved far out of town, but, as he knew himself, the Bronx was a million miles away from Manhattan if you were looking for somebody. Iggy looked across at her again, refilling the coffee pot behind the counter. He felt a silly disappointment that she had not stuck around in the area for him.

He went up to the counter to pay. Katie had left Sheila to deal with him.

She came over with his check. He wasn't interested in her. She'd blown it. Guys like him didn't go around giving people second chances, even when they didn't know that they wanted one.

So she was absolutely astonished when the great Iggy Morrow handed over two dollars and said, 'You want a job?'

She wanted to lean over and hug him. But hugging wasn't her style and so, instead, she found herself saying, 'A job doing what?'

Her lower lip was trembling. Iggy could sense the tension in her voice and see her eyes lose some of their determined hardness. She was desperate. She needed work, the Mafia were after her, she'd be a lucky woman if he offered her a job, even selling cigarettes or working in the cloakroom. Would she go out to dinner with him now? he wondered. He knew she would, but he didn't know if she would want to. And he wanted her to want him.

In that moment he knew that, while she was keeping up the tough façade, she would take anything on offer.

In that moment Iggy knew that he had complete control over Sheila Klein.

'I would like you to come and manage Patrick Murphy for me. You were right. The kid's got talent, but I don't have time to bring him on.'

Inside, Sheila was screaming. Was this happening? Was this guy for real? She kept her face as impassive as she could and narrowed her eyes. Persuading herself they looked as hard as concrete, she said, 'Fifty-fifty – straight down the line.'

Jesus, Iggy thought to himself, what am I taking on here…

'Sixty-forty – and I pay his salary. Best I can do. Take it or leave it.'

She made him wait for five beats, then nodded. 'You've got a deal, Mr Morrow.'

Iggy went straight back to his hotel, told them to keep his room for an extra two days and cancelled his flight to Boston.

23

ROSE PASSED a very pleasant evening with Donnie and Marisa Jones. Especially when she learned that Donnie had arranged for the local Irish Catholic priest to introduce her to an Irish gentleman the next day who might be able to help her find Patrick. Given a choice, she would have called on him that very evening, but basic good manners required that she stay with this nice family for one night, at least, as she had arranged – leaving money for them that she sensed, more than saw, they probably needed.

'I feel so lucky,' she said, when Donnie got back from his shift and told her about the priest.

'New York's not so big as all that,' he said, 'when you are churchgoing people. Ministers and priests in this city know just about everyone.'

'Time for bed,' Marisa said, scooping up the baby from Donnie's lap.

'Can the white lady draw me another picture?' she cried.

Marisa smiled apologetically.

'The white lady is called Rose – and no, she can't draw you another picture. Goodness knows you've worked our guest hard enough today!' Marisa felt bad taking money off the girl now that she had grown used to her.

It was immediately clear that this blonde, delicate-looking creature came from money. Those pearls were real. But this chick was also tougher than she looked. Stealing from her parents and chasing all the way across the world looking for her man. Marisa knew tough. Her mom had raised Marisa and her older brother, Christopher, by herself, holding down three jobs. Marisa went out working in a hair salon at fourteen, and between them she and her mother sacrificed everything to put Christopher through art school.

While Donnie put the baby to bed, Marisa went around the room tidying, carefully picking up the dozen or so drawings that her children had been pestering out of Rose. One was of the youngest child. Plump cheeks and sparkling eyes, her features captured perfectly, her nut-brown skin shaded in soft charcoal smudges.

'You're good,' she said.

'Thank you,' said Rose. She knew she was good. Praise meant very little to her.

'You been to school?'

'Art school? No. Not yet.'

'Why not?'

Rose felt a little irritated.

'I haven't had a chance yet. I only just left regular school. My parents were going to ... Well, you see I'm over here now ...'

Chasing after some damn-fool man, Marisa thought. 'My brother was in art school.'

'He's an artist?'

Rose didn't care, she was just being polite.

'Kind of. My mom and I paid for his studies, we never thought we'd see our money back but… now he has a really good job in an advertising agency.'

'That's nice.'

Was there any point in even talking to this girl? She was so caught up with finding this guy. However, Marisa hated to see talent go to waste.

'It's just he uses a lot of illustrators and you seem really good.'

'Thank you,' said Rose. She wasn't sure what Marisa was driving at. A job? But that hardly seemed likely. She hadn't even finished school.

'Once I find Patrick I'm sure everything will be fine.'

Marisa smiled, tightly. Rich white people. They really were different.

'Well, you know where I am,' she said.

'Yes,' said Rose. Even though she did not have the first clue where she was at all.

The following morning Father Moran came to collect her in his black Ford car. She thanked the Joneses and as she was getting into the car, Marisa handed her a piece of paper with their address on it. Rose stuffed the note carelessly into her coat pocket, trying to keep herself in check as the old priest drove slowly across the bridge out of the city into the suburbs of the Bronx.

The priest was not only old but rather grumpy. As soon as he drove off he began to question Rose about why she was here and what on earth she thought she was doing leaving Foxford and demanded to know where she got the money for an aeroplane ticket.

'My father gave it to me,' she lied. 'He's a doctor.'

Rose shuddered as she realized she sounded exactly like her mother. 'Doctor's daughter' gave her an elevation in status that could, if not excuse her behaviour, then at least might soften the priest's attitude.

'And you came here chasing after a man, I suppose?'

'My fiancé,' she pronounced, 'is working in New York. I came to surprise him, but now it seems he left his previous employment. It's just a question of finding out where he is gone.'

Father Moran shook his head.

'And what is this fine fellow's name?'

'Patrick,' she said.

'An Irishman in New York called Patrick? Goodness me, I never heard of such a thing.'

She really did not like this priest. However, he was the only person she knew right now that would be able to help her.

'Patrick Murphy.'

'Well, that narrows it right down. There are hundreds of thousands of Irishmen in New York. It was very irresponsible of you to come looking for one of them without making proper arrangements. And now, do you see, you are putting all of us out. '

A terrible despair crept over Rose. Perhaps the priest was right and she would never find Patrick after all. What would she do? How would she survive?

She went very quiet and when the priest glanced across at her, he saw tears pouring out of her large blue eyes and down her creamy cheeks. He was immediately sorry to have upset her. It was just that sex and all that nonsense led to such trouble between people, and there were so many other things to be concerned about, people suffering genuine hardships, that it was hard not to lose patience sometimes.

The girl could not have been more than seventeen or eighteen, not much more than a child really. Perhaps he was being too hard on her. After all, she was a long way from home, and she obviously came from an educated class of people.

'There there,' he said. 'Tom Brogan is a very good man. He is chairman of the Connaughtman's Association, so if your... fiancé... is still here in New York, there is a good chance he'll help you find him.'

Rose wiped away her tears and gave him a glittering smile.

'Thank you, Father,' she said in a heart-melting tone that made him wish everyone would address him with such devout reverence.

Rose stared out the window, feeling fearful and worried that she had come all this way for nothing. Worse was the idea that she might go home without seeing Patrick.

This place felt so strange, so foreign. Everything looked so new, so modern. Even new houses in Ireland looked old. Everything in Ireland was touched by history, personal or political. Everyone knew where everyone else was from. If you tried to build a new house, or a new life, the past would always catch up with you. Over here, the past meant nothing. Perhaps she meant nothing to Patrick any more. The thought terrified her more than the idea that she might never see him again.

After what seemed like an age, driving endlessly through neat, swept streets with polished gardens, they came to a wide road and pulled up outside a rather grand house.

Father Moran lifted her bag out of the car and a nice man, about the same age as her father, wearing horn-rimmed spectacles and a benign expression, greeted them at the door.

'This is Rose,' the priest said. 'She has managed to find herself alone in New York, and I was hoping you'd be able to help her out.'

'Hello, Rose,' the man said. 'We'll see what we can do for you. Won't you come in, Father?'

'No, no, Tom – thank you. I have urgent business to attend to…' Truthfully, he had had enough of this rather mournful young woman's company and was anxious to get back to the city and the good cooking and jolly ramblings of his comely Kerry housekeeper.

Tom took Rose straight into the kitchen. It was a Saturday and Nessa was in the city shopping. The house had not been the same without Ava, and while they both missed her dreadfully, Nessa was still disappointed and upset over her marriage. Tom had hoped Ava would have called in to see him at work sometimes, but even if she had, it would have felt disloyal of him to meet her without Nessa.

It was nice to be in the company of a young woman again. Although it was very unusual for a young Irish woman to arrive in New York and not immediately go into the care of employers and/or family. The young men were the ones that came here speculating for work and found themselves getting into trouble.

He made her tea, and within a few moments they were talking about where she was from, although not the full circumstances of what had brought her here. After the priest's unsympathetic reaction, Rose was nervous about confiding too much in strangers. These people could help her to find Patrick, but she was also entirely dependent on them. She was in a strange place without her parents there to look after her. She needed for this kind man to like her, so she moderated her story. She told him that she had always dreamed of coming to New York. 'And what do your parents make of it?' he asked. How could she begin to explain? So she just tightened her lips, and looked across at him with her big, blue eyes and let him draw his own conclusions. Some part of Rose knew that Tom would assume her parents had committed sins against her that were too harsh to be spoken but she *was* still angry with them. Rose justified the assumptions that would be made by her coy silence by telling herself that her parents had acted cruelly and unreasonably. When Tom asked where she got the money to come, she told him the truth and said she had stolen it from her parents. She then said that she knew it was wrong and she hoped that one day they would forgive her. She just wanted to have an independent life. That last part was a lie, but she wanted this kind man to like her. She needed his help.

Tom flinched. Ava had an independent life now. A life independent of them, anyway. Tom did not press Rose as to precisely how her parents had been cruel to her but experience in these matters told him it must have been severe enough for one so young, and clearly so delicate, to have run to the other side of the world to escape. He knew, too, that cruelty was not the preserve of the poor, and that snobbery often let psychopaths from the privileged class go unpunished. Her parents, probably her father, must be truly despicable.

'I have a friend in New York I would like to find,' she said. 'His name is Patrick.'

Tom smiled. She was such a sweet thing. 'I'm afraid every Irishman in New York is called Patrick, my dear. Even me, occasionally,' he said.

'Patrick Murphy,' she said. 'We were engaged. Well. Sort of.'

A small cloud wandered into Tom's mind.

'Again,' he said, 'Patrick Murphy is a very common name.'

It was unusual that his new son-in-law (it still felt unnatural calling him that) was from the same part of the world as this girl and his name was Patrick. However, both were common and if, by some remote chance, they did know each other, the last thing his daughter needed was more complications in her already very fraught situation. So Tom pushed any idea of further investigation to the back of his mind and concentrated on where to place this needy young woman.

He could see that she had never worked behind a bar and would not be fit for cleaning bathrooms or waitressing with her rarefied background. In all honesty, he had not got a clue what to do with her. She needed to be advised and looked after by women. Maybe pointed towards a secretarial course of some kind. For the time being, however, the best place for this innocent young woman was, clearly, with the nuns at St Agnes on the Upper West Side. Tom took Rose out to his car, lifted her unopened bag into the trunk and, as he settled her into the front seat of the Lincoln, apologized at the swiftness with which she was on the road again.

'Where are we going?' she asked.

'Back to the city again, I'm afraid.' Honestly, he thought, Father Moran didn't have the brains he was born with. The priest could have organized all of this himself.

'I think you'd be best off with the nuns, dear. Don't worry, they are not all old fuddy-duddies. The sisters at St Agnes are all quite young and very kind. They'll help you get a job and fix you up with an apartment in due course.'

Rose felt quite sick. She had not travelled all of this way to live with nuns. She could do that at home.

'So you don't know anyone called Patrick Murphy?' she said again.

Tom felt irritated by the question.

'No,' he said, quite firmly, 'I don't.'

Rose looked out the window at the wide roads, the lattice bridges, thousands of cars and people. Patrick was out there somewhere but she was as close to finding him as she had been at home in Mayo. With a rising sense of panic and dread the magnitude of where she was and what she had done began to hit her.

She was broke and utterly alone in big bad New York City. Worse than that, now she was going to live among nuns.

24

THE KID was sitting on the edge of the stage with his legs dangling down in front of him. He was wearing a suit and his hair was slightly frizzy as if it had been freshly washed. He was handsome, but he needed to look a whole lot slicker than this if Sheila was going to do anything with him.

She had been home to change out of her work clothes before coming back to the Emerald. She had put on a fresh uniform of black pants and polo neck sweater, but made herself look smarter by backcombing her hair into a high ponytail, applying some eyeliner and lipstick, then throwing a smart trench coat over the top. Gerry, the lousy manager, had opened the door for her and said that Iggy was in the office and she could call in on him later, when she was done.

Holding out her hand as she walked across the room, Sheila now said, 'Hello, Patrick, I'm Sheila, your new manager. I am so excited that we're going to be working together.'

When Gerry had told Patrick the news that Iggy had hired a manager for him and he was to come straight over and meet them, Patrick had not been expecting a woman. He didn't know that women were music managers. Perhaps they were like secretaries and Iggy didn't think he was important or good enough to have a male manager yet. Patrick was disappointed but immediately decided it didn't matter. A few weeks ago Iggy Morrow had noticed him, and now he was making an investment in him.

The boy was gawping at her with his mouth slightly open. It made him look somewhat gormless. Had he never seen a woman before? With those good looks, she doubted that was the case. He really was a distractingly pretty boy. Anyway, she didn't need him to be bright, and she didn't need him to like her, she just needed him to look gorgeous and sing. She had remembered his moody good looks, but she needed reminding of the voice.

She said, 'So, Patrick, let's get straight down to business, shall we? Why don't you run me through your repertoire.'

'Now?'

Sheila smiled. The very brittle 'management' smile she reserved for shoddy cleaners and lazy barmen.

'Is there a problem, Patrick?'

'Well, it's just that my wife is pregnant and I said I'd take the day off.'

A wife? Sheila's heart sank. The number-one rule for aspiring young pop stars was 'no wife, no girlfriends'. You belong to your screaming fans. Iggy had kept that one quiet from her.

'And yet,' she said firmly, 'here you are.'

'Yes well, Gerry said that Mr Morrow asked if I could come in and meet you, and now I've met you, so…'

Patrick's new manager pursed her lips, her dark eyes glowering with a barely veiled threat. The expression brought to mind Patrick's Aunt Biddy, when she had walked into a pub back home and caught him breaking his confirmation pledge. The silence seemed to last for ever until she finally said, 'Patrick.'

'Sorry,' he said.

'Shall we get started?'

'Of course.' What else could he say?

For the next three hours Sheila put Patrick through his paces.

He had the raw material, but there were plenty of pretty boys out there who could sing. Sheila knew she had a lot of work to do to get Patrick on track to stardom.

First, she made him run through every song he knew, unaccompanied.

Patrick felt very uncomfortable at first. He had got used to singing in front of an audience, and although he often practised on his own, this woman stood squarely at the front of the stage with an imperious expression on her face. It was most off-putting.

For the first two songs, he was so nervous he kept stopping, forgetting the words, hitting bum notes. He moved on to one of his best ladykiller tunes, 'Only You', but ended up so off tune that he thought he might cry. He then moved on to a couple of Irish ballads that he had been singing since he was a child and knew completely off by heart. Sheila seemed particularly uninterested in them, checking her nails and chain-smoking with obvious boredom.

During his rendition of 'The Galway Shawl' she walked across to the bar and poured herself a whiskey. Patrick found himself so addled and insulted that he stopped singing.

'Why have you stopped?' she said.

'You don't seem to be enjoying it,' he said.

She took a long drag of her cigarette and blew it out in his direction.

'It's not about me enjoying it, Patrick. It's about both of us figuring out where your strengths lie. Keep singing to the end of that song.'

Patrick was feeling frustrated. He had never had such a dreadful, unappreciative audience, and it was shattering his confidence.

'What's the point if the audience doesn't like it?'

'I am not your audience, Patrick,' she said, 'I am your manager. Don't ever forget that. No, I do not like those schmaltzy Irish ballads, although I'm sure they make lots of Irish ladies go weak at the knees. However, unless I've listened to you sing every damn line, I can't be sure that I'm not missing something...'

He didn't have the first clue what she was talking about. Neither did she really.

'Look,' she said, inviting him to sit down on the stage next to her. 'You are a good-looking kid and you can sing. Now that you have a nice regular gig here, you can call yourself a professional singer. That's a lot. That's more than a lot of kids get.'

Patrick nodded and tried to look sage. Inside he was thrilled. He was a professional singer!

'But it's not enough for me.' She lit a fresh cigarette from the old one, which she stubbed out on the stage.

'Let me tell you something, Patrick. You're my only client. Just you. Nobody else. I saw something in you a few weeks ago and I hounded Iggy Morrow to let me manage you.'

Patrick didn't know whether to be pleased or not. He thought he was Mr Morrow's charge. He was the one paying his salary.

'Mr Morrow may be paying your salary, Patrick, but believe me, I am calling the shots here.'

This woman was scary, it was like she could read his mind.

'So what I need to do now is take that little special some-thing I saw in you, nurture it, make it grow until it is big. Really big. So big, that everyone in this country knows who you are. Elvis big. Jerry Lee big. There's a lot of copycats out there, and right now you're one of them. You've got the Elvis moves but here's some news for you...'

Patrick flushed.

'You are not Elvis, Patrick, and you know why?'

Patrick shook his head politely. He felt a bit sick.

'You are not Elvis because you are not different. Elvis was different. Bill Haley was different...'

Patrick shifted around uncomfortably. He wished to hell he had just sung all the songs like she had asked him to do.

'... Little Richard? Different. When I heard you sing a few weeks ago, on this stage, I thought I saw something, some little spark, that might set you apart. Something that could make you different too. Something that could make you big. But what I'm getting from you right now, Patrick, is run-of-the-mill. Are you with me?'

'Yes,' he said. He could feel tears building up in the back of his eyes. He swallowed hard.

'What I'm getting is regular, dumb-ass, white Irish-boy bullshit. Is that who you are? Just some regular fool kid who happens to be able to sing good?'

'No, ma'am.'

'Good. Because I don't need that. I need a star. Could that be you?'

'Yes, ma'am, it could.'

'I want to you sing every single song that you know how to sing, as best as you can, to me, just me, right here, right now, so that I can figure out what is special and different enough about you that I can use to help make you into the kind of star that I need to get on my books so that every bullshit man in the music management business will take me seriously. Are you going to do that for me?'

This woman was truly crazy and he was going to do every single thing that she said.

'Yes, ma'am, I most certainly am.'

For the next two hours she cajoled and coached him through every song he knew and some he didn't. They played every record in the place and she put him through his dance and microphone moves, making him sway, and throw his mike from hand to hand a thousand times until it was as natural to him as gunslinging to the seasoned cowboy.

She instructed him on just the right way to tilt his head and where to set his eyes to get that gazing into the distance mooning about his true-love-ways look. She taught him to loosen his hips so that he owned his 'Elvis', and made him drop the raised-lip snarl so that he didn't look derivative.

By the time Sheila sent him home sweating and exhausted, Patrick felt he was just getting into his stride. He had worked harder than he had ever worked in his entire life, even when pulling in the hay on the farm during the hottest summer days, and yet it felt liberating to be told what to do. He was honing his craft, and he would have stayed all night inching through each improvement. Sheila, however, was glad to send him home so she could regroup. The kid had everything: talent, looks, willingness and ability to learn. What he lacked was an edge. Every act needed an edge, and Sheila was not sure that Patrick truly had one.

'Send my apologies to your wife,' she said, as he was leaving.

'Ava would love to meet you,' he said. 'Perhaps you will come round for a meal soon.'

'Perhaps,' she said, although they both knew she was just being polite.

The wife thing was not good. Fans liked their stars single. Sheila would have to figure out a way around that one too. Iggy had given her the opportunity to work with Patrick but, although Sheila sensed something special about him, for the life of her she could not get it out of him that afternoon. He was good, but 'good' wasn't good enough. She would have to work with him a lot more before he was ready for her to bring out into the world. Until she had a recording contract, Patrick couldn't earn any money for her outside the salary Iggy was paying him to sing in his venues.

Iggy had worked that out too.

He had a plan: Gerry clearly couldn't manage his place on his own so he would put Sheila in as joint manager.

However, it was tricky because Iggy had a policy of not putting women he fancied on his payroll.

And he fancied Sheila.

There was no getting around it. Around six o'clock he went into the manager's restrooms to have a shower and change into a fresh shirt. As he stood in front of the mirror patting after-shave on his freshly shaved cheeks, he thought to himself how hollow and haggard he looked. Beady eyes glared back at him, accusingly. Even though he was a self-assured man, certain about almost everything he said and did, Iggy always looked perplexed and slightly annoyed. It was one of the great injustices. He was not handsome. He never had been and while it had bothered him as a boy, when he started making money it stop bothering him at all. Women liked money and power. They liked looks and talent too, but Iggy's money and power put him on a level playing field with his handsome young acts. The problem was not that women didn't find him attractive, the problem was that Iggy didn't always trust their intentions. So, while he found a lot of the women he knew sexually attractive, they were simply not interesting enough for him to want to spend time with them outside the bedroom.

Sheila was different, and as Iggy was preparing himself for the evening he could only hope he might be spending in her company, he could feel a hint of fear creeping into his heart. He had never been in a position where he felt nervous before seeing a woman. He worried that he might become diminished if he allowed himself to fall in love with her. He had cancelled his travel arrangements to Boston the following day. His whole month's schedule had been compromised because of a woman. This was not good. And yet, Iggy knew he had to follow it through. The fact that she had turned up like that, after he had been looking for her, was a sign that fate already had him in her grip. A smart man knew when the wind was too strong to fight. Sometimes, in life as in business, Iggy thought, as he tightened the knot on his silk tie, and grin-checked his teeth in the mirror, you had to let yourself get blown around a bit, just to see where you landed up. The true test of a man was where you would take it from there.

Sheila's spirits fell when she walked into the office and saw Iggy perched on the side of the desk, freshly shaved, in a three-piece suit. One look at him was all it took to tell her Mr Morrow was planning to take it all the way this evening. Dinner and a nice hotel. It would be a nice hotel because he was rich. But that really was not the point.

Sheila was exhausted after working so hard all afternoon with Patrick, and now her boss wanted to sleep with her. Not simply wanted to. He intended to. There was no other possible explanation for the deliberate way he was standing, cigar in hand, trying to make himself look as powerful and important as possible.

'Things went well with Patrick?'

The formality was gone now. It was straight down to business. Sheila liked that, at least.

'Very well,' she said. 'I think we'll work well together.'

'How would you feel about joint-managing the place with Gerry? As you can see, he's a bit overwhelmed. He could use a helping hand.'

Sheila was less insulted than disappointed at how predictable he was. Having him turn up like that and then offering her the job of managing Patrick had turned her life upside down in a day and set her on a path which had felt, until a few seconds beforehand, like an unforeseen adventure. Now the sense of adventure had been replaced with the dull inevitability of sex. Sheila was not a romantic soul. Often, if the opportunity to sleep with someone came up, she was happy enough to run with it. She thought that Iggy was an interesting and attractive man, but never before had Sheila felt offended by the idea of having sex with somebody.

'Two jobs in one day, Mr Morrow. You're a very generous man.'

'I rang around town and I've heard you're a good manager. I'm no fool.'

'Neither am I...'

She let that hang in the air for a few minutes but he didn't flinch. If he had been ringing around asking questions then he knew about the Balducci brothers. He also knew that she had slept with her last boss.

'How come you're all dressed up?' she said, raising her chin at him.

It was his turn to flush, although he made pretty certain he didn't show it. Jesus, but she wasn't making this easy. Whatever 'this' was. Iggy decided to play it straight. That was always the best hand to play in business if you were not sure.

'I was going to ask you out to dinner and if it went well, back to my hotel.'

His eye was unflinching. His gaze was steady and remained cool, and yet she felt it sear through her like white heat.

'Pretty fancy suit for dinner.'

'Was planning a pretty fancy dinner.'

She opened her palms and looked down at her outfit.

'I'm not dressed for dinner.'

'It doesn't matter.'

Sheila didn't know if he meant 'It doesn't matter what you're wearing' or 'It doesn't matter because I don't care that much'. She couldn't read him, and suddenly the distinction mattered.

'What doesn't matter?'

Iggy took a deep breath. Sometimes you had to take a risk.

'It doesn't matter what you wear and it doesn't matter if we don't go out to dinner.'

Nobody had ever been that straight up with Sheila before. Nobody had ever been that straightforward, that honest in their intention. She didn't know what it meant, and she didn't care what it meant either.

She just walked straight across the room, took the cigar out of his hand, stubbed it out on the polished mahogany desk then kissed him. Iggy stood, steady but utterly powerless as she pulled her sweater over her head. She clambered up on his desk and whispered, her voice heavy with desire, 'You don't own me.' Knowing as she said it, in some part of her, that it wasn't true.

25

THE CONVENT was in a large old house in the Upper West Side. It was clean and warm and the nuns were friendly and many of them were quite young. The building itself was jolly, for a religious institution, with fancy wallpaper as a backdrop for all the religious statues. The girls slept in dormitories, with a tall locker each where they could hang a small number of clothes. There was a curfew of ten p.m., but apart from that, and a short morning mass at eight a.m., the girls could come and go as they pleased. Rose was put to work cleaning and cooking in the convent itself. For the first few weeks, it was decided, the nuns would get the measure of what her capabilities were before they tried to get her a job out in 'the real world'. Tom had told the mother superior, Sister Augustine, that Rose was escaping 'an unnamed abuse' at the hands of her parents, back home in Ireland. The nun did not prod for more information. These things were best left unspoken. Propriety would be recovered, in time, through prayer, good food, hard work and kindness. Sister Augustine put Rose in a small dormitory with two other Irish girls: Eileen from Cork and Una from Connemara. Eileen was twenty-three, and at secretarial school. She had been unable to find either a husband or a job in Ireland so she had been packed off here to New York to live with an ancient aunt who had died while she was en route by boat. The nuns had offered to sponsor her secretarial training and she would pay them back after she started working. Una was still recovering after giving up a baby for adoption at another convent, where she had been so brutally treated that kindly Sister Augustine had taken her in.

Her room-mates were good fun and she liked them but Rose was not in the humour for making friends.

'So, what brought you to New York?'

It was the first question they asked, but Rose felt too foolish to say why she was here, so she smiled and said, 'A new start, you know?' She felt lost. Everyone here knew where they were going. Even poor Una had dreams of training in a hair salon as soon as she felt well enough to re-enter the world. Rose had no plans. Her plan had been to find Patrick and live happily ever after. It had failed. Now what? There was nothing. Just a void. So, she just kept her head down and did as the nuns told her. Rose was happy for them to tell her what to do because she felt broken. Lost. She had no spirit left in her. Sister Augustine had a soft spot for the beautiful girl who looked so much like the film star. Grace Kelly was a good Catholic and, even if this young girl did not seem particularly devout, she looked the part at least, even though she did not feel Rose belonged in New York. Rose decided to simply sleepwalk through her chores and try her very best to forget about Patrick Murphy until something else presented itself. Although she did not have much confidence that anything would. Without Patrick, her life was over.

A few days after her arrival at the convent, Rose went back to her room after her morning chores were finished to find Una and Eileen plotting a night out.

'They won't be on stage until nine, and sure we have to be back here by ten. It'll take us an hour to get home from Yonkers. We can't do it!'

'How about if we get a taxi?'

'That takes nearly as long,' Una complained.

'You're "in" with Sister Augustine, Rose. Ask her for a special dispensation.'

'What for?'

'Urgh – you are so not with-it, Rose,' said Eileen, thrusting a leaflet into her hand. 'The Dolly Butler Band are playing the Emerald in Yonkers on Saturday. They are the biggest thing back home in Cork – I have to be there…'

But Rose wasn't listening. She was staring down at the leaflet as if she had just seen a ghost. On the left-hand corner of the page, in the black-and-white picture of smiling Dolly sitting in the middle in front of her all-male seven-piece band in their smart sweaters, was a small picture of Patrick. His hair was different, set into a quiff like Elvis, but it could not be anyone but him. Next to it the caption said, 'Supported by the Emerald's popular resident singer, Patrick Murphy.'

Rose was beside herself and it took every inch of energy she had to maintain her composure. Although she was fit to explode with excitement, she didn't want to share her personal business with these strangers.

'What is a resident singer?' she asked, keeping her voice as light as she could.

Una snatched the leaflet off her.

'Patrick Murphy – he's a dish, all right. Resident singer means he is there all the time.'

'You mean during the day as well?' Rose said.

Una looked at her sideways; their new room-mate was a strange fish.

'Actually, I think he probably is. Doesn't Patrick work behind the bar there sometimes, Eileen?'

'Never mind that – Rose, will you clear Saturday curfew with Sister Augustine?'

'I'll do it now,' Rose said, flying from the room, grabbing her purse and jacket as she left.

She didn't go and see Sister Augustine. She ran straight out the door and grabbed a taxi for the Emerald in Yonkers.

The place was all locked up, and she banged and banged and banged on the door until, finally, a man came and answered it.

'I need to see Patrick Murphy,' she said.

'Who are you?' Gerry asked. A mad fan? Lucky Patrick. She was a looker. Anyway, he couldn't let her in. Iggy and Sheila were in conference with Patrick, and Gerry had been put under strict instructions to keep everyone out of their way for the afternoon.

'I'm a friend from home. I need to see him urgently.'

That was another poster of Patrick up outside the door. It was him! It was really him! And now he was a big singer, and she had found him, and everything would be as it should be! Rose could hardly believe this was happening.

'Afraid he's not here. Have you tried him at home?'

Gerry was sure Ava would be back at their apartment. Great girl, Ava. Patrick was one lucky guy. She would entertain this girl for Patrick. No better woman.

'I left his address in my other purse,' she lied, scrabbling for a scrap of paper and a pen in her bag. 'Could you give it to me again?'

Gerry jotted down Patrick's apartment details and Rose hopped straight back in another taxi into town. All these taxis, all this money. It didn't matter a damn any more.

Soon they would be together and he would hold her in his arms and everything would be all right again.

26

PATRICK WAS on a high when he got home from the Emerald that evening. He had learned so much about himself as a performer during the afternoon. Those few hours in the company of Sheila had been more productive than all the weeks he had been singing on stage and, indeed, the twenty-five years he had been singing before that, thinking he knew what it was all about. He knew nothing. But he didn't mind one bit because Sheila was going to show him how to do it right. Sheila was going to make him a star. It was late, but there was still time to take Ava out for that spaghetti dinner. She would be angry with him for staying away for so long, but once he started to tell her about the day he had had, and all the wonderful things that were ahead for him, and, of course, them, she would certainly forgive him.

As soon as he got in, Patrick ran straight into the bathroom and put the shower on. Back out in the hall he started to strip off his clothes so that by the time he was in the kitchen, his shirt was on the floor behind him, and he was already pulling his vest over his head, saying, 'I know, I know I'm late, Ava, but I've got so much news. You would not believe the day I've had but I can just tell you that everything is going to start happening for us now. All the dreams we ever had are about to come true...'

He had unbuckled his belt and was scrunching his vest up into a ball for the laundry basket when he walked into the kitchen and saw her. It took everything in his power to stop himself from letting out a yelp of shock and shouting out her name. For a second, although it felt like an hour, Patrick just stood there, unable to move. The sun-kissed-blonde hair, the piercing blue eyes looking across at him, pleading. Rose. From Foxford. Sitting in his kitchen, talking with Ava. Could this really be happening? It was like he was in some kind of a weird nightmare. And yet, she *was* here. The questions how and why could barely form themselves out of the intrusion of her just being here. Even so, Patrick could feel his body begging him to go across the room and embrace her. He kept his arms firmly by his side and tried to hold his face as naturally as possible.

'Darling,' Ava said, smiling at first, and then laughing at the ridiculousness of her husband, accidentally stripping in front of another woman. He would be so embarrassed, especially when he saw it was somebody from home.

Ava and Rose had become great friends in just a few hours. At first, Ava had been taken aback by this breathtakingly beautiful young woman arriving at her door saying that she knew her husband. Her nervous manner had made Ava feel uncomfortable. However, she was only in Rose's company for a few moments when she realized there was nothing for her to fear. Rose had such a delicate, open face and her manner was so gentle and sweet, so lady-like, that Ava instantly took to her.

Rose had not known Patrick very well, she assured Ava. She had led such a sheltered life – it was more that Patrick's name was known to her as a young man from her village who had gone to New York.

'I just wanted to meet someone from home. Not having any family here. I am staying in a convent.'

Rose was keen to wait until Patrick got back from work. Ava explained she was in the middle of some chores and asked if she would like to help her sort through some clothes for a charity package. It was so nice to have another woman to talk to. These days, Ava saw very little of Myrtle, who had a job and spent her evenings and weekends in the Emerald. Ava got the feeling that Myrtle was annoyed that her plain friend had got married before she did. There was not a hint of that kind of nastiness from Rose. She was a real lady. All charm and smiles as she helped Ava pick out the clothes to keep until after her pregnancy. She was particularly taken with Ava's Sybil Connolly suit and discussed the Foxford Woollen Mills tweed with her at great length. She reassured Ava that she would fit back into the suit after her pregnancy, and helped her pick out other clothes that would be suitable to send back to Ireland.

'How do you send them?' Rose asked.

'I don't know,' she said. 'My mother organizes it.'

As soon as she said it, Ava realised she sounded rather pathetic, especially to this brave young woman who had travelled across the world to rescue a new life. Ava determined, in that moment, that she would write to her mother and ask advice about where to send the package. An olive branch. Life was too short.

After they had sorted out the clothes and discussed Ava's plans for the nursery and the baby, the young women prepared supper together and waited for Patrick to come home. And here he was. Although he looked somewhat discombobulated.

'Of course, you know Rose?'

'Oh yes. Hello,' he managed to say.

Patrick could not have been more thrown. Immediately, he checked Ava's face for signs of anger or upset. How much had Rose told her about them? Ava looked quite happy so it couldn't have been much. More importantly, what the hell was Rose doing here?

Ava was disappointed that he seemed unimpressed to the point of being rude. Really, he was so caught up with work all the time, he could think of nothing else.

'Rose has come to stay with us for a while...'

'Good – erm...'

Ava was so embarrassed by her husband's behaviour she couldn't even look at Rose. Sometimes she wondered if she would not have been better off marrying a gentleman, someone with proper manners. Dermot flashed into her head and Ava quickly reminded herself that you could teach a man good manners but passion was something that could not be learned.

'You remember Rose? Of course you do!' Ava kept her voice sunny.

'Yes' was all he could manage.

Throughout the meal Patrick's strange, dark mood continued. Ava was secretly fuming, trying to draw conversation out of him on the subject of his new manager and work but with little success. Ava was mortified. She liked Rose and Patrick was making things positively uncomfortable. He might not have known her well, but Rose was the first person who knew Patrick from Ireland that she had met, including his family.

After they had eaten supper, Ava decided to go across to the ice cream parlour to get some dessert. Perhaps if Patrick was left alone with Rose for a few moments, he might find his manners!

As soon as Ava was gone, Patrick turned on Rose.

'What the hell are you doing here?'

Rose immediately burst into tears. This was not how she had imagined their reunion would be. She had come all the way across the world, only to find that the love of her life had married somebody else. That was bad enough, but it might almost have been accepted for the disastrous mishap that it was. In the hours that had passed since she got this terrible news, as she was nodding to his wife, talking about charity clothes and being as brilliant an actress as she could be, covering her horror with charm and polite chitchat, Rose had thought of every possible scenario to justify his betraying her. He must have been lonely and believed that she didn't love him any more. But when his first words to her were so cruel and cold, Rose could not bear it. It simply wasn't possible that she had come all this way for nothing. It wasn't possible that Patrick did not love her any more. It was unthinkable.

'I came to find you.'

Patrick had suspected that to be the case but, even so, he was frightened. He didn't even ask how she had got there or whether her parents knew where she was. All he could think of, right now, was that Ava could not find out.

'Well, now you have found me. You can't stay here. It's out of the question. Ava does not know that we were sweethearts…'

'I haven't told her.'

'Good.' He stopped short of saying thank you.

'It was my parents, Patrick. My father tricked me, he tricked both of us. I didn't get your letters, I found them in my father's desk and as soon as I found them I came straight away. I thought you didn't love me any more…'

'I don't love you any more.'

Rose took a sharp intake of breath. It was as if she had been stabbed. She looked at his face. He had to love her. He must be lying. For a terrible moment she imagined that perhaps she was just believing that to save herself the pain of having chased across the world on a whim for a man she thought loved her. If he didn't love her then she was the greatest fool that ever lived. If he didn't love her, it was so much more than the humiliation and the hurt. Patrick was everything to her. If Patrick didn't love her everything would be gone. Life would not be worth living.

'I'm with Ava now. We're married.'

Patrick was as white as a sheet and his gaze was flitting around the room.

He was lying. Rose felt a thin veil of relief.

'Say it again,' she said. 'Look me in the eye and tell me again that you don't love me.'

He looked at her – pitiful, pleading.

'I don't need to say it again. I love Ava. I married Ava…'

If he stayed hard and tough Rose would go away. He wanted her to go away, although now that she was here, sitting in front of him, in the flesh, his beautiful, delicate Rose, close enough to him to reach out and touch her hair and feel the soft lips at the end of his thumb, Patrick was no longer sure of anything.

'You have to leave,' he said. 'You must see how impossible this is.'

He had thought he would never see her again. He had,

perhaps, hoped that would be the case. Her father had sent him to America to keep them away from each other. He understood that now. In some small part of himself, Patrick feared that perhaps that had been the case all along. Perhaps, in some hidden part of himself, he had traded his love of Rose for the opportunity to come to America. Now, when everything was working out so well, his past had turned up to punish him.

Ava opened the door, abruptly, and they both started slightly.

'How have you two been getting along?'

Ava stood looking puzzled at them both until Rose said, 'Just fine.'

Patrick smiled, his best, most convincing stage smile. This was a nightmare, but if he didn't play along, he feared Rose would tell Ava everything. Aside from the fact that he had been in love with Rose, Patrick knew that the way in which he had abandoned her might upset kind-hearted Ava more. Even if he had thought to tell her the truth, the moment he saw Rose in their house, the lie had begun and now he had no choice but to follow it through.

'Although,' Rose added, 'I do not want to be a burden on you.'

'Why, there is no burden at all,' said Ava. 'Is there, Patrick?'

'No,' he said. Everything out of his mouth now was a lie. Curse Rose. What was she playing at? Where would this end?

'No, thank you, I'll stay at the convent, but if I could just get a job,' Rose said, 'something small, anywhere. I suppose, in a way, I'm being selfish.' She added, 'I have not seen anything since I got here and I would just love to work somewhere that I might see a bit of the New York life I've heard so much about.'

Rose knew, in some part of herself, that she was being cruel, manipulating Ava's good nature in this way. She was, truly, a lovely woman. It was not her fault that Patrick did not love her, could never love Ava, the way he loved her. This was something Ava had got caught up in. Something she could never understand. Rose felt bad for her. Worse, she felt bad lying and wheedling to get her own way. But what choice did she have? Patrick was, after all, the love of her life. After talking with Ava it was clear that she had not stolen him from her. Rose was confident that Ava had not even known she existed. That, in itself, gave Rose some comfort. The fact that Patrick had lied to Ava, and never explained to her about their love, their engagement, was testament that she must still mean something to him. The fact that Ava was pregnant made it even worse. But Rose knew that her love was pure and true. Great passion meant great sacrifices. And the passion Rose shared with Patrick was not the ordinary love of everyday life. It was something so much bigger than marriage. They were soulmates. Nothing could part them. Not her parents, not the great Atlantic Ocean, not even marriage to another woman – however nice she was. They were meant to be together. And even if Patrick did not have the courage to face that right now, in time he would.

'I've got an idea,' Ava said, taking up her guest's cue. 'Patrick, why don't you take Rose into work with you tomorrow? You can collect her from the convent, I'll call Gerry now. I'm sure he'll be able to find some small job for her.'

'I don't want to be any trouble,' Rose said.

'It's no trouble at all, is it, Patrick?' Ava said, looking at him firmly.

He really was being insufferably childish. Ava could not

imagine why he was behaving so badly, but while she was irritated by his taciturn manners, she was, at least, comforted by the fact that he obviously did not have any particular ghrá for this beautiful girl from back home.

27

'AGAIN!'

Patrick had sung 'It's Only Make Believe' half a dozen times, and he still could not get it right.

Sheila had decided that, like Conway Twitty who had made the song a hit, Patrick's voice was best suited to contemporary ballads. His being Irish, he had a country twang. However, she was anxious to get away from the Irish ballads and pure country – she would never get a hit out of that. 'It's Only Make Believe' was, she felt, the perfect song for him. But it was also Conway Twitty's song, and Patrick was performing just like a poor version of somebody else today. No matter what she gave him to sing, he seemed to turn it into a dirge. His voice was as strong as ever but his eyes were completely dead. There was no life in him, no passion. The voice was passable, but he was an unconvincing performer. Sheila was starting to get annoyed. She didn't need a copycat, she needed an original star, but Patrick was letting them both down with these lacklustre performances.

As his voice reached for the crescendo, Sheila waved her cigarette at him.

'Stop, Patrick. You sound awful. I don't know what's wrong with you today…'

'I'm sorry, Sheila.'

At least he knew something was wrong himself.

'Would anyone like some coffee? It's just finished brewing.'

It was that irritating Irish girl again. She was a kid from Patrick's hometown. Some kind of a runaway. Patrick and the girl had come in with his wife, a plain-looking woman who, although friendly enough, kept insisting that her father was some Irish big shot who knew Iggy. That irritated Sheila far more than it impressed her, but she took on their sad case anyway. For no other reason than she thought her pretty face about the place might put a bit of life into Patrick. Having her young star married with a child on the way was an unnatural state of affairs for an aspiring pop singer. Girls and drugs and parties were what made great rock and roll singers. Not nagging wives and weeping children. However, it was clear that this girl was madly in love with him. Every time Sheila turned around she was there offering coffee or lazily wiping down a booth, while gazing up at him with a sometimes frightening intensity. Frankly, the girl seemed a bit nuts. Sheila had hoped she might provide an adoring audience. However, it seemed more likely that the simpering admiration was putting Patrick off his singing rather than adding to it. She had thought she should probably get rid of her, but at the same time it was important that Patrick learned how to sing the same, whatever else is going on in his life. The kid needed to man up and not let his life being run by a bossy wife or the lovelorn attention of a pretty girl. He had to get used to singing to crazy fans if he was going to be a star. Although by his performance today, that was seeming less likely than ever.

Sheila really needed Patrick to become a star.

In the past couple of weeks she had begun to feel unnerved by her situation. Here she was, again, managing a club and sleeping with her boss. Iggy wasn't married, although he was so distant and secretive he could just as well be and nobody would ever know it. He was, when he was around, an attentive and caring lover. He gave her small gifts, although they were never insulting (underwear) or extravagant (jewellery she would never wear), as many of Dan's gifts had been. He was careful in his manner too, and Sheila understood his reticence as respect. There were certainly no insistent professions of love as there had been from Dan and she was grateful for that. Sheila hated being lied to more than anything else, but this meant that she had a tendency to believe men when they told her they loved her; the alternative – that they were lying to please her – being too dreadful to contemplate. Sheila had believed Dan was in love with her, and that silly belief had prolonged the affair, making it more than it should ever have been. Now, here she was in the same situation again. Iggy was as straightforward and honest a person as herself; she trusted that. However, he was pathologically secretive, and that was, in itself, a kind of lying. Nobody knew where Iggy would be from week to week. She knew that was how he ran his business and how he kept control of his empire, but nonetheless, Sheila felt uncomfortable always living on the edge of his life. Iggy himself admitted that it was a 'strange way to live', but he could see nothing wrong with it. Indeed, Sheila had always lived life on her own unconventional terms. However, they were her terms as part of her life. Living on the edge of somebody else's was a completely different matter. From day to day, Sheila did not know where her lover was or when he would be back in New York again. She was being sucked into his footloose, routineless way of living and she didn't like it. This uncertainty had led her to stay with her aunt and uncle in Riverdale for the time being. They did not ask about her comings and goings. Auntie made up cold plates for her supper and left them in the Frigidaire for whenever she might be around. They did not know she had a lover, and the nights that she spent in hotels with Iggy they put down to late working hours. They were so grateful for the time that they had with her that, although every week Sheila intended to leave and find her own apartment again, somehow she returned to the comfort of sharing some semblance of a domestic life – standing at the sink washing out somebody else's cup, listening to the radio with her uncle – however fleeting it might turn out to be.

In addition to that, she did not want to tie herself down financially to rental lease when she had no idea how long she would be around. She knew, already, that history was repeating itself and that she did not intend to stay managing the Emerald and being Iggy Morrow's mistress indefinitely. As soon as Patrick's career was up and running and he had a recording contract she would be able to leave and start expanding her portfolio. However, she had to find him a hit record first, and songwriters weren't cheap. She didn't want to have to charm that money out of Iggy; not, indeed, that charming anything out of Iggy was possible, but if she didn't come up with something soon, her dreams would start to disintegrate again. And Sheila could feel she was close, so close to success now, she wasn't going to let it go again.

'Let's wrap it up for the day, Patrick,' she said, ignoring Rose. Then, more to punish him than anything else, added,

'I'm sure Patrick could use a coffee, sweetheart. You guys go ahead. If Gerry needs me, I'm in the office.'

Sheila went into the office then nearly jumped out of her skin when Iggy suddenly appeared standing next to the filing cabinet as she shut the door.

'Christ! What the hell are you doing in here?!'

The curse came out before she even knew what she was saying. Iggy laughed. He loved when this happened. It was the closest he came to having fun in his job. Once people had been working for him for a while they got used to his sudden appearances, and that took the amusement out of it.

'This is not funny,' she said. 'I could have had a heart attack.'

'Well, you didn't,' he said, putting his arms around her waist and pulling her into him, 'although your heart is beating kind of fast. Just let me check in here…' He placed his hand gently on her breast.

Sheila's eyes fluttered closed, and she leaned back, unable to help herself. No matter what time of the day or night he suddenly appeared like this, she always wanted him.

She made herself pull away.

'I'm busy. If you can turn up like this to check up on me, you can't expect me to drop my pants every time you come into the room.'

Iggy flinched. He hated when she referred to work and 'them' in the same sentence. It made what they had seem cheap. And it wasn't cheap. Not to him. Iggy had never been in this situation before. Sleeping with somebody that worked for him. He made a point of never doing it. Sheila was an exception. She had been an exception since that first night, he knew that now. Although he did not like to admit it, Iggy was in love. All the signs were there. When they were alone in a room together all he could think about was making love to her. Everything she said, even the banal, everyday business of their work together, was fascinating or amusing just because it was Sheila saying it. When she cursed him, he laughed. When she berated or belittled him, he couldn't feel angry. Instead, it felt like a knife in his chest. She weakened him, and in her company sometimes he felt powerless. At the same time, however hard she appeared, some nights after they had made love, when she could be persuaded to spend the night with him in his hotel, he would watch her sleeping and his breath would catch at how delicate and vulnerable and warm she was. In life, Sheila was feisty, a livewire. In her sleep, and in some of the quieter, gentle moments in their lovemaking, Iggy sensed a tenderness, a sensitivity he found too compelling to name. Sheila was, in her lithe figure and her hidden spirit, he believed, like a child-woman. She was tough and it was no game, he knew she was no pushover, he could not pull the wool over her eyes in business or in their private life, and nor would he attempt to. However, on some level he knew that she needed looking after. For the first time in his life, Iggy felt that was something he wanted to do. But he mistrusted that instinct and pushed it to one side. Partly because he knew she would never concede, and partly because the idea of loving someone that much, being tied to somebody else's life, somebody else's needs, was beyond him.

While Iggy counted the days until he would see Sheila again, he was grateful for the incessant travelling because it enabled him to keep control over himself. If he gave in to his feelings, he would have spent every day and every night in her company and let his great empire crumble to the ground. The fact that he could never let that happen was, he believed, his saving grace. To allow such romantic instincts would be dangerous, particularly with a woman like Sheila, so independent, so cool, so reserved, so very much like himself. He knew what level of detachment he was capable of and he believed she was capable of the same. However, when he was with her, he found he was unable to help himself from wanting more. Not more sex and more amusement, but more of the thing he could never admit to wanting: the intimacy of love.

'I thought we might eat in the city tonight?'

Sheila was furious. Furious at him for creeping up on her like that, furious at herself for her impulsive, shocked reaction which made her seem foolish, but mostly furious with the irrational impulse she was now feeling, to simply grab Iggy by the collar, kiss him, then make love to him in the office in the middle of a working day.

'Well – I can't tonight,' she said coolly. 'I'm busy.'

She could tell by the look on his face that he didn't believe her. She had half a mind to lie and tell him she was seeing another man. He would believe that. Sheila knew she had that much power over him at least.

'I promised to have dinner with my aunt and uncle.'

For the first time in her life, Sheila was aware of using her family as a kind of trophy. Iggy had no family. He had told her about his life in the orphanage. She had never confided in him about her parents and brother. How could she? She had never spoken about anyone. And yet, here she was, triumphantly proclaiming what little family she did have. What was this impulse to be cruel that he brought out in her? We are both orphans, but at least I have some family.

'Why don't we bring them with us? I would love to meet them.'

As soon as he had said the words, Iggy knew that he had gone too far.

Sheila blushed and coughed. She seemed as awkward as it was possible for a person of her cool demeanour to be. Her smile was apologetic, pained.

'I don't think that's such a good idea. Do you?' she said.

At once, it seemed like a dreadful, hurtful thing to say to him. At the same time, she did not see what else she could possibly say. The idea of her lover meeting her family, her precious aunt and uncle, was anathema to her. He must have known, as much as he seemed to know her at all, that she was not the marrying kind. She had never brought anyone home to meet them before, and to do so would be making a statement so broad, so sweeping, she could not possibly justify it.

Iggy felt the knock-back as a kick of rejection.

'I suppose not,' he said. He was back on the sports pitch of the orphanage, in the sidelines of the football game, nursing a bloody leg, waiting for the jeering in the changing rooms. He left there promising himself he would never be slapped around again. And yet here he was, having his heart and his ego bruised by this woman. Letting her do it because, underneath it all, he believed she was as sweet as he was.

As he turned his back on her, pretending to tackle the papers on his desk, he hoped it was true.

'How is Patrick going along?' he asked without looking at her.

'To be honest,' she said, 'I think he would be better if he was working with some new material.'

'Original material?' Iggy said, his eyes resolutely on his paperwork.

'Yes,' she said. 'He's got real potential. I'd love to try and get a recording contract.'

I bet you would, thought Iggy. Then the pair of you would

fly out of here in five minutes. He resolved to get proper contracts drawn up on his next trip to Boston to see his lawyers.

'Well,' he said, ready to look up at her now, 'when the audience out there get sick of hearing every song in the hit parade, here and in Ireland, come back and have a talk with me then.'

He was angry and she had bruised his ego, Sheila knew that. All the same, she was annoyed that he rejected her suggestion so quickly, and annoyed with herself for not being more coy and manipulative in her timing.

Iggy began fiddling around with his paperwork again and as Sheila left, saying, 'I'll see you later,' he barely grunted a reply, and did not look up from his desk, although he did hear her mutter, 'If you're still here...' She closed the door rather sharply behind her.

Heading back into the ballroom, Sheila paused at the door for a cigarette. As she was lighting it her attention was caught by a heated argument that appeared to be happening at the side of the stage. It was Patrick and his simpering fan. Fascinated and not wishing to be seen, she lowered her cigarette and eavesdropped.

'You said you loved me!' the girl shouted at him.

'Shhh – somebody will hear us!'

Too late, somebody already has, thought Sheila to herself, smiling.

She stood stock-still, so she wouldn't get caught in her hiding place.

'I don't care who hears me, Patrick. I love you and I know you love me! We can make it work.'

Silly girl, thought Sheila. Still, the kid was a dark horse after all. She didn't know he had it in him. Although he was handling it very poorly. He seemed very agitated. The colour in his cheeks rising, his hands opening and closing as if hoping to release his anger.

'How many times do I have to tell you, I am married to Ava now. We have a child on the way. Things have changed. This is going nowhere.'

'I know it's a terrible situation, Patrick. You know your marriage was a mistake. At least if you can admit it we can move on. Nothing is impossible. We can work it all out—'

'There is no "we"! You have to stop talking like this. It's over. Please, Rose, stop acting crazy!'

The girl was enraged now. 'What about this?' she screamed at him. She waved a sheet of paper in his face, and then started to read from it.

'"There's nothing in this world that makes me feel the way I feel—"'

'Stop it! Stop it, I'm telling you...'

'"When I'm with you because I know this love I have is real..."'

He reached out to grab the page from her. Tears were streaming down the girl's face. This is all too dramatic, thought Sheila. Two children having a lovers' tiff. It all seemed rather overblown and silly to her. In fact, she began to wish it would end, so she could come out of her hiding place and light her cigarette.

'I suppose none of this means anything to you, I suppose I never meant anything to you...' Then she scrunched up the piece of paper and threw it dramatically aside. 'Perhaps it was all lies, Patrick. Maybe it was always just your plan to get to America. Maybe you just tricked my father into giving you money and were delighted to get away from me? Is that how it is?'

Patrick closed his eyes in frustration, seeming to gather himself for a few seconds before opening them again. And when he did, from her hiding place it seemed to Sheila that he was looking straight at her, although, in fact, he was looking straight through her. Back into a past when it was just the two of them, kissing, in a field.

'You know that's not true, Rose. You know how much you meant to me.'

In the young singer's eyes Sheila saw a passionate pleading look. If only he could put on that look when he's singing, she thought.

'Then there *is* hope for us, Patrick.'

Sheila raised her eyes to heaven. If this nonsense didn't come to an end soon she have to go out and stop it herself.

'No, Rose,' he said again, storming off with the crazy pretty girl in close pursuit.

Sheila came out from behind the curtain, shaking her head in a mixture of amusement and frustration at what she had just seen. Patrick really was a hopeless case. For such a good-looking, talented and ambitious kid, he was still such an ingénu. If he was going to sleep round on his wife, well, he needed to learn to lie a bit better than he was doing. And not just to his wife, but his lover too.

She lit her cigarette and walked across to where they had been standing to pick up the piece of trash that Rose had thoughtlessly thrown on the floor. She looked around quickly before opening the crumpled page, to amuse herself by reading the love letter that seemed to have caused all this trouble.

Immediately, she saw that it was not a love letter, but a handwritten poem. Her eyes quickly scanned the words.

It was a love song.

Sheila smiled, carefully folded the paper and put it in her pocket.

At last, she had struck gold.

28

A COUPLE OF days after Rose came into their lives,
Ava had received a reply from her mother in the post.
It was a mass card, presumably to pray for the recovery of her sullied soul, getting pregnant before marriage etc.
However, Ava was nonetheless glad to get the peace offering. In the past week Ava had become aware that there
was a life growing inside her. She was only just beginning
to show, but she had begun to feel that she was pregnant,
and not simply fat. The awareness that she would be a
mother soon made her conscious of her own mother's love
for her, and Ava felt softer towards her. And she began to
understand that Nessa's anger had been based only on the
worry, fear and betrayal she would no doubt someday feel as
a parent.

The letter contained a formal introduction to an Irish
priest in Manhattan with whom Nessa had volunteered her
to do some charitable work. Her own priest had told her that
Father Moran, who worked in Hell's Kitchen, was looking

for a respectable woman to help coordinate a 'Parcels to Ireland' programme. Nessa had suggested Ava as she had some volunteering experience in their own Yonkers parish. Also, she was her 'father's daughter' when it came to such things. Reading between the lines, Ava felt the note itself was acknowledgement that she was now living an independent life. If Nessa did not wholly delight in her marriage, she was, perhaps, coming to accept it. The note was also a not very subtle assurance that the continuance of Ava's good Catholic habits would help bridge any gaps in her mother's approval.

The church was in the heart of Hell's Kitchen. The last time Ava had been to this part of town was with Dermot, the night he had proposed. The night she had first met Patrick. She brushed the thought aside as she pulled the car up and parked it on the sidewalk at the bottom of the church steps, so that she would not have far to carry her heavy bags of clothes. She felt curiously independent and brave coming to this part of town on her own. However, the experience of helping Patrick's friend Rose get on her feet with a job in the Emerald had made Ava see that, like her father, her mission in life was to make herself useful to other people. Ava had taken it upon herself to contact Gerry at the club and ask if he could get Rose a job. He had said they were always in need of reliable Irish girls and had passed the message on to his new boss, and Patrick's new manager, Sheila, who had given Rose a few hours cleaning during the day, and occasional work covering the cloakrooms. The next visit she made was to Sister Augustine to see if Rose could be allowed to come home late on certain evenings, if her new job required it. The nun was very accommodating, and impressed with the pragmatic, pregnant young woman, especially when she learned she was Tom Brogan's daughter. When she told Ava that it was her father who had brought Rose to the convent in the first place, Ava was taken aback. Had he not known that Rose was a friend of Patrick's? The nun also explained, on the quiet, that it had been some 'awful' experience with her father that had sent the girl chasing halfway across the world to escape them. Ava could not imagine what that terrible thing would be, but the information just made her feel even more warmly towards the young woman. It made Ava feel even more fortunate to be in the position she was in. She was married to a good man with a baby on the way. Although their life was modest, they loved each other. Despite Patrick's great aspirations for fame, Ava did not feel she needed much more than they already had, except perhaps more of her husband's time. Although, she determined, if she were to spend her own time more usefully, doing good deeds, she might miss his company less. One had to make sacrifices in life and getting pregnant out of wedlock had been a dreadful sin. So, it seemed only right that Ava should make amends by helping people who were less fortunate than herself. Helping Rose had given her a small start and today, volunteering for the church, could be the beginning of a new, positive phase in her life.

The church was quiet for a Saturday, with a dozen or so people occupying the pew opposite the confessionals. Ava was irritated with herself for not having remembered Saturday-morning confessions would probably be underway at this time. She really had been very remiss in her religion of late. The feeling of sadness flooded over her briefly as she thought how far she had fallen from her faith in the past few months. However, she reminded herself she was here now to make amends to God, her church, her parents and herself.

She wondered if Patrick felt the same way. She had noticed him moving away from her in the bed lately. She was hurt, but she could understand it. Her body had changed and no man would want to make love to a woman knowing there was a child inside them. She still had the same urges surging through her body despite the fact that she was pregnant. If anything, they were stronger than ever. That, Ava now believed, was God's gentle way of punishing her for not keeping a check on her passions. So, she didn't bother Patrick, had a cold shower every morning and had now resolved to be the best person she could possibly be.

Knowing that Father Moran would be in a hurry, Ava left her two heavy bags at the door and hurried up to the sacristy to catch him before confessions began.

Dermot was having a wretched morning. First of all, he had been unable to find a clean shirt. His ironing service had not delivered the day before, so he had been forced to wear yesterday's crumpled and slightly stained one. This was just one of many small domestic disasters that he had been having of late. Work had been busy and he had not had time to do all the chores that, if he were a proper man, he would have a wife doing for him. Dermot did not mind doing his own laundry and, as a matter of fact, he was rather a good cook. However, at the age of thirty, he felt the failure of his bachelor status more sharply now than ever before. Before he met Ava, Dermot had been resigned, if not entirely satisfied, to being on his own. There had been a rhythm about keeping the apartment tidy, a routine in putting the trash out, going to the grocery store, leaving money out for the cleaning woman. However, the very moment he and Ava got engaged, with the promise of marriage, Dermot allowed his entire domestic routine to fall apart. No woman wants to be married to a fuss-budget of a man. A decent woman will want a man she can take in hand. So instinctively Dermot began to let his domestic life go to pot. It seemed the right thing to do. Even though the engagement went on for only a matter of weeks, he had been unable to recover his meticulous, organized home life. Ava had been the love of his life. Losing her had meant losing everything. If his life went back to the way he was before he met her, to the man he was before he met her, surely that would make the loss even greater because it would be as though she had never happened.

Better to have loved and lost – and all that.

In his scruffy shirt Dermot had to go down to Hell's Kitchen on what he had been led to believe was a straightforward document-signing mission. When he got there he found that Joe Higgins had arranged a meeting with one of the Balducci brothers. Some business about some woman who had slept with somebody's husband. Dermot had been dragged in to 'mediate' the situation, which was gangster code for 'if we do something really terrible can you get us off?'

Dermot had spent his morning listening and nodding sagely as some of New York's most terrifying gangsters set before him convoluted scenarios of premeditated violence: 'If a guy were to… say… lose his footing and accidentally fall into a large hole…' 'If a guy were to accidentally shoot himself in the knee – and say there was another guy in the car with him when it happened…', and trying to find a way of responding that would not result in him playing centre stage in one such scenario.

All of this in yesterday's shirt.

By the time he got out of there, Dermot was so stressed

there was no way he could get into his car and drive. He walked around the block a couple of times, but he was more nervous of running into one of his clients, a highly likely scenario in this end of town, so he decided to pop into the church. He was not a good practising Catholic: Christmas, weddings, keeping his mother happy was about the strength of it. But occasionally, when he was passing, he popped into this church. It was a peaceful place to come during a crazy day and he always managed to clear his head when he came here.

Dermot sat on the end of a pew near the back of the church then closed his eyes and let himself sink into the incense-scented silence. Peace. At last.

When he opened his eyes, however, he got such a fright that he nearly jumped out of his skin.

Something more terrifying than any gangster scenario that he could possibly imagine.

It was Ava. She was walking directly towards him.

Dermot froze. He had not seen Ava since that night she ditched him. He knew she had married that singer, after becoming 'disgracefully' pregnant, as his mother described. Dermot had been beyond hurt. He knew he had to deal with it and, being part of the same Irish community, would certainly have to face her again one day in the future. But not today. He was not ready. He was not prepared. He was wearing yesterday's shirt.

She had not noticed him so he would have to act quickly. Dermot leapt to his feet and ran to the nearest hiding place. The confessional box.

Father Moran said goodbye to the lovely young woman, who turned out to be Tom Brogan's daughter. She really was a charming thing. The ladies that worked in his parish were a very tight-knit, older gang and she would be a real addition. A breath of fresh air. There was something, however, troubling him about their meeting, which he could not quite put his finger on. He was musing on that as he sat down in the box. First penitent in would be Bridie Flaherty. She was always first on a Saturday. Bridie would have been here since nine, doing the stations and firing out a few decades of the rosary. With a bit of luck she might have murdered her husband this week to make up for the years of sinless Saturdays she had made him endure. He engaged in his preparations, a good scratch followed by a pre-confession hearty cough and nose-blowing ritual. Bridie always gave him a few seconds before she came in.

'Bless me, Father...' said a low man's voice.

'Jesus Christ!'

The Irish priest made a habit of never swearing, unless he was drunk. Certainly never in a place of such holiness as a confessional.

'You are not supposed to be in here,' he boomed. 'Get out and wait your turn!'

Bridie heard him and was delighted. She, along with the other penitents, had been horrified to see the young man leaping into the confessional. They assumed he was, at least, a murderer looking for urgent penance.

Dermot was mortified but, at the same time, he wasn't going out there to face Ava. Especially not under this new, embarrassing circumstance.

'... for I have sinned.'

'You most certainly have... now get—' But Dermot was going nowhere.

'It has been ten years since my last confession.'

'Humpf,' Father Moran said. 'Clearly.'

Now that he had started, the priest had no choice but to let him continue. Anyway, he consoled himself, a break from Bridie couldn't be a bad thing. Men of his age in suits in this area often brought in great confessions. Sex and drugs and the odd maiming – occasionally a murder. No priest really liked to hear of terrible crimes against God and man happening on one's doorstep but at least, Father Moran thought, it gave one a sense of purpose. The devout Bridie Flahertys of this world were two a penny but a good gangster could really turn a Saturday morning confession around.

Unfortunately, this was not one of those men.

Once Dermot started saying the confessional prayers, he found that the floodgates opened and it all came pouring out. Father Moran got the whole story. About how he was in love with this girl, and how he had been so happy, and then he had asked her to marry him, and she had said 'yes!'. Oh joy! But then she had let him down by falling in love with somebody else, needless to say, a cad – a no-good singer called Patrick Murphy who deflowered her (he said, haltingly) – and now she was pregnant and married to this Murphy but he was still in love with her himself and what was he going to do?

Patrick Murphy? Hadn't Tom Brogan's girl mentioned that name to him earlier? Good heavens! Ava was married to Patrick Murphy and this young man was in love with her too. Father Brogan wondered who he was. He would ask Bridie later. Now then, that was a nice piece of gossip to pick up on a Saturday morning. But he felt certain there was something else. Something about that name, Patrick Murphy, that he couldn't quite remember. He had thought it earlier when Ava had mentioned it to him. There was some connection he wasn't quite making. Ava had said there was a girl newly arrived in the city and she might get involved in the parcels to Ireland. From Mayo...

'What should I do, Father? What do you advise?'

Oh God. He was still here.

'I am not here to advise, only to give penance. Say two Our Fathers, a decade of the rosary and a Glory Be.'

When the young man didn't get out, Father Moran realized he was stalling because he was afraid of running into Ava. He could be here all day!

'What I suggest you do, young man, is get a firm grip on yourself. Stop sitting around moping, get out there and find yourself another woman. There are plenty of fine young women in all the dance halls in New York and once you get out among them you will find that one is much the same as the other.'

'I can't dance.'

Even to Dermot's ears it sounded pathetic. The priest sighed deeply. This lovelorn idiot was really trying his patience.

'Well go and take some lessons then. Young Ava Brogan is married now and that is all there is to it. Now hop out of this box and give somebody else a turn.'

When Dermot didn't get up he barked, 'She has left the building!'

Dermot got up to leave so quickly he banged his head on the way out. A line of old ladies glowered at him so murderously that he didn't even kneel down to say his penance.

Back outside, when the cruel snap of daylight hit him, Dermot realized he was furious. This was why he had stopped coming to mass, this Irish-American nonsense where everybody knew everybody else's business. It was worse than any gossiping small town in Ireland.

His heart was broken and nobody cared. Not even, no, especially not, his priest.

Dermot decided to go home to sit in his apartment and feel sorry for himself for the rest of the day. But first he would head up to Saks on Fifth Avenue to buy himself a dozen new shirts.

29

S HEILA WENT to the Lexington club where Frankie the Sax worked and managed to catch him on the kitchen phone.

'Who was that kid you said got some other kid to write that tune? Turned up in a Benz, got signed to Decca?'

'I hope you ain't still in town, girl?'

'I'm staying with my folks. Out of town. In Riverdale.'

'Riverdale? Nice. I didn't even know you had folks.'

Sheila didn't know if Frankie had family either. She was guessing there weren't too many of them if he did. That was the way the scene was. They were each other's family, except there were no questions and no commitments. That was how she liked it. Freedom. Now she was living with her aunt and uncle and embroiled in some kind of a strange scene with Ignatius. The quicker she got Patrick's show on the road and got enough money to move on, the better.

'His singing name was Johnny Blue – I don't know who the writer was. Some English kid, I think he said. The song did

OK but not as good as Johnny hoped. I think he had to give the car back. As far as I know, he's still gigging. You can catch him at Mo's on a Wednesday.'

'You got a number for him?'

Frankie laughed. 'I ain't even got a phone, sugar. Got no place to put one neither. Call Mo. He'll put you in touch.'

Sheila thanked him. Was she crazy doing all this? Frankie's tone certainly implied she was. But Sheila could feel her break was coming. She had to keep going.

It took a few calls before she eventually tracked down the songwriter. He was a kid called Malcolm English who worked out of a music factory in Chelsea. It was a large loft space where half a dozen young guys all worked and lived together. They spent their days writing music and jamming, and their nights partying and fooling around. They were hipsters, rebels. Some of them were trying to break into the music industry, others were already out of it, disillusioned with the big business.

There were any number of well-known songwriters that Sheila knew she could approach, but they were all expensive and she doubted any of them would be happy to work with another man's lyrics.

'Man, this is schmaltzy stuff,' Malcolm said when she handed him a piece of paper where she had freshly typed Patrick's poem. 'Did you write this?'

Sheila stood in front of him in full skinny black beatnik gear, her dark eyes glaring at him from behind her long fringe.

'Do I look like I wrote it?' she growled.

'I guess not,' he said sunnily in his London accent. He smiled to himself as he realized she was trying to intimidate him. Malcolm didn't even know what intimidate meant. He was twenty-four and the world was at his feet. He had

already written half a dozen hit songs in the UK before deciding he didn't want to be part of the music establishment and
splitting for America to start again. The world was changing.
A cat could move from one place to another – all he needed
was cash. Malcolm chose who he worked with and when.
He certainly didn't usually work with other people's lyrics
but he liked this woman. She was kind of cool for an old bird.

'The kid that wrote this has a lot of passion, but I need to
get it out of him. Can you help me?'

Malcolm liked a challenge.

'You want a ballad?'

'No. I want *the* ballad. I want the best, most painful, most
passionate ballad anyone has ever goddam written. I want
something that will make every single woman in the world
fall in love with this guy.'

'It'll cost you…'

'… and I want it for free.'

'You're kidding, right?'

Now Malcom was intimidated. Hell, he was scared. This
woman was sitting on the edge of his desk and now he knew
she wasn't cool after all, but crazy.

'Look,' she said, offering him a cigarette. He took it, shaking his head slowly. 'You're good, I know that. If I had a
load of money I would give it to you to write the music for
this song. But then, I would be crazy not to, right?' Now the
woman was admitting she was crazy. 'But listen to this, Malcolm. If the song's a hit, I stand to make a fortune. I should go
and steal the money to give to you to write this song for me
so that every penny that it makes belongs to me. That's how
the record companies do it, right?' Malcolm nodded. 'So
how about this. You write a song, with these lyrics, with no fee.
Then, I give you a contract saying you have fifty per cent of the

copyright, and as such you get fifty per cent of all record sales. Does that sound reasonable?'

From experience Malcolm knew that music managers and record labels were making a fortune out of his work. He got paid a one-off fee, albeit a very good one, but by the time his songs were marching up the hit parade, he had already spent the money. He had hoped the system in America might be different, but it seemed it was just the same. This woman was clearly interested in operating outside the system. She was one of them.

A week later, Malcolm delivered the song.

Sheila could read music but Patrick could not so Sheila arranged for Malcolm to stay for one rehearsal to work through it on the piano with the singer.

She had called both of the young men into the Emerald for a rehearsal at three in the afternoon, making sure that Malcolm would arrive twenty minutes before Patrick so that she had a chance to look at the song and give it her approval. The band would join them for a full rehearsal at six when the doors of the Emerald officially opened for business. The dancing crowd didn't start coming in earnest for at least two hours after that, and the band didn't really consider themselves 'onstage' to their audience until eight.

Malcolm handed Sheila the sheet music and she scanned it, humming along on the first read. He was impressed that she grasped the notation so quickly. Even more impressed when she sat down at the piano and, falteringly, played it. 'I like it,' was all she said. Malcolm gathered from her demeanour that that was high praise. Then she stood up and gestured him to take her place just as Patrick arrived.

Sheila could not imagine two young men who were both the same age and probably equally musically talented and yet were so very different. Patrick, with his Irish good looks, so earnest and passionate, wearing his heart on his sleeve; Malcolm had that sneering, slightly cynical edge, but was as earnest and devoted when it came to making music.

'Patrick, this is Malcolm,' she said. 'He's one of Britain's best songwriters and I got him to write you a song. Hopefully, a hit song.'

'Cool,' said Patrick. He tried to look pleased. He was trying to look pleased for everyone these days: Ava, Sheila, Rose. God! Rose! What the hell was he going to do about Rose? That thought had been occupying his every waking moment and Patrick was finding the strain of living a lie terrible. Things were becoming unbearable with Ava. He felt guilty and trapped all the time. He hated Rose for doing this to him. Worst of all, Sheila was not happy with him. Their last session had not gone well, and he was beginning to believe she might get rid of him. He could not blame her if she did. She wanted him to sing with passion but Patrick felt all stodgy inside. Singing had always made him feel free, as if it was a release. But since Rose had come back into his life everything inside had become clogged up with all the lies and guilt and confusion. Sheila had commissioned a song for him but all he could feel was this fear he would not be able to sing it.

She handed him the sheet. He glanced at it briefly and said apologetically, 'I can't read music.'

'Listen to Malcolm sing it, and look at the notes while he does – you'll pick it up.'

Malcolm played a brief intro and as he began to sing, the words *It Was Only Ever You* burned up at Patrick from the sheet. What was this? His poem to Rose?

'Where did you get this?' he wailed at Sheila.

'I found it on the floor after you had a row with your girl-friend,' she said dismissively.

Malcolm looked over, worried.

'Carry on playing,' she said, nodding at him.

'I won't sing it!' shouted Patrick. He felt on the verge of tears. Was this some kind of a terrible joke? 'You have no right...'

Sheila's lips tightened and she held out her hand, signalling Malcolm to stop playing.

'I have every right,' she said. 'I am your manager. You entered into a contract with me to sing any song that I gave you and do whatever I thought was necessary to get you on the ladder to being a star. So far all you have given me is Irish schmaltz. We had an agreement, Patrick – I do the thinking and you do the singing. I don't care how embarrassed you are right now, how humiliated you feel. I do not care how much of a mess your love life is in. All I care about is what you sing and how you sing it. So either you sing me this song the very best you can or you walk out that door, right now, and I will find me another Patrick Murphy.'

Patrick's face was burning. He felt like walking out, he really did. But he also knew he had come this far and if he turned back there would be nothing waiting for him. This was the end of the line. Pleasing Sheila was his only hope.

And so, after Malcolm had sung through 'It Was Only Ever You' and begun playing the intro again, Patrick opened his mouth and he sang. He was so embarrassed, the first line came out in a whisper.

'Louder,' Sheila said.

He pushed the sound out from his chest.

'Louder, I said!'

He threw his voice into the words. Had he really written them? O God, on the plane. Rose had thrown them back at him...

'Louder! LOUDER! Jesus, Patrick, where is your voice? GIVE ME YOUR VOICE!'

Patrick felt like punching her for all this badgering. This was just the worst thing that had ever happened to him. He hated her more than anything in the whole world. As Patrick was singing the words he thought how much he hated her, so he sang as loud and as hard as he possibly could. Then, when the song hit its towering crescendo, he missed the note, and it came out in an angry squawk. He sounded terrible.

When the song was finished, Sheila stopped pacing, looked up at him and smiled.

'That was good,' she said.

'It sounded terrible,' Patrick said. Had she lost her mind?

'Of course it sounded terrible. But the performance had emotion, and that's all I care about. Now we've just got to teach you to sing it as well.'

Despite his anger and humiliation, Patrick felt something fall into place. He did not know what that something was, only that he had something to reach for.

And reach he did.

For the next three hours solid he sang the song over and over and over again.

Sheila roared at him: 'Higher!' 'Lower!' 'Faster!' 'Slower!' 'More feeling!' 'Put your heart into it!' 'Rubbish!' 'Start again!'

She interrupted and criticized and pleaded with him until he felt his throat dry up and Malcolm over on the piano thought his hands would drop off. The composer was now so sick of the song it made him regret ever having written it.

And still Sheila shouted, 'Again! Not there yet.'

Then, as the afternoon wore on and the band were given their sheet music and began to join them, her tone softened. 'Nearly there.' 'One more time.' 'Good performance' and 'We're close to it now.'

Finally, at six thirty, Patrick gave her what she had been waiting for.

Each note was perfect but it was the passionate innocence in his delivery that gave the song its uniqueness. The thing that would make the song a hit, its singer a star, and its manager, finally, a success. As Patrick reached for the high notes in the penultimate stanza, the final 'you' of 'It Was Only Ever You', the one that all those hours ago he had thought was impossible, Sheila closed her eyes and felt the notes reverberate through her entire body. This was music. This was what it could do to you. She opened her eyes and looked at him, her young star, and noticed that the passion that had been lacking even just a few hours ago was miraculously returned, and in greater measure than she could possibly have imagined. Marvelling at how he was able to drum up such emotion looking out into an empty room, she followed his eyes.

There, standing in the direct line of his gaze, was the pretty young blonde girl, Rose.

He was singing to her, and she was sobbing her heart out.

The club was virtually empty, apart from a half-dozen regulars who had come in for the early bird cocktails, and the luxury of practising their dance moves on an empty dance floor as the band rehearsed. Such a small crowd was all but invisible to the performers and staff who were used to seeing large crowds. To them, with only a half dozen regulars scattered across the vast room, the room was more or less empty. A smattering of committed dancers would hardly notice the young singer kissing the bargirl.

Unfortunately, one of those regulars was paying them a good deal of attention. Myrtle had come early on a promise to perfect her jitterbug with a hopeful young man she had been dancing with the past three Thursdays in a row. Quite used to seeing her friend's husband Patrick on stage, she was stopped in her tracks by the beautiful song he was singing.

'It was only ever you...' he crooned across the room, gazing off behind her to some imagined true love. Even though he was her friend's husband, not for the first time Myrtle felt herself go weak at the knees. When Patrick sang, he really was an absolute dreamboat. Although, offstage, she found him to be a bit of a sap, this was the dreamiest dreamboat song she had ever heard him singing. She was quite carried away with herself and when he had finished she waved across at him. As he climbed down from the stage Myrtle was fully expecting him to come across to her and exchange a few pleasantries. Instead, he walked, as if in a trance, straight past her to the spot where he had been looking as he sang. Myrtle turned around and saw that blonde hussy, Rose. She had always suspected the tart had designs on her friend's husband. If Myrtle was married to a man like Patrick she certainly wouldn't be encouraging him to have pretty, female 'friends from home'. Ava would never suspect such a thing could happen, of course. She was too good. Everyone thought Ava was terrible leaving Dermot and going off with Patrick and getting pregnant, but Myrtle had known Ava all her life and understood that she wouldn't have done something like that unless she was truly, madly in love. Patrick had seduced her into getting carried away with herself. It had been out of character, and she probably would have been better off marrying Dermot. They were certainly more suited. But then, Myrtle reasoned, what girl doesn't want a love so romantic, so powerful that she gets carried away? That was what happened to her friend and now she was being punished; her worse nightmares were coming to pass. Sweet, stupid Ava had entertained that girl Rose, becoming friends with her, and now she was kissing her husband. Kissing him! As if it were the most natural, beautiful thing in the world. The same way, no doubt, he had kissed her. Myrtle was boiling. She lit a cigarette and stood, glaring at them, willing them to turn around and see her. What a fright they would get.

Except they did not turn around. They were too lost in their kiss. Lost to the world. Myrtle could not have been more hurt and angry for her friend, but seeing them, standing there, locked in each other's arms, Rose's delicate blonde face leaning up towards Patrick's willing mouth, her small hands desperately clutching his shoulders, his long arms wrapped around her body at the waist, recklessly, openly kissing in front of everyone, Myrtle had to admit it: they did look terribly in love.

30

AVA HAD not been feeling well all morning. She had been sick after her breakfast, and when the nausea had abated it was replaced with a nasty cramp that came and went.

Knowing that if she went to the doctor he would tell her she should probably go to the hospital and get checked out, Ava reassured herself that this was simply a return of her earlier sickness and decided to go ahead with her plans anyway.

This was a very big day for Ava. Father Moran had sent out a circular with the previous week's church news sheet asking all of the ladies of the parish to bring in clothes for the Parcels to Ireland project, along with names and addresses of people in their parishes back home for them to apply to have the clothes sent to.

This was the first time that Ava would be meeting many of the ladies from the parish. She knew from experience with her mother that the older more established ladies of the parish did not always welcome new faces. Especially not a younger one who might be seen to be taking over their territory. Ava didn't mind this. She rather enjoyed the idea of buttering up and charming the old guard. Ava got on with most women. This was, she knew, because she was not pretty enough for the younger women to feel threatened and she also had a sensible way about her that the older women liked. However, by now, everybody in the Irish Catholic community would know about her shotgun marriage. Ava felt nervous about facing them, in spite of telling herself she was married now and so had nothing to be ashamed off. Giving a good first impression was important if she wanted to overcome their prejudice.

Deciding what to wear was the big thing. Ava had quickly sewn herself up a smock dress the night before, from some expensive cream wool she had bought on sale. It was a simple, unfussy garment, but it sat neatly over her small, but growing bump. If only she had something nicer than a plain cardigan to cover her arms. Looking in her closet for inspiration, Ava saw the rose suit. It was out of the question, of course, but the pink weave was a perfect match for the cream dress. She tentatively reached for the jacket, then, taking a deep breath, tried to fit one of her arms through the sleeves. It was a tight squeeze. She could barely bend her arms at the elbow, and, of course, there was not a hope of closing it, but even left open, it set off the cream dress and made it look special. It transformed her from a dumpy pregnant woman into an important, dynamic church lady.

The suit had transformed her life once before, and now it was doing it again. Ava smiled as she ran out the door and headed for the church.

* * *

The church ladies loved her straight away. They all knew Tom and Nessa Brogan, by reputation at least, and the fact that this respectable couple's daughter had fallen somewhat, before redeeming herself through a speedy marriage and a desire to do good works, made her all the more adorable to them. Ava was under the impression that Father Moran had given one or two of them a firm talking-to beforehand, but if it made her job easier, so much the better.

Ava's job was to gather and coordinate all of the clothes and put them into piles that were of equal value. There were, as she knew there would be, objections.

'I would like to make sure that that yellow jacket reaches my cousin in Kilkelly.'

'This bag here simply must reach Cork in the next month. It contains a dress for my grandniece's first Holy Communion.'

'My brother is a farmer and if we don't make sure he wears a respectable suit for market day, he'll never get a wife.'

'Ladies, ladies,' Ava commanded them. 'Can I just remind you all that these clothes are intended for the most needy? And while I understand that we all want to look after our families back home, we really must be mindful of spreading our privilege equally.'

They nodded at her wisdom, as she assured them that the programme would give them the opportunity to do their own personal packages as well as charity ones. She remembered her mother once telling her: 'Half the time they just want to get together with other women, show off the clothes they can afford to give away and talk about their families back home. It's as much of a charity to the women giving the parcels as those receiving them.'

By late afternoon there were thirty parcels ready for dispatch. Ava had eaten nothing all day, despite there being a table laid out with a tea urn and an impressive array of sand-wiches and cakes. She had taken a mouthful of tea earlier but was unable to keep it down. The cramps had been coming and going, but Ava found when she was busy and distracted she could ignore them better than if she was at home.

However, around five o'clock she got a wave of pain that forced her to sit down. The ladies immediately gathered around her in a concerned group but she pleaded with them to leave her alone for a few minutes to gather herself. Pregnancy was a funny business, so they left her alone.

She held her head down for a few minutes and breathed into the pain. It was so intense she felt like crying out but she did not want to make a fuss that would draw attention to herself. So she kept her eyes closed and breathed until the pain subsided. When she looked up again she saw Myrtle walking across the room towards her. What a wonderful surprise! Had she come to join the parish? Ava didn't care. She had come at just the right moment when she was feeling vulnerable in front of a group of strangers she was anxious to impress. If she was sick her old friend would find a way to get her out of there while maintaining her dignity. Myrtle looked determined, sweeping through the other women, as they wondered who this assertive gatecrasher was, assuming she must be something to do with their charismatic new leader. For a moment Ava wondered herself how Myrtle, with her rescuing demeanour, had known she was sick.

'I need to talk to you, Ava,' she said, plonking herself down beside her. She stayed quiet for a few seconds, with her eyes lowered, wringing her hands. Ava realized she was not here for her, after all, but had some problem of her own she wanted to share. She felt the bite of resentful disappointment. Then Myrtle looked straight into her eyes and grabbed her hands.

'I don't know how to tell you this, I have been going over and over it wondering if there is a way I can not tell you – but you're my oldest friend and you have to know the truth. And I am the only one that can tell you...'

Ava felt a knot tighten in her stomach. She did not know if it was fear of what Myrtle was about to tell her or the baby-wind cramps she had been experiencing all day. The threat of a pain was so intense, she felt as if her head was in a guillotine waiting for the blade to drop.

'... but yesterday when I was... Oh, hell – I'll just come out with it – I saw Patrick making love with Rose.'

What happened next was so shocking that Myrtle and the ladies would not be the better of it for years to come.

Demure, stoic Ava threw her head back and let out a scream so bloodcurdling and terrible that it reverberated through the sacristy and up the centre of the silent church like an invasion of demons.

At the same time, a gush of blood came pouring out of her, running down her legs, and spreading in a violent, crimson puddle on the linoleum floor. As Ava slumped forward in a faint, her shocked friend caught her body, shouting, 'Quick! Somebody call an ambulance.'

When Ava woke up she was in a hospital bed. Myrtle was holding her hand, looking both concerned and frightened. Ava remembered the reason she was here like a bludgeon across her head.

'The baby?' she managed to say, although she knew the answer. Myrtle shook her head. There were tears streaming down her face. Ava, despite her situation, felt she should comfort her.

'This is my fault,' Myrtle said. 'I should never have told you.'

'It would have happened anyway,' Ava said. 'I had been having pains all morning.'

She should have gone to the doctor. They might have saved the baby. This was her fault. The business with Patrick and Rose, she did not want to think about that now. She couldn't. It was too painful.

'I called your parents,' Myrtle said, 'they are on their way. Do you want me to call...'

Myrtle couldn't even say his name out loud.

Ava shook her head, then closed her eyes tightly and let her bitter tears burst out of the corners. As her old friend held her hand, Ava sobbed quietly into her growing grief and waited for her parents to arrive to take her home.

31

'OH DEAR, oh dear – this really is the most unholy mess,' Father Moran lamented. And he wasn't simply referring to the bloodstains on his new linoleum floor.

Breda, one of the more eagle-eared ladies, had been arranging a plate of flapjacks behind where Ava was resting and had heard her friend tell her about her husband's indiscretion just before the miscarriage took place.

A rather zealous old-school Catholic, the lady believed it some form of divine intervention.

'The Lord works in mysterious ways,' she said to her priest, sagely.

'He certainly does,' said Father Moran. Although his withering look implied he wondered how the Lord expected him to tolerate such superstitious nonsense from some of his less erudite parishioners.

The poor girl. He wondered if there was anything he could do for her.

'That Patrick Murphy,' he heard one of the women say. 'Carrying on with some girl from home right under her nose. And out there on the stage at the Emerald every week as if butter wouldn't melt.'

Something began whirring in the old priest's memory.

'What's the girl's name?' Father Moran asked, before catching himself engaging in idle gossip.

'Rose,' Breda said, delighted to not have to pretend she had not been listening closely. 'She definitely said, "Patrick and Rose" – then the dreadful thing happened. The blood! The screaming! Goodness me but I shall never forget it! The Lord works in mysterious...'

There it was now. The full story. That wicked girl that he had picked up in Harlem had deliberately come over here to take away lovely Ava Brogan's husband. The lad himself was hardly to blame. Sure, what could he do about it? Once a siren like that set her sights on an ordinary man, he would not be able to help himself. Ordinary men were different from the likes of himself who were destined for a higher order of behaviour. Even so, Father Moran had seen many a cleric fall prey to the seductions of a wicked girl. It was important for all men to be vigilant. The girl might have been forgiven if she had simply been seduced. But she had obviously come here on a premeditated mission. Father Moran felt somewhat guilty that he had not made the connection before now. He might have stopped this from happening if he had done so. It was hard to think now what to do for the best. In any case, he should give Tom Brogan a call and see if there was anything he could do to help the family.

* * *

Kissing Rose last night had been a mistake. He had not meant for it to happen, but while he was singing, Patrick had found himself overcome with emotion. He got caught up in the words of his song as if they were really true. And it wasn't hard, because they had been true, once. He remembered how he had felt when he first wrote them, the desolate unhappiness he had felt leaving his true love behind. 'Feel the words' Sheila had said, and that was what he did. So, when he saw Rose standing in front of him, weeping with love for him, he understood for the first time the heartbreak he had caused her. In singing the words 'it was only ever you' he was genuinely pleading for her forgiveness and understanding. Coupled with this sadness was the elation that he knew he was singing better, and truer than he ever had done in his life before. When he walked across the room to kiss Rose he was in a trance of his own making. It was as if his own heart had drugged him. While they were kissing, he was carried back to the fields of Foxford and it was as if there was no one else in the room. No one else in the world. It felt as if they had never been parted. It felt so natural that it could not be wrong.

'Do you really think this is a good idea, Patrick?'

Sheila had sneaked across the room and asked the question right into his ear with mocking pragmatism. It was over. The spell was broken.

He quickly broke away and went to the bar. When Rose tried to get him on his own again later that evening in the club, he avoided her.

Patrick was angry with himself for having given in to his old feelings. What had he done? What had he been thinking? Not only was he married to Ava, but he was not in love with Rose. Not any more. Over the past few weeks Rose had been making his life hell. Following him around at work, constantly trying to get him alone so she could persuade him to come back to her. He had held firm, but now, it seemed he had ruined everything in that stupid moment of weakness. Patrick had allowed himself to get carried back to who he once was, who they once were together. He was not that boy any more. He was a married man, soon-to-be father and a successful singer. Once enough money started coming through he would send what he owed back to Rose's father and ask him to come and take her back to Ireland so she would stop causing trouble for other people.

Patrick left the Emerald early to go home and get changed before the evening shift. They had been rehearsing 'It Was Only Ever You' all day and Sheila had given him the evening off. 'I don't need you until about ten tonight, Patrick. We'll just warm up your voice with a couple of numbers, and put the new single out to the audience. But I don't want you to overdo it. I want you on top form from now until we break you out.'

'Yes, ma'am,' he said. She gave a swipe to tell him not to be cheeky. Sometimes Patrick wished he could just tell Sheila what was going on with him. She was, in her own way, kind and he did feel that, singing aside, she cared about him. But he knew Sheila didn't like hassle, and right now, that's what his whole life felt like.

As he opened the door of the flat Patrick concentrated on how much he had been looking forward to seeing Ava all day. She would be back from her church work by now and they would have a couple of precious hours alone together.

But when he opened the door and walked into the bedroom, where he thought he heard her, Myrtle was in there. She had one of Ava's suitcases on the bed and was filling it with clothes.

'What's going on?' Patrick asked.

Myrtle didn't even look up at him but continued folding and throwing clothes into the suitcase in a rather violent, pointed way.

'What does it look like? I am packing a bag for Ava.'

'What's the matter? Where is she?'

Myrtle stopped and looked at him. For a second he saw the terrible look of pity cross her face. Then, seeming to think better of it, she bared her teeth at him and said, 'What the hell do you care? Philandering bastard.'

That could only mean one thing. She'd seen them. She'd seen him kissing Rose.

'I can explain—'

Myrtle shook her head and carried on with the packing.

Maybe she hadn't told Ava yet?

'Myrtle, please. It was a terrible one-off mistake. I've been under a lot of pressure – Ava would be heartbroken…'

'Huh!' she exclaimed in a sharp huff. 'She's a lot more than heartbroken, Patrick, *she* is broken. She is in the hospital…'

'The hospital?' Patrick stared at her in shock. What did she mean?

'Yes, Patrick! The hospital! Congratulations for ruining her life…'

'Which hospital? I have to get there now – is she all right?'

Myrtle looked at Patrick and his face was a mess. It was contorted, horrified. This was not how she had expected him to react. She took a deep breath and for the second time that day delivered ruinous news.

'She lost the baby…'

'Jesus Christ no.' Seeming to lose the strength in his legs he sat on the side of the bed. The baby? He had not really thought about the baby that much since Ava got pregnant.

It was really her concern, her joy. He just went along with it. But now, suddenly, this thing, this person that he had not even come to know in any way, was gone. Why did he feel it with the shock of death when it had not even been properly alive to him? How must Ava be feeling? He had to see her, right away. He had to put his arms around her and tell her everything would be all right.

He stood up. 'Come on,' he said, 'let's go.' He knew he had to act fast but everything seemed vague, abstract, as if none of this were truly happening. 'I'll drive us to the hospital...'

'Patrick, sit down,' said Myrtle. He was in shock. This was terrible. She wanted to hate him, for her friend, but she couldn't. He was broken. And if there was anything more pitiful in the world than a broken man, Myrtle did not know what that thing was.

She put her hands on his lap as she had done with his wife earlier.

'Ava knows about you and Rose.'

'You told her?' he said. He could feel a bulb of anger open in his stomach. Then he remembered the baby was gone – their baby – and the bulb rotted away to nothing.

'I told her,' she said. This was the bravest Myrtle had ever been in her life. Twice in one day. She wished, more than anything, then, that she had kept her mouth shut about Rose. Patrick loved Ava, that was clear to her now. He was eaten up. What had she done?

'Look. She doesn't want to see you right now. Her parents have arranged to collect her from the hospital. I am going directly out to the Bronx with her bag. I will tell her how upset you are and how sorry you are and perhaps you can call tomorrow and go and see her then?'

'I'm coming with you now,' he said, standing up. 'I have to see her, Myrtle. Please, you must help me. I promise, if you can just tell her to see me, I can make all of this right.'

Even though, in his heart, in this moment, he could not feel that was true, if he was able to get Ava and say it to her then perhaps everything could be made right again.

'Please, help me,' he said, again.

Myrtle had no choice. She finished packing the case and let Patrick drive her out to the Bronx.

They drove quickly and in silence. Patrick did not ask any details. He did not want to know. He was still in shock. All he wanted was to see Ava. He would hold her in his arms and let her pour everything out on to him. He would explain about Rose, tell her everything. He would say he was sorry over and over and over again, and he would keep saying it until she gave in. He would tell her the truth and she would forgive him. He would make everything all right again.

Tom Brogan met them at the front gate.

When Myrtle had told him she would go back to the apartment to get Ava's clothes, he had thought this might happen.

He was not long off the phone to Father Moran, who explained about Rose. Patrick and she had been engaged in Ireland. He had promised to marry her, to send for her when he was on his feet. Instead, the rogue had married his daughter. Doubtless, as his wife had always suspected, for money and gain.

Who knows, but perhaps Patrick and his girlfriend had always planned to run off together when they had the money to do so. Tom Brogan barely cared what they had been planning to do. He was just horrified to have allowed his daughter to be part of such a treacherous manipulation. Tom Brogan was not a man given to fury. He was liberal and forgiving. He was always willing, perhaps too willing sometimes, to give the benefit of the doubt. This was not one of those times. Tom Brogan had no doubt whatsoever that Patrick and Rose had lied to his family and hurt his daughter, immeasurably. His wife believed that the news of Patrick's betrayal had brought on Ava's miscarriage. Perhaps she was being dramatic, but it pained him to think that, in insisting that Ava's relationship with Patrick was ill-advised, Nessa had been right.

Tom felt that he had failed in his duties as Ava's father. He had failed to protect her from a bad marriage, and from a bad man. Not only that, he had been responsible for putting the cuckoo into her nest.

The only thing left that he could do for her now was to make sure that she never saw Patrick Murphy ever again.

He marched down the drive, and taking the case from Myrtle said, 'Go straight up to the house, Myrtle. I want a word with…' Patrick's name crumbled in his mouth, 'him.'

The moment she was out of earshot Patrick started babbling.

'I am so sorry, Mr Brogan. I know this is all my fault. Is Ava all right? I need to go and see her. I need to explain everything to her. I need to.'

Tom Brogan could not remember ever having been so angry in his life as he held his palm up in front of the young man's chest to stop him walking on. He was not touching him, and was afraid if the young man stepped forward, he could not be responsible for his actions.

'I do not care what you need. I do not care what you want to do. You leave my daughter alone, you hear? You are never to see her again. Go back to your poisonous girlfriend and look for some sympathy, you will find none here.'

'Mr Brogan, please, I need to see Ava. Our baby...'

When he mentioned the baby, Tom saw red. He closed his hands into two fists and cocked his head sideways in an angry stare. In that moment, Tom Brogan could have been one of the gangsters he so despised.

'I'm warning you, boy – if you take one step further on to my property I will call the cops. Do you understand me?'

He looked at Patrick in a way that left him in no doubt that he meant what he said. The kind eyes of the man that helped had disappeared and been replaced with the burning fury of betrayal.

Patrick nodded that he understood and turned back.

He stumbled more than walked the few steps to his car. His hands and legs were shaking so hard he did not think he would be able to drive. But Tom Brogan was standing watching him go. Patrick drove the car to the end of the road, then, still shaking, pulled his vehicle up on to the sidewalk.

There he sat, quietly, waiting for the tears to come.

When they came Patrick felt his soul had been turned inside out. He cried for his baby, for his lost wife, for the family he had left behind in Ireland. For an hour he was just a man, sitting in a car on his own, crying his heart out. Nobody troubled him, and when he was all cried out, Patrick started his car again, and drove around the city until he was nearly out of gas. He did not know where to go. He knew that he could not face going back to the apartment. The mere thought of sitting in their home, being surrounded by their life, was too much to bear. Then he remembered. He was an Irishman and what did Irishmen do when their lives fell apart? They drowned their sorrows. So Patrick started the car again and headed for the Emerald.

Meanwhile, back in the Bronx, Tom Brogan was sitting in

the kitchen. Nessa was upstairs, sitting by Ava's side. Their daughter had barely said a word since she came home. 'She's in shock,' Nessa said.

All that anger had disappeared from his wife, melted away the minute she saw her frail, traumatized daughter come through the door. Nessa had lost two babies before their precious 'keeper' Ava came along. Nobody was better equipped to look after a grieving mother.

Tom felt helpless as his wife prepared tea and toast, filled a hot water bottle and went to sit in uncharacteristic silence by their daughter's bed for the rest of the night.

'She has had the baby keeping her company day and night for four months,' Nessa said. 'She shouldn't be left alone.'

'I'll sit with her,' Tom said.

'No,' said Nessa, 'let me.'

This was women's business and he was banished. There was nothing he could do but sit around feeling utterly helpless. Tom was a helper. Not being able to do anything to help his daughter, or indeed his wife at this time, was excruciating.

But it was as if, in the serenity of her new, understanding self, his wife had handed him her petty grievances about Patrick and their daughter marrying beneath herself. As Tom poured himself a whiskey, he found himself unable to let go of the unjust way this young couple had treated his daughter.

With a sense of resolve he picked up the phone and a few minutes later he was speaking to Mary Geraghty in the post office in Foxford, County Mayo, Ireland.

'Could you put me through to Dr John Hopkins?' he said.

An American accent. She'd not heard that voice before. Maybe it was something to do with the daughter?

'May I say who's calling please?' she said brightly.

'No,' said Tom, 'you may not.'

Despite himself, and the awful nature of his call, Tom Brogan could not help a small smile. Things back home in Ireland never changed.

32

'THEY FOUND her! She's safe! Oh, thank God – thank
God!'

Eleanor Hopkins was beside herself. Over the last
few months Eleanor had been shattered with the disappearance of their daughter. On a number of occasions, her hysteria
had risen to such levels that John feared he might have to admit
her to Castlebar mental hospital. He tried to quell her fears
as best he could with assurances that he himself had come
to believe.

When Rose had first disappeared they were both shocked
and worried. Shocked that she had stolen the money from
them and worried that she would not be able to manage on
her own in the big wide world. John knew that she had found
Patrick's letters and assumed that she had gone to New York,
and doubtless had found him. Whether it was a wise decision
or not, he had not confided this to his wife. He set before her
prettier scenarios. That their daughter had gone to Dublin,
or London perhaps. That she had taken plenty of money and

would get in touch when she felt that they might have for-given her for stealing from them. It could be a year or more, he assured her. 'Rose is a big girl, she can look after herself very well,' he said.

'She is a *child*,' Eleanor screamed at him. 'What kind of a father are you that you won't go and find her…'

What kind of a father indeed, John thought.

If he had not interfered in Rose's life the way he had none of this would have happened. His daughter and her young man had fallen in love. In all likelihood, if they had been left alone, they would have fallen out of love, as young couples often do. If they had got married, they might have fallen out of love when it was too late; either way, it was fool-ish to interfere with fate and meddle in other people's lives in that way. Even if they were your only child. Even if you were only trying to do what was best for them. People had to do what was best for themselves. John knew that now.

'My girl, my darling girl! Now you can go and get her and bring her home. Pack your bag right away and you can go and stay in Dublin until the next flight out. She could be home in a few days! This is wonderful news.'

'I'm not going to get her, Eleanor. She is alive, that's all we need to know. If Rose wants to come home, then she can call us and make arrangements to do that. I will even send her money, if she needs it. It's up to her now.'

Eleanor went white. This could only mean one thing.

'Merciful hour, John – she hasn't married him, has she?'

John lost patience. Of all the terrible things that could have happened to their daughter, alone, in New York, all Eleanor cared about was that she may have married 'beneath her-self'. In actual fact, as that very decent man on the phone had made clear, Rose had acted beneath anything either of them could have imagined possible of her. She had stolen from them, destroyed a marriage and created a level of distress and hurt in a respectable, good family. Truthfully, John had no desire to see his daughter. He was glad she was safe. But, for the time being, until an apology was forthcoming, that was enough.

'No, Eleanor – Rose has not married Patrick Murphy.'

He didn't even want to tell his wife what Rose had done. He was afraid her reaction might throw him further into despair.

'Thank goodness. Well then, there is no reason for her not to come home.'

'She is leading her own life over there. When she is ready she will call us.'

'Did that man give you a telephone number for her?'

'Yes he did but—'

'Give it to me at once.'

John stepped aside and nodded at the pad next to the phone where he had written down the number of the convent where Rose was staying.

Eleanor grandly picked up the receiver and asked to be put through to the exchange.

Inside, she was shaking at the idea that her daughter might not want to come home, as Tom said. What would she do then? These past few months had been occupied utterly with her daughter's disappearance. She had forced the information about her stealing money out of John, after believing that the child had been abducted from the house. At least she knew she had the gumption to go, although she had not imagined in her wildest dreams that she had followed that young vagabond to America.

'Putting you through,' said Mary Geraghty. Eleanor closed

her eyes in preparation for speaking to her daughter, saying a quick prayer that Mary would not listen in.

It was not Rose that picked up the phone but some American girl.

'Can I please speak to Rose Hopkins?' Eleanor asked in her posh, telephone voice.

'She's not here,' said the girl rudely.

'Ah – this is her mother. Can you tell me when she should be back, please?'

'Never – I hope…' Insufferable rudeness, but then, they were American.

'Can you at least tell me where she has gone?'

'I have no idea – but to hell, I hope. Congratulations on raising a prize bitch, lady,' then she hung up the phone.

Eleanor had lost her again. She looked across at her husband, her face collapsed in disbelief and despair.

Perhaps, John thought, it was time to tell Eleanor a few home truths about her precious daughter.

Rose got off work early. She knew that Patrick was planning to spend the afternoon at home before coming back in for his evening shift. Perhaps, if she arrived unexpectedly, there would be an opportunity for them to be alone together again. They needed to talk about things, make plans. They needed to talk about the kiss.

Rose started to believe that Patrick did not love her after all. He was married to Ava, and Rose, despite herself, could see what Patrick saw in her. Ava was a warm, kind woman, as kind and sweet a person as Rose could imagine anyone being. As Ava befriended her, part of Rose wanted to believe it would be possible for them to be close. But, no matter how hard Rose told herself it was the right thing, the sensible thing, the decent, and eventually, the *only* thing to do – she simply could not let go of her feelings for Patrick. Her love for him was embedded too deeply in her. Although, she wondered, surely this was not what love was all about? All this chasing around? All this lying? When Patrick said he loved Ava and not her, in her heart Rose simply could not believe that was true. However, she did believe it was possible, that he loved both of them. And that being the case, then as he was married to Ava, Rose knew that she should do the decent thing and let them be.

But then he had kissed her and everything changed again. How could he not love her when he wrote that song?

Rose had just arrived for the evening shift and was putting on her uniform when she heard him. She could scarcely believe her ears. After they had had that fight and she had thought it was all over. But he must have picked up the sheet of paper that she had thrown on the ground and written music to the lyrics. Now he was singing those words he had written for her: 'It Was Only Ever You'. His message could not have been clearer if he had written above the stage in ten-foot letters, 'I still love you, Rose Hopkins'.

As she walked through the club towards the centre of the dance floor and stood in front of him, he sang directly to her. There was no mistaking his feeling, his love, his longing. Everything she had been through in the past few months; stealing the money from her parents; chasing across the world, persisting in her love for him, even when he pushed her away; the guilt of deceiving his wife after Ava had been so kind to her; all of those terrible things faded away to nothing when he walked across the room and held her in his arms and kissed her.

He had, of course, chased her off afterwards. This was a very complicated situation and she knew that Patrick would want to do the right thing. Perhaps that was staying with Ava, after all. But even if that was the case, Rose owed it to herself, and him, to acknowledge their grand passion. In her darkest, most selfish moments, Rose determined that if she could get him on his own and kiss him again, she would make him see that their love was strong enough to get them through whatever was coming down the line. That their passion was strong enough, deep enough, to sacrifice a marriage for.

When she got back to her room in the convent, she found Rose's friend, Myrtle, sitting on her bed. Myrtle came quite often to the Emerald and had made a point of introducing herself when Rose first started working there, although she had had very little to do with her since. Rose sensed Myrtle didn't like her, and the expression on her face now suggested she hadn't changed her mind.

'Hello,' Rose said, trying to keep her voice light, 'what are you doing here?'

'The question is surely,' Myrtle replied, 'what are *you* doing here? Oh yes, that's right – stealing my friend's husband and causing her to have a miscarriage.'

Rose gasped.

'Ava lost the baby?'

'… and her husband, thanks to you.' This was terrible, shocking news.

'Where is she?' Rose asked.

Myrtle stubbed out her cigarette and looked across at her with a nasty sneer.

'Not that you care but she is at home in the arms of her loving family. And before you ask – Patrick is with her sobbing his guts out. It seems you have ruined his life as well as hers.'

'I don't know what you mean,' said Rose. She felt sick. All these lies were bunching up inside her, poisoning her.

'Of course you do. I saw that pathetic show you put on at the club. That kiss.'

'You told Ava?'

'So what if I did,' said Myrtle. She had felt guilt gnawing at her ever since breaking the bad news, but justified it by insisting to herself that it was all Rose's fault.

'It wasn't a proper kiss anyway, I could see that right away. It was all for show. Us pretty girls all know how easy it is to seduce a man into kissing you. But it doesn't mean anything. I could see right away that Patrick was playing with you. He is completely different with Ava, you can see how much he cares for her. Besides, Sheila told me she had encouraged him to do it. She was trying it out as part of the act. Make the girls swoon.'

Myrtle wasn't as good at lying as Rose was, but she was learning fast.

Rose felt a wave of nausea. Her head was spinning. Could it be true that Patrick had been playing with her? Could it be true that he loved Ava and not her? That his kiss was all part of the act?

'But still,' Myrtle continued, 'I found it quite disgusting. And so did Ava, and so, by the way, did her family, especially after all they have done for you.'

Rose was burning with shame.

'I also saved you the trouble and filled in your room-mates, Una and Eileen, nice girls – I know them from the Emerald. Oh yes. Everybody knows what a slut you are now. Also Sister Augustine who, as you can imagine, was *thoroughly* appalled.'

Myrtle stood up and reached down beside the locker and

picked up the bag Rose had travelled to America with, and handed it across to her.

'I assumed this was your grubby little case so I have filled it with your grubby little clothes and you can run away back to Ireland to your mammy and daddy, who, by the way, also know where you are and what you've been up to. Tom Brogan filled them in on all the nasty things you've been getting up to since you arrived in New York.'

Rose stood there in shock. She did not know if she would be able to move her feet.

Myrtle shook the bag at her.

'Are you taking this or would you like me to kick you out with nothing?'

Rose reached across and took the bag. She felt she should say something, 'Goodbye' or 'I'm sorry', but there were too many people to say sorry to and the goodbyes ran too deep.

Myrtle walked her down the front steps of the convent and watched her until she had cleared the block. Where would she go? The only other place she knew was the Emerald, but humiliation would be waiting for her there too. She stood under the awning of the apartment block and looked up and down the busy sidewalk. People rushing about, busy in their lives. Men in hats rushing to and from work, women pushing buggies towards the park, old ladies wheeling buggies full of shopping. Everyone in New York had a life. She had been clinging on to somebody else's, trying to steal another woman's husband, another woman's life. Rose checked her purse. She found one five-dollar bill. As she rifled through looking for another, she pulled out the slip of paper that the taxi driver's wife, Marisa, had given her when she first came here.

Rose had nowhere else to go, so she hailed a cab and asked the driver to take her to the address in Harlem.

33

PATRICK SAT in the bar of the Emerald and drank himself into a stupor for nearly three full days, under
Gerry's watchful eye. The bar manager put him in
a quiet corner at the end of the bar then filled him to the
brim with drink, listening, as much as his work would allow,
as the young singer's pain came roaring out of him. Tearful regrets about the beautiful family he had left behind in
County Mayo, and the simple life he should have followed,
taking a job in the Foxford Woollen Mills like his father. Then
his own stupidity in losing his wife, and when it came to the
baby, he would become crippled with a regret so heartbreaking that, once or twice, Gerry simply handed him the whiskey
bottle and let him take it from the neck. When he was done
crying, Patrick would rant and rave, ruing the day he had laid
eyes on that wicked blonde temptress, Rose Hopkins, cursing
her snobbish parents from the high-heaven. When he became
too rowdy and began to upset the other customers, Gerry
would call one of the doormen to help bring him down to

the cellar where they would lock him in a stockroom to cool off. His fellow Irishmen set up a bed with blankets and cushions and brought him down food and coffee until, sobbing and regretful, he would go back upstairs to start again. Sheila was horrified with the ritual, but Gerry explained that it was important for Patrick to 'drink it out'. It was like lancing a boil, Gerry explained. 'Otherwise, it'll fester. And once an Irishman starts to fester, you'll never get him back the same way again.'

After three days, it was over. Patrick took his breakfast and coffee and did not go back to the bar. His hands were shaking and his head felt as if there were a dozen goblins in there, hammering. He was, in some ways, grateful for the physical hardship because it took from the emotional pain that the drink had masked, but not cured. In his dedicated grief, Patrick had, at least, come to understand with absolute certainty that his marriage to Ava was over. Her family had never fully approved of him in the first place, and, after what had happened, there would be no going back. Rose had ruined his life. He had ruined his own life then by allowing his pathetic heart to lure him into kissing her. The reality was, he was on his own in New York. All he had now was his career. Although, without somebody to share it with, that hardly seemed to matter any more.

'How dare you contact the Decca scout about the kid? He rang me earlier about some deal you are trying to fix up. Who sanctioned you to get a song written for him?'

When Iggy had asked Sheila to meet him in his office, this was not what she had been expecting.

Sheila had put out her cigarette at the door and unbuttoned

the top button of her new black shirt in preparation for the assignation. Iggy had been away for nearly six days, visiting his properties in Ireland and Britain, so this trip had been longer than most. She had missed him, and she knew he had missed her. Within an hour of getting back into New York her lover always took the opportunity to show her just how much. Usually prefaced by a stern invite to meet him 'in the office'.

Except now he was giving her a telling-off? Not a sexy telling-off either – a real one.

Who sanctioned the song? Was he kidding? She knew that little bum from Decca wasn't used to dealing with women. The fact that he had called Iggy at all was humiliation enough, without Iggy not standing up for her and telling him where to get off.

'Nobody sanctioned the song. The kid wrote the words and I got some other kid to write the music...' As he opened his mouth to object, she filled it with the words, 'for free.'

'Nobody works for free.'

'OK – I gave him a percentage of record sales.'

Iggy put his head in his hands before looking up at her. His face was angrier than it should have been. Maybe he had had a bad flight.

Actually, it had been a great flight, and one of his favourite Aer Lingus hostesses, Belinda, had given him the number of her hotel room. He would not take her up on the offer, but it had briefly irked him that he shouldn't, or rather couldn't, even if he had wanted to. The truth was, he didn't want any woman apart from Sheila. That alone gave her a power over him that made him feel uncomfortable. Iggy had no idea if Sheila felt the same way, but she acted sometimes like she could take him or leave him. The way that air hostess threw herself at him, she knew he was the boss. A man needed to be in charge of his own destiny but, in his intense feelings of fondness towards Sheila, and his growing dependency on seeing her, Iggy could feel his destiny slipping away from him.

He needed to show her who was boss. Thankfully, she had given him the perfect opportunity to do so.

'So, tell me, how are we expected to get a record deal if you're giving away sales percentage to some songwriter?'

'We own half the song because Patrick wrote the words.'

'So now you are going to tell me that Patrick owns half the song and the songwriter owns the other half. What do we get out of it?'

'A percentage.'

It occurred to Sheila that maybe she had acted too hastily. After all, Iggy had a lot more experience in this field. He was managing and touring acts, many of whom had record deals, but she had wanted to do this on her own. She had wanted to prove to herself that she could do it alone. She certainly needed to prove to him that she was her own woman. Taking help from a man like that could lead to him walking all over you. At least losing her freedom. Just standing here, Sheila thought, is a loss of freedom in itself. He didn't care about Patrick's career, she knew that. He just wanted a piece of the action so he could keep her beholden to him. Well, that wasn't going to work.

Once she had Patrick launched, a record deal secured, 'It Was Only Ever You' in the charts – she was out of here. And no man was ever going to tell her what to do again. Iggy could go to hell.

'A percentage of nothing, Sheila, is not a percentage. The only percentage you can take to a record company to make them listen is a hundred. Artist on a salary, writer on a fee.

When they play a venue, it's a different story – but when it comes to recording that's still the way it's done.'

'Well I think it's fair.'

Sheila could not quite believe that she had said something so lame. But she had.

'Fair?' Iggy was looking at her, his eyebrows raised in amusement, waiting for what she was going to say next.

'Look – the kid that wrote the music to this song has already bagged seven hit singles in the UK. He's a smart kid, he's done the math, and he's sick of working for fees. No matter how high they are he knows he's getting ripped off. You know it's the song that can make or break an artist. You can put out a good band with an average song and they'll do OK. You get a good artist and give him a great song, you can make some serious money. Sooner or later the writers will come round to hanging on to their copyright. And when they do? We've already set our own bar and built up a stable of material. There's a lot of average out there, Iggy, but if you want the very best – you've got to pay.'

Iggy thought about it. Damn but she was making sense.

'And this guy is good?'

'The best. And he's fresh off the boat from England and ready to deal.'

'The song?'

'It's a heartbreaker. A real gut-wrenching ballad. It will make Patrick a star. It will change everything.'

Iggy looked at her intensely. She was so hard to read. A fat ball of smoke from her cigarette drifted up towards her eyes. They were, he noticed, glittering. Ambition? Intent? Desire? Love even? For him? Patrick? He couldn't tell and that bothered him. When the pretty air hostess had batted her glittering eyes at him, he had known exactly what was on her mind.

KATE KERRIGAN

'I will call my man at Decca and try to rescue the deal.'

That sentence, Sheila decided, summed up everything that she found offensive about the world in general, the music industry in particular and, as a man and an individual, Ignatius Morrow. 'My man', 'rescue', and not her deal but 'the deal'. No matter what she did, he would want a part of it. As long as she was here, under his roof, he was calling the shots. He was the same as every other guy she had ever worked for. Possibly worse. The fact that she had feelings for him was certainly making it worse.

'Great,' she said. 'Thanks.'

There was a pause before he asked, 'See you later?'

Without missing a beat she said, 'Not tonight, I'm afraid.'

He raised his eyebrows in surprise.

'Other plans?'

'Yes,' she said. Then gave him a sharp, curt smile and left the room.

She had no plans. She never had any plans that didn't involve him any more. She had to pull back and stop being at his beck and call. She had to start clawing back some control over her own life.

Sheila went back out into the ballroom to look for Patrick. He should be there now. It was a big night tonight with the scout coming in. She wanted to get in a few rounds of 'It Was Only Ever You' to make sure Patrick was on top form. Maybe the little blonde might come and stand in front of him again – that was some performance she drew out of him before.

When she got there she found him sitting on the edge of the stage. His body was as stiff as a board and he was rocking gently backwards and forwards. Something was very badly wrong. As soon as he saw Sheila he began blabbing, sucking in air between the words to stop himself from sobbing.

'I've messed up so badly Sheila. I've got nobody left...'

Then, unable to stop himself, he began to wail like a child. Sheila tried patting him on the back but she was lighting a cigarette in a hurricane. A dead baby and a thwarted, absconded wife was a lot to deal with, even for a soft kid like this one. For a second Sheila wished she'd come down on the blonde home-wrecker, but she guessed it wouldn't have made much of a difference in the scheme of things. At least he had stopped drinking.

'I've got nowhere to live! I've got nowhere to go!'

'We will fix you up. Don't worry, everything is going to be all right.'

'I can't sing tonight. Please don't make me sing. Don't make me sing that song...'

Sheila reached for a cigarette and realized she already had one in her mouth. She lit the fresh one and gave it to him.

'OK,' she said. 'Just wait here.'

She was not equipped to deal with this emotional stuff, but she knew she had to look after her boy.

Sheila ran to the office, banged on the door and entered before getting a call. Iggy was on the phone.

She ignored that fact and said, 'Patrick is having a crisis. His wife left him. He has been out in the bar, drunk, for three days, so I'm taking him home to the folks with me for a proper meal. Can you call *your* man (she couldn't resist it) in Decca and put him off until I get this sorted.'

Before he had a chance to respond, Sheila was gone.

Dropping everything for pretty Patrick? Bringing him home? Sheila had never invited him to meet her family. In their warmer moments he had dropped hints about home-cooked

meals and never having had his own family. She always found
a way of ignoring him, adeptly pushing the suggestions aside
in that cool way she had.

She was pouring everything into the kid, and nothing into
him these days. She was using him, just hanging around to get
her act on the road. She was the same as all the other women,
after his money and his power; she was using it to do something else. Sheila thought she was so smart. She thought she
was better at hiding it than most women, but she wasn't.

To hell with her, Iggy thought. He threw down his cigar,
then picked up the phone and called Belinda the air hostess.

34

S HEILA DID not call ahead to warn her auntie there would be an extra person for dinner.

Anya was so excited when she saw Sheila come up to the front gate with Patrick she began shouting, 'Samuel! Samuel! Sheila has a man with her. Quick! Hurry, put on a tie.'

As she ran to the door, removing her apron as she went, she raised her eyes and hands to heaven and thanked God that there was a fine piece of brisket that had been braising in her oven since that morning. It had been intended to last them the week and now God had sent Sheila a man to eat it with them!

She opened the door, grinning from ear to ear and holding out her hands to embrace them both.

'This is Patrick, Auntie,' Sheila said, opening her eyes widely to tell her to calm down. Patrick held out his hand. 'Good evening, Mrs Klein. I'm so pleased to meet you.'

He was very young and, Anya was disappointed to hear from his accent, Irish. Still. He was a man.

'I hope you like brisket?'

'I don't believe I've ever had it before,' he said, 'but I'm sure it'll be delicious if it was cooked by you.'

Such lovely manners! The Irish weren't so bad. The boys loved their mothers, like the Jews.

Sheila was pleased to see that Patrick's spirits had lifted. Although Auntie's attention was excruciating, it was amusing and she would calm down once she was told who he was.

The moment the old lady greeted him, for the first time since he had come to New York, Patrick felt at home. The small, suburban house, with its chintzy net curtains, profusion of ornaments and soft, dark carpets was very different from the bare cottage he grew up in, but he recognized the warm welcome and the instant hospitality. The troubles of his day were forgotten and he was overcome by a feeling of gratitude for being taken to such a safe place. Samuel came out and instantly understood who he was from what Sheila had told him about her business.

'So? You're going to marry my niece?' he said, holding his hand out.

'Samuel!' Anya scolded him. 'I'm so sorry,' she apologized to Patrick. If he carried on like this, Sam would chase him away and Sheila would never get a husband.

'Patrick is my singer,' Sheila said, laughing. 'The one I was telling you about?'

Anya waved her hands in the air and walked into the kitchen. Again, they were talking about things she didn't understand. Another small humiliation. What did it matter if he sang? He was a man!

Sheila could see she was upset and followed her into the kitchen as Samuel brought Patrick into the drawing room to see his records.

Auntie was hunched, her frail arms lifting the huge pot out

of the oven. 'I'm sorry, Auntie. Patrick and I are just friends. He is having problems in his marriage so I brought him home for some brisket. That's all.'

'He is married?' Anya said.

'Yes,' Sheila said firmly. Then, sensing her aunt's disappointment she asked, 'Why do you want me to get married so much? Why is it so important? Am I not enough for you as I am?'

Auntie put down her pot and snapped angrily, 'How can you say such a thing? You are more than enough. You know you are everything to me and your uncle.'

Sheila smiled.

'Then why with The Husband, The Husband all the time? It's so old-fashioned!'

Anya was not stupid. She knew when she was being teased. She turned to her niece and put her hands around her face, her long, knurled fingers framing Sheila's sallow cheeks. Those dark eyes, heavy, knitted brows. She looked so worried all the time. It was the same since she was a child. Auntie wanted, in that moment, to tell her everything. How she had seen her niece so lonely for her family from the moment she got here. That she and Samuel had tried to make up for her loss but they knew they would never be enough. That, despite what she said, and how hard she tried to hide it, Auntie knew that Sheila was sad and did not want to be alone. A husband was not so important as family, but when you have no family, and if she and Samuel died, which they would soon, Sheila would have nobody in the world. Selfishly, Auntie did not want to die leaving the child she loved completely alone in the world. But she could not say all that. So, she looked into Sheila's eyes and said, with as much sincerity as she could, 'Every good Jewish girl needs a husband.'

'But I'm not a good Jewish girl, Auntie.'

Auntie gave her a playful slap on the cheek and told her to peel some potatoes.

While the potatoes were cooking, Samuel introduced Patrick to Mahler (to little effect) and Sheila persuaded Patrick to sing the first two verses of 'It's Now or Never' to show her uncle how her fortune would be made (to even less effect). However, Samuel was delighted with the company. This was the first person Sheila had brought into the house since she was a child.

Patrick helped the women lay the table, but just as Samuel was saying grace, the doorbell rang.

Even though he was the boss, Joe Higgins had decided to do this house call and sort out the Jewish broad himself, for a number of reasons. First of all, he felt bad because Dermot had let him down at the meeting with the Balduccis. His lawyer had not given his questions the gravitas they deserved. At one point, Dermot had contradicted Joe and said that this was not a legal matter 'in any sense I can get involved in'. He had also questioned Joe's motivation in making forensic distinctions between 'manslaughter' and 'murder', questioning his moral stance. Joe was a good Catholic. He went to mass every Sunday and confession once, sometimes twice every month. He did not like having his morality questioned. Bottom line was that Dermot had made him look like an idiot in front of Antonio Balducci. However, he could not afford to lose Dermot, he was the best defence lawyer in town. So, he persuaded Antonio to let him handle this important family matter. 'You don't want to be – pardon the expression, Antonio – shitting on your own doorstep.'

It wasn't a big job. Antonio just needed to assure his sister that the woman was scared and wouldn't be back. He didn't need to kill her or anything. Just scare her, and if that didn't work, give her a slap.

The Italians agreed because they felt this was an Irish matter too. Their brother-in-law, Dan McAndrew, was half-Irish. If he knew Joe Higgins was involved he would get a nice fright, and that might help the lowlife keep his wandering dick tucked away a bit better. Then he might stop upsetting their sister who, in turn, was driving them crazy. Wasting their time when they had more important business to attend to. They had 'spoken to' every damn club owner and scared her out of the city, but the Bronx wasn't far enough away for Angela. She was one vindictive bitch, their sister, but the Balduccis weren't going to have the broad murdered for her. It was too risky. Joe Higgins saying he would deal with it was ideal.

Joe had one other motivation. Iggy Morrow. Iggy was an Irish businessman, like himself. But despite having reached out to him several times over the years, Iggy had always ignored him. Joe didn't like that. It made him look small. Now, he had learned that some kid that had washed dishes in his golf club was working for Iggy. The kid was being groomed for stardom by, guess who? This Sheila bitch. Information had come out through the meeting with the Balduccis, which was very embarrassing for him, as they had assumed that Morrow was in his pocket. It was time for Iggy Morrow to be sent a message.

Joe got into the car where Aiden, his right-hand henchman, had been watching the house for the past couple of hours.

'Only the old couple in there. Then a woman arrived about an hour ago. She had Patrick Murphy with her.'

'Who the hell is Patrick Murphy?'

'The singer! He sings at the Emerald every week. He's fantastic. They're calling him the Irish Elvis. All the old stuff, but he can rock and roll too. The ladies...'

Joe gave him a murderous look and he shut up. He forgot they weren't allowed to go to the Emerald.

Joe didn't bring his gun in with him. He didn't want to be tempted.

'You wait here,' he said to Aiden.

'You don't want me to come with you?' He sounded disappointed. He had been kind of excited about meeting Patrick Murphy.

Joe figured he might end up just talking. He was a reasonable man. But then, if the bird was feisty, and he figured she was, she might make him angry. Then he might lose his temper. A lot of men, Aiden among them, were squeamish about hitting women. Joe didn't like to make a habit of it either, but sometimes, if they drove you to it, there was no other way to get your point across.

The street was quiet, too many neighbours for his liking, so Joe walked quickly across the road and tapped on the door impatiently. An old man answered the door.

'Good evening,' Joe said. 'May I come in?'

Then he stepped in, shoving the old man to one side slightly and closing the door behind him.

'Who are you?' the old man said. He was bristling. Best to ignore him. Ah – here they were. Dan McAndrew's bit and the dishwasher who thought he was somebody. Joe recognized him. He had smartened himself up for Iggy Morrow. The adrenalin was pumping through Joe now. This bit was what he enjoyed the most. Confusion. It was like introducing yourself to guests at a party they didn't even know they were invited to.

'I am so sorry for the intrusion. I just didn't want to be standing around in front of the neighbours, you know? This is kind of a delicate matter.'

'What do you want?' said the old man. His voice was shaking. Joe could tell right away he was as weak as a woman, and as for 'Elvis'...

'I am sorry, sir. My name is Joe Higgins and I have come here to have a chat with a lady called Sheila. I'm guessing that's you, my dear.'

The woman looked across at him defiantly. Joe smiled, sharply.

She should look scared. She wasn't a respectful woman.

'I have come to relay a message from Angela Balducci, although you may know her as Mrs McAndrew. You really want me to say it in front of your father, dear?'

'Go to hell!' she said.

Joe didn't need more of an invitation. He pushed the old man away, so he fell down, then began to lay into 'Elvis', who was foolishly standing in front of the woman. The kid managed to throw out one protective thump, giving Joe a nasty clip to the side of his mouth which really hurt, but it barely gave him pause as he laid Iggy Morrow's 'star' to the ground and began kicking him. He was about to set his foot down on pretty boy's face when he was assaulted with a pungent smell of meat, then whole world went black.

The moment Anya heard the fear and confusion in her husband's voice on answering the door to this stranger, she knew there was trouble, and watched the drama unfold from the dining-room door. When the man began to hit Patrick she did not pause. She picked up the hot brisket from the dining-room table where she had just laid it, then took the five steps it took to get into the hall, stepped over her husband and slammed the cast-iron pot into the side of Joe Higgins's head.

There was brisket everywhere.

For a few minutes they stood there in shock. They thought perhaps he was dead.

'We should call the police,' Samuel said.

'Don't,' Patrick said. 'Joe Higgins is a gangster and you don't want to get involved.'

He looked out the window and saw Aiden, Joe's henchman whom he knew from the golf club, sitting in the car across the road. He signalled across for him to come.

'Jesus Mary and Joseph,' he said, when he saw his boss unconscious and covered in hot beef. 'He won't be happy about this.'

'Good,' said Anya. 'Tell him I am seventy-eight years old and he can come back for more any time he likes.'

Aiden smiled and apologized for the trouble before throwing his boss over his shoulder and carrying him out to the car. He thought about going back to get Patrick's autograph but decided against it. Another time.

When he had left, Anya and Samuel fell into each other's arms, too stunned by what had just happened to even ask questions. Sheila was sitting at the bottom of the stairs. She had collapsed there in shock as Joe landed his first blow on Patrick. She had sat there, helplessly watching the violence unfold. Sheila had imagined herself the sort of person who would have fought back. But the guttural grunts of kicks and fists being administered, the spitting vicious anger of the attack and then finally, as Auntie slammed the heavy pot down on the gangster's head, the way he had fallen to the floor and the shocked look on his face, had affected her in an entirely unexpected way. As the first blow was struck, something inside Sheila began to unfold and she was overcome with a feeling she recognized but had buried all of her life. Terrors she had written down in her dreams, the unspoken-of horrors that had befallen her family, unseen but clearly imagined. Those fears had been folded and folded and folded away into some dark recess in her soul. In the years since she had learned of their death, whenever they threatened to emerge, Sheila would throw a blanket of cynicism and insouciance over them to keep them hidden, from herself and anyone else. Then, as she watched Joe Higgins's face in the second when he believed death had grabbed him, the curtain had lifted. Her darkest thoughts began to unfold and flutter chaotically like black butterflies. Now, the gangster was gone and her family were safe.

But the fear was still there.

Patrick sat down beside her, put his arm around her and kissed her hair. It was as instinctive as his stepping in front of her as he saw Joe coming towards her. He had wanted to protect her. And as Patrick went down with the second punch, he had felt nothing for himself, only fear for Sheila's safety. Then Anya felled his attacker and Patrick got to his feet, and the first thing he felt he needed to do was embrace Sheila.

Sheila gasped, and shocked by the intimate gesture, flinched. Patrick tightened his grip, then put his broad hand over the shaking fingers on her lap and said, 'It's all right, Sheila. You're safe now.'

He realized, then, how much this woman had come to mean to him. How much she had helped and nurtured him. How much she meant to him.

Sheila looked up at Patrick and, for a moment, she saw her brother's face as it might be now. An earnest young man, endlessly hopeful, but, in this moment, full of concerned tenderness.

Sheila's face crumpled and seventeen years' hard-held tears came pouring out of her. The black butterflies were stilled and in their place was an almost overwhelming feeling of love.

35

AVA'S RECOVERY from her late miscarriage was long and hard won. However, it was not as long and hard as it would have been without her mother's unstinting support. For three weeks Ava stayed in bed. The doctors had said there was nothing physically wrong with her and that she was more than ready to get up, but only her mother understood her seeming lack of motivation. The baby was gone, her husband was gone, she had nothing to live for. Nessa knew from her own experience that the devastating effects of losing a baby were rarely given the attention they deserved. The focus was always on trying again for a new baby. Ava did not want to go back into her marriage. Not yet, at least. Nessa remained silent. In truth, she had lost any of her opinions on the subject, good or bad. She had lost her fervour about controlling Ava's future. Instead she remained focused on getting her through each day, keeping her calm and as at ease as possible. With daily care Nessa pulled Ava out of the despair and depression she would have certainly fallen into had she been left alone.

Tom was distressed and panicking at his daughter's tardiness in getting herself 'back to normal'. He was still angry with himself for the way he believed he had let her down. Nessa defended her daughter's unwillingness to rush her recovery, ministered to her every day, bringing her up food and ensuring that she ate, just a little. During the brief times she was out of the room herself she left her distracting magazines and books which, for the first couple of weeks Ava did not look at, but then gradually came around to.

As three weeks stretched to four, Nessa called Myrtle, warning her not to make any mention of Patrick or Rose, unless she was prompted. Myrtle brought make-up and rollers and candy with her and said, 'You look a fright!' when she walked into the room, and pretended that everything was normal. She stayed overnight, as they had done when they were children. By the following day, Ava was ready to get up and go downstairs.

Myrtle stayed that second night, and they put on 'Rock Around the Clock' and danced around the living room.

Ava was pretending to be happy, but she was grateful to find she now had enough strength to pretend.

The baby was gone and nobody could bring it back.

She would always be sad about that, but she knew, too, that life would go on. Ava was glad to find the will to live again, even though she thought it had been lost to her.

'Will you ever come out dancing with me again?' Myrtle asked. 'I'm still looking for a husband, even if you're not. Of course, we don't have to go to the Emerald...'

It was a clumsy prompt for Ava to talk about Patrick's betrayal with Rose. She wasn't ready, and felt she might never want to talk about it at all. It felt like an old wound she did not want to pick over. Her handsome husband had been making love to a beautiful girl who had the kind of film-star beauty she could never hope to aspire to. Now, it transpired, he had been engaged to Rose when he married Ava. Patrick had, she was certain now, simply used her to get along in America. Her mother had been right. It had never been true love. Vanity had tricked her into believing she was the kind of girl he could fall in love with, but she wasn't. She was plain old Ava, as she had always been. For a period of time she had thought she was, if not beautiful, then at least attractive. Dermot had certainly thought so. She had been thinking about him a lot these past few weeks. Wondering how her life would have been if she had never fallen in love with Patrick and had stayed with him. They would be married now, and living comfortably near her parents, no doubt. She might even be pregnant.

The problem was, of course, she didn't love Dermot. She had thought she loved him and she might have been happy, but then Patrick had come along, swept her away and shown her what true love was all about. Dermot paled in comparison with the passion she felt for Patrick. Not, indeed, that Dermot would come near her ever again after the sluttish, cruel way she had behaved towards him. Just thinking about it made her shudder. If Myrtle had her way she would spend the rest of her life raking over the dramas of the past, relishing every ghastly moment.

Myrtle gave her a look that said, 'Trust me. You've had long enough.'

'I don't know if I ever want to go dancing again,' Ava said. 'Honestly? I don't know what I want any more.'

Myrtle grabbed her hand and squeezed it. 'Don't worry, Ava, you'll get another one.'

Ava did not know whether she meant baby or husband and

she didn't want to ask. Myrtle had meant both, but she didn't want to push it either. Ava wasn't ready. So, she leant across the sofa, switched on the TV and the two of them escaped into an episode of *Father Knows Best*.

Nessa, who had left the kitchen door open, listened in to the two friends. Above the canned audience laughter, as clear as if it were the only voice in the room, Nessa heard Ava laugh. A little tear ran down her cheek. She could tell, from the tone of her voice, that her precious daughter was, finally, on the mend.

The following week Myrtle was volunteering at Quinn's Ballroom Dancing School in Yonkers. Once a month there were 'men only' evenings where the more atrocious of her students could step on the toes of hardy volunteers of the opposite sex. The humiliation for a man-who-couldn't-dance was that the volunteers were generally women on the edge of spinsterhood, resigned to seeking out the fresh blood of a bachelor who had neither the courage nor the ability to hit the dance halls yet. This was Myrtle's first time. She already felt desperate enough without seeing somebody she knew.

'Dermot Dolan,' she shouted brightly across the room. 'What are you doing here?'

Dermot put on his best criminal lawyer smile but Myrtle could tell he was not one bit happy to see her either.

'I am learning to dance, Myrtle. Well, trying anyway!'

After that awful time in the confessional, Dermot had decided that the ill-mannered priest was right, after all. It was time for him to get back out there and find himself a wife. Knowing that his two left feet were holding him back from entering the only place where a man might meet a woman these days, the cursed dance hall, he signed up for lessons. Dermot was embarrassed to see Myrtle but she was equally embarrassed to see him.

Breaking the ice with happy exuberance was, Myrtle decided, the best way to approach it for both of them.

'I'll take this one,' she shouted across to Mary Quinn, marching over to him. Then she draped her hands over his shoulders for the opening waltz and added, 'Unless you're already taken?'

Dermot shook his head and laughed. He had always liked Myrtle.

The music started and they shuffled around a bit, he assiduously letting her lead so he could avoid her feet.

'God, you really have not got the hang of this yet, have you?'

'No,' he said. Then he laughed, and she laughed and, for a moment, Dermot thought how nice her hair smelt and wondered...

'How is Ava?'

It just came out of his mouth. He had not been going to say anything. Ava was the reason his heart had taken an unpleasant dip when he saw Myrtle, and yet he was compelled to ask.

'Ah.' Myrtle was surprised to find herself feeling a little disappointed. After all, a man was a man, and just recently she had come to wonder how important it was if he could dance or not. Dermot was nice. Certainly, Ava would have been better off if she had stayed with him instead of letting herself get carried away with a handsome cad. It had given Myrtle pause about her own preferences.

'So, you've not heard?'

'No,' Dermot said. Oh, why had he been so stupid and asked that question? Now she was going to tell him about Ava and her wonderful life. He didn't want to hear it.

Myrtle paused. She could tell Dermot the whole nasty story. About Rose trying to steal Patrick and showing the whole marriage to have been a sham. He could tell him about Ava's 'women's problem' that men were so squeamish about: how she had collapsed in the church, spilling blood everywhere, losing the baby, then had lain in bed, depressed and miserable for nearly a month, even when the doctors said, officially, there was nothing wrong with her.

If she told him all that, he might be glad to be away from the whole sorry mess. He might be happy to settle for a nice, cheerful, pretty, sensible girl who would teach him to dance. But then again, Dermot's brother Niall was still single...

'She broke up with Patrick. The marriage is over. Didn't work out.'

'Really?' Dermot's heart soared. What about the baby? Had she had it? He didn't care. It didn't matter. Maybe there was hope. Why that fool Patrick had left her did not occur to him. How any man could leave such a wonderful woman was beyond him. Surely, this meant there was a chance, again, for him? Perhaps – but it was too much to hope for – some residual feelings for Dermot may have contributed to the marriage not working. He could barely contain himself with excitement, but kept his voice light and steady as he asked, 'Is she still in the city?' He looked up and took his eyes from his feet.

'Ouch!'

'Sorry.'

'No. She's been back home with Tom and Nessa for nearly six weeks now.'

That wasn't long off two months. Was it too early to call on her? Was two months a respectful amount of time after a break-up? Would she still be interested? Despite his reservations, Dermot knew that he had to go and see her. It would be embarrassing, potentially humiliating for him, but he had to find out if he was still in with a chance.

In the meantime, Myrtle had made her own mind up about something else.

Volunteering at Mrs Quinn's was not for her. Not even in pursuit of a suitable husband like Dermot. Niall was way better-looking than his brother. And he didn't step on toes!

'Ah, Dermot.'

Tom's heart sank when he saw the smartly dressed man standing on his front doorstep, his nervous smile almost entirely concealed by a huge bouquet of pink roses.

His daughter had just seen off one disastrous romance and now here was another one, seemingly determined to turn their family tragedy into the plot of a Jane Austen novel. Tom wished everyone would all go the hell away and leave his family alone. He just wanted things to be back the way they were before, when it was the three of them. Before his daughter had met Dermot Dolan or Patrick Murphy. He knew it was stupid, and untenable, but things were so much simpler and happier when he was the only man in Ava's life. Was that such a terrible thing for a father to want for his daughter? To be able to protect her for ever? To have her wit and good humour all to himself?

He stepped aside, saying, 'You had better come in.'

'Thank you, Tom.'

He smiled, nervously.

Stupid fool. If Dermot had been enough of a man to hold on to his daughter in the first place, instead of letting her chase off after that gutty-boy, none of this would have happened. The only saving grace in this scenario was that Nessa was out shopping, so would not get to do the 'Mrs Bennet' act which had got them into all this mess in the first place.

'Ava?' he called out to the kitchen. 'You've got a visitor.' He nodded at Dermot's flowers and said, 'I assume they're for Ava?'

'Ah now, they're not really your colour.'

Tom smiled, despite himself.

Ava got a terrible shock when she saw Dermot standing in the hall. She had thought it was Myrtle and had not even bothered taking off her apron. He looked so smart in his blazer and slacks. More handsome, less rounded than she remembered him. His eyes were sparkling in that slightly amused way he had. Although they had always sparkled when he looked at her. 'I'd get these in water quickly, if I were you,' he said, handing over the flowers. 'Your father thought they were for him.'

As she took the roses from him, he turned to her father again and said, 'Sorry, Tom, next time, I'll bring you a cigar.'

He really was a wit! Ava felt like laughing out loud, but she didn't want to give him the wrong idea. Was it possible he was still in love with her? After all she had put him through? She dipped her face in the flowers and in the moment of sniffing their divine, sweet scent she felt – there was only one word for it – happy! Such an ordinary feeling, once, but of late, it had become extraordinary.

'OK, very funny.' Tom was a lot more amused than he was letting on as he pottered out into the kitchen. He had forgotten how much he liked Dermot. He just hoped there wasn't more trouble ahead.

'You look well,' Dermot said.

Ava smiled, self-consciously. She looked a mess but again, she knew he could not see it. She had not even dressed properly. She was wearing no make-up and an old dressing gown over slacks and a light sweater. She could not think of anything to say that would not raise his hopes. Everything she wanted to say, a joke about his shiny buttons, a quip on how he was 'wearing his hair' (even though it was thinning), or even a comment on how well he was looking himself, might slide them back into the comfortable familiarity of how they had once been. How were you supposed to be with a man you had cruelly dumped? A man who had the right to gloat over your misfortune, and yet, in his kind face, she could see so clearly that was not the case. Dermot, sensing her awkwardness, stepped in.

'I was just passing...'

Ava held up the roses and smiled at him.

Dermot's heart ached, just looking at her.

She looked so beautiful to him. He didn't care if she was wearing a dressing gown and her hair looked as if she hadn't brushed it for a few days. She looked like a queen to him. His queen.

'Ah yes. The flowers. I found them on the sidewalk on my way in... They must've fallen out of a florist van.'

Ava laughed.

'You know how careless delivery men are.'

She was grinning now. Her face lit up like a beacon when she did that.

'Look,' he said, 'I heard you were back home and—'

'It's OK,' she said. And, to her surprise, Ava realized that it was.

'Can I take you out to lunch?' he said. 'It doesn't have to be anywhere fancy...'

'Now?'

'Well, if it's...'

She put him out of his misery.

'Great,' she said. 'Let me run upstairs and get changed.'

She left the flowers on the hall table. Tom came back out and picked them up.

'Ah – I get to put them in a vase at least.'

Dermot smiled. He felt he should be saying something to Tom, explain himself somehow. He just wasn't sure what that was. He broke the silence anyway by saying, 'Ava is upstairs getting changed…'

Tom was staring at him intently.

'… I am taking her out…'

Too intently.

'To lunch…'

Then Tom said it. What he had been bottling up for weeks.

'Ava is very delicate right now. If you hurt her…'

'I understand—'

Dermot knew what he was trying to say and wanted to spare him, but Tom would not be interrupted.

'If you hurt her, so help me God, I don't know what I'll do.'

Tom's face was tight with contained rage. Dermot recognized the feeling because he also channelled his masculine anger through the filter of reason. It was how respectable men did things.

'I would never hurt Ava,' Dermot assured him. He would have added more about how he felt about the likes of Patrick Murphy and how he would welcome the opportunity to protect Ava from such men in the future, but she came down the stairs.

They drove as far as Getty Square and had lunch in a diner. Nowhere fancy, just somewhere impersonal and cheap where they were not likely to run into anybody they knew. They talked as easily as they had always done. No mention of Patrick, or lost babies. Dermot told her about his disastrous meeting with Joe Higgins and the Balducci brothers, and Ava was horrified, and impressed, but mostly – amused. She had forgotten how much Dermot made her laugh. What he lacked on the dance floor or in dashing good looks, he more than made up for in personality.

'Actually, I've got a confession,' he said. He took a chance and told her about nearly running into her and hiding in the confessional box. He made it sound so funny that Ava actually wept with laughter, although he didn't tell her about confessing his love for her to the priest. That would have been too much and he needed to hang on to some semblance of dignity.

Once or twice during the lunch Ava felt her hand wanting to creep across the table and take his. She was grateful that he did not reach out in the same way. It would have been too much. But, at the same time, she felt perhaps, if he had it might have felt as if they had never been apart.

After they had eaten and Dermot had settled with the waitress, Ava said, 'Shall we go for a stroll? I've hardly been out of the house for weeks.'

Dermot felt ludicrously happy. He was trying to keep himself in check but his spirit was soaring. This afternoon was going better than he could have ever expected. She was as warm and loving towards him as she ever had been. And, he believed, he had cheered her up and made her happy. Making Ava happy gave him more joy than anything else. Could it possibly be that they were starting again?

As they walked, Ava took his arm. As he felt her hand settle on the crook of his elbow he reached down and rested his own hand on top of it. She did not move away.

They walked in companionable silence, not taking much notice of what was going on around them. Dermot was lost in a reverie of romantic love. He was afraid, in fact, to open his mouth in case he said something foolish like 'Shall we get married?' or 'I love you' and of course it was way too early for that. Dignity was the thing now. Dignity and respect... and then Ava stopped walking.

Dermot rejoined the world and his heart gave a jolt when he saw where they were.

They were standing outside the Emerald dance hall and in front of them was a huge poster advertising, 'Patrick Murphy sings his debut single, "It Was Only Ever You". Saturday, 8pm.'

Dermot began to panic. Ava seemed paralysed. Her hand loosened on the base of his bicep.

Dermot did not know what to say. Did she expect him to say something? There were any number of barbed comments forming in the back of his mind, the most obvious of which was to simply mutter the expletive 'bastard!'

But he was too much of a gentleman to do that. So he simply put his hand over Ava's again, and picked up the stroll. He kept the talk going with silly chit-chat but inside his head he was saying, 'You stupid idiot! You led her straight to him! Stupid, stupid idiot.'

They went back to the car and Dermot drove her home.

The spell had been broken but then, as she was getting out, Ava turned, looked him in the eye and said, with all sincerity, 'Thank you for a lovely afternoon, Dermot. It was really good to see you.'

'Maybe we can do it again?' he said.

She looked at him, seeming to pause, then said, 'Maybe sometime, Dermot. I'm glad we are friends, but...'

'I understand,' he said. Then he smiled, said, 'Goodnight,' and pulled the door shut.

He had given her his heart and, for the second time, she had broken it.

'But'. Dermot knew exactly what that meant. But you are not handsome. But you are not exciting. But you are too nice. Too funny. I love you *but* I am in love with somebody else. Let's just be friends.

All the way back to the city Dermot worked himself up into a rage. He knew he could make Ava happy, but if she was going to persist with being 'in love' with this cad, well then, he was going to have to do something about it.

He had had enough. There were going to be no more 'buts' for Dermot Dolan.

It was time to man up and take action. Dermot ran up the stairs to his apartment and grabbed the phone book from the hall table. He found the number he was looking for and dialled.

A woman's voice answered.

'Is that Myrtle Milligan?'

'Yes.'

'Myrtle – this is Dermot Dolan. I need your help.'

36

ROSE PUT the finishing touches to her illustration. It was a lavish party table with platters of vol-au-vents and steaming apple pies laid out on a gingham tablecloth with the logo 'Molly's Party Platters' emblazoned across the top in copperplate typescript. She was still learning to measure out the stencils, but it looked even to her.

She straightened the A1 sheet on her drawing board and waited while Christopher, her boss, the creative director in Gimble Advertising, checked it over.

Man, this girl was good. In just two months she had picked up the basic rules of advertising design, in addition to being able to draw, always to the brief and close to perfection.

When his sister Marisa had rung Christopher and asked him if he could find a job for some Irish girl she knew, he was sceptical. She did not have an art education or any art training, but Marisa rarely asked him for anything, even though he knew she and Donnie were hard up, so he couldn't say no. The pretty, blonde, demure creature, clearly middle-class, was very different from what he had been expecting. But Christopher took his sister's word that she was 'needy' and put her to making coffee and buying in lunches for the art studio. The kid got lucky on her fourth day in the job. The studio was snowed under with deadlines when a last-minute pitch for a new brand of cigarette came in from the sales team. Chris had no one else, and decided to give her a try-out. It turned out he was the lucky one. Rose had a rare talent for drawing. Less than an hour after he gave her the brief she came back with a life-like drawing of a Hollywood doyenne, smoking with such style that the client bought it straight away. From day one, Christopher had found Rose to be the most efficient, accurate artist he had ever worked with. She was his shining star. Unlike many of the brilliant illustrators who earned a fortune in advertising, Rose was not arrogant or demanding. She was not only an excellent employee but a popular member of the team. The men were all a little bit in love with her, and, because she was so young and innocent to the ways of the big city, the women all felt protective of her. Rose had a bright, friendly way about her, doing the secretaries' jobs for them and always anxious to be helpful and cooperative. She now shared an apartment with two of the secretaries on the Upper East Side. As a fine artist, Rose's salary had already outstripped that of Christopher's brother-in-law Donnie. He felt bad about that, but he had to pay her union rates for the job she was doing. Marisa told him that Rose called around to them every week, without fail, with gifts for the children and themselves. Marisa would not take any money off Chris, so he was thinking of recruiting Rose in his efforts to get his sister set up in a hair salon as soon as this next baby was born. He was beginning to consider her a friend.

'Looks great, Rose,' he said now, leaning into the picture and marvelling at the detail. 'I'd like you to come into the client meeting after lunch.'

Rose loved her work. Christopher telling her what to draw all day long, and having to produce drawings to a deadline, was the perfect job for her. Not least because it offered her constant distraction. Rose needed distraction more than anything else.

'You're my lucky charm, Rose,' Chris said. 'Go out for lunch and I'll see you in the boardroom at two.'

Rose smiled sunnily and said, 'See you then!'

She knew she had been lucky. A whole life in New York. In just two months she was settled into a great job and an apartment in the city. She was making new friends and a whole world was opening up to her.

However, Rose felt that if she was charmed, it was by the devil. She had intended to run away from all the bad things she had done in the past few months. From stealing the money from her parents and leaving them to go out of their mind with worry about her. Impulsively chasing across the world to find Patrick and determinedly pursuing him even though he was now married to somebody else. Lying to Ava and encouraging him in the deceit was the worst of all. She might have been the cause of the loss of that baby, she had certainly been the cause of a broken marriage.

From the vantage point of her new, lucky life, Rose could see the hardship and pain that she had caused. Not only could she see it, she could feel it now. Every day, not one minute went past when Rose was not filled with regret at the intense, determined madness that had overtaken her in her pursuit of Patrick Murphy. Because that was all it was. Madness. When they said 'madly in love' was that what they meant?

She had come to the taxi driver's home in Harlem in a very different mood from the one she had left it in. Almost immediately she confessed to Marisa the terrible things she had done since she had left them. Marisa had not thrown her out on the street, but offered a kind, sympathetic ear and contacted her brother.

The ease with which Rose had fallen into this new life, and seemingly been forgiven for her sins, far from making life easier for her, was making it harder. Aside from the time when she was lost in her work, she felt guilty all the time. A sick dread clung to her conscience. The inescapable knowledge that she was, despite her pretty looks and polite ways, a bad person. Rose hated herself for what she had done and was beginning to hate herself for the person she was because of it. Everybody liked her, but that was because they thought she was a nice person. Only she knew that she was not a nice person. She was a bad person masquerading as sweet. She was a fake and she knew it.

As soon as Rose had begun her new job, she had written to her parents. She had kept it brief, apologized for all the worry she had caused them, and promised to pay back all of the money she had stolen.

She received a letter shortly afterwards from her father, apologizing himself for having chased Patrick away. He assured Rose that while he had forgiven her, he was still trying to persuade her mother that it was a good idea for Rose to stay in New York for a while. Her mother was still very anxious that she come home and missed her terribly.

Reading between the lines, Rose understood that her mother was suffering from depression. She knew that if she was not entirely the cause of it, the disappearance had certainly been a catalyst.

Short of returning home, there was nothing she could do to comfort her parents. She also knew that if she did return home, there would be no comfort for her.

In the meantime, she had to try and enjoy this new life, despite the terrible things she had done to Patrick and Ava. She knew that apologizing to them would not be as simple as it had been with her parents. She had caused a lot of pain and it was better for her to leave them alone to deal with it. To try and offload it on to them would be a selfish act. At the same time, she wanted to try and find a way of living with it, of living with herself, with more comfort.

The offices had been so busy lately that she decided to get out on her own, get some fresh air and try to clear her head. There was a corner café that she liked two blocks from the office, midtown towards Hell's Kitchen. She took a window seat and ordered herself a salt beef sandwich on rye bread and a coffee. Rose gazed out the window, watching the world go by, feeling a little sad at how separate she felt from it all.

As the waitress laid down her coffee she paused with her hand on the cup and looked off into the middle distance as a song came on the radio.

I ask myself are you the one I dream of night and day
Are you the reason why this yearning never goes away...

'Turn that up, Freddie!' she shouted out.

The music became louder, as the waitress sauntered to the next table, slowed down by the romantic, crooning voice:

I ask myself are you the one whose face I can't forget
Your name hangs gently on each breeze I still can hear it yet

Rosie felt her stomach turn inside out. It was Patrick, singing that song. Their song. The song he had written for her, telling her, 'It was only ever you.'

She threw some dollars on the counter and ran out. It had been a terrible shock, hearing his voice like that. What did it mean? She had known that his manager had been planning to release it as a record, but it seemed inconceivable that it had actually happened. Emotion pumped through her, fear, excitement, shame, shock, but underneath all of them emerged the untrammelled thrill of having been loved by him; of being the woman he had written those words for. It was wrong, so wrong, but she could not help it. Would this cursed feeling ever go away? The feeling of being in love with somebody who cannot love you back.

Rose found she had been wandering aimlessly in the opposite direction to the office. Afraid she might be lost, she stopped to check where she was, and saw she was standing outside a church. She had not been to mass since she had come to New York. She stood for a moment, looking up at the imposing building, its ornate steeple reaching up into the grey, Manhattan skyline, competing with the office buildings either side of it, and thought that perhaps her loss of religion had contributed to her wayward behaviour. She had not given a thought to the right or the wrong thing to do in her pursuit of love. She had been too single-minded, too passionate. Perhaps if she talked to a priest and confessed her sins, Rose might get some relief.

She had forty minutes before she had to be back at the meeting at two, so she climbed up the steps. Inside, the church seemed much bigger and grander than on the outside. She immediately regretted the idea of finding a priest and making her confession in such a large, intimidating place.

Then, walking towards her, she saw a familiar face. She struggled to remember who it was before finally recognizing him as the priest who had taken her out to the Bronx. A friend of Donnie and Marisa. Father…? She smiled and walked slowly towards him, desperately trying to remember his name.

He remembered her, though, and marching determinedly towards her he barked, 'I hope you're here to do a confession, young lady.'

Rose started. How did he know? She remembered, he knew Tom Hogan – but it was too late to turn back. He had her in his sights.

'After all the trouble you caused. You should be ashamed of yourself…'

Rose did feel ashamed of herself. She was about to tell him as much when he continued.

'…coming over here, chasing after some man you think you're in love with. I have never heard of such nonsense…'

As he continued, Rose said, 'I'm sorry. I'm sorry, Father…'

Perhaps it was because of the way that she had found herself saying 'Father', even though she was simply addressing a priest, but Rose was taken back to that moment in her father's study where she had seen the letters that Patrick had written her. The letters that her father had hidden. The words of 'It Was Only Ever You' that she had heard earlier in the café. And Rose realized she wasn't sorry for having followed Patrick to New York. She was sorry about what had happened since she got here. And she was sorry that her parents had been worried, she was sorry that she had pursued Patrick when he had not wanted her to, she was sorry that she had kissed him when she had known he was married to somebody else. She was sorry that she hadn't simply told Ava the truth and then walked away, and she was deeply, deeply sorry for having betrayed a nice woman who had been nothing but kind to her.

However, when she looked into the face of the angry old priest, Rose realized that she was not sorry for having loved. She would not apologize for having been true to her heart, and she never would.

37

SITTING ON the stairs of her aunt and uncle's house in Riverdale, Sheila clung to Patrick. She was so raw and emotional that, for a moment, she thought she had fallen in love with him. Then, the shock passed and, as she saw the faces of her aunt and uncle she realized that the love she felt was the all-encompassing love she had felt as a child. The love of life itself and everyone around her. Standing in their hall, shattered with shock, the old couple looked into the face of their niece and immediately recognized that something significant had happened to her. The light in her that Hitler had extinguished was back. It was as intangible and mysterious as love itself. As the couple embraced her after the ordeal, they both felt it in the softened commitment of her arms around them and heard it in a barely discernible mellowing of her voice. Anya saw it first: the child had returned to Sheila's dark, once impervious eyes. The transformation felt as instant and as shocking to Anya as hitting the man's skull with the pot. Why such a terrible event should have had such a positive, transforming effect none of them could guess. Except that an old, sharp edge that had been twenty years in the making had been hit with a hammer and a soft curve left in its place.

Over the coming weeks Sheila polished that curve by encouraging and nurturing Patrick's talent.

Nothing developed between them, except for, on her part at least, a warm sense of sisterhood and mentorship. However, her caring for Patrick did go some way to filling the gap Iggy had left behind.

Her lover had pulled away from her. They had not slept together in weeks and Iggy's attitude towards her had reverted to a respectful employer–employee arrangement. No confrontation took place, just a quietly created distance separated them physically, and emotionally. Professionally, they remained in close touch. Sheila felt that Iggy had come to respect her way of doing things. Under her management, the Emerald was making more money than ever, and he had relinquished all control over Patrick's career and was letting her get on with it. Iggy resumed his rigorous travelling schedule. As he spent more and more time away, into that space emerged an assumption, with Sheila, that it was over. Once, in the office, she had picked up the phone to a woman. An air hostess, the girl had been keen to tell her. It hurt. But Sheila, for all her new vulnerability, could not give in to it. She had to keep herself moving forward, more now than ever. So she focused on her career and channelled that hurt into Patrick.

Iggy had allocated Sheila a budget to spend in whatever way she saw fit. The usual way of doing things for a manager was to engage the interest of a producer and then let them deal with the record company. Sheila had decided that she wanted to retain as much control as possible. Iggy, having set up the recording deal, allowed Sheila to go directly to the record company, setting herself up as producer, even though she had no track record. Sheila approached Malcolm, the songwriter, and asked if he had a young producer in his coterie who might be looking for a break. Declan was a year older than Malcolm, Irish, a technical music buff, bursting with talent and zero cash.

Sheila hired them the biggest, best studio in New York for the day.

'I want big!' she told Declan. 'A big, big sound. When the chorus comes, I want it to be like an avalanche of music. Like Mount Everest collapsing...'

Sheila filled the studio with musicians. They brought in the resident band, and bumped them up to a half-orchestra with some of Malcolm's rock and roll buddies, and Sheila's old friend Frankie and his friends provided some extra wind. She even invited Iggy along so he could see where his money was being spent.

She didn't expect Iggy to come, but he did. She did not notice him arrive and when she did spot him, sitting in his unobtrusive way at the back of the room, watching them all from a distance, Sheila felt a shot of pity for him. He seemed so out of place, so formal, in his straight-from-the-airport suit. She nodded at him and he nodded back, solemnly. He seemed sad and she longed to go over and talk to him. But she pushed the longing aside, reminding herself that they were no longer lovers, or even friends – simply business associates. She had work to do and he was here to make sure that she did it. She was determined not to have him distract her. However, when she looked around for him an hour later, and saw the grey office seat left empty, her heart sank.

Patrick, in contrast, was in his element. He had the song nailed. Every inch the star, he knew every line so well that, at one point, Sheila caught him singing it backwards to try and impress one of the guitarists.

Sheila told him that she needed him to put his heart and soul into every single take. As the day progressed, he did not let her down, as she strove to get the very best recording.

Past lunchtime and into the evening, Sheila cajoled the tired musicians into yet another take as Declan layered the sounds on the complicated deck. The young producer was in his element, sliding and pressing all the knobs and buttons, waving instructions and smoking frantically as coffee cups and bottles of beer gathered all around the edges of his deck. With the intensity of a true composer he altered treble and bass, building and building the sound until the ballad fell gently into heartbreaking, cavernous valleys and rose up in yearning crescendos. As Declan managed the sound, Sheila made Patrick reach, reach, reach for those high notes. She wanted so much emotion in this recording that it would draw tears from a stone.

By six o'clock, everyone believed that the song was in the bag. Except Sheila.

'I've got a half-dozen usable takes here, Sheila, at least two outstanding ones. We're done,' Declan said.

'One more time,' she pleaded.

She felt there was some small thing missing. She could not put her finger on it but she was sure she could get to it, if they would just try one more time.

Tired and hungry, everyone went for one last shot at it.

Sheila sat down, for the first time that day, next to Declan at the producer's bench. She leaned back and closed her eyes, allowing herself to get lost in Patrick's voice.

As his smooth baritone caressed each word, Sheila felt as if she was hearing the lyrics for the first time.

I ask myself are you the one who filled me with desire
Are those the eyes that once searched mine and set my soul on fire

Then, when he came to the crescendo, 'it was only ever you' Sheila suddenly felt it. The feeling she had been waiting for. It was as if her heart had been punctured, and whatever was inside released. A truth came flooding out of her. It was beautiful, certain and yet terrifying, because she had been neither wanting nor expecting to feel it. She loved Iggy. That strange, remote man was her other half, after all. The only man that could ever truly understand her. She had never met another like him and she knew she never would again.

She realized, too, that she had known she loved him all along but had been afraid to face up to it. Because, running alongside the certainty that she loved him ran the knowledge that he was utterly unavailable to her. He would, could, never love her back in the same way. Iggy was a lone wolf. He had never promised her anything different. He had got involved with her because she had been as cold, as hard as he was. When she had started to get close, he had backed off. Now that her heart was open, she could never be with him.

As the band came down on the last note, Sheila wiped away her tears. Everyone assumed she was crying for the song.

'It's a wrap, boys,' she said, clapping. 'Well done – we've got a hit on our hands!'

Sheila seemed happy, smiling and smacking everyone on the back and congratulating them. Inside, though, a bleak feeling had taken hold. Once 'It Was Only Ever You' hit the charts, it would be time for Sheila to move away. Joe Higgins would be back, as he had promised, and to stay any longer would be to put her family and Patrick in jeopardy. Patrick was on the road now. He did not need her any more, not in the same intense way he had needed her up to now. In any case, the kid was becoming way too dependent on her. He needed to stand on his own two feet. She was his manager, not his mother, and the quicker he came to terms with that the better.

More importantly, Sheila still had enough pride not to hang around New York yearning for a lover who did not want her.

Iggy had been hoping to get in and out of the Emerald within the hour. He had one or two things to tie up with Gerry before leaving on a more extended trip.

He needed some time away to think things through.

That day in the recording studio had opened his eyes to just what a great businesswoman Sheila was. Her handling of Patrick's career had really impressed him. She was, much like himself, a trailblazer, arranging this recording of 'It Was Only Ever You' in a completely different way from any that had been done before. Later that evening, the record would launch at the Emerald. Patrick would sing in New York while the single itself would be played simultaneously in each of Morrow's clubs across America, Ireland and Britain. They had been advertising it for weeks and each club would be packed with punters ready to spread the word. As soon as the record had been cut, Sheila had gone out there and bribed all the right DJs to give it airtime. Most of her upfront money had gone into ensuring the right DJs were in her pocket. Iggy had never had the stomach for paying people off, but Sheila had no such qualms. Decca would make a number of the records available in each venue for sale on the night. Sheila had brokered the deal. Record shops were up in arms at the bold move, but she asked Iggy to assure them they would not be making a habit of selling records in this way again. It was a promotional tactic. A way of getting Patrick's name out there in an aggressive, one-shot manner that would lead to greater sales down the line.

Iggy admired Sheila. She was not like anyone else he had ever met. She was creative and dynamic and she got things done. He even thought her to be a lot like himself, but when he saw her in the studio that day, the way that she handled the musicians, and her devotion to Patrick, he realized she was more than him. Sheila was an unknown entity to him. He felt she was extraordinary but there was an edge to her that he felt he didn't know. Could, maybe, never know, and the not knowing made him feel uncomfortable.

To Iggy, discomfort was the opposite of love. He knew that unsettled feeling from his boyhood. Not knowing where you are going or what you should be doing. It was a feeling he had been chasing away all of his life with his meticulous scheduling and his secretive ways, keeping everything so close to his chest that nobody else could get in. Iggy had organized his life so that he remained always separated from other people. He kept himself safe in his quiet isolation. The safety of solitude. Now this uncomfortable feeling was back. Sheila had brought a disquiet, an uncertainty with her.

He admired her, he wanted to be with her. But not if it meant losing himself in the process.

'Did you hear the news?' Gerry said as he walked into the office.

Iggy was in bad form this evening. You could tell from the cold way that he had nodded at him as if to say, 'In my office, now.' He had not even bothered to take his coat off.

Gerry guessed the reason for his bad mood, and his pro-longed disappearance. The boss and Sheila had been having an affair. Iggy had wanted to cool it for a while, so he had made himself scarce. Gerry couldn't really understand what the big deal was. As far as he could see, Iggy and Sheila were as strange as each other. They were a match made in heaven! Maybe if he got married he might be less of a strange fish. Hell, he might even get happy and cut back on the miserable, poker-faced arse act.

'What news?' he said, only half listening. He could not even pretend to be interested in gossip.

'Joe Higgins called around to Sheila's family home and came the heavy. He was acting for the Balduccis, stupid eejit. Anyway, he gave Patrick an awful pelt on the cheek...' Then, seeing Iggy's extraordinary expression of terror and fury, quickly added, 'Sheila's auntie threw a pot of roast beef at him and laid him out. Made quite a mess, it seems. Aiden was in here last night and said Joe is still mad as hell...'

'Why didn't you call me?' Iggy said, although he knew the answer already. Nobody had his number. If something bad happened, or if somebody got into trouble, the managers had autonomy to deal with it themselves. Iggy had no attachments to anyone or anything. Business was just business.

Until now.

Joe Higgins was surprised to see Iggy Morrow turning up in his club. Surprised but secretly pleased. He had doubtless come to plead for his girlfriend. Joe had taken a fall that night, that was true. It had taken him a little time to recover from the nasty gash on his cheek, but more time from the rumours that he had been felled by corned beef in the hands of a seventy-year-old woman. Joe laughed it off, but it wasn't over. Nobody humiliated him like that. The Jewish broad was still around and Joe had plans to send somebody else down to Riverdale to get rid of her once and for all. However, he had to hand-pick them. Aiden and his lads didn't do old people and women, but there were a few guys out there that were less discerning about their clientele.

Just the sight of Iggy Morrow being all manners to his doormen made the fact that his plans had not yet taken shape all the sweeter.

'Mr Morrow,' he said, walking towards him holding out his hand. 'It's a pleasure to see you.'

Iggy paused before raising his right hand. Joe noticed his reluctance and it really got his blood up. This guy had always got on his nerves. He just couldn't make him out. He was a successful guy and Joe could respect that. But he was too straight, if there was such a thing; at least, if he was bent, Joe didn't know about it, and that made him feel uncomfortable. Joe could not help feeling that Ignatius Morrow looked down his nose at him. Plus, nobody knew anything about him, where he was from or who his people were. It just wasn't how things were done. It just wasn't... Irish. He was a man of mystery. Joe figured that was probably a construct. Maybe Morrow just kept out of everybody's way because he was a coward.

'We need to talk,' Iggy said.

'Let's go into my office,' Joe said. 'It's out the back.'

As he guided his guest through the bar with a flourish, Joe noticed Iggy looking around, his lips curling at the abundantly green decor. He made a mental note to get it changed. At the same time, he had half a mind to call a couple of the guys into the meeting to help bring down the great Ignatius Morrow and show him who was boss. Morrow was a powerful man. He could probably pay to get people whacked but he didn't go in for violence. If he did, Joe would have heard about it. He was shorter than him, Joe happily observed. He didn't know what all the fuss was about. Joe could show him a few moves of his own. As they walked through the bar he drew some pictures in his head of how it might go. Joe would get things started with polite chat, explain about the Balduccis and reason with him. Morrow would probably get all uppity with him, Joe would seem to let it go, then you would have to pull a gun. He wouldn't even have to touch Iggy. He was a straight guy, and with guys like that all you needed was a gun in your hand and the kind of face that said you had the intention to use it. He would be frightened out of his wits!

Joe was allowing himself the indulgence of how it was going to be as he turned the handle on his office door. But before it was fully open, Iggy had grabbed Joe's arm and twisted it until he was lying on the floor of his office, face down. Iggy was sitting on his back and had something sharp trained at the corner of Joe's neck.

'I am not going to waste my time reasoning with you, Joe. If you ever come near any of my staff, ever again, I will personally kill you. But I'm guessing that you don't believe me, so I'm going to cut off your ear now just to make my point.'

'No, no, no!' Joe cried out.

He had been threatened enough times in his life to know when somebody meant what he said. Morrow had the cool voice of the guy who means business. He wasn't a hothead like Joe. He was one of the others. The really crazy ones. The ones you avoided. Shit.

'I hear you, I hear you!' Joe pleaded.

'The problem is, I don't believe you're a man of your word,' Morrow continued, not moving the knife an inch, 'so I'm just wondering if I should go ahead and do it anyway...'

'Please, please don't cut me. I swear I'll stay away from the whore and the kid. I promise.'

'Good,' Iggy said, putting the knife back in his pocket.

As he moved his knees from the small of Joe's back, the gangster heard a deafening crippling crack and screamed out in pain.

'That's for calling Sheila a whore,' Ignatius said as he broke Joe's arm at the elbow.

As Aiden ran to his boss's rescue Iggy added, '... and upsetting her family.' Then, as he walked out the door, 'Although I understand the old lady can look after herself quite well.'

He was shaking so hard when he came out of Joe's club that he could not trust himself to drive his own car and had to hail a taxi.

He was not shaking for fear of what he had just done, but the fear of what he was about to do. Even though he knew that it was the right thing to do, the only thing to do, his fear of failure was greater than it had ever been.

Iggy had not been afraid since he was a small boy. That was because he never wanted anything badly enough to be afraid of not getting it. He had a lot of money, but it meant nothing to him. If it all went in the morning he knew he would be fine with that. The great empire he had built up was simply a way of keeping control over his place in the world. It was as much to do with the lifestyle of moving from office to office, country to country, place to place, people to people – keeping separate – as it was to do with a sense of satisfaction of all he had 'achieved'.

Iggy knew that he could achieve anything he set his mind to, and with all his money and success, he could have anything he wanted. The one thing, the only thing Iggy Morrow believed was beyond him, that had eluded him, was love. All his life, ever since he was a little orphan boy, Iggy had wanted a family. Sheila was as close as he had ever got to one in forty years. As he said to the taxi driver, 'Third and Mill Street, Riverdale,' the address he had memorized since their first night together, Iggy still believed it was beyond him, but he owed it to himself to try.

As the taxi drove up the leafy streets Iggy could feel his fear rising. All these comfortable houses, filled with comfortable families, eating their meals at the same time every night, watching TV together, leading small, ordinary lives. It was another world to him. And as the taxi drove deeper into suburbia, on every street corner he thought about telling the driver to turn back. Finally they pulled up outside the house.

'Is this it?' the driver asked.

'I don't know,' he replied, but he got out and threw twenty dollars at him anyway.

The taxi driver decided to wait. The guy was a generous tipper and he might want to be brought back to the city if it was the wrong place.

Anya opened the door and started slightly. She had been expecting Ruth from the bakery who had promised she would drop by with the cheesecake. The sight of a strange man at her door threw her, especially when he said, 'Is Sheila there?'

Immediately, Sheila appeared behind her. As he stepped inside, Iggy noticed two large cases in the hallway.

'Yours?' he said to Sheila.

She nodded, awkwardly. What was Iggy doing here?

She had decided to quit town before tonight. The big launch would be high profile, and she didn't want the wrong people hearing about her being the manager. She was going to take a leaf out of Iggy's book and stay out of the limelight. She'd written Patrick a letter explaining as much to him, because she knew that he would try and persuade her to be there. Possibly even try to protect her if there was trouble. And that wouldn't do his career any good. Once she was out of the way, Patrick and her family would be safe.

'I just called to let you know,' Iggy said, 'that Joe Higgins won't be bothering you any more.'

She believed him. Iggy was a force to be reckoned with. Way more powerful than Joe Higgins, but all the same she would never have asked for his help. Who had told him?

'So you can put those bags away and come back to work.'

Work. That was all this was.

'I'm not coming back,' she said. 'I always said I would move on, and it's time.'

'I see,' Iggy said, but he didn't move. He couldn't. There was something that he felt he wanted to say but whatever that something was it had eluded him completely. Or rather, it was so terrifying he could not even put words to it.

Anya was standing near the kitchen door. Utterly enraptured with the scenario, she was keeping as still as she could so that Sheila would not notice her eavesdropping. Sheila saw Iggy's eyes move shyly across her, turned around and said, 'Auntie!'

The old lady jumped and Iggy, despite the grave situation he found himself in, laughed.

He leaned past Sheila and held out his hand. 'You must be Sheila's Aunt Anya? She's told me so much about you.'

She virtually ran towards him to take his hand.

'You're the big boss man, so nice to meet you,' she said, almost genuflecting. 'Why don't you come in and have some tea? I am expecting a cheesecake delivery at any moment.'

He smiled again and said, 'That would be delightful.'

'My husband is out at present, but he should be back at any moment and—'

'Auntie!' Sheila said. 'Please, I need to talk with – Mr Morrow.'

It was painful having him there, standing in her hallway, just as she was about to leave. It was difficult enough leaving Auntie and Uncle. She had not been planning to say goodbye to him as well.

'Mrs Klein, Anya,' Iggy said, 'I would love some tea but first, I have something I need to ask Sheila...'

Sheila turned and gave Anya a wide-eyed stare that said, 'You see?' and as she did her aunt's jaw dropped open and she pulled her hands up to her mouth in a shocked gasp.

When Sheila turned around again, Ignatius Morrow was kneeling in front of her.

'Sheila Klein,' he said, 'would you do me the honour of becoming my wife?'

For a moment, Sheila stood there, unable to believe what she was seeing. Initially, she actually believed that this was some kind of dreadful joke he was making in front of her little old Jewish aunt.

Then she looked at his face. His expression was grave and slightly cross, as it always was, but kneeling, looking up at her, there was not a hint of scepticism in his eyes. Only a tender pleading. Iggy wasn't simply asking her to marry him, he was begging her to love him.

She leant down, pulled him up to his feet and glared at Anya until she went away.

'You don't need to marry me, Iggy,' she said. 'I love you, anyway.'

'Then you'll stay?' he said.

'Yes,' she said. 'I'll stay.'

And they kissed, both knowing that Anya was watching from the kitchen door.

'Will we go back to the Emerald?' he said. 'It's your big night.'

'Maybe later,' she said. 'Patrick can fend for himself for a few hours at least. I think we should stay here and eat cheesecake.'

So that's what they did.

38

AVA HAD been unsettled and had barely slept since her afternoon out with Dermot, a week ago. Nessa was beginning to worry that her daughter was sliding back into the listlessness.

In fact, quite the opposite was happening. Ava was thinking about getting her life back on track, and what her next step ought to be.

Seeing Patrick's poster outside the Emerald had jolted her back down to earth. Not that Dermot's attentions had her floating on a pink cloud, but she had been enjoying his company. The intrusion of seeing her husband's smiling, handsome face on that huge poster had immediately given her pause about the wisdom of gadding about with her ex-fiancé.

She saw that Patrick was releasing his first record later that week. So, his dream of being a famous singer was finally coming to fruition and Ava knew she had been an important part of that. How must he be feeling now? she asked herself. Just as everything was coming together for him, his marriage ended and he lost a baby. Ava had not even said goodbye to him, left a note or anything. She had been hurt by what he had done, the terrible betrayal, the way in which she had found out about it and the subsequent terrible loss of the baby, which she had managed to get through without his support.

She began to see that it was not entirely his fault, either. He had come to the house but her father had chased him away. Perhaps if Tom had let Patrick into the house that day, and they had talked, all of this would be behind them now.

Rose was out of the picture. She had left town. When Myrtle had told Ava about how she had confronted Rose, Ava had been quite upset. She felt quite sorry for the girl. After all, the only crime she had committed was loving Patrick and following him to America. She knew that Myrtle was only acting out of loyalty and kindness to her, but there was something humiliating about her husband's lover being banished on her behalf. There was no doubt that Patrick had loved Rose once, enough to get engaged to her. But then, Ava remembered, she had been engaged to Dermot and had left him for Patrick. If Rose and Patrick truly loved each other nothing would keep them apart. Certainly not a threat from Myrtle.

But, whatever he had done, Patrick was still her husband. He had made a mistake, one mistake, albeit a very serious one. But, underneath it all, he was a good man, and Ava knew he would have been suffering. Patrick had always told her that he could never be a success without her. And now that his dream was coming true, the very foundation on which it was built had crumbled. He must be feeling dreadful. Ava, for all the pain she still felt at his having betrayed her, still felt a deep loyalty to the love they had shared and to the baby they had made and then lost. They were married. Surely that meant they should stick together, no matter what?

All of this was swirling in a confusing soup of conflicting thoughts and emotions in her head as she sat down for breakfast that morning.

Nessa put the cornflakes packet in front of her and asked, 'When are you going to see Dermot again?'

You could tell from her voice that she had been clinging on to the question since their afternoon out, a week ago.

'Really, Ava, he is such a nice man.'

Ava felt like screaming at her but instead she just nodded and said, 'I know.'

There was no point in trying to explain any of her thoughts to her mother. In any case, Nessa was right, Dermot was a very nice man. But then, he always had been. He had just never been quite 'enough' somehow. That was something that she could never hope to make her mother understand. In truth, Ava struggled to understand it herself.

In any case, Ava had a feeling that Dermot would always be there, but if she wanted to hold on to Patrick, and their marriage, she would have to act fast.

Whatever the future held for them, Ava knew that she should be there for him on his important night. She would simply go along as a member of the audience. Maybe they would talk. Or maybe he would just see that she was there to support him. Whether they would be able to put the past behind them and reunite was a matter for later. However, Ava knew she had to at least try to make it work.

'Anyway, I'm going out tonight,' she said to Nessa. She did not tell her where or who with and Nessa had the good sense not to ask. Although, as she stood at the sink facing out the kitchen window, she beamed heartily, believing it was Dermot. Wait until she told Tom!

Ava telephoned Myrtle while her mother was out of earshot

to see if she would come along as her partner in crime. She did not mention Patrick, just that she would like to go dancing at the Emerald. If Myrtle told her that it was Patrick's gig, something she would surely know about, Ava would try and persuade her it didn't matter. But, she didn't.

'I'm busy tonight,' she said.

'A date?' Ava asked. If Myrtle met a man now and left her, Ava did not know what she would do.

'Maybe,' Myrtle said mysteriously, then quickly rang off saying, 'Got to go, I have a crazy day!'

Ava tried to keep her head straight for the rest of the day. To her parents' astonishment, she took a train into the city for the first time since her recovery began, and walked round the stores looking for an outfit to wear that night. However, she was so filled with nervous excitement, she could not find anything and took the subway back to Yonkers, where she went to a local salon, getting her hair styled and her nails manicured. In the early evening, she opened her wardrobe to find something to wear. By this time, she was irritated with how she was feeling at the prospect of seeing Patrick again. It was a very different kind of excitement to the lusty nervousness of when they had first met. This stomach-churning was closer to dread than passion. She was not thinking of seeing him with any particular joy in her heart. She only knew that she should be there, and that, if she ended up being on show as Patrick's wife, she should, at least, look her very best. Not simply for him, but more to prove something to herself.

Opening her wardrobe she flicked through endless mediocre, casual ensembles, flinching as her freshly painted fingernails brushed the maternity dresses. Then, she came to it. The rose suit.

She had lost a great deal of weight in the last few weeks. Would it fit her?

She quickly took it out and tried it on. The zip on the skirt ran up like butter. Every button on the jacket closed snugly across her breasts.

Nervously, Ava looked at herself in the mirror. She saw the elegant young woman who had surprised her, a year ago, in front of Sybil Connolly's Plaza suite mirror. Except that her transformation was no longer simply in the suit. It had been earned through a year of love and loss. Life was written on her face, now, and it had made her beautiful.

She drove down to South Broadway and parked outside the Emerald.

Even though it was early there was already a long queue. Taking a deep breath, Ava marched to the top of the queue, as she had done in the old days. Gerry happened to be at the door. His eyebrows raised slightly in surprise. 'Ava. Good to see you,' was all he said, before ushering her in himself.

'You going backstage?' he asked, gently.

'Not tonight,' she replied, and he sat her at a booth near the stage, instructing one of the bar staff to bring across the red VIP rope and wait on her all evening.

Ava appreciated his recognizing her status, but his respect-fulness also made her feel a little sad. This did not feel like her life. Aside from that one night when she had got Patrick up on stage, she had never been a part of his work. He had said that she was his rock, but, in reality, Patrick had done it all by himself. His manager, Sheila, had been the one to encourage and support him. Ava certainly did not resent her for it. She had never had any real interest in the music, beyond dancing to it and enjoying it, just the same as everybody else. She was his audience. No more, no less. In a small, shocking moment she wondered if she had been the inspiration for this record that Sheila had arranged for him. 'It Was Only Ever You'. Surely not. It had never been only Ava. In some part of her, she had always known that. She had always known that she was not the first girl he had been in love with. That was why she had never asked. If she had he might have told her that he was in love with Rose. And although Patrick had been the first man she had gone all the way with, Dermot had been the first man she kissed. If she had married Dermot, before she met Patrick, he would have been the only man she might have known her whole life. And that, even though it was wrong, might have driven Ava half-mad with wondering what might have been...

The compère came out and introduced the resident band. Patrick would be on stage at eight o'clock, less than half an hour away. The place was really filling up fast, and, as the band struck up Bill Haley's Saturday-night anthem, 'Rip It Up!' couples began flooding on to the dance floor. The air was electric with the start of the weekend and everyone was letting off steam. Ava was sitting there, demure with her cigarette and a just-delivered martini, with no intention of dancing. She watched on as guys threw girls over their shoulders, spinning them around, with feet going heel-to-toe faster than was feasible. This had once been her world, but tonight, all that felt like a lifetime ago.

'Wee-ell I got me a date and I won't be late...'

As the song took off Ava's friend Myrtle came into view. She was ripping it up like crazy, right in the middle of the floor with some guy who Ava assumed must be her new mystery man.

* * *

Dermot had begged Myrtle not to make him jive. After his frantic phone call where he had asked Myrtle to come and teach him, once and for all, how to dance, Dermot had immediately regretted the decision.

He never felt more of a bumbling fool than when he was on the dance floor. The baggy, long-line suits, coupled with his complete lack of coordination made Dermot look, and feel, like the greatest idiot that had ever drawn breath. Dermot was at his best in a courtroom, and an old-fashioned three-piece suit like his father, pontificating cleverly. However, Ava was never likely to see him in that light. And if she did, it was unlikely to impress her. He had tried, and failed, so far, to win Ava's heart and, out of desperation, imagined that learning to dance might do the trick. However, he now realized a few lessons wasn't going to fix his broken heart. And, in any case, he had been attending Mrs Quinn's dance classes for months now, and he still had two left feet. He was beyond help.

However, to the indomitable dancer Myrtle, nobody was beyond help when it came to romance.

So, on the phone that day, she did a deal.

'I will teach you to dance and fix you up with Ava if you put in a word for me with your brother.'

Niall, that little tearaway – what would she want with him?

'Fine,' he said. 'I'll put you in his path.'

'And your mother?'

Myrtle knew from Ava that Mrs Dolan was a hard nut to crack.

'I'll tell her you are a real lady from an excellent family.'

'Which I am.'

'Of course you are.'

'We have a deal. See you tomorrow at your place, six p.m. I assume you have a record player?'

'Of course!' Although his records were mostly Mahler.

'I'll bring the records. Roll back the sofa and don't be late.'

In their first session, she laid out the ground rules.

'Rule one: do everything I say. Rule two: listen closely to the music. Rule three: keep going no matter what.'

For the next two hours Myrtle dragged, cajoled, persuaded and prodded Dermot around his living room. Dermot was a nice guy. She liked him. She was glad that he loved Ava and she was sure that, if she could just fire a little jazz into him, she could get Ava to love him back. But when it came to being fun, of which dancing was the top qualification, he was a washout. Finally, after a lacklustre cha-cha, she sat him down, looked him straight in the eye and called him out. 'Do you love Ava?'

'Why?' he said.

'Don't look at me all embarrassed. If you don't know by now then...'

'She is beautiful...'

'And?'

'She's smart, and funny. She makes me laugh...'

As he was talking Dermot began to feel as if Ava was there, in the room with them. 'She is full of energy and life...' God he loved her, 'and she is just about the most capable woman I know...' It was all true. How he wanted her back! He had to win her back!

'Yes, Dermot, she is all that and she loves to dance. So, if you want her back, you are going to have to step up to the plate, loverman. Because Ava is not going to settle for some lousy grey lawyer who is as stiff as a board. Is that you, Dermot?'

'No, it's not!'

'Can we do this, Dermot?'

'Yes!' He was going to jive his way back into Ava's heart if it was the last thing he did!

Myrtle stood up and put on 'Rock Around the Clock' for the umpteenth time.

'And remember – it's only a bloody dance. Don't let it get the better of you. Now. Let's try it one more time. With some feeling, yes?'

As Ava watched Myrtle giving her all on the dance floor, getting stuck into 'Rip It Up!' she felt a twinge of regret that those days seemed to be behind her. She did not quite know how that had happened. Only that the carefree impulse to jump on to the dance floor and let herself go had left her. She had become so distracted by her passion for Patrick that dancing had seemed childish somehow. It was who she had been before she met these men. It was no longer part of her life, and she felt that, more keenly than ever, sitting separate from the crowd in her private booth. Alone, struggling to recover from the aftermath of her broken marriage. Dancing was something you did when you were happy, did not have a care in the world. Perhaps she would be happy one day. As Ava was thinking these thoughts, her eyes fixed on Myrtle.

She was wearing a beautiful sky-blue blouse tucked into a black skirt, which hugged her curves, and a pair of stilettos. It set off her slim figure perfectly and she was dancing very elegantly, and without her usual wild abandon. Nonetheless, her face was glittering with joy, and she seemed very pleased with herself indeed. He must be a very special guy, Ava thought, if he is eliciting this kind of effort from flirtatious Myrtle. As they spun around in a restrained, but perfectly timed turn,

Ava strained her eyes to get a look at him. As he came into focus she was astonished to see that it was Dermot.

That was not what she had been expecting. Dermot? Dancing? He wasn't the best dancer in the room, but he wasn't the worst either. When did this happen? Could Dermot really be Myrtle's mystery date? It certainly looked like it. She was beaming like the cat that got the cream. Dermot was a free man, he could date whomever he liked. But Myrtle? Everyone knew she was desperate to find a husband— Wait – was Ava jealous? As she watched the couple weave in and out, their arms sliding seamlessly over each other's body, smiling, jumping about, having fun, Ava felt a stab of sadness for all she had lost. Then something happened. The band hit a particular part of the song that she loved. Ava felt the music tingling through her feet, then moving up her legs, filling her chest, her arms, every inch of her body until she got up from her seat and began walking towards the couple. As she walked, Ava felt the beat slamming through her, driving her on. 'I'm gonna rip it up…' There was only one thing on her mind: This is my dance, this is my man and, as she pushed Myrtle aside and slid seamlessly into a side swing, This is my life and to hell with the world. I'm gonna shake it up!

Dermot was surprised and almost lost his step when Ava butted in. He had practised every move of this dance meticulously with Myrtle and wasn't sure he could carry it off with anyone else. But Ava was so determined, so glorious in her smiling, smooth energy, that all he wanted was to keep her there, with him. Dermot found he was able to stay one step ahead of her, pre-empting her moves, being the steady presence guiding and leading her into looking good in her favourite place, the dance floor. It seemed that this was what made Ava happy, and Dermot loved making her happy.

When the jive ended, the band moved on to a slow waltz. Ava was utterly distracted by the adrenalin that was still pumping through her. The delight of dancing again. The thrill of it being with Dermot. She paused, briefly remembering that she was here to see Patrick, but then Dermot put his arms around her and pulled her into a tight, chest-hugging waltz hold. Patrick had never held her like that, with such firm determination. Then, without giving her time to breathe, Dermot leaned in close to her and whispered in a voice that was deeper, more masterful that she remembered it being.

'There is no other woman in the world like you, Ava. You are the only one for me and you always will be. Please. Let me make you happy.'

Dermot knew he should stop there but, uncertain he had fully got his point across, he decided to drum his message home with a quote he had recently come across, although he was not sure where from. 'Ava, my darling – you know that "it was only ever you" I could love. Will you give me another chance?'

Ava's stomach did a sideways turn. Dermot was setting himself up in direct competition with Patrick. Using the title of her husband's song to woo her. What an outrageously confident thing to do. No wonder he was considered one of the best lawyers in the country! She was impossibly torn. On the one hand was Patrick, with whom she was passionately in love, and on the other was stalwart Dermot, although, it seemed, that had all changed. In fact, standing here in Dermot's arms, with the heat of the jive still pumping through her, Ava could feel the same powerful stirrings Patrick had brought out in her. Plus, Dermot said Ava was the 'only one' but she saw the way Myrtle had been gripping him during that jive. Imagine if Dermot ended up with Myrtle Milligan.

Her mother would go half mad. Then, Ava realized with something of an emotional jolt, so would she.

She had to act fast.

She brought her voice down to a breathy whisper, and leaned into his ear and asked, 'Have you got your car outside, Dermot?'

Taken aback, and somewhat disappointed at the change of subject, he answered, 'Yes.'

'Good,' she said, reaching for his hand, 'because I want you to take me for a drive.'

Dermot was delighted that Ava wanted to leave with him, alone, and not stay on to hear her wretched husband sing his silly song, whatever it was. However, he was slightly confused about the car. Where was it she wanted to go? What on earth could she mean by 'drive'? Not... Oh now, surely not. How could he even dare think of anything so unseemly of Ava? Not that he had never thought about it but... No, it simply wasn't possible.

Ava dragged her new lover silently across the dance floor and out of the Emerald. She smiled to herself as she thought about the thrills that were ahead of them that night and how shocked Myrtle would be to think what she was up to, especially after she had set her sights on him.

She did not know that Myrtle was with Dermot's brother Niall in a corner booth, engaged in a determined kiss.

39

PATRICK HAD never been more nervous in his life. There was about an hour to go until he was due on stage and he had just read the note that Sheila had left in his dressing room.

It said she was leaving town for a while and would be basing herself in Boston, 'for the next few months, at least, maybe longer'. She would be forwarding her phone number within the next two days, and, in the meantime, his gig schedule was all set through Mr Morrow's venues, and Iggy's secretary would be in touch to firm up any queries.

Patrick could not believe that Sheila had abandoned him in this way. How could he manage without her? He had no wife to look after him, no family to fall back on. Over the past few weeks Sheila had become everything to him. If she were younger, he might even have fallen in love with her. That evening, when he had taken a fall for her, he had thought that perhaps he already had. However, he knew that the warm feelings he had towards her were more gratitude than anything else. Without the help she had given him since he got here, he would be nothing. He owed her as much as, if not more than, he owed Ava.

He looked up at his mirror where Sheila had pinned the words of 'It Was Only Ever You'. He felt a sting of regret for Rose but quickly pushed thoughts of her aside. That was what he always did. He had sung the song so many times now that he had almost forgotten why he had written it. Almost.

He picked up the Max Factor panstick and dabbed a little over his skin as Sheila had taught him to do, covering up any small blemishes on his face. Then he picked up the Brylcreem and comb and began to set his hair into a quiff. There was a time when, looking in the mirror like this, he would have felt secretly proud of how handsome he was. Perhaps, even, thrown himself a charming smile, trying it on for the audience. But tonight he was not in the mood. When he looked in the mirror all he saw was the empty room behind him. A space that should be filled with a wife or a lover. To lose both of those things in one year had been careless and stupid of him. Now, his manager had abandoned him as well. He struggled to hold his hand steady to put the last strand of his quiff in place, his big blue eyes staring angrily back at him. They were glittering with fear. He would not be able to do this tonight. Not alone. He needed someone else there to bolster him, to egg him on. Sheila had been the last one who could offer him the support he needed to get on stage. This was the biggest night of his life, he could not go through it alone.

Through the heavy walls Patrick heard the thump of the visiting showband starting up. He couldn't sit there any longer fizzing with nerves. He had already drunk the two beers that had been left backstage for him and he needed another. He could try to sneak over to the bar, as he would do on a normal night, but this was his big debut and it would be bad form for him to be seen out front with the punters. Patrick decided to go to the heavy fire door that led from the office area to the dance hall. He could try and get the attention of one of the waitresses. Staff were trained to make sure the door was closed at all times, so if it was ajar somebody would notice him peering out. As he looked through the door, he half expected to see Sheila flying around the room in her black hipster garb, bossing people about. However, even if she had been, the huge room was so thronged with people he would have been hard pushed to find her. It was early for it to be so crowded, even for a Saturday night. With a rising wave of nausea Patrick remembered that all of these people were there to see him. He was shaking and badly needed another drink to calm his nerves. He narrowed his eyes and searched the crowd until he saw Gerry serving somebody at a booth. Waving frantically, his eyes moved to the booth itself and with a shocked jolt he saw Ava sitting there. He could hardly believe it. Had she come to see him? Was it possible? Why else would she be there? Again, Patrick waved frantically at Gerry, trying to get his attention, but Gerry walked away without seeing him. Patrick was considering sneaking over to her himself when Ava got up from the booth and moved across to the dance floor. Where was she going? He couldn't see from where he was, and he could not follow her into the crowd, so Patrick ran backstage to look through the side curtain from where he would get a bird's-eye view of the whole floor.

A small ray of hope opened inside him at the thought that, despite everything, perhaps his wife was returning to him. Perhaps he would not be alone this evening, after all. But then, as he looked out, Patrick saw that Ava was dancing a wild jive with some man. He vaguely recognized him, but could not say who he was. As the jive stopped and the music slowed down to a waltz, Patrick said a small prayer that Ava would move away from the dance floor to come and find him. But she didn't. As they waltzed, the man's arms wrapped around Ava. Ava was smiling as she leant into the man's ear and said something. Hot tears poured down Patrick's cheeks as the man's face came into view and he saw it was Ava's ex-fiancé. The man she had jilted to be with him. He had known that she was gone to him before tonight, but this seemed like a special, cruel reminder of all he had lost. After a few moments, Ava and her partner left, hand in hand.

Patrick felt all the old hurt flooding through him. Weakening him, poisoning his desire to sing. He had known that Ava did not love him any more, but the fact that he had hoped, made him feel impossibly sad. Nobody loved him. He had taken everybody's love and ruined it. Abandoning Rose, betraying Ava and finally, he knew, clinging to Sheila like a child – needing more than she was willing to give.

Patrick wanted to run away, out the door, back on to the streets of New York, down to the docks and on to a boat back to Ireland. Back to his Saturday-night gigs in Ballina town hall, squabbling with his siblings over the leg of the Sunday chicken, gathering hay with his father, and those secret summer assignations with sweet, blonde Rose. He began to cry at the very thought of how his life had failed him, and he was just calculating if he had enough money to make a run for it when he heard Sheila's voice in his head: 'Stop crying, Patrick! You're streaking that panstick. Just get out there and sing.'

Patrick wiped his hands across his face just as he heard Gerry bash his door shouting, 'You're on!'

There was still time. He could run past Gerry, through the back exit and leave it all behind.

Walking back to the office that afternoon Rose knew that she had to see Patrick again. She could not move on with her own life until she had resolved what had passed between them. She was no longer certain if she truly loved him any more. She only knew that the madness that had taken her recently had left her, and that she needed to apologize to Patrick for all that she had done.

The client meeting went well, but Rose was unable to get the need to see Patrick out of her head. Since hearing that song on the radio earlier, it was as if he was calling to her.

The image of Patrick, as he had been to her once, kept floating into her mind. His jet-black curls falling into his eyes, singing her some sweet love song as they lay on the grass at the back of her parents' field. Those sharp blue eyes softening with desire, as he pulled her up to the surface of the lake that day. Rose did not need to be rescued any more. In the past two months she had learned to rescue herself, but she felt terrible about all that had happened in the past few months, and needed to, somehow, make amends. As much as she had pursued him before, Rose now felt the need to see Patrick to apologize, face to face, for all of the hurt she had caused him, and Ava. Only then would she be free to get on with her life properly. Perhaps, she thought, Patrick too needed her to set him free? Whatever the case, it was time to, literally, face the music.

Rose finished work at six and got straight on the subway to Yonkers. In all likelihood, Patrick would have moved on from the Emerald Ballroom by now. Certainly, if he had a record on the radio he would be hitting the big time. However, wherever he was, and whatever he was doing, the Emerald would be the best place to start her search.

'Come on, Patrick.'

Gerry had been warned by Sheila that Patrick might get a fit of nerves. Without Patrick knowing it, Gerry had kept a close eye on him all evening. There was no way Gerry was going to give his charge more than two drinks or bring his estranged wife over to cause him a load of emotional upset before going on stage. Aside from anything else, Sheila would kill him if tonight didn't run smoothly. Gerry felt bad for betraying her when he told Iggy about the Joe Higgins incident. He felt sure that was what had chased her out of town on what should have been her big night, as well as Patrick's. It was up to him to make sure that kid got on stage and sang like a pro.

So, when there was no sign of Patrick, Gerry did what he thought Sheila would have done. He opened the door, grabbed Patrick by the arm and dragged him up on to the stage, literally giving him a sharp kick on the behind to propel him in front of the band.

Patrick had no time to question if he wanted to be here. The band had played the opening bars and he had to start singing. As he held the microphone to his mouth, he was aware of the audience, hundreds of people looking up at him, expecting something brilliant. Expecting entertainment, emotion, the evoking of love. 'It Was Only Ever You' was coming out of him automatically. He had sung it so many times before that as soon as the music came on he would start singing, despite himself. He crooned and moved the microphone backwards and forwards and swayed and made all of the right movements. But he wasn't feeling it. As he went through the motions Patrick was actually glad that Sheila was not there to see him giving such a lacklustre performance. Halfway through the first verse he remembered Sheila once advising him to, 'find a pretty girl in the audience and sing the song for her'.

So, Patrick looked out into the crowd.

There, like a vision – and Patrick believed that it was only a vision – in the middle of the dance floor, stood Rose Hopkins.

Could it be true... could it really be you... the one I search for in a song and waited for so long... was it only ever you?

As he sang to his 'vision' of Rose, Patrick began to feel the power of his voice. He remembered the first day he had fallen in love with the doctor's daughter and how his song had stopped a bull from charging. His voice had saved a life and started a love story so great it had crossed an ocean.

Then, as he sang the words, 'I tell myself you are the very reason I exist', Patrick realized the whole truth of his life lay in that sentence he had written. It was not about Rose, after all. He did not need Rose or Ava or even Sheila to make him sing. He had been singing before he met any of them and he would be singing long after every lover, wife or manager had ever left him.

Music was his first love. It was 'only ever' about the music. Music had been the lover that had ruined his life. The promise of a career had lured him away from Rose. The stability and security he needed to build that career had been given to him by Ava. Sheila had elevated him from singer to star. Of all of them, Sheila understood him the best. He was an artist. His art would always come before human love. 'It's the way you're made,' Sheila had once told him. 'Put the music first, life later,' had always been her advice.

Patrick had only known one other person like that in his life. Someone who could get so lost in their work, so lost in their art, that it was as if nobody else existed. Somebody who seemed heedless of the feelings of others when in pursuit of something they loved.

That person was Rose. The song was not about the love he had for Rose, but the thing they shared in common – their love of music and art.

As the song rose in a crashing crescendo,

Because it's true… it was only ever you… the one I love with all my heart… and have done from the start…

Patrick kept his eye on the beautiful blonde vision, although it was not until the song came to its soft, teasing, close,

It was only ever you… my love… yes… It was only ever you

that he realized she was real. It was, actually, Rose standing there, in the flesh. The last time he had seen her in that spot he had walked across the empty room, kissed her and brought his life to an end.

Yet, he was still here, and so was she. Along with nearly a thousand other people, all screaming for him.

Patrick barely saw them as he hopped down from the side of the stage and walked towards Rose. The crowd surged around him so that he became trapped, the people pawing at his chest, congratulating him, girls telling them they loved him, everyone begging for his attention. Patrick panicked as he found that he could not move. He was drowning in adulation.

Then he saw Rose's white-blonde hair emerge through the sea of faces, like a beacon rising to the surface of a stormy ocean.

She reached in and grabbed his hand, and Patrick knew he was saved.

HISTORICAL NOTE
FROM AUTHOR

For the post depression years up to JFK's visit to Ireland in 1963, it was possible for the Irish to enter America with a passport and an assurance there would be a person to meet them at the other end. They did this in their droves until, in the early 1960s, Ireland's Taoiseach (Prime Minister) Sean Lemass asked President John F Kennedy not to give Ireland an allotment of US visas in an attempt to stop the brain drain in Ireland. This led to the introduction of a rigorously policed visa system that remains to this day.

ACKNOWLEDGEMENTS

Thank you to Judd Ruane for his invaluable research on the showband scene.

Helen Falconer for use of her big brain.

Ella Griffin for daily writing support.

Joe Queenan of Foxford Woollen Mills for research.

Elaine Tighe for writing the lyrics for 'It Was Only Ever You' and wonderful Tommy Fleming for bringing the song to life and recording it.

My assistant Danielle, on hand always, brilliant as ever.

My student Frederique Bresson for her sterling work.

Brendan Hoban for swift replies to 'priest queries'.

My mother Moira for her cheerleading and unconditional love.

My husband Niall, for his endless tolerance and respect.

My sons Leo and Tommo – for giving me the reason to work.

My agent Marianne Gunn O'Connor and Pat Lynch for their faith and constancy.

Amanda Ridout and her Head of Zeus team: Nia, Liz, Clémence, Madeleine, Jessie, Suzanne, Victoria and, of course, Anthony Cheetham for starting up such a vibrant, creative, supportive house in the first place. I feel very lucky indeed.

Last, but certainly not least, my indomitable, awesome editor, Rosie de Courcy. I value your opinion above all others and thank you for taking the time to make this book come alive. It was a close one, but we did it! Thank you for making me a better storyteller and a better writer.

Truths, Half Truths and Little White Lies

Truths, Half Truths and Little White Lies

NICK FROST

HODDER &
STOUGHTON

First published in Great Britain in 2015 by Hodder & Stoughton
An Hachette UK company

1

A CIP catalogue record for this title is available from the British Library

Hardback ISBN 978 1 473 62087 2
eBook ISBN 978 1 473 62085 8

Typeset in Sabon MT by Hewer Text UK Ltd, Edinburgh
Printed and bound by CPI Group (UK) Ltd, Croydon CR0 4YY

Hodder & Stoughton policy is to use papers that are natural, renewable
and recyclable products and made from wood grown in sustainable
forests. The logging and manufacturing processes are expected to
conform to the environmental regulations of the country of origin.

Hodder & Stoughton Ltd
Carmelite House
50 Victoria Embankment
London EC4Y 0DZ

www.hodder.co.uk

follow Nick Frost here:
Twitter @nickjfrost
Instagram @friedgold

To the many I lost who broke me.
And the one I found who fixed me.

For Mac . . .

Introduction

How does one capture the nuance of a human life in a book? Is it even possible? (Of course it is, you helmet, have you not read *Long Walk to Freedom*?) Sad as it sounds, I always thought if there was a book about loss and tragedy they'd probably ask me to write the foreword.

It has not been easy being me sometimes, but please don't imagine for a second this'll be all doom and gloom. How could it be? No life can really be all black, right? Even during the darkest, poorest, shitest, hardest times, what got me through that bleakness was laughter and time, lots of time. With enough of both of these things I reckon you could get over just about anything. Just about.

It was a difficult decision to write this though. Am I willing to lay out my total being in all its ugliness for the potential of selling 1,500 hardbacks? Do I just want to produce another 'celeb' autobiography, written by a ghost, telling you about the time I met David Attenborough? (He was lovely.) No, I didn't want to do that. If you're going to tell the story of a life, my life, tell it warts and all. That, to me, is a better reflection of a person. If the tale you tell is too saccharine sweet what can the reader take away from it? What do they learn about you? About a life? Fuck all. Write everything down. The shit, the death, fun, naughtiness, addiction, laughter, laughter, laughter, tears and lots of love and happiness. Surely this is a better reflection of what a person is and if someone can read the book and take something away from it then all the better.

These are themes that anyone can relate to. (Apart from all the foie gras, private jets and money fights obviously.) Who really cares about a story where a well-paid actor's feet hurt after forgetting to properly break in their new handmade shoes at a massive film premiere. It's bullshit.

Despite the job I currently do I would hope I'm just like everyone else reading this. Just like everyone else who will never read this.

So why now? I'm only forty-three, it's no age at all. I had lunch with two old people yesterday, friends of my eighty-year-old ex-father-in-law (gorgeous, gentle gentleman) and they laughed when I told them I was writing a memoir. I felt slightly embarrassed.

I think I'm writing this for my son. My boy. The best thing I ever did and the most important thing to ever happen to me. By thirty-nine I was an orphan. It's not that young compared to some but very young compared to many. I have a seventy-two-year-old friend, an actor I've worked with a few times, a good man, a gent. I asked him once what he was up to for the weekend. His reply:

'I'm off to Manchester to see Mum and Dad.'

It floored me and I couldn't help but blurt out, 'You got a fucking mum and dad!!!'

He laughed, fortunately.

That, I think, encapsulates the great randomness of life. You just don't know. Some of you may not even finish this book, you may be so engrossed one day by the narrative that stepping off the bus you . . . BANG!!! You never know.

Having had a relationship with my parents that one might describe as tempestuous and now having no parents at all, I often think of the stories they had that will never be told. The things I'll never know about them, about their time before each other, about their time before me, their courtship, their passions, their love. What did they like? What were they afraid of?

I know lots of things about them of course but there are holes in their story and I think that's why I wanted to write this book. I want my son to be able to read this at some point in the future and know what his dad was all about. The good and bad, because both are valid.

I'd also make a plea to you lot, you glorious 1,500; ask your questions now! Once they're gone, they're gone and those answers you crave can be lost for ever. I've kept a journal or a notebook for most of my life. Usually during the times when I was down, but I found writing a great way to escape and lick my wounds. It also makes remembering things pretty easy – that and music. Music helps. Some things are gone from my memory for ever sadly. I don't remember much about secondary school. There's also a bit of my late twenties missing. But mostly it's all up there, somewhere.

I've written chronologically but there are jumps in time and flights of angular fancy. Some of this is as it comes to me, randomness of thought, brain tics. Those of you who know me well, please forgive me if I've got it wrong or my timing's off. Bear with me, be gentle and please save your questions to the end. Let's do this.

Part One

I was born in a hospital in Hornchurch, near the sleepy village of Romford in Essex. The first house I remember was 111 Lindsey Road, Becontree Heath, Dagenham. There was a flat before this in a place called Harold Hill but I was too young to remember it. My parents, John and Tricia, told a story that when I was two and a half I climbed up on the railings of the balcony of the flat, some thirty feet above the concrete below, and stood there gurgling until my mum found me. She had to lie on the floor and crawl towards me, fearing that if I saw her I'd get excited and fall. I turned round at one point and laughed, she sprang up and grabbed me as I fell backwards. This book would've been a lot simpler to write if I'd have fallen then. Definitely shorter.

No, Dagenham is where my first memories begin to bubble up. There were always lots of people in that little terraced house on Lindsey Road. It was the mid-to-late seventies, which meant floor-to-ceiling brown and orange. I lived just with my mum and dad, with the occasional stay from one of my half-siblings. Dagenham felt like a community to me; we were always in and out of each other's houses. Kids playing outside, wandering off, knock down ginger, even the old bag of burning dogshit trick on one old bastard's doorstep once. Naughty.

When it was hot the whole street would gather outside to play cricket. I got run over once by a man on a bike as I reached to take a beautiful catch on the boundary. When I say boundary I mean the patch of dirt outside 105. It hurt like hell, as he seemed to run right over the middle of my body. That's the kind of place Dagenham was. You'd be playing cricket in the street and a big man on a child's bike could run you over.

Our neighbours on that street were lovely. Auntie Joan was on our left (not a real auntie). She had a very fat chocolate Labrador, and her house – always dark and mega hot – smelt like boiling tripe (it was the East End in the seventies after all). On the other side were Auntie Elsie and Uncle Harry (again, no relation). Elsie was old and looked like the actress Yootha Joyce. Harry was small and meek and always wore a tank top. After we moved away they stayed in our lives a long time. They were good to Mum and Dad.

During a rainstorm in 1974, Mum and Dad were dashing back to our house from Elsie and Harry's when Dad (who was holding me over his shoulder) lost a slipper, slipped, and flew into the sky. He landed on top of me on my face from a height of about five feet. Dad, of course, was distraught. They said my head swelled to the size of a pumpkin. What kind of pumpkin I guess I'll never know – this is why you should ask these questions now.

Dagenham was also the place where I hospitalised my dad for the first time while doing DIY. I was five and Dad had stupidly given me a large claw hammer to drive a nail into a piece of timber. His last words to me were, 'When I nod my head hit it.' He nods his head and I bludgeon him across his pumpkin with the hammer. When Dad regains consciousness he is in an ambulance on his way to King George Hospital. That was the last time we ever did any DIY together. I think this episode severely dented my own DIY career.

Shortly after this a second terrible tragedy strikes my family. While cleaning out his cage my budgie, Bobbi, escapes, flying out of the window and away into the filthy air over Dagenham. Two weeks later while whacking a bush with an unstrung badminton racket I find Bobbie's headless corpse. It is my first brush with death and one I struggle to get over my whole life.

Dagenham was also the place I had my first cigarette. It was Christmas Day, 1980. I was nine. After pestering Mum and Dad for ages, they finally crack. They falsely believe that by giving me a cigarette (a Piccadilly filter) it will turn me off smoking for ever; they were so wrong. I smoke it in silence, they watch me smoke it in silence, and I put it out in a style I'd seen them do, a kind of tamp down, fold-over thing. A beat, a moment, I turn and ask for another. Dubious parenting. If they were alive today my parents would be horrified I'm telling you this.

There's no doubt I'm Tricia Frost's son though, defiant and stubborn as a bloody mule. My mum was so beautiful, even at the end when she was nearly sixty but looked eighty she still had something. She was always well turned out. Lots of gold jewellery and a ton of Elnett hairspray. She used the same hair dye for years and years (Clairol light ash blonde) with perfect white smile (dentures) and perfectly manicured nails. She had a wheezy but infectious laugh and she was small (five foot two) like her sisters. Hobbits all.

As I got older, I started to become more like my dad, more of his traits, thank god. He was gentle. If the Bee Gees were in one telepod, and eighties Noel Edmonds in the other (the Noel Edmonds when he looked nice and not like a wrestling promoter), Dad would pop out of the third telepod. Back then he was a happy man, always quick to laugh or tell some corny joke. Dad was a pun man. He'd do that thing where he'd stop proceedings by saying something like 'Hey, guys . . .' and then drop some awful gag. Groans all round. He'd laugh and his eyes would crease up making him look like one of the Mr Men.

I still have Mum's temper, that fiery red fog that descends; she left me with that and after reading this book you'd be forgiven for thinking she'd also left me her penchant for excess. This, for me, is a work in progress, a chance to not make the same mistakes.

When I was nine or ten I was getting bullied, not at school but on the bus. The journey there was usually cool; coming home was a different matter. Two brothers who lived round the corner, right little meatheads, they were. They'd wait at the bus stop for me, I can see them now, smiling, nudging each other as they see me. They'd kick me in the back of the legs and pull my bag. I hated it and it went on for months. I became a recluse, not wanting to go to school or to walk home.

Mum probed and prodded as to what was wrong but the stupid code of silence kids must live by forbade it. Snitches get stitches. I wish they didn't get stitches. I wish they got Snickers. Snitches get Snickers – there'd be a lot less bullying, more diabetes sure, but a lot less bullying. Looking back now and having a son myself, I'd have to say no matter what the fallout, tell someone! Do not suffer in silence. Tell someone.

The brothers always seemed to be there and because they lived round the corner they usually ended up following me home. One day they grabbed me just as I reached my front gate. Big mistake: Mum was looking out of the window. They aimed a knee for my young balls but instead thudded me in the thighs, then grabbed my jacket, pulled at my ears, laughed at me.

The front door opens and my small yet fearsome, big-armed mother comes thundering out. Before the meatbags know what's happening they're grabbed by her merciless hands and slapped dizzy. They squeal and beep as she kicks them down the road. What a woman. She grabs me and shoves me towards the house.

Sitting in the front room she looks cross and sad. She cuddles me to make me feel better. Watching those boys get theirs was a wonderful feeling. Mum goes into the kitchen to make tea. Looking through the window I see a big woman careening towards the front door. She knocks on it so hard it rattles in its frame. This will not be good. Mum tells me to get it. I stand and traipse over. I open the door.

'Is your fucking mother in?'

'Hang on. I'll get her.' I close the door gently and walk to the kitchen.

'Mum, it's for you.'

'Who is it?'

'I don't know.'

Mum walks through the sitting room wiping her hands with a tea-towel and opens the front door. She is immediately set upon by the big lumpy woman who is the mother of the two bullies. She punches Mum in the mouth as soon as the door opens.

After you've endured years of physical abuse at the hands of a very big man I suspect the weak right hook from a flabby Dagenham Madre feels little more than being hit in the mouth by an egg-heavy she-moth. (More on Mum's life before she met Dad later.) Mum shakes off the initial shock of the sneak attack and sets about systematically dismantling the woman bit by bit, ruining her hair, then her face, and finally her coat.

It was a hell of a thing to watch. It ended after Mum kicked her opponent deep in the vagina. She lay in a heap on the front lawn, her dinner ladies wobbling. Mum pants, knackered but victorious.

The woman gets up, angry still but not because of the justice my mum meted out to her disappointing bully-kids but because her coat has been ripped to shreds. During the scrap all the buttons have pinged off her coat and the pockets flap low and loose like elephants' ears.

'You ruined my farkin' coat, you cunt!' the lady screams at her.

Mum sets off towards her. Fearing another hefty boot to the baby-machine the lady stumbles backwards.

'Give me the coat! Give me the coat!' Mum gestures to the tattered garment. Big Arms is suspicious at first, Mum pulls at the sleeve, and the woman cautiously lets it slip off. Together they search the front garden and pick up the coat buttons.

'Give me two days and I'll have the coat mended.' Mum's words confused me. What was all that about? Some kind of secret fighting credo between working-class women?

'Fuck me up but don't touch my coat, it's my good one I wear to the towel market on Sunday.' Two days later that coat was good as new.

After Mum shut the front door I got it in the ear. She was cross I hadn't pre-warned her about the impending fury. I understand her anger now. After the fighting chemicals ebb away, Mum's upset. She cries and we have a cuddle, it cheers us both up a bit.

* * *

As well as Dagenham and Essex where lovely Uncle Brian and Auntie Francis live with my cousin Paul, my life extends to the south as far as Kent, home of cousins Caroline and Simon and their folks Uncle John and lovely Auntie Rosemary. My scope also extends west two hundred miles to where my mother was born. To Wales. To Pembrokeshire and the town of Haverfordwest to be more precise. This, even now, I consider my second home.

My gran and grandpa, Eileen and Arthur, live in a solid stone house called Millbrook. It's at the end of a long lane set in a dense forest. As far as idyllic locations for a child to be brought up, this was it. It was perfect. Every Saturday my mum and her sisters, Marion, Sandra, Betty, Melanie and Linda, would congregate at my gran's house. On top of the sisters and my mum's brother Emmy, all my cousins were in attendance too, me, Mathy, Simeon, Ceri, Naomi, Siobhan, Anoushka and Marcello. And then there were the friends, boyfriends and husbands too. The weekends at Gran's were fantastic.

I have the nicest memories of Millbrook. Everything seemed perfect. Apart from the bees. My gran's house had the biggest bees' nest in the roof space. Every summer me and the cousins could probably expect to be stung upwards of thirty times each. The bees would hang around waiting for us in a little bottleneck round the back near the kitchen. Striking our faces and soft necks.

The house in the forest and its small stream running through the garden meant this place was a haven for dens and general pre-teen hijinks. We were master denmakers. We'd leave the house early in the morning, *Star Wars* figures in tow, and spend the whole day out walking through the forests and splashing in the rivers. At some point we colonise a small island we name Rickmelbon and the Nettle Cutters Club is born.

At one point we decide to build a long, high zip line from a tree up on a ridge down into the raspberry patch. It takes us ages securing the rope and pulling it tight. Eventually we're ready to go. We draw straws – no we don't, we bully Simeon into doing it. He's pretty high. Twenty or so feet. He's nervous. We're nervous. The wind drops and he's off. And down. The rope untethers and he drops like a sack of shit into the soft earth below. He survives.

I think being at my gran's house as a young boy surrounded by my extended family, having my foul-tempered grandfather swiping at me with his stick for being half English, was the happiest time for me. I've been happy since then obviously but when I think about that place and the long endless summers it's only ever good. It's innocent, and it's fun, baking gets done, baby chickens hatch, berries are eaten off bushes, fish get caught and dogs get patted. The older I get the more things change, things always change, but back then it was perfect.

By the time my grandad came swinging into my memory he was already pretty old. I always remember he looked how men looked in pictures from the forties. Baggy trousers, white shirt, sleeves rolled up, braces. This was his uniform. His hair was wartime too. Classic short back and sides, maybe even a little Brylcreem. Grampie walked with a cane and would use it to attack us grandchildren at any moment. We'd play a game of roulette where we'd creep towards him as he slept – our aim was to twang his braces. He was never really asleep. As soon as we got within range he'd explode awake and scythe us down with his stick. It was all bluster. Sometimes we'd bundle him en masse and shower his scratchy unshaven chops with kisses.

We'd laugh as he feigned disgust. He smelt like whisky but nice whisky.

My gran was a white-haired joy straight out of central casting. She was compact and sturdy, a no-nonsense lady who loved to laugh. She smelt amazing and I loved running in from the car on those days I got to spend with her and burying myself into her smell. She mostly wore a kind of cleaning dress with deep, apron-like pockets in the front, the pouch always full of treats and tasty tidbits. To finish off her ensemble she wore wellies with the tops turned down. The only exception to this look was when Gran either went into Haverfordwest to shop or when she went up to Tre-wyn to play bingo – then she'd get dolled up. I loved staying at her house with my cousins, being looked after by Uncle Emmy while Gran and Mum and the rest of the sisters went out for the night. He'd tell us ghost stories and frighten the hell out of us. I'd lie in that massive soft, hot bed, in that creaky, windy house, breathing hard until fear eventually led to sleep.

Gran was quick to use her big rough hands to mete out country justice. In a good way of course. Those hands were so strong, she loved laughing and giving you a pinch or a little dig. Mum and Gran's hands looked exactly the same. I loved holding those hardworking, hard-slapping meat gloves.

Mum and the other Hobbit women of Dyfed had a weird connection with the occult, the supernatural if you will. This shit's hard for a kid to be around. One night back in Dagenham my mum is woken by a tremendously bright light; she tries to wake up my dad and failing to do so she sits up in bed only to come face to face with Jesus Christ himself. Not a spirit or a malevolent poltergeist but Jesus. She said he was talking to her but she couldn't hear what he was saying, he was just moving his lips. She turns to try and wake Dad who's lifeless, but when she turns back the baby Jesus is gone.

Looking back now as an atheist it's clearly an alcohol-induced hallucination or an ultra-lucid dream. She wasn't a massive drinker back then, that came later, but as her seven-year-old son and raised a Catholic I had to believe what she said. Why would I disbelieve it? My mum was completely convinced. She fled the house that night and sought sanctuary with our family priest Father Dodd. She stayed there for almost a week, drinking whisky, smoking cigarettes and trying to get to grips with what she had seen.

It changed Mum, she became slightly more devout after this (when it suited her of course). It was weird going into her bedroom while she was away and looking at the chair Jesus had sat on. It was a white high-backed thing with a purple cushion, very uncomfortable, classic Jesus. I stood and looked at that chair, touched it. I remember sniffing the seat cushion a bit, hoping that he'd left the scent of flowers behind. It didn't smell like flowers, it'd been too near Dad's arse and his dirty socks for too long for even Christ's sweet bum scent to permeate. Still, it felt creepy. I'm not sure why it would be creepy. Surely Jesus is anti-creepy?

My Auntie Linda, a small fiery woman with a jet-black bob, tells a story that used to chill me when I was younger. She went to work as a chambermaid in a big hotel in London and stayed with an old friend of hers who had a two-year-old son. Upon arriving she found all the rooms of the house empty, all the furniture from the flat crammed into one room.

The baby had his cot in the empty room next door. The mum, Linda's friend, hardly went into that room after the baby was put down for the night. At one point during their conversation that evening my aunt's friend described to her a thing that had been rampaging in their house at night. As Linda told it to me it always sounded like a classic poltergeist.

Linda told me that just then they heard a noise, a rhythmic thumping. They edged into the baby's room and saw the child standing in the cot watching a rubber ball bounce from wall to ceiling back to wall and so on. Like Paul Newman with the baseball in *The Great Escape*. When the baby saw them he laughed and the ball stopped. Telekinesis. It went on for a few years. The older the baby got the less it happened.

Then there's Auntie Melanie (Melons). All the cousins are sure she's either (a) a witch, (b) some kind of night dweller, or (c) has a Dorian Gray thing going on, because she's fifty something and is still pretty fit in a kind of Kate Bush way. She always has been, and she doesn't seem to age as she gets older. Maybe it has something to do with never being awake during the hours of daylight.

She lives in a house on an estate on the outskirts of Haverfordwest and she too has always been surrounded by supernatural happenings. When I was seventeen/eighteen I spent a lot of time in that house and it was there where I've been nearest to things unmentionable.

I'd lie on the couch at night trying to sleep, my ears thumping, hair on the back of my neck standing to attention. There were things in that room with me. I'd hear the noise of our empty coffee mugs being gently pulled across the table. Porcelain sliding on glass. Stopping. Then sliding back. I'd bury myself under the blanket, I was so afraid.

What didn't help was that Melons's daughter, my beautiful cousin Siobhan, was a keen sleepwalker. Sometimes if I crept up the stairs to wee between phantasms I'd be met by a small girl with long blonde hair, wearing a Victorian-style nightie pointing at me. Terrifying.

* * *

When I was about ten my half-brother Marc came from Wales to live with us in Dagenham for a while. He was eight years older than me. I loved it having my big brother there. Debbie (my half-sister) would also come and stay for extended periods back then. Never Ian though; Ian was/is my other half-brother who died while I was writing this book. I'm so gutted. It was a phone call I knew would always come but it still punched me in the balls when it finally arrived. He was a man who struggled with grief and anger and alcohol and depression for most of his adult life. Taken away by a booze-related illness, exactly the same as my mum. I miss you, mate. I'm sorry I couldn't make it better.

I think Ian was too cross with Mum, believing, quite wrongly, that she'd abandoned him/them, Marc, Debbie and him. She'd really had no choice if she wanted to live. I wasn't sure at the time what the 'half' bit meant. As far as I was concerned these people came out of my mum. They were my blood.

My dad tried to be a father to my half-siblings. As much as he could anyway. I always felt he was very sensitive to his place in the food chain of their family. He was good like that. I think Marc and Debs quickly warmed to Dad. It took Ian longer to come round; that said, it was never tense or moody. There were never furious rows, just the odd stand-off from time to time.

When Debbie lived with us in Redbridge there definitely was the odd argument. She was moody and Dad wanted to stick up for Mum and let Debs know that she couldn't just do what she liked in his house etc. I guess similar conversations go on with step-kids every day. She was difficult though – boys, drinking, weed, boys, boys with motorbikes, thrush. Teen girl shit.

They loved my dad though. He was kind and funny and fair and adored their mum. What's not to like. When Dad died Ian made the journey from Haverfordwest with my cousins up to east London to attend his funeral and cried like a baby. He loved my old man.

* * *

It was 1980 when we started our fractious relationship with Barking rugby club. I say our, I mean Mum and Dad's. I think it was because of Marc staying with us and wanting to play for a local team while he was living in London that Barking RUFC became a big feature in my life. The coach journeys to away matches, the old clubhouse full of stolen trophies pinned, nailed, screwed on the wall, proud relics of battle.

Playing for Barking Youth was a treat, it was the camaraderie and physical contact young me needed. I don't mind saying I was pretty good. My brother Marc loved it there too, and because he was much older than me he seemed exciting and dangerous. Sometimes the door knocked at three or four o'clock on a Sunday morning and Mum would get her dressing gown on, cursing as she descended the stairs.

Opening the front door she'd be picked up by fifteen drunken rugby boys and bundled inside. It was Marc and his hammered teammates. My mum loved boys and men, she was a real man's woman. She'd never be cross but that wouldn't stop her from at least feigning anger. Slaps were dealt out but the charm and enthusiasm of the drunken lads meant she was easily swayed.

Mum, without fail, would always cook. She was like Martin Scorsese's mother in *Goodfellas* but Welsh. A 4 a.m. feast of sausage, egg and chips or bacon sandwiches was not unusual. She loved the fact that they all called her Mum. I'd stand in the corner and watch these boys. Once we woke up to find a bus stop in our front garden they'd cemented in overnight as a prank. Stuff like this happened all the time. I loved my big brother. He was courageous, generous and honourable.

In the mid eighties there was a new style of crime on the tubes and trains called 'Steaming'. Gangs of youths, ten or so strong, would get on a train at one stop, steam through the carriage taking everything they could, before getting off at the next stop and legging it or getting on another train to do it all over again. Devilishly simple, impossible to predict and difficult to combat.

Marc was sitting on the train eyeing up a woman when a gang of steamers boarded the carriage ransacking the place. When a youth grabbed this chick's bag and headed off, apparently Marc uttered the words 'This one's mine' to the woman and set off after them. He managed to get hold of her bag and began rampaging into the shocked gang like a drunken man-rilla. Sadly he ran out of steam pretty quickly and they fucked him up. Using his skills as a prop forward he lay in a ball clinging onto that bag until the attack was over. Bleeding and bruised, he gave the girl her bag back. I suspect, knowing Marc, he may have even given the lady a wink as well. He got hurt, not too badly, something broken, some stitches, but that was Marc all over. Gosh I miss him.

When Marc left us he spent a few years travelling the world on the lucrative sheep shearing circuit. If I remember rightly the 'circuit' was Australia, New Zealand, the States and somewhere in Scandinavia. Marc told me a story once. In the off-season from shearing, by all accounts a thing he was brilliant at, he took a job working in an abattoir, something he was really cheery about. The picture he paints of the place was horrendous, but he didn't seem to mind. I think the après-murder more than made up for the killings.

Lots of like-minded lunatics holed up at night in some dark, alcohol-fuelled Scandinavian abattoir bar. It sounded like one of the circles of hell, but with music. One day an old bull was brought in to be euthanased. After the grizzly act Marc thought it would be hilarious to de-cock the retired stud. Later that night after work when the lunatics were smashing it up in the bar, Marc waited until a number of people had gone off to the toilet. He hid the bull dick down his trousers and went to the loo. His friends made room as he edged into the trough. I imagine there was some casual chatting before Marc reached into his pants and unravelled a giant twenty-pound beef stick. It crashed into the steel trough splashing piss everywhere. People gasp, momentarily believing this titanic wang might just be his. There is screaming which ebbs into howls of laughter, which become tears. The way he told it, that beef willy was paraded around the place like a returning war hero. They propped it up at the bar and all night bought it drinks. I imagine it sitting there, fat and slumped over slightly, tired and triumphant like Hemingway himself.

At Barking RUFC one of the highlights for me was the food we got in the clubhouse after a game. Pie and mash with beans, or sausages, shepherd's pie, hearty grub suitable for the returning warriors all served through a mysteriously low serving hatch. Sometimes I'd sneak into the kitchen, the sweaty, steamy room on the other side of that low hatch, and watch the big-armed kitchen dollies sling out post-game delights. If I was lucky they'd wrap up a fantastically hot sausage in a napkin and give it to me to eat, and I'd rush outside and eat it under the bridge round the back of the club.

I was too young to fully understand what was happening in that clubhouse but I remember witnessing a fair amount of lunacy. It was always good natured and I enjoyed watching adults get silly. My dad loved it; he never really had many male friends that I can remember so I think he enjoyed the bullshit and camaraderie with the other blokes. I think that was part of my mum's problem: she lost control of him when he hung out there, he became one of the boys. Dad wasn't like that generally – he was a homebody; they enjoyed each other's company. They were together most of the time. But Mum was high maintenance. Dad was Mum's. That sounds mean but this isn't my intention.

On Saturday nights the clubhouse would be rammed and raucous. I don't think it really mattered whether we won or lost. If the first and third teams played at home the second and fourth teams would play away. At some point in the evening the battle coaches would return and the club heaved. Most of the time people would end up naked, steaming, frequently spraying Ralgex or some other heat-based embrocation on each other's balls and anuses. (That was just the women.) I've been fortunate enough to spend some time in the Sergeants Mess in the military hospital at Headley Court, Surrey over the years and it reminded me of the clubhouse at Barking.

Even during the chaos and the mayhem there were still rules and regulations to be adhered to. Failure to do so resulted in more and more drinking. A lot of this revolved around toasting and the wearing of correct clothing at all times, asking to go to the toilet. Not picking up on minuscule signs the others were secretly showing you resulted in drinking and balls being plucked or shaved or sprayed with a napalm-like substance intended to be used only in the event of a human being's spinal muscles going on strike.

Pints of beer would be flung everywhere, on the floor and all over each other. People would then fling themselves down the length of the clubroom, often leaving giant torso- or head-shaped holes in the plasterboard at the other end of the room. As a child this was amazing. I could do literally anything I wanted and a drunk man with no trousers on, balls the colour of a baboon's summer-rectum, would throw a pint on me, ruffle my hair, and tell me I was a good boy. Amazing. Maybe it was here that the seed of my love and terrible fear of mass lunacy was planted.

Round about this time, due to Dad and the office furniture company he worked for doing well, he got a new car. It was a really big deal – we'd never had a new car before. I seem to remember some of our neighbours coming out and cooing while the kids sat in the driver's seat making high-pitched engine noises. It was a brand-new Jaguar XJS V12, metallic mint green with a plush cream leather interior that smelled like wealth. He was a man going places.

He once drove that car on the motorway with me in it at 142 miles per hour. I whooped and egged him on. (I loved and still love the speed and roar of a very fast car, something my son has picked up, enjoying it when I stick my M5 into second gear and rev hard.) Dad had been cut up by an urchin. He looked at me, eyebrows waggling.

'Shall we take him?' I nodded excitedly. There's only one way to deal with an urchin on the burn-up. We hammered past him doing close to one hundred and fifty. I was later to beat his speed record by 13 miles an hour – on a closed circuit I might add! Eat that, dead Dad's speed record!

* * *

After an afternoon, an evening and a night at the rugby club, Mum and Dad had the first massive fight I can remember. It started simmering and boiling in the car and exploded when we got home. I could not escape it, I couldn't go around it and I couldn't go over or under it. I stood there in the corner eating a banana while a foulness in a black cloak, an ebony-wrapped tornado, raged all around me.

At its height, Dad, so frustrated by my mum's drunken belligerence, punched his fist through a door, breaking it badly (both fist and door). This is where I must have picked up *my* annoying and very painful habit of breaking my own hands. I've broken three or four hands stupidly over the years. That sounds weird – I only have two hands but I've broken them both several times. It's a way to unload a terrible need to hurt someone other than yourself while only hurting yourself. The last time I did it – and hopefully the last time I ever do it – was during the shoot for *Paul* in New Mexico.

I once had a big fight with Chris, my baby's momma, soon to be ex-wife, a good loyal woman and the best mother you could ever wish to meet. It erupted from a misunderstanding and a lack of emotional flexibility on both sides. I decided to take my frustration out on the thick, unyielding stone walls of our rented casa. I swing a giant right around, and immediately I connect with the wall I hear the sound of a man striking an oven-ready chicken with a heavy lump hammer, an explosion, the sound of bones snapping inside a fatty shroud of meat.

Pulling the hand away the first thing I note is my little finger's hanging off, hanging free, halfway down my palm like an unused Swingball. I automatically grab it and crunch it back into the position it should be in. It lolls free again preferring its new home midway down my paw. This is really bad. I pull it once more and an ice cold sweat begins to leak into my eyes. I rush slightly. Chris goes to bed. I set the dislocated finger back in position, I can feel the fractures clack together, before finally the snapped pieces marry and the finger stays put. Thank god. I pray that perhaps it's only dislocated. Tomorrow we start shooting. It really couldn't have come at a worse time.

I take a roll of thick gaffer tape and secure the finger with roll upon roll of sticky fabric. Perfect. Perhaps I can attend my 9 a.m. tennis lesson after all. I never make that lesson. I wake up in the spare room at 3 a.m. heaving with pain. My hand is the size and colour of a well-used griddle pan; the tape is buried in the fat, swollen meat of what used to be my hand. What a fucking idiot. If you're ever so angry you want to punch something, punch the air or a man of feathers, don't punch walls. If you watch the film *Paul* carefully you can see the character I play, Clive Gollings, is left-handed.

While Dad struggled to free his arm, Mum saw her chance to finish him off. She picked up a giant crystal ashtray, the type which was de rigueur in the late seventies, square, heartless and angled to fuck, and smashed it over his head. I think he's dead, at least he looks dead. He's actually slumped unconscious, hanging out of the door. At some point an ambulance is called. Not by me. I feel neighbours may have intervened, Elsie and Harry maybe. I sat, wide-eyed with fright, banana in hand, feeling terribly guilty. Why was I guilty?

I remember Dad telling a joke when he got home about the tetanus injection he'd had at the hospital. The nurse says to Dad:

'This shouldn't hurt, it's only a little prick', to which he responds:

'It may only be a little prick to you, love, but it's all I've got'. He booms his lovely, wheezy laugh out, grimacing as he feels a twinge of pain from his fucked-up hand. That was the kind of person my dad was. Even at his lowest ebb he always had a shitty joke or pun to hand. What a trouper.

So Dad loved his puns and his lame wordplay. I was always more into the physical comedy. I'll give you an example from back then. One Christmas when we lived in Redbridge, we were sitting chatting and laughing round the table after one of Mum's big beautiful Christmas dinners (she was a great cook). Mandy, my neighbour, and her family were there and I started flirting outrageously in a boyish kind of way. It peaked when I picked up a jar of pickled beetroot and pretended to drink from it. The jar had no lid. Me, the white tablecloth and our fine mint-green carpet were doused in litres of bright red juice and balls of earth fruit.

* * *

I still love a beer but I can't hide from the fact that alcohol, more specifically alcoholism, seemed to tear at and ravage my family like a coyote with a hen carcass. I see more and more of its casualties the older I get.

As a child, though, I'm completely unaware that this isn't normal. The flip between someone who likes a drink and someone who has a terrible problem is often difficult to pinpoint, even for them. As a young boy I didn't notice it happening. I didn't see it, such was the sophistication of its cloaking device

I had an inkling things weren't perfect. I'd even summon up the courage every now and again to say something to Mum, but I was immediately cut down and told off. It was none of my business, she used to say. But it *was* my business. I understood my place in the family hierarchy pretty early on though, so I'd shut the fuck up.

The way I describe my parents in this book, particularly later on, you'd be forgiven for thinking it was a terribly dysfunctional, co-dependent relationship. Which it was. At least at the end. To get to that point though where Mum looks after Dad after his collapse and Dad looks after Mum for the ten years it took her to finally drink herself to death, that takes groundwork. Years and years of groundwork and the laying of foundations of trust and a shit load of love. Mum and Dad were completely in love for as long as I could remember which made what came later all the harder to stomach. They were so romantic. Dad was a flowers-and-notes kind of guy which was great because Mum was a flowers-and-notes kind of gal.

With them holed up in a pub most of the weekend – something Dad grew to hate but due to his loyalty to Mum would never challenge – it meant I was allowed to rent any VHS film I wanted to watch at home. For a young, gore-hungry boy such as myself this usually meant *The Hills Have Eyes* (the original), *The Shining, I Spit On Your Grave, Poltergeist, The Howling, American Werewolf in London, Alien, The Living Dead at the Manchester Morgue,* etc. I remember me and my big sister Debbie giggling loudly one afternoon watching the credits to Dario Argento's *Suspiria*. We howled when we saw the soundtrack was by a band called Goblin.

I became numb to the images I saw, they were gore-filled and exciting. I liked it. I imagined everyone would feel the same. I showed *The Exorcist* to a mate of mine once, we were both eleven or so; he ran off thirty-five minutes in, muttering something about hearing his mum calling. Poor lad hardly slept a wink for a week. The screaming. We didn't play much together again after that. Shame.

* * *

When I first became aware of my mum she was a bookkeeper of sorts, but I never remember her keeping any books. Before that she worked in an electrical shop called Stanwoods, that's where she met Dad; he was some kind of manager and I guess with smiles and laughter and flirting they fell in love.

Dad had been married before to a lady who I think had suffered a terrible breakdown of some kind. Nowadays, the things that blighted that poor woman would have a name. From what my dad told me it sounded like a form of extreme OCD. Back then, sadly, such a malady was nameless. It was just something that ended a marriage. Dad had two daughters from his first marriage. They're my half-sisters. He bloody loved those girls.

She had a problem with my dad's new relationship with the woman I'd eventually pop out of. I completely get it. When Mum got pregnant it was too much for her to cope with. Shit happened and it got ugly. Soon after this she took her kids – Dad's kids, their kids – and moved to New Zealand. I understand it was what she needed to do. I'm not sure my dad did though, not then anyway. Over the years he suffered from not being with his girls. Having a child now myself I can only imagine what that feels like. I don't hold any kind of grudge against her in any way, shape or form. But it was a sadness he kept to himself. I've met her many times since and she is absolutely lovely, a warm caring mother and grandmother. Being under a terrific amount of pressure and losing love and face and dignity can make people, good people, any people, stumble.

* * *

After keeping books – again, no idea what this means – Mum worked at The Napier, a pub in Ilford. I remember getting a bus to the pub after school and sitting on a crate underneath the bar waiting for her to finish. I'd eat crisps and drink bottles of Coke through a flimsy paper straw which would collapse if over-sucked. I remember watching her flirt with the old regulars; she was the classic brassy barmaid, perfectly adapted to cope with pervy pissheads, she was quick, funny and tough. The punters loved her.

At the time I was attending St Peter and St Pauls Junior School in Ilford. It was a nice school but I do remember some turmoil. I didn't like it. The first week was a real nightmare. Poor Mum. I was a real mummy's boy and she doted on me something crazy. Mum had to drag me into school. When it was time for her to leave I kicked up the biggest fuss. It was like I was possessed. There was a red cage that wrapped around the staircase in the school so kids couldn't commit suicide I guess. I hung on to that cage like a demented ape for an hour a day for the first week screaming, while Mum and assorted teachers tried to prise me off, convincing me to stay. I did not want her to go. My little boy's a bit like that now. Still I'm stronger than him so

I'm ready for the fight. I think I'll bring a small lever and work on his fingers one by one until he's finally off and in school. I imagine me and Chris will need a deep coffee after this.

I don't know why I always hated going to school as much as I did – maybe the rules, being told what to do. I mean I came to like aspects of it, but generally school could've sucked my dong.

I think the beginnings of my current life as an actor started here. Getting off school by pretending to be dangerously ill takes skill, courage and commitment.

I had a lovely little technique where I'd take the thermometer Mum was using to check my temperature and rub it hard with my tongue, and blow hot air on the mercury-filled bulb. Anything to get it over the golden number, 101 degrees F.

The sickness gig was very to and fro with Mum, she'd threaten to call the doctor out, I'd say I was fine, and that it was just a bug etc. She always came round to my way of thinking. I was good, often interrupting a conversation with a round of coughing and dry heaves. I'd lie on the sofa pretending to be ill. It was a Bifa-worthy performance. Utterly compelling.

My enjoyment of *Jamie's Magic Torch* however was one day rudely interrupted by a brusque knock on the front door.

As a fake sickman there are times when you need to deeply immerse yourself in a role. Factors need to be considered. What do I have? What is the timeline for said viral infection? How sick am I? Last time we spoke how sick was I? Have I become dramatically worse? Am I feeling slightly better? What's the longest possible time I can eke this out for? Getting sick on a Wednesday means I will not be back at school till the following Monday. Come Friday at 4 p.m., I'd be feeling much better. The answers to the above questions give you the level of illness you need to pitch. It's pretty simple really. Stay in character. Commit.

This was a Wednesday and as such I was in the grip of a nasty Asian ape flu that had been going round.

In response to the door knocking I pulled my blankets up and moaned, as if deep in a Bronte-esque, soaked-by-rain-on-a-dark-heath-fever-induced daymare. I moaned, brilliant touch.

'MUM!!! DOOR!!!'

I could hear Mum talking to someone, I strained to hear snippets of a conversation: 'Thanks for coming . . . He's in here.'

I shut my eyes, and moan, shivering, so cold, so sick. The only way a human would be as sick as I was pretending to be was if he/she had eaten a rotten monkey-brain omelette in the central market in Liberia, West Africa. I hadn't.

My arms contorted in spasm and I woke with a start. Too much. Too big. Hammy performance. I opened my eyes to see our GP standing there. Tit bags. She actually called the doctor. I'm ruined.

The doctor, a big man, towers over me. Tough it out. Commit. You're one of the best poorly child actors in Europe.

'Has this child been to Liberia in the last ten days?'

'No.'

Maybe I'd pitched my performance just right after all.

The doctor takes my blood pressure and temperature, he listens to my chest with his stethoscope. I can see my smug mum behind him, smiling. She's called my bluff, what a dick.

Doctor's brow furrows, I drop out of character for a second, he sees this. He tuts and shakes his head. Mum and I lock eyes briefly. I pretend to get suddenly very cold.

The doctor slowly pulls his bookish, half-moon glasses from his noble Hippocratic face. (He didn't wear glasses.) He fixes my mum with a hard stare and barks out these words, 'Mrs Frost, would you be so kind as to call an ambulance please?'

I suddenly feel a lot better. Is this part of Mum's bluff? No, she is rooted and white as a sheet. This is actually happening. I'm actually sick. The doctor has diagnosed a potentially dangerous heart murmur; my dream of being a deep sea diver hunting for booty now lies in tatters. I was in hospital for three weeks. I never pretended to be sick again.

As the school 'postman' I went to church every day and afterwards I would pick up the letters and take them to the office (in hindsight I'm not sure why the school couldn't have just got the letters sent directly to the school and not via the church).

This was before Thatcher took away our milk. We drank a lot of milk in little bottles with blue straws, played a lot of crab-football. At the age of six or so we were called into the music room and all given an instrument to learn. I was so happy when they decided to give me a shiny trumpet like Miles Davis. So happy.

After several weeks of struggling with this shiny knot of brass the Head of Music called me and my mum into his office. He talked to Mum as if I wasn't there. He told her my lips were too big and I would never make the grade for a trumpeter. What. The. Fuck. Had this dick never heard of Satchmo? He took the trumpet out of my hands – *pulled* it out of my hands – and as I grasped at the thin air that used to contain a trumpet he stuck a trombone into my hands. *He gave me a trombone.* Apart from the tuba, it ranks as the fattest sounding of all instruments. If a tuba wasn't available and someone needed to soundtrack a mega-fatty struggling down the street with a big bucket of chicken, the trombone would be the instrument they'd use.

My stubborn streak – cheers Mum – surfaced at school one lunchtime. For whatever reason, although I suspect I may have been showing off a bit, I decide to get three portions of jam roly poly and custard, all piled high in one bowl. My friends laugh as I prod at the jammy suet. The bell rings and I make to leave. I'm stopped at the door by the lunch monitor.

'You're not leaving that.'

'But I don't want it.'

'Then why did you get so much?'

'Dunno.'

'You're going to sit down and finish it.'

'But I can't eat any more.'

'I don't care. Sit down please.'

I was giving some major attitude in front of my homies. Fuck this dude. I sat down. The teacher plopped the pile of stodge in front of me.

'When you finish this bowl you can leave.'

'I'm not eating it.'

'We'll see.'

'We will see. I'm not eating it.'

'You will.'

'I won't.'

And I didn't. I sat there from one o'clock until half-past four, when my mum was forced to come and get me. She was not happy. She was fine with me, but she wasn't happy with them forcing a little boy to miss a whole afternoon of lessons to try and prove a point. It was great having a woman like Mum on my side.

Paul Eaton was my best friend at the time; notable others include Sean Creagan and a kid called Peter who dipped toast into tea – it used to make me heave. I had my first kiss with a lovely Irish girl called Patricia Dugan, she had a shiny black wedge like Pam Ayres's. Rachel Cosgrave was the fittest girl in school; she had two different-coloured eyes – one blue, one green. It was amazing. I'd never seen anything like it. (Except for Dave Bowie.)

Around about this time Pope John Paul the Second got shot. Being a Catholic school it was a really big deal. We were asked/made to write 'get well soon' letters. Being a young funnyman I decided to include a joke. Poor bloke got shot for Christsakes, I thought he'd need a laugh. Off they went, my letter one of among thousands of well wishes from young Catholics all over the world.

A month later a letter plopped through our letterbox. The envelope was like nothing I'd never seen before. White, padded, rich smelling. Embossed on the front of the letter was the cross keys of the seal of Vatican City. WTF. My hands trembled as I opened the letter carefully. It was from the effin Pope! Actually from his personal secretary to be fair but close enough. It said the Pope was happy I had written to him and my joke had made him laugh! Holy (literally) shit.

My other best friend was a fiery loonie called Vincent Heggarty. He had an older brother called Brendan, who much later would become a really good friend and help me make my important choice to escape the UK to live in Israel.

That though was ten years away. At this point I was just his little brother's mate and he'd spend his time shooting us with an air rifle loaded with phlegm and tin-foil wrapped needles. Disgusting and painful.

They lived in Seven Kings near Ilford. One night when I stayed over in Vincent's hot, packed, Irish house all hell broke loose. We heard it floating up through the floorboards;

someone had died. I think this was the first time I was exposed to grief, Irish grief at that. Drinking, singing, crying, laughing, anger. This really affected me as a little boy, I cried my eyes out, although I wasn't sure why.

There are only fragments of memories about that school and my time there. Dad started working with Dennis Bennett, his old school friend, at Comida Contracts, a company that designed and manufactured high-end office furniture. He began when the company was tiny, first as a driver and then as a trainee upholsterer. He gradually worked his way up, eventually becoming managing director, hence the Jaguar XJS V12 (metallic mint paint, cream leather interior).

We got to the point in our lives back then, through Dad's hard work, hard work that bordered on the workaholic, where we had the chance to move away from the mean streets of Dagenham. Mum and Dad found a lovely double-fronted, three-bedroom house with a massive garden in Redbridge, Essex – 27 Babbacombe Gardens.

I was nervous, all my friends were going on to Canon Palmer, a secondary school in Ilford, and I was going to a place called Beal High School in Redbridge. I never saw anyone from my old school again more or less. That chapter closed and I was forced to move forward.

The new house was a two-minute walk away from the new school, which was nice. The place in Dagenham had been two buses and a long walk away from school; 27 Babbacombe was a real palace compared to our box-like and very terraced Dagenham house. For fun recently I looked it up on Zoopla. Two things struck me: one, I didn't remember it looking like that at all. My brain has completely made up a view of that place that the Zoopla image doesn't match, and two, it was pretty bloomin' cheap. (Relatively.) I seem to remember it was some kind of mansion. But no, it can be picked up for £400k.

The neighbours on our right were Dave and Jane. Jane was a stone-cold MILF, although the term MILF was a long way from being invented at this point. I reckon she was in her late twenties/early thirties. Lots of low-slung, tight jeans, flat, hard tummy and bellybuttons, long fronds of loose blonde hair, no bra, bending over to pick up a well-chewed dog toy – this was too much for a young boy to take. I remember Dave liked knives and Rottweilers, a frightening mix that should've guaranteed I kept my young horny eyes well away from his wife. It didn't, my burgeoning sexuality – I was twelve for godsakes! – and real need to see what a woman looked like was to get me into terrible trouble while perving on Jane as she sunbathed topless in the garden.

I'd cleverly worked out that if I stood on the toilet, and angled a CD (acting as a mirror) I could see her knockers. I'm ashamed writing this, ashamed and proud at the level of invention my perverted determination drove me to.

I thought this discovery was amazing, she was my first fantasy and I needed to confide this naughtiness to someone. Sadly I made the mistake of telling a big-mouthed friend who, literally the moment I finished telling him, ran up to Jane, who had conveniently wandered round the corner, and told her. (She worked as a dinner lady at lunchtimes at the school.) 'Miss, Nick perves on your bangers when you sunbathe.'

I couldn't believe it. This was the first time I experienced what has become known as a Heat Flash. I was/am to experience it many times after this. It begins in my feet, moving north, it flashes up my body at three times the speed of sound, leaving me momentarily deaf. The deafness is replaced by the sound of my blood pumping through my ears and then slowly, gradually, normal service resumes.

I imagine it to be a similar physical sensation to standing slightly too near a car bomb as it goes off or driving a heavily armoured vehicle over an IED. Once I've recovered enough to move, I set off at pace, running for home. I fly through the front door screaming to Mum that I wasn't very well and I get into bed. It's one o'clock in the afternoon and one of the hottest days of the year. I lie there wishing I were dead. (This is a perfect example of Karma in action and totally serves me right for being a horrible little pervert.)

Then there was a knock at the front door. I'd been half expecting it, the blood pressure whistles loudly in my ears, I knew what was happening, who it was, it was Jane. I hear her talking to my mum and then I hear the front door closing, someone coming upstairs. There was a tap on my door.

'Hello,' I croaked, pretending to be dangerously ill. Jane comes in and we fuck violently (we don't). Actually she was absolutely lovely about it. She very quietly, calmly and peacefully told me that what I had done was wrong. And that was that. She went off and it was never mentioned again.

Next door to Jane and Dave lived the Ellicotts. They were a nice family with four strapping sons. Dad was a copper and their mum was a lovely, lovely Irish lady called Peggy, with a need to constantly feed people until their stomachs split. The house was very messy and the kitchen was packed to the rafters with bumper packs of food, cases of soup, cereal, eleven thousand slices of packet ham, fifty litres of margarine, a ton of Quavers on a pallet, chocolate, peanuts, chocolate peanuts, and the world's biggest private collection of tinned fruit. I guess having four sons means you need a lot of food. I have one son and I'm constantly amazed by how much he eats.

Every year the Ellicotts had a New Year's Eve party. It was always fun and crazy and was the chance to stay up late and steal cans of lager. It was at one such do that we all sat and watched Michael Jackson's *Thriller* video directed by the great John Landis. It was absolutely amazing. I'd never seen anything like it.

The Ellicotts's 1987 New Year's Eve bash provided the setting for a moment of young weirdness for me.

Sexy neighbour Jane had got over my earlier sexual misdemeanour, and asked if I wanted to go upstairs and smoke a joint with her. Course I did, the fact Mr Ellicott was the police didn't bother me much at all to be honest. Jane and I stuffed our bodies halfway out of a tiny window and hung out of it puffing, it was nice. There came a sharp knock at the door, I suffer a low-level panic, I frantically whisper at Jane to not open it, she tells me it will be fine. I trust her. Jane opens the door, her face softening.

'Who is it?'

'It's fine . . .' I relax. Jane continues . . .

'It's only your mum.'

WHARRRRRRRRRTTTTTTT!!!!

It was very odd, Mum was pissed, and I was frankly too high to care – in fact I even recall at one point relishing showing my mum how to smoke a joint properly. Weird scenes inside the Goldmine.

The next morning was awkward. I came down to find Mum washing up. I cleared my throat.

'Hello.' I was casual.

'Hello.' Mum was casual.

We didn't make eye contact. I grabbed my stuff and left for the day. Do you know that feeling when you end up French kissing an uncle while camping? It felt a bit like that.

* * *

On our left, at number 29 Babbacombe, lived Chris, Alan, Ian, Mandy and Martin. They become pretty important. My mum and Chris soon become best friends. Me and Chris's son Ian who was four years older than me also became good mates. Ian loved *Cagney and Lacey* and Status Quo and we spent a lot of time playing golf at Hainault municipal golf course. I kind of idolised him a little bit.

Mandy was Chris's daughter; she was my first proper love I think. Mandy was three years older than me, not much in the big scale of things granted, but when you're twelve it was a love forbidden.

Me and Mandy would play a game where we'd stand on the corner of the street kissing to see how many people would honk their horns at us. It never went much further than kissing but then it didn't have to, it was enough. I really liked her. She had other, older boyfriends; I didn't mind, I knew our thing was transient and just for giggles.

Mandy's year in school had their own common room, I was a few years below and being in that room flirting outrageously with the fittest girl in her year was taken by some as a major slight.

There was a guy in her class, the older brother of a mate of mine, who really fancied Mandy. Seeing her cuddling and kissing cute old me drove him crazy. He made the mistake of confronting me in front of everyone, an OK Corral kind of thing. He told me I didn't belong, that I should 'get lost'. He then made his final mistake, trying to knee me in the Goolie Bag. (As an aside he actually got my inner thighs.) This I couldn't take. Everyone was looking while he towered over me smiling like a cunt. My ears rang, my fist clenched itself up. (You'd be forgiven for thinking this was the plot point in *BTTF* where McFly clumps Biff.) I stand and begin moving a solid, powerful right towards his fucking head, I sit into it moving my body round so the arm whips around quicker, it pludges into his face, his neck whips back, and the world speeds up again. He slumps to the floor. Nunight.

This is the first time I ever did anything like this. I felt good slugging that pompous jerk-off. I felt good, for about a second. I've always been someone who overthinks things, works shit out and imagines the consequences of actions, my actions. Fighting left me cold. What if I hit him and he falls and hits his head and dies? He didn't die. There was a collective gasp. Is Mandy looking at me with a newfound pride and attraction or does she have the beginnings of slight conjunctivitis? I don't hang around to find out. My plan didn't include what might happen if he gets up with fight still in him, so I run. There is no come back. He never bullies me again and nor does anyone else. I guess a secondary school is a bit like a prison in so much as once people know you're happy to sling a fist or two they tend to stay away from you.

These people, our neighbours, were the closest friends we had. Up the street a little way lived my new best friend, at least for the first couple of years of school; he was a peculiar fellow called Brett Colley. He had perhaps the best and biggest train set I ever saw. It took up his whole room leaving a tiny space in one corner for his little bed. His brother Ricky was a much bigger boy who could ride really fast on his bike. His mum was like Dog Chapman's lovely wife Beth and I seem to remember his dad was a Fred Dibnah-style man, always stuck down in his vast shed/workshop taking apart and putting together old cars and engines. There was lots of that back then. Essex seemed to be a real hotbed of taking apart and putting together old cars. Me and my later crew had our own workshop in Peter Ashton's shed, we'd spend a lot of time sanding and filling old car panels and hanging them back on whatever shitty banger Pete was working on at the time.

I begged my dad to buy me a shitty banger and after weeks of me hassling him he did just that. It was a powder-blue Escort MKII. It was beautiful and fucked and I loved it. I think I was fourteen at the time. My intention was to work on it until I passed my test and then I'd have a car straight away.

It sat outside the back of the house in the alley for several months. I didn't do much to it. I think once I hit the engine with a hammer, maybe I sanded a wing. A few weeks later I try to jack the thing up. The car creaks and slumps and finally emits a loud cracking sound. The jack rips through the floor pan and lodges itself deep into the underbelly of the car. Try as I might, I could not get it out. Like the sword in the stone I was not worthy. I soon lost interest in that car and it was eventually pushed into a river and set alight. Don't judge me, I'm from Essex.

I often wondered what happened to Brett. He got a lot of stick but I liked him. He'd always have an angle and was a pretty savvy businessman, buying boxes of Mars bars at trade and selling to the other kids well above market place. I bet he's some kind of tech billionaire now.

Beal High School also had an ice cream van, a kind of mobile tuck shop if you will, that'd come in at lunchtimes for all the eager fatties. Brett worked out a deal where he would essentially do litter patrol at the end of lunch and get free sweets from the ice cream man. Brett was the only kid I knew that had all of the NatWest Piggies. He looked like a thirteen-year-old Freddie Mercury complete with partially formed bumfluff moustache.

I remember playing hide and seek in his house once; it was dark and we had our school uniforms on so I imagine it was winter. I found a place on top of a cupboard where I curled up and waited. While I was lying down wanting to piss – this is a sad side effect hide and seek has on me – I noticed the bulb-less light socket hanging from the ceiling and an odd plan of action made itself known to me. The voice in my mind said this . . .

'Stick your finger into the light socket to see if it's on or off.' I had to know and sticking my finger into the socket was the only way I could think to find out, so I did it. The whole room popped and for a moment the darkness became bright like a supernova. I woke up on the floor, muffled voices filtering into my consciousness; I'd been flung across the room, what a fucking idiot. I was absolutely compelled to stick my finger into that live socket, perhaps this is a valuable insight into my powerful lack of impulse control.

Brett also went on the school canal trips, and was the main reason really that I wanted to go. From my first year at secondary school until the fifth year when I left we went on the annual canal trip. It was a week over the Easter holidays with the groovy gang from the school's canal club travelling different routes around the highways and byways of Britain's majestic canal network. We were the uncoolest people in the world, but it was fab and I friggin loved it, especially the feeling of responsibility.

It was run by science teacher Mr Fisher, a big, bearded man who always creeped me out a bit. He had large hairless hands with big pores and was always a bit too touchy feely; because of him I now have a distrust of men with hairless big-pored hands.

In the run-up to the trips we'd attend a class after school a couple of times a week for about a month, teaching us the technicalities of narrow boats, how locks worked, safety on board and general waterway etiquette. Usually four boats would be hired, a twelve berth, a couple of tens and an eight. After a safety briefing from the hire company we were off. We were allowed to steer, operate the locks, and we all took turns cooking and cleaning as we pottered down the canals at 4 miles per hour (bliss).

On the canal trips there was always some kind of drama going on, lots of falling in love with people, drunkenness, little arguments, people falling in. One year a kid called Amit and a teacher called Mr Green had a major beef, fuck knows why. Amit could be annoying and a little bit hyper but he was essentially a good bloke. Green really had it in for him, I think at one point he pushed Amit over into some nettles. Nettles for fucksakes! I even seem to remember him holding Amit down in a muddy field and struggling with his conscience whether or not to punch Amit in the chops.

I remember the thrill of the Tardebigge flight and the terror of the mighty Pontcysyllte aqueduct, an iron trough two hundred feet in the sky with no safety rail. I remember smoking and laughing a lot with Peter Ashton, eating eggy bread, walking miles at night with a torch trying to find a phonebox! Finding a fucking phonebox. (I'm glad I straddle this era between phonebox and mobile.) I fell into the canal twice. I fell in love more than that.

The most memorable thing to happen to me though was on my last trip. I was fifteen and the trip fell on my sixteenth birthday. As it was my birthday they made a real fuss of me. It was day two of a seven-day trip. That night we were moored up in the Gas Street Station in Birmingham – a place I'll never forget. We had a small party on Mr Green's boat and I drank too much whisky. Too much for a sixteen-year-old anyway.

I begin to get a whisky rage on, the first inkling I may have Celtic Twilight in me. In a fit of rage and teen despair I smash a bottle and attempt to punch a bridge. It hurts and I trudge back to Green's boat; someone suggests I should stay and not stumble back to my own boat up the dark towpath. I find myself in the female teachers' cabin. I'm drunk on the floor on top of a thin mattress in a sleeping bag. I hear the words, 'Why don't you come in here, you'll be more comfortable.' Then something about it being cold.

How did this begin? What sparked it? When had it become this? What led up to it? Was there flirting? I don't remember guffing on her so maybe not. I was sixteen and she was at least thirty-seven. At school we called her Lumpy Linda. We used to joke about the way she walked, a kind of bouncy half tumble, and how she always wore these long pointy shoes, shoes a Turkish soldier might wear, while guarding the shrine of Atatürk.

I allow myself to be pulled into her tight bunk and then, space being a premium, I end up on top of her. I'm hammered and confused. The vast expanse of her big white tummy spreads out beneath me, an icy field of wrong. My head swims. How did we get here? Things become vague. I remember snippets of things, sure, but nothing concrete. I think I'm losing my virginity to a woman called Lumpy Linda. This is not how I imagined it to be honest; that said, I'm not sure I *had* ever imagined it.

Almost the second it's finished, Lumpy Linda leans her head out of the bunk and projectile-vomits all over the tiny cabin. It's like I just lost my virginity to Mr Creosote. The fact I ever had sex with a woman again absolutely amazes me. With the noise of the – whatever it was – and the puking the whole boat comes thundering into the cabin to help out. They fuss around and help with the vomit, torches are shone in to illuminate the scene. Shouts of 'Back to bed everyone!' Am I naked? Am I in my trademark Tanga briefs? Mr Green's there too, what did he think with his stubby legs, gappy teeth and desert boots?

The next day, and in fact the rest of the whole week, was fucking awful. Everyone knows. She keeps trying to catch me alone at the locks to talk about what has happened. I'm totally unprepared for this, talking about feelings is not what the sixteen-year-old me wants to do, can do. I'm completely without the tools to cope with this.

After a while it slips from the front page to page eleven and then it's chip wrappers.

* * *

Between fourteen and sixteen I spend a lot of time down in Wales. It's a place where I feel like I'm treated like a grown-up a bit. From the age of eleven I'd been taking the train or a National Express coach on my own to Haverfordwest. I loved being down there. Things at home had taken a turn for the worse and Mum's drinking was getting out of hand. I'd use Wales as a place to escape to. Staying with Auntie Linda or at Auntie Melanie's house on that little council estate up near the cemetery was a dream. It was in Melanie's house I first saw *Close Encounters of the Third Kind*.

They all found me hilariously funny and I loved showing off, making them all laugh. Despite the shit there was a lot of laughter at home, at least early on. I was the funny so and so. Impressions were my thing and mimicking voices. Dad was a pun merchant and Mum was dry as a bone. Guffs got a lot of airtime. Lotta guff comedy at home. I remember as a young boy I'd ripped my underpants pretty badly. I decided to use this tatty garment as a prop. I ran into the kitchen in my gran's house and did a very loud fart which I then pretended had blown my underpants to bits. My gran and four or five of my aunties howled with laughter at six-year-old me dancing around, arse scorched from a flaming pump. Maybe I should try and resurrect 'pant explosion' in a film sometime.

At sixteen, though, because of the pressures of home I was a miserable so and so. Many was the time I'd sit on the bus driving from Haverfordwest to Fishguard and back again with my Walkman on listening to the Smiths and watching the rain trickle down the fogged-up windows. It felt right to be there. What a moody little twat I was.

I'd hang out in a pub on the square. Some people knew me, most didn't. I liked that. I'd write in a little notebook and be miserable, I thought it was attractive to be mysterious and sullen. When I was there I was definitely from London, I made a point of not hiding it. At the weekends I was allowed to go to the club with my aunties. RJ's was a real shit hole. On a Sunday as part of the entrance fee you got a free sausage and chips. What a place.

One weekend I managed to persuade my London mates to drive down to Haverfordwest to stay with my gran for the night, then go clubbing. I wouldn't say it was a disaster but it was a long way to go for a night out. We smoked joints on the way down and when we got nearer I told a story about an evil dwarf that lived with my grandmother. I managed to lay it on pretty thick and put the willies up them.

We were silent while we drove through the pitch-black lane, and a sigh of relief washed over them as we saw the welcoming lights of my gran's house. Now, the story I told them was not actually completely untrue: my Uncle Emmy had suffered from a terrible bout of scarlet fever as a child. It stunted him mentally and physically. He never really grew up. Emmy was amazing. Me and all my cousins loved him so much. He was small and wrinkled like a prune with the spirit and heart of a child. I knew the weed had bent their minds and I wanted to use this.

My lovely gran welcomed us into the kitchen. The guys, stoned off their minds, huddled around her big Aga cooker in silence; it was the same Aga that years before I'd seen her use to hatch half a dozen hens' eggs.

Uncle Emmy was a creature of habit. I knew exactly where he'd be, sitting in his chair, the one behind the door, watching the big old TV Gran owned. Knowing this, I sent the boys into the front room to sit down. They opened the door and essentially hid Emmy from their view. Once settled, Emmy kicked the door closed so he could see the TV. He omitted one of his funny trademark noises, a kind of long, loud hum.

From inside the kitchen I heard the boys shriek. Poor things. That night didn't go so well. The club was cool although at some point we thought someone had spiked our drinks. I have a vague memory of one of us getting punched too, or threatened with a punching at the very least. At one point walking down the lane deep in the forest on the way home I decide I need to shit more than anyone in the world. So I do, by the light of someone's Zippo. Bleak.

In the morning the terrible truth is revealed to me. While crouching to plop I had not cleared my own jeans. I had shit into my jeans and all down my white AS Roma away shirt. Oh dear.

I always had a vague notion I'd end up living in Wales. It was a dream, that's all. For all the issues and faults I had with and in London with Mum and Dad, it was still my home. But it was difficult. Things were difficult. Mum continued drinking, Dad's business was failing, leaving school with and for nothing, no job, a sadness descends. Looking back now at the age of forty something, I'd pinpoint this time as the beginning of a lifelong battle with depression. A battle I didn't understand was being waged in me until years after.

* * *

Although no longer at school, the boys and me were still mates at this point. It was just before Mum and Dad lost everything, before I was cut loose by my friends and forgotten, ignored. I spent a lot of time with the fellas in a shit car driving around smoking hash. We did that a lot. Our range was fairly big, from Gants Hill and Barkingside all the way to Romford and Southend. We'd just drive around listening to pirate radio or Public Enemy, Shut Up and Dance, Jungle Brothers, Doug Lazy, Twin Hype, getting off our heads.

There was a place up in Epping Forest near High Beach where we'd go and park and smoke joints. It was a tiny lane deep in the forest in the middle of nowhere. Early one evening the four of us were sat in a mate's shit beige Escort estate. I was in the passenger seat. So and So always drove, bullied and guilted into driving, poor fella. We'd smoked so much shit that I couldn't see the driver, we'd created what the Dutch call a Grade 5 'hot box'. Down the lane we saw two headlights slowly bumping down the track. 'Old Bill!' I joke. We all panic and then laugh like drains. Some paranoia flashes over us.

'Don't fuck about.' Another peel of laughter that's immediately cut short when we realise a police car has pulled up beside us and the coppers are silently peering into the smoked-filled car full of red-eyed lemurs looking back at them.

I whisper loudly, 'Don't open the windows.' They mishear me and the windows are opened immediately. Forty cubic metres of bright blue smoke are emitted into the low atmosphere around the vehicle and for a moment it looks like the car has a foggy afro. The police move off slowly, eye-fucking us. A terrible panic breaks out among the lemurs. Everyone fires off an opinion at once, and eventually in about one millionth of a second a conclusion is unanimously reached . . . DRIVE!!!

Why the fuck did we do that? That was one of several ropy decisions we made that night. The car, now clear of smoke, moves off at pace (7 miles an hour). I look back, praying I don't see lights, praying they don't turn around, the 1.2-litre engine screams under the bonnet. I see lights. On our left we see a parking spot full of early-shift doggers. In front of us a small hill, beyond that, the safety of Epping Forest.

We are all shouting our opinions, I catch flashes of sentences, 'pull in', 'let's run', 'the woods are our new home now' and 'they'll never catch us' among other things. What the fuck were we thinking as we come hammering into the car park, skid to a halt, exit the vehicle and make off across the field and up towards the safety of the trees?

Realising we'd forgotten our carrier bag full of snacks we turn back. We grab our Frazzles and the giant Fruit and Nuts we'd need to survive and shunt it up the hill. No one ever stopped and thought for a second what we'd do once we got there. I actually remember hollering out, 'If we get to the safety of the forest they'll never find us!'

The whelp of the siren throws my life into slow motion, the trees in front of me bathed in the flashing of a shade of blue light that can only mean one thing. You're fucking nicked, my son! I look across at H, we both have the same weird, almost peaceful look which is somewhere between 'having witnessed a rapture' and a 'dynamic young veal in an abattoir'. I recall us both laughing, although neither of us seemed at all happy.

The police shout something, I know not what although if I had to hazard a guess I'd say it was probably something like: 'Stop, you little fuckheads!' I do the only thing available to me at that point and I open my Frazzles. After the twenty-metre shuffle up the hill I'm absolutely knackered and happy to stop. I hate running and eating crisps at the same time, it's pointless, like a pub-crawl. Just stay in one pub and drink a lot. Why combine drinking with cardio? We turn and slowly trudge down the hill. People who'd been fucking in their cars quickly speed away. We are restrained but it's fine as I've finished my crisps.

Lots of things, confusing things, happen in the next twenty minutes or so. We're searched, the car is searched, souls are searched and discussions are had. The word 'arrest' is bandied around, some wee plops up, but oddly it's all pretty jovial, the atmosphere, not the wee. I wish this story had a better ending but we are let go! We were all completely amazed. They took our big lump of hashish and our Liquid Gold and threw it into a patch of long grass. To stop us spending three hours looking for it they made us drive off first. The deafening silence was broken by an eruption of wheezy laughter. What a fucking lucky escape. Thank you, lenient policemuns.

I have hash at my house so I suggest we spin round and grab it. This is exactly what we do. We pull up. 'I'll be five minutes.'

I let myself in and immediately notice that the TV is off. This is a terrible sign. Something's happened, someone has died. This first time I feel the dread of a silent room is when I'm 10 and we're staying in my Auntie Marion's house, in Broadhaven. I used to be able to do a weird thing where I'd lie in bed at night and make the light switch move around the wall just by looking at it. I'd stare and it would tremble and then move. Sometimes I could get it up on the ceiling. I'd seen *Carrie* so I thought it was a form of telekinesis. I wasn't telekinetic in the slightest and, I won't lie, was partly disappointed by the fact.

In the early morning I could hear a commotion coming from Auntie Marion's kitchen. I inch down the stairs peering through the banisters and notice the telly is off. Deborah had died. She was my dad's oldest child and my half-sister from his first pop at marriage. She was a beautiful eighteen-year-old, a talented up and coming actress and singer who lived so far away I'd only ever met her twice. One night after a show she came home, lay on the couch and had a massive asthma attack. She never recovered. No matter, my dad's anguish was now mine. To this day I can't bear to be in a silent room. Something always needs to be on.

* * *

Back home, high and cocky from my brush with the law, I poke my head around the door to the lounge and Mum and Dad are sat in silence, telly off. How long had they been there? How long were they planning on being there? In the middle of the room, in the middle of our mint-green carpet, was a giant lump, my giant lump of hash. It looks exactly like a brown Rubik's cube but obviously a lot easier to solve. Trouble now breaks out. Not a row, just a kind of Category C rumble with a drug pro and con to-and-fro-type parent deal. To be fair they make a compelling argument but I'm high, the guys are waiting, and I'd like to be higher. My counter comes in the shape of a rat out.

I decide to point out to Dad that me and Mum have indeed smoked hash together. This should relieve some of the pressure. It does and they turn on one another, it enables me to brazenly grab my gear and fuck off. I jump back into the car, I've been six minutes thirty-five seconds: 'Sorry I was so long.' We drive off.

What an absolute little prick I was. Writing this makes me feel bad. Yes I was young and naughty but this feels like something and someone else. Makes me feel like a schemer. I think it was the beginning of a turn in me and drugs seemed to be the catalyst and the accelerant. Of course my life at home and the things going on were the driving force of this escape but still . . .

I go through a heavy drugs phase round about now, lots of hash, poppers and tons of LSD. These were the times when I started going to my first, and indeed *the* first, raves. Raindance at Jenkins Lane was my first. I was terrified and I loved it. Others followed, unused farm buildings, weird old dilapidated manor houses near Basildon, industrial units near Tilbury, sometimes wine bars in Loughton. It was exciting. I was a little Essex druggy tearaway, an urchin, a scoundrel if you will but a scoundrel with a good heart.

For me it was all about the music and getting high. Getting to a place where the sun would collapse into itself, there'd be a tremendous flash, and I'd wake up in a white room surrounded by all the other most fucked-up people in the world. An orbital way station for people on a chemical vacation. Psychonauts fleeing their earth land.

This time coincides of course with bad shit personally. It was my escape from my mum's alcoholism which was a huge problem for me. I hated it and I hated her and I hated myself for feeling that way. Around then Mum and Dad decided to separate. A lot of my friends' parents were splitting up so for once I didn't feel behind the curve on a current social trend. This is a perfect example of why I wish I'd asked more questions even though it would've made for a difficult conversation. I can't remember why they separated. My overwhelming hunch was drinking. It had to be, right? What else could it have been? I've thought maybe one of them strayed but it just doesn't feel right. Dad was deep into his workaholic phase. I wonder now if this was to get away from Mum and her drinking.

Don't get me wrong – it wasn't like she was arseholed from morning till night at this point, god no. That was unacceptable to Mum. She was a woman who believed it was unseemly for a 'lady' to smoke a cigarette walking down the street. Oh no, with her it was all about public perception and image. Me and Dad would often crack up listening to Mum answer the phone using her posh voice. This feels dangerous to me now, caring what the neighbours thought. This is why things became hidden. No, Mum was a fully functioning drunk then. A mother and a home maker. Still I wonder if Dad coming home late every night to a G-'n'-T-soaked, angry, emotional firebomb was the thing that made them split. It feels right but I'll never know.

This was a time of weekend visits from Dad while he lived in Uncle Brian's spare room. I didn't feel like I was being denied a father, in fact I probably saw him just as much to be fair. We went on what felt like functional trips to places like the newly opened Thames barrier and the *Cutty Sark*. We both hated it really. He wanted to be home and I didn't really want to be forced to lose a weekend on my hot BMX.

We had a big fight one Saturday when me and Dad went to buy rugby boots. He tried to fob me off with bad boots with moulded rubber studs. Oh no. All the forwards from my team that season were wearing Adidas Flanker and that's what I wanted. He was so cross. He slammed the cheap boots down and walked out of the shop without me. I was in trouble. He really screamed at me in the car.

After almost a year Mum and Dad had worked things out and Dad moved back home. What a strange episode. I guess their years and years of relationship groundwork and the fact they had me meant eventually they couldn't be apart. They were in love, right up to the end. I think you have to be to go through what they went through. Sometimes it's just easier to keep going forward together than to leave.

My dad had gone through a big change. He'd left the company that he'd helped to build from the ground up when he realised he was not getting everything he should've been. Yes we had a nice house, and a nice car and blahblahblah but it wasn't what the others had and in terms of a work – life balance there was none as he was always working.

Dad decided to start his own company. Clover! It was the happiest I remembered him. (Not completely true but you know what I mean.) He was moving on and forward, he was doing something that would make sure we had the big house in Essex and the horses and the tennis court and the Ferrari and endless summer barbecues where we laughed and stuffed ourselves with meats prepared over open flames. What a life. If anyone deserved that life he did. Dad had worked from the ground up and had taught himself everything there was to know about the design, manufacture, sale and distribution of high-end office furniture. He was a good man who had made a lot of friends in the business and people wanted him to succeed.

Being a sixteen-year-old boy-man I was shielded from certain aspects of our family life. Things that might worry a young brain. Things kids don't need to know about, don't really care about until Christmas gets cancelled and you end up all alone in a shit council estate . . . Oh.

The things I was shrouded from was how Dad got the money to start the company. Essentially everything was up for grabs. The house was remortgaged up to its balls to pay for this venture. In hindsight it's a massive risk and it's easy for me to sit here at the free laptop Apple gave me because I'm a 'celeb' and criticise a man, a good man, trying to do the best for his family. Could I do what he did? I doubt I'd have the bollocks to be honest.

My mum and dad turned our shed at the bottom of our garden in Redbridge into a workshop to make high-end office furniture. They worked so hard. Dad spent the first few weeks out on the road selling Clover. He spent so long drawing little designs for logos and beautiful sketches for amazing chairs. He was so talented, such an amazing draughtsman. Dad was also

a fantastic watercolourist. So technical, creating perfect buildings and landscapes. I have all those paintings. People went
crazy for his designs but that's all they were at that point, just
designs, pictures on a pad.

Once they had enough orders in, Mum and Dad set to work
making the chairs themselves. Let me just write that again . . .
They made the chairs themselves! All the individual pieces were
manufactured off site then delivered and put together by Mum
and Dad in the garage. Some nights they'd be down there until
two or three in the morning putting together handmade chairs.
After a couple of hours' sleep Dad would load up the van he
rented and deliver the things himself.

I think a business of this kind needs to expand quickly and
take people on, otherwise you get swamped and can't actually
fulfil your orders. This was exactly the case with Clover. They
got a big order from a major company to make chairs for a new
HQ. This was it. Fulfil this order and we were fucking laughing. We didn't and we weren't laughing.

As I said, I didn't know and still don't know all the whys and
wherefores, but we failed. The order was just too big. The bank
sent notices, the creditors circled and we were finished. When
the end comes it's horrible. Everything my dad had worked his
balls off for was taken. Assets and dignity stripped away. In the
garage the frames of chairs, the skeletal remains of a dream
wrapped in sheets of soft Italian leather, lay waiting to be
reclaimed by creditors. Behind closed doors voices are raised.
Tears. Fists are pounded into tables. In public there is silence.
Dad gazes into the garden. Deep sighs. Thousand-yard stares.
Mum busies herself around Dad, cajoling, geeing him up,
trying to ignite something in him. Everything is gone, and with
it my beautiful father's dignity. He never recovers.

We were out on the street. The bank takes our home away. How can a bank be allowed to turn a family out onto the street? It's criminal. The council refuse to rehouse us at first, so we live next door with Chris and Mandy and Ian and Martin. They do what real friends do and they step up.

From our lovely double-fronted house in Redbridge where so much had happened to us, we now lived next door in one tiny room that used to be Mandy's bedroom. Three of us lived there with our massive Alsatian Sheba. It was weird to think that only eighteen months before I'd been sat in that room on Mandy's bed sniffing her novelty rubbers trying to think of new inventive ways to kiss her. Apart from death, I can't think of many things worse than losing everything.

We were all so stressed and sad and angry. I spent a lot of time suffering at the end of a Rizla or hiding under the saggy tumtum of a laughing Buddha.

To be fair the atmosphere in their house was always nice. Tea was always being made, *Dallas* was usually on, and Mandy was there which was a bonus. One night I came in fairly early. Everyone was up and about except Mum. She'd gone to bed early with a bit of a headache. Despite all our shit, I loved, still love, my mum with all of my heart. I pop into the bedroom to say goodnight.

Literally as soon as I push the door open I hear a very inhuman and yet totally human noise, a scream, a hollow roar, the noise of a mother hearing her son has been murdered. It isn't right and my spine and brain twitch. It's dark and I don't know what's happening but noises like that never mean anything good. Never.

I flick on the light and find her fitting violently. Her arms tight and thrust into the sky like a boxer knocked out with the perfect punch. Arms thrust upwards, defending themselves from a nightmare. Their brains are malfunctioning. My mum's brain is malfunctioning and it's the oddest most frightening thing I've ever witnessed. She's having a stroke.

I watch for what seems to be an age, one of her eyes focuses on me, pleading for help. I don't move, I can't move, I'm stone. She emits a growl and it snaps me out of my terror. I crash through the door with the little slats and pick up the phone.

I'm making a strange noise, which gets people off the sofa. They peer at me. I literally cannot talk but my noises leave little doubt that something is very fucked up. Chris sees me and sees my panic and as an ex-nurse knows exactly what's happening. Chris always had a very cool head.

I have the phone in my hand and 999 answers. I can't speak. I groan and feel tears tumbling down my cheeks. I try and talk but someone takes over and once again life quickens. An ambulance turns up, groaning Mum is rushed into hospital. The stroke was bad, and the doctors suggest it was brought on by drink and stress. It could've been a lot worse, we could've easily lost her that night. After three days of touch and go, her prognosis finally improves. Her speech returns – this has its good and bad points. Eventually her facial paralysis disappears too. Mum was so fucking lucky.

After this point with the company folding and us losing everything I feel truly alone. It's a sobering feeling the moment you become your parents' parent. For some people it's not until they're in their fifties or sixties but I was sixteen and it was too much for me to bear. After Mum's stroke my lovely gentle dad had a massive nervous breakdown and he was never the same again. The man I knew, the workaholic, the joker, always laughing but often absent through hard work, had disappeared. I never saw that man again. There were glimpses every now and then, especially after Mum died, but it wasn't the same.

I'd only seen Dad cry once up to that point, when Deborah died. After the collapse of us I saw him cry every day. The fact that my dad had failed, failed in business, failed as a man, to support us, his family. It killed him inside. The truth is not this at all, he didn't fail me. What I saw was a brave man who gave everything he had to make things better. I watched a man get beaten down time and time again and get up, slowly some-times, but get up and trudge forward. He has always been my inspiration.

He was different when he came out the other side. Not neces-sarily a bad different but different. He was quieter, gentler, softer, he needed Mum now more than ever and she gave him what he needed. Mum was a good wife and a fucking strong woman despite her issues. She held him when he cried, soothed him when he was frightened, and when it was needed she bullied and cajoled him into action. What that action was is hard to say. Dad never really worked again. At first he'd just leave the house in the morning and would spend all day out, just walking. He'd take the dog and walk along the River Roding sometimes for seven hours a day.

He started fishing through the river and reeds for lost golf balls near a local course. He'd come back with carrier bags filled with hundreds of balls and sell them to a local driving range. This was what he did for a long while. He just couldn't take it any more. He couldn't find it in himself to get smashed up by the baying, hungry rat race again. His heart was broken and he was a fragile thing, and if all he could face was collect-ing golf balls then that was fine by me.

Eventually, after a couple of months, the council rehoused us in a place called the Ray Lodge Estate in South Woodford. The first time I went there my blood ran cold. The room that eventually became my bedroom had human shit smeared all over the walls. There was also a big red puddle in the middle of the floor which the council woman suggested nervously was 'just paint'.

It was the worst place in the world to me. Hard kids with dead, hard eyes bogged me down, smashed-up washing machines and fridges lay everywhere, needles and burnt-out gutted cars littered the underground car park. How the mighty fall. As a sixteen-year-old it was a bad time to try and fit in. I'd missed the window. If I'd have moved here when I was younger I'd have just become a part of it. I never became part of it. Thank fuck I had a big dog, a big Alsatian, the gorgeous and talented Sheba. No one fucks with you when you have a big dog. She was my furry flick-knife.

Once we moved into the mouth of heck – so dramatic – my 'mates' distanced themselves from me. After everything that had happened it hurt me so much. They'd play games with me, not answer their phones (house phones I might add, this was a long time before mobiles). They'd not call me back, they'd say they'd come round and they never did and I don't know why. What had I done to deserve this? This was one of many cata- lysts that led to a descent that seemed to be unstoppable.

I was alone in a terrible place with an alcoholic mum and a father broken by failure. I think I probably wanted to be dead at this point. One day I'm very drunk at home in my room. I'd started stealing and squirrelling away Dad's pills, he had so many barbs and squeakers and downers he never noticed any missing. I liked the way they made me feel when I took a bunch with booze.

The drunker and higher I got the sadder I became. I took a handful of pills and washed it down with more booze. I write a goodbye to Mum and Dad apologising for what was about to happen and I try and attempt to lie on my bed. I don't make it. The *Close Encounters* soundtrack, a favourite album I find in a junk shop, blares out, my head fogs up and I collapse on the floor. Dead. I'll definitely miss everyone but I'm glad, to be honest.

I wake up the next morning. Balls. I'm still alive. My room has literally not been touched. My note has not been found, my *Close Encounters* album is still revolving on the record player. No one came in. No one lifted me onto my bed or called an ambulance. I feel like shit. I'm seventeen.

I leave school when Mum and Dad collapse. Partly because I hate school (apart from rugby) and partly through a sense of duty: we have no money. Nothing. We live off of Mum and Dad's benefits. I felt like I needed to contribute.

After a lot of interviews and looking in the papers for jobs I find myself employed. I start working at a shipping company in Ilford called Cowell Nicola. I have no experience but it doesn't seem to matter, they employ me and I like it. I really like working in that office.

I'm the youngest one there and they treat me good, the girls think I'm cute, and the blokes talk to me like I'm a football hooligan. At this point I was earning five thousand a year! It seems like fuck all now but back then it was loads, loads to me anyway. After I'd paid housekeeping to Mum and Dad I was free to spend the rest. Spending my money meant booze and petrol for our mate who drove, and McDonalds and raves and hard-house weekenders and hash and squares of paper with mystical symbols etched into them. If you ate the squares the wonders of the universe would be unveiled to you. Not bad for a fiver.

There were some great people at that company. Big Terry Musk, our office manager, heavy smoker, nice easy laugh. Kerry, who looked like a sexy poodle with her mound of heavily curled hair, heavy smoker. I fancied her a bit. Dave, a big brutish ex-hooligan, great at tennis. Dean, suave and heavily receding. Sue, busty, saucy and a real den mother, and Neil Driver, a Cooganesque section leader who made us all laugh a lot.

I liked the fact they treated me like a grown up, which I wasn't. The work was easy and they introduced me to the joys/regrets of afternoon drinking. Nipping out at lunch for a couple. A couple often turned into four or five. How could people work like this? Once a girl got so hammered at lunch we had to cover her in coats and hide her under our desks. That company felt like a little family, we'd do things together a lot after work, softball tournaments, tennis tournaments, parties, drinking in shit pubs in Barking. It was a good time for me, professionally anyway.

Home was somewhere I did not want to be. I'd work then I'd do drugs, mostly on my own. Mostly weed, sometimes other things if I needed to be really away. I needed to escape that place mentally if not physically. When I was there I was locked in my room listening to music, music was one of my escapes. I loved the Happy Mondays, loved the Stone Roses, Inspiral Carpets, Charlatans, Spacemen 3 and the illegal exciting world of pirate radio. I also began writing poems and painting. Could I have been any more of an angsty teen-twat cliché? My poor parents, my poor me.

At this point I fall for a girl who I knew from school called Lee Morris. She was so beautiful. She lived near work on her own and knew what I was going through; she was kind and let me stay with her sometimes. It felt intense and grown up, confusing. She lived in one room, a bedsit, she had a little TV and a black kitten that would flick cat-litter all over the floor at night. I have no idea why a seventeen-year-old lived on her own. If I did know the reason it's now gone. We sleep in the same bed but nothing ever really happens although I seem to remember trying a bit.

Lee was the first in a long line of girls who were way out of my league. I fell for them, hard, but they didn't feel the same way. They saw me more as a friend. Shit. Not good for a falling-in-lover like me. I feel the first delicious pain that only unrequited love can bring. I grow to oddly like that feeling. Sometimes you fall back to something you know and understand, even if it's something that hurts. You get used to it and at the end of the day it's better to feel something, even if it's pain, than feel nothing at all.

Eventually Lee and I stopped whatever it was that we were doing. We contacted each other recently on Twitter. She was happy and apparently makes amazing soup! All's well that ends well.

After a year or so at Cowell Nicola I began to think about moving up the ladder. I needed to be more than a Junior Freight Assistant. I think the truth was I actually wanted a bit more money. Cowell Nicola was a small company but well thought of and it looked good on my CV. I found a job – or was I headhunted? Maybe. That sounds good so let's say yes, I was headhunted, and began working at P&O Containers in Hainault on their Africa desk.

Again I meet good people. It was me, Iain Brymer, our team leader who we all love. Denise, a beautiful cockney firebrand who had a thing with Iain for a bit. Lydia, who's sexy and brassy as fuck, I'd literally never seen a girl like her before, she wore suspenders! This is my first brush with lingerie. Sometimes if you were lucky you'd get a cheeky little flash. Pervert. Me, not her. Last but by no means least the brother of my junior school mate, the one and only Brendan Heggarty.

We had such a laugh. I loved them all and I loved working there. I also got a pay rise, I was now earning a stunning £6,400 (p/a) which was frigging great!

Living with Mum and Dad in Ray Lodge, I took the train every day to Hainault, where the offices of P&O were. I loved going to work because it meant I could leave the confines of my council prison. I hated leaving the office at night as it meant I'd have to go back to Ray Lodge. Whenever I got close to that place my heart would beat a little faster, especially if I didn't have the dog.

It says something about the estate that I was relieved when I finally shut that heavy multi-locked PVC door behind me. Inside was a different type of nightmare but one I'd grown used to.

It wasn't all doom and gloom in that tiny five-room flat. For all the drama and alcohol there were times when we laughed and danced and forgot. The walls in that place were so thin I could hear when my dad ripped off a powerful guff. I'd laugh and then Dad, hearing me laugh, would join in. During this time the smell would waft up into my mum's sensitive nose and she would begin a series of very high-pitched dry heaves. This would send Dad and me into fits of hysterical laughter. Every time she heaved we would lie there on the other side of the gossamer-thin walls laughing our arses off. Mum would struggle to speak. Hearing her heave her way through the sentence 'John, you dirty bastard' was too much to bear. Sometimes I'd laugh so much I'd have to leap up and do a wee. I think it says something about my memories of that place that the best thing

I can muster is listening to my mum heaving to one of Dad's eggy farts.

I began hanging out with Iain Brymer more and more outside the office. He was my direct superior and a bloody good egg. I think he had problems with his mum too in their tiny flat in a tower block in Tilbury. Often I've found myself drawn to people, sometimes without even knowing it, who have similar issues to me.

Even though he was our boss, Bifta (Iain's nickname) often got into trouble for not wearing socks and his anti-establishment vibe meant he was a bit of a hero to me. He was a raver, a renegade and charming as all hell. Don't get me wrong, when we worked, we worked; even though we laughed a lot there was no fucking around. It was important to him and therefore to us that we had the best, politest, most efficient desk in the office and we did.

One day at lunch while Iain flicked through his copy of the *NME* (so fucking cool) he stopped us mid-sandwich and declared that we were getting tickets to see the Stone Roses at Spike Island. So this is exactly what we did.

We took a coach up to Spike Island, which was somewhere near Widnes. It was to be my first time in the Great North. Heck, I even made my own flares. Making flares is simple really, if you ever fancy it, essentially you cut sections out of the bottoms of your jeans and insert big triangles of another fabric, in this case yellow corduroy, simples. Apart from Bifta and Denise and I think Brendan, I have no idea who else came. It was a long coach trip up from Victoria with a real bunch of weirdos, us included. When we finally got there Widnes looked like a frightening shit hole.

The Stone Roses gig at Spike Island has now passed into legend, a defining moment for a bunch of floppy-haired revolutionaries demanding the freedom to party. The zenith of a cultural upheaval and a new Woodstock for what was called the second summer of love. Of course I remember next to nothing about it. Well, I remember bits, I'm not a complete morom. Microdots were ingested, things get wobbly, it was a very hot day I seem to remember, and at one point they play the noise of a freezing cold wind through the PA. I watch about twenty thousand people stand and put their coats on. I also see a man who had no feet, but hoofs, clip-clop by. This wasn't just me, everyone in the group saw him.

I do however remember the Stone Roses themselves; we were some way away from the stage so it looked like a flea circus to me but it felt amazing. Standing in that field on that island in the middle of the River Mersey surrounded by all the weird fuck-ups my subculture could muster belting out the words to 'I Am The Resurrection' was pretty fucking awe-inspiring. Those moments of complete synchronicity are rare and fleeting and pass so quickly. Embrace it when it happens.

On the drive home we listen to a man screaming about a baby being on the roof of the coach for two hours; it's weird and frightening and does nothing to aid sleep. I get off the coach in Victoria at dawn, wide-eyed, freezing cold and shattered. Being with Brendan and Bifta made me feel happier and I could almost forget about home and the fact my friends had abandoned me. I return home and cry.

I really should describe to you all the injuries my mum received while she was drinking. I've no idea why but I feel it's important for you to realise what I see growing up.

One evening during a holiday in Wales, Mum and Dad go out to a party. I'm there too but I don't remember much about the party but I do remember leaving. It was cold, icy and misty. Mum, drunk, took a tumble down some stairs. It was brutal. She lay there a while, silent, then she began laughing and, by this time, people were out helping her up. She was embarrassed and waved them off. We went home and went to bed.

The next morning I hear a moan coming from their room. I was frightened so I ran in and found Dad trying to help Mum up onto her feet. Both of her legs were black, she'd broken *both* of them in the fall and she didn't even realise. Poor thing.

I have a terrible phobia of porcelain dolls. I come in from school one day, aged about twelve, people were there, I think my half-sister Debbie among them. There was a kerfuffle of sorts, a tall box on the floor. Not bothered, I go into the front room and take my shoes off and switch the telly on. I turn to look into the kitchen and I see my mum staggering towards me, tottering, teetering, pissed up, arms outstretched, she's coming towards me holding a large, white-faced porcelain doll with curly blonde hair, Victorian dress, bonnet of lace. She's also covered in bright-red blood, it pumps from a deep wound in Mum's hand. The doll is crying tears of blood, its gaze and jagged smile fixed as Mum stumbles towards me.

On hearing I'd returned from school she panics and tries to hide the abomination. Leaning on the back of a chair, it over-balances and she tumbles backwards, slashing her hand on a sharp metal edge on the top of the radiator; she didn't even know. She had to have lots of stitches.

When we lived at Ray Lodge, Mum was in bed early one evening, pissed. Me and Dad had a perfunctory conversation.

'Where's Mum?'

'Upstairs.'
'Is she asleep?'
'Yeah.'
'It's six o'clock!'
'Yeah.'
'Right.'
'Do you want any tea?'
'No. I'm going to my room. You okay?'
'Yeah. You?'
'Yeah.'

I run upstairs and put my music on low, headphones plastered to my head. I'm hiding, hoping she doesn't wake up. When you're the child of an alcoholic parent more often than not you breathe a sigh of relief when you come in and they're asleep. You pray they don't wake up. Suddenly I hear a noise that sounds something like a forty-seven-year-old woman falling down a set of steep wooden steps. I fly out of my room to find a forty-seven-year-old woman, my mum, lying at the bottom of a set of steep wooden steps. Dad runs out of the kitchen and we stare at each other. She lies semi-conscious at the base of the stairs groaning. We wait for an ambulance and in the hospital later they tell us she has snapped the bottom inch off her coccyx.

One day Mum bought some false fingernails and couldn't work out how to secure them to her existing nails. Under the influence, she finds superglue and bonds them onto her fingers. A few hours later she comes into my bedroom – we still live in Babbacombe Gardens at this point – the same house where Mum would let me and all my friends sit up in my bedroom smoking at lunchtime. The door would kick open and a chorus of 'Hello, Mrs Frost' would ring out, she'd bring us all cake and sandwiches, mugs of hot sweet tea. Her rationale? She'd rather us be safe and warm at home where she could keep an eye on us than out on the street. Cool.

Anyhoo, she knocks and comes in, she is in pain and crying. The ends of her fingers have swollen around the plastic nails and the superglue means she cannot get them off. Pleading with me to help her, my thirteen-year-old self now has to perform a kind of light home surgery. I think about the task in hand and settle upon three different-sized needles and a slim steak knife. I sit Mum down and put her massive red hands on a soft pillow. I put two bags of frozen peas on her hands and leave her for a bit.

After a while we begin. I start with the smallest needle and I try and push it between the falsie and her existing nail. (As an aside my mum always had lovely hands and nails, and had no need to use false nails.) Anyway, after much shrieking and tears I get the needle down there. I waggle it about until the small needle moves freely, I then put the bigger needle under and do the same, then the biggest needle and finally the steak knife, which I use to prise the nail up and off. Mum's relief is palpable. I repeat this ten times in total. What a palaver. It does however give me a taste for home surgery. Something I still do to this very day. If any of you ever need a skin tag or in-grown toenail removed give me a bell.

Finally, the big one . . . Death. She died. I think for a long while I couldn't shake the feeling that she killed herself. I was so cross. I was so cross for years and years. Being angry at a dead parent is such a destructive thing it will eat you up and eventually end you too.

I'd hate for you to read this and just imagine my mum being some horrible drunk monster. I'd also like to point out that for everything she did, everything that happened to her, and us, she was the only mum I had and I loved her and still love her with all of my heart. She was a good woman who had a very hard life and in the end just couldn't go on.

Before you judge a person it's important to realise and understand what may have happened in their life to make them become what they eventually become.

My mum was one of many from a very poor family. The older girls were expected to look after the younger ones – I think sometimes at the expense of their own liberty and education. Mum told me it was a hard life. Gran and Grampie were strict but they knew nothing else and that's what they had, in that cold house up on Hazel Grove.

When she was still just a girl my mum left home and married a man who was older than her. I think she must've thought she was being saved from her life as it was. She was wrong. Isolated high up in the hilltop farm in the tiny Pembrokeshire village of Maenclochog, she was trapped and isolated. That's when her punishment began. She quickly had three children, Marc, Ian and Debbie. My half-siblings. My mum was strong and opinionated and feisty, cheeky, mouthy, she didn't, wouldn't, couldn't ever back down. These traits are sadly a red rag to a bull when you're living with a violent alcoholic. He beat the shit out of that girl time and time again. Along the way my mum lost all her teeth. He'd knocked them all out. *He knocked them all out!* This is the reason my blood boils when I hear about a man hitting a woman.

One day when Mum was in her twenties the police parked outside the house. They waited for him to leave, came in, told her to pack a bag and they took her away, frightened that her husband would kill her. The police put Mum on a train to London. So after years of physical and mental abuse she had escaped. But at what cost?

She'd been forced to abandon the children she loved. She had to take what she could carry and go. Having a child myself I can only imagine how heartbreaking that must have been. It must be a million times harder for a mother. It was one of the things that changed her for ever. I don't think she really ever got over it. How could she? How could anyone? That's why drunk Mum was so overly protective, so overly affectionate. I hated it.

She clung on to me so tightly and in the end she lost me too. I found it hard to forgive myself for a long time. I couldn't help it though, that drinking of hers. I couldn't watch her kill herself and there was nothing I could do to help her. I couldn't, wouldn't, watch her die. Maybe a better person would've tried harder?

I was on the *Shaun of the Dead* DVD tour in Los Angeles in 2005 when my mum died. It was the night I'd met Tarantino for the first time. Edgar, Simon, QT, our beautiful friend Greg Nicotero and me. I think a few others popped in along the way too and it would get most raucous.

We met in a little Thai place on Sunset, opposite El Compadre, for me the best Mexican restaurant in West Hollywood. Steer clear – or not – of their giant strawberry margaritas. The weather was terrible – torrential rain, Angelinos are shit drivers in the rain. I heard that there were six hundred crashes on the highway that night.

I call my mum and dad that morning, Mum is drunk. She sounds hammered, slurring, stammering – fuck, I was angry with her. Short, curt, I wanted to wrap her quickly and talk to Dad. I was angry with him too for letting this happen. As I tried to sign off from her she said the last words I'd ever hear her speak.

'You'd love it here, Nins. It's snowing in the kitchen.'

'You what?'

'It's snowing in the kitchen.'

Lunacy. I was cross.

'What are you talking about? Put Dad on.'

Dad came on the phone.

'Is Mum okay?'

'Yeah, she's all right.'

'Is she pissed?'

'No.'

'Right, I only ask because she just told me it was snowing in the kitchen.'

There's a pause.

'Oh, right, okay.'

'I got to go, Dad. Love you.'

'I love you too.'

And that was the last time I ever spoke to my lovely, troubled, anguished, beautiful, passionate, funny, angry mum. I had a phone call from Dad while we were at dinner; I was relieved in a way because it meant I could excuse myself from Edgar and QT's baffling conversation about obscure Japanese cinema. I feared they'd unmask me as a fraud and I'd be banished from the table. Don't get me wrong, I like films, I really like films, but they LOVE cinema. They are true cinephiles. I can hold my own with any movie geek or film buff but they are something else. It's baffling to listen to, like mathematicians talking about triangles. I excuse myself and take the call. Dad's voice trembles.

'Mum's sick.'

I feel my heart beating in my mouth.

'How sick?'

'She's really sick, Nins.' Nins is what they called me.

I paused. There's a long silence. I take this information with a pinch of salt. Her drinking had put her in hospital many times. A couple of years before, I was told to prepare for the worst, an artery had ruptured in her throat after a coughing fit and they couldn't stop it bleeding. Doctors believed that she would bleed out right there and then. She didn't. They saved her. I think my parents went to hospital a lot without me knowing, without wanting to worry me.

With all this in mind I tell Dad I love him, tell him to keep me informed, I hang up and go back to the table. It takes me a while to shake off the call. Simon notices, of course, and quietly asks what's wrong. I tell him but he's been through it all with me before so he does his best to tell me it'll be cool. I relax, the night I was about to have with the boys and QT would do its best to erase the call pretty good.

Being there on Universal's dime doing press for the DVD's release meant we had a driver for the night. It's a lovely thing having a driver. It doesn't happen that often but when it does it's a real treat. It means you can really tie one on and not worry about cabs or distance or time. This is exactly what happened.

We finished dinner and nipped next door to a 'British' pub for a few pints; it was packed and people went crazy for QT and, by association, the *Shaun of the Dead* guys too. It was crazy, we decide to bail, and someone suggests we head to a strip club that QT knows. We bundle into the SUV and head to East LA.

After a while cruising through the city the car pulls into the parking lot of a rough-looking shit hole. Nervously we step from our fancy, chauffeur-driven car and are immediately eye-fucked to death by a gang of fearsome-looking Cholos hanging around a low rider. (This cliché may or may not have actually happened.)

The tension eases slightly when QT jumps out. The Latino community love QT. The owner bustles out and we are greeted like family. Hugs, hands shaken, slaps on the back etc.

This does nothing to calm me. I feel fucking queasy. I've always had a great trouble detector, often leaving a pub or club moments before it kicks off. My 'danger – you may be killed by men' alarm is screaming, I can't silence its buzzing. I stop sweating and my hands and feet become ice cold, my body is preparing itself for battle. If I think the alarm was loud outside it was nothing compared to when we went inside. My danger alarm explodes.

There are close to four hundred of what I guess I'd have to call, reluctantly and not wanting to play to an obvious cultural stereotype, Gang Bangers. They have face tats, hair nets, and gang signs are being flicked all over the place. Latino machismo is literally being squirted all over me.

We are stuffed, stuffed, into this large, low-ceilinged, red-walled strip club. In the middle of the place was a raised runway packed with attractively chubby Mexican strippers. Along the back wall runs a very long bar packed with one-eyed lunatics. It is, without doubt, one of the top five roughest places I've ever been in.

It's about to get a lot rougher as the owner decides to shut the club early and turf out four hundred drunk, dangerous, very horny vatos, so we can have this deep-red hell all to ourselves! For a moment I'm slightly concerned we might get shot. I glance across at Edgar who looks pale and weak. Simon and I hold hands secretly for comfort.

We relax now it's just us and realise just how big the place is. Friends of friends have joined and all in all there are probably twenty of us. It's a good gang of blokes and we have a great laugh.

At one point QT sticks a big roll of dollar bills into my paw and assures me I'm going to need it. He smiles and waggles his brows suggestively. I smile. It begins. I spend two hours stuffing George Washingtons into the knickers of sexy brown girls. Much tequila is drunk, we laugh like idiots. My dinnertime phone call ebbs away from my memory with every dollar bill I twang into a G.

The MC brings us to attention, a show is about to begin. We gather around the stage and he announces the next girl, she is small, chubby and sexy. Music kicks in, it's a song I know, I've heard it before, it's a track on the *From Dusk till Dawn* soundtrack. If you've ever seen *From Dusk till Dawn* you'll know there's a scene where our heroes, now unwittingly trapped in the Titty Twister, sit up at the runway watching Salma Hayek do a horny snake dance. The thrilling denouement sees the sexy Vampire Queen Hayek sticking her foot into QT's mouth and pouring whisky down her leg straight into his gob. It's a sexy scene. It's also a scene that is now getting a twenty-five-cent re-creation right in front of me. I exchange looks with Simon and Edgar. We all laugh so hard.

At the height of the dance the chubby girl in the yellow bikini sticks her foot in QT's mouth and instead of pouring whisky down her hairy leg she opens a can of Tecate beer. It was amazing. I felt honoured to have witnessed this. I'm happy and for the first time actually begin to like the Hollywood thing. I like QT a lot. He's always been really good to me.

We leave this beautiful hell as the sun is beginning to rise. By the time I get back to The Standard I'm glowing and hammered. I get into my room, collapse on my bed and sleep.

I'm asleep a couple of hours before the high-pitched vibrations of my silenced phone wake me up. It's Dad with an update no doubt.

'Hello?' Nothing.

'Dad?' Silence. I get *the feeling* ringing in my ears. An orange flash that begins at my feet and moves north at the speed of light.

'Dad?' He breaks the silence.

'Mum died, Nins.'

'When?'

'Just now.'

It's my turn to be silent. I listen to the sound of my world collapsing in on itself.

After Debbie died I had counselling for a while although it didn't last long. I was smarter than the therapist and he offered me nothing new by way of personal insight. Although he did ask me what I'd like to happen, what I'd like to happen to Mum, to Dad, to me, to us. At the time, Mum was really sick and I loved Dad so much, it was hard seeing him having to care for this old woman. He was a remarkably selfless person. I thought about the therapist's question and I answered honestly. I told him that I wished my mum were dead. It was an answer that has haunted me ever since I heard Dad tell me that she was dead. I didn't mean it.

'I'll have to call you back, Dad. I love you.'

'I love you.'

My hands shake. My ears ring. I let out a noise. It is primal, it is guttural, I heave grief all over the floor, all over the toilet.

I can't believe it. I stand blinking, naked in the middle of that room, trying to talk, jabbering, jabbering, turning around in a circle, my computer is misfiring badly. I need someone, I need

Simon, I have to call Simon. I dial his room. Please be awake. He answers. He's groggy.

'Hello?'

I can't talk. I know exactly what's going to happen when I hear my boy's voice. I knew it would send me over the edge. I make a noise, the noise sounds like a gorilla punching me in the solar plexus. He knows. There's a level of instant knowing at the sound of a person who's lost someone close, really close, one of the big seven, Brother, Sister, Mother, Father, Husband, Wife, Child.

I drop the phone and slump to the floor. Simon couldn't have been more than two minutes but it was a fucking long, lonely two minutes.

I'd already lost two half-sisters and a half-brother at this point so I thought I was getting good at this grief thing. I was so fucking wrong.

Grief, like strong LSD, comes in waves. There are moans, weeping, tears, laughter, silence, random thought processes I have no way of controlling. I have no control. Simon grabs the situation by the balls and phone calls are made. Arrangements. Flights changed. Meetings are cancelled. The *Shaun of the Dead* press tour is over. My sense of responsibility and work ethic means I'm sad it's over but I can't go on. I can't do it. Nothing matters to me anymore except being with my dad.

Simon and me are on a BA flight that night. Sitting at the gate people ask us for photos. It's hard to say no to a fan especially if it's a kid, we had photos. I'd hate to see those pictures.

We board the 747 and sit upstairs in Business Class. While waiting for the doors to close a funny thing happens. A man, young, English, early thirties maybe, is also sitting up in Business Class, and he's what cockneys might call a Proper

Cunt. My backstory for him – I create a backstory for almost everyone I meet – was this: he's the young up-and-coming director of promos, ad campaigns, that sort of thing. He's arrogant and thinks he's entitled because he has a bit of money. That said, there's no way he paid for his own ticket. No way. People up in First and Business hardly ever do.

He's with an American girl, tall and very beautiful, catwalk model beautiful. A fit girl like this will always multiply the arrogance of a proper arsehole. He'll always feel like he needs to be edgier, more outspoken, more opinionated than anyone else because deep down he knows that she may jump ship at any second.

They were both being very loud, complaining noisily. They'd been denied an upgrade and now he finds his shitty, wide, tons of legroom seat has a tiny smudge of melted chocolate on it, he wants – no, demands – to be moved. The attendant sighs, she doesn't need this shit. Model girl still wants an upgrade but there are no seats. The flight is still full! The attendant, calm, professional, quietly spoken offers to put a blanket on his seat. It is literally all she can do unless he wants a downgrade? Model is starting to blame Dickhead for this terribly unfair business. He needs to save face and fast. He stands. This is going to be good. I forget my woes for a moment and look at Simon who gives me a 'this is going to be good' look. Dickhead looks around, takes a breath and declares . . .

'Fuck this. We're getting off.'

Wow. Big move. Big statement. She'll love that, I bet she has a wide-on. The Model agrees. After a lot of 'look at me'-style kerfuffle, they leave accompanied by some light applause.

We are now forced to sit at the gate for a further forty minutes waiting for their bags to be offloaded. Finally the doors are closed; we push back and take off. I'm going home. I'm frightened. The ding noise dings and the seatbelt signs go off. We are now free to walk about the cabin.

Two minutes later the lovely stewardess who had been through so much shit with that pair of pricks swings by and reveals two passports! One British, one American. What she is showing us are their passports that he'd shoved down the side of the seat! In the rush to get off the plane they'd left their fucking documents on board! Karma right there! BOOM! My mum died, fuck you, you Chocolate-Seat Helmets.

* * *

I digress. This is all to come. For now I was still in fucking Ray Lodge. Only one thing helps me escape my fucking pain and I start to hit that shit very hard indeed.

I really liked my P&O teammate Brendan Heggarty. It's amazing how a few years make all the difference in terms of friendship. When I was his younger brother's friend, Brendan hated us because we were little jerks. Ten years later, it all changes. I was still a lowly freight rookie while Bren was a man going places in the shipping world. But during our time at P&O he never once fires a phlegm-centred foil ball at me. Not once! On the contrary, I think he was the person who helped save me from myself.

Working was my escape from a totally shit home life. I hated my life, I felt so alone, so lonely. I didn't know what to do. I found it all too much watching my mum kill herself. Watching my dad, a shell of a man, broken, quiet, absent. My friends absent, no girlfriend, me having to live in a shit estate.

'Oh boo hoo! Poor me.'

I think it broke me though. I was seventeen or eighteen years old. I didn't realise what depression was for another twenty years or so.

One afternoon in the office Brendan pulled me aside, suggested we go and have a beer after work. It's what geezers do when they need to put the world to rights. I met him in the Valentine in Gants Hill, a place I used to frequent when I was fifteen or so. We all hung out in pubs back then, playing the endless game of cat and mouse to see who could get served.

I think Brendan saw in me something he might've had in himself. After a while and several beers later he talks to me about his time abroad, talks to me about his travelling adventures. He tells me about a place he went to that helped him sort his shit out.

Like the French Foreign legion, this socialist commune accepts people from all religions, all colours, all creeds, no questions asked. All you need to do is work. He's talking about a kibbutz. My mind starts to race. I could go. I could leave and start again, be someone else. Leave this fear and paranoia here in England.

If it hadn't been for Bren's intervention I think I might have died. Everything was killing me.

The problem was I had next to no money. Fortunately for me, back then in the early nineties we didn't have the instant connectivity there is now, banks didn't talk to each other as much, this was perfect for what I needed. I found a place that had four or five different banks pretty close together. I started at 11.59 p.m. and stopped at 12.01 a.m., going from one cash-point to the next drawing out all the money I could. I managed to get almost £700. Minted. Let's roll.

I found a company called Project 67 in Edgware Road that could get me to Israel and place me on a kibbutz.

I don't remember what my mum and dad's reaction was to me leaving. I think they were shocked but they didn't try and stop me. If this is what I wanted then they'd support my decision. We had a little farewell BBQ at Uncle Brian's house where I was presented with a shiny new backpack.

Mum kept a stiff upper lip until we got to the airport where she crumbled slightly. Poor thing. Dad's wounds were beginning to scab over so he was on good form, cuddling Mum and cracking shit puns. We had a three-way cuddle and that was that. I was gone. When you share joy and tenderness and sadness at the prospect of a long time away from people you love it's easy to forget for a moment the reason you're leaving.

Part Two

I had NO idea what I was getting into. No idea whatsoever. That said, I was happy to be away. I immediately felt lighter, my soul felt lighter. I liked being on my own. Anything that happened to me now was completely my own doing and completely my own responsibility. I had no one else to blame but me and I liked it.

The El Al plane landed late at night in Tel Aviv's Ben Gurion International Airport. Wow. My mind was completely blown. What a place. It reminded me of Mos Eisley spaceport. It was the hottest, most alien place I'd ever been. I couldn't believe you could reach somewhere like this by simply flying east in a plane for four hours.

It was amazing, frightening and utterly beguiling. The noise of mopeds, alien languages being coughed up into the air. Crowded mouthfuls of brown and broken teeth. Hundreds of cigarettes being smoked by men in long white robes. And then there were the soldiers, which of course meant guns. Lots and lots of guns.

A few of us who'd come through with the same operator bumble together, terrified, shuffling around, not knowing what to do at all. We wait alone for ages, we're approached by men who raise their eyebrows and finger our shirts. Some of the blonde girls have their hair sniffed. Not me though, no one tries

to sniff my hair. Not then! By and by, Project 67 (the tour operator) vehicles turn up, names are shouted out according to
kibbutz. Goodbyes and good lucks are uttered and one by one
they disappear. It feels like waiting to be picked for football. In
the end the van that was coming for me and three or four others
didn't materialise.

The rep sticks me and the leftovers in a hot, loud taxi. It
takes us to a youth hostel behind Ben Yehuda Street. I'm led
with the others through a maze of hot, humid alleys into a
tiny lift in an art deco building. I generally don't like staying
over at other people's houses, I hated it as a child and even
today if there's a chance I can have my own bed, I'll absolutely
take it.

Now, however, I have no choice. I stand in the reception of
my first ever youth hostel. I actually feel homesick, I want my
mum, it's an unfamiliar feeling for me. To want my mum.
Maybe it's not weird for me. I think I always wanted my mum
really. Just not the Special Brew version.

All around reception are seasoned, battered-looking travellers, all dust and beaded goatees, they sense the freshness of
my meat. They know something I don't, they have the look. I'd
get it eventually but it would take a while. To be fair they may
have also been looking at my brand-new Berghaus rucksack
(65L), a gift from Uncle Brian and Auntie Francis. God, I must
have looked so young. I *was* so young.

I got checked in for one night – the next morning I'd go to
the Project 67 office and be assigned a new kibbutz placement.
For tonight though I'd be free to kick up my heels in Tel Aviv!

I'm assigned a space in a dorm. Four hard, metal, functional
bunk beds in a very dark room. Wet towels hang from a spider
web of twine strung across the room. Bags litter the floor. I see

the shape of people sleeping under thin sheets. It's so hot, and so smelly. I find a bed with a free mattress and haul my bag up. My bunk was the top one, there's someone's stuff on the bed beneath mine but they're not there. I don't unpack. I grab my secret bum bag, the kind you hide under all your clothes and reveal to would-be robbers the moment you have to haul your new shirt up to pay for anything, and meet the others in reception.

I buy a cold can of beer. It is called Goldstar, she is a stranger to me at first but would soon become my friend and part-time lover. She is so cold and so wet and delicious I devour her right there in the lobby. I don't care who sees or hears my groans. I must imbibe her.

I think there were four or five of us in our little team of refugees, other forgotten souls like me, left over from the selection process. I don't remember anything about them. Soz. Not names, not the girl:boy ratio. I'm not even sure what we did, not really. I vaguely remember walking around, eating a fucking great falafel and drinking beers. Then at one point we're all on the beach. It felt so strange and different to me. Who knew that by taking one flight everything I had on my shoulders would be gone. It was that easy. (Of course it wasn't, but sitting on that warm night beach, flirting and drinking beer felt a world away from Ray Lodge.)

We go back to the hostel, a small group of tipsy, noisy kids on holiday. I stumble into my assigned cell. Beds that had previously been filled with human-shaped lumps were now empty and empty beds now full of breathing, snoring human-shaped lumps.

Being a Bigmun there are universal truths you must quickly accept – limitations, one might say. Climbing silently up a flimsy bunk bed while a bit pissed without it shaking to fuck is one of those things. And volleyball.

Sure I made a bit of noise, and you can't just climb into a bed and lie completely motionless, there's always a period of adjustment and re-adjustment. It's how it is. Maybe the bolts were a bit loose? The bed did look very old, worn. It did wobble, though, I'll give you that. It wobbled. In hindsight I accept that now.

The motion of my ascent settles by and by. I lie there knowing what was coming next, knowing what I have to do, I don't want to but I'm compelled like a Wolf or Chihuahua and it begins, I roll and turn a while trying to get comfortable. I come around for the third or fourth comfort roll and I notice an old man standing five inches from my face.

He has long white hair in a loose plait and a white beard. He is shirtless although he wears a fetching denim gilet. I then note that in his left hand is a shiny ten-inch hunting knife. I say ten inches – it could've been eight. We regard each other in silence for an age.

'Hello.' I babble, he stares, unflinching, then speaks.

'I was in Vietnam.'

'Oh, an American!' Why did I decide to play it so chipper, it was an odd choice. His cold blue eyes blink for the first time and he heads back down to his place.

Fuck it's hot! Don't move. You'll be killed. When I was little I'd wake up and run to get into bed with Mum and Dad. It was always a massive mistake but I never learnt my lesson. Once in the bed they'd fall asleep leaving me wide awake, sandwiched between the two of them unable to move. This was me now. Don't move, for fucksakes don't move. I lie there most of the night terrified John Rambo might push that long piece of cold, forged steel up through the series one boxset-thin mattress and into my ribs and soft, fragile organs within.

At some point I nod off, when I wake up it's morning and I'm still terrified so I lift silently into the air and still horizontal I levitate off the bunk and gently land on the floor, silent like an autumn leaf. There's not a wobble in sight. The bunk beneath mine is empty, the bed is made with a coin-bouncing, military precision. My nightmare has gone. He was so lucky.

Later that morning I appear at the Project 67 office in Tel Aviv. Apologies are made, as are phone calls, and I'm shown a list of kibbutzim with available places for volunteers. Some of the others have places already in mind: a couple want to go down near Eilat for the beach and constant sun, some near Jerusalem for the history, Haifa for the . . . container port? I chose one at random. I say random – I really fancied living high up in the mountains, all the other would-be volunteers wanted the relentless organ-frying heat of the Sinai Desert. That was not for me so I chose a kibbutz called Bar-Am, high in the mountains in the far north of the country about two hundred metres from the Lebanese border. I'd considered climate over safety. What a bell-end.

I was given enough shekels for the bus ride north, a set of instructions and a contact list. An hour later I was in the old Tel Aviv bus station, hung-over and famished. It was here I stumbled into my first piece of good falafel-fortune. I find one stand among many and it does great falafel, they have a unique selling point and it's this: as long as your pitta bread is intact you get free refills of the crispy falafel balls. What a joyous discovery! I find the secret is applying the minimum amount of tahini. It's not easy but it ensures you keep the bread intact for longer. I think I had three refills. It's enough. Three is more than enough for even the chubbiest of Rabbis.

It's almost time for my bus. I grab a cola-style drink and a bar of chocolate with cartoon basketballs depicted on the wrapper and get on the coach, which dreamily is air-conditioned, lovely! I settle down for the ride, I like bus journeys in foreign countries, it gives you a chance to see a lot relatively quickly. The journey takes about four hours. Sitting alone on that bus gave me a chance to think about where I was and why I was there.

Tel Aviv, apart from the art deco sections, which are beautiful, and the beach, again Copacabana-esque in its loveliness, was a bit of a hole. Don't get me wrong, I saw less than five per cent of the place but none of it looked finished to me. Maybe it wasn't? Bomb damage? The Intifada? First Gulf War? I guess these things all take their toll on a place.

Once out of Tel Aviv things brightened up a bit. The weather was great, on my left I could see the bright blue Med and I was heading north fast. I like moving, north, south, whatever, just keep moving. Between Tel Aviv and Haifa is a dense corridor of industry, a busy, heavily populated strip of land sandwiched between the sea and the desert. That's Israel all over.

We stop in Haifa and I have to change buses. I'm stood loafing around eating another falafel, of course. I watch a car, can't quite remember which type, but if I had to hazard a guess I'd say a white Peugeot 306, it hammers into the station at pace and an elderly, kindly-looking Palestinian man jumps out and leaves the engine running. A small amount of hell breaks loose, a light panic rises among the folk, soldiers begin hesitantly to remove their battle rifles from their shoulders and start shouting things in Hebrew. People swarm away from the car, sirens begin. This is a fucking car bomb.

I'm about to be torn apart, first by the concussive blump of the pressure wave and then by razor-sharp sections of the white Peugeot 306. The panic begins to reach a crescendo and the kindly Palestinian man comes running back out of a shop holding an armful of bread. He is immediately surrounded by twenty IDF soldiers pointing Galil assault rifles at him. It is now the Palestinian man's turn to panic. Poor fucker. He only ran in to get some bread, he's now one bad decision, one quick movement away from being killed. He's roughly pulled from the car and led away. The mood immediately lifts as people laugh at the crushed loaves on the pavement. I'm stunned. I stagger onto my bus and leave, heading north towards the mountains.

My bus stops, it'd been nice and quiet before now. The doors hiss open and the bus fills with essentially thirty or so catwalk models. Sexy sexy sexy women in army uniforms carrying a selection of sexy assault rifles. I was frightened and nervous and terribly horny. The hot girl warrior that sits next to me senses my horniness, she doesn't return my desperate attempt at a smile, she moves her Galil assault rifle around so it's now sitting between us. Bit rude.

The warm weather and the gentle bumping of the bus sends her to sleep pretty quickly. As we bump along the muzzle of her rifle comes to rest on my thigh (as a rule heavy assault rifles don't really come to rest, they dig in and this one was really digging in).

I'd never seen a gun until two days ago and now there are probably sixty on this bus alone, one of which is leaving a red circle on my chubby white thigh. I decide to push it off a bit. As soon as my paw brushes the unrelenting iron of her Jewish killbroom her eyes spring open and her finger skips off the trigger guard and onto the trigger. How did she know?

'The, the, your, um, your gun is digging into my leg, miss.'

She huffs loudly, she's starting to fall for me, I can tell. The rifle's pulled and repositioned away from me. Please don't go off. I fidget nervously. I press my head against the vibrating window and doze off.

When I wake up the bus is quiet and almost empty. The war models got off at a kibbutz called Sasa. I wish I could go there. The next stop is me.

I'm always a bit sad arriving somewhere after a long journey when it's dark. I want to see what a place looks like. That said, I like the surprise of seeing it the next morning but I guess I'm impatient like that. Night is falling rapidly and the bus belches me out. The doors hiss and it rumbles away leaving me stood on my own, surrounded by sticky warmth and a cacophony of the loudest night sounds imaginable. It's the first time I've ever heard cicadas and it's fucking loud and beautiful.

In the failing light I shuffle downhill towards a brightly lit guard hut. Seeing me, the soldiers inside trudge out, rifles slung low, they clearly don't see me as much of a threat. What they're guarding is a massive gate, thick steel, bright yellow. Fences run off left and right to who knows where. The ten-foot-high perimeter is topped in acres of razor wire. It looks like a category A prison, a place where only the hardest fuckheads need apply, but it wasn't that, it was simply a farm.

When I see the rifles I slow, then stop, there's a slight standoff while I'm worked out. After speaking Hebrew to one another they wave me forward. More Hebrew is spoken. I show them my passport and the letter from Project 67. There's head nodding. This is good. The soldier inside does something to a lever or a button and an orange light starts spinning on the gate. The giant portal slowly pulls back. I wonder briefly if they have a T-Rex. I'd like to say I remember a giant siren making an ERR URR-ERR URR noise as the gate withdraws but that would be false.

I'm given directions to a work office, a small room under the dining hall in the main building of the kibbutz. Even in the tightening twilight I could see the place was covered in trees. It was dark and warm, the whole place smells like pine and forests. I'm not in Kansas anymore.

The release and relief from my responsibilities mean the tiredness has caught up with me. The bright lights hurt my eyes, and people stare. I was lost and new and gleaming white and everyone could see it. I was relieved to be there, proud at what I'd done but feeling very alone. A sudden dawning of what I'd done shuddered over me.

I knock on the door. Someone shouts something from inside and I enter. A woman who looks like Nana Mouskouri sits behind a table that's stacked high with paper. She stares at me through her thick, black-framed glasses. She is the embodiment of the seventies. It was 1991.

'*Ken!*' (Hebrew for yes.) I shuffle in, my rucksack banging the frame of the wooden door. She smokes and tuts and refuses to look at me. She gestures at a chair. I struggle to sit. I give her my letter. She reads it and finally she regards me. Softening slightly.

This is Vicki. Over the next couple of months I get to know her and really like her. She was a hard woman, blunt, direct, no fucking around. She wasn't everyone's cup of tea and didn't suffer fools gladly but I was always really cheeky and she liked it.

Vicki was the leader of the volunteers, our mother away from home. She drew up the work schedules, gave us what we needed, at times told us off. She was an avid smoker. She also had a little dog that followed her everywhere, a mean and nasty little dick. I'm getting ahead of myself but the little dog was later badly injured after being hit by a car. I think it must've severed his spine, he followed Vicki down to her office one Tuesday as normal but the little thing was dragging his back legs behind it. Limp, dead. It didn't seem to dampen his spirits anyway. He was still a mean son of a bitch. I asked Vicki what was going to happen to him. 'I have to put him down.' I laughed, disbelieving her. She didn't laugh. She meant it. Two hours later there's the noise of a single shot from a high-powered 9mm handgun. We never see him again.

This was a way down the line though. For now she looked at me like a sweaty human shit sitting behind her desk, which is exactly what I was.

Kibbutzniks have a wariness of volunteers, the travellers so necessary to them at the busy harvest time but generally overlooked as just a bunch of sex-crazed alcoholics who needed to be avoided at all costs. In hindsight they were actually spot on. It takes a lot of hard work and time to gain the trust of the Israelis.

The details of what happened after this point are a little hazy. I have a memory of other Israelis getting involved and me being led up to the dining room. It was massive, more than capable of fitting all six hundred residents in comfortably, which it did every Friday during Shabbat meal and various high days and holidays.

I sit alone watching other people eat supper, I enjoy the pleasant murmur of a conversation I can't understand. Vicki returns with a housing list and I'm assigned a bed in a four-man room, she offers me dinner, and I accept. I wish I hadn't the moment I see the horrors on offer. I have never seen so much veg and salad and unknown grains and pulses in my life. I never realised that food came in so many colours. For me food had always been brown and beige and a crossover between brown and beige, a colour I'd come to know as Broige. Also some yellow. The bread was nice though and the butter was diamond white in colour, I should say that ice-white butter takes some getting used to for an English like me, for the first few weeks it feels like I'm eating dripping.

I eat, I try and eat, I pack up my tray and then I'm led down to where I'd be living. It was a nice gentle stroll down-hill to the two, two-storey blocks that housed the animals, us. They were squat white-ish buildings with an area of tattered lawn in the middle. People sit around swigging from bottles, laughing, a fire blazes. I see a young man with a guitar and I panic slightly, fuck it. I steady my ship. A new start means it was a time to accept new things, new people. Just let it go, Nick, please, please just let it go, it's just a guitar for fucksakes.

I'm introduced to people. New people. Something I'm not really very good at.

'Hello,' someone says.

'Also hello.' It's standard basic human interaction. I'm terri-ble at it and it frightens me. I smile a bit, I seem like an oaf, I'm embarrassed and shy.

'Where you from?'

'London.'

'Cool. See you later.'

'Okay. Goodbye.'

The blocks are tatty, paint peels and there's broken glass on the floor, a million fag butts, a dented kettle lies dying in one of the hallways. There's very loud music, chatting, laughter. I buzz a bit, the first inkling that I could grow to love it here.

My new room's upstairs, first on the left. The door's blue and covered in stickers, they do a bad job of hiding the odd boot and fist hole. There are three other boys in that room and by god I can't for the life of me remember who they were. Please forgive me. In that tiny room were four beds, four tiny metal-framed beds with pancake-thin mattresses. The bed in the bottom left of the room is free. I unroll my new sleeping bag and stick it on the bed.

I get shown around, the shower room has many cracked tiles. The toilets are thick with limescale, like a Mother Shipton's cave of chuds if you will. The place is dirty, cobwebs everywhere, vast cathedrals for our arachnid overlords. Other rooms are visited, cheery 'Hellos' are waved. People come and look. It was always a thing when someone new turned up. I was led to the common room. Wow, what chaos. What a shit box. I love it. It was two rooms knocked into one; the walls were covered in graffiti, there was a kettle, a toaster and a big old TV bolted into a large wooden box on the wall.

About thirty people were lying on the floor on cushions watching MTV and drinking heavily. Some girls made toast and passed it around the room. I did a lot of awkward, what I like to call Edgar Wright-style waves. It's basically mouthing the word 'Haloo' silently and waving at the same time.

The deal on the kibbutz is this: you're there to work! That's it. You work for six days a week, six or seven hours a day, and in return they feed you, clothe you, give you alcohol and cigarettes and anything else you need/want, you even get paid a little bit, almost £30 a month! Sweet. They didn't necessarily care what you did, except fighting and drugs – fighting and drugs were out. Anything else as long as you worked hard seemed to be fair game.

In the summer you started early to avoid the crushing heat of the day. It meant you finished early too. Your working day was 6 a.m. until 12.30 p.m. and then the rest of the day was your own. Simples.

In the winter it was cold and dark in the morning so you'd start a bit later which meant you'd finish later. Some jobs, like picking cotton or working in the vast fishponds, were about an hour's drive away in the superheated Bekaa Valley. You'd start at 4 a.m. and be finished by 11.00 a.m. Lovely.

That first morning though my little travel alarm goes off and I groggily get up and follow the others. My first ever job was to work in the apple-packing factory. If kibbutz jobs were the army, apple packing was definitely the infantry. A boring, easy, tedious, meat and potatoes kibbutz job.

The factory was pretty big, exciting, it was the first factory I'd ever been in. The main section was a cavernous warehouse with a brick room on one side and offices up to the left, in the centre was a giant machine. The apple packer. I was instructed to sit at a low stool on one side of a long conveyer belt. Above was a machine that channelled empty apple boxes down to us ready to be filled. We all sit waiting.

A round and chunky Israeli man with tight permed hair bustles to the front of the conveyor and utters the words I will hear many times, 'Guyth come to thee pleath.' This is Eli Azer and he has a lithp. He's one of the good guys, quick to laugh, and heavy handed with the volunteers he liked. I was to receive over six hundred dead arms from him in the next few months.

Later I'd do impressions of Eli Azer to make the other volunteers laugh. Boom! Dead arm! When the phone rang in the office a loud bell would ring across the whole factory, it was always for Eli Azer. A voice on an intercom would cut the radio and the factory-wide PA squeaked to life, 'Eli Azer, Eli Azer, *telefon mer ve shtayim*.' Essentially it means 'Eli Azer, telephone line 102.'

I discovered I could do a pretty good impression of the voice from the office, so sometimes I'd sneak off the work line, use the phone as an intercom and say the words, which would then blare out across the factory. We would laugh so hard watching Eli Azer trot to the phone to find no one there. Eventually they caught on and I was rumbled. Even Eli Azer found it funny in a kind of 'now you're going to get a really fucking dead arm' kind of way.

That was to come. For now he kept his distance from me. I was an unknown. He, like all the Israelis, had to ascertain what my work ethic was. Am I there to work or am I just going to drink and fuck about? I guess it's also some kind of defence mechanism; being raised and living on a kibbutz means that people leave, volunteers by their very definition are bound to be transient. Don't get close to us. You'll be hurt when we go.

We gather round and watch Eli Azer pull apples from a hopper; he packs them with a speed I never could've imagined from sausage fingers like his. What a talent. There I was thinking you'd just stick them in a punnet. Each different size and type of apple had a different technique. A technique designed to fit exactly the right amount into each punnet. Clever. Easy. Boring.

After the lesson a buzzer sounds and the machine creaks into life. The apples tumble down onto the conveyor, you pack them, face them up real pretty then you do it again and again and again. Once you'd done two boxes, you'd drop your little packing plinth down and roll them onto another conveyor that led to a workstation we called Wrapping and Stacking. This was where the cool kids in the factory worked. Jobs on the kibbutz were very hierarchical. The longer you'd been there, the harder you worked, the better job you got.

Later in my kibbutz experience I myself would become a Wrapper and a Stacker. I'd intercept the apples as they thundered down the roller thing and sling the boxes, with great accuracy and just the right amount of power, onto a pallet until they were seven or so feet high. Four cardboard corners would be secured around the stack and then you'd use a really annoying ratchet machine to bind the whole wobbly lot together. It was a good fucking job. If you worked strong and fast you could move thirty tons of apples a day. It was a point of pride to see how many tons you could shift. After doing this job for a couple of weeks you got giant, well-defined forearms and shoulders. Furious wanking also helped.

Whatever jobs you did – except if you worked down in the fields – you'd work for a couple of hours before breakfast, and it took some getting used to. When I wake up I usually need to eat immediately. A hooter would sound and we'd hammer up the hill towards the dining room to feed. Breakfast was rushed and primal; as a volunteer I was hungry most of the time. We'd spend a lot of time talking about the food we missed and what we'd love to eat right now – weirdly it was usually roast dinners or McDonalds with the odd Full English thrown in for good measure.

I was a fussy little sod back then when it came to food. Crisps aside, I essentially didn't eat any vegetables. It was like this until I was thirty or so when my taste buds changed and I couldn't get enough of the things. At this point though I'm a strict carnivore, crisps aside, so being in Israel surrounded by nothing but crisp, fresh salads was an absolute fucking nightmare. I eventually found things that worked for me and stuck to them.

Breakfast was all about the eggs on toast, soft boiled eggs, mashed up in a bowl with mayo and plenty of black pepper. The problem with breakfast eggs on kibbutz though is they never seemed to be fully cooked. I love yolk and I think yolk with cracked, black pepper to be one of the greatest flavour combinations known to man, but I hate food which is gluey or snot-like or shrouded in jelly. I was in Japan once with the lovely Joe Cornish and had to eat a lot of McDonalds as everything came shrouded in gluey phlegm. (A slight over-exaggeration but you know what I mean.)

Sometimes at breakfast I'd open nine eggs just to find one usable egg. Let me tell you a 9:1 usable egg ratio is a really poor egg ratio. All those wasted embryos! The food was generally bad, not bad per se but bad for me. That said, the longer you were there the more scams and angles you could find.

If you knew where to look in the kitchen, what pots or pans to peer into, you could find the delicately poached chicken breasts they cooked specifically for the elderly Holocaust survivors. This insensitive scam, though delicious and meaty, was essentially a bit naughty. It was fine when it was just me on the sniff but when the other meat-craving volunteers caught on the gig was up. We were warned off and rightly so. Imagine surviving the horrors of Auschwitz only to have some fucking Herbert half-inch the only food left you can stomach.

Still, you could supplement meagre rations a few ways, toast and ketchup being one of them. I still to this day love toast and ketchup. Another was to befriend the guards in the guard house. They always had tons of food. On a Friday night after the disco (more on the disco later) I discovered that the soldiers would cook chips. Wonderful handcut, proper chips. The Israelis would fry half an onion in the oil first before putting the potatoes in. It gave the chips a unique oniony flavour that was delicious and quite unforgettable.

If you were nice/pissed enough and hilarious they'd give you a big bowl of those lovely, oniony bastards. A few times they'd even drop me back to the block in their battle jeep afterwards. I'd usually try and ponce fags en route too. Naughty.

After breakfast we'd amble back and pack more apples until the coffee break at about ten-thirty. Coffee break was fun, we'd gather in the break room and the Israelis would bring out nice biscuits for dunking. It was a chance to chat about packing apples and have a laugh with our Hebrew overlords. After break I'd have another couple of easy hours' work and that was that, the work was done.

Essentially every day, every week, on the kibbutz was the same. It was like being in a prison for alkies. Any deviation was to be mistrusted and embraced. Apple packing was the first job most people did. Generally you did one job for weeks, if you showed a natural flair for one thing chances are your gang boss would want to keep you there.

Before apples could be packed they had to be picked and that meant working in the orchards which were lovely. This was one of the kibbutz's main jobs in the summer. They'd need all the volunteers they could get to bring in the harvest. I liked working in the orchard, it was hot, the sun was always shining and you could eat all the apples you wanted.

You also got these lovely buckets made of canvas that you'd strap on with a harness (I love a job with equipment). Once the basket was full you'd shout the Hebrew word for basket, '*SAL!*' Someone would turn up, take your basket, give you a new one and on you'd go. It was great, you'd chat, talk about food, who you fancied, who was fucking whom, music, family, anything, sometimes silence would reign and you'd enjoy that, it was sweet.

The volunteers, like me, were fuck-ups from all nations. Adventurers, drifters, gap-year kids or people just heading through. Swedes, Danes, South Africans, Kiwis, Australians and loads of Brits make for a heady mix of ideas, cultures and boozing styles. As a guy on kibbutz the holy grail was a new group of Swedish girls arriving. What a treat, so blonde and shiny, hair glinting like freshly cut gold.

Water and coffee were very important things in the orchards, if either was left back in kibbutz it'd cause a real stink. Someone would have to go back. We'd take our midmorning break sitting in the shade of the apple trees, they'd bring ice creams, what a wonderful treat. Sometimes while picking you'd hear a volunteer shriek loudly. It'd be one of two things, either chameleons, which took great pleasure in grabbing on to the hands that reached into leafy canopies looking for apples, or little furry grey tarantulas that would nestle under the stones and logs at the base of the tree. Terrifying. Sometimes if you were lucky you'd see volunteers stumbling backwards screaming with a chameleon attached to their arm. Big funs.

The kibbutz had acres of orchards; one of my favourites was right on the border with Lebanon; actually most of the kibbutz was on the border with Lebanon, but this orchard was *right* on the border. We'd heard a rumour that if you threw something at the security fence (a fence that runs the entire length of Northern Israel, Lebanon, Syria and Jordan) tanks would come! Working in the closest orchard our curiosity got the better of us. After much hysterical debate, one of us did it. A big apple was found and we – notice I'm saying we – flung the fucker over the kibbutz fence and into the security fence beyond. The first time we did it we absolutely shit ourselves panicking, we lay trembling under the trees, I needed the toilet so badly. After some silence and nothing happening, we first heard and then watched two tanks rumble up to where we'd tossed the apple. Holy Balls. This was the coolest thing ever. After the first time it got less stressful and slightly less fun but we endured. I thought it important for the defence of Israel that the tank crews be well drilled.

I've always thought that if I didn't do what I do now I'd want to work on the land or as a water sheriff. The kibbutz was generally perfect for this, plenty of chances to be outside.

So when I looked at my work rota for the week and saw I'd been assigned to work in their plastic factory it was a real blow. The only upside, it was air-conditioned. Lovely, lovely, cold, really expensive air. The plastic factory had two basic jobs you could do. One was done dressed in a white clean-room hygiene suit. You looked like the Oompa Loompas that send Mike TV across the studio in *Willy Chocolate and the Wonka Factory*.

It wasn't a fun job, the stuffy Israelis in that factory meant chatter was not encouraged and the day always seemed to go on and fucking on. The plastic factory, Elcam, made one thing and one thing only, the little plastic valves they'd put in your arm if you were unfortunate enough to ever need a drip. Essentially it's a small plastic chamber with a needle at one end and two wheels the other end so one could direct or restrict the flow of intravenous medicines. (Where did that come from?) And that was it. For six hours we'd turn a tiny valve onto a tiny screw. For six hours. Not much talking, just screwing. A few clever people brought Walkmans (if you're not sure what they are, Google it) but generally we'd work in silence, save for the odd inevitable giggle outbreak.

The other job in the plastic factory was worse, much worse. The shift would run from midnight until 6 a.m. and it was a job for just one person. Tonight it was just me. Me and my mind, which can be difficult at the best of times, to be honest. Joining me tonight is a giant machine that does something and the soothing *ping* of their onsite reactor. The reactor was used to irradiate and sterilise the product. The *ping* was an indication that everything was okay. Why the *ping* couldn't just happen when shit gets fucked up I'll never know. If I was lucky someone would let me use a cassette player so I could try and blank out the *pings* and *beeps* of the factory with a well-worn tape of house mixes.

Being in that place alone at night made me nervous, especially if the gap between the *pings* suddenly lengthened, even by a fraction of a second. My imagination being what it is, I'd often see myself in the centre of a Three Mile Island-style melt-down, immolated in an atomic power throb. STOP THINKING!!! Near enough every five minutes I'd spin around convinced there was someone sneaking up behind me. It's the same feeling I get snorkelling in the Med.

The job was this: you'd sit on a stool peering through the window of the giant machine, every two seconds the machine would hiss, a hydraulic head would spin round and you'd have to put a tiny, threaded, plastic head onto one of the valves. The machine would hiss again, take away your valve and replace it with a new one. That was it. That's what you did all night, for six hours.

I think I've always been able to shut parts of my brain down and thus nullify certain brands of monotony. Which was very useful for this type of work. On the right of the machine was a small white counter, it told you how many valves you'd done in a minute. It helped with my boredom. I spent hours trying to break my own record.

I must admit I've always kind of loved every job I've done no matter how shit it was. Whatever, I've always given it my all, a trait I inherited from watching my dad over the years. However, there were two exceptions to this:

1) Working in a warehouse that dealt with car parts. Hated it. Itchy shirt. Lasted two shifts.

2) Barman in Tony Roma's (St Martins Lane). Hated the manager and told him to fuck himself after four hours.

I've always felt life is too short to stay in shit jobs. Fortunately my dad was very supportive of this view. He'd say, 'There's always a job somewhere if you look hard enough.' I still believe that to be true.

The plastic factory has a small kitchen, little Plancha grill, hob, kettle, tea, coffee, milk etc. However, in the fridge was a veritable Aladdin's cave of delights. Cheese! Fucking cheese! Amazing. Some kind of ham, turkey, chicken, eggs and meat, delicious meat! Steak to be more accurate, beautiful thin minute steaks. Part of the deal of this shit shift was you could take, prepare and eat whatever you wanted. I'd usually make a big omelette with lots of cheese and ham, or I'd have a rare steak with a fried egg on top and mill of fresh black pepper.

Those breaks were actually pretty nice, sitting alone, silent, save for the comforting *ping* of the atomic reactor, enjoying a cheese-heavy omelette. After my shift ends and before leaving I grab a bag and stick some cheese and ham in it. I wrap it up and stuff it down the front of my boilersuit for later.

I'm not sure when it starts or how but I think I know why, the dangling twin carrots of boredom and hunger. I become a cat burglar. I never burgled houses for money or jewellery, no, the only thing I'd ever steal, the only thing I wanted at the time was food and my quarry was the fridge inside that plastic factory.

The old disco on the kibbutz was under the gymnasium and the walk home led me past Elcam. One night I am walking home pretty drunk when I see the factory looming up before me. An idea crackles into existence. I was fucking hungry after all that drinking. That was the thing about kibbutz, there was no food anywhere after hours unless you'd squirrelled shit away or bought Cup-a-Soups from the shop. Eating after disco usually meant all of us crammed into the common room eating round after round of cheap ketchup and toast.

But tonight would be different. In my state I decide to see if the door is locked. It isn't. The factory is silent, no night shift during the Sabbath! The door to the kitchen is also unlocked. The fridge is full and I begin my raid. I make lots of sandwiches; rifling through a drawer, I find a carrier bag and stuff it full of cheese and Jewish turkey-ham, there was so much they'd never notice. I make my exit and casually trudge back to the common room and plomp the sandwiches down onto the counter. It's gone in moments and there is much happiness and rejoicing! I feel like Robin Hood but with sandwiches.

Over the next weeks I raid the factory twice more in this manner, filling up with sandwiches and cold cuts. It was a dream, as a group we were in clover. We had all the sandwiches we'd ever need. One drunken night I set off on a raid. I try the door to find it locked. Locked? WTF? Questions reverb around my mind. Why, why was it locked, why now? I would not, could not, let this deter me. I had customers that were relying on me, that needed the good shit I could get.

I knew of another door in another part of the factory and thought I'd give it a go. Bingo. It was open. Suckers! I found a set of dark stairs that took me up to the plastic factory and completed my raid. Would this be my last? Were they catching on to me? Did they keep count? Take stock? No? They might? They might now? I should stop. I can't stop. I won't stop. I need it. I need cheese and curious white ham-style turkey meat. NEED IT. I need that buzz of burglary, and the curious white ham-style turkey meat. Nothing's gonna stop me. NOTHING! HAHAHAHAHAHAHAHAHAHAHAHAHAHHAAHHAH! Meat.

Next time I try the door, it's locked again, no fluke, those fuckers know. The downstairs door is still open though, what chumps. I sprint silently up the stairs taking two steps at a time, through the dark corridor to the break room. I turn the handle to the kitchen door. It's locked! This is a problem. I panic briefly then shut it down. Think. Turn back, end this now. I can't. At this point I question whether this is about the cold cuts or the thrill of the crime. Go home, you've had a good run. In the kitchen door near the bottom is a panel probably twenty-four inches square. In the panel are slats of frosted glass. I have an idea. I gently tug upwards at one of the slats, joy of joys, it gives, it simply slides out, I lay it gently on the floor and get to work on the others. That done, I crawl through the new hole, fill up with booty, re-slat the hole and I'm gone. Textbook meat theft.

This could be my life's greatest work. In fact, I'd say apart from my son and my accent in *Hot Fuzz* (which was flawless and for which I received no recognition), this series of robberies was the greatest thing I've ever done.

The last one I do ends in stalemate. I get to the door and the slats have been removed, replaced by a square of plywood nailed over the hole. Who was the genius that'd bested me? I considered mule kicking the plywood away and doing a crude snatch and grab. I didn't, I couldn't, it wasn't my way, and it wasn't elegant or clever enough, not for me. I learnt a valuable lesson that day about the business of cold-cut theft: know when to walk away. This was my time. My career as a thief of cold meats and cheeses was over. The Case of the White Ham was closed. Or so I thought . . .

The next day there's a message on the notice board. An unscheduled volunteer meeting had been called that afternoon, after work. Balls. My creeping fear is confirmed. It is a meeting about the theft of food from the plastic factory. They didn't know who had done it but whoever it was should stop immediately. I'm sure Vicki's gaze lingered over me for a second. Paranoia. It was over. For days after, lots of us suffer comedowns, cold turkey, cold ham, cold cheese. It was okay. We were okay. For a time, I'd been someone, I'd been a champion of the people, a hero to some, villain to others. Now? Well now I was just like every other civilian craving a sandwich. I still have the memory though, the memory of those heists, and it still tastes so fucking sweet.

After assignments like apple picking, apple packing and plastics came the more specialised jobs, jobs you got if either the Israelis liked you or you'd been in the country a while. Working in the fishponds and in the cotton fields were both great jobs. Each offered a great deal of kudos. I should probably offer up a note on kibbutz fashion here. There wasn't any and therein lay the fashion. Newbies wore their own clothes to work, jeans, shorts, Ts, tops, dresses, and skirts, whatever. Oh,

I have a theory on why English holidaymakers always stand out so much while abroad. We always buy brand-new clothes! We look ridiculous. Anyway, on kibbutz everyone gets issued with work boots so usually they got worn; however, trainers were also acceptable.

The longer you were on kibbutz, the more you wanted to look like an Israeli; this transformation happened pretty quickly for me, I bought in. I loved it from the off. There was a big box with old secondhand work clothes in Vicki's office that we were allowed to rummage around in. I found some absolute gems. Ideally you'd want to wear a T-shirt with Hebrew writing on it, something from a factory, something denoting heavy industry, a happy apple in a hat, perhaps a giant tractor tyre smiling? This would be combined with blue canvas work pants tucked into work boots (military style) and a blue canvas work jacket. I looked like a poster boy for Chairman Mao's dig for victory campaign. The clothes always had to be worn with a healthy covering of earth or dust. Instead of wearing a belt, I had an old shoelace that I'd cleverly knotted between two belt loops. I've never looked cooler or felt more comfortable. I'm not a fashionable person so to live somewhere where everyone essentially dresses the same was absolute bliss to me.

Looking like a farmer also set you apart from the newer volunteers. It was a badge of honour. The only time you changed out of this garb was during disco night when everyone would get dolled up. Which in itself was also kind of fun.

Although my hair was long and parted in the middle I made the decision one day to shave it all off. Bald. Number zero. It was a decision I quickly regretted. After being 'in-country' for months I'd got a lovely tan everywhere except for under my raver's bob. For weeks I had to suffer the embarrassment of walking around looking like I was wearing a grey swimming cap.

Working in the cotton fields was some of the hardest physical work I've ever done. Cotton was an hour's drive north-east. I loved that drive. Because of the travelling time (which was included in our workday, bonus!) we had to leave really early (4 a.m.). The cotton fields were down in the Bekaa Valley so it was much hotter than our mountaintop kibbutz. We'd usually finish by 11 a.m. and at that point the temperature was already into the low hundreds.

The drive from the kibbutz was beautiful. We hugged the Lebanese border until we were south of Kiryat Shmona (the Town of the Eight). There was a great bar there called Bar Hash. Buses from all the kibbutzim across the north would bring volunteers to party. The place was pretty spectacular. It seemed to be a vast amphitheatre, an open-air stadium for lunacy. Through the middle of the place ran a small river. The DJ booth was a VW Beetle covered in thousands of tiny mirrors. It was very, very cool.

Once I ordered chips at the bar and when they came I ripped open packets of salt and sprinkled them on top. The Israeli bartender looked at me weird.

'What?' I asked.

'Why are you putting sugar on top of the chips?'

Balls, it was sugar. Front it out. I leaned in and shouted over the music.

'It's what we do in England.' I winked and headed off to throw my sugarfries into a bin.

During the drive down to the fields most people would catch up on their sleep. I tried not to, I preferred to sit in silence and watch the stunning sunrises. Those dark blues and vivid oranges as the sun shimmered through the atmosphere over Syria were the nicest sunrises I think I've ever seen.

I spent two weeks working in cotton and I only did one job. Sadly that wasn't picking the cotton itself, wrong season. What I did was less fancy and a lot more gruelling. There were five of us and for six hours a day we walked behind a tractor pulling giant rocks out of the sun-baked earth and tossing them into a trailer. I loved that job. It was a big fucking field, by my reckoning I'd say a kilometre wide by three of four kilometres long, it really was the hardest work. I love any job where, when I finish, I'm shattered and gasping for a cold one. This job, like many on the kibbutz, guaranteed both. We had such a laugh, I felt like a prisoner on a chain gang plus you finished work at eleven o'clock! Brilliant. I'd heard by all accounts that harvesting was pretty nice too, they let trusted volunteers drive big fucking tractors. Foolish.

Fish was also totes sweet. A similar gig to cotton in terms of time, workday and location, fish was also kudos-heavy! It was a chance to hang with the Israelis, smoke dangerously strong cigarettes and drink thicker and blacker than thick, black coffee.

The kibbutz had several giant fishponds, each housed fish at different phases of their development. Once the inhabitants of a pond had reached maturity, they lifted up giant nets from the base of the lake and funnelled the delicious carp into a corner, up a conveyor and into the back of large water-filled trucks. My job was to stand in neck-deep water hauling the net in and helping the fish up the chute.

When the temperature is over 100 degrees, the best place to be is in neck-deep cold water, it was heaven. If there was a downside it would be the stink of fish, which was difficult to remove. You'd also find large, shield-like scales in the weirdest of places. Every now and again big, heavy carp would try and escape. These rogues, some weighing almost 30lb travelling upwards of 20 knots, smashing you in the chops can be really painful. The final downside and the worst one for me was their screaming. I can still hear it sometimes at night. Apart from that, it was ace.

There were three other jobs I did, two were amazing and very cool, very kudos-heavy. One was absolutely awful, where to start? Good first. The kibbutz had a small museum and art gallery. I thought at the time (and probably still do secretly) that I wanted to be a painter, an artist like my dad, he was such a talented watercolourist. I painted some childish pictures and became friendly with the tiny old man who curated the collection; they were shit paintings but he seemed to like them, seemed to like the fact I showed some interest in art. He supplied me with paper and acrylics and one day offered me a job. Sweet! No more hard labour for me, no more intense heat or 6 a.m. starts. Instead I was to be surrounded by cool cool culture. Jubbly.

I was essentially an odd-job man, which was great and I was eager to learn. Back then I was much better with my hands than I am now. I'm terrible now, I think I just can't be arsed.

My job was varied, anything from digging holes to fixing toilets, sometimes I'd help collate the collection, sometimes I'd whitewash wooden cubes ready to display the museum's many sculptures. If I was a good boy I'd get to help hang the new exhibitions. Sometimes Old Tiny – I call him this as he was old and very tiny, a bit like a Jewish Yoda – would bring in cookies and cakes for us to have with our coffee at break time. It was very nice. Nice work in a beautiful building in the middle of a forest.

Often, and this was my favourite part, Old Tiny would go out and leave me to my own devices. There was a little radio that wafted out classical music, the only music allowed to be played in the museum. I'd sneak into the storeroom and look through the hundreds of canvases they had there. I loved it so much. Sometimes I'd play a game where, turning up the radio, I stalked the silent, empty galleries holding a large claw hammer pretending I was Patrick Bateman. HELP ME.

My other favourite job was with Michel. Michel was the most laidback man I'd ever known. Sometimes speaking seemed like too much of a bother – instead he'd gesture and make noises. His eyes were mega droopy and he had a massive red Afro of loose bouncy curls, he also loved reggae. It's amazing now looking back that I never imagined he was a pothead. How did I not see it?

He was the kibbutz plumber and heating engineer. I was essentially his plumber's mate. We had a tiny van and we'd bomb about fixing radiators. It was sweet, after the summer and before autumn we overhauled the boilers ready for the winter. Any job where I get to use Swarfega at the end of a shift is all right with me. Eventually I'm trusted enough to drive the van and have my own tools.

I dressed like an Israeli. I spoke some Hebrew; I had my own van with tools. Finally my transformation was complete. I felt like I belonged. I was an Israeli heating engineer and plumber, I was happy. Home seemed like a million miles away.

The Girls' toilet and shower had a savage blockage at one point during a hot day at the end of the summer. The place had become like a Woodstock for bluebottles. I was tasked with crawling under the building, which frightened me anyway (the thought of snakes and big fucking spiders a constant fear in my mind, even now), finding the main sewage pipe, opening it and clearing the blockage. It really couldn't be easier.

I find the pipe in the intense heat and fiddle to get the elbow free, it pops off and I shine a torch inside. I see nothing. Michel finds a coat hanger, unfolds it and hands it to me. Suspicious. I stick the bent wire inside the pipe and I ram hard. There's a hiss, a rush of dead air grabs hold of my features like a Face-Hugger, a gurgle, the sound of a thick liquid now moving freely and in a moment I'm covered in a foul broth of shits, pisses, condoms and almost a thousand used tampons. Holy. Fucking. Christ. I lie there for about thirty seconds while this fluid glues itself to me. After a while it stops, I casually screw the elbow cap back on and shuffle out. Michel laughs at me. Hilarious. I'm hosed down while people point and laugh.

This was nothing compared to the hen house. Chickens was the worst job in my life. It was terrible. They knew no one wanted to work there so they'd wait outside the disco at 3 a.m. and snatch people as they came out. It's what the old navy would call a pressgang. We'd become crazed, senseless ship rats, leaping this way and that, over hedges, under vans, anything to avoid working with the chickens.

There were four houses, two hundred metres or so in length. Each housed chickens at different stages of development. The birds went from little chicks to fully grown hens in three short months. I'm no bird farmer but this seemed very quick to me. They weren't battery hens in the truest sense I guess – they weren't caged – but there were almost twenty thousand birds crammed inside.

We wore white coats, and white dust masks that would usually be soaked in cheap cologne. I was told the reason for the 3 a.m. start was so all the chickens would be asleep. It felt like clearing a ghetto, the irony was not lost.

We'd sneak into the hen house, the smelliest, hottest place in the world, to be confronted by a sea of white feathers. Thousands of hens sat in their own acrid shit fast asleep. The large double doors to the mega-coop would open. The lights would be put on but dimmed so as not to rouse suspicion among the hens. A low caging vehicle would then be driven into the house and it'd be game on.

We were usually pretty hammered coming straight from the disco, you had to be, and sometimes a collective insanity erupted. The noise of the machine and eight of us a-hootin' and a-hollerin' meant the chickens began to wake, but not all at once; the nearer you got, the more of them would rouse.

I used a technique that's known in the trade as the four-bird lift. If you had to breathe it was in deep hard gasps through the mouth. No matter how drunk you were the smell of all those hens crammed into a shit-filled shed in ninety-degree heat was too much to bear. I'd run in and grab the birds by the legs, four in each hand, they'd then be transported to the vehicle and stuck into a metal crate. Grim.

We mostly encountered little or no resistance. Mostly. Some of the bigger, bolder roosters would rally and slash at us with their razor-sharp talons. The defence of their hens, though noble, was ultimately futile.

Small running battles would break out all across the front which had formed across the width of the hen house. Every now and then you'd hear the word 'cunt' shrieked out as an angry cock slashed at our soft white hands with his ankle daggers. It would be a point of honour to pursue the male who had cut us and dispatch him into the vehicle.

Within four hours it would be over. The house would be clear. Sun rising, we'd stand, breathing heavily like Gomer Pyle, vodka wearing off, ashamed, confused, some considering veganism. The Israelis kindly let us keep all the dead and dying birds we found, they allowed us to eat them. Not raw – we'd BBQ them and serve it with a kind of simple chimichurri sauce we'd invented, we weren't barbarians.

All this work and high jinks soon led up to my first Christmas in Israel. It was actually really nice. We'd become a little family at this point. A rag tag bag of emotional refugees, fleeing who knows what. These were my friends and through my own choice the only family I had or wanted.

Arrangements were made for a proper Christmas dinner and a carol concert, not usually my kind of thing but fukkit, vodka. The Israelis screened films for us all day, they asked us what we'd like to see and the answer was simple. Bond, James Bond.

We all got up early and exchanged gifts. (Vodka.) Then, still in our jimmy jams, we made our way to the common room where we snuggled in to watch a Bond triple-bill. I loved this time in Israel, where you'd all just hop into bed and have a cuddle. It was fairly innocent in a kind of 'tops and fingers' sort of way.

The English girls spend half the day preparing a fantastic Christmas lunch. We have a tree and some decorations and the Christmas dinner itself is absolutely delicious.

Eventually I have to speak to Mum and Dad. It's Christmas. I can't remember the conversation but I remember crying a lot. Our lovely Welsh den mother Mary came and cuddled me. Lots of people came and cuddled me. Sorted me right out. It felt amazing. I'm not sure I'd ever felt so loved. (Not true but I know what I mean.) I think I was crying because I finally felt like there was enough distance between me now and me back there to afford myself a moment of Yuletide acceptance. I came out of my foxhole, Mum came out of hers and, with Dad refereeing, we played football in no-man's-land.

* * *

A little while after Christmas the weather turned bad. Until that point it'd been hot. Not chilly, not wet, not cloudy but hot. Then it started to rain. A lot. Which was nice, torrential and cooling, and it meant no flies, which was also nice. The flies were terrible. At times we were forced to shit in an old paint tin and cover it in syrup. It would then be left some way from the house so the flies would feast on that instead of the liquid in our eyeballs. It's an old Berber trick apparently.

The downside of the cooling rain was the hordes of giant black spiders it would drive into our living quarters. I remember watching ten stout men do battle with one of them in a shower block one night. It was horrible and it was weird. I watched the beast bristle and shimmer forward, the shirtless men panic and run here and there. To and fro the battle went. Why? It was a thing so heavy it made a *pudpud* sound when it walked. Eventually it fell. No one ever mentioned it again.

By mid January the rain stopped, and it started to snow. I never imagined, stupid young man, that it would snow here in Northern Israel but it did. It snowed loads and that meant one thing for hungry volunteers. Chips! Lovely, lovely chips. When it snowed on kibbutz they served chips. What an amazing rule. Chips, proper, handcut potatoes, deep fried in sun-hot golden oil. It was a very special thing. I still didn't have a great relationship with the food on kibbutz. Too many vegetables. I know chips is a vegetable but it was deep fried so fuck it.

At times – and when I say at times I mean most of the time – there was a shared lunacy among us, among the volunteers. Our life was so monotonous you'd be forced to focus on and cling to the smallest things.

Apart from six hours of hard labour a day you had the other eighteen to do what you wanted. Usually those precious hours of R and R revolved around drinking, heavy bastard drinking. I had left my junior drug fetish behind and had effortlessly slipped into the guise of a semi-professional alkie. Mum would be so proud.

At one point during chip season and the spider battles the DVF was formed. The Drunk Volunteer Force was an unofficial paramilitary (paralytic military) arm of the Israeli Defence Force. It meant that we drank a lot but unlike the other drinking that went on this was officially endorsed by us. Lovely.

The drinking club invented some fun called 'the Shotgun Challenge'. You take a can of beer, cut a small hole in the bottom of it, hold it to your lips, pull the tab and suck down the turbo-charged brew. Easy. It starts off as a bit of fun, something to do. But with the official formation of the DVF shit became real, we sat and wrote rules, we knocked it into shape.

An official table was constructed, essentially a cardboard league ladder where competition drinkers could be moved up and down according to official timings as the season progressed. I'll try and explain the rules as I remember them.

A shotgun was only official if it was witnessed by three or more members of the DVF. It could only be counted official if it was timed using the official DVF Alcometer, essentially my watch, a simple Casio. Once the hole was cut into the can it had to be scrutinised by two DVF officials. The size of the hole was important. There's a set of stringent measurements. The hole could be as small as you wanted but it couldn't be bigger than the rigid specs laid out in the DVF bible.

The officials, once satisfied that the regulations had been adhered to, gave the nod and the drinking could begin. Almost. The competitor would raise the beer gently to his or her mouth, being careful not to overflow the shotgun can's newly jagged aperture. As the official timer I would say the words that every official shotgunner heard.

'In your own time, when I hear the click.'

I'd stand, fingers ready on the buttons of the Alcometer, a collective hush hangs, all betting stops, a small cancer-ridden Vietnamese man screams 'Diddi Mao!' And this thing is fucking on. Once I hear the first hiss rush out of the can I'd press start.

An eruption of sound and immense noise, pushing, screaming, weeping, two or three other emotions. Generally the best technique and one that, like the Fosbury flop in high-jump, completely revolutionised the sport, was the 'Suck and Squeeze'. As the name suggests you'd open your throat – not everyone can do this – and suck the turbo-charged beer down while squeezing the golden piss out of the can.

The shotgun challenge was quick, fast and explosive. At the time there wasn't another spectator sport in the world as fast-paced and exciting as the Shotgun Challenge. We were it. The only game in town. Once the competitor was finished the can would leave his or her lips and the Alcometer was stopped. The can was immediately handed to me; failure to do this would result in instant disqualification. I'd then place the empty can on an officially endorsed flat surface, a step or something, and the precise measuring could begin. The can is swarmed by DVF officials scrutinising the vessel.

If any liquid could be spilled out of the can, even as a thin vapour, it was immediately classed null and void. If nothing dribbled out of the can it was a good shotgun and all eyes moved over to the official timer, moi. The time would be read out, cheers or commiseration would then follow. Your tab would be moved up or down the league table dependent on your time. What mindless larks. Everyone loved it.

Being a face around there and a world-class drinker I was close to the top of the table. It was a long hard season and your surge for glory had to be timed just right. I was competing against some real fucking animals, big strong boys all vying for the crown. Top of the league was a powerful Dane called Hans Jacob Jespersen. He tweeted me a few years back. He was doing great, a big shot in the Danish army. Towards the end of our time together he admitted that he dreamt only in English, which I found amazing as I dreamt entirely in Danish. I once asked Jacob what was the worst swear word in Danish he could think of. He pondered and told me he'd have to think about it.

Later that evening there was a soft knock on my door. It was Jacob.

'I've been thinking about what you said.'

'About what?' I'd forgotten.

'About the swearing thing.'

'Oh, go on then.'

He stumbled slightly, ashamed that he now had these awful sounds inside himself.

'I don't really . . .' He trailed off.

'Come on, cunt, out with it.'

'Okay, the worst insult I can think of in Danish is this . . .' Even I had reached a point where I wasn't sure if I wanted or needed to hear these mystical killing words. I tremble.

'Look, if you don't want to it's fine . . .'

'No, I need to.' After a moment he swallows and says it. The most insulting thing he could think of in Danish was . . .

'Long-haired communist fag,' he blurted.

I lay in bed, stunned.

'What did you fucking say?'

'I won't repeat it.' He nods shyly and leaves, shutting my door quietly behind him. I can hear him on the other side, breathing. After a moment he pads off and that was that.

Swearing aside he's a giant of a man and a damn fine shot-gunner. I liked him very much.

The last day of the championship was upon us; a long hazy season had almost drawn to a close, Jacob sat on top of the table. The final shotgun of the season was mine. And it was massive. All or nothing, death or glory. Something or another something. The lights go green; I hear the words, 'In your own time, when I hear the click.'

BOOM!

I power that motherfucker down. I care about nothing and no one at that moment. I'm deaf and I'm blind, sucking down that cold can of Maccabee like nothing else mattered.

My lips undocked from the can, I reeled backwards, eyes wide, grunting and held the can aloft, an official taking it off me. By the ripple of cheers erupting from the crowd I knew it was good, it felt good, it felt really good. People crowded the timer, confusion reigned. The can was offi-cially stepped and to my absolute horror a tiny bubble of lagery foam bleeds from the hole. NOOOOO!!! The championship had gone. I knew then that it was gone. What was the time?

1.92 seconds. A new world record. A clear second faster than Jacob, but it didn't count. I didn't count. It was the shotgun heard around the world. My career as a shotgunner was over. It hit me hard.

Things in the DVF become darker. I'm becoming a kind of Colonel Kurtz-style character. I spend a lot of time wearing a multi-coloured towelling robe, sleeveless for comfort and convenience. I've also taken to carrying around a metallic blue kettle I call the 'Kettle of Doom'. Where it came from I shall not say. The kettle was our holy grail; our piece of the true cross, our Alma Mater, and wherever it went, alcoholic mayhem ensued. Inside the kettle was a vodka-laced punch and about a pound of rotting fruit, slowly fermenting. My own micro still. I never took the fruit out, and I never washed the thing once.

At volunteer parties the drink of choice was a terrible fruit punch. Fuck loads of it. We'd borrow a massive pot from the kitchen, fill it with bottles of weak squash, fruit would then be added and then the booze, vodka, shitty shitty vodka. It was our drink, it was cheap and plentiful. For special occasions and shots we'd have lemon vodka but there was another kind. Another altogether darker kind. The fathers of the DVF – me, Kiwi Shaun, Little Pete and Dave – one day stumbled upon a new pain. A pain so powerful it had to be purchased in a hardware store. It had a plain white label and always reminded me of the bottle of booze Belloq gives Marion in *Raiders*. On the plain white label written in Hebrew and English the legend said simply, *Alcohol*. That shit was 95% alcohol, not proof, alcohol. Bear in mind whisky and vodka are usually 40%. Now with hindsight being 20/20 I can only assume what we were drinking was turps or paint thinner. Agreed it seems like total lunacy but it really wasn't that bad when you mixed it with Coke or Sprite.

Do you know that feeling when you spill white spirit onto your hands when you're cleaning a paintbrush? It doesn't trickle off, it just kind of goes in. That's exactly what happened when you drank it. It's making me heave slightly to remember this. I never swallowed a mouthful of that shit, it just kind of went in. A triumph? A disaster? Heave.

If there was a party people would draw lots to see who'd go on the booze run. Usually it needed three of us, not always the same three, but three was the minimum number needed to carry all that booze back. Those going would have to ask permission to leave work five minutes early in order to catch the bus to the nearest town, Safed, the jewel in the crown of the Galilee region.

With the hour there and the hour back it gave you about two and a half hours to get what was needed before the last bus returned. It wasn't just booze, we'd have a long list of things people wanted, needed: good shampoo, chocolate, nail clippers, nail varnish, Pot Noodles, tights etc.

It was always a special treat to leave the kibbutz. Safed was pretty in a bullet-ridden kind of way, built up into the hills overlooking the Sea of Galilee. It's mentioned in the Bible apparently too, if you're into that kind of thing.

For the booze run itself it was important, no imperative, that you shopped as quickly as you could, booze booze booze then shampoo. Get it done fast, then kick back and eat.

Compared to that healthy muck they served on kibbutz, Safed with its numerous pizza places and falafel stands was heaven. One place stood out though, a pizza restaurant serving perhaps the greatest NYC-style cheese pizza I've ever tasted anywhere in the world and that includes New York.

I'm not sure if it was actually that good or just because we were all desperate for it but it was amazing. Crispy, cheesy, buttery. My tongue has a hard-on. Sometimes a couple of us would save up and take a day off, jump on the 10 a.m. bus and spend four or five hours eating slice after crisp buttery slice and downing litres of ice-cold Goldstar beer. It was absolute bliss.

The parties we had were fucking mental. So much so that all I really remember was wearing a toga, and that's it. Once during the festival of Purim I thought it would be fun to dress up in my friend Eli Azer's Israeli army uniform. I woke up at 6 a.m. outside somewhere after having the shit beaten out of me by two drunken soldiers. Eli Azer forgot to tell me he was a Military Policeman, generally disliked by the other regiments in the IDF. Unable to talk, I was too pissed to explain I wasn't an Israeli soldier.

Every Friday was the volunteers' disco. It was a big night. First you had to get Shabbat meal out of the way. The whole kibbutz would sit together in the main hall eating dinner. The volunteers were ghettoed up one end. The Israelis generally wanted to keep their distance, afraid they'd catch what we had. That was not always the case. If, like me, you'd been there a while you sometimes got invited to sit with a family to eat Shabbat meal. Not me, that never happened to me but I was told it was most pleasant.

Shabbat meal was generally a lot of fun, food and, foolishly, free wine on the tables, sweet, spine-vibrating Shabbat wine. Silly Israelis.

Friday after work I'd swim, play football for two hours and then sleep until about five o'clock. You'd wake up, shower and, for perhaps the only time that week, you'd wear clothes that you'd brought with you from home. There were exceptions, long-time volunteers could rifle through Vicki's box of old seventies clothes. Clothes would also be handed down from volunteer to volunteer. People left, clothes stayed.

It was a treat seeing the ladies get all dolled up. During the week they usually looked like part of a socialist land army, sexy in a Marxist kind of way. Friday night though . . . Hello! Make-up, perfume, the lot. Sometimes even shoes!

Once dressed we'd do shots, not too many as you still had a big formal dinner to sit through and Shabbat meal was important, you had to behave. Public drunkenness on kibbutz was frowned upon. As a volunteer you had to behave. Up to a point. Friday was the only time volunteers got table-served by the Israelis. We loved that. Loved making it a bit difficult for them, especially if the Israeli serving us had been a ball/boob breaker during the week. The food was always good too, much better than the usual rations.

There was usually a candle lit, a prayer or prayers, a song, a poem. This bit tended to drag, we just wanted to eat and drink wine. Trying to be quiet would just make us worse. Giggles stifled. People coughing loudly. This high-pitched noise emitted by people trying not to laugh, Errrrrddddd! I'd do this thing where I'd let a long string of gob hang off my tongue and then at the last possible second I'd whip my tongue up and a chandelier of phlegm would arc up and plop onto my forehead. Big lolz from the boys. Admiring glances from the girls. Phlegm chandelier got me so much pussy.

As soon as prayers are over, eating erupts. The drinkers among us had a very important job to do. It took planning, clinical observation, patience and stamina. While hammering through the wine on our table me and the other DVF members would be constantly scanning the other tables around us. How much have they drunk? Are they drinking? When are they going? It had to be played just right though, the locals would frown upon blatant wine collection and hoarding.

The key to a great haul of free wine was simple. Sit near the old people. They never drank much if any and they'd fuck off early. Cool. You tried to stay at your table as long as possible, even while the room was being cleaned around you. Once most of the Israelis had gone you essentially had your pick of about three hundred bottles of shitty Shabbat wine. Time it right, get up and casually stroll out grabbing bottles and sticking them wherever you could. That wine would then either be drunk immediately pre-disco, or stored underground for when the lean time came. (Monday.)

Between the end of Shabbat meal and the disco opening there was a two-hour wait. It was a tricky period. If you went off too soon you'd be so hammered that you wouldn't make the disco, and it was the only chance to go out in the week. Not good. A couple of times going off too soon meant I even failed to make Shabbat meal, which was a terrible shame. I got so pissed that I fell asleep outside a small warehouse leading up to the dinner hall. I was shaken awake by a furious Vicki who sent me home and banned me from the disco that night. She'd received a couple of complaints from elderly members whom I'd apparently growled at, although that doesn't sound like something I'd do at all.

For an avid cockroach like myself Fridays were a good opportunity for more foraged treats. The Members Club near the dining hall would allow volunteers in to drink coffee and eat biscuits on the Sabbath. We'd rarely drink coffee; instead, while browsing the English novels on one of the shelves of the small library, I'd be stuffing biscuits or little cakes into my mouth, pockets and sometimes even turn-ups.

Ten minutes before the disco opened we'd trudge up the hill towards the bar. When I first arrived at the kibbutz the disco was in a giant room under the gymnasium. A month or so into my stay the disco was moved into an old bomb shelter under the Members Club. It was much nicer. I must point out that the word 'nicer' in this case was relative. It was a big concrete room that had a sound system and stank. We loved it. I had some of the best times at those discos.

The DVF would always post up at the bar for the first hour or so. It felt nice, normal, a bit like home. Sitting at the bar bullshitting with the Israelis, laughing with good mates, drinking tall, cold, draught Goldstar. Even better perhaps it was all free. Free. All free. Ha-ha. Free. The. Beer. Was. Free. And it never ran out. Never! (Well maybe once or twice but you get my point.)

After a while we'd spin our stools around and break ranks to flirt and chat and dance. Dancing was important. Everyone would dance like crazy. House of Pain's 'Jump Around' and 'The Sign' by Ace of Base were both favourites. It was totes bacchanalian.

I remember a lot of injuries and mishaps in that place. Beer spilled, skiddy floors, trips, slips. You soldiered on, alcohol-based injuries and not making work because you were pissed or injured or hung-over were not tolerated. My poor friend Theresa, a tall, broad, Irish lunatic of a woman, fell over one night and knocked her two front teeth out. She couldn't afford to get them fixed so she stayed like that for weeks. This horrified the Israelis.

When the disco was over, it was usually well past three in the morning. There were no sneaky afters or cheeky lock-ins. We'd leave and either I'd break into a factory for ham or stumble back to the common room to eat ketchup on toast and drink vodka, usually with a juice of some kind, although mixing it with water and drinking chocolate was not uncommon. Filth.

Saturday was never without a hangover. It was our day off so that was cool. I once woke up covered in a hundred partially digested cherries. I'd obviously fallen asleep eating cherries and had woken up, honked and gone back to sleep. It looked like a bloodbath. Waking up with the bed and walls covered in red liquid was absolutely terrifying. I believed my kidneys had been removed while I slept. Another time I woke up with my head plastered so close to the wall that I screamed and rolled off the bed thinking I had been struck blind.

It was all high jinks until the DVF discovered the pain of the 95% and things took a more sinister turn. It took us over. We had become a coven of drinkers. It was no longer a big group of us laughing and joking around, it was like we'd stumbled into the darkness. The alcoholic occult. We took the pomp and verve of the shotgun challenge and x'd it by a thousand and crammed it into a Ouija board. It was like *Jumanji* with crying.

Four of us would sit in one of our rooms. The door would be locked. Tea lights were lit. A small ornate table would be positioned in the centre of the room, on it the official ashtray would be placed.

We'd sit at the cardinal points on the compass, north, south, east and west. The four were usually me and the aforementioned Kiwi Shaun, Pete and Dave. These were my best friends. The term 'best friend' is perhaps a strange concept on a kibbutz. People you grew to love, who when their time was up would pack up and leave, move on, go home, go somewhere else. It's the way it was. I think I got good at being left. You had to really.

But these three were my best friends and I loved being with them. By now my time on kibbutz meant I'd been upgraded to sharing a two-bed with Shaun. We were really close. Many were the times I woke up from a boozy coma to see Shaun humping off on his lovely Danish girlfriend Margritte.

Shaun and I would also, from time to time, have the odd drunken altercation. It would start off as a competition to see who could slap the hardest, or some other lunacy, but it would soon become serious and more often than not we'd have to be separated. The next morning he and I were always thick as thieves again, eating a hangover breakfast and laughing like idiots. It'd confuse people but it was our way and we kind of liked it like that!

The other two players were Pete and Dave, friends from home who had travelled to kibbutz together from Scotland. They were alcoholic fuckheads and total degenerates. Just like me. I loved them and we laughed a lot.

Not one of us ever questioned why we were doing the 95% séance. What possessed us to dabble into the occult? We just did it. It just emerged into existence. It created itself. The first bottle – I say first, it was normally the only bottle – was usually, brought to the table under a veil of lace. A bell would sound and the shroud would be lifted. At this point the cardboard game wheel would be revealed. (Of course there was a game wheel, we were bored and clever.)

I think the wheel and therefore the game was called the 'Wheel of Destiny'; it'd be retrieved from its dusty sarcophagus and the fun would begin. The only other things allowed on the table were a small chalice (big shot glass) and a two-litre bottle of red death (Coke).

Let me tell you a little more about the Wheel of Destiny. It's important you know so you can avoid the mistakes we made. Avoid the regret, the tears, the confusion.

The wheel was divided into twelve sections, each home to a ratio. Either 80/20 or 60/40 or 20/80, 90/10, 70/30 and so on. The first number was the amount of 95% in the chalice, the second number the amount of red death. There were also some fun curveballs in there too: one said 'Don't Drink'. Why? Why would it say that? Another decreed 'Everyone Drinks'. That's better! Some had a small 's' in the corner. These were fun, the 's' stood for 'shake'. You essentially did a slammer inside your own headbox. You take the drink and shake your head until it felt like your eyes had come out and by that time the liquid had vaporised across the blood/brain barrier and gone into your mind.

I was going to call those nights fun, but I'm not sure fun would be correct. Sure we laughed a lot but it didn't feel like fun.

That shit was so strong, we'd drink about 250ml each in shot format with a mixer and it would be goodnight Tel Aviv. The night went like this: laughter, laughter, laughter, death. That's how it went. It turned us into babbling zombies, lunatics. We'd begin at 6 p.m. and by 7.15 p.m. we were absolutely ruined. Complete blackout. People would tell me I'd been mobile, shuffling, spitting but making no sense.

Places I woke up after drinking 95% (all true): up a tree, on a large flat rock, in an empty, pitch-black bomb shelter (it took me an hour to find my way out), lying on the border fence trouser-less being licked awake by a giant Rottweiler. These and other such shenanigans meant that eventually the use of 95%, much like chemical weapons in wartime, were banned by the DVF. It was too dark, too many people – good people – were hurt. Here endeth the lesson.

* * *

About a year or so into my first tour I decided that I'd had enough and I wanted to go home. God knows why. I seem to remember a little light pressure from people to stay, to become a member of the kibbutz. That meant either joining the army or getting married to an Israeli girl. The army wasn't interested in a drunken Catholic, albeit lapsed. And in terms of Israeli women, they were very hard to woo, you had to be in it for the long haul, the ones I knew on kibbutz anyway. No, I was strictly a Friday night Euro-banger at this juncture.

I packed my stuff, Vicki arranged for me to get a lift down to Tel Aviv and I went. The only thing I remember from the flight was the smoking. It was the last time I ever saw smoking on a plane. It's so weird to think, and I say this as a smoker sadly, that at one point in the not so distant past one could smoke in a plane, with kids there too, or on the tube, on buses, in restaurants for godsakes – as if the notion that a small, low wall separating the smoking from the non-smoking sections made a blind bit of difference to where the smoke would float!

* * *

In fourteen months on kibbutz and with the help of very little food, tons of exercise and ball-breaking labour I had gone from nineteen stone to eleven! This was a big shock to my parents who were waiting for me at the airport. I stood straight in front of my mum and she didn't recognise me. She craned her neck looking for her chubby little soldier. Eventually she realised this tanned, thin, shaven-headed kibbutznik standing before her was me.

'What have they done to you?' she sobbed.

She grabbed me and hugged me so hard. Dad got involved at one point too and I think we all had a little cry. It was really nice to see them.

I'd almost completely forgotten about 214 Ray Lodge Road. It was a real shock to be back there. I felt that big, wet, black blanket drape itself around my shoulders almost instantly. I say home. It was a house and my parents lived in it. I just couldn't be there.

After being away for so long and blooming, breathing, changing, growing, I'd half expected it to have happened to everyone here at home too. This was not the case. It was exactly the same. Nothing had changed. Nothing. I had to leave. I took my passport, the one with the stamp in it that said I couldn't come back to Israel. (I was arrested at the airport for overstaying my visa by eleven months and effectively deported.) I wasn't going to let this stop me. I tore my passport up, went to Petty France and reapplied for a new one. Cunning twat.

I have an odd relationship with passports. (I wonder if these words have ever been written before?) Years later Simon and I made an arrangement to spend five days writing in Helsinki. We wrote nothing by the way. I love the film by Jim Jarmusch, *Night on Earth*. The Helsinki vignette always fascinated me, it made me want to go there. So we did. The promise of snow was too much for me and Peggy to bear. We love snow. We were very excited.

Two days before we leave I try and find my passport. I can't. I look everywhere. It's gone. Lost. Balls. My personality is such that losing things is bad for me, it unsettles me, makes me feel disappointed with my brain. I don't want a glitch in my matrix. I turn my place upside down looking for that fucking document. After a while I call Simon, tell him regretfully we'd have to cancel. He was furious.

I think the problem was we'd built up such a picture of this winter wonderland over the previous couple of weeks that to have it snatched away like this was too much to bear. He was so cross. I hung up saying, 'Leave it with me.' I couldn't let my little soldier down. I remember I had an old passport in an envelope in a box in the shed. After rooting around I find the thing. It's musty, out of date, cancelled and also cut in half. Clean through. Two pieces. Oh. As I sit at my desk I feel like Donald Pleasance in *The Great Escape*, headlamp blazing, scalpel and a roll of clear Scotch tape in hand. It took me almost three hours but I'd surgically taped that thing back together. We were going to Helsinki!

This was pre 9/11 so security was pretty lax, but still I was shitting a brick. If I had a kilo of squidgy-black taped to my calf I couldn't have felt any guiltier. Cut a long story short, we got there, just. Being poor at the time, our cheap tickets meant we had to trans-ship via Amsterdam so this meant three sets of checkpoints; they looked at the passport, looked at me and waved me through. Fucking hell. So illegal. In Finland it didn't snow once. We drank about 700 Lapin Kultas, laughed a lot and had brandy for breakfast – it was cold, so well deserved and purely medicinal, we believed.

Once again I said goodbye to M and D, took a train to Gatwick and flew back to Israel. I'd spoken to Israeli friends on kibbutz and they were happy to have me back. There'd been a change of administration in the weeks since I'd been gone. Vicki had left her post and a lady called Yael Arnin had taken over. She was tiny, beautiful in a Dana Scully kind of way and most formidable. I loved her and thanks to my cheekiness we got on well. She was really good to me.

Even though I'd only been gone a month the turnover of the volunteers was such that I hardly knew any of them. No matter, they knew me, I was still a Master Sergeant in the DVF and that meant something. I get back to work, keep my head down, drink, flirt, laugh, make new friends and don't think about the future. I loved the day in day out of kibbutz life, same thing week after week. Four-forty a.m. alarm goes off, teeth brushed, work, lunch, swim, sleep, dinner, drink, sleep, four-forty a.m. alarm goes off.

Friday was Shabbat meal and the disco, this you know about. Wednesday we were allowed to use the shop. On Tuesday Yael opened her office. We'd get a hundred fags a week and five aerogrammes, which I never used; I'd stockpile mine and use them to trade for extra ciggies with some of the Danish girls, many of whom were avid letter writers.

I'd drop my dirty laundry off in the office and it'd be returned on Thursday all folded up in a little canvas bag, clean but essentially smelling of nothing. These were the routines I lived my life by and I liked it. I could do it with my eyes closed. I need routine. Even now, I'm shit if I don't have a routine, really bad.

My twentieth birthday was approaching and my mum called to ask me what I'd like. A few people had planned a trip to Tiberias and I really wanted to go. I told Mum about the plan and she assured me that she'd sort it. Great!

Money, generally, was never an issue on kibbutz because no one had any. You didn't need it. It was only when you wanted to venture outside that you ever needed to think about cash. On kibbutz, we had something called funny money, essentially coloured squares of paper assigned a value by the inclusion of a number on one side.

Tiberias is on the western shore of the Sea of Galilee, deep in the heart of Jesus country. I liked it there, great food, and amazing falafel. Outside the city's central bus station there was a long row of lovely falafel stands, colourful, beautiful; with giant bowls of salad, chopped vegetables, beans, pulses and the smell of chickpea patties frying in golden oil. Yumfuckingyum.

A couple of days before my birthday a parcel arrived from home, I eagerly tore into it. This is going to be good, weekend away here I come! Out of the package tumbled forty Benson and Hedges (Result!) and a fiver. Five pounds. Five. A fucking fiver. Sorry to sound ungrateful, I know they didn't have a pot to piss in but still. Why assure me? I didn't feel assured. I laugh a bit, confused, look back into the parcel, empty. Oh. Gutted. I laugh when I think about it now but I was definitely crestfallen.

I had unconsciously prepared for this kind of eventuality. I'd scrimped and saved up bits here and there and just had enough to get to Tiberias and back. The fiver actually came in handy for a few beers once I'd exchanged it so I was happy enough.

A bunch of us bussed it down to Safad and then hitched from there to Tiberias. We grabbed supplies of fresh pitta, cans of tuna, cheese, ham, vodka etc. and headed north around the top end of the Sea of Galilee. It was a long way and very hot but it was my birthday and we were in high spirits.

By the time we arrived at the campsite it was late afternoon. It wasn't strictly a campsite, it was a beach dotted with life-guard towers, and if you could find one that was hippie-free you could sleep on it. Which is exactly what we did. We laid out the sleeping bags and had a little picnic on the beach; we drank a little and swam in the Sea of Galilee. It was pretty magical. I felt free and happy. We stood in silence in the black, tideless water and watched the sun go down.

Later we lay around in our nest eating crisps and, taking long swigs of lemon vodka, we chatted and laughed. At one point I have a vague memory of one of the boys deciding it would be a good idea to piss all over us. The lemon vodka was beginning to darken the mood, I needed to be alone and so I wanderstumble off.

I sit on the beach, hearing europop drift across the sea from Tiberias, campfires up and down the beach fill the air with smoke, I hear the noise of a guitar, girls giggling, the soothing 'AchAch' of ancient Hebrew.

At some point I make the stupid decision to wade out into the Sea of Galilee. It starts off innocently enough as a little paddle, then I witness myself wading and then marching out further and further. There comes a point when I can barely touch the bottom. What a fucking stupid thing to do. So drunk I can hardly see, neck deep in the unknown.

Two things happen to me at this point, one is a realisation, the other is a physical incarnation of my deepest primal fear. The realisation is remembering how terrified I am by deep, unpredictable water. The sea hates a coward and in the sea I am most definitely a coward. I'm not a good swimmer and the notion of currents unseen, of tidal ebb and flow, makes me afraid – I'm just not good in the sea. It's a primal environment and far too much for my imagination to cope with.

On holibobs I'll happily wade and I'll even have a little snorkel in the warm, clear Med, lovely. But I'm not in the warm, clear Med. I'm here, on my own, three hundred feet from shore in the pitch-black Galilee. This is not a good place to be. I blink and instantly become sober enough to understand the predicament I'm in. Breathe.

My Jiminy Cricket is now sober too, he's really cross and shouts at me, 'Chop-chop, dickhead, back to shore!' That guy's always shouting at me.

I turn and begin my swim/doggie paddle/terrified bounce-run back to the beach when the second thing happens.

Under the water an unseen entity brushes against me. Something of enormous size and power. It is massive and it is silent. I don't or can't move and plips fall out of me. The top of the thing brushes against my chest, the base of the leviathan brushes against my shins, for a moment we have full body contact, it glides through me. I feel the scales on its flanks, big as saucers. It's so big and powerful that the current it creates when it pulses its tail and glides off picks me up and spins me further out to sea, away from the shore and to a place where I definitely cannot touch the bottom. I've never been so frightened.

I'm going to either drown or be eaten by a monster, they'll find nothing of me but my fat head on an Israeli lake-beach and it'll have a little crab living in the eye-socket. I don't want a little crab living in my eye-socket. Not yet. I'm treading water, panicky, terrified. Jiminy punches a button on a panel in my control centre. A flash of an idea. 'Swim, you fucking dick!'

I explode into action and doggie paddle back to shore. I beach, exhausted, gasping, frightened. I check myself all over and find I'm fine although the ring I wear, a ring my dad gave to me, is gone. It's a beautiful green-and-black signet ring with flecks of fiery red and it was now lost at the bottom of the Sea of Galilee. Maybe the ring falling off my finger was tariff enough for Neptune that day. I'm bummed but totally alive.

* * *

The second time on kibbutz was different from the first. Not worse necessarily. It's all about the people. Obviously different people give off different kinds of vibrations. Some are nice, with a pleasant frequency, you yearn to be in the company of that person. Some are high-pitched, twangy, jarring; it warns you subconsciously to stay away.

It's like dogs or bees or rats picking up the scent of cancer or landmines. People have no control over the vibes they give off. It can't be disguised by a shallow smile or a pat on the back, you just sense it, it's a gut instinct and it should *never* be ignored.

At that time and generally, volunteers were a tight-knit bunch. We knew each other, we loved and looked after one another. It's how it was, how we liked it. There was little or no trouble. When new volunteers showed up it was usually in small groups, ones, twos, the odd three. People generally made the effort to integrate and we embraced that and they were then part of the gang. Easy. There were no cliques and although you'd naturally get on with some people more than others, we all generally got along.

This changed one day and it affected us all. The vibes got dark. Four boys, mates who'd known each other a long time, pitched up. They were already a crew and had no need to make the effort to blend in. I have a very well-tuned aggro-sensor and it went off the moment they showed up.

Over the days and weeks there was a certain amount of natural cultural osmosis. They softened slightly, or at least appeared to soften, they made friends, sort of, but I never trusted them. Their vibes were rotten, they made me feel like a hen in a fox coop. The primal-fear alarm bleated every time they got close.

Before coming up to us in our mountain kibbutz they'd spent a couple of days in Tel Aviv. Apparently they had 'befriended' a kindly Israeli man who offered to let them crash at his place. In the morning before their hung-over host was awake they opened his closet and decided to take a shit in all his shoes. Who the fuck shits in a man's shoes?

I got on with everyone on kibbutz. I liked everyone and hopefully most people liked me. I worked hard, I was loyal, I was funny, and I liked making people laugh and generally people like laughing. All these likeable qualities had sadly put me firmly in their cross-hairs.

Out of the four, one was nice. He was good at heart and he knew that I knew it. I could see that he was using kibbutz as a way to start again perhaps, try new things, and meet new people, distance himself maybe. One of them was on the fence; on his own he was fine but with the others and a drink in him he changed. The other two were different. The one who was their self-proclaimed Boss was cunning, volatile and violent; he was a controlling bully trying to keep a crew together, a crew that perhaps had seen that maybe there was another way. A way that didn't include shitting in the shoes of a kindly stranger. The other was an ex-junkie, very paranoid; he could be controlled, manipulated, have his will moulded, have his mind fucked with by the Boss. To be honest, I didn't mind the junkie. He was all right. We got on and when we worked together he laughed a lot. The Boss had a problem with this. I sensed he knew his control was being diluted by volunteer life. Culture, art, music and laughter can do that really easily. His hold over them was loosening, and he hated that loss of control. The Boss was unpredictable and he frightened me.

One Friday night at the disco I'm having a slash, Bossman comes in and starts pissing next to me. He's happy and smiling, banter ensues although I'm always guarded. As I zip up and leave, this aside takes place.

'Oh, mate, meant to say, Junkie wants to see you.'

'Oh, right. What's that about?'

'Dunno, he was just looking for you.'

'Where is he?'

'Downstairs. You should go and find him, it seemed important.'

Lots of smiles and nods from Bossman. I leave and head downstairs. I find Junkie sitting in the corner on his own in a booth. I go over and sit down. He's different. Pissed, stony-faced. My alarm goes off. His opening gambit sends a red pulse up my feet and into my ears.

'Bossman told me you've been telling everyone that I'm a fucking queer, you fat cunt.'

Oh dear. He is nervous and jangly, his body jerks involuntarily, he looks down and my eyes follow. In his hand is a Stanley knife. I'm fucked. He's going to open me up, I have no doubt about that and I have no doubt I'm not his first.

What follows over the next twenty minutes, a twenty minutes that seems to go on and on, is some very quick, clear talking. An honesty and a truth he had not been expecting. He tenses and wants to cut me twice during this conversation. I can see the battle inside him. Eventually I talk him down. I see him soften, see his eyes change and I know I'm going to be okay. He retracts the slicer and sticks it back in his pocket. I get us a beer each, we clink and it's done. Inside I'm crying. I breathe a secret sigh of relief.

I look at Bossman and see that he's livid. His plan to get me wasn't meant to go down like this. It reinforces to me just how dangerous he is. I feel like someone has just tried to assassinate me. Junkie's failure to carve me up sets off a chain of events that'd lead to the senseless assault a couple of weeks later of a quiet Swedish boy. That boy did nothing to deserve being fucked up. I don't know what happened to kick it off, I don't think with people like that anything needs to happen. The bent perception of an insult is often the only thing needed to spark off a kicking.

The police come, an ambulance, but he refuses to press charges. It's too late though, the Israelis have seen enough and they're expelled. Two leave and two, Good Heart and Junkie, can stay. Over time they're assimilated, they become like us. I hope they stayed that way.

From time to time during my extended stay in the Middle East there was a little armed conflict. Obvs, I lived on the Lebanese border. Sometimes security got beefed up for one reason or another, more tanks and jeeps than usual would rush around. Sometimes shots would zip overhead, bright tracer rounds pinging off into the night. I'd been at a safety briefing once where I was told that if I received packages that smelled like almonds (Semtex, the plastic explosive, smells like almonds), I should stick it in a bucket and alert security. I was glad Mum never sent me that marzipan.

Sometimes on a Saturday I'd be sitting outside on the lawn, chilling, smoking, whatever and I'd watch jets and assault choppers, heavily laden with missiles, roar overhead, quick and very low. Thirty minutes later they'd head back, unladen and very high to avoid enemy surface-to-air missile batteries. I quickly got used to the sound of jets tearing overhead smashing the sound barrier. At first that noise sent the fear of god up me but, like most things, you get used to it. It was exciting to me.

One morning I had a special work detail in a new orchard working with a volunteer called Steve. He was sleazy as fuck and probably thirty-five, which is pretty old for a volunteer, and he emitted a Gary Glitter kind of vibe I couldn't ignore. Steve always had some kind of tummy bug or a boil or explosive diarrhoea. He had a thick sheen of sweat dripping off his heavily receding hairline, and his smoker's cough, and his need to hawk out ball after ball of smelly brown phlegm only added to his sexual allure.

They dropped us in a field, a shadeless brown rectangle fifteen minutes from home, and left us. To find out we were the only two people working in the orchard bothered me. Steve gave me the willies. Still it was hot, the sun was shining and the work was honest and hard so who was I to complain. We had our polystyrene cube filled with cold water and we had our tools. It was all we needed. Steve and I sat and smoked a ciggie and eventually began our day. We dug holes in the ground and popped saplings into the earth. Digging, planting, watering, so sweet. I would've rather been on my own of course but I wasn't so what the fuck. Crack on, big boy.

Later that morning a formation of attack helicopters roared overhead, whatevs. It wasn't unusual but I'd always stop what I was doing and look up, it was exciting. The choppers entered Lebanon and attacked a convoy of vehicles. In the vehicles were the leader of Hezbollah and his extended family. I didn't know this though. I was planting apple trees with Steve who was doing a series of really dribbly guffs. I heave. I hear pops and rumblings – it's not Steve, it's the sound of tanks and artillery on the move. This is normal, normal to me anyway.

Steve tells me the dysentery he contracted in Cambodia has returned. He limpjogs off and does a noisy shit. I heave again. I understand more than most that if you have to go you have to go. I get it. The problem I have now though is we're in a big field, there's no cover, no big tree or ditch to do it behind or in. There's nowhere to hide. I'm forced to watch sweaty Steve, throbbing boil on his neck, hanging off a young sapling grunting out jet after jet of broige liquid terror. I want to die. After five minutes or so I've seen enough, I have to turn around. I cannot watch another plip. I close my eyes but I could still hear it. I *can* still hear it.

From the security fence a very loud siren begins to wail. I'd never heard that siren before and it unnerves me. Steve joins me, rubbing soft earth into his hands to de-clag his slim, hairless fingers. They are stained brown, it could be tobacco, although it didn't taste much like tobacco.

While we look north into Southern Lebanon the siren continues. Probably just a drill. I see a small shape arcing high into the air – to quote my darling Jimi Hendrix it's 'a giant lipstick and pencil tube shaped thing'. It's silent and quick and beautiful. Clearly it has somewhere it needs to be. It's a missile. It passes overhead and drops beneath the horizon into Northern Israel. Thud. A concussive boom. An explosion. Then another.

All over the sky from the north I now see similarly shaped things heading our way. This is Hezbollah's response to the convoy attack. Steve and I instinctively lie down in the field. We have no other plan. The Israelis will come to get us, right? While we're lying there we have a cigarette, why not, nothing else to do. I don't feel afraid at this point. My fear comes later, much later, maybe twenty years later, to be honest.

This shit is too trippy to be afraid. It was more unbelievable than fearsome. After thirty minutes or so an army jeep roars into the field, angrily sounding its horn. Eyal, who is Yael's husband and the kibbutz's head of security, jumps out, he's a handsome bugger and definitely not to be messed with. He has a cheeky grin and likes to laugh so we get on well. He motions for us to run to him. I finish my fag and scarper.

We'd been the only two volunteers working on our own and we'd essentially been forgotten. When I get back to the kibbutz I'm cross, I also find out they've decided against serving lunch, I don't understand. I kick around the car park fuming, grumbling about being hungry. A rocket screams overhead. Eyal shouts at me to run and get down into the volunteers' bomb shelter. I kick my heels and walk at my own pace. What a helmet.

When I shuffle into view of the shelter the Israelis shout at me again! Twice in one day. How rude, I'm hungry! They're amazed at my stubborn moody shuffle as missiles rain down all over the north of Israel. I'm ushered into the shelter, I continue my grumble about lunch.

The bomb shelter deal was this: if it was an air raid we'd be put into the shelter. If it were an incursion by terrorists we'd have to go to our rooms and lock the door until an all-clear was given. The logic behind this was simple and stark. Terrorists could kill more of us at once if we were all in the same place. There was brief mention of a bag of grenades being stuffed into air vents.

The bomb shelter was a thick concrete square sunk thirty feet into the ground, dusty stairs led to the outer giant steel door lined with heavy rubber seals in case of chemical attack. That led to a small chamber on the left and a storeroom on the right, this led to another massively heavy blast door, through this the bomb shelter proper. Our home for the next two weeks.

On the walls around the shelter hung metal bunk beds, suspended from thick chains and stacked three high. There were probably thirty-two or so bunks in all. The rest slept on mattresses on the floor. It was fun at first, novel, but that soon wore off – fifty people in a damp dusty shelter getting bombed by Hezbollah gets old really fucking quickly.

Despite the bullshit and bravado we were afraid and nervous. Outside, rockets thudded into the holy earth, inside we'd hear the concussive thud and the sound of dust raining onto the crispy polythene outer shells of our sleeping bags. No one sleeps that night. The next three days were bad. The IDF move heavy artillery close to our position. It was no longer just Russian-made Katyusha rockets heading south, it was now also the relentless *thump thump thump* of the IDF's merciless response heading the other way.

Again sleep proves difficult. I lie awake listening to the boom and counter-boom of the exchange. I think someone got killed in the next kibbutz over. We were lucky. One or two degrees clicked either way on the rudimentary sighting mechanism and it could've been us. It could easily have been us.

The days pass, we rally, our spirits lift and fall. The nights are still shit and weird but during the day we are allowed to leave the shelter and go to our rooms or work inside the kibbutz a little bit. Sometimes the sirens would begin again and we'd be forced back underground.

There's a security meeting one afternoon to review the situation. If the Israelis were serious you could guess the situation was serious. The Israelis were serious. They spoke about potentially evacuating us south to Tel Aviv. There was a murmur from the volunteers, not one of us wanted to leave. We were all really close and needed to see this through together. The kibbutzniks never forget that. We were treated differently after the war.

At night when all seemed quiet, me and some of the other boys would creep up the dusty concrete stairs and sit outside on the roof of the shelter smoking. One night we watched a missile streak overhead, its engine burned hot and blue across the night. We watch in silence, the engine flickers and the flame dims. It falls from the sky some way across the horizon. A silent flash. A thud and it's done. We finish our ciggies and decide to go back inside.

This sustained bombardment is bad for my nerves, everyone's nerves. A decision's made, the Israelis move us south for a couple of days, relieve the tension. Our work boss, Michel, the laidback afro-cowboy, invited a few of his faves to ride in the VW Caravelle with him. Sweet, I loved those Caravelles. With Michel at least you could be guaranteed a nice bit of reggae on the radio. What you need during a bombardment is some 'Bam Bam' from Sister Nancy, it's good, it helped.

We leave at pace heading down the side of the Bekaa Valley on a hairpin-heavy road onto the baking valley floor below. The Bekaa Valley in the north of Israel is the northern limit of the giant fissure, which eventually travels south and becomes the Great Rift Valley. It's amazing.

Once we're down Michel pulls into a petrol station to fill up. We all get out of the van and following the Israelis' lead smoke ciggies right there on the forecourt. I love a lack of health and safety. I smoke and casually drink a cold Kinley, it's a kind of

Fanta. Michel pays and leaves the shop. The moment he exits the air-raid sirens sound.

A forecourt packed with smokers filling up their cars empties in twenty seconds flat. Some people run towards the nearest shelter. Others speed away heading south. I panic slightly, we all panic slightly except Michel who pats his pockets looking for a lighter. Do we run to the shelter? Do we run into the vehicle and flee? I'm essentially standing on top of a concrete box filled with thousands of gallons of a highly flammable accelerant. I don't feel comfortable standing here.

Michel, who's the most unflappable man I ever met, is now stood looking at something in the middle distance. He casually flicks out a ciggie from his soft pack and lights it up in one smooth motion.

'Guys, come to see.' He points north as his lazy, semi-closed eyes scan the horizon, it's the most animated I've ever seen him.

'There!' He points at something, sure enough a long, sleek, black pencil, with a very basic computer and a nose packed with high-explosive, sharks over the lip of the valley. It skims the geography with no effort at all. It's beautiful and deadly and I can't take my eyes off it. It ghosts its way towards us before swerving left, jinking hard right and slamming into the road we'd just driven down ten minutes earlier.

I love it when you actually get to see the difference first-hand between the speed of light and the speed of sound. I'm fascinated and afraid. I see the missile pummel into the mountainside and a large section of earth silently slumps into the air and slides like water down the valley. A second or two later a giant bang. A supersonic shockwave hammers around the valley. Its noise amplified by the steep sides. It leads me to think about how it'd be great to be assassinated by a highly trained sniper with a Barrett .50 cal sitting 400 metres away, high in a clock tower or minaret. I think that's how I'd like to go. No pain, no awful illness. That giant cartridge would turn my soft computer into a sticky pink foam in a thousandth of a second, long before I ever heard the bang of the gun. You would literally be dead before you knew it. Cool! I digress. I've just watched this science right in front of me, live.

'We should go,' mutters Michel, and we go.

I'd been in Israel, give or take with my first bit and now, for twenty months. I have my own room now, it's real 'big-dog' shit, no more sharing for me. I'd taken all four single beds and I'd lashed them together with zipties to form a single mega-bed. That's real power. Colonel Kurtz was back. It was time for me to leave.

Easier said than done. I was in a rut and I liked it, it was what I knew. I was comfortable swaggering around like I owned the gaff. Something had to change and naturally the catalyst was a girl. I met her and fell for her and when she left my heart wasn't in it any more. Three weeks later I was gone.

I didn't actually like Rachel very much at the beginning. I was sitting with Dave in the common room and she swanned in and turned the TV over while we were watching it! That's not on. You don't do that. She drove me bonkers (a sure sign I liked her).

From the off I was always fighting a losing battle, but I didn't really care. I liked her. I knew she kind of liked me too but I probably understood from the get-go that long term it wouldn't work. I was so different then, confused and very jealous, wanting someone to cling to. She wasn't it. Not then, we were both really young. Rachel, originally from the depths of Virginia Water, was a free spirit. A traveller, and the most sociable person I knew. Everybody liked her. She also spoke fluent Hebrew.

We'd been hanging out together, having a laugh, not having a laugh, being together, not being together and definitely not having sex. It was a confusing time. One day Rachel invited me to spend a night with her down in Tiberias. I was excited and nervous. This had never happened to me before, a weekend away with a girl! I felt a bit grown up. It was Passover and she had to meet her grandmother who was an Israeli. I wasn't Jewish and could not be relied on to behave so I wasn't invited to meet Granny. Which was fine by me.

She'd meet her Bubbie, I'd hang around drinking and we'd hook up later and spend the night in one of the lifeguard towers. As ever, food was a big draw for me, I was happy to leave the culinary monotony of Bar-Am for a couple of nights. The thought of rich, crispy, buttery pizza plus the chance to hang out with this nice girl who liked me was a dreamy notion. I talked at length on the journey down about that pizza.

When we arrived in Tiberias I had my spirit crushed pretty fucking quickly, my dream lay in tatters. This had nothing to do with Rachel. This had everything to do with Passover and kosher law. It meant pizza places couldn't use leavened dough. Instead of thin, crispy, buttery NYC-style pizza it was kosher cheddar and tomato puree sprinkled on a stack of matzo crackers. This was a bad omen. I should've turned round and gone straight back to kibbutz. No woman was worth this.

She said shalom and we arranged to meet later. The year 1992 was a time before mobile phones, for me anyway. To think of a time before mobile phones now seems utterly ridiculous. Life was different then. You made an arrangement and you had to stick to it, there was no texting a raincheck an hour before. I found a bar, post up and ready myself for the wait.

I was a long way from having to meet her grandmother. During an earlier trip we'd tried to meet members of her family. It didn't go so well. We were in Jerusalem on a kibbutz trip, all the volunteers, including Rachel and me. It was great. She had family in Jerusalem so while the rest of us went on the piss she went off to visit them. We'd arranged to meet Rachel and her cousins in a bar called The Underground.

The Underground was like an Israeli version of the cantina in Mos Eisley. It was a place where one could do shots, have a shit falafel, eye up the birds, punch on, piss yourself and quaff litres of cold draught beer. I'd done all of these things by the time Rachel turned up with her handsome teetotal cousins. I was not good when they arrived. I was shirtless, jeans around my ankles soaked in my own wee-wee liquid. I lay semi-conscious over a large wooden barrel, dribbling. It's all about first impressions, isn't it?

I completely understand Rachel's decision to not allow me to meet Granny. It was probably wise. I wasn't ready, I'll be the first to admit. I'd never really had a girlfriend, sure there were crushes and teen fumblings but this felt like next level potential girlfriend shit.

A couple of hours later we hook up, and keeping my promise I was definitely not pissed. We got our shit together and headed south out of the city on foot in search of somewhere to stay. It was getting late and the more we walked the more we could tell our plan of sleeping on a lifeguard tower had a few flaws.

That winter there'd been a very heavy and prolonged snow-fall all over the north. Which was great, I loved snow because as we know on kibbutz snow means chips. It also meant that the melted snow had added almost fifteen feet of water into the Galilee, this meant no beaches and the lifeguard towers we were planning to sleep in were half covered with floodwater. I heard a story about a biblical zoo on the banks of the Galilee. It houses all the animals that lived in the Holy Land at the time of Christ. They had a few Nile crocodiles. Sadly in the spring their enclosures became deluged by almost fifteen feet of melt water, and simply swam out.

It took us an hour or so to realise our plan has gone to shit. We turned and headed back towards Tiberias. We're tired and end up squabbling a bit. It's close to 1 a.m. and we're not really talking. In the distance we see the lights of a car coming towards us.

All good slasher/hitcher films start the same way. A car pulls up fifty feet away. Stopping slowly. It's brightly lit from the front so we see a nice silhouette through the back window of the faceless driver. We look at each other, excited that we have a lift and run towards the Zodiac Killer – I mean our lift. He leans over and opens the passenger door. We crane to peer in. He's a heavily decorated soldier. We're saved! Rachel lifts the front seat up and I jump into the back, she sits up front and a conversation in Hebrew begins.

I now get my first look at the Zodiac and ironically he actually looks a bit like John Carroll Lynch. He's a major in the IDF, fancy! He also has an Uzi in his lap. No biggie. He speaks to me in broken English, he seems all right, he opens the glove box and slings me a bottle of vodka. Brilliant. Free vodka. I like this guy. We pull off and I take a big swig and pass it forward. He swigs too which is unorthodox but what the fuck. We drive in silence except for the odd Hebrew from time to time. More vodka is quaffed.

After about twenty minutes we turn down a pitch-black dirt track, he pulls up, turns the engine off and we sit in silence for a time. Some more Hebrew breaks out. The major is looking back at me smiling, talking Hebrew to Rachel. I happily smile back and nod and continue my assault on his bottle. To say I was totally oblivious to a growing weirdness would be a little inaccurate, I had sensed the beginning of a minor weirdness. Rachel suddenly jumps out of the car and ratchets the seat forward. She shrieks at me.

'Get out now!'

'Why? Free vodka.'

'Get the fuck out of the car.'

I bumble out of the back seat, grumbling. I was so sick of walking.

'What the fuck's going on?'

'Just walk, go, right now.'

I was starting to get the point. I half walked, half ran away from drunken Major Zodiac with his curly hair.

After some running we stopped and turned to see him still sat there, lights on. He was making a decision. Thinking things through. The car starts and slowly begins to reverse. Rachel relaxes enough to tell me what happened. When Zodiac was talking to her in Hebrew, even though he was looking back at me and smiling, he was propositioning her. Trying to convince her to fuck him, even suggesting I could stay on his couch while it went on, which was nice of him I guess. He was fairly insistent towards the end, forcing Rachel to leap out. Poor girl. What a blind idiot I'd been.

We trudged back into town. Our common enemy meant we were actually in a bit of a better mood. We walked round the city a bit and eventually found some stairs leading up to a large flat roof. We checked it out. It was clean and quiet so we made our bed up there. It was nice to finally be together. We snuggled in and fell asleep.

After a few hours we were awakened by the sound of a Muezzin calling the Muslim faithful to prayer. It was fucking loud. We'd inadvertently slept on top of a mosque. We were also now surrounded by thirty cats. It was nice, I like cats.

* * *

When Rachel left Israel I missed her so much. I felt hollow. I wanted to leave. I'd been there long enough. So I left, again. When I got home Mum and Dad told me of their plan to move to Wales. Back to the place it all began for her. I think it was the right thing to do. Mum and Dad were not well, they'd got the council to rehouse them in a little place called Letterston, it's a small village on the main road into Fishguard. This news meant I had eight weeks to get my shit together and find somewhere to live. Great.

I'd made a mate in Israel this last time out, a man called Pat. He was a lot older than me and kind of a serious person. I liked him though. He was Irish and loved the Craic. One day on kibbutz I noticed a big red scar under one of his arms, near the chest. Me being nosy I asked how he got it; at first he wouldn't tell me, he seemed sheepish and quickly covered it up. So I left it.

Weeks later, after a few bevvies, he starts to tell me a story about what he did back in Ireland. I'm made to promise not to tell anyone. I'm excited, my interest definitely piqued. He tells me he's an officer in the Anti-Terrorist police in Northern Ireland and the scar is a result of being shot in a firefight with the IRA. During a pause in the battle, Pat rolls over onto his back to grab a fresh magazine which is strapped to his chest and he's shot by a sniper in the only part of his body not protected by his armour. Right under the armpit. Holy fuck. Tough break. Poor him. That was that. He never mentioned it again except to say he'd come to Israel to convalesce. After that we became mates. I completely trusted him.

A couple of weeks after I got back from Israel I get a phone call from Pat. Amazing. He's in London and wonders if he can come and crash at mine for a couple of days. Absolutely you can. He turns up, we embrace, hugs, laughter. I introduce him to Mum and Dad, he's charming and funny, brings a bottle for Dad, something for Mum. Real textbook shit.

Pat stays, we have a laugh. I like and trust him. He's my mate. Most mornings he'd head off to use the phonebox on the corner, he needed to check in with his commanding officer. Cool. Our flat is so small that having a big Irish lump on the sofa is making the place feel even smaller.

Mum and Dad start to hassle me, rightly so. A few days has turned into two weeks! I think Pat senses his time is coming to an end here. I feel bad for Mum and Dad but awkward about asking him to leave.

One morning Pat heads out to make some calls. When he comes back he tells me I have to rent a car. His C/O has given him a job while he's here and he needs my help. I'm afraid and excited.

'What do you want me to do?'

'There's an old pub in Peckham, there's a package that's been left there for me. I need to go and get it.'

'Right . . . Um, sure.'

'There's a house. We need to park up the street and see who comes and goes.'

This seems way above my pay grade but he seems to know what he's doing so fuck it. I'll be a spy for the day. I hire a car. He tells me it has to be powerful in case we need to get away. I squeak a bit inside. We drive down to this old boarded-up pub. I don't fancy talking very much.

'Pull in here. Keep the car running.'

'How long will you be?'

'Don't know.'

Pat leaps out. He looks around to see if we've been followed. Classic spy stuff. He walks off and disappears behind the back of the pub. I need to shit so badly. After ten minutes he comes out holding a small package.

'Drive!'

I leave at pace revving loudly. After a while I ask him what's in the package. He tells me it's a handgun. My shit comes out. This is way too much for me. I'm actually properly afraid. The next day he tells me he doesn't think I should come on the stake-out. I'm thrilled. He leaves very early and comes back late afternoon. I ask no questions and he tells me nothing but seems happy. He wants to celebrate. His treat. Cool. I'm still on edge but a night in London makes me feel better. It'll also give Mum and Dad a chance to have the place to themselves for the night.

We spend the night tearing it up in town, this is great, this feels like we're back on kibbutz. This feels like the old Pat I know. I relax into him again. At one point we cross a packed Leicester Square when a rangy kid, all ribcage and long arms, approaches us.

'Pills pills pills . . .' He's got pills apparently. I make that kind of 'hmmm, yeah, um, sure' face. I pull some money out. He pulls some pills out. I look at Pat to see if he's up for it. I've forgotten the job he does. I turn to see him grabbing hold of this kid round the neck. Balls.

From out of nowhere two of the dealer's mates run towards Pat, he gets hammered by flying haymakers. Pat grabs the dealer even harder, his head deflecting the fists of these kids. I see others approaching.

Pat screams at me. I am literally shitting myself. 'Run to a phone and dial 999. Tell them Anti-Terrorist police officer needs back up.'

I do not need asking twice. I fucking sprint out of there. I'm being followed. I find a phonebox on the east side of the square and dial 999. I tell them what I'm told to say. Even before the phonecall is finished I start to hear sirens. The door to the phonebox is jerked open, I'm punched. I grab the door and pull it closed. I'm shouting down the phone. Three youths, mates of the dealer, associates, are trying to get into this phonebox. Through the window I can see police vans and cars and officers pouring into the square.

It offers little or no relief to me. These kids are tearing at the door to the phonebox. They've seen me in the square with Pat. The door's flung open, I pull it back closed, through the gap, fists, punches and knives are trying to scythe their way in, trying to cut me. Street vengeance. Four coppers pound their way towards me. The kids see them and bounce. There's a brief scuffle outside, I see my chance and head out, running. All around me the scene is absolute mayhem. I can only estimate the number of Old Bill but I'd have to say more than fifty. Easy.

I find a copper. My hope is they'll stick me in a car and take me away. My fear is I'll be followed and stabbed, killed in an alley outside the back door of a theatre. I'm so fucking mad with Pat right now.

I explain to the policeman what happened and that I was the one who made the call. Instead of taking me off the street and out of danger he tells me to run to Vine Street, 'it's where they're taking everyone.' I don't pause, or wait or hesitate. I just run and run and run. My feet snap against the concrete, my heart pounds, my lungs are so fucking mad with Pat right now.

I leave the din of shouting and screaming and sirens and fury behind but I don't stop until I find the Nick. I run in headlong and burst into words. Pat is here. He's bloodied and bruised. We're taken into a custody suite. We sit in silence. I can't even look at him. The door begins to open.

He spit-whispers at me, 'Don't say a fucking word.' I couldn't be any more sober right now if I tried.

A detective comes in and he and Pat speak for a moment, it's terse and business-like. It makes me nervous. Pat reaches into his pocket and pulls out his warrant card, the thing that identifies him as a policeman. The detective softens at this. I relax by 4%.

A conversation happens, it's full of language I don't or won't understand. A document gets signed. I sit and say nothing. Then it's over. The cop stands, Pat stands, they shake hands. It's done. We can go. What has just gone down? What the fuck is going on? I'm so afraid I avoid Leicester Square for almost six years. I feel bad for the dealer.

When I get home I'm angry and confused. We don't talk. I think I want Pat to go now. I know we're mates and shit but enough is enough. I'm not a copper, in fact at this point I'm probably completely the opposite. Pat senses this.

The next morning he heads out to make his secret phone calls. When he comes back we're all there. I sense something is really wrong. His eyes are red.

'Are you okay, mate?' I forget about last night. He stumbles and stammers.

'My mammie's dead.' He releases a noise like a fat boar struck by a javelin and falls into my mum's arms crying like a baby. Shit. Poor him. There's no way we can ask him to leave now. I watch him grieve his way through the nice bottle of scotch he bought Dad upon arrival. We leave it for a while, imagining he'll go home and take care of what needs to be done. He doesn't though, not immediately.

A couple of days later he gets up and goes to make his daily phone calls. Strangely, after two hours he's not back. Six hours later he is still MIA. He doesn't come back that night, he doesn't come back the next day, or the next, in fact he never comes back. He never comes back. I never see him again. This, to me, is the most frightening thing of all, the not knowing.

After a couple of days my parents decide to search his bags and phone the police. He left everything he had at my house. Left it all. Just ran. He even left his passport, one of three he had which are all in different names. What the fuck was going on?

My mum is genuinely concerned, she files a missing person's report, the police come round, take his stuff and promise to make enquiries. Mum decides to let his work know. His work being the Anti-Terrorist police in Northern Ireland. She makes a lot of calls and tracks down, eventually, a man who Pat claimed was his C/O. This man knew nothing about Pat. He had never heard of the man Mum described.

I thought he was either a spy or a member of a terrorist organisation. A sleeper. Either was bad for me. For a long while I truly believed someone would knock on my door and I'd be killed. I'd seen too much. Also what was all that bullshit when he busted the pill dealers? How the fuck did that go down? The coppers there treated him like one of their own. And the scar! What the eff was that? Who was this man I'd befriended in Israel? I didn't know him at all.

It didn't help my conspiracy paranoia one bit. The trail then goes cold. Days become weeks become months. My fear subsides. My mind quietens. Years later and I mean, like, six years later, I get a phone call from Mum. She'd heard something about Pat. The police had contacted her after all this time. Pat was not a copper. Pat was not a terrorist. Pat was a professional conman. Holy. Fucking. Balls. A conman.

It turned out I was not his first stop after Israel and I wasn't his last. After he fled mine, leaving everything, he made his way to Sweden, obviously with another fake or forged passport, to hook up with a girl he'd met in Israel. She was a lovely woman. She was gentle and quiet, and suffered from a severe lack of confidence, probably due to the fact she was really quite big.

He seduced that poor girl, told her he loved her. Once she was in love that's when he closed the trap, got her poor gran to sign stuff over, lend him thousands of kronor. Then he left. I don't know who he went to after that but it went on. Eventually he'd been caught and ended up going to prison for a fairly long time.

Part Three

At some point Mum and Dad get the nod from the council to say their house in Wales was ready. She was going home, I was homeless. Nice. I know it wasn't as cut and dried as that but that's how it felt then. But despite the fact that I was soon to be on my own, I was thrilled Mum and Dad had the chance to leave Ray Lodge – a stark, modern construct and a reminder of their failings as people and as parents.

Rachel, the free spirit, had come to live in London, in a kind of squat-thing in Golders Green known to me simply as 'Golders'. I want to be near her so I head there. I've no friends and no mum and dad back in Woodford Bridge and I need somewhere to live, somewhere to work and I definitely need some cheddar so I go to Golders Green.

The house was a big old lump of a place sitting on top of a kosher bakery. It was a madhouse and a shit hole, but it smelled nice. It had four large bedrooms and a kitchen that was usually the centre of high jinks. The loft had also been converted into a living space. I never went upstairs and never met anyone who lived up there. I knew they *were* there because at night I could hear them moving around, whispering.

All in all I think twenty-five people lived in that place, crammed inside on top of one another. Each room had five or so people plus the whispering loft dwellers. That meant the house was always happening, it was noisy, the place never slept. (Except at night.)

The people who'd been at Golders the longest got the best rooms; when someone left everyone moved up a space, better room, bigger bed.

I was the last to arrive so I got the smallest bedroom although it wasn't actually a bedroom, it was a cupboard. It had no windows and instead of a door a kind of plastic shower curtain. It was a shower curtain. The room was so narrow that the thin single mattress which was my bed bent up the sides of the walls. I felt like a hot dog sleeping in a bun.

I wasn't in that cupboard long. There was a fairly swift turn-around of folk with people coming and going. It's what I'd become used to. A space came up in one of the rooms and I took it. I was enjoying life at Golders and my on-again off-again thing with Rachel. There were five of us crammed into a bedroom, but a good five. Me, Sarit and CJ, Lauren and, I think, Jo, Rachel's mate.

Sarit was a beautiful but very fiery Israeli. CJ was a tall, beautiful male model from Socal with an easy smile and big booming laugh. They were girlfriend and boyfriend. Like a lot of beautiful Israeli women, she was hard work. She often sent CJ out at three o'clock in the morning to get treats. He always obliged. What a good egg. I'm not sure I would've.

Lauren was nice, she was a London girl through and through with West African heritage. She was chippy and had a laugh that always made me smile.

For a young man, living with Lauren could be tough. I'd never met anyone who was so brazen and open about their body and nakedness before. After showering she'd come back into the room where I was trying to plough my way through Solzhenitsyn's *Cancer Ward* and towel dry *and* oil her bare, lovely, giant African breasts. It was amazing. I didn't know where to look. I was barely out of my teens at this point and although Israel had opened my eyes I still had a lot to learn.

One night Lauren and I decided to take a shit load of mind openers and explore the mysteries of the universe, laughing like fucking idiots. We sat in the kitchen looking at each other change and morph as the sun came up. Briefly I became an African girl and briefly she became an overweight white man. How we laughed. The door to the house opened at about 5.30 a.m. and a complete stranger walked in. This wasn't odd, the door was never locked and people would often come and go.

This stranger was a woman in her thirties, pencil thin with a big helmet of bright orange hair. She smiled and joined us at the table. Was this happening? It was. Cope. Breathe. I'm African once more and I cluck and suck my teeth. We both look at her, eyes wide, she fumbles uncomfortably. One of my eyelids droops down and briefly obscures my view. I lift my eyelid up with both hands and the woman then makes a noise. It is long and it sounds like she is saying the word *buuuuuuuurrrrrrrrrrddddddddddddooooooooo*. There is no such word in my language. I don't think there is such a word in any language. I look to Lauren for reassurance and support and discover she is no longer there.

Lauren runs away screaming at about the third 'u', leaving me sweating and trying to lift my big floppy eyelid back over my head so I can see. I smile and back away into a cupboard, the cupboard is tiny and it forces me to re-emerge briefly. I smile and a tooth falls out. I turn and run up the stairs. Later I sadly find out the poor woman was there to meet a friend who was taking her to the airport, she was also profoundly deaf. It was too much for our brains to take. Poor girl. What idiots.

* * *

I began working at Chiquito Mexican restaurant at Staples Corner when I was twenty. Let me, off the bat, state for the record that when I began working there it served the finest Mexican food to be found anywhere in London. All the sauces were handmade fresh every morning by an army of brawny Ugandans. Now, sadly, it's an absolute abomination, just my opinion you understand. What a shame we live in a shitty world where the phrase 'Brand Standard' is commonplace. Anyhoo . . .

I began working on the bar at Chiquito sometime in the summer and really liked it. I only planned to stay there for three months until I got my shit together, whatever that meant – it felt more like something to say to convince myself that I wouldn't be there for five years, which of course I was.

It would also be the first place I actually set eyes on my heterosexual life partner, best friend and godfather to my son, Mr Simon Pegg. I'm jumping ahead of myself though.

Restaurants, like kibbutzim, have a high turnover of staff or 'Fresh Meat' as we liked to call them. At this point I was fresh meat. At first I was partnered with another bartender, known as Wavy Davy. An angry Kiwi who seemed to hate his job, his life and especially the customers. That said, he was a good egg at heart and certainly fun to work with. I'd never known anyone be so cheeky to customers. It was all about the tips. I loved his catchphrase 'you flaming ball-bag', it was a real winner.

Dave showed me around the big walk-in fridges and freezers, it was a place I'd get to know intimately over the next few months. Sometimes if I was mega hung-over I'd pull a chair into the fridge and sit there wishing I was dead.

The first time he showed me round the big freezers he pulled out a tray of frozen ice cream balls covered in cornflakes and bit into one like an apple. These were the deep-fried ice creams, an important part of Chiquito's elaborate birthday treat that all customers got if it was their birthday. He bit into it and stuck it back on the tray. I'd never seen lunacy like it. A few days later I found myself alone in the freezer. Wanting to be as cool as Dave I grab an ice cream and stuff it in my mouth. Sadly though it wasn't an ice cream. It was a ball of frozen shrimp butter. It was horrid and I vowed I would never randomly eat frozen balls of unknown matter again. It's a promise I have never broken.

The most fascinating part of the whole place for me was the kitchen. As you kicked open the flappy 'In' door you came upon the kitchen proper, we called it the Line. It was not for the faint of heart. Many was the time I'd seen bad waitresses made to cry by good cooks. A bad waiter can fuck shit up very quickly in a busy kitchen. A couple of times too I'd see some low-level violence, angry waiters pulling cooks through the line. People would have to jump in to stop it going any further. When, years after, I worked in the kitchen myself, I lost my shit with a waiter one Sunday and ended up pulling him through the line! The key is to strike fast, get a nice tight grip and then lean back and stand up. The waiter comes right through; if you're lucky you drag them across the beans and sauces and they end up looking like an oil painting.

On the far right of the line was starters, next to that the section where all the dishes were garnished, and just behind was the heart and anus of the kitchen, a very big, very hot griddle. Next to this there's a section where soft tacos and burritos are prepared. Throw in a couple of big ovens and the odd salamander grill and you get a picture of what the line looked like. On the far left was the pot wash. This was the home of Karim, a stick-thin Ugandan man who had the singing voice of an angel and spoke little or no English. The only thing I ever heard him say was, 'Can I have cheeseburger' – they fed us a staff meal every day and a cheeseburger was always his. I caught him lots of times eating scraps off the plates, something we'd all indulge in every now and then. Who could resist a juicy shrimp?

The only other interaction I had with Karim was a curious one: he'd hunch over like an old man and shuffle towards me in his ever-present Wellie boots, he'd then grab me in his thin but exceedingly strong arms and pretend to jerk me off, while making this noise, *dibbydibbydibbydibbydibby*. We'd all howl with laughter. Why?

But for now the bar was my realm, it'd be three more years before I made the move back of house. There were two sections to the bar, customers and service. Service meant you only made drinks for the waiters and their tables. On the weekend it was bedlam. The little bar printer would beep and puke out a ticket and another and another and another; if you weren't fast enough you'd end up with a bunch of very cross waiters all demanding their drinks first.

Wavy Davy never had a problem with demanding waiters, he was more than happy to tell those 'flaming ball-bags' to get fucked. On a busy weekend I liked it very much, I liked the buzz and the pressure. Double shifts were cool but long as it was busy most of the day. The bar was not the place to legally make a lot of tips. If you wanted to potentially earn £100 a day for a busy double the floor was where you needed to be. That's where the action was, the glamour.

I started working for £1.92 an hour plus tips. It was nothing but I didn't need much as I paid hardly any rent. Any money I earned went on weed, drinking and cabs. I never went on holiday, I didn't have a car or kids, I didn't really need or want much. Chiquito was my life right now, I needed nothing except what it gave me.

Unlike people I went to school with, faces from the old neighbourhood and even most people from kibbutz, some of the people I met in Chiquito became friends I still know today.

Big Red was a man with the words 'Fuck You' tattooed inside his lower lip. Red was a cunning little silver fox, he always had an angle, a way to make a quick buck, a way to stick it to the man with a scam. He was with a girl called Chicky, a real beauty with a great laugh, she was lovely and we got on well. She was like my big sister. They were a great couple, great people and they really looked after me. Chicky and Rachel were great friends who knew each other before Israel, so we all hung out a lot. I think I attended my first dinner party in their house. It was a very mature thing for me to do, I may even have managed to wear trousers. They had a small flat down Kilburn way crammed to the rafters with cool shit. They were stylish, cool people.

Chicky was there the day me and Rachel split up for good. Rachel was going to LA to pursue her dream of becoming an actress. The day before she left there'd been a horrible misunderstanding about a used condom she found in my bedroom. She accused me of cheating on her. I hadn't but she found my 'posh wank' excuse hard to swallow.

Racked with sorrow, me and Chicky sat up all night drinking in their flat. Red, who'd left the restaurant to become a milkman, got up at four to do his round to find us still up. At about five and after many tears Chicky convinced me that going to Heathrow to say goodbye was a good idea, a grand romantic gesture. Yes! I was all about those, great idea. I have a vague recollection of us being in a car at one point, and then we were magically at Heathrow.

Rachel was really happy to see Chicky. Not so much me. It could've had something to do with the ironing board and bottle of Captain Morgan I'd insisted on bringing. Rachel's mother was also there. She hated me. I hid, trembling behind the ironing board until Rachel had gone. That board definitely had its uses.

On the way past, her mother hissed at me, 'I feel really sorry for you.'

I wasn't sure what she meant but I took it to heart and cried all the way home. What was I crying about? Stupid drink.

Sometimes on busy nights Chicky, a trusted employee, would work in the cash booth, a little cupboard in the corner of the kitchen where we'd drop off the bills and money after the tables had paid. Once you were in there you had to stay in there. Security, you understand.

One particular Saturday, and this was rare for me, I had the whole day off. I arranged to meet a mate who also happened to be my general manager at the time. We went to drink in a shit pub up in North Finchley, pints and pool being the order of the day. After about an hour a shifty cunt approaches and offers me a magical and ancient laughing compound. I gratefully accept.

He limps off, returning ten minutes later, and discreetly drops the package into one of the pockets of the pool table. Real cloak and dagger shit. The package rolls into the body of the machine and is lost. He returns ten minutes later and, forgetting all the subterfuge, decides to simply put it in my hand. We consume the HaHas and wait for Christ to arrive.

At one point my GM suggests we go back to the restaurant and drink free shit and have a fajita or two. The Toucan and me agree this is a good plan and we float off into the sky. When we get there the place is calming down a bit, still busy but manageable. I wonder for a moment if anyone else can see this Toucan?

We sit in a corner of the bar. He drinks beer and I gulp a giant strawberry margarita. Delish. Someone comes and tells me Chicky wants me to go and say hi. In the kitchen it's bright and hectic and all the Ugandans shout the word 'Woomla' at me. This is actually true. The Ugandans on the line refer to me as the Woomla King. I can't remember why but I like this alter ego.

My big dumb grin arrives before I do and knocks on the cash booth door. Chicky opens up and beckons the rest of me to come in.

'How fucked are you?' she howls, laughing.

I loved Chicky's laugh, part dockworker, part geisha. My eyes roll and then focus on a button sort of hidden under the cash desk.

'What's that?'

'Panic button.' Hahahahaha . . . we laugh.

I'm panicking a bit so I jab at it. Janine now panics a bit too, but she's laughing and is quickly calmed by my confidence that it doesn't do anything. As she's laughing I jab at it again and again. We chat briefly and she reminds me I shouldn't have my spirit bird in the kitchen. I understand. We have a little cuddle and I move out to finish my giant red drink.

As I kick open the swingy both ways door I'm met by the sight of twelve armed policemen steaming through the front door of the place. The button worked. I look to the boss who seems really cross with me. The Toucan stifles a giggle and pecks a nut open on my head.

'It was me! I leant on it by mistake!' I fess up immediately. Honesty is definitely the best policy when confronted with firearms I find.

I'm frogmarched outside and given a very stern dressing down. I'm so glad they can't see the Toucan. A rare and endangered bird such as this could bring me a shit load of trouble. The Toucan winks at me and pops a nice ripe berry into my mouth and we smile, he nuzzles my ear with his beak and right then I know we'll be okay. They buy it and leave. Sorry SWAT team, totes my fault.

This sadly was not my last brush with armed police, there was to be what has now become a legendary story – when I say legendary it just means I've told it a lot. In terms of the timeline I'm jumping way ahead here but what the fuck, I like telling it.

We were shooting series two of *Spaced* and there's a scene where Mike Watt TA strips an MP5 sub-machine gun blindfolded. Being a bit Method and knowing Edgar would take great pleasure from me learning how to do it properly they got one of the on-set armourers to take me through the process of stripping and rebuilding the weapon. He'd even kindly taken some Polaroids at every step for me to follow when I got home. They were letting me take this home . . .

I shoot the first scene of the day and then wonderfully I'm wrapped. Incidentally, the word WRAP on a film set is an acronym for Wind Reel And Print. A throwback to the early days of film-making. Yawn. Sorry, but I find all that a bit cool, some continuity in film-making that runs across the generations. That sound I hear of film running through the gate, or used to hear before film started being used less and less, is the same sound Harold Lloyd or Buster Keaton heard when they filmed. I think there should be a button on the new digital cameras that reproduces that sound. Anyway . . .

I stuff my sub-machine gun, spare clips and a handful of dummy rounds into my bag and jump into my car to head home. I discover the house – a big, ground-floor flat I share with Michael Smiley and Simon – is empty. It's right next to Highgate Station and the back garden is huge with an area of woodland beyond that's a real hotspot for European Jays.

It's a very hot day, the kind a tabloid might refer to as 'a scorcher'. I open the back door that leads directly into our lovely back garden and allow some much-needed breeze in. I change into some tiny house shorts and mince around with the gun for forty minutes or so. I take turns raiding the other guys' bedrooms. Tossing a balled-up pair of socks into the room, stunning the terrorists inside with a flashbang before moving in and cleaning up with a series of devastatingly accurate double-taps. PapPap! Tremendous.

After a while it's time to put some time in on the task at hand, stripping this firearm. I retrieve a giant bag of icky, smoke a bowl and get to work. At first I follow the pictures, slowly pushing out the pins in the correct sequence, stripping the receiver out, barrel, ejector port etc. It's going well and I decide to start stripping it with a blindfold on, hone my martial skills properly. I blindly strip and rebuild the weapon three or four times. Pleased with the way it's going I decide to smoke another bowl and take the rest of the day off.

I remove the Bluetones scarf I'd been using as a blindfold and straight away something feels wrong. My spider-sense tingles. I look to my left as it feels like someone's watching me through the window. I'm right – someone *is* watching me. Actually six someones, six armed police officers.

Two of them are already in the room pointing Glocks at me. Great handgun. The other four, armed with rifles and, ironically, actual MP5s, are outside. Once we'd laid eyes on one another it was on. I tensed. They tensed. This is really bad and very dangerous. One wrong or quick misplaced move – hell, even a deep breath – could end in me being killed.

They see their opportunity and stream in like a big blue tsunami. They holler various things at me, like 'don't fucking move' etc. I'm now working on instinct, my anus clenches and a small cough is released. I, slowly and in one silken movement do two things: I take my hands off the replica and raise them, palms and fingers spread, high into the air above me. I then shuffle backwards away from the shooter and further onto the settee. I couldn't have been more submissive if I'd tried.

I'm hauled off the sofa and hogtied. Once immobilised they stop pointing their killy guns at me. Still, I'm not allowed to move or speak. They search the house methodically, laying out everything they find in a logical and pleasingly symmetrical manner.

Mine was not the only firearm-shaped thing we owned. With the weed and still smoking bong, the table now looked like a snapshot from a raid on a Triad girl farm. I was oddly thrilled.

By and by the mood lifts. They'd set out ready to kill a lump with a skinhead and having not had to kill anyone they relax slightly.

I could hear them shouting and talking to the girls in the flat next door. I was embarrassed by what they were saying, I'd rather they'd lied and told them I was some kind of hardnut. I heard snippets of this conversation . . .

'What's going on?'

'—blah blah blah—'

'Actor.'

'Silly little boy . . .' etc.

Some laughter, they were clearly flirting with these girls – still if it kept them from shooting me in the mind then go for it.

Forty or so minutes passed. My voice, which at first had been high-pitched and squeaky, returns to normal. When they'd streamed in, and while I was sitting back and opening hands up to the heavens, I was also shouting, 'Don't shoot me, I'm an actor!' but in the highest possible voice. I called it the übersoprano.

The lead officer screams back at me, 'If you're an actor what's your Equity number!!!' I stumbled, I did not have this information to hand. That was when shit was bad. Since then I'd recovered somewhat and my story had checked out and shit was less bad. That said, I never in a month of Sundays with the replica and the big lump of green believed I'd stay out of custody. No fucking way. I imagined the call to production from a young, court-appointed lawyer. Not good.

I then wondered how they'd known about the gun. Apparently a poor old lady had seen the barrel sticking out of my bag as I got out of my car. They'd blocked the road off and had sent scouts in to watch me hop around the house like *Die Hard*'s John McClane but in short shorts. What a dick.

The team's chief told me, with some jollity, that in their pre-raid briefing they'd decided to take me down, to shoot me if I'd had the gun in hand. It was so close. I actually think in this rare instance being stoned helped me.

The guy in charge picks up my 'erb bag, sniffs it, zips it back up and leaves it on the table.

'You'll deserve a nice stiff drink after this, son, and you may want to knock this shit on the head, eh?'

Police laughter. I couldn't believe this, it actually appeared that I would not only escape custody but get to keep my 'erb bag as well. What the fuck!

They stride towards the back door from whence they came and leave me with a final piece of wisdom . . .

'You did well, mate, a lot of people piss themselves.' Much laughter from the Blue Tsunamis. I was thrilled I hadn't pissed myself.

* * *

When I wasn't setting off security buttons in cash booths I was still working on the bar. Wavy Davy had gone and in his place were two South African guys, Dion Sampson and Tony Lindsay. I still know Tony, he's one of my best friends, I was best man at his wedding and godfather to one of his children. He looks like a skinny, white Dwight Yorke. His initials are tattooed on my arm (along with Simon Pegg's, Michael Smiley's, Danny Brown's, Edgar Wright's and Nira Park's). Sadly I don't really see Dion any more. It's one of those horrible drift-aways where six months becomes a year and a year becomes five becomes ten. I regret this.

I'm a pretty good mimic of accents, particularly South African, and for two days with the help of my voice skills I completely fool Tony into believing I'm from Durban. It's a story Tony still tells today.

I don't remember leaving the big lump of a house in Golders Green but I do. I move in to a house on Cricklewood Lane, number 142. I live there for a long time. With whom and in what order I have no idea.

It's a small, three-bedroom maisonette with a wonderfully large balcony. I had a great time living there and again people come and go and rotate but I finally had my own room and I loved it. Number 142 was a revolving door of lunatics, alcoholics, actors, singers and artists. I'm not sure which tag suited me best, definitely not actor though. I never wanted to be an actor. The thought of being an actor was a terrible nightmare to me then. Having people watching me show off seemed a horrendous notion. Don't get me wrong, I had my moments but usually that was in small groups of high friends, not un-high in a studio watched by eighty people. I really had no idea what I wanted to do. I had no long-term goal.

Down the way at 148 lived the wonderful Kiwis Keith and Michelle and Michelle's sister Rebecca. I still keep in contact with them to this day and occasionally see them when I'm down in Wellington. I invented a thing called the Cheese Eagle, a raptor that only eats cheese that Michelle used to love. I'd swoop down and grab her Edams. That sounds weird. Sorry, Keith.

At work I'd moved from the bar onto the floor and found that I was a great waiter. My unflappable, logical mind found it easy to prioritise sometimes up to twelve tables. (Not easily, waiting twelve tables is very hectic.)

I've said before in interviews that being a waiter was how I learnt to become an actor, that and my long training since I was a child in pretending and mimicking accents and doing impressions and copying what I saw on films and adverts and television. I quickly understood that if you wanted to make big money as a waiter you had to adapt to every customer that came through the door. I think generally there are only seven or eight different types of people in the world so it wasn't too difficult.

If 'Geezers' came in I was a farkin' cockney barrow boy, I was a chirpy, cheeky, cockles and friggin' mussels 'big old boy outta Repton' kind of toilet. They loved it. If a rich Indian family came in I'd bow and scrape and only talk to the oldest man in the group or the most glamorous lady. If businessmen came in there would be lots of 'yes sir no sir'. Out of all the groups I served, businessmen were by far the rudest. I was literally shit to them. Their self-importance was boundless. I had to frequently remind myself they couldn't be that big a deal otherwise they wouldn't be having a shit hamburger at Chiquito while discussing unit cost on lengths of PVC piping. Anger at rudeness aside, I started to make some pretty good money.

I liked working in the restaurant. I never had a thought about my future. I never really had, even as a child. (A trait I hope my son doesn't inherit.) That said, this stupidly blasé attitude has served me well over the years.

At this point I had little or no contact with Mum and Dad. I was too angry and too sad. I'd been left alone when they moved to Wales and alone was how I considered myself mostly. Of course from time to time there'd be phone calls. As soon as I heard Mum on the other end of the phone, literally the first two words she spoke, I could tell that she'd been drinking. I hated it. As soon as I heard the tiny slurs of speech I turned off. 'Is Dad there?' I'd talk to him instead and usually I was pissed off with him for letting it happen. He didn't let it happen by the way, he had no choice. Mum's all-powerful character and illness within meant it was easier to go with it than fight against it. I feel ashamed that I treated them this way but I didn't know what else to think or do. So usually we just didn't talk.

Being a dad myself now and knowing what they'd gone through I can't imagine how hard it must've been to not see or speak to your son for months at a time. I think it has and will kind of haunt me for ever now they're not here. 'I could've done more.' In reality though there was nothing more I could've done.

What I really wanted to do was write novels. Thanks to Rachel I'd discovered a love of moody Russian literature, the works of Milan Kundera and other eastern European existentialists. I longed to sit in a chilly, carpetless garret eating a watery potato soup, itchy blanket slung across my shoulders, writing about lost love and how grim and pointless life was. Thank you, Comrade Solzhenitsyn.

Copying Red's example I trawled through the myriad junkshops and secondhand places in Edgware and Golders Green hoping to strike gold. What gold meant was a first edition hardback book. I think in all my time doing it I found three, one by Norman Mailer, one by Aldous Huxley; the third one, my prize possession at the time and more so now I've worked with Steven Spielberg, was the first edition novelisation of *Close Encounters of the Third Kind*. I loved that book. Still do. I love the film and I loved the soundtrack that fifteen-year-old me used to listen to at night to frighten myself.

Years later I find myself on the set of *The Adventures of Tintin* directed by the lovely Mr Spielberg – Uncle Steven as Simon and I take to secretly calling him – I've got the book with me and on the last day of the shoot he signs it! Such a nice personal inscription. Funny how things work out. That first edition I found in a junk shop is now priceless, to me anyway.

When I wasn't trawling secondhand shops for rare first editions I was working. I worked most of the time. Thing about that sort of existence is if you don't work you don't make money. Simple as that. I had a vague concept at the beginning of my foodservice career that I'd save some money and travel again but it wasn't working out that way.

What I earned I spent. After most weekend shifts and some weeknights we'd end up in a Nepalese restaurant in Cricklewood called the Pink Rupee. To this day I still think about the perfect Butter Chicken they served. We'd sit there sometimes until three or four in the morning pissed and laughing.

There was a lovely old man who looked a bit like Fu-Manchu who'd come in late at night and read his paper, he was nice, we'd chat to him and mid conversation he'd fall asleep into his curry. Fu-Manchu was the only person I ever knew with bona fide narcolepsy. It was so shocking it wasn't even funny. It was a bit funny, obviously not funny if he were piloting a container vessel, but here in the relative safety of the Pink Rupee, some-times it could be a bit funny. A couple of times I had to fish him out of a particularly saucy Pasanda to stop him from drown-ing. I'd gently lift his face out, move the plate away and pop his head down on a napkin. Seconds later he'd be awake again, wheezing his sixty-a-day laugh and tucking into his supper.

I drank, I partied, and I worked serving mediocre hamburg-ers to fucking horrible businessmen. This was my existence and it was a rut that I liked being in.

At Chiquito we had a thing called the Birthday Song – if someone came in and it was his or her birthday we'd be forced to sing the following ditty:

Happy happy happy birthday,
Happy happy happy birthday,
Happy happy happy birthday,
To you, to you, to you, Olé!!!

Some fucking genius got paid to write this. I'd heard it was Chris de Burgh but I've never received confirmation on that. We used to have a better birthday song but TGI Friday's took them to court for infringing birthday song copyright. It was basically the same song but someone had cunningly changed the word 'Friday's' to the word 'Chiquito'. (Probably the same genius that got paid a Trillion Turkish Lira to write the new birthday song!) Who knew the rules surrounding theme restaurant birthday song law could be so tricky to navigate.

The birthday song generally made me sad. For someone who got embarrassed easily and had/still has a little working-class chip on his shoulder, having to sing for rude dickheads who were essentially lauding up the fact they did jobs where they weren't forced to sing for a stranger's birthday made me cross. Busy Friday and Saturday nights were the best for the birthday song. All the waiters would grab spoons and pans to use as percussion instruments and we'd really belt it out. Part of this was about defiance, not wanting to be broken. Sometimes instead of the last 'Olé' we'd mumble the words 'fuck you'. It was so quick and hidden among the rest of the cacophony people never twigged. Hardly ever.

The birthday song was very popular, punters lapped that shit up. Sometimes annoyingly customers would pretend it was someone's birthday even if it wasn't, just for the embarrassment factor and the free fried ice cream.

On a quiet Monday afternoon having a couple of young kids demanding the birthday song when I'm the only waiter and Wavy 'Flaming ball-bag' Davey was the only bartender was another matter. You had to do it so you'd suck it up and belt it out. If you were lucky they'd leave you a thirteen pence tip.

Tiny tips were always given back. At first I didn't have the balls to do this but after a while getting a pound tip off twenty women who'd eaten and drunk 400 quids' worth of burritos and margaritas, who also received great, fast, efficient, friendly service, was too much to take. Sometimes I'd follow them out and give them their pennies in the car park . . .

'Oh, thank god I found you, you forgot your change.'

They'd smile, confused . . .

'Oh, it's fine, it's for you.'

I'd smile . . .

'I think you need this more than me. Thanks though!'

Outrageous behaviour. Waiters live on tips. Fact. But . . . As a waiter, to expect a tip is wrong wrong wrong. It needs to be earned. Tips is actually an acronym – To Induce Prompt Service. I think Dr Samuel Johnson, the inventor of the modern dictionary, coined this.

Late one night almost as my shift was about to end I was given a table of surly Middle Eastern gents. Getting a table at the very end of a long shift was a pretty mean thing for the host/hostess to do. If you'd been cross and shouted at the host you were generally punished at some point.

A clever host has the power to make your shift very easy indeed. It's about gently filtering tables into your section bit by bit. If you've twelve tables all at different points in their meal it's easy to cope. Sit four tables all at once and you have a problem. I wasn't generally a shouter but illogical people who are shit at their jobs make me cross.

Tonight it was my turn to face the hostess's wrath. I'd snapped at some earlier lunacy and I was to be punished. Or not, as it turned out. I'd almost finished cleaning my section and just about to ask my GM if I could close when the hostess, Melissa, who was actually pretty good and absolutely lovely, sat a group of surly men at my table. It essentially meant that a half-ten close would now become a half-twelve finish. Maybe later. The repercussions were great, it meant that I wouldn't be smashing the granny out of a Butter Chicken and eight pints until at least one in the morning. Not cool.

Middle Eastern businessmen want one thing from a waiter: to be treated like kings. If you can identify the richest one in the group and pander to his needs then you might hit the jackpot. Pander too much though and you're perceived as a snivelling worm and they're more likely to set their hawks on you at the end of a meal than give you a big tip.

They sat and drank bottles of spirits; the thing about buying bottles of spirits in a restaurant is you get charged by the shot, thirty-three shots per bottle at £6 a time, that's almost £200 a bottle, and that was the cheap shit. They drank jug upon jug of margarita, they feasted on nachos and fajitas and delicious, deep-fried chimichangas, in fact everything on the menu, and everything good Texaco-Mexico cuisine had to offer.

They ran me ragged. After the desserts, which they were too pissed to eat, Prince Money Bags, who smells of deep Italian leather and Aramis, raises a perfectly threaded eyebrow that denotes he'd like the bill. It was £2,400! The biggest bill I'd ever seen in that place. He pulls out a pack of fifties big enough to choke a pig and rolls off three grand in cash. I thank him, nod to the party and leave the table. I'm stopped, I feel a firm, manicured hand on my arm. I turn, his deep mahogany chocolate eyes blaze and crackle, he smiles gently. I think I'm in love with the handsome Omar Sharif-a-like, he mutters the words every waiter longs to hear: 'Keep the change.' He just told me to keep the change! I am in love. He just gave me a £600 tip and I didn't have to suck ONE cock. Not one! KER – FUCKING – CHING!!! That was the biggest tip I ever got and like most of my money at that point it went pretty quickly. Six hundred quid buys a lot of beer, green and king prawn madras.

At some point along my meandering timeline a girl came to work in the restaurant who would eventually and inadvertently change my life for ever. She was a wee Scottish thing I'll call Charles Mouse. I really liked her a lot. She was quick to laugh, funny as fuck and so smart. At that point I'd never met anyone like her. I must admit for a moment my heart sank when eventually I found the nerve to ask whether or not she had a boyfriend. She did. All the best ones do. I caught a glimpse of this sexual Tyrannosaur one night. It was the first time I'd ever seen a man under thirty-five wearing elbow patches on a corduroy jacket.

A few weeks into knowing her we had a party at 142. A big sound system was brought in, the front room was emptied of all our shit-brown furniture and a big bag of crisps was opened. This party promised to be a roadblock.

I'm a bit nervous to be honest, her boyfriend – her stand-up comedian boyfriend – was coming. I'd heard a lot about this guy, I felt any man would have a problem living up to this kind of expectation. The Mouse felt sure we'd get on. (As an aside, if you want me to dislike anyone tell me we'll really get on.) Happily though this was to be the exception to my brain's stupid stubbornness. I wasn't working that night so we began the party a little early, with half-pints and shots first in the pub across the street. By the time people start turning up I had become, with the aid of Red Stripe, either a charming bon viveur or a lumpen jelly bag, I can't remember which – no matter.

I was actually really nervous waiting to meet Mouse's boyfriend. Sure I was funny, perhaps in the top five, maybe even top three, funniest people at Chiquito Staples Corner. That's no mean feat when I was working with Flea (the template for Mike Watt). And Harry, a Nigerian arms dealer who looked like Rango.

We offered an open-door policy at 142 and at some point Mouse walks in, I crane to look, and there he is. I hide in the crowd, I'm not ready, I flit from inside to out, I host, I avoid, I spread confusion, a little fear. Mouse catches up with me in the kitchen and we say hello.

'Are you coming outside to meet him?'

'Sure.' I'm hammered and think WTFN.

She leaves, I follow. He's there chatting to some of my friends and they're really laughing, some of the girls are even tossing their heads back, really guffawing.

I realise, oddly, I now have a toothpick in my mouth. No idea how or where it came from. I gob a foul brown liquid from my chewing tabbacy into a bucket, it dings loudly. The crowd part and that's when I see him for the first time, Simon fucking Pegg . . .

For the next two hours we spar, jab and comedy counter-jab, our eyes narrow as we size each other up, we drink and, at points, we go separately to the toilet. In truth I remember very little of this meeting. I know we laughed a lot and that there, on that balcony in Cricklewood, was where our (at this point) twenty-one-year best-friendship began. We did impressions, Rick from *The Young Ones*, Matthew the kindly Nigerian from *Desmond's* and of course sports commentator David Coleman.

Things then get dark and blurry, party business takes over, and in the confusion and flirting with Simon I've neglected my job as host. Other faces come and go, drink is quaffed, girls are kissed or not kissed, people become shapes and silhouettes and eventually sound is the only sensation to remain until that gradually drifts away and I die.

I'm glad people were there to tell me what happened. Apparently and actually pretty early in the night I drank myself to a standstill. Sitting to take a breath and to gather my thoughts I fall asleep, cross-legged, leaning against a giant Bass Bin and that was where I stayed all night. People had to step over me to get out. Simon tells it that I was slumped against the speaker while the speaker rumbled me to pieces, reggae and Red Stripe will do that to a man.

HAHAHAHA!!!

'Stop laughing, Nick! It's not funny. Didn't you realise you had a terrible and burgeoning drink and drug habit?'

'Stop shouting at me!'

Peggy Poo and me see bits and pieces of one another over the next couple of weeks. A drink after work here and there, the odd house party, but it was at the Pink Rupee where our love truly blossoms.

A bunch of floor staff had gone out after work one Friday night for a nice Butter Chicken and a few cold ones. The management had pushed together a number of tables and Simon and me found ourselves sat opposite one another. We'd reached a place, pretty quickly actually, where we could make ourselves laugh like drains. We still have that today. We'll find something funny and work the shit out of it until it reaches its zenith comedically and then it dies. Game over. Next!

As we talked and laughed drunkenly that night Simon did something that would change me for ever, change us for ever. He picked up a condiment and moved it across the table making this sound: *Birbirbigitt Birbirbigitt bigitt.* I knew exactly what this was. Time slowed around us, a warm bubble of light inflated and for a moment I couldn't see or hear anything but SJP. He was making the sound of the mouse droid that Chewbacca roars at in *Star Wars.* It was as if we were the only two people in the world. He got it, whatever *it* was. I understood him completely and he understood me.

I'm not sure how long we were in that golden bubble of self-indulgence but once it popped our mains were on the table. It must have been a while though as my naan bread was floppy and cold. This was the beginning. From this point on, me, Simon and at first Miss Mouse were pretty much inseparable. I didn't know what was happening but I'd made a new friend really quickly, and I wasn't afraid or nervous, it didn't feel weird – on the contrary it felt great and it's been that way ever since. I guess one could argue we fell in love that day. It's never really left us either, it's obviously changed and evolved as all long-term relationships need to do if they're to survive, but we still make each other laugh more than anyone else.

We can also fall into fits of laughter without talking which some people find unnerving. I always know exactly what he's thinking. An eyebrow cocked or a brow un-crinkled at just the right time can be like an A-bomb going off for us comedically. Not talking can be just as effective as repeating over and over again the phrase 'Would you like a white eel?' Let me explain.

We were on a plane a couple of years ago coming back from the Dublin leg of the *World's End* press tour. We were sat together at the front of the plane, we'd been delayed for some time so by the time we boarded we were tired and emotional. After take-off a lovely old flight attendant shuffled up to us and almost whispered in the softest Irish brogue, 'Would you like a light meal?' We both declined but there was something about the phrasing that got us going – once it happened it couldn't be stopped. I imagine it's probably how David Banner feels before turning into the Hulk; it can't be stopped so the best thing to do is to embrace it and enjoy the helplessness that comes from laughing so much you cry, laughing so much that eventually no sound comes out accept the odd 'Eeerrrrffff'. I turn to Simon: 'Would you like a light meal?' The change begins. We have a thing that others call 'Rainman', it's where we say the same thing or a variety of the same thing over and over again.

'Would you like a light meal?' suddenly became 'Would you like a white eel?' And on it went. At one point we imagine that she's vigorously woken us from a deep sleep to offer us refreshment.

'Oh, I'm so sorry to wake you, I noticed by your eyelids flickering that you were in a deep state of REM sleep but . . . would you like a grey seal?' We had this from the start and it's something that's never left us. Some of the in-jokes and lols we have now are based on and evolved from things that started all the way back then.

We were a cool little crew at the restaurant round about this time. Being a waiter was good but unrewarding, it was easy, I was good at it and it was never much of a push. I was a big fish in a small pond and that was cool. I was cool like this. It was enough for me. At that point I wasn't sure what I wanted, I never felt like I had to make a decision in terms of something long term. My parents never pushed me to get into a career. It literally never came up once.

Every Thursday Miss Mouse and I would rush back to the place she shared with Simon. Expecting our arrival he'd set up a kind of nest in the living room and we'd run in full of excitement, open some wine and watch *Northern Exposure*. We loved it. Even now if I put on an episode and see grumpy Dr Flieschman or Ruth Anne in her 'Born to bingo' jumper it takes me back to that nest. It makes me happy.

It wasn't just *Northern Exposure*, it was *Reeves and Mortimer* and *The Day Today* as well. I'd never seen things like this before. I'd felt them, felt that they were possible and that they might exist out there but I'd never seen them. I guess this is what happens when a university-educated Rik Mayall-a-like and a Dagenham bell-end hook up. The pot gets stirred.

The three of us really were inseparable. We did everything together. Mouse and me would work, Simon would gig and come to meet us, and we'd eat and drink and fuck about and laze around in Soft World and laugh. It was like *Y Tu Mamá También* without the rimming.

This was also the time where the character of Mike Watt TA, or roly-poly gun-mad Mike from *Spaced*, first fell out of my mind. He was a bit different at that point though, older, an actual veteran whose combat experience had driven him underground, a woodsman with advice on a million different and exciting ways to kill a man. Covering a foe in Tizer and then letting fire ants eat the flesh from their bodies being just one.

Another was finding an enemy asleep, cutting his legs off, while still asleep, replacing them with table legs and letting termites do the rest. That kind of stuff. Simon and me laughed a lot at Mike. We loved his misogyny it wasn't really a fear or dislike of women, it was more like they didn't ever show up on his radar. He didn't know how to deal with or talk to them. 'How you doing, little lady? Mike Watt TA.' This was Mike's seventies-style greeting to Woman.

Mike was a mixture of two people I knew at the time, one was a really close mate called Lee, although people called him Flea. He was a curious one. A big, giant, baby of a man, tall and heavy with long greasy hair. He was bonkers and made me laugh a ton. I know he wasn't a Nazi but he liked Nazi memorabilia. It confused me. It was wrong but he was a lovely man, kind, gentle, an alcoholic lunatic but definitely not a racist or a fascist and absolutely not an anti-Semite as I'm sure his Jewish girlfriend at the time would attest. He just liked the design of the stuff. We hung out and got drunk together a lot, sometimes we'd head out to some dark shit hole in Camden and drink two bottles of JD while listening to some band called Stinkpipe or Ovaryfart. I once saw Flea slide down the middle ramp-like centre between two escalators in Camden tube station. He probably flew fifteen feet off the end of that thing.

The other man responsible for the other half of Mike was a brawny lump we called Kippy. He was a member of the TA by day and a mediocre bartender by night; someone my dad might've referred to as a Bullshit Merchant. He was tall and muscular and the girls loved him. Me and Tony and Dion would tease him about his part-time army career. Kippy was to have the last laugh though: years after our time together he actually made the regular army and went on to do several tours in Iraq and Afghanistan. Who knew? All that bullshit was actually true. I opened the paper one day and saw our glorious leader David Cameron being protected by Kippy. He had dark Oakley shades on, a PLO neck scarf and a fat M4-style battle rifle. Amazing. Good for him. What the fuck do I know?

Pretty early on in Simon's, Mouse's and my time together I casually mentioned to Mouse, in a moment of reflection, that maybe I could be doing something more with my life. Simon had moved down to London from Bristol to pursue a flowering stand-up career, and she suggested I try stand-up too and that Simon could help. I wasn't sure. The very notion of performing made me immediately frightened.

Simon kindly wrote me a note, which I still have somewhere, telling me where I should go to do open spots. (Open spots are the little five-or ten-minute bits that new stand-ups do.) This unpaid gig was the chance to hone your skill. To feel real terror in a relatively low-pressure environment. I remember on the note he'd written, 'Don't be afraid. Audiences smell fear like sharks smell blood.' It was so fucking true. I didn't like the idea of doing stand-up, it filled me with unease, but I went home and began thinking about writing a set. I had no idea where to start.

* * *

I'd called a bunch of the promoters and comedy bookers on Simon's list and secured my very first open spot at the Cosmic Comedy Club on Fulham Palace Road. I'd worked on a little set and was as ready as I would ever be. This seemed very unlike me, putting myself out there, but I'd reached a point where I kind of said, 'Why the frig not?'

Simon thought it would be a good idea to go and see some stand-up before I dived in. I'd never seen live comedy before, naively I didn't realise it even existed, or that as a scene it was so big. I had no idea, apart from *The Young Ones*, that there was an alternative comedy scene. Yeah, I knew about Bernard Manning, *Wheel Tappers and Shunters*, Norman Collier and the like, but my life up until that point had been deals for tiny amounts of hash in shitty pubs, watching Irish men fight, a father who was a workaholic cum nervous wreck and an alcoholic mother who died a bit more each day. I had never before tasted these delicious little cutlets of culture that were now, thanks to Simon, being served up to me. I liked it, they tasted sweet like barbecued lamb.

The Cosmic was a big place, much bigger than I'd been expecting. I thought most comedy was done in grubby basements or upstairs in shit boozers. The Cosmic was part of the new wave, built using the swelling coffers that a hungry audience desperate for a laugh brought in. It was like a small theatre but instead of rows of chairs facing the stage there were long benches and tables. It was pretty dead that Tuesday night, twenty or so people, maybe thirty if I squinted my eyes a bit.

The room was really quiet too, the only noises I could hear were the low rhubarb of chatting and the clatter and squeak of knives and forks as the sparse audience hacked their way through chicken and chips. These are perhaps some of the worst conditions for comedy to thrive in.

We stood at the bar and the guy who ran the place came to say hello to Simon who was fast becoming a major player on the London circuit; they chat for a bit and he bustles off. Simon and me have a couple of beers. It fills up a little more but it was no way what you'd call busy. The booker came back over, another chat. He heads off again, Simon turns to me.

'The compere hasn't shown up. They want me to do it!'

I would've been so nervous but he took it all in his stride. He left me at my booth drinking beers and disappears through a door, emerging on stage five minutes later. There's a polite ripple of applause although some seem cross that a comedian would spoil their supper by coming on and trying to do some stand-up.

After some classic Pegg-style jovial banter he brings on the first act. I've no idea who any of the stand-ups are that night but they were all pretty brutalised. It certainly didn't make me want to do stand-up. Simon returned looking down. He didn't think it went too well. In fact he states that he died on his arse but I thought he was good. I don't remember him dying.

Tomorrow I'd be on the same stage doing my first ever stand-up gig. What an idiot. Don't do it!

The details of how and why it happens elude me now but for some idiocy I'd been entered into an open-spot competition as my first ever gig. Sadly, lots of people from work had been invited – I don't think inviting people would've been my thing at the time. I would've been happy doing it quickly on my own and running off into the night from whence I came. No, inviting people sounds like it might've been Chicky or Jo's doing. The kind of thing where you tell them quietly looking for some gentle support, and before you know it most of the restaurant was involved. Looking back though it was a good thing. I was glad of the support.

My lot take up two whole benches, maybe twenty people give or take. After my gig we were having a big party back at 142 no matter what the outcome. I couldn't wait for the party. Several hours before the gig I'd begun to feel something I had rarely felt before, nerves. Real terrifying, shit your pants nerves.

It made me sick to my stomach. The only time I think I'd felt anything near this was the moment before the referee blew his whistle to start a rugby match. This wasn't a rugby match though, this was going to be much rougher.

I was there predictably early. I'm always early. I can't help it. I stand around not being able to talk or eat, friends come and talk to me, I barely respond. I smile weakly and shake a hand, my hand, why am I shaking my own hand? In the end I hide behind a curtain silently going over my routine in my head. Simon's there but knowing what I'm going through he keeps his distance and advice to a minimum, he watches me like a great corner man, assessing me, geeing me up where necessary.

The lights go down and the competition begins. This is the first competition of any kind I've ever entered. I'm second on the bill out of ten or so terrified souls like me, which is something at least. I think it's always best to get it over and done with. I develop a mantra at this point, it's a kind of countdown to release: 'this time tomorrow it will all be over' becomes 'in twelve hours it will be over' then an hour, then ten minutes, you get the idea. I still use this method today if I'm ever going through something stressful or unpleasant. I never quite understand why all the speeches at a wedding come after the meal. It's stupid. I've given two best-man speeches and one groom's speech in my life and they both took place after dinner. Like all the other A-list top-table speechmakers, I'm too nervous to eat. By the time you finish and you're hungry again everything's cold.

'Nick Frost . . .'

The food was nice too, at Simon's there was haggis and I love haggis. Love it. All oats and stomachs and pepper. At my wedding we had Moroccan lamb, crispy on the outside and pink in the middle with a delicious tzatziki-style thing. Not traditional wedding fayre but fuck it.

'Nick Frost . . .'

At Tony's wedding in Africa I think we had dik-dik, at least it tasted like dik-dik – that said, it could've been any number of gamey bush meats. I was best man at that wedding and I think it's safe to say at that point the first best man in the world to give his speech reading from a BlackBerry. I'd never seen so many one-armed men at a wedding – I asked and was told something about drunk driving. Terrifying.

'Nick Frost . . .'

'What? Stop shouting!'

'You're on!'

I *was* on. The compere's calling my name. It's now or never. The ref blows the whistle and the ball is coming straight at me through the glare of the sun. I take a deep breath.

Backstage is a cheap plastic and metal chair, the type you get on hospital wards and public libraries. I pick it up and throw it out across the stage. Why? I pretend, using the microphone offstage, that I'm having some kind of unseen fracas. After a moment I run on, looking offstage, and make some shit joke about me owing Mother Teresa some money. I'm embarrassed just writing this, to be honest.

It gets better. My material wasn't great but I was enthusiastic and showed no sign of nerves once I'm on stage. Simon's advice about sharks and blood still rings in my eyes. I'd decided that if I wasn't going to be the best comedian in the world I'd be confident and in these situations maybe confidence can get you pretty far. If you can't be good be lucky. I wear a pair of white Nike Hi-top trainers, jeans, a white fifties-style bowling shirt kind of thing with a slight beige stripe running through it, and a pair of terrible thick-framed Ray-Ban glasses. Buddy Hollies I think you can call them. As a young waiter I got a lot of shit for those glasses. Shit from tables of lads. Pricks. Now they're being used as part of a comedy uniform.

I'm trying to remember parts of my routine now, and like most things in my mind it's pretty hazy. (It's not, I'm just too embarrassed.) There's some cutting edge stuff about a man who has a Treet for a face (Treets later went on to become peanut M&Ms); there's also a 'joke' about stealing an orang-utan from London Zoo and hiding it in my rectal cavity and that's all I'm willing to tell/can remember.

It seems to be going really well. There's a lot of warm applause and, more importantly, lots of laughter and not just from my noisy lot, although I'm sure their infectious noise helps grease the wheels. After eight or ten minutes I reach the end of my material. I'm so happy it just about bursts out of me. I say thanks and say my name, I pick up the chair Mother Teresa's thrown at me and that was that. I did it. I can hear people clapping and a whooping and I couldn't help but beam. I was so happy. Simon's there waiting for me and he's smiling. The look he gives me was one that I've seen him replicate many times with me over the years. Pride. He was proud of me.

I come off stage and feel the tension pour out of me like a sonic bleat. It was amazing. I get a weird rushy migraine. I got a migraine after every gig. I think it was a release, a relief of getting through this most alien of things. Even though people say I was funny, getting up on stage and being judged was still difficult. Still, I'd finished and I could sit back and relax with the gang, who were now quite pissed, and watch the other poor saps.

I'm not really a competitive person, at least I pretend to myself I'm not. I've never trusted people who are overly competitive. I don't get it. I get the drive and commitment needed to see something through, a work ethic, what I never got were those people who are desperate to win at any cost. It's just not in me. I think also when it comes to something as subjective as comedy or literature it's difficult to accurately pick a winner. I feel if you're willing to put your heart and your all into something as emotional as art in all its facets and forms then you're a winner from the get-go.

After the stand-ups finish we all have to endure a nervous wait while the scores are totted up. I go and have a piss, it stinks, I gaze into the metal trough and I'm joined by a man who comes and pisses next to me. He waggles his eyes suggestively; this, I discover, is the chief judge of the competition. His waggling puts me off. I'm not sure what he expects. I finish and wash up. He joins me at the sink, waggling.

'I shouldn't tell you this but . . .'

'What?'

'No, I shouldn't.' He turns and dries his hands. I don't push.

'Okay, I shouldn't tell you this but between you and me . . .'

'Yeah . . .'

His face softened . . .

'You've won the competition. Congratulations!'

He leaves and I lean on the sink. I can't believe it. I'd won a comedy competition at my first attempt. It meant that I'd now go through to a regional heat. What. The. Fuck. I went back to Simon. Sat down, he noticed something.

'What's up?'

I told him what had happened in the bogs. He was so happy. I think I made the mistake of telling someone else, and before long all my lot were coming up and congratulating me.

The lights drop and the compere takes to the stage. This was it. This was my night. It was the first time that I could actually, justifiably call a night mine. There was applause and the room fell silent.

'Blahblahblahblahblah. Comedy. Comedy, blah blah, comedy, and the winner is . . .'

I smile, it's totally Robbie Williams in its smugness. My leg muscles get a premature message from my brain. It says:

'Prepare to stand and receive your accolade, bigman.' They twitch. This is it. Here we go . . .

'And the winner is . . .'

A girl on the table next to mine stands – no, leaps – into the sky. She's screaming, her crew rush to embrace her. It looks like the famous Iwo Jima flag pose but with chicken in baskets on the table.

What the actual fuck. Boos ring out around the venue. People are angry. My legs are angry that they even bothered getting their coats on. They go back to bed and I slump into my chair. I watch the girl skip onto the stage and collect her book token. My spirit sags.

I'm told later by an impartial third party that there was a great deal of impropriety and vote rigging from the winner and her posse in the final moments of the count. I'd been robbed. Cheated.

A similar thing happens years later at some kind of shitty comedy award. We're sat near the stage, always a good sign. A producer tells us minutes before the show that *Shaun of the Dead* has won. I'm so fucking proud and happy. In between that premature announcement and the award being handed out they'd managed to secure Jack Black on a live video feed from LA.

Desperate to add Hollywood credence to the event they'd given the award to *School of Rock*. Gutted. Not that *School of Rock* won, it's a great film, but who doesn't like to win every once in a while?

Me and the crew leave the club. I'm crestfallen but happy, I'd done my first ever gig. I was proud and I proved to myself that I could do it. There was a big party at mine and everyone came. They all made me feel like a winner that night. I think I even signed an autograph for Keith and Michelle, just for fun like, but it was nice.

This was the start of my career as a stand-up comic. I did twelve gigs in all. It was a short career. Six were great and six were, perhaps, the lowest points of my life. The good ones generally went very well except for my post-gig head pounder. Some were just okay – did the open spot, got a few laughs and off I went. The bad ones were really bad, really terrible. I think my problem with stand-up was this: I was a funny person but not a good stand-up. I find it hard to explain. It was mostly the same material give or take but the reactions of the audiences were completely different. There were so many variables, not least of all the confidence or lack of from gig to gig. Stand-up for me was a bit like golf. I wanted to be good straight away and when I wasn't I lost heart. Like everything in life these things take time and effort.

Although I had great gigs I never once found my own voice. Being a fan of *Reeves and Mortimer* and the stand-up of Harry Hill, Sean Lock and Simon Munnery, I really wanted to be a weird surrealist and the problem with that is I wasn't using my own voice. Get me in a small group and I could be frigging hilarious. In a room full of people looking at me expecting something funny I found it tough. Often my voice would crack or when heckled I'd forget where I was and stand there saying 'ummmm' for what felt like six hours, blood pumping out of my ears until the slow handclaps would begin and I would die a terrible terrible death.

The shortest gig I ever did happened at a pub venue in Ealing one Tuesday night. I was on a day shift at Chiquito and from early in the day I could feel the panic rising, 'In twelve hours this will all be over.' The day shift was busy so at least I could throw myself into the work. This coincided with a time when for some reason I was taking a lot of Pro Plus. Not a good idea. The day shifts were always chilled out, more or less, there'd be a slight rush from noon until three and then you had a couple of hours to kill until the evening staff came in. Once you had a tidy-up and a restock of clean, polished cutlery, you'd stand about doing fuck all – hopefully there'd be a bartender on so you could have a chat and a laugh but usually you were on your own. Sometimes a couple of very young Indian lovers would come in and you just knew they were not meant to be together. They'd naughtily giggle and laugh in fear that they might get caught at any time. I liked that. Young love will always find a way.

This day there was boredom and, thanks to the handful of Pro Plus I'd fisted down with four cups of strong espresso, anxiety. I had to leave at five o'clock sharp. There was a saying an old manager of mine used to have. It was fucking annoying but sadly true and I was always early anyway so he never aimed it at me, but hearing it would make me want to strike him in his fat ginger head with an oar. It went like this:

'blubblubblub early, blahblahblah, on time, blah blah bluch, late'.

I struck him hard and he fell backwards into the turbulent ocean. He blubbed, his wide, white face fixed with an 'I can't believe you did that' look. He jolts and is pulled down. He rises back to the surface briefly but is wrenched downwards once more by an unseen Goliath, he smiles, not at me, it's just his brain turning his mouth up at a sweet memory long forgotten. One more jerk by fuck knows what and the foaming water blooms deep red, his sweaty ginger bonce was gone for good.

I once watched this mirthless Honeymonster of a manager give the chefs and me an early morning masterclass on how to make the perfect green tomatillo sauce. He made us stand around and watch while he stirred a massive cauldron with a giant metal spatula. That day four poor Ugandan men and myself were forced to witness six litres of salty fluid drip off his nose and forehead into someone's meal. He was so wet by the end of it that he had to go home and change. And what had we learned? Nothing. We had learned nothing. Those men had fled Idi Amin's brutal dictatorship only to be met with this new, more sinister brand of fuckery. Poor men.

At a quarter to five I had still not been relieved. The phone rings and someone in the office answers before I have a chance to. It's also getting busy. I can feel a rage building within me, a tiny baked bean-size rage.

A voice shouts from the office, 'So and so can't be in until six!'

Fuming! More Pro Plus, another triple espresso, more tables, more ear steam. Where in the human body is ear steam generated? At six-ten the waitress saunters in, I change out of my uniform that smells like old milk and I bolt into my pre-booked cab.

We turn left out of Staples Corner and slam into a traffic jam three hundred miles long. A hiss of steam pisses out of my brain. I sit still for as long as I can, I pay angrily, and run out of the taxi. We'd travelled less than a mile. My head pounds, fists itchy with rage. I run and try to board several buses that are bulging at the seams. It begins to rain heavily. Balls.

I eventually find a bus that takes me to the tube which then takes me to another bus, and then from there it's a simple thirty-minute walk to the venue. This is not going well. I should've turned round and gone home there and then. I should've known that this was a bad sign. An omen of the most terrible portent, like a crow shitting on your hat. I was so fucking cross. I'm soaked to my skin. I take a breath and try and get my shit together.

The venue was an old hall attached to a shitty fucking pub. From inside I can hear a noise that begins to fill me with dread. The noise sounds like an inexperienced compere starting a vicious heckle war with twelve cunts all from the same Sunday league pub football team.

As I push through the swing doors I see an empty hall save for an inexperienced compere starting a vicious heckle war with twelve cunts all from the same Sunday league pub football team. A crow shits on my hat. The compere sees me, understands who I am and waves me up. I'm not ready for this. I'm totally unprepared. I haven't even taken my coat off. I scamper towards the stage, I can feel angry low-browed meat bags eye fucking me. I may not even get as far as the stage. The compere introduces me as Nick Roast! I should run, that's what my eyes and legs are compelling me to do. I don't.

I still have my jacket on as I mount the stage, the compere passes me, thrusts the mike into my hand and whispers, 'Good luck.'

I look at these hate-filled baboon-rapists and open with a tried and tested goodie.

'Hello!'

I notice a big man stand up from somewhere in the middle of the pack. He must have something really important and insightful he needs to share. I'm all ears. Two ears. Here goes . . .

'FUCK OFF, YOU FAT CUNT!!!'

Oh. He seems so very cross. I slowly clip the microphone back into its stand and hop down off the stage. I feel deaf, it's a mixture of intense rage and heart-crushing grief. A terrific heat flash ensues. I trudge out of the hall still soaked and out into the deluge. Inside I hear them laugh and roar.

It was gigs like this that made me want to stop. A half-decent stand-up would've taken those men to pieces. After the day I'd had and the build-up and the transit and the rain and the Pro Plus, it was all too much for me.

I had another gig where two businessmen sat in the front row chatting and laughing at me. Not with me, at me. Throughout most of my set. It got so bad that at one point I dropped my microphone and leapt into the crowd. I managed to grab one of them round the throat and subdue the other with my big right leg before security put me in a choke hold and bundled me down the stairs. I wasn't asked back. There were one or two more gigs but my heart wasn't in it. I stopped. I was disappointed in myself. At that point I wasn't what you'd call a starter finisher. That came later.

During this time though Simon and I became closer and closer. We really were a mismatch in terms of background. It worked though. I was a bit rough and had no idea what PC was or meant. Simon went to Bristol Uni and was all about feminist cinema. He even knew what an acronym was. He showed me things and I taught him that it was okay to say the word 'black'.

While my stand-up career died, SP's bloomed and I was happy to be along for the ride. I loved watching him gig. We worked out that one year I saw him gig over two hundred times. We'd drive all over the country in his little white Renault 5. One wintry afternoon we were about to settle in for the evening when Dawn his agent rang to make sure he hadn't forgotten his gig in Hull that night. He had forgotten. We threw our shoes on and ran out of the house. This was a time long before sat-nav. We used maps. Maps are basically static versions of a satnav but printed onto large sheets of paper and bound into a big book and, do you know what, they actually worked pretty well.

It took us an age to get to Hull. Part way up the country it started to snow really heavily; eventually we got to the gig at Hull University students' union, which sadly was virtually empty. He still did his gig, the show must go on darling, and he put just as much effort into this as any he did, full or not. Good lad.

He finished, we jumped in the car and fucked off. On the way back the snow was so thick and heavy we were forced to pull over onto the hard shoulder. While there we began to get the fear that a lorry, unable to see us in a small white car in heavy white snow, would plough into the back of us doing one hundred and forty miles per hour. The car and everything inside it, us, would be completely obliterated. They'd have to identify me by using my dental records. It was close, lorries would thunder past us and we'd scream and grab onto each other. We became hysterical and laughed till our tears froze.

We couldn't stay there. Eventually we got the courage to start the car and drive home.

Simon would soon be going up to Edinburgh to do his first Fringe solo show. It was a really big deal. He put a lot of effort into that tour. It really took it out of him but predictably he smashed it. While he and Mouse were in Edinburgh I got to stay in their little flat in Cricklewood. Absolute bliss. The only job I had apart from taping *Reeves and Mortimer* and *Northern Exposure* was to look after Simon's lovely big goldfish, and what a noble beast it was. I'd never seen a plumper, longer-tailed, more beautiful fish. I think he'd had it for a long time, a firm friend and confidant throughout his university education. What a fish.

They were due to return on a Monday; I returned home from a day shift on a Sunday to find the fish dead. It was dead. Oh god. Any pet looked after by a friend or relative will always die the day before the owners return. Always. One day before. So it was the case with mega fish. I fell to my knees and sobbed, more for me than for the fish actually. I pulled it out and gently blew into its gaping mouth hole. Nothing. I placed it back into the tank and used my hand to create a turbulent current with the hope I could push some oxygen through its pale, lifeless gills.

It's still dead twenty minutes later when I give up trying to bring it back to life. The fish was well and truly dead. I slump onto the floor exhausted by the efforts that went into the revival attempts. After a while my pragmatism wakes up. I need to arrange the funeral. How does one deal with the earthly remains of such a stoic aquanaut?

I lift him (I'm guessing it was a he) onto a piece of newspaper and mummify him ready for his journey down the toilet to his spiritual father, Poseidon. When push comes to shove I can't do it. I evolve my plan slightly and I decide to bury the beast.

I look for a suitable coffin. I empty the curdled liquid from a milk carton and gently lower him in. He doesn't quite fit, his tail is so long and beautiful that it sticks out of the top of the carton by a good three inches. What to do? I grab a pair of scissors and neatly cut the tail off, plopping the two long fins in either side of his body. I close the carton up, Sellotape it shut and bury the poor mite. I say a prayer in the beast's own tongue and that was that. Simon wasn't happy and I think a small part of him believed that someone murdered that fish on purpose. I guess we'll never know for sure.

Him and me spent more and more time together, Mouse not so much. She got a job touring with a play and off she went. When she came back terrible things happened. When the considerable ash plume settled Simon and I were all we had left. I never saw Mouse again. I got him and he got me. It was imperfectly perfect. I picked him up and he picked me up, so began our time living together.

After moving out of Mouse's flat Simon had nowhere to go so he came and moved in with me at 142. At first he lived on the couch for a bit, then he slept next to me on the floor but soon he became chilly so we topped and tailed. One of our favourite things to do was sit up in bed and read a big book together, usually a big glossy atlas or a book about Christmas. He'd hold one page and I'd hold the other. After a while he'd just stay in the bed. It was cold at night and we'd just snuggle down and sleep. It felt right.

So much has been written about us sleeping together like some kind of modern Morecambe and Wise that it now feels pretty boring talking about it. At the time though it felt nice.

There was never once a sense that at any point we'd start making each other's bananas cry. We often use the phrase 'Some mornings I didn't know where he ended and I began.' That makes me laugh so much. I think it made it into our wedding speeches.

I often get a suspicious narrow-eyed look from 'Real Men' who hear we used to sleep together in a single bed for nine months, but we were great friends and then like now we've never had a problem showing affection and love for one another.

This arrangement didn't last long though, thank god, for as much as I liked it I enjoyed the nights I got the bed to myself. Simon was offered the opportunity to travel to Australia as part of a comedy tour. He took it. I was sad for me but happy for him. It was exactly what he needed. Of course I was still work-ing in Chiquito. I must have been twenty-four by now, I was starting to get bored on the floor, starting to yearn for some-thing else, what that was I had no idea.

It's tough sometimes when you deal with the general public and you realise there are a lot of fucking bell-ends out there. One lady asked if I could put more ice into her drink, as it was too cold! Whaaaarttttt! Another man complained, as he'd found a bone in his rack of ribs. It is bones. Ribs is bones. The bit that's delicious is the bit between the bones. That's the bit you eat. Sometimes there was a strange phenomenon where once one table complained about the food all would start to complain. I think it was a kind of shared psychosis.

On a couple of occasions someone would complain about something small. This is how I'd deal with it. Big smiles. Big bowing apology. I'd take the offending plate back into the kitchen, count to five and bring it straight out again. Exactly the same meal. Sometimes I'd regarnish it, sure, or stick it in the microwave but in essence it was exactly the same meal. They'd tuck in happily, chuffed a waiter, someone of lower status, had apologised to them. That's the key to dealing with complaints at the table. Many apologies.

You have to make them think they're completely right, apologise, remove the offending dish straight away and offer something else. Nothing should be too much trouble. If they're really acting up sling them a free pitcher of margarita. No one can resist a free pitcher of margarita. Even if one of their party dies choking on shrimp a free pitcher of margarita makes everything okay.

Some people though were absolute monsters and deserved to be punished. One man who was so disgusting got his car scratched to fuck with the two pence tip he'd just tossed at me. I stood in the window and watched him discover the offence. Fuming. Good. Don't fuck with the waiters.

If the person I was serving was both a monster and a vegetarian, I'd handle it a little differently, I'd take a different tack, a silent revenge if you will. While their burrito or soft taco was being made I'd nip behind the line and pop in the tiniest, microscopic speck of beef into their meal. They never knew a thing. I'd smile while they shovelled it down and abused me knowing they'd be turned away from their heaven by their vegetarian god once they'd passed. Sometimes revenge tastes just fine served piping hot.

Late one Saturday night I receive a table. I was very not happy. I was six minutes from closing and they get sat in my section. I must've really pissed Melissa off that night. Fifteen rowdy drunks who are loud and aggressive, lots of swearing, lots of nipping back and forth to the toilet, lots of sniffing. When it comes to the food, some order one starter between two people as a main course. This was not going to be a good table tip-wise. On top of everything else these folks were finger clickers. I was tired and pissed off. I took all their shit knowing there'd be little or no reward at the end of it.

No matter. Suck it up, do your job, get rid of them, go to the Pink Rupee. After a while I get clicked at by a belligerent old fucker wearing stained tracksuit bottoms and a dress shirt. Not a good look.

'Oi!'

Fuck, here we go.

'Oi!'

He repeats it again but this time louder. His angry relatives have taken some kind of offence that I didn't react immediately to what I imagine is their elderly father and they are now giving me a kind of death stare that makes my feet ache.

'Yes, sir, what can I get you?' His voice stumbles and cracks, his eyes close then flicker, he seems way fucking gone.

'Get me a fucking beer!' Woah.

This man's far too pissed, he's so pissed it's actually illegal – no, morally *wrong* – for me to serve him any more alcohol. As a waiter I have a responsibility to this poor man and his family while he's dining here at Chiquito Mexican Bar and Restaurant plc.

I also think it's a great way for me to get them out as quickly as possible. At first my voice shakes. I know the reaction to this will be bad. British people tend to react really badly when you accuse them of being drunk. Even if they're so pissed they're shitting in a hat.

'I'm afraid I can't serve you any more alcohol, sir, I think you've had far too much already.'

His son looks up at me with half a chimichanga hanging out of his mouth. His eyes fixed wide with a disbelief his brows never knew existed. The women at the table tense up. It'll go like this: first the kids get chippy and call you a cunt, then the big-armed women wade in and attempt to smother you with their bingo-wings, lastly the men punch you in the temple with a Clipper lighter until a fluid that smells like freshly cut hay dribbles out of your ears, all this for the chance of a £1 tip.

I grow more confident. Legally I have the law on my side. Rumbles around the restaurant at my denial of alcohol mean my GM has come out to watch, to observe from a distance this family killing me.

'I'm afraid I can't serve you any more alcohol, you're too drunk.' Silence.

The stick-thin dad with the stained tracksuit bottoms, drunk and so angry, struggles to get to his feet. He stammers, fuming.

'I'm not pissed . . . you, cheeky . . . prick . . . I've . . . had a fucking . . . stroke.'

Oh. My. God.

Some heck breaks out. The women stand and tuck their war-gunts into the top of their jeggings. The men get their stubby Clippers out ready to jab into my paintwork. I edge backwards really slowly and turn, running into the kitchen. My manager follows me at pace. I can hear shouting.

'Just go quickly and hide in the break room.'

My plan has worked perfectly. Sure people have been stabbed but I'm out of there by midnight with a great story, noshing down on a Butter Chicken.

* * *

Rachel had gone and I'd been single for a while. Sure there had been kissing and second base visits but it wasn't very fulfilling.

I'd never been the type of man to just fuck around, not then, not later. I didn't like it. It felt weird and I always ended up falling for one-night stands. I'm a romantic at heart and I think what I was really looking for was love.

One afternoon, a bright, clear spring day, a girl walked into the restaurant, a new hostess who completely blew me away. This was Stevie and she was amazing. Tiny little floral print dress, long bare legs, glossy brown hair, rich chestnut-coloured eyes and the most amazing smile. Butterflies and bluebirds surrounded her. She was the most amazing girl I'd ever seen.

'Hello.' She was Scottish. She bit her lip. (She didn't but it adds to the erotic charge.)

I just stare at her. She giggled a bit and I scurried off to fetch the manager.

That's how it began. I was completely enchanted by her. I'd never felt anything like it before. Over the next few days and weeks I played it cool, well, cooler than I had during our first meeting. She was so out of my league. To use one of my lines from *Cuban Fury*, 'It was like a butterfly going out with a parsnip.' Again I was the parsnip. I had something that the parsnip didn't have though, I had the funny, I could make her laugh.

I flirted with her so outrageously over the next few weeks she felt compelled to tell me she had a boyfriend. I was sad, she saw I was sad too. I'd played my hand too soon. She knew. I didn't care. The dance begins. We up our flirting. I can't believe this. It never goes this well. Never. She told me she wasn't in love with her boyfriend any more. That made me happy. She saw I was happy. That was a green light to me.

The usual way of courting here in Britain involves alcohol and lots of it. You go out. You have a drink, a dance, another drink and then you try and kiss, then you decide to go out or not at a later time. It can be that simple. It can also be a fucking disaster. A few times you'd get too pissed to close the deal or you realise that she's a complete helmet when she'd had a few. Or I was, entirely possible.

The problem I had was this. A year or so before meeting Stevie I'd decided to stop drinking. Holy Fuck. Big shout. I did not see that coming. It'd just got all too much for me, the hangovers, the anger, the aggro, the crushing shame of a wet bed. I couldn't do it any more. I went to AA but chose a really hard-core meeting in Hendon. The people there, the brave people, frightened me. Their stories and tragedy frightened me. These people were at the end, they'd hit bottom. I kidded myself that I wasn't like them, that Mum wasn't like them. I honestly never made the connection between what those people at that meeting had and my mum's own illness. Later down the line Mum attended two AA meetings in Fishguard. After the second someone pointed out two women there who came not because they were alcoholics but because they wanted to gossip about who in town had a drink problem. I wonder how many people those two blabbermouths drove away from help. I never went back to those meetings. I decided to try and do it on my own.

So far I was a year dry and as such I didn't have the tactical advantage of using alcohol to woo Stevie. No matter. We still laugh a lot, our hands brush together, the air between our fingers ignites spontaneously. She bites her lip. (She actually did this time.) It was too much to bear.

Eventually after weeks and weeks of intense build-up it happens. We lie on the floor smoking joints (I know, I know) and reading passages from *The Prophet* to one another, what a cliché! At one point I turn and kiss her. She kisses me back. It was amazing. And that was that. We fell in love. I fell in love. We were an item.

Stevie became my girlfriend. The more I knew about her the more I liked. We walked around London hand in hand, lay in the park, laughed, went to museums, the lot, proper boyfriend/girlfriend stuff. I told her about my exploits in Israel and promised one day I'd take her there. I told her I intended to write a book about my adventures, she liked that, liked the fact I wanted to be a writer.

Some afternoons if I wasn't working I'd take the bus into South Kensington and wait for her to finish university (she was studying biology). I'd never been to a university so it was always a thrill to push through the big old doors and enter the Gryffindor Quad from the east side. I'd watch the boffins running here and there with their abacuses. It was nice. For a moment I regretted my absence from tertiary education.

Stevie and I hadn't moved in together but I spent a lot of time at hers in Cricklewood. We planned our trip to Israel and worked hard to pay for our tickets. We were actually in love. It felt amazing. She was fresh and funny and fit and beautiful and every day I was with her I found myself a moment away from fighting with perverted men. Going out with a hottie has its downside. The letching chimps hanging out of vans making 'fuck' noises at her was too much to bear. Poor woman. Poor women. If you go out with a hottie you better be good at looking like you're good at fighting.

At one point in our sexually frantic courtship I began to write my book. I called it 'The Alcoholic's Guide To The Holy-Land' and it was a fictitious account of a boy's time on a kibbutz. It was based on my own time there but trippier, more psychedelic, with a really tragic ending. It was also tragically, really shit. When I tried to read it a few years ago I was struck by how infantile it was. The imagination was there but everything else was truly awful. Leaving school at an early age hobbled me slightly, grammar wise. I still don't know what an adverb is. True. The only reason I wrote that book was to impress Stevie.

I had no table to sit at and certainly no such thing as a laptop. I wrote it using a creaky old typewriter with an ironing board as a table. I didn't plan the thing out, instead I wrote the whole book like a big story a child might write at school.

With our lovely young relationship getting more serious it was time for us to pay a visit to her parents in Glasgow. I began to sweat at the thought of parents. My last parent hadn't gone so well. The rum and the ironing board shit. I planned to learn from my mistake and be cool. Be on my best behaviour. I'm not drinking so this should help a lot. We took the train up and we're met by her mum and younger brother at the station. It's my first trip to Scotland and with Stevie on my arm I felt great.

Even though her family are Rangers fans they live in the shadow of Parkhead, the home to the city's traditionally Catholic football team, Celtic. This, I sensed, was a secret pain for her father.

Stevie was greeted at the door the way you'd expect a returning daughter, the apple of Daddy's eye, to be greeted. I was also greeted the way you'd expect, a sharp nod, an impossibly firm handshake and that was about it. He knew, as a father and more importantly as a man he knew, and as a younger man I knew he knew and he knew I knew he knew. It was unsaid and it simmered. She was eighteen, I was twenty-five and we were boning like rabbits. I was a scummy, overweight English waiter who smoked way too much weed. She was a porcelain-skinned ray of light receiving a fine university education with the aim of becoming a scientist, a fucking scientist for godsakes. She was gorgeous and clever and saucy and I totally understand her dad's negative vibes.

It was cordial to begin with, the first inkling of an issue arises when I refuse a beer. Suspicious. They have a few, we chat and then Dad decides to put *Braveheart* on. He goes upstairs and returns wearing a fine Glengarry with a long feather stuck in the top. I was beginning to feel uncomfortable that said, the DVD player's sound system belted out a tremendous noise with an impressive depth of clarity. I could literally hear every drop of English blood spilt on the battlefield in crystal clear 5.1 digital Dolby surround.

I'm definitely in the spare room that night. At one point the door opens and Stevie creeps in. I'm terrified our angry noiseless fucking would wake Dad and he'd come in and cleave me with *his* fat broadsword.

In the morning Mum introduces me to the wonders of the square sausage. Ironically I'd been doing exactly the same to her daughter the night before. (I have no idea what that means.) The Saturday was nice. We visited the sight of the battle of Bannockburn where Robert the Bruce routed the English, then we drove to Sterling and I was forced to climb the William Wallace monument, erected to the memory of a man who'd spent years routing the English. I started to get the feeling I wasn't welcome.

We drove through the Highlands and Dad stops the car and makes us all get out. I'm forced to drink from a small stream running off the heather-clad hills to prove Scottish water was the cleanest and best in the world. It gave me terrible diarrhoea.

I still sensed a simmering anger from Dad. To smooth things over I ask if I can cook them dinner. My mum's fantastic recipe for Beef Stroganoff is sure to smooth over any cracks. Food and the eating of it I feel can be a great weapon in the war for peace. I've been cooking the Stroganoff since I was twelve and feel its soft beef and rich sautéed onions would work a treat.

Me and Stevie hung out and laughed while I cooked. Her brother keeps an eye on me while Mum and Dad laugh like drains watching an old video of English people being killed in car crashes. As I was about to serve up there's a slight issue: unknown to me her brother has a weird phobia of people touching food with their hands. I wish he'd said something while he stood and watched me cook it. Mum fortunately intervenes and makes him something untouched by me. This was the beginning of an uncomfortable dinner.

They sniffed the food with suspicion while me and Stevie hungrily tucked in. The conversation gradually turned to the future, our future, a future that included our forthcoming trip to Israel. We'd mentioned it in passing the day before, enough time for the parents to cogitate the information. I was now grilled about my time there and the current security situation, I could tell they weren't happy.

They put their collective feet down and insist Stevie would not be going to Israel with me. A loud argument begins between Stevie and her parents. I'm blamed for this, this change in her. I'm the scapegoat. At some point Mum pushes her chair back and storms upstairs. Dad stands.

'See what you've done?'

I try and make it right but my flustered assurances about terrorism and separate beds only seem to make things worse. Mum's upstairs crying, Dad is fuming. It's then I notice his left fist is clenched and leaning in the rice, poor Stevie is in tears. This is terrible.

Father's last words to me as he thunders up to bed were these: 'I want you gone first thing.'

I think I'd be out with a rice-fist in my ear that night if Stevie hadn't liked me so much. Why did parents hate me so?

The next morning a cab arrives at 8 a.m. After much arguing Stevie insists on coming home with me. Her parents are angry about this. I want her to stay, I think this would be for the best but still we leave together. I could see she was sad and I regretted this. There were tearful hugs on the doorstep for Stevie, she breaks away and walks to the cab, I smile weakly and look doe-eyed, maybe we can salvage something from this. I hold out my hand, the front door is slammed in my face.

I lean down, open the letterbox and shout through, 'Bye then!'

This does not go down well. Dad opens the door and thunders out. I leg it into the car. It was only Stevie's plea for leniency that stops me eating a gob full of his angry rice-covered fist. Why was it still covered in rice?

At some point over the next few weeks I move in with her, much to the annoyance of her flatmate Edna. At first we're blissfully happy, at least I was blissfully happy. Sometimes Simon would ring me from Australia and we'd bullshit and talk and it'd remind me how much I missed him. He wrote me a really long letter once but customs opened it and took out several pages so it made little or no sense.

Things had got past the honeymoon stage and Stevie was in class at uni more often than not. I hated not seeing her but we were arguing a bit and my policy of non-drinking was really beginning to put a strain on our relationship. She and her best friend Tim would spend more and more time drinking together. I grew jealous and suspicious.

Being forty-three now I look back at that time and curse myself for being such an idiot, for not seeing the signs, the blatantly obvious signs. I was blinded by love. If someone I was seeing spent the night out with a boy I think I'd be very cross and absolutely suspect the worst. Then I was just desperate to keep hold of her. I wrote her a book for fucksakes, a really terrible book. God, I fell hard for her. Often the compulsion to hang onto something so badly leads it to slip through your fingers like a separated egg yolk, indeed this was the case here.

Stevie had gone to a weird science camp in Surrey to study worms. I was invited to spend a night there. It was awkward and she was a bit cold but then so was I, I think fearing the worst. I'd drawn back a little bit. I watched her drunkenly flirt with Tim all night. You know when you watch two people and can just tell something has been shared. A line has been crossed. If not physically then certainly emotionally. We argue and I leave the next day.

When she gets back it's pretty awful. She says she wants to move out, even though it's her place. We agree I'll take the flat over. That said, I didn't think she meant moving out that day. Her 'friend' Tim comes to help her. After a bit of persuasion I get her to admit to me that she'd been having an affair. Heart. Crushed. I was so sad I wasn't even sad. Again I was numb.

With tears in my eyes I sniffled out a final thought: 'Just fucking leave, take everything but my books and go.'

What a pretentious art-helmet I was. I had about ten books. I stormed out to work and when I arrived home six hours later she was gone. She'd literally taken everything in the flat except my ten books which were in a neat pile in the bedroom. I cried as I made a cup of tea in a wok. It was the last time I ever saw or heard of Stevie.

I was left in that flat on my own. I hated that place, you had to walk through the communal downstairs hall to get to my front door. The place stank and a drunken, aggressive Irish loony lived there. He frightened the shit out of me. Creeping in late at night was the worst. The lights would be off and the hall illuminated by the silent TV that was still on, flickering. If you were lucky you'd hear him snoring. Perfect, unlock the door and go home. If you were unlucky he'd stumble into the hall and threaten you with his thick, Irish Hulk hands. My mate Dion got hold of him one night and threatened to fuck him up. He slumped to the floor, terrified. Good. I hate bullies.

The other downside of Stevie leaving was our trip to Israel. I'd booked our tickets and I couldn't get them refunded. I was still keen to go. Ten nights in the sun was exactly what I needed right now so fuck it, I went.

I've got a lot of thoughts about this holiday. Maybe holiday's the wrong term, I went there to mentally convalesce. I decided to keep a journal and get down all my thoughts and feelings about what happened between Stevie and me. Being alone was tough, I loved and missed her so much, and Israel wasn't how I remembered it but that was my problem not Israel's. I went up to the old kibbutz. It was nice to hang out with some old Israeli friends but my heart hurt and I felt really lonely. After a couple of days I said goodbye and bussed it down to Tel Aviv.

The rest of my time in Israel was spent walking around the city, trudging down the beach to the Arab section in old Jaffa. It was nice and cool down there near the sea. I'd sit in a café and write my journal for most of the day. As ever I was pretty much skint. At lunch I'd walk over to the bus station and have a falafel. Fortunately they were still offering that great deal – if the pitta was intact then you could get it refilled with fresh, hot falafel as much as you liked. Remember, the key was to keep the first couple relatively dry. Once you reached the ultimate tummy fullness you could moisten (sorry) the whole thing up a bit with tahini and other exotic Middle Eastern sauces.

Falafel aside, I was sad and skint and bored. My diary however makes for very interesting reading. I looked at it fairly recently and was surprised by the amount I wrote. I filled up a whole book with my filthy melancholy. You can see as it grinds on how my emotions change. The first half of the book is me, grief stricken and broken physically and spiritually. Then there are some juvenile ramblings about life and love. Then about halfway through there's a passage where I break away from my sadness and ogle at a passing girl's lovely bum. Naughty. My spirit picks up from there. I begin to write about other things not connected to Stevie.

When you split up from a girlfriend or boyfriend, things like life tend to get in the way of truly understanding what's just happened to you. It slows the healing process. I found the good thing about being away and alone was I had time to think about Stevie and us and the break-up. I had time to work it all out. And as a result I think I got over it pretty quickly. Don't think for a second that was that. It still hurt like fuck but I could see a way out.

My boredom and depression and no fucking shekels got the better of me however. I go to a travel agent on Dizengoff Street and tell them, using some fabulous acting, that my grandmother has died and I need to get back home immediately.

They couldn't be more helpful. They mistake my tired eyes, light beard and the shadow on my spirit for actual grief. The next day I am on a flight.

Years later not long after my dad died I went away on holiday. I thought it would help. It didn't. It was a terrible mistake. I wasn't ready for it. Me and Chris (Baby Momma) argue terribly – completely my fault – and we decide to go home early. Before changing our flights the airline insists upon seeing my dad's death certificate. Karma in action maybe, too many Herberts pretending Granny has died. Still, heartless pricks, also who carries their dad's death certificate with them on holibobs?

I get home from Israel and go back to the empty house with no furniture in it. I boil a wok, sit on the floor and decide what to do next.

My first brush with House music had been as a sixteen-year-old. Basically, apart from the odd flirt with indie, metal and alternative styles, it lasts a lifetime. Don't get me wrong, I love all types of music except ragtime but House music, and in particular Hard House, is something that has stayed with me until now. While at Chiquito and through my friendship with Tony and Dion I hung out with a lot of South Africans and Kiwis. We all had a shared interest in Hard House. These were Tony and Dion's mates from back home, all in all a good bunch of girls and boys. We started clubbing a lot. It was the boom time for Hard House in the summer of 1997 and I was there at the front blowing my little horn. Hard House was everywhere and I had no idea after my first brush with the embryonic scene back in 88/89 that it was still happening – not just happening, but absolutely going off.

Dion and Tony started going out almost every weekend after shifts in the bar at Chiquito. At first, and I'm not sure why, I didn't really fancy going clubbing. I think I had a weird kind of agoraphobia. Simon was still away in Australia on tour but I was happy in Cricklewood and the thought of leaving it and going into London put the willies up me. Still, after hearing about this thing happening my curiosity eventually got the better of me. It was safe to say I was hooked from the start.

The first place I went to was a club called Sunny Side Up. It was set in a long wet tunnel under a viaduct in Vauxhall. It was frightening and amazing in equal measure. This was not strictly my first brush with HaHa beans but it was close. I never had it during the Second Summer of Love, too expensive back then for me. The sum of £25 for one dose seemed like lunacy. No, back then you needed something weird and long lasting. Lysergic acid diethylamide. Cheap and cheerful.

A few months before my first Sunny Side Up I went out with a mate of mine called Sean. He was tall and impossibly thin with long glossy black hair. He looked like a Navajo. We puffed a bit together and he suggested we go to the Ministry of Sound. I was nervous but thought fuckit, why not. While in the massive queue to get in he gave me a small glowing pebble. I take it and, using my watering fear-spit that was pooling in the depression under my tongue, swallowed it down.

I was so frightened about taking this new rave canape, after hearing bad things about them on *London Tonight*, I thought my heart might explode there and then. By the time we got to the front my feet were tingling. The security apes look us over and tell us to fuck off. Oh. There's clearly no waggle-room in this statement. We trudge away disappointed. Sean knows another place but I feel sick and trembly so I decide to head back. It's still early to hook up with the team at the Pink Rupee.

I'm sitting on a night bus passing through Kilburn when something strange happens to me. The 'thing' has dissolved inside my tummy and is now giving my brain a gentle massage. I rush as it jets up from my feet and into my brain so hard it makes my eyes roll backwards. It was like someone had flayed me alive and was blowing a fan over my freshly exposed nervous system. The old fella next to me shifts nervously. He gets up and stands by the door. It was my stop too so I get up and stand next to him.

He's a small well-dressed Indian man, I begin to notice the jacket he's wearing, it's so nice, a soft brown tweed-like fabric. Really lovely and so inviting. It pulses and throbs at me. I rush again slightly and I realise I have this man by the arm and I'm rubbing my face on his shoulder. My eyes are as wide as bin lids. He's frightened and I'm horrified and apologetic. I let go of him and he jumps off the bus and runs up the street. I follow briefly but my heart's not in it. Instead I cross the street and stumble into the Pink Rupee. It's bright and people look afraid of me.

That was then. Things felt differently now. I'm not on a bus on Kilburn High Road, I'm here at Sunny Side Up under a viaduct in a drippy tunnel. It felt right. It felt like home. That night on the bus opened my eyes. It was the beginning of a long relationship with that scene with its smiling people and the myriad possibilities that mind-altering things propose at three in the morning: world peace, laughter collectives the government couldn't touch, chemical stasis and what have you. It started off great. I wanted to be frozen in these moments. Eyes rolling, cuddling strangers to the most amazing music imaginable. We were the few. Our scene was underground and people were afraid of it and, by association, us. Me.

This was a dangerous time for me. It'd be my undoing. Not just yet but eventually. Tony, Dion and me would work our arses off in the week, skimming a little off the top here and there, at weekends we'd smash it up. The whole gang. We'd start Saturday night, then onto Sunnies at eight o'clock Sunday morning. After that we'd maybe head into Soho or go back to 142 Cricklewood Lane.

The girls would have baths or showers and change into warm, fresh clothes and the boys would smoke and continue to greedily ingest powerful chemicals. Sometimes we'd go to the Spotted Dog in Willesden and I'd watch them drink the edge away, usually though we'd just lie around talking and trembling. The girls would look after us and play with our hair, give us massages, feed us orange juice. It was nice. I used to sit, eyes wide, and watch the juice inside the glass transform into a pint of rice.

The spirit liberators always made me see the weirdest things, things civilians would've found frightening. I wasn't frightened. I liked it. I yearned for it, yearned to be in that place where anything and everything happens. I embraced it fully. At the height of the lunacy I'd often get a thing where everyone I looked at would be wearing glasses. I'd have to run my hand over their faces to know if they were real or not. People didn't mind, they knew what was happening. Unless they were real glasses and then I'd have to apologise profusely.

Once I saw a hot glow like a laser or a spot welding arc under a man's skin in the middle of his forehead. It just hummed and crackled while I looked at him. Another time a beam actually broke through and shone an intense light out of a man's back.

I followed him. The thin beam moved across his shoulders, slowly tracing a shape I couldn't make out at first. The faster it got the easier it was to see as an image. Have you ever seen pictures of the Nazca Lines in Peru? It was that. It was one of the hummingbirds drawn on the floor of the desert, so big they can only be seen from the air. It didn't freak me out. I considered it a spirit guide. I smiled and it told me I should eat another peanut. So I did.

These were my weekends. It wasn't just Sunny Side Up either. We went to a place called Sunflowers, we went to the Aquarium in Old Street, a club with a swimming pool in it! Disgusting. We went to the O bar in Soho and on and on and on. My favourite DJs were Tony De Vit, Pete Wardman, Skol, Roosta, Darren Poole, Darren Pearce, BK, The Tidy Boys, The Sharp Boys, John 'OO' Fleming, Tall Paul and Luke Brancaccio. These were the gods on the scene at the time. You didn't just go to specific clubs, you followed the DJs around. Wherever they played we went.

Tony and Dion decide they want to go to the States, that was always their plan from the start but the mayhem and the rut one inevitably gets into working in the food service industry meant they'd been here longer than they'd envisaged.

They left and went to live in Huntington Beach, California. Shit, I missed those jerk-offs. I enjoyed hearing of their exploits and was jealous I couldn't be there. Girls, surfing and getting high seemed to be the order of the day. Simon had left Australia and had gone to spend some time with Tony and Dion over there, then travelling around on his own and getting his shit together.

When Simon got back we begin our lifelong 'I love Agent Dana Scully' phase. God we loved that woman. By this time I'd sourced a TV and a cupboard and we were pretty happy with this. Simon and I would lie around watching endless *X-Files* box sets dreaming and hoping that one day we'd watch Mulder and Scully kiss. That's all we wanted.

This was the time of the infamous Piegate drama. Piegate's something bad I did to Simon. Something I regret. Even though he says it's cool I know deep down he's never forgiven me, probably never will.

We'd spent the day puffin it up. We're at a point, between episodes of the *X-Files*, where we get the munchies something rotten. I'd invented a meal, which, apart from the staff food at Chiquito, was the only thing I seemed to eat for years. It was called simply, Pies in a Bowl. It consisted of two Findus chicken and vegetable pies, cooked, in a bowl. I'd then mash the pies up, add Bisto gravy, lashings of white pepper and ketchup. It was fucking lovely. I miss Pies in a Bowl. It was a big hit, it was cheap, nutritious, and suited my lifestyle perfectly. We were Pies in a Bowl kinda guys back then.

I don't know what made me say the thing to Simon that I said. I think it was the Devil or Hitler. Yeah, that's it, it was Hitler. I found myself taking a loud breath like I'd just remembered the most important thing in the world, his ears pricked up!

'What?' Simon was mine.

Slowly I drop my knowledge bomb on him . . .

'I've got chicken fucking pies in the freezer!!!'

His eyes widen. We both cheer! What was I doing? Stop this now. I didn't stop. We got to the kitchen and we pause, harvesting the anticipation. In forty-five short minutes – just enough time for another *X-File* – we'd be feasting on Pies in a Bowl. Simon looked at me. I egged him on.

'Go on . . .' I pushed him to open up the freezer. His little face looked so young and excited. It was like watching eight-year-old Simon open up his Stretch Armstrong on Christmas Day. Simon opens the freezer. Once the icy fog clears he sees nothing. There is nothing in the freezer but an icy emptiness. It's like a diorama of Hoth. There is nothing at all in the freezer. There are no pies. What's more I knew there were no pies. He looks around with a weird smile on his face, understanding perfectly what was going on yet at the same time understanding nothing. He can't believe that I would've, that I could've, done such a thing.

'What's going on? Where are the pies?' He's clearly heartbroken. What have I done? I've completely misjudged this.

'There are no pies,' I regretfully advise.

He slumps, spirit crushed. I begin laughing manically, taken by the evil spirit that inhabits my kitchen. It instructs me to scream and rip my shirt in half. So I do. Simon looks terrified.

Simon didn't stay with me for long in Ivy Road. In Australia he'd met and toured with a Northern Irish bloke called Michael Smiley. They'd decided to move in together as they were both stand-ups and had become very good friends. The first time I meet Smiley I'm terrified. He has a skinhead, bad teeth and scars from a bicycle crash on his face. He's by far the most energetic, aggressive, funny lunatic I have ever met. I loved him and still do. He's one of my best friends sixteen years on. Michael was a great stand-up, audiences loved him and were frightened of him in equal measure. He'd escaped the ravages of eighties Belfast and moved to London and fell into the world of cycle couriering. He loves cycling. Me and Simon used to tease him about what gear he had on his bike, he'd laugh because we were idiots.

. The first time I saw Michael do stand-up he started his set like this: 'I'm not actually a stand-up comedian [ripple of laughter], I'm just here to tell you you've got fifteen minutes to clear the room!' With his thick Belfast accent it got a big laugh. Sometimes when he did it the laugh was a nervous one at first that developed into a relieved roar when people realised he wasn't from a terror agency. I think Michael was a bit suspicious of me to begin with, two working-class men circling around each other, I understood.

Somewhere in the mishmash of my timeline Michael and Simon find a flat in Kentish Town and move in. It's a cool place. I still wallow in my Ivy Road flat for now. I'd moved from being a waiter on the floor and into the kitchen. I started working on the line. I was the only non-African and I loved it! I'd known a lot of these guys for a few years when I was a waiter, now though I was part of an elite crew. The kitchen brigade.

I began at first in the prep kitchen. I'd come in early each day and start my shift at 8 a.m. I'd check in all the deliveries, put them away and crack on preparing the sauces and salsas and marinades the restaurant would need for that day. By far the best thing about that job was the fact I didn't have to deal with customers. It was bliss and I actually felt like I was learning something. I'd spend hours slicing and chopping vegetables. Stirring sauces and preparing crispy tortilla shells for the nachos.

Being in the restaurant first thing with just the cleaners and the duty manager was sweet. We chatted, we had music on, we drank coffee, ate stuff we shouldn't have been eating and laughed. During my time in the kitchen I really got to know a lot of those lovely Ugandan men very well. At one point a year or so in I'd picked up enough of the language to be able to do a small stand-up routine in Swahili. They bloody loved it. I'd watch them clap and howl with laughter as I portrayed a man, stopped by police, having to explain why there's a monkey in the boot of his car. Monkey in a car boot comedy must be pretty big in the comedy clubs of downtown Kampala judging by the level of rich African laughter it would elicit.

Me and my friend Yusuf, a Ugandan ex-international footballer turned line cook, worked on an elaborate and very false backstory of my time as a child in the remote Ugandan town of Mukono. The story revolved around the fact my father used to be the manager of the Mukono Collins Hotel and this is where I grew up. It would freak out new Ugandans when they arrived at the restaurant. I loved that game. I guess it was like acting. I loved Yusuf. We went to a party one night where I met the wife of deposed and exiled Ugandan dictator Idi Amin. She was all right.

There was a big manual at the back of the kitchen, it told you in very simple steps how to make every sauce they used in the restaurant. That was my job and eventually I didn't need the manuals. Sadly for me that knowledge no longer exists inside my brain. It's a shame as I often yearn for the rich and creamy queso sauce or a sharp and spicy green tomatillo sauce for my homemade burritos. I can make my own versions but they're not quite the same. The only recipe I remember is the one for guacamole, I love it and it's something I still make to this day.

I was moved out of the prep kitchen and onto the line. This is where I really wanted to be. Cooking, although it was definitely not cooking. Not really. Not in the truest sense. It was putting together pre-made elements of a dish, not doing every dish from scratch. It was still tough and needed a great deal of skill on certain sections. I started, predictably, on the starters section. The waiters took a while to get used to the fact I was now a Linepig. Some of the sneakier foodservers, the ones who'd do anything for a tip, would try and approach me to sort them out free shit for their tables. I didn't. I couldn't.

A tiny machine would beep and puke out an order. It was then my job to gather all the bits together. Easy. I moved from appetisers to mains and from there onto the grill. The grill was where the action was. The weekend on that broiler, Friday to Sunday, was crazy. It was so busy. From 12–4 p.m. you were slammed and from 7–11 p.m. you were slammed.

One of the differences between the bar and kitchen was you could shout and swear in the kitchen and no one in the restaurant could hear you. Some of those poor waiters got sworn at so much. Bad waiters could potentially put some really bad fuck on your night. It could take the kitchen a long while to recover. I was responsible for anything that was cooked on the grill, steaks, fajitas, ribs, and every kind of burger. It's the kind of stress I like. The whole kitchen can fall or thrive on the strength of their Grill Man. At times on busy nights you could have fifty things on that griddle all at different points of readiness.

Like most things that involve a lot of people, communication is the key. When it's flowing and going well it feels amazing. We're all one beautiful Ugandan hive mind moving as one, making sure all the items the waiters need find their way onto one big tray all at the same time. When it wasn't that, you were fucked, hard and quick.

Although I liked working in the kitchen more than I'd liked working on the floor, it had its downsides. The worst one was the clean-up after a busy night, having to degrease that griddle and the floor and every other bit of your section was a pain in the potty-hole.

I'd done every job possible in that restaurant and for the first time in five years I began to have an itch I needed to scratch. This was something I'd never thought of before. I began to think that maybe I should leave that place and move on.

I was living a weird double life at this point. Working in the place had now taken a back seat to hanging with Simon and Smiley and other loonies, watching tons of stand-up and meeting good, funny people. My mind was being fed and this new sense of possibility made working at Chiquito more and more of a drag. There were so many great comics at the time and London culturely, comedically felt so fertile.

I was definitely different back then to the person I am now. I felt comfortable and relaxed and myself with Simon and Smiley and my friends at the restaurant, people I'd known for a while and trusted. Anyone else though and I retreated into myself. I became the silent shadow on Simon's shoulder, ever present but hardly talking.

I'm not sure why. Chip on my shoulder maybe, a suspicion of these types of flamboyant arty folk? I think the simplest answer was probably the truest. I was a bit shy and I thought, wrongly it turned out, that all these funny, smart people would just not be interested in what I had to say. Not true.

I think my working-class thought processes were a lot different to theirs though. A lot of the time I was silently working out whether or not I could take these people in a fight should push come to shove. How would I escape should there be a small fire? Does anyone have drugs? That kind of thing, but mostly it was just shyness.

This was the time I met Edgar Wright, the sweetest little ball-bag you'd ever wish to meet. I remember going out with Simon one night to the Battersea Arts Centre to see some stand-up and afterwards we stood around drinking in the bar, and that's where I saw him – a small and delicate little hair bear with skin as fine as wedding porcelain. He was a young director doing stuff with Alexei Sayle and Lenny Henry. He talked a lot and quickly (this has never changed), his passion and knowledge of all things TV and film meant it took me a while to fully get to grips with him. Not that I didn't like him, I just couldn't find a gap in the conversation to say anything, and even if I had I wasn't sure at that point if it'd be valid or funny enough.

As well as Edgar I met cool young bands and musicians, editors, costume designers, actors, writers, comedians. I was really lucky. I felt myself growing inside. Something had been awakened. The restaurant didn't seem enough, it was basically all I knew but I just couldn't do it any more, so I left. There was no fanfare. I just left. Five years. Goodbye. I knew I'd only leave to go to another restaurant but it felt good anyway. It was positive.

After five years of stability now came a time of job-hopping. Moving from restaurant to restaurant. Work was no longer the most important thing in my life, it was raving and comedy and Simon and Smiley and my mate Danny and Maxwell and all the other new people I'd met who'd enflamed my throbbing art gland. That took money though. I think if the truth were told I was a little bit embarrassed that I had to wait tables while my new mates did comedy. I had no reason to moan, these guys were skilled and worked bloody hard.

Simon and Smiley were living together at 9 Busby. It was a fantastic place. If you could avoid the violent racists or dangerous street gangs that littered the walk from Kentish Town tube you were laughing. It was fine in the day but coming home from work after midnight was sketchy. My trick when walking past groups of youths on bikes, hoods up, spitting, is always to either be totally invisible or act like a loony. I'd much rather mime eating some of my own fudge than get myself all stabbed up.

The house, if you ever made it, was a big lump of a place and because of Simon and Smiley's generous souls they took pity on me and let me live there. I paid very little rent. This meant though that I was morally obliged to get a Smiley talking-to about the virtues of 'Pulling your own weight, big lad!' I've had lots of these, even fairly recently – we call it getting 'Smiley'd'!

Michael had the room at the top of the house, he was very Bohemian and had his bike hanging on the wall and a pair of Technics 1210s set up, no bed just a mattress, bongo drums, big record collection with the odd picture of George Best in his prime here and there. It was mostly off limits but we were allowed to go up and play records when he wasn't about, which was often – Michael was a very good, in-demand stand-up who'd tour the country most weekends.

Simon had the big room downstairs next to the kitchen, two big floor-to-ceiling windows illuminated the place and there was a lovely original Victorian fireplace on one wall next to his futon. It was really nice, he too had a banging sound system.

My room was the place where the other two left boxes of shit they didn't want or need any more. In fact you could be fooled into thinking that freezing, damp room was a storage area for a tramp's mortuary. If you pushed aside some of those boxes and made your way past the binliners full of shoes and faux furs, you'd see that some poor soul, me, had made a rudimentary bed. No mattress, just cushions held together by a thin cotton blankey, two flat, yellow pillows without cases and a duvet without a quilt cover. This was the Crab Pit. This was the bedroom where I lived. A sordid shit hole.

The room was so cold in the winter that when I woke up an icy fog would hang low, hugging the floor like mist in an Arctic pre-dawn. I think this is where I got my superhuman resilience to the cold. I have to be cold at night. I know human beings are split into two camps in this matter, warm room or cold room, but I am definitely firmly encamped in the latter. The colder the better. What's the duvet for otherwise?

My need for extreme cold has driven wedges between me and some girlfriends in the past. I say wedges, we argued about it and then in the night they'd die of exposure. I lost three of them like that. Shame.

I went to a wedding in Ireland once with Chris and was forced to stay in a B and B, first and last time by the way. Don't get me wrong, lovely little place, new build though, the owners were nice, very welcoming but the house was like a fucking sauna and the windows were locked shut. It was immense. I awoke at 6 a.m. so hung-over and hot that I had to walk four miles into town topless in the rain to cool me down.

* * *

After three years of not drinking I have a weird notion pop into my head. I'd been really strong up until this point and hardly ever thought about alcohol. Still, the voice in my head had now begun to tell me it would be all right to have one beer. Just one little ice-cold pint. It can't hurt, can it?

I had to push these thoughts from my mind remembering the friends' rooms I'd pissed in and the countless times I'd borrowed a hairdryer to use on yellow, wee-stained sheets. There's a kind of shame we don't have a word for in English, I suspect the Germans do, they have a word for most things grim. It describes the embarrassment one has at being caught dumping a wet mattress in the street. Combine this with fights and anger and the dreadful quilt of fear that frequently hung over me days after heavy drinking occurred and you can see why I wanted – no, needed – to ignore this voice that had begun to crackle inside of me.

I don't know what started this man ringing his bell in my head but I felt like I needed to have a drink, just one, just to try, just have one. Okay? Just one. No! Yes, do it. Stop! I can't stop. The din and screaming of my Weakness being fucked loudly in the room next door by a young stud with a giant dick became so loud I fled the house to escape its wanton moans.

I left our house in Busby Place and walked past the old Jewish school that's not there any more. A few times after massive benders we'd find ourselves standing on the balcony in sarongs and balaclavas drunkenly toasting the horny sixth form girls who'd laugh at us as they went into class.

The din turned into a sinister whisper as I wandered into Camden Town. The shouting made me angry. The whispering made me frightened.

I stood and paced up and down outside the World's End. I stopped and looked up, the name of the pub was not lost on me. I spent an hour outside cogitating on what was the best thing to do, all this time the hiss building in my head like the rumbling in Tommy Lee Jones's 1997 hit film *Volcano*. I went into the pub. I'd never been in it before and was struck by how shit it was, how the clientele were either down and outs or stick-thin Italian tourists with futuristic haircuts.

I walked around that pub looking at those people, those guilty day drinkers, and I go to the toilet to do a quick line of tears. Standing at the bar now with that noise roaring out of my brain I start counting out change and finally order a beer. A Foster's of all things. The barman places it on the counter and turns to put my sweaty coins into the till. By the time he turns back I'm gone. I left the pint on the bar and ran outside.

All in all I spent nearly two hours in turmoil at the thought of that Foster's. Fighting this urge. I was tired and it laughed knowing how unrelenting it could be. I'll fucking show you. I strode back in and the Foster's was still there. The barman has put a beermat on top to denote the pint is still active. Oh god, it was still active. I took the hat off the glass and looked into the golden column. The crescendo of noise was deafening now, but as I lifted the jar up to my lips the noises and clatter, clank and chatter, ceased. Anne Heche and Tommy Lee Jones look up, it's awfully quiet?

BOOOOOOOOOOOOOOOOMMMMMMMMMMMM!!!

I drank that pint down in one go, it was cold and it was fizzy and it was amazing and the guilt and disappointment I felt at that moment tasted fucking great. What had I done? Emperor Yamamoto looked up from his map of Pearl Harbor and uttered his now legendary words, 'We have awoken a sleeping giant.' That old, dead Japanese bastard was right. The AA has a saying: One drink is too many and a thousand's not enough. I ordered another. This time I watched the trace as the bubbles fled up, it was a real *Ice Cold in Alex* moment.

I gulped that one down too, not as quickly as the first but in four big shunts. Then another. I needed to call Simon, racked with guilt and excitement I wanted to tell him about what I'd done. I was still a year or two away from getting my first mobile, my main Christmas present from Peggy that year. I'd made a massive Christmas error by searching the house looking for my pressie haul. I'd found a bag under some coats deep in a cupboard. I shouldn't be doing this but I can't stop myself, I open the bag and holy fucking shit the Ericsson mobile phone of my dreams! Bosh!

Sometime between that point and Christmas Day Simon made a decision to change the phone so when I opened the gift, full of excitement, my crestfall was plain for all to see as I set my eyes on a giant lump of a Samsung mobile. A lesson there for every naughty boy and girl.

But this terrible moment was still a couple of years away. I go outside and call Simon Pegg from a red phonebox. He came straight away. I think he was pretty pleased I'd started again, to be honest. It meant we could now get right on it.

After four or five pints we stumbled back through Kentish Town with our trousers round our ankles. We got home hungry for more and smashed up a bottle of Blue Label Smiley had been keeping for special, he wasn't in so we went for it. That next morning I woke up with one of the worst hangovers ever. I find a large, rabid badger has shit into my brain and down the back of my eyes. It's horrible. That was the beginning of my second coming as a drinker. If you're expecting a PS to this where I go through some kind of primal pissmageddon then you'll be disappointed. Things were different from then on with drink for me. Yes I got pissed and beaten and swore at people and got sworn at and puked, passed out and blood-farted bacchanalian havoc all over the place, but I wasn't the same person I was when I stopped four years previously and that made me happy.

The house at 9 Busby Place had a garden that we couldn't access. We could see it but we couldn't get to it. The only access was through the downstairs flat. We'd been told that the place used to belong to our landlord's father who'd sadly died there. I can't really remember our landlord but I remember a feeling of dread if we knew he was turning up. I feel like I want to say he was a mean skinflint who never wanted to spend any money on the place but he had it in his power to let us have the key to downstairs and in turn the garden, so we played the game. Smiley, our working-class hardnut and spokesperson in residence, put the shit eye on him and the landlord tentatively agreed. We were thrilled. It meant we could have a garden for the summer.

There were a few of us at the house that morning when we first decided to use the key to the Dead Man's flat. We'd heard noises drifting through the floorboards before but I put that down to the 'erb I'd been smoking. We used the Dead Man as a thing to frighten us, he was a cautionary tale, a fishwives' yarn. We knew it was rubbish and stuff we'd say just to freak each other out but standing there at his old front door making a spooky *ewwwwwwwwhhhhhheeeeoooohhhhhh* noise I couldn't help but feel anxious.

The door stuck and we all pushed it open, our noses assaulted by the whiff of things old and foul. It was day and the sun struggled to make a dent through the brown net curtains. As we stepped inside the yellow-dark room our eyes strained to focus on the horrors within.

The Dead Man's flat was exactly as it was left the day he died. Nothing had been cleared. It was a mausoleum, a memento mori covered in a thick layer of dust and it was fucking creepy. There were still plates in the sink, food in the fridge, clothes, cutlery, pots, pans, dusty hats, furniture.

Poor bloke. We walked around for ages like CSI: Kentish Town, we looked in every drawer and every cupboard, on a calendar he'd marked dates well into the future when he'd be taking his pigeons to their next race.

We'd forgotten all about the garden. Our focus had turned to a very dusty but completely functioning La-Z-Boy recliner. Smiley was brave and gingerly sits and uses the sturdy lever to recline, fully. Simultaneously our minds link and we all accepted that in spite of its creepiness this would be a great addition to our house. This was the green light for low-level looting to begin. It felt like a bad idea, I could feel the dusty spirit fingers of a pigeon fancier jabbing his bones into my eye. We survey the garden for a second and all hastilly agree on what needs to be done to make it nice and went back upstairs.

The chair was dusted and hoovered and it was good as new. We had a fucking La-Z-Boy recliner! This was the best day ever! The chair though had the last laugh, the chair and the Dead Man. The malevolent spirit of that old pigeon keeper sadly haunted the chair, we should never have taken it. People who slept in that chair, and there were many, all shared a similar dream. They awoke in our front room in the chair, unable to move, the Dead Man would be on them, over them, moving and looking into their eyes. If it was a girl asleep in the chair he would often rub himself off on them; once he finished the spell was broken and the girls could finally wake up. Weird and horny shit I'm sure you'll agree.

Over the years Simon and I had many other brushes with the occult, it was something we loved to flirt with. We loved the fear. We loved the spirit world. Often the pair of us would head into the wilds to hunt for ghosts and ghouls.

The first time we did this was deep within the Essex country-side. We pulled up outside a thirteenth-century Saxon church he'd read about. The church sat in a freshly ploughed field and we switched the engine off and sat in the cold dark, our breathing, shallow and quick, the only thing that could be heard. We got out of the car eventually after winding each other up a lot and tried the door to the ancient church. It was locked. Lights from a slow-moving vehicle on a nearby lane and my terrible overwhelming urge to wee forced us to run back to the car and drive away at high speed laughing like idiots.

When we lived in Highgate our house had a massive garden that bordered on a piece of woodland. For months we didn't really pay it much mind other than it was a nice thing to look at and the busy comings and goings of the cheeky European Jays was most cheery.

Simon and I were alone one night drinking litres of strong cider. It was dark and drizzling and having discovered a hole in our fence earlier in the day we decided to go through that hole and see what was in the forest. It was a mistake that almost cost one of us our life.

The forest was dense and the ground covered in a tangle of logs, vines and slippery ivy. We could see the lights of the cars on the Archway Road and hear the *clickclack* of the pedestrians streaming out of Highgate Station. It was exciting to be an unseen watcher, it pushed us deeper into the woods.

Eventually we find ourselves alone in the rain in a forest in the middle of London. We'd left the noise of the road behind. It felt like we were the only people left alive. It was a feeling we liked.

That house in Highgate was where we talked about what we'd do, how we'd cope during a Zombie outbreak. It took us a while to refine our plan but eventually we settled on this:

Using the backs of the houses we'd garden hop down the Archway Road until the houses became terraced with balconies along the front. We'd take to the balconies fifteen feet above the undead horde and silently make our way to a place called Pax Guns. A shop we'd reccied many times. It sold high-powered air rifles, optical scopes, ammo etc. but we suspected it had tastier stock out back for naughty little bastards like us. Climbing down through their extension skylight we'd raid the shop for whatever they had and arm ourselves with shooters.

Our plan has changed and evolved slightly over the years to include the use of edged weapons and pieces of pointy metal. The last thing you need when you're facing a gang of bitey fucks is to run out of ammo, then you got wampum big problem. A knife does not run out of bullets. That said, using a rifle as a club or stabbing a long blunt barrel through the eye bulbs and into the brain would also do the trick.

Once we'd secured our weps (weapons) we moved on to stage two of the plan. Heavy weps. (Heavy weapons.) You can't have too many heavy weps. (Heavy weapons.) I'd heard of a British army base in Enfield, which was essentially a giant arms cache. This was our second destination. After finding a truck or large van we'd head there to raid it hoping we were the first. Other desperate survivors will kill you just as quick as a mindless Z-Bag.

With the guards either changed or long since gone, it would be easy to break in and upgrade to the standard British Infantry L85A2 assault rifle in 5.56mm, its troop support version the L86A1 LSW and a long-barrelled .50 cal sniper's rifle for weekend field clearance. Then our plan changed gear. We needed to think about friends and family and a long-term solution for living the rest of our natural lives in relative comfort.

The answer was an easy one. We'd use one of London's many stadiums. As we were closer to Arsenal this is the one we chose. Once inside it gave us everything we needed. The stadium was a circle of lockable gates. Security was assured. The many hospitality boxes gave us somewhere to set up a kind of home, there'd be supplies, food and plenty of bottled water. More importantly for our long-term survival, half the pitch could be turned into fields for the cultivation of fresh food, wheat, corn, potatoes, apples, pears, plums, tomatoes, and the other half could be used for the grazing of the livestock we'd need for fresh meat. Easy.

However, this plan was a long way from needing to be utilised (2029) and right now we were soaking wet, pushing through an urban forest looking for goblins. What we found was a tad more exciting.

The forest clears slightly and we see the big brick arch of an old tunnel. It was caged and gated but in the far distance we could see a tiny speck of light. An entrance or exit depending on which end you're standing. We turn and follow what used to be the train tracks deeper into the woods. After a couple of minutes struggling through the forest we both stop, our mouths fall open. We have just unearthed the find of our lives. An old abandoned tube station. The remnants of the old Highgate High-level station, closed in 1954.

We stood in silence not quite believing that this had been here all along and we never knew. After a moment we climbed up off the tracks onto the old platform. It was amazing and perfect in every way. We patted ourselves on the back, finished our big cider and opened the back-up we'd brought in case we ran out, which we had. Good fucking times. Running around that place peering into the locked rooms and rattling the old platform dispensers selling things long forgotten like Hutchinson's Original Phlegm Pastilles and Miss Cunty's Titwax felt like heaven to us.

The rain began to lash down and fearing we'd soon run out of back-up cider we turn and head for home. It's heavy-going on the way back, muddy, slippy, very treacherous indeed. I lag behind with the dwindling cider rations. I could hear Simon in front telling me to hurry up. I pick up the pace and seconds later I slip on some wet ivy and smash my head on a log. I'm out cold. I think I'm unconscious for thirty seconds or so. When I wake I can hear an angry Simon call-ing my name. He thinks I'm fucking about. I can hear him shouting.

'I'm not fucking about, Nick! You better answer me!'

I couldn't speak or move.

'Nick! Fine! I'm going home and I'm ordering Chinese because I'm really hungry and I will see you later.'

He pauses . . . Nothing.

'Okay, I'm going. Seriously.'

I hear him tramp off into the woods towards our house. I cannot move. I'm badly injured and slump into unconscious-ness again.

When I come to it's raining heavily still. I'm drunk and hurt and wet, this is a very dangerous triumvirate. I could kill or severely maul someone to death in this fragile state. I pull myself up into a sitting position and from there the next thirty minutes is spent dragging, tumbling and crashing my way through the forest towards home. Falling face first again I sleep for a while. A hundred metres or so in front of me I can see the welcoming lights of our front room burning in the darkness. I compel myself towards them. Finding the hole in the fence I crawl through and

I'm in my own garden. I roll onto my back, relief floods through me. The wolves turn back, afraid to pursue me any further.

I hoist myself up onto my feet and stagger, jaeger-like, up the garden and towards the house. I can't believe he left me. He bloody left me. Could this be revenge for Piegate? I fill the window soaked and covered in leaves and mud and shit and blood. Eventually Simon tears his eyes away from the TV and cheerily waves me in. I'm speechless and stumble into the front room, Simon sits happily watching telly and eating a massive Chinese. I'm angry and try to tell him as much but I'm stammering badly.

'Sorry bud, I thought you were joking. I was really hungry.'

I wasn't joking. I was also really hungry, hungry for medical assistance. Next day at the hospital it was revealed that as well as the massive lump on my head I had suffered a heavy concussion and a light hypothermia. This was the penultimate time we ever hunted for ghosts. Like Piegate, my near woodland death is a section of our lives we rarely talk about.

The last time we ever messed with the occult was in December 2002. We'd read about an old abandoned stately home in Surrey called Tilford Manor. It was the seat of the Duke of Guildford until a fire gutted the place and killed the fifth Duke's wife and his six children. After the tragedy the house was left to fall into disrepair.

This sounded perfect for us. We drove down late in the afternoon and arrived just as the sun was beginning to set. The main gate, at one point a fine structure, now dilapidated and dense with weeds and brambles, had a space large enough for the both of us to push through.

The forest on both sides seemed untouched and completely overgrown, no birds sang, no wind blew, this was the perfect storm for both horror and the desperate need for me to do wee wee.

We walked up the drive, now pierced by grass and weeds, until we got our first glimpse of the shattered remains of Tilford Manor. I felt a surge of cold from my feet up to the top of my head and we stopped, briefly unable to move. It was the creepiest place I had ever seen. Me and Simon discussed just going home but eventually, laughing like drains through terror-nerves, we decide to push on. I'm not sure we were ever going to go in, I think we were just going to walk around the outside and look through the windows, shit ourselves up a bit, that's what we enjoyed.

The windows on the ground floor were boarded up. We made our way around the back through a tangle of overgrown hedges and trees. The back of the house stops us in our tracks. It was absolutely beautiful, with a half decent gardener this place could be knocked into shape in no time at all. A vast, over-grown lawn spread out downhill from the house to a lake now covered in weed. A frog and newt haven for sure.

We walked down the lawn a little and turned to look back at the house, it was only now we see the place in all its glory. In its day it must have been fabulous. Now it's remembered only as a house where six children died.

I began to feel we'd done enough on this ghost hunt, we should go home, my almost constant need to wee was begin-ning to change into a solid yearning to make a plop. If push came to shove I could dump in one of the outhouses and use my pants to make clean and it'd be blamed on a loose-bowelled junkie.

Hidden in among the bushes was a set of stone steps leading to a battered old door. Simon pushed at it and with little effort the thing shuddered open. We deployed our head torches. *Paul anyone?* When ghost hunting we'd always have our head torches, it was a great way to leave both hands free if you needed to punch an amorous hobo.

The wind howled and the door slammed behind us. Inside that room was freezing cold. We stood in what I believed to be an old servants' kitchen or pantry with stone floors, butler's sinks, hooks for cloaks and on one wall, high up near the ceiling, a long row of bells. Underneath these shiny brass flowers were little handwritten notes to tell the old maids what room was ringing what bell. Down here, this place seemed untouched by the fire.

I assumed it had started in one of the bedrooms and spread, sparing the lower levels. Our fear was briefly overwhelmed by our curiosity about this piece of forgotten history we found ourselves in. Pushing through another door and up another set of stone steps we arrived at the foot of a great wooden staircase, ahead of us was the old front door, massive and boarded up with planks. On the left double doors leading to who knows what.

Here, there were signs of both Mother Nature's seizure and the fire which had taken six young lives. The ornate plaster cornices above the great staircase blackened and charred, had cracked. The wooden balustrade wrapped in long tendrils of ancient ivy. At this point one of the kitchen bells tings. I piss and we spend an age looking at one another. This is a shared aural hallucination, right? We wait. The fear subsides and we begin to theorise in whispers. It rings again, this time it's slightly more insistent. We hold hands and drops of sweat pitter patter fear all over our trainers.

We sprint back into the pantry and look at the panel of tiny bells, willing it not to ring. It rings again. This time it is long and angry and sustained. The sign beneath the bell reads Miss Emma's

Room. It honestly feels like we're possessed because we both make the decision to go and find her room. To this day I wish we hadn't. We should've run there and then. We should've run away.

We creaked up the stairs. Branching off the first floor landing there are two corridors leading to the back of the house. Each corridor has five or six doors. We walked down the first corridor, downstairs the ring of the bell, angry, insistent, continued. Every door is locked. Turning back we hear a loud creak coming from upstairs. We feel compelled to go up. We find charred wood, smashed brick and plaster; here half the house had given up and slumped in on itself.

Trees and bushes spring out of the brickwork making this part of the house look like Shockheaded Peter. We see the clouds racing by. Peering down into the hole we see what must be a hundred dolls and teddies littering the rubble beneath. All are headless.

Towards the back of this burned and broken corridor we see a door. As we approach it we see it has a cracked chalkboard hanging off the black door handle; in spidery, faded writing we see the words, Little Miss Emma. Simon and I look at each other and the bell downstairs stops ringing. I know what we shouldn't do but we do it anyway. My hand, trembling, reaches out to the dented and smoke-stained knob. I turn it and the mechanism inside the lock clicks and the door swings open.

The room inside is black with soot, the remnants of a fierce fire evident. There is a cupboard, a bed, burnt and charred, and a small dressing table, its combs and brushes melted and warped, its mirror cracked. We enter the room and kick and stand on what must be a hundred dolls' heads. The fear shakes itself loose and jangles up my spine and into my brain. We shouldn't be here. Once again the bell begins dancing down in the pantry. Whatever, whoever, is pulling that cord is in this room with us.

I turn to look at Simon. His eyes are wide as saucers, his mouth is agape and he trembles. I cannot see what he sees. I don't want to see what he has seen but I must. I have to see what he's seen. I turn and look at the spot on the wall where the bell pull dances and after a second I see it. It is black on black. The burnt wall here is not flat and it is not a wall but it is burnt and black, her nightie is black, charred, her face is black, her hairless head is black, her hands are tiny and black. She stops pulling the cord and the distant bell falls silent. Her face crinkles and her burnt, brittle eyelids spring open. She looks at us, right at us, her eyes, white as box fresh cue balls, are the signal for us to go. Flee now . . . RUN!!! And we do.

The wind roars through the house. We hear Little Miss Emma laughing and laughing, it is loud and terrible. It vibrates inside me and I slump against the wall and vomit. Simon grabs me and heaves me down the main staircase, we turn and head down the steps into the pantry. All the bells begin to ring, the inhabitants of the rooms long empty, angry and now pulling with all their might. We claw at the door and surge outside into the garden. The pantry door smashes closed behind us and inside the bells stop.

We don't stop running until we reach the car. We get inside and Simon revs the engine hard and we spin away as the wheels struggle for purchase. We don't say a thing and eventually we have to stop. Simon shakes so much I'm afraid we'll crash, he pulls the car over and we cry. It is uncontrollable. We never speak of this again. I will never forget Little Miss Emma's white eyes.

* * *

At some point two friends that Simon and Smiley had made while on tour in Australia came to stay. I'd heard a lot about these two. Greg Fleet and his then girlfriend Janei Anderson were both performers, actors and comedians. Greg was the person responsible for killing Daphne in *Neighbours*, he played a drunken yahoo who killed her in a car crash. Janei can be seen as Jacqui in the film *Romper Stomper* screaming up a right storm when the Koreans start handing out revenge beatings to the nutty skins.

I liked those guys from the start, I mean really loved them. I was struck by the amazing relationship they had at the time. I say amazing – it was terribly co-dependent but I'd never seen anything like it before so to me it was amazing. He was so naughty. He'd been a heroin addict for years and years by the time I met him but she just forgave him any indiscretion. Janei had so much bloody love, she was a sexy, funny, den mother. She cleaned with a finger of spit, she'd advise, she'd listen, cuddle, kiss, whatever was needed. She was also fucking funny. What a gal.

Greg, or Fleety as he was known, and me got each other immediately. We understood, not just each other but also the need to push things to their very end point, both socially and chemically. I'd never known anyone who did heroin before. I was frightened and fascinated and, to be honest, pretty confused at first. I think I was taught to be afraid of 'smackheads'. I didn't think they could be normal, amazing, beautiful, creative people who just happened to do heroin. Then again my tolerance for addiction and addicts was pretty high anyway because of my own experiences with it. I was more than ready to accept people for who they were, not what they did.

I didn't realise at first what was happening with the heroin, Greg would slope off to the loo and stay in there for ages. When he came out he was so sleepy. We'd sit and watch the morning cartoons, Greg would sit in the Dead Man's chair and smoke, he'd nod off and would come to as the hot end of his ciggie burnt him awake.

With Smiley and Simon and our two new arrivals the house bloomed and blossomed. It felt amazing being there, it was like a Lars von Trier collective but with less trumpets. Some mornings we'd all put faux fur coats on and shoot music videos. We were always creating something. I still had to go to work and wait tables or shake Martinis but it gave me a reason to forget my folks and my sadness and enjoy myself. This, of course, meant drugs, although I never tried H. I always hated needles so for me injecting was way beyond my limit.

This was my Camden Town time and I loved it, I looked forward to it, it made me feel special. Every Sunday I'd get up at whatever time, shake off whatever was still in me, and dress up. I'd try and look cool to impress Janei, it was difficult for me – the others made it seem so effortless. Janei was a very stylish woman and I tried to impress her whenever I had the chance. We all did. Smiley has always dressed well. He has a great sense of style. He's one of those fellas where clothes just hang so well on him. Greg was an H pony so he seemed not to care much about fashion, yet in his not caring it made him very stylish and cool. Lucky prick.

After breakfast/brunch/lunch we'd stroll into Camden Town. Camden Town then on a Sunday was very happening. It still is but now it seems more corporate-sponsored, cleaner, less dangerous. It's still nice though, even a little edgy I guess if you're a Danish teen on an exchange trip. Back then it was a dirty, dangerous breeding ground for bands and drugs and laughter and fighting.

We'd walk around the stables for ages, buying T-shirts or new screens for the bongs or sunglasses. It made me feel like an extra in *Blade Runner* walking under the railway arches that heaved with tourists, Rastas, wide-eyed Ravers and back-combed Goths as we trawled the stalls looking for nice fresh falafel. It was exciting.

Under the bridge by the lock was the place to go if you wanted to buy the shittest drugs in the world. The dealers were men used to cutting at thin tourists looking for something to blaze up through the window of their two-star Paddington flop house. I'd been burned a couple of times but sometimes after a few drinks on a Sunday it was hard to resist the temptation.

One afternoon I pushed past a group of Polish kids who were waiting to be threatened. A frightened young Swede with deep cuts to both his arms bumbled back up the towpath crying. In the canal there were two corpse-shaped things floating just beneath the surface. It seemed quiet for a Sunday. No matter, I fancied a smoke and this time I had a surefire way to not get burned.

As I neared the stick-thin one-eyed Rasta I took an approach I was hoping they'd never seen or heard before. Honesty. I was going to be honest and just lay it all out there.

'All right?'

'Whauwan?'

So far so good . . .

'I need some bush.'

I'd heard some white Trustafarians in an earlier exchange say 'Me need some bush, mon.' They got cut and rightly so. The exchange progressed and I see One-Eye reach into his jacket to fish out Sir Stabsalot. It's at this point I spring the trap:

'Wait!' He tenses up. I continue:

'Can I be honest with you?' A fog of confusion descends upon the trader. His hands tremble as he works out what's happening. I think he thinks I'm Old Bill. I'm not. I continue:

'I'm from London, born and bred as, I think, are you.'

'Fucking right, blud. Islington.' His patois drops for just a second. This is good – for the moment my body remains watertight.

'Can I be honest with you?' I repeat.

'Go on but be quick I got Spanish kids to slash at.'

'I understand. I live in Kentish Town, I'm here every week and I've been burned in the past by people that trade under this bridge. I'm a bit pissed and I'm desperate for a smoke, I don't want to spend £40 buying something that'd be better suited going into cannelloni.' I hear someone drop a knife behind me in utter disbelief. There's a long pause, he's debating how to open me up: tummy jab maybe, bleeds a lot, takes an age to die if it's shallow enough I guess, how about a . . . facial slash? Facial slash is good because it sends out a very visible warning. Maybe a few short sharp stabs to my bum and upper thighs – I'll shit standing up in the shower for the next eight weeks but I'll live. Who knows. Let's find out, he stares at me . . .

'Yeah, okay, fair enough, follow me.'

I follow One-Eye back to his flat on the outskirts of Camden. I'm slightly nervous but we've begun to chat and like a trusting fool I go with him. The atmosphere lightens somewhat when he lifts his patch to reveal another fully working, bright clear chestnut eye. I shouldn't have but in the atmosphere of honesty and trust I do. He invites me in, I accept. By and by we have a glass of semi-skimmed milk. He pulls out a carrier bag of stinky shit, I hand over dollar bills, he hands over the fat buds and the deal is done. Simple as that. We shake hands and drift back into town together. As he nears the bridge he explains, pulling down his patch, he has to put his game face on.

'I've gotta get back to work. It was nice to meet you though.'

'And you, mate.' I go to shake hands, he pulls away.

'I can't, the guys are watching.'

'I understand. How do you want to play this?' He thinks for a minute.

'I'll shout loudly calling you a Bumbaclart, I'll go through my pockets looking for my carnival knife and you flee into the crowded market place.'

'Sounds like a plan. Thanks, Ian.'

'BUMBACLART!' He winks. I run.

Sometimes honesty is the best policy.

Camden on a Sunday was something all the crew liked. Usually it was me, Fleety, Janei and Simon, later we'd hook up with Smiley and his lot, the stand-ups, proper stand-ups, dark, edgy, wonderful loonies. Later still Dion and Tony and the South Africans would roll into town and shit would get weird. These were not exclusive combinations. For a long while we'd hit the World's End, the place where I broke my neck falling off of the wagon, and sit there for a long-time session. Once hammered we'd drift off into the market for fun and cheap Chinese food that made us all need to do semi-solid toilets really quickly. We loved it.

There was a club in the market on a Sunday evening run by the legendary DJ Goldie called Metalheadz. We weren't into Drum and Bass that much, Hard House was our thing, but we weren't snobby and after fifteen pints it was nice to have a joint and a jump. The guys came a couple of times but their hearts weren't in it. Mostly – and when I say mostly I mean the five times we went – I went on my own. I loved the music but the clientele seemed a bit too serious, they seemed to want to be seen, it didn't feel like anyone was having that much fun. Not like Hard House, that shit was all about fun.

Sometimes, and I liked these sometimes, I'd have a mooch with the gang and we'd stop to drink a coffee under these arches deep at the back of the market. Dub reggae would rattle my eyes, my nose assaulted by the smell of 'erb and incense. We'd sit and watch tourists drift through. It was so nice sitting there, it felt like being in a futuristic space souk.

Afterwards we'd bowl over to meet Smiley at The Stag's Head pub just across the street. I liked it here a lot. It was a proper Irish boozer, packed with hipsters and locals. It also had an amazing Thai kitchen. Like I said, traditional Irish. It was always exciting in that place. Smiley obviously bossed it, he's so fucking cheeky and gets away with absolute murder, it's thrilling to watch. He'd often leave me open-mouthed by his naughtiness. The first time he met my mum he goosed her slightly and asked if she had knickers on. Lolz! She loved it. They all did.

As well as Smiley he was often joined by a big dangerous northern man called Danny Brown. Danny quickly became a good mate to me. He lives nearby now and I see him all the time. Danny, along with Smiley, Simon, Nira Park, Tony Lindsay and Edgar, all have their initials tattooed around my arm around a crown. Kings and queens among men. I couldn't have done any of it without them.

Danny and Smiley were the two toughest sons of bitches I knew and I couldn't help but feel slightly indestructible when I was out on the piss with that pair. There was also a small wiry fella called Andrew Maxwell who could talk the back legs off a donkey. He's funny as fuck and sharp as a razor, smart and dashing to boot. Great stand-up. When I had my stag night Maxwell turned up with a massive glass bottle shaped like the Eiffel Tower, it was full of absinthe. Pandemonium ensued.

Often other friends and family would turn up at the pub, children too; naughty and mischievous, smart, loved and clever, they would run around stealing sips from pints. It felt like these people in this place were my family. It was all I had and it was enough. After drinking and doing whatever else, the crew would walk back through Kentish Town back to Busby Place. We'd wind down listening to Smiley mix or watching new episodes of *The Simpsons* smoking fatties and sitting in the Dead Man's chair. I'd often snuggle up and nod off with my head on Janei's lap, she'd stroke my hair and call me Bubbie. I think it was the happiest I'd been.

This was the time me and Simon started to make our first little films. They were shit and amazing. Little horror films we shot on Simon's video camera. Our films, shot on location in 9 Busby Place and almost entirely in French, had the potential we thought to rock Hollywood to its very core.

Aniseed Du Peril was the story of a man killed by a possessed bottle of the antacid drink Gaviscon. Thrilling stuff. *Il Slash Mon Guts (He Slash My Guts)* was a grizzly stalk and slash which became an advert for Gaviscon. Smiley had a plastic retractable knife that we used in the film, and in the thrilling dénouement when a bad me killed a good me, the blade snapped. During the only take we filmed you can see how frightened I am exactly at the moment the knife breaks. It adds a dimension of realism to the scene if you know that Smiley will be so mad when he finds out you went into his room and took something without asking which you then broke.

Me and Simon rewound that moment about a hundred times and screamed with laughter every time we watched it. It's funny when my dying screams turn into a 'oooh' noise when I realise how much shit we'll be in.

Our last horror short was a black and white effort called *Dinner For Two*. A tense psychological thriller starring the excellent Greg Fleet and the Alluring Janei Anderson. There was a chilling twist at the end which I won't give away. The funniest part of that film was watching Greg trying to stick an LP record into a CD player. What a wally. So simple but boy we laughed.

My double life continued apace. I'm never sure what me I was. I know there were lots of naughties in my life. I was clubbing at every opportunity I could and spent my time planning for weekends or getting over the weekends. This had gone on for so long that I was beginning to feel jaded, dirty, even a little bit bored of it. My head was everywhere. The fantastic and magical had become the grubby and malignant. I was paranoid and the consumption of more and more was beginning to feel like a hollow mission. I never stopped to enjoy or breathe.

I found myself one night in a club somewhere in South London. I'd heard stories, rumours on the scene, that government agencies had infiltrated circles of dealers and that dodgy bumbles were being sold to break the movement up. I didn't believe it. I was sure our government has better things to do than fuck with hedonists and independent thinkers. Right?

That night a packed club full of happy people became an empty club within three hours. Everyone became very ill. I stumbled around until I found an overground station. Getting onto a train that was headed fuck knows where, I puke onto the floor of the empty carriage. My eyes roll, I couldn't believe what

I saw. I was covered in a thick black foam. What the fuck was going on? I was puking thick black foam. What organ in the body is responsible for producing black foam? I was unaware of the black foam gland in the human stomach up until that point. What was happening to me? I passed out and when I came to I was standing on a beach looking out at the sea. It was flat and calm. I closed my eyes. The sun was shining and it felt lovely.

I realise now I had been deaf, the noise of gulls and children screaming tickle my eardrums and I fully awaken. I have no idea how I got there, what time it was or even where I was. In my hands I have two books, *Cancer Ward* and *The Gulag Archipelago*, both by Solzhenitsyn. No idea how I got them.

I'm in Brighton. It's the first time I'd ever been. I make my way home and spend the day trembling. This was the start of the end of that section of my hedonism. It continued, sure, but it was different. It took its toll on me. My glass shattered. I wouldn't call it a massive breakdown as such but it was a tiny bit of a breakdown. A Nervy B as my mate Paddy would call it. I had a little Nervy B.

When I was coming down off shit I used to feel sounds. Sounds would transfer into nerve commands and rattle up my pathways into my brain. It was terrible. I hated it. I always said to Simon it felt like my mind was a very thin veneer of glass resting on four old, red bricks. Every now and then someone would drop a piece of gravel on that glass. The fear I had of it shattering and its noise transforming into a bolt that raced up through my nervous system and into my brain was too much to take. One day my glass shattered.

I stopped working, I stopped going out, I couldn't really eat. I lay in bed or on the sofa smoking weed, feeling fucking sorry for myself. Feeling my brain frighten itself whenever it could.

Weed didn't help me of course but I never knew that back then, that's a fairly recent realisation. It's probably been the thing that fucked me up the most over the years and I failed to acknowledge it until it was almost too late. I think I refused to accept that it was the HaHa biscuits making me feel like this. How could something I love so much be hurting me so bad? I couldn't get my shit together. I was afraid and I was shit.

Simon and Smiley and a few of the girls I knew were amazing at this time, always popping in and bringing me Weetabix. I like Weetabix. The boys gee'd me up and financially sorted me out. I really owe them so fucking much. After a few weeks I started to pull up out of my dive, the darkness cleared slightly and something started to drag that big, wet quilt off my stubborn bonce. Smiley is always great in these situations. He Smiley'd me one night and told me how it was. It was exactly what I needed. In the absence of my own dad, due to our alcoholic exile and my sad bitterness at the whole 'Mum' situation, he was it. He was the kick up the hole that shook me out of my chemically induced mind funk.

Smiley was the guy who made me realise that it was all right to succeed. No one had ever told me that. It was something I'd never considered before. That's stayed with me ever since. It's okay to succeed. I knew what it felt like to hurt and fail, those things were familiar to me. But the thought that I was allowed to succeed was something new and scary and something I needed to hear.

* * *

I did not want to go back to working in restaurants. I looked around for other things first before I was forced back on the floor. A cabbie maybe? I liked driving but couldn't afford a car, I didn't have a pot to piss in. What could I do? Me and Dion thought about starting a garden-clearing business called Busy Bees. It never came to fruition.

I needed to do something so I took the first job that I saw. I spent a week working in a call centre off Great Portland Street. Telesales. It was not for me at all. It was full of *Wolf of Wall Street* wannabees. Guys with headsets on selling, selling, selling. At points they'd stop yabbering to use the telesales professional's greatest tool . . . Silence. Let the other fucker speak first. Take away every opportunity the guy on the other end of the phone has to say no until the only thing he can say is, yes. Boom! There's your sale. There's your commission. I hated watching those cocky twats. I lost count of the amount of smug winks I got from helmets about to make £50 in commission.

I found it really difficult. I couldn't do what they did. I didn't care enough and it felt like a scam. I'd sit in my booth, head down, cold-calling people, reading my lines off the ready-prepared script. People who'd been there a while didn't need the script, they used it as a frame and hung their own shit off it. There was a skill involved certainly but I didn't have it. I'd mumble into the headset and get hung up on. NO NO NO! I heard that a lot. I made no sales. In that business you live and die on bottom line. No sales? No commission? Then you're out.

After a few days chasing leads I sensed a sale was on the cards. I used the silence and chiselled away every opportunity for the customer to say no until he finally said yes! I leapt up and punched the air. I had my first sale. The company procedure for a sale was this: you took a sales form and faxed it over to the other company, got them to sign it, faxed it back and then boom! The sale and the commission was yours.

I gathered the documents together and rushed to the fax machine, I wrote the fax number on the back of the last sheet, stuck it in the machine and dialled. A moment, some squeaks, and the fax went through. I was about to get paid. Yes! I was chuffed to bits. Maybe I was cut out for this after all.

Colleagues now full of pride, and seeing my immense potential, came and patted me on the back. I did it. I shuffled the papers and re-ordered them, placing them in a little file marked 'Successful sales'. It was at this point I realised I'd actually faxed him my script covered in explicit doodles of giant helmeted dicks and big-titted women, legs spread ready to gratefully accept the aforementioned giant helmeted dicks.

The guy was furious and complained. I didn't come in the next day and was unemployed again. Good. I hated that fucking horrendous, windowless, smug-filled anus farm.

So obviously I went back to the only thing I was good at. I wound up back in a dining room having an interview at a restaurant called Frankie and Benny's. It was a bad interview as I still struggled slightly talking to people and being outside but I had to do something so fuck it.

Having to work in a restaurant again after hanging out with my friends who were my family, these funny, complicated, beautiful, creative, angry fuckers, and knowing there was another life I could be leading was a real pain in my helmet.

I got the job and was now working in East Finchley. I could do the work in my sleep but I began to enjoy it as I always seemed to.

It was the same drill. A fiery crew in the kitchen, this time all Portuguese, dishing out pasta and pizza, and a nice manager, Sam Baker, who swore like a trooper and laughed a lot. I liked her. One day I saved her life when we stole a pizza and wolfed it down laughing like drains out the back, she sucked a piece of sausage down the wrong hole, and choked. I intervened when I saw her lips turning blue, performing the Heimlich like a champ. We both watched the Frisbee-like pork assassin fly up and out of her throat. She gasped and we hugged and laughed.

There were a couple of boys on the bar who I became friends with. They were up to no good. By this time Autoglass had been round and replaced my shattered mindscreen. The Nervy B now long forgotten, I jumped in with both feet. As was my wont.

One day a new waitress came into the restaurant. Her name was Callie and she rocked my little world for a while. What is it with me and gorgeous waitresses? So silly. I think I was still quite shallow at this point. I didn't care enough about what was up top or in the heart, I cared about how they looked and something so superficial will only ever bring one thing. Pain. Pain for me anyhow. I've left this behind, now as I've gotten older but then I was crazy for the perfect nose and glossy red hair of this girl. This would be no flash in the pan. I fell hard.

Apart from a few bonkers parties with the hardest, naughtiest kind of chocolate buttons, Callie was the most memorable thing to happen to me during my time at that restaurant. That and *Spaced* of course. Callie had a boyfriend but I sensed they were off-again on-again quite a lot. She wanted to be an actress, I still had no idea what I wanted to be.

I made Callie laugh and I could feel us getting closer but she was still in love with her boyfriend. I knew from the beginning it would hurt, I suspected she was using me to get back at him, although I'm not sure he ever knew about me, thus defeating the purpose I guess. I wasn't the kind of hunk girls used to make other hunks jelz. He was, I imagine, a big, handsome fucker, to get her you'd have to be. (Unless you were funny, like me.)

I think the mistake I made was fairly early on telling her that I loved her. Error. I think I did. I felt like I did anyway. Now obviously looking back it was nothing like love. It was my balls trying to convince my brain that I loved her. As soon as I told her this it was game over and I'd lost. Again.

This affair went on for a while and coincided with a heavy consumption of dangerous and psychoactive lolflakes. The lolflakes I think helped and prolonged my 'relationship' with Callie, added another level of mystique to me. I may not have been a looker in her eyes but I was funny, smart, complicated and troubled. This was almost enough to keep her interested. Almost. I used a cracking technique when we first met, although to say technique would imply some kind of thought process behind it; there wasn't. What I did was I simply forgot her name. It made her mad that this plain lump would, could, forget *her* name.

We had some lovely days. Once in the morning I brushed her hair and we went to the zoo but I could see her heart wasn't in it. We worked and I made her laugh and I wanted her to love me and it was complicated and I guess secretly I liked it. The fact I ever got her to stay in the Crab Pit was amazing to me. How would any young lady in her right mind ever want to wake up in Tramp Henge? I knew how to treat a woman back then. Once I bought her a lettuce as a present. I woke up and she was gone. Only the lettuce remained. I panicked slightly.

I think if you took 9 Busby Place as a whole, its inhabitants, the vibe – sorry, me – it was a fairly attractive place for Callie to be. We had some amazing parties in that house. I don't remember much, which is probably for the best. I once saw two burly northern women holding onto each other for balance while they pissed off a high balcony onto the street below. It was a very dangerous manoeuvre.

That same party saw the police try and secrete a plain clothes officer into our rave. The police had come round earlier in uniform asking us to turn down the music. We didn't. So later in the night they pulled up the street a little way in a marked panda car and dropped off an undercover man. Silly tactic. We were all stood out on the balcony and watched the whole thing unfold. The young officer, wearing tight, stonewashed jeans and a fleece – what did off-duty police wear before the invention of the fleece? – hopped out of the vehicle and grabbed a four-pack of generic lager. He set off to infiltrate and realised he'd been rumbled. We laughed and barracked him from the third-storey balcony. He turned tail and got back in the car.

Some of my favourite times at Busby Place came on Sunday mornings when we had been clubbing hard. Smiley's records and deck set-up meant it was a perfect place to chill out as the sun came up. Sometimes twenty people would come back, the sexy Antipodean babes would bath and get into some kind of snuggie, while the boys smoked biftas and talked loudly.

We'd wake Smiley up and pester him to mix for us. He'd be absolutely furious for a second and then his spirit chimp would kick in and the need for him to create a little mischief would overwhelm his urge to kill us. Pretty soon after a Norn Irish breakfast (tea and a fag), he'd start to play records and the night would begin again.

Eventually we'd run out of steam and we'd all lie in a heap, the girls in their snuggies and all freshly showered smelt and felt amazing. We were naughty, greedy boys and secretly the girls liked it. They'd play with my hair and massage my hands while my eyes rolled. They were perfect Sundays. I think this is a fine dynamic when you're in your twenties. The longer this goes on the more boring it gets. Especially for the girls. Girls don't want those types of guys into the mid-thirties and beyond. Very unattractive.

One afternoon Smiley arrived back from gigging upcountry, I hadn't been out and Simon wasn't in. Smiley was acting very weird. He was quiet, not like Smiley at all. He came in and made a cuppa. A few words were exchanged, not much though. He goes upstairs to shower, I light another bifta. When he comes back down his skinny little body is wrapped in a towel and he's wearing a big cardie. He sits down and watches telly not saying a word. Something bad has happened. I don't pry at first, the weed gives me a sixth sense that says 'not now' so I leave it. A little bit later my weed says 'now'.

'Hey, mate? Are you okay?'

He nods silently and gets up and leaves. My feet feel hot. Something's wrong. Ten minutes or so later he comes in again and turns the telly off. ALERT. ALERT. ALERT. I push my legs back and move the Dead Man's chair from horizontal into a high vertical position. The weed stutters . . .

'Don't, don't, please don't turn the telly . . .'

'I need to talk to you.'

'Right.'

'You know I said I was gigging up the country?'

'Yeah.' Oh god help me, I know what's coming.

'I wasn't gigging.'

'Oh. Right, where were you then?' I didn't want to know.

Me and Smiley have a long history, Smiley more than me to be fair, of flirting with Simon's lovely mum. It drives Simon slightly mad and makes Gill laugh, it's all in good spirits. She is absolutely lovely. She's one of the nicest people in the world and has been so good and kind to me ever since I first met her twenty-one years ago. We have a kind of mother/son thing going on, but Smiley's a big flirt and likes to make me and Simon feel uncomfortable so he always pushed it that much further.

Smiley continued but inside I knew what was coming.

'I spent the weekend in a hotel.' he said.

'Oh right.' I pretended to be dead but he continued anyway. Why had I smoked that joint?

'I spent the weekend in a hotel with Gill.'

BOOOOOOOOOOOOOOOOMMMMMMMMMMMMM!!!

My left brain shuts down, my right hand shuts down and I piss-fit slightly. Smiley gets up, pats me on the shoulder and leaves me alone downstairs, terrified. My liver hurts.

I remain paralysed, shut down, dormant for over an hour until I hear the downstairs door open. Simon is home. I know the worst secret in the world and it's killing me. Our dream, our little collective, is gone and dead and I know and I can't say.

Simon senses weirdness from me and it's all I can do to stop myself grabbing a giant kitchen knife, touching the point to the place on my chest where my heart lives and falling forwards until it's sticking out the other side and one of my feet is twitching.

'What's up?'

'Nothing.'

'Smiley in?'

I nod. Simon puts the kettle on. I'm wearing a sarong and an orange shirt that I love, it has the legend 'Down By Law' etched on the back; being a big Jim Jarmusch fan I was very proud of this work shirt. I wear thick-rimmed black glasses and my hair is set in a high backcombed pompadour. The guys used to call it The Goose. I'm almost constantly high, something I'm regretting right now as I lie there unable to speak, hoping Smiley has somehow died in the last hour.

I hear his door open. I hear his bony little feet padding on the stairs. He's coming.

'Hey, mate.' Smiley puts on his butter-wouldn't-melt voice. Simon smells a rat immediately.

'Hey, mate.' They cuddle. Smiley pushes it.

'You wouldn't make me a nice lil cup o tea, would you?'

'Sure,' says Simon. 'Everything okay?'

A pause. I look at Smiley. He looks at me.

'Aye.'

Simon sits and we all drink our tea in silence. This is too much for me to bear so again I click into a vertical position, stand, retie my sarong and bumble around trying to act casual. Smiley's watching.

'Where are you going, big lad?'

Simon's slightly confused, he senses wrongness.

'What's going on?'

'Nothing, I'm going up for sleep.' It's one in the afternoon. I have to leave. I run into the Crab Pit and pull a box of musty towels across the door. I listen for Simon's grief-ridden cries as he finds out his best mate has violated not only the sanctity of a lovely friendship but also his mother. I pace and pound around my Crab Pit. Eventually I am forced to go downstairs. I ghost down silently and note the TV has been muted. Simon and Smiley sit next to each other in silence. Oh god. Poor Simon. Will Smiley eventually become Simon's new stepdad? That could be awkward.

I walk into the kitchen, fluids pumping around a brain, flabby and numb, make a whooshing noise every time my heart pumps, which, right now, is a lot. I do what I believe is the right thing to do. Let's have a cup of tea and talk this through.

'Tea anyone?' I turn to see them both smiling. Oh. Then Smiley waggles his eyebrows, Simon chuckles.

'What's happening?' I wish I was gone.

They both start laughing. This, it turns out, is a very cruel trick. A very cruel trick indeed. Smiley, seeing me high, had decided to play a joke of such life-rocking proportion I had internally peed into my own bladder. Why would you play a trick like that? Simon wasn't in on it but when I fled Smiley saw his chance to rope him in. What a willy. We laughed.

* * *

Our time at Busby Place came to an end. We knew our time was up one afternoon when me and Simon were watching TV. With no warning at all the ceiling of the kitchen/living room simply detached and fell onto our heads. We could easily have been killed. After a second, once an internal health diagnostic had been run, we laughed. The landlord never really had the drive or the gumption to do the place up. I think eventually he decides to sell that big lump of a house. So we move out.

Simon's career had gone from strength to strength. A couple of years before he found himself touring with Steve Coogan on his live show, *The Man Who Thinks He's It*. It was a great show. Steve and Simon became mates off the back of it and I guess, through him, me and Steve got to know each other a bit too. I like him a lot, he's funny and very generous.

When he found out we were being put on the street he offered us his mews house in Archway. What a Mensch. Next door lived either Pepsi or Shirley, from the band Pepsi and Shirley. They started out as a backing group for Wham! in the eighties but went on to have a nice little career of their own. I never found out which was which and we never really saw them very much so it didn't matter. It was a really lovely house and we paid very little for it.

I was still half seeing Callie, still in love, still working in the restaurant but something was about to change. Simon, along with an ultra-talented loony called Jess Stevenson, had been approached by Channel 4. He'd met her making a TV show that Edgar directed. They really enjoyed each other and Simon thought Jess and Edgar were friggin geniuses. He was right. They hung out a lot and came up with the idea for a flatshare comedy which became the show called *Spaced*.

It was great seeing Simon potentially get his own series, he was cockahoop. After a lot of meetings with the channel they agreed to commission seven episodes of network television. What a great thing.

Me and Peggy went to Camden one day to drink cocktails and meet Jess. Once she'd arrived they put a proposition to me: 'How would you like to come and be in our show *Spaced*?'

He wanted to use a slightly tweaked version of my character Mike Watt in the show and wanted me to play him. I'd never acted before and didn't ever think it would happen so I shrugged, 'Fuck it, I'll do it.'

That was that. Anything to get out of waitering. I never thought it'd happen and I'd ever have to do it so what was the harm in saying yes?

This gave me the chance to lord it up a bit over Callie at work, she wanted to be an actress so badly, she seemed amazed that I'd be so casual given an opportunity like this. Maybe she was a bit cross that this thing had flopped into my lap when I didn't really give a fig about acting or being famous.

I put the meeting in Camden out of my mind until I started to receive phone calls about costumes and sizes and my availability etc. What was happening? Simon would come home every night buzzing about what he and Jess had written that day, jokes they'd laughed at, characters they'd crafted. It was exciting. Still I waited tables.

In the evenings we'd sometimes all hang out together, go to a pub, party, dinner, drinks. I knew everyone more or less by this time and I wasn't afraid any more but I still didn't have much of a voice. Who cared what I had to say, what I thought was funny? I was good in small groups. Fortunately Edgar and Jess had seen me in small groups so they had got to know me better.

That said, it was only fairly recently that I discovered Edgar had had a conversation with Simon one day shortly before the pre-production of *Spaced* began. He questioned whether or not Simon was sure I could do it, whether I could act, whether I could perform in front of people. It's a perfectly understandable question to ask. I think Simon said yes – I think. What a gamble, what a risk to take. I hope I've repaid that trust over the years. I'm glad Simon was confident because I sure as shit wasn't. I didn't want to be an actor in any way, shape or form. No sir. It seemed too much like showing off for me and if there's one thing I'm not it's a show-off. (Maybe a little bit in the kitchen.)

What was I going to do? I'd never acted before. I say never – I did have a tiny part on BBC2's *Big Train*. Dressed as a builder I had to fall in love with a horny puppet bird as it bounced past me. That was it. It was short and sweet but I think Simon arranged it with Graham Linehan to give me a taste of what shooting was like. I got to meet the lovely Julia Davis and also a man who's become a very close friend over the last fifteen years or so, the very lovely Mr Kevin Eldon. Gosh he makes me laugh. He's the nicest Buddhist I've ever met. And that's saying something. Our children are betrothed to be wed someday.

It was only after I'd gone to my first costume fitting with a Scottish firecracker called Annie Hardinge that I began to real-ise this thing may actually happen. Annie and I have worked together a lot since then. She's a fantastic costume designer and a wonderful woman. Always well turned out with long curls of rich auburn hair. She's the kind of woman an American airman would've painted on the side of a B52.

Simon, Edgar, Jess and Nira Park – enduring friend, godmother to my son and perhaps the world's greatest producer – went into Channel 4 to have a meeting with someone high up. During the meeting my name was brought up, the exec wanted to know who I was, what I'd done and whether or not I was in *Spotlight*. (*Spotlight* for those of you who don't know is essen-tially lots of very big books with pictures and brief resumés of thousands and thousands of actors.) Simon and Jess lied and said I was in *Spotlight*. Fortunately for me there was another Nick Frost and we said he was me. The exec seemed happy and let it slide.

So this was me. A man with a complicated history, a past littered with overindulgence and family alcoholism, on the verge of making a TV show. The issue I have, and I think it's kind of a biggie, is I have no idea how to do the actings. Even though people had been calling me from the production office I still didn't think it would happen. I didn't want it to happen. I wanted things to stay as they were. I didn't really, I knew this was the change I needed, but I could've done without this ball of anxiety bouncing around inside of me.

Living with Simon I had the chance to get the scripts in advance and start to try and learn them. The thought of not knowing my lines and fucking up in front of people I didn't know made me want to die. I'm not too bad now, I just got better at learning lines, and after twelve years I'm pretty good. I still have that terrible fear of fucking up, but it's not all-consuming any more. Day to day I put a lot of time and effort into making sure this doesn't happen.

Sometimes though it just does go wrong. Actors are not computers, if a script has no melody or flow then it's tough to learn no matter how many hours you put in. Also, it's not live, it's not the end of the world. Audiences don't need to know how it's made, the process; what's important is the finished product.

Back then I was terrified. The Big Waiter on campus would soon be taken out of his comfortable restaurant, the place I knew and loved, the place that fed and housed me and supplied me with money for chemical vacations and an endless stream of horny waitresses to flirt with. Soon I would be thrown from the comfort of the above into the uncomfortable world of British Television. I didn't deserve it and I didn't want it. I did, however, need it.

About four weeks out from the beginning of production I was told to appear at so and so a place in town for my first ever read-through. Whatever the fuck *that* was. I had no agent although Simon's lovely rep Dawn Sedgwick (bloody good egg) agreed to take care of my paperwork. More importantly, I had no acting experience. Save for those 5 seconds on *Big Train*.

A read-through is something that's done around a big table with every cast member present. It's usually to help the writers get a feel for what's working and what's not. After the read-through the scripts are tweaked a little, sometimes more work's necessary. Then shooting scripts are released and you're ready to go.

I was so shy and nervous. I don't think I talked to anyone much. I knew Mark Heap and Katy Carmichael a little bit through parties and gatherings over the last few years but I didn't know them very well. We'd read through the script once all together on our own in a big room and then after that we'd grab a sandwich and then be joined by the big cheeses and heads of department, and other honoured invitees who'd all sit and listen to the scripts being read aloud.

These things never start on time. Actors, not all actors but some actors, are always a little bit – or in some cases a lot – late, often rushing in, cappuccino in hand, sometimes wearing a pompous hat or silken pashmina, items of clothing that alert potential street robbers to the fact that these people are actors and as such have no way to defend themselves whatsoever. It was ever thus.

I find read-throughs a lot of fun now. Unless the thing you're reading is shit. Also if none of the decision makers laugh you can leave the room feeling like it's your fault. It's soul crushing to see a Commissioner sending or reading an email mid read-through.

I've also seen the opposite happen, people laugh so much

that it's difficult to ascertain whether or not the thing is actually good. Actors love the sound of Commissioners laughter. It often means the louder the laughing gets the bigger the performance. It's an ugly thing to watch but completely understandable. Who among us doesn't like the taste of fresh laughter?

If you have the world's most amazing read-through it's often tough for the actual film or TV show to live up to the expectation of that read-through. I always think it's like spending a hundred grand on a dream wedding. Once the dust settles it's going to be tricky for the actual marriage to live up to the expectation of that massive knees-up.

We sat around the table and read the scripts. I don't think we read the whole series. I think we read three episodes or so. I was afraid but kept my head down and tried to interpret what Simon and Jess had written in terms of comedy beats etc. As Mike was my invention, written for me by two fantastic writers, directed by a hairy boy genius, I would've had to have been a complete fuckhead to not get laughs. I was funny, what I wasn't was an actor. Not yet, that comes much later. Right now I was a lucky waiter pretending to be an actor.

The first read-through with just us went great. It was relaxed, it was fun, and watching people, great people – great actors like Mark Heap and the sexy, beautiful Julia Deakin – work, and seeing what their process looked like, was exhilarating and fascinating to me.

I think throughout my whole life I've done a lot of this. Watching, seeing how things worked, seeing the shape of the food chain, who does what etc. I've asked a lot of questions too. As I never trained as an actor every department was equally interesting to me and I think that's really held me in good stead over the last twelve or so years. Especially as long term my aim is to direct and produce more. (Fingers crossed.)

After some light refreshment Nira, our fearsome producer, entered the reading room. She's not so fearsome now, not to me anyway and not after all these years, but back then I'm not sure she thought I deserved this shot or if I could even pull it off. I don't think she talked to me properly for two years. Many was the time in a pub after a few I'd turn to Simon and ask if he thought Nira liked me.

Nira's arrival means one thing, Big Wigs are en route. Assistants came in and set up chairs in a formation that was definitely gladiatorial. The chairs were shoved up close behind us. People filtered in, heads of department, well-wishers, agents, channel bods and other VIPs responsible for the show. Please note the most important person at a read-through will always be late. Always.

My heart begins to pound. I sit, frightened, quietly sipping on a water. This was the most alien thing I'd ever done. I think I remember catching Simon watching me, he looked nervous, we nod, he came and gave me some final words of advice. A light squeeze. It was all a blur. I must have looked like a frightened WWI tommy about to go over the top. Looking at it now I think this was the beginning of it all really, my career, this career that chose me. If I'd fucked up and the channel insisted they recast Mike that would've been that. I've no idea what I'd be doing today. Maybe I'd be an area manager for a chain of Mexican restaurants? Maybe I'd have a company car and play golf?

Nira stood and said some words, which is the one thing she hates doing more than anything. There's a little light applause, a laugh or two, and she threw it open to us. At the beginning of a read-through: words are said by the director and/or producer and then you go round the room saying who you are and what you do. I watched the introductions roll round the venue until it was three away, then two, one, now me! The blood pumps like fuck in my ears and I make these words fall out of my dry, baggy mouth:

'Hello. I'm Nick Frost and I'm playing Mike Watt.' That was that. Introductions over, everyone clapped and we were off.

The next worst bit was waiting for my first line to come round. Reading down the script and seeing it approach was awful, here it comes . . . here it comes . . . say the line . . . say it . . . NOW! And out it came. It got a laugh. Oh. Nice. They laughed, people laughed! That felt pretty good. The read-through finishes and people clap. Nice. Simon was giving me that look I liked. Pride, mutha-fucka, pride.

After the read-through there's always a little debrief, tea, pats on the back. I think after that, at least I hoped, Edgar and Nira might begin to believe that maybe, just maybe, I could do this.

Part Four

My social life and things outside of starting to make a TV show were still the same. Being naughty, powerful potions, and falling in love with fit girls who liked laughing but, long term, didn't see any future with me. The sex was cool, but I always wanted the love. I wanted them to fall in love with me. I wanted to properly love someone.

On top of that I still had my self-imposed exile from Mum and therefore Dad, which was a shame. Mum was a shame too, don't get me wrong, but seeing my dad look after this woman who was slowly dying was tough to take. It made me cross, therefore it wasn't too hard for me to exile the both of them.

It sounds hard I know. I'm not sure how it happened, me getting so hard, but it did. The more people died the harder I got. It was gradual, like the calloused skin on a builder's hands, the more trauma, the harder they become.

I've really had to watch this over the years, but therapy helped a bit. Everything's relative. People have a harder life than me. People have an easier life than me. After lots of mine had eventually departed, I'd find it difficult to hear someone bellyaching about the small shit. I had to work that out, that's my problem though, not theirs. It's big for them. All relative.

There were conversations with my folks semi-regularly on the phone, though yet again as soon as I heard that slur I wanted to hang up. I became impervious to Mum telling me how proud she was. It didn't mean anything and at the same time it meant everything.

By day I'd rehearse and by night I'd wait tables. It was an odd existence. Rehearsals were strange, reading stuff out, not knowing what was going on, what things meant. Learning my lines was the thing I feared most. I was also afraid of letting people down, and by people I mean Simon. If he thought I couldn't pull this off he never let on, which was either really clever or really nice. Maybe both, he's good like that.

The best thing about rehearsal was getting to hang out. Just sitting about, chatting, laughing like drains felt so good. I never felt I belonged, not at that point, but I felt welcomed. I had a lot of work to do to belong. I was meeting more and more new people and the prospect of having to leave ChickenPasta-McFuckheads or whatever it was called filled me with absolute joy. Once I left waitering to be an actor that was going to be it, fame and fortune awaited me.

My affair with Callie was getting complicated. I'd made the terrible drunken mistake of sleeping with another waitress, one who was actually pretty lovely. I mean as a person as well as being fit, which was a novelty for me. She was in a Spice Girls tribute act. I really liked her. What a shallow greedy dickhead I was. Maybe I got everything I deserved. I think I frightened the Spice Girl off a bit by being drunken and unpredictable one Christmas Eve. We worked in the day then got pissed once the restaurant had closed at 6 p.m.

We found ourselves frenching in the bogs. Then frenching on a night bus while a man dressed as a nun watched, then frenching on Simon's bed, frenching *in* Simon's bed etc. etc. etc. You get the picture.

I was in a bleak Russian novelist kind of mood. In between pumps and bouts of sobbing I'd swig from a large bottle of red wine. After we finished I threw the bottle across the room, it smashed. She seemed afraid and confused. I thought women loved that moody shit, that ennui.

The next day was Christmas Day, this was the best Eve I'd ever spent, all crying and sexing up a Spice Girl. I wanted it to go on. Tomorrow I'd be alone, Simon and Smiley were away, I couldn't be at home so I asked Spice Girl to stay. She didn't. I think the crying and bottle smashing mid-doggy was the death knell for that short-lived thing. I think I also might have told her I loved her too. Which got back to Callie. Shit gets complicated. Still, I have my work. My new work, as a TV actor. Ha Ha.

My friend Andrew Maxwell (the one that brought the Eiffel Tower of Absinthe to my stag do) calls me the world's luckiest waiter. Which I guess is right. Was right. Since the beginning, though I've always worked my cock *AND* balls off to make sure I didn't have to wait tables again.

I feel I ought to finish the Callie thread as when it actually finishes we won't be here. The book will be over by the time we get to that bit. I'm not sure I'll ever get the chance to write another one so I should end this now. I'd hate to think you'd never get to find out what happened.

After months of falling and chasing, hoping this could be the time a fit, shallow girl finally falls for a tubby jokesmith, we were approaching the end. It wasn't all bad which I guess made it worse. There were times when we did things that made me believe we could work. Once in the afternoon we went to see the film *Happiness*. She didn't get it and seemed offended watching Phil Hoffman jerking off. We left and sat in a café eating bacon rolls. It was so nice. We laughed a lot.

Please though don't imagine it was all her. Fuck no. I was far from perfect. My issues were many and complicated. Issues no pretty young girl from Leeds could or should ever have to cope with. This I understand.

There's one thing that happened that told me without a shadow of a doubt that I had to turn away and not look back for the sake of my own sanity and dignity, no matter how sweet this patootie was. I had to man up and bite the bullet.

One night we're lying in bed. In my new bed in the house in Highgate I'm to share with the boys. She utters to me words that have stayed with me for ever.

'I really like you but I wish you looked more like David Beckham.'

Wow. That hit me for six. It was the bucket of cold water in the face my dignity needed. All my instincts, finally singing off the same hymn sheet, hollered in unison.

'Get the fuck out of there,' they chorused. 'For your own sake, get the fuck out.'

I could barely speak, I looked at her perfect body for the last time. My balls wept, dropped to their knees, implored me to keep going, they told me things would change, she just needed more time. I'd heard enough, I slapped my dick round it's face. I was sick of listening to that fat liar.

I try to exit with a grand gesture, an overly verbose post-script she'll think about in fifteen years' time when she's wiping her tenth baby's arse and cursing the TV or cinema screen every time she sees my happy yet vulnerable face.

I need to say something which means I *couldn't* come back even if I wanted to. I think this technique was my psyche's plan of escape if all else failed.

In the end, as I struggle to pull my jeans up over my now striking balls (striking as in on strike, not visually stunning, although it has been noted before that I have very attractive Willy Balls. I digress), I manage to utter a shaky 'fuck you'. That's all I have, all I can muster. I leave at a pace, slamming doors, and stand on the street looking for a cab to take me away from all this heartache, when I remember that this is my house. She walks past me in the hall as I trudge back through the front door. And that's that. Well almost. I've never been one to just turn off emotions the way a fishmonger might simply turn off a running tap. For me shit lingers, which means small arguments tend to hang around. Shadows bang and holler upstairs as I try and work things through; things other folk would quickly forget tend to stick around a little with me. I need to learn to let things go, move on. Stop analysing every tiny detail. That shit be destructive yo. I, like you, am a work in progress. And I hope I'm never finished.

* * *

I have one more brush with Callie, in fact that's not quite true, there's two. A few weeks later I go and see her in a play. It's bad. She's okay but the play's not good. I think I'm drunk and sad she's shut me off so I leave at half time. I go back to the house in Highgate with Simon. We're watching REM live from Glastonbury. I'm drunk, I may have started into my first bottle of Night Nurse.

Me and Callie start texting, it's hard and cold. We're at that point where everything that went before, the niceness, the hair-brushing, Phil Hoffman jerking off, softness, laughter, they've all gone. They're replaced by a sharpness and a tightness of mouth. Silent tension reigns here now. I'm not sure how the end comes but it comes and I end up in tears.

I'm sitting on the sofa. Simon's watching me. 'Everybody Hurts' comes on. I cry solidly for an hour, my heart well and truly broken again. Simon fulfils the tricky job of cuddling me and telling me things I needed to hear right then. What a guy.

The second brush came years later, I'm in my house in Twickenham when a girl who looks exactly like Callie walks by pushing a pram. I don't move. Weeks later it happens again. I leap up and track her down the road. Nice arse. Days later I'm taking my bins out and she comes out of a house four doors down pushing a cute baby in a buggy. She's moved four doors down! From a completely different part of the city, Callie has moved into a house four fucking doors down. I'm amazed by this cosmic pull.

I don't run inside as my instinct tells me to. I stop and smile as she walks up. She smiles a bit too. Only a bit. It's awkward. I'm famous by this point so it must be hard for her. The man that never wanted it, never cared, standing there in house shorts holding bags full of stinky filth. Things are utterly different this time, there's no sense of a flicker, no match being held up to a short piece of fuse, no histrionics, no light flirt for old times' sake, nothing. We exchange a few words. I go in, she goes off. That's that. It's the last time I see her.

Days later a sign outside her house says 'FOR RENT'. Now I feel bad. Had I really been that bad? Does she really hate me so much? I have to believe this is not all about me. Months later I bump into a mutual friend. My suspicions are confirmed. It wasn't about me. It never is. Well, hardly ever.

* * *

All this was yet to come. Right now I'm leaving the restaurant and starting my career as a TV actor. Easy. The rehearsal process ends. The numerous meetings with hair and make-up and costume mean my character's look was now set in stone. Mike Watt TA would wear combat gear and polarised shooting glasses, the legacy of a childhood injury. He'd wear big combat boots and have a very short haircut. Perfect.

The scripts have kind of been learnt, I had no idea how to do it other than by saying the lines over and over again. I've got better over time and don't now feel the need to learn the whole thing in one like a play. That's what I tried to do at first. It expends so much energy. Now I learn a week at a time with a general 'loose' knowledge of the thing as a whole, it's so much easier.

I begin to receive paperwork, a shooting schedule comes through, money has been agreed upon, hands have been shaken, contracts signed and countersigned. A moment of clarity flashed into my pumpkin, a bean of truth that makes me heave. This shit was about to happen. *Spaced* was actually going to happen. The great Channel 4 swindle had been a success and I now have to walk the walk. Balls.

The night before the first day on set I spend puking my ring up. All night, no sleep, just being sick, such is the level of my nerves. As an aside, this feeling stays with me for years. There's hardly a job I do where I don't spend the night before being sick with nerves. I hate it. Now though, like line learning, it's better, I know the feeling and I've come to like it. Over the years, with knowledge and the odd technique and a lot more faith in myself that I've earned my place here at the table, the feeling has gone away.

On Monday morning, very early, the doorbell rings to Coogan's place and it's our driver. We get a bloody driver! Me and Simon get into the car. We drive and arrive at the studio in silence. The only time I now feel like this is before red carpets for one of my films. Not all of them, a *Paul* or a *World's End* or a *Cuban Fury*. You get the gist. The drive from the hotel to the cinema is one that I dread. I do the film for free, you pay me for the red carpets. It's not fun and it's not glamorous. That's the real work for me. The car pulls up through crowds of people craning to look at you, slightly disappointed you're not someone a little more famous. The car stops, a lovely grey-haired man called Paul opens the door. I breathe and BOOM . . . It's on. Nerves go, game face on. Let's smile and sign stuff and pose for selfies!

If Edgar had been unsure whether or not I could do it, meeting me that morning probably made him feel a lot worse. I was a fucking wreck. Seriously. I try and keep it subdued by not opening my mouth but sometimes there's so much of it, whatever *it* is, it kind of bursts out. Panic.

My eyes feel sweaty. I immediately meet loads of new people. Everyone's job title seems to be contracted down into letters, ADs HODs, DOPs. The studio was busy. Studios are always busy the first day of a shoot.

I barely touch my full English breakfast except for the sausages, eggs, fried-slices, bacons and mushrooms. I barely manage to wash it down with two strong coffees. I sit in my dressing room, dressed far too early in combat fatigues waiting for my execution to begin. Time passes quickly. I don't want it to. I want it to stop. I want to be back at Chiquito, flirting, laughing, not having a TV licence.

There's a knock at my door. A girl sticks her head in.

'Ready on set to line up, Nick.'

'Thanks.'

What the fuck does that mean? I stand and look. I'm in fatigues, I have a beret on. I've grown a big ginger moustache. What had I become? A charlatan moments from being found out.

A line-up is usually the first thing you do on any given shoot day. You get on the set and you walk the scene through. I didn't know that then. My credo at this point was say nothing and listen, don't fuck up. The first thing I ever shot on *Spaced* was the party scene where I supply security. I stand behind the door and appear shaking my side-arm happily.

All the guys are there. Lovely, weird, funny Mark Heap, lovely Katy, bloody lovely Julia Deakin, lovely Jess, smashing Edgar '8-ball' Wright and my darling home boy Simon 'Simon' Pegg. I relaxed slightly. It was only us. We talked a bit about how shit would go down and then we do a crew rehearsal. It's no longer just us. The crew streams in. My cold fear pops my top bulb and I panic. Simon stays me. We do the rehearsal and my little comedy pop-out makes the crew laugh. I think I suggest I'm found with the barrel in my mouth, as if Mike had been thinking about what it would feel like to end it all there and then.

It was a thing I did at home to make Simon and Smiley laugh, Edgar loved it too. It was essentially a charade I did for the guys where I'd load and discharge lots of different kinds of guns, shotguns, assault rifles, pistols and machine guns. Essentially a spree killer. (Grim.) It always ends with me doing a weird smile and offing myself. The guys would laugh at the dark dénouement. Sometimes imaginary gunfights would break out as locals fought to contain me. A lot of my darker comedy ends with me killing myself. Help . . .

The tension builds and for a moment I wish this gun was real. What must Simon have been thinking? This was his gamble. If I scream and run off, never coming back and they have to go on hiatus for two weeks while they recast my role at considerable fiscal cost to the production, which means a knock-on effect where no one gets wrap gifts, it would be his fault. It would also I imagine put a ding into our friendship. Or would it?

Back then I bailed on shit. I started things, I got all the gear and then I stopped. I couldn't be bothered. A couple of years before all this began – my new career – I decided I wanted to do an A-Level at night college. So I did. I was pretty skint at the time so a guy I knew, another Simon, who was my GM at the Mexican place, gave me the money for the course and off I went. Twice a week I'd take the tube to Old Street and attend a course to get me an English A-Level. I'd done so shit at school in terms of grades I felt like I needed an actual qualification. This is the first inkling in me that I couldn't be a waiter for ever.

I didn't know then, obviously, how things would turn out. I enjoyed the course and stayed for quite a while but as the exam drew nearer I got nervous and I stopped going. Classic me. I did the A-Level but never took the exam. That was me all over. Until *Spaced*.

The first AD says the words I will hear many times over the years to come but this first time dread punches me in the spleen.

'Final looks please, shooting this time.'

A burst of activity as every cast member is checked over and preened, brushes on faces, collars turned down. A lady puts what feels like Rizlas on my face and leaves them there for a while.

'What are these? They feel like Rizlas.'

'They are Rizlas. We use them to soak up the sweat.'

'Oh. Am I sweating that much?'

'Yeah.' She bustles off leaving three Rizlas glued onto my drippy five-head.

The AD then shouts something else.

'And turnover.' The floor is cleared. My Rizlas are ripped off. I'm powdered briefly. Other voices from other departments pipe up.

'Sound is at speed.'

'Rolling.'

'Mark it!'

Someone rushes in with a clapper board, hooray, finally, something I recognise! I love having a laugh with the clapper peeps, generally they don't answer you back or talk at the point of the clap. This is their big moment. That doesn't mean you can't talk to them though. Simon does it too, you give them a brief pep talk and then rate the board. Sometimes you do it really quietly.

SNAP – 'what a lovely board'. Or 'what a terrible board'. It makes the camera teams laugh, one of the main actors gently ragging on a young clapper loader.

There's none of that today though. My blood pumps into my hearts and for a moment I feel really weak.

'And . . . Action.'

From my vantage point, hidden behind the door, I can hear the scene unfolding but sadly any memory of my cue line is long dead. Oh fuckballs. When do I come out? Did we ascertain that? I'll just stay here. Maybe they won't notice. That's what I'll do, just stay here. A minute or so passes and I hear a line I feel I remember. It's the beginning of the cue, of my cue! This is it. Do it. Do actings now!

I pop out and wave my little gun. Say my line. I blush inside, then outside, and I retract back behind the door and wait for the scene to be done.

'And . . . cut!' Edgar sounds chipper. People emerge from their hiding places off the set and tweaks begin. Little lighting issues are dealt with, costume bits, make-up brushes are deployed. Edgar hops around giving notes if notes need to be given. He comes to me, excited.

'That was great! Let's do another one.'

'Okay!' So we do another one. And another.

You can always tell what Edgar thinks of a take by the way he says 'cut'. If it's bright and chipper then he likes it. If it's slightly elongated and unsure you know he has reservations about something.

We finished the first set-up. A wide. It's usually always a wide, or 'Master', then the camera pushes in for tighter coverage. It works great this way, it's economical usually, and sets the continuity for the rest of the scene. I felt good, in fact I felt great. I'd done it. I hadn't burst into flames causing a terrible fire, I hadn't turned to dust or melted. I did it. We crowded around the monitors to watch the take back. It was good. People laughed as I popped out. All I needed to do was know my lines and be funny. That was it.

* * *

As time passes Simon and I find our little routine. We like having a little routine. We'd shoot all day and then get dropped off at the pub at the end of our street. We'd have a couple of beers, debrief a bit, laugh at things that made us laugh during the day, then we'd look at tomorrow's work. I liked the rigidity of that. It gave me purpose. Something to focus on. I liked that.

I keep this kind of routine now when I shoot. It takes a lot of work and a partner who knows and accepts that this is the most important thing in your life for the next four months or so, longer in some cases. It takes its toll – sadly, when your partner sees you give your best on a set and then not much in your home life, it takes its toll.

For a big film all I do, literally, is work. I'll get up and do ninety minutes' line learning, then I'll shoot all day, come home, bit of food, then bed. I'll lie in bed reading the next day's work. I want to know everything. Everyone's role. Everyone's lines. I then read the call sheet from front to back. Every word. Who's working? What scenes are we doing? How many extras? What time is lunch called for? What props are needed? What's the weather going to be like? Everything. I want and need to know it all. If there's a unit list on the back, read it. Learn everyone's name. Bill Nighy taught me how important this is. It's really important. Why shouldn't an actor know everyone's name? It's just good manners. I started this method twelve years ago and I still do it today. I served and continue to serve an apprenticeship in this business that I hope will last for my whole lifetime. I hope it never ends.

Spaced continued. I got my head down and concentrated. I loved it. I loved the crew most of all I think. The crews thrill me and continue to thrill me. Day in day out they bust their humps making film and television. I only have to come in to do the shooting bit. Eight weeks, twelve weeks, a bit more, a lot more actually if I'm writing or producing something. Then I'm done. Crews maybe get to take the weekend off and then they start all over again. Actors, even successful actors, rarely go from job to job to job without a nice big sunny holiday in between. These brave boys and girls do it week in week out. The 5 a.m. calls. The weeks of nightshoots, being away from home and family in shit hotels that cast would never dream of staying in, and all because they have decided to follow a career in film and television. I've literally never seen any crew member fuck up on anything I've ever done then or since. They're amazing people.

With a fantastic crew, great cast and lovely script, the atmosphere on set was smashing. I fed off it. I grew, I got bigger, more confident. People couldn't believe I'd never done it before. What helped me was my friendship and chemistry with Simon. Apparently you couldn't then and can't now 'buy that shit'. People loved us together on screen. I loved us together anywhere.

The weeks bled into one another. My focus intensified. I saw bits of Callie but not much. My issues seemed to ebb away for a while, I still smoked the 'erb and drank a bit but I was happy working. I didn't need anything else.

Coming back to Steve's place was an absolute treat every night. It was a lovely open-plan, factory-style mews house and was done up beautifully. On the top of the house was a little roof garden. It was here Simon and I perfected a thing we loved called the 'bloodclart assassination'. It was simple but made us laugh. We'd fill a big champagne bottle with water. (Don't

judge.) Then load a fake 9mm with a small steel ball bearing
and conceal the weapon behind our backs. The game was then
to pretend to be a fearsome Yardie gangster: you'd casually
stroll up to the champagne bottle, say something in Jamaican-
style patois, and then you'd pull the nine out and drill a ball
bearing into the bottle.

'BLOODCLART!!!' we'd shout.

God, we laughed. The first time we did it we were amazed
that the steel sphere penetrated the bottle leaving a perfect hole
behind. No cracking, just a perfect hole. Little things please
little minds I guess.

People often ask if me and Simon ever fight. The answer is
very rarely. Of course we've had tiffs and barneys, we've been
together for twenty-two years, it'd be strange if we hadn't.

Real big fights though are pretty rare. I can honestly only
remember one face to face. There was another on the phone
once during my honeymoon and one or two spats, I guess
you'd call them, but that's about it. It hasn't been all sweetness and light though. I remember a time when we were
living together in Kentish Town when we really didn't like
one another. Seriously. It was serious. I think if we'd actually been boyfriend and girlfriend we'd be thinking about
going on a break or moving out altogether. What was that
all about?

I didn't think about this at all back then. Not when it was
happening; I've thought about it since and I suppose the thing
I put it down to was jealousy, plain and simple. What a terrible
thing. I'm ashamed to say I wanted what he had. Hanging
around with all these new people, seeing how happy he was,
how success was starting to tickle his lovely plums, how popular he was, I thought it was as easy as that. I forgot how much

work he'd put into it. Forgot how much he'd suffered for it. What he'd sacrificed. He earned everything that came his way. Shame on me. I worked my hole off too but for what? To what ends? Where was I heading? What was my fucking future? I was funny, people liked me, so why wasn't I earning big dollar? What a horrible chip to have. For days and then weeks and then months everything he said to me, everything he did, annoyed me. I know the same was true for Simon.

The money thing was an issue for me. I was pretty skint half the time and I didn't want him to have to lend me money so I could go out with him and his lovely, cool new friends. Even though I was desperate to go. I think that meant I spent a lot of time indoors being a weed hermit.

My delight at potions and smokeables I suspect played their part in our blip, our unmeshing. Things came to a head, we knew we had to sort things out but neither wanted to take the first step. This is how things never get better, when people refuse to take the first step, refuse to apologise. God, it was so close to being so very different.

We went out clubbing one night, me, Simon, Tony, Dion, the gang, South African shitheads and scumbags. Lovely. I went hard, got hammered, pissed, you know the deal. The club finished and, for whatever reason, missed rides and taxis meant me and Simon found ourselves together outside. We started to walk. It was a long way. I think we walked from Covent Garden all the way back to our place in Kentish Town.

It was silent and, as the sun rose, the day revealed itself to be grey and weatherless. We walked in silence. I love the early mornings in big cities. A place where a few hours from now millions of people will emerge from pots of steel and holes in the ground to earn a living and try to justify their place in the food chain. We were in that third shift. Just us, ravers, aliens and big-bummed African cleaners chatting and laughing on their phones. These are the people of the third shift.

As we walked something lovely happened, our hearts waved white flags and we started to talk. During that stroll we cried and shouted, laughed and held hands and by the time we pushed our heavy front door open we were back!

We were friends again after that. All the tension was gone and we moved forward, thick as thieves. We've continued to evolve with each new incarnation of our friendship, whether it be girlfriends, moving out, marriage or kids, we evolve and we work.

We did have one other row, I'd say it was Jeremy Kyle-like in its intensity. Drink played a part. And weakness, mine. I'd decided to stop smoking fags. I found it really hard. Simon was keen that I give up. I fancied giving it a go and I stopped. I'm not sure how long for. I want to say days but realistically it was more like hours.

It was the early afternoon and I think I'd had a couple of Night Nurse margaritas. We had people over, I know that much. Something happens, Simon says something, something about my weakness for giving in and having a ciggie. He calls me weak. Oh no. Oh god no. David Banner walks into his bedroom and shuts the door. His eyes pulse and throb. He loosens his tie in savage expectation. Oh fuck. Weak. Fuck. I get up and steam into his room. There are people there, who I don't know, don't remember or can't see. I explode. (Close up on green mushroom cloud expanding in eyeball.)

Right there and then we have a massive screaming match. Huge. The drink and Night Nurse combined means it's all pretty nonsensical. I have to hold onto a door frame with two hands because I'm afraid if I have a hand free I may grab at his throat meat. I have a vague notion of people standing around open-mouthed, some kind of intervention, and then it blows itself out. I wake up some time later. All is forgotten. Simon says sorry for calling me weak. He feels bad.

All the rest were just little bullshits. We had a barney once during *Hot Fuzz*. We're sat in a car, watching Martin Blower and Eve Draper speed past us. It was awkward because we were miked up and all the crew could hear us rowing. We sat in silence for three hours in that car while the crew eggshelled their way around us. What a pair of dicks.

One night years before when we were still living at Ivy Road, sleeping together on this shitty futon I owned, I got up to grab something from the end of the bed and Simon thought it would be funny to kick me off. It wasn't very high but it hurt and Simon's hysterical laughter as I floundered on the floor made it hurt a bit more. I fumed as we lay in bed in the dark in silence. Eventually it broke. I turned to him in the dark.

'I've got a job interview at Trebor tomorrow.'

We both laughed like idiots and it was over.

Simon's hurt me a lot over the years. The futon thing hurt; he's also slashed at me with a knife while we were fucking about on set one day, I still have the scar to prove it. The worst injury though was not all his fault. We'd had mates round and the day had got to the point where me and Simon were swigging Harvey's Bristol Cream out of the bottle. I suspect it wasn't our first either. Me and Simon find ourselves in my bedroom wrestling topless on the bed. (I promise you we've never had sex.) We had people round for fucksakes, why we were wrestling in my room seems weird now, and from a hosting point of view downright rude.

Anyhoo, at one point Simon flies at me, foolish, very foolish, my immense strength means I'm great up close. I do most of my best work up close. He's now in my arms in a perfect position for me to deploy an Atomic Power Bomb. I hesitate a second, fuck this, deploy! From a standing position I slam him onto and then through my bed with terrific force. The sound of smashing and cracking is frightening but the power bomb has been utilised with such force and elan we're both pretty fucking proud. We're also laughing like drains. The bed is completely destroyed. All the legs have fallen off and the mattress struts have shattered into splinters. A moment to get our breath back and we rise, surveying the damage.

It's at this point Simon notices the thumb on my right hand is hanging off. It's dangling loose. Just flapping there like a windsock. Oh. There's no pain so I pick it up and jam it back in. Hooray, I'm cured. It lolls off again, swinging like a catflap. Balls. Being a keen home doctor I prescribe for myself gaffer tape, and lots of it. As we've already seen, it's a technique that has served me well although one the British Medical Council tends to foolishly ignore. Imagine the savings the already creaking NHS could make with my self-care proposals.

While I'm securing the thumb into position our guests, upon hearing the Atomic Power Bomb and the smashing of a bed, come to investigate. There's the usual mix of horror and laughter. Andrew Maxwell is here and some girls including Chris, my future wife. Maxwell's attention immediately turns to my shattered bed. He talks ten to the dozen. There's a large group gathered in my room, and the girls fuss over my loose thumb while the hunky men work out how to fix my bed.

I hear Maxwell holler a command: 'Let's put the bed up on its side so we can see how fucked it is.'

It's only at this point that I realise what's going to happen in about one second. In about one second, these people, these fine Samaritans, friends, lovely comedy fun-girls, are going to see about five hundred hardcore porno mags under my bed. They're barely contained by two massive Ikea bags. Some of my Wank Du Jour are loose on the floor, close to hand. I panic – something I tend not to do any more, my embarrassment gland seems to have withered and died the older I've got. Back then, though, I panic. I start to flap about and fluster.

'Leave it, guys, I'm fine. I'll just sleep on it like it is, please, yeah? Leave it, leave it, please, put it down, I'll sleep on the debris, seriously, it's not . . .'

WANK MAGS!

The room actually goes silent for a moment. I laugh a bit. Mortified. It's only porn at the end of the day, no one was bothered. I think the boys were impressed and the girls were worried that I wasn't getting laid enough, which at this point was probably true.

Years later I do a show called *Danger! 50,000 Volts!* (which I'll cover in book 2). There's a lovely young lad working as a production assistant; I'm not sure how it came up but we start talking about porn one day. I'd moved in with Chris who was my gf at the time. She nudged me, and rightly so, into maybe getting rid of these mags. I didn't want to at first, and it was only after meeting this little Welsh fella who literally fell off his stool in his eagerness to get hold of this nearly pristine catalogue that I gave in. That was the thing. I could've got rid of them bit by bit, wrapped in a carrier, under a bridge or in a derelict factory but I couldn't bear to split the collection. Too much spunk went into these things for me to just fuck them off near a river for kids to find. No way.

This Welsh production assistant was a breath of fresh air. Once I explained my conundrum he sprang up.

'I'll have 'em!' he said.

'I'm not splitting up the collection.'

'You don't have to. I'll have 'em all.'

And indeed, he had them all. One evening after work he came round in his little red Nissan Micra and we silently moved the two bags from my place into his boot. It felt like moving a gorilla's body. We nodded, then shook hands while never really making eye contact.

'Look after them.' I said.

'I will.' he smiled

He got in, started the car and was gone. They were gone. Ten years' work, gone. I often wonder what happened to those guys. Fuck. Happy days . . .

I wake up with a scream at 3 a.m. I was having a terrible nightmare that I'd broken my thumb and had gaffer-taped the thing back together. Oh. I struggle to turn the light on and when I do I wish I hadn't. I'm lying on a mattress supported by columns of porn. Splinters and shattered pieces of bed lie all around. My hand is throbbing. Bits of black hand meat throb out through the gaps in the gaffer. Oh shit. Hospital for me. I'd broken my thumb pretty badly. Why did Simon keep injuring me? If I was his wife I think I'd have him put on some kind of register.

* * *

The thing about working on a show that everyone loves is you know eventually it's going to end. This is what was happening to *Spaced* right now. It was ending. It'd been my first job and the thought of it coming to an end made me feel very sad. I was also tremendously proud. I'd done something I'd never done before and I think I bloody nailed it.

I had no idea how popular *Spaced* would become. No idea if we'd do another one. No idea what to do with my newfound skill in front of the camera. Where next? I did think about these things briefly but I was still concentrating on getting this shit done. Not letting anyone down.

Making what I guess can be classed as cult TV and films is an odd thing. For the fans it's really important, it's their escape, the thing they set their Tivos for. It shouldn't be under-estimated. Look at the massive convention circuit for godsakes. That tells you all you need to know. For me the geek, it was *Star Wars*, *Indiana Jones* and *X-Files* (to name but three!) but for me the actor, it's something you work on, love, have a hoot making, and then you move on. My brain tends to dump old content pretty much straight away so I can fit more dialogue in.

I think this is difficult for people to understand: why wouldn't you remember doing *Spaced*? Of course I do but that was the first thing I did and I've done countless TVs and fifteen or so films since then. That sounds like a boast, it's not meant to. Sorry.

* * *

During the shoot we were forced to move house yet again. Steve's dream mews was only ever a temporary measure, as much as it would've been nice to stay there living next door to Pepsi or was it Shirley? One day on the way back from a shoot Simon drives past an estate agent and notices a house to let in the window. He gets the car to stop so he can see it and then calls Smiley. Smiley goes up and looks and arranges a viewing. It's perfect.

Sometime later we move into Shepherds Hill in Highgate. It's amazing. I have, mostly, the nicest memories of that house. We had the whole bottom floor of a large Victorian mansion. It had a massive garden, which, as I've said many times before, was a real hotspot for European Jays. It felt like a big boys' house, new carpets throughout and its own fridge. It was really lovely.

The rent was split three ways at this place. It would be the first time I could properly pay my way. I spend a few hundred quid getting the bed me and Simon would later kill, some shelves, a simple table, a lamp. I felt so grown up. I had my money from *Spaced* and I thought the salad days would never end.

We finished shooting the show and it was a fabulous experience. It was the first time in my life I realised what I wanted to do. What I wanted to be. Thank heaven, I'd left it so late. All those years I'd lain in bed at night listening to my Jiminy Cricket tell me everything would be okay were finally justified.

For the first time ever in my life I had money in my bank. Not a lot but . . . I think people assume if you do a TV show or a film you're immediately a millionaire. I think I got paid a high four-figure sum for *Spaced*. It was more than I'd ever been paid before in one lump! I was earning £1.92 p/h at Mexican Restaurant Inc. It's all relative. One would be forgiven for thinking I'd been paid 600k the way I was living though. I was in a nice house with my best mates, money in the bank, just finished a TV show that everyone said I did great in. What could possibly go wrong?

I have no idea what I thought I'd do immediately after *Spaced*. I guess I imagined the work would just roll in. Right? Well maybe after the thing gets aired, but that wouldn't be for another year at least. I paid this no mind however. I also, through complete ignorance and the misguided belief that I, Nick Frost, someone who was above all this kind of shit, thought I wouldn't have to pay tax on it. What was I thinking? I just spent. I raved and drank and fucked about and had a great time.

During this period I was invited by Adam and Joe to a fancy party. I was chuffed and began to feel included in the scene. I'm not sure what the occasion was but my party instinct tells me either wrap or Christmas. No matter. For some reason I'd spent two months regrowing a big Zapata moustache after shaving my *Spaced* one off when we wrapped. I gave it to Edgar in a matchbox as a gift. He still has it although now it looks like a red marble. Gross.

I'd left the party at around two o'clock to get home in time to watch the first Evander Holyfield/Lennox Lewis fight. I was pretty pissed up as I walked around Farringdon looking for a taxi. I was outside a BP garage on the outskirts of an estate when I turned to see five youths bowling up towards me. Fuck!

As a man I had always been terrified of this happening – one on one fine, fair game, but this was different. This was the thing where, despite your best intentions of a noble fightback, through sheer weight of their numbers you would be completely emasculated and there was nothing you could do to prevent this. Nothing.

Many times as a younger man I'd mulled over the eternal question. Stabbed or slashed? For the record I'm all for the stabbing. Here's my logic: for someone who is terrified of having stitches the thought of having two or three hundred in a gaping chest or back slash is unthinkable. But the thought of being stuck and having an operation under a general anaesthetic was complete bliss. How did we get here? Oh yeah, the guys surrounding me. The great stab or slash question now flickered through my processor. It was rudely interrupted by this . . .

'What are you fucking looking at, you fat cunt?'

As an opening remark it leaves little or no confusion as to what their intention is; as direct approaches go it's actually quite refreshing.

I'm fucked. I quickly formulate a strategy, this buys me the precious seconds I need to figure out a Jack Reacher-style plan to get me out of the pickle that's come to be known as 'The incident of the wrong moustache in danger town'.

Here's what happens next . . . With a powerful, fast-paced right hook I knock the main cunt out. Sparko, gone, jaw pops, eyes roll, he does the thing boxers do where their arms spasm into the sky, flapping at white ravens unseen. He might be dead. Gutted.

This completely throws a fox into the hen house. This has never happened to them before, their random victims never fight back. It's not the done thing. The toilet muffin behind me beeps and starts to panic. Whatevs. I spin, laying a pointy elbow into his soft human temple. He vomits and groans like a grieving widow. He collapses into a puddle of his own council estate honk. Three left.

A handsome, long-limbed simpleton swings one of his rangy paws at me. Christ he was slow. I step left and one step forward quickly rotating. I flick out a shattering back fist. Poor lad, he'd have to undergo four hours of painful NHS dental surgery.

I pull one of his oversized incisors from the back of my hand, I toss it to the floor and giggle like a wet Geisha, I close my eyes, and let the man chemicals flood through my brain. I cum.

The last two combatants are completely horrified. I get the feeling they've never seen a man involuntarily ejaculate during a Fatty Bash before. I see them think twice. Seeing me on all fours tasting my own seed they decide to fuck off. I survey the pile of human shit around me, and pulling Willy out I take a post-fight piss on them. I notice one of them has a Cadbury's Double Decker in his pocket. I reach in, open it and feed. Fuck, it tastes good. A black cab pulls up and I jump in.

'Where to, Guvnor?'

'Highgate please, Driver.'

'Good night?'

'Excellent.'

Job done . . .

My fantasy ends and to my horror I find I'm still surrounded. Skins, geezers, faceless, mirthless, dead behind the eyes. I mutter a cowardly retort to his original quesion:

'Nothing, mate.' My eyes cast down at the pavement.

The tension builds to a point where I think my femurs might snap and to my utter amazement they just saunter off. The ringleader gobs on the floor as a goodbye and they bowl off into the garage. Deep breath, big boy. Important decisions are now made quickly, decisions that could save my life. Don't run, this will trigger their chase response and you'll be killed, pray for a taxi.

A taxi doesn't come and I'm still there when they stalk out, all bogging me down. I should've run, they didn't need to see me still there. It's some kind of diss. They wander off. I breathe easy. I may have even smiled a bit. I'm free, you lucky twat.

From behind my right shoulder I hear a powerful haymaker whizzing past my ear. It catches me square on the button. Right on the chin. Flat footed. Pop. Lights out. Gone. Down like a sack of shit. No defence, no chance, knocked the fuck out.

I'm asleep for quite a while. Fortunately I come to just as they're changing shifts. Punches have now been replaced by penalty kicks to my head and its face that lives around the front. A refreshing change in martial techniques. Through all the violence and punch-guffing I can sense them tiring. I recall a weird calm descend on me, I'm either dying or I've just wet myself. After years of being terrified of this kind of thing happening I actually remember thinking that it wasn't too bad. This block of abstract thought lasts two seconds, no, one. Then I remember thinking that I'd quite like to go to sleep. One last giant boot to my face granted me my wish. I'd finally tired them out.

As I lay on the street in a puddle of my own claret, blind – they'd kicked my contact lenses out of my head – I remember a maroon car pulling up, screeching up, two men jump out, and chase these fuckheads off. What a brave and noble thing to do. I never got a chance to thank those men. I truly feel if it wasn't for them I would've died that night.

I miss the Lennox Lewis fight. Simon arrives to pick me up. He puts me to bed and soaks my once-beige now-claret jacket in a bath of cold water. What a sweet sweet man. He really looked after me.

I didn't feel afraid after that, didn't feel like I couldn't leave the house. On the contrary, I felt like statistically I'd had mine. I think I was relieved that the person who got the fuck kicked out of him was me and not some frail old lady. Like my brother Marc, I could take it. Just.

* * *

I begin to realise my massive *Spaced* pay cheque had all but disappeared. I'd pissed it up the wall. It was all gone. I don't even remember what I did. I wish now I could see that as a good thing. I don't. I think now, looking back, it fills me with shame. A little bit of shame.

I try and eke things out for as long as I can. It's not long. I have no money, no job, a girl who wished I looked more like David Beckham. What am I going to do? I know what I have to do but I deny it, deny myself, pride punching me in the tool at the very notion of what I was thinking.

I'd found a great little pub just round the corner called The Shepherds. Me and Simon walked past it a few times but it looked old and piss-soaked, so we avoided it for quite some time.

Being an unemployed actor now, I had most of my days free. Walking past one day with an *Evening Standard* under my arm I thought, 'Fuckit, go in.' And I did. If I ever write another one of these I'll go into it more, but that pub was massive. It became a massive part of my life. Of Simon's life. But back then it was a place to eat a lasagne and chips (lashings of white pepper), drink a pint of Stella, and look at the job vacancies in the back of the paper.

A few days later, it's a Saturday night, about half-past twelve, and I awake with a start from my wonderful dream of being an actor. I'm wearing a tight red polo shirt and I have a mop in my hand. I may or may not be wearing a corporate baseball cap. A single tear falls into my grubby mop bucket as I clean a floor covered in puddles of spilt cocktail and pieces of fractured bottle. I've just done my first return shift on the bar of Old Orleans, Finchley Road. (A taste of the Deep South.) I was right back where I started.

Can I tell you that things picked up for me? Professionally yes, of course they did. I got to write my autobiography – they just let anyone write autobiographies, you know. Shame, some real smart waiters and bartenders are out there with amazing lives. Not just bartenders, people, normal people with amazing stories to tell. Stories that'll be forgotten once they're gone. What a shame.

My professional success (relatively speaking) comes at a price though. I want to tell you that things got better for me emotionally but I can't, they didn't. Seemingly every time I did a film another member of my family died. Was this the price I had to pay for success? (Relatively speaking.)

Back then when I was in the midst of all that shit with friends and family, drink and other unmentionables, I never thought I'd be here. There were times, long, horrible, black times, when I just didn't want to exist. I would never kill myself but the thought of just, bing, disappearing was really attractive to me. What changed? I think one thing was I learnt to forgive. I forgave my mum. I was too angry. What is the point of being angry with an amazing woman who loved me more than anything but had a terrible disease she had no control over. Why be angry at that? It's too destructive.

One day about six years ago on a whim and with the crazy notion that by doing this I may free myself of something bleak, I took my car and drove the four hours to the small windy cemetery overlooking Withybush hospital where my mum's buried. I wasn't sure what I hoped to achieve but I knew what I wanted to do. I wanted to tell Mum that I had forgiven her. And that's what I did. I stood and sat and screamed and cried for ages. Me and Mum really hashed it out. An hour later, amazingly, I felt a million times lighter.

By and by shit goes down to fuck all this up again, but I'm not one to sit down and give up. Not any more. I think one could be forgiven for reading this book and shouting, 'You can't blame your mum, you hypocrite! You're just as bad!' I'd understand that. I'm not one for spoilers but I will say this, there have been lots of times since then when I feared I may tread the same path as Mum and Ian and Debbie, to trudge blindly into a genetic imperative, bound for a destruction I have no control over. I was afraid for a long time until something happened that changed me overnight, and I hope for ever. I say 'hope'. With the best will in the world none of us can tell the future.

After doing IVF a couple of times and being told potentially it'd be really difficult to conceive, me and Chris silently decide not to have kids. We justify this to ourselves by saying we can have eight holidays a year.

Then four years ago while I was shooting the BBC drama *Money*, Dad is diagnosed with terminal cancer. Nine months later my beautiful, soft, fragile, hero of a father is dead in my arms.

Everything I'd endured up to this point pales into insignificance compared to right then. An orphan at thirty-nine. It's not that young compared to some but very young compared to many. For months and months I grieve and drink and try to choose a suitable tree in Richmond Park that I can drive my powerful car into and obliterate this silent anger. What drama, poor Chris. Thankfully I never find my perfect Death Oak.

Some weeks after Dad dies, me and Chris are in her brother's house on a gorgeous island in the Baltic Sea. I have literally had a complete meltdown. This is it. If there's a god he will now intervene and take me away, if not for me then certainly for Chris. Enough is enough. I cry myself to sleep that night.

The next day I watch Chris come out of the toilet with a pregnancy test I had no idea she'd bought. Her hands tremble so much. My eyes widen. She is crying. I jump off the bed and leave my black duvet behind. I look at the test. Pregnant. Chris was pregnant. Instead of taking something away I was given something. I was going to be a daddy. My switch got flicked. This was now about someone and something much bigger than me. I promised that day that I'd do everything in my power to make sure Little Boy had a better time of it than me.

A lot goes on between the end of this book and my son popping out. Things change for me, to me, for the best and for the worst, but him popping out that day in June changed me for ever. I wrote this for him. So maybe he can one day read it – when he's much older, says Mum – and have the answers I've now sadly lost.

My family, my lovely, complicated, fun-packed, fucked-up, laughter-filled, tear-drenched, utterly devoted family, were now gone, replaced by one little boy, that gift. The past now had passed over, totally forgiven but never to be forgotten.

You have been watching…

The 70s! Me, Mum and Dad after my First Holy Communion at St Peter and St Paul's.

The Frost clan! From left to right. *Back Row*; Uncle Simon (Rosemarie's husband), Dad, Grandad Frost and Danny from Holland (Auntie Hazel's ex). *Middle*; Auntie Rosemarie, Mum, Auntie Francis, Helen (Grandad's wife), Cousin Simon. *Front row*; Auntie Hazel, Cousin Caroline, me, Cousin Paul and Uncle Brian.

Me and Mum outside at 214 Raylodge Road. This was when I came back from Israel for the first time.

My brother Ian. What a little bruiser.

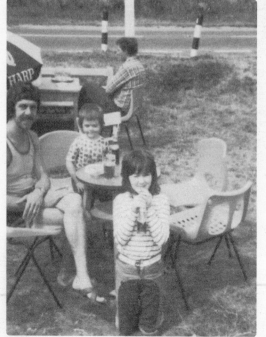

Me, Dad and my sister Debbie outside a pub called Corner Piece. This was Uncle Emmy and Grampie's favourite pub.

Uncle Emmy with
Auntie Betty,
Auntie Marion and
Auntie Melanie.

Me, Mum and Dad
circa 1972. Look at
Dad's lovely dimple.
His lifelong beard meant
it was never seen that
much. Shame.

A goodnight kiss from
Papa Bear as Teddy
Edward looks on.

Auntie Sandra
and my Cousin
Matthew, (Fergs).

Me and Marc
on the beach at
Broadhaven.

First day of school
1976. Cute.

Marc, Ian
and Debbie.

Grampie, Mum, me
and Gran outside
Millbrook.

Mum with a
massive shotgun.

Me and Cousin Paul at his 4th birthday tea. Grandad offers some sage words of wartime advice.

Mum and her boys AKA Peggy and the Mitchell Triplets.

My beautiful sisters Deborah and Sarah.

Me and Mum.

Grampie on the beach. Kickin' it 1940s style.

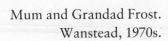

Mum and Grandad Frost. Wanstead, 1970s.

Me strangling
Mum. Christmas
in Highgate.
Circa 1999.

My lovely
Uncle Emmy.

Me and Pops.
Why's my hair
blonde. I look
demented.

Acknowledgements

Mum and Dad. I miss and love you more than you could ever know.

My boy and his fantastic mother Christina. Mark and Emma Lesbirel. Big Vern, a giant of a man in every way. Trudy, one of my surrogate mums, thank you.
Gill Pegg, my other surrogate mum, thank you!
Sarah and Gary and the boys.
Sweet Sheba.

Simon, Mo, Smiley, Bunny, Tony, Jax, Dion, Edgar, Danny Brown, Vicki, Fergie, James, Nira, Jeremy, Beevs, Hayley Stubbs, Kevin Eldon – I love you all. Bad Boys for life.

Hannah Black and the Hodder crew. Thank you.
Big Talk Productions.
Working Title.
Public Eye communications, Nate, Libby and the gorgeous Ciara Parkes.
Tom Drumm. Josh Katz. Christian Hodell and Mikey.
Conor and Sam and the Troika crew. Dr. Christina Romete.

People I knew well but now don't. Waiters and food service professionals all over the world.

Rugby. (The sport not the town)

Israel/Palestine.

Wales.

British Waterways.

Stella Artois. PG Tips.

Ciggies.

Coffee.

Sweet sweet Mary Jane, gone now but definitely not forgotten.

Hard House I love you.

Ravers I love you.

Jimi Hendrix. Hunter S Thompson. Jim Jarmusch. Woody Allen. Mulder and Scully. Steven Spielberg. John Williams. *The Simpsons*. George Lucas. Roy Neary. *Indiana Jones*. *The Young Ones*. Bill Nighy. Martin Amis. The Smiths. The Bluetones. Shit pubs. Sunny Side Up! Aleksander Solzhenitsyn. Alexander Shulgin. Timothy Leary. Milan Kundera. West Ham Utd.

Close Encounters of the Third Kind. Falafel. McDonalds. Meat Fruit. Good curries. Global knives. Non-stick pans and decent ovens. Onions. TV.

AHL forever!